LAST DAYS OF THE CONDOR

JAMES GRADY

FORGE®

A TOM DOHERTY ASSOCIATES BOOK
NEW YORK

LAST DAYS OF THE CONDOR

A Forge Book
Published by Tom Doherty Associates, LLC
175 Fifth Avenue
New York, NY 10010

www.tor-forge.com

Forge® is a registered trademark of Tom Doherty Associates, LLC.

ISBN 978-0-7653-7841-5

Our books may be purchased in bulk for promotional, educational, or business use. Please contact your local bookseller or the Macmillan Corporate and Premium Sales Department at (800) 221-7945, extension 5442, or by e-mail at MacmillanSpecialMarkets@macmillan.com.

First Edition: February 2015
First Mass Market Edition: November 2015

Printed in the United States of America

0 9 8 7 6 5 4 3 2 1

for

Desmond Jack Grady . . .

. . . running toward tomorrow

RAVE ON

Wonderful artists & colleagues & inspirations, plus loyal fans & friends & trusting sources helped Condor *fly.* *THANKS to all of you, especially:*

Jack Anderson, Rick Applegate, James Bamford, Richard Bechtel, David Black, Hind Boutaljante, Jackson Browne, Buffalo Springfield, L.C., Michael Carlisle, Tracy Chapman, Tina Chen, Stephen Coonts, Citizen Cope, Dino De Laurentiis, Nelson DeMille, Sally Denton, Sally Dillow, Tom Doherty, The Doors, Faye Dunaway, Bob Dylan, Jean Esch, Bob Gleason, Bonnie Goldstein, H.G., Nathan Grady, Rachel Grady, John Grisham, Francois Guerif, Julien Guerif, Jeanne Guyon, Jeff Herrod, Seymour Hersh, John Lee Hooker, Richard Hugo, Stephen Hunter, The Kingston Trio, Starling Lawrence, L.M., Ron Mardigian, Mark Mazzetti, Maile Meloy, Lee Metcalf, *The New York Times,* Roy Orbison, J.P., George Pelecanos, Otto Penzler, Seba Pezzani, Walter Pincus, Sydney Pollack, Kelly Quinn, David Rayfiel, Robert Redford, *Rivages Noir,* Cliff Robertson, S. J. Rozan, Derya Samadi, Roberto Santachiara, Lorenzo Semple, Jr., Yvonne Seng, David Hale Smith, Bruce Springsteen, Steely Dan, Jeff Stein, Buffy Ford Stewart, John Stewart, Roger Strull, Max von Sydow, Simon Tassano, Richard Thompson, Shirley Twillman, Paul Vineyard, B.W., Jess Walter, *The Washington Post,* Tim Weiner, Les Whitten, David Wood, Bill Wood, The Yardbirds, Jesse Colin Young, Warren Zevon, and Anlan Zhang.

LAST DAYS OF THE CONDOR

1

A cover team locked on him that rainy Washington, D.C., Monday evening as he left his surface job, flipped up his hood and stepped outside the brass back door for the Library of Congress's John Adams Building.

A white car.

Indicator One on the white car as a cover team: Tinted windows and windshield.

Indicator Two: A car engine suddenly purred to life as raindrops tapped the blue mountaineering coat's hood over his silver-haired skull. He spotted the white car parked illegally at the Third Street corner of A Street, SE, a townhouse-lined road that ran from Congress's turf through Capitol Hill's residential neighborhood.

Indicator Three: The chill in the rain let him see wisps of gray exhaust from behind the purring white car. As it didn't pull out into traffic. As it sat there, wipers off, heaven's tears dotting the tinted-glass windshield.

Indicator Four: No one hurried to the white car from a nearby home. No commuter leaving work splashed through the rain toward it to be greeted with a spouse's kiss.

Indicator Five: He felt the cover team. Chinese martial artists talk about the weight of a stalker's eyes, feeling the pressure of an enemy's *chi*. Kevin Powell—who got his throat cut in an Amsterdam brothel the year the CIA-backed Shah fell in Iran and the Soviet Union invaded Afghanistan—Kevin insisted you must pay attention to your guts, your feelings. Or you'll get butchered on some midnight street. Or wake up screaming in a windowless steel room. That Monday D.C. evening, the silver-haired man standing on hard cement in the chilly spring rain knew what his tingles meant.

One, two, three, four, five. Like fingers of a hand, a hand that meant *cover team.*

He looked to his left along the sidewalk running past the Adams Building with its six stories of white stone plus basements of knowledge and secrets. The brass door behind him could withstand a car ramming into it or a giant gorilla banging on its locked metal.

Walking down Third Street as if to pass the Adams Building came a man: Caucasian, dark hair, late thirties, white-collar-warrior suit and tie under a tan coat, brown shoes not built for running, holding a black umbrella in one brown-gloved hand, the other holding a cell phone pressed to his face as he said: "Where are you located?"

Could have been a cover team communications ploy.

Feed data via a phony phone conversation.

But the silver-haired man didn't think so: *Too unnecessary.*

Suit & Tie Cell Phone Umbrella Man walked closer, now nearly perpendicular to him, brown shoe step by brown shoe step rippling puddles on the dark, wet sidewalk.

A stream of strangers joined Mister Cell Phoning Suit & Tie, all looking like innocent Americans headed somewhere after work on a Monday evening.

If your cover team is there for wet work, sometimes a

better option than running from them is to imbue your assassination with Elevated Exposure Costs.

The silver-haired man in the blue hooded coat put his hands in its storm pockets as he stepped away from the Adams Building. Run, he did not run. He joined that stream of eight pedestrians, five of whom walked under umbrellas. Like a blue penguin, he wove a crooked course to the center of the umbrella group—innocent bystander casualties being a classic EEC.

The smart move.

Unless the cluster of strangers he'd slid into belonged to the cover team.

The Israelis used a twenty-nine-member cover team for the Dubai hotel room assassination of one Hamas executive back in 2010.

Of course, a cover team didn't necessarily mean a hit or mere surveillance: these strangers walking with him under their umbrellas on a Washington, D.C., Capitol Hill sidewalk could be a snatch crew who he'd now let surround him.

But none of his fellow pedestrians vibed *hunter* as they marched toward the restaurant row on Pennsylvania Avenue just up from the House of Representatives' three castle-like office buildings. He flashed on sixth grade, walking to school with other kids. He remembered the smell of bicycles.

We're all kids on bicycles, he thought. *A flock of birds.*

Wondered if *whoosh* his flock of umbrella strangers would sense a shift in the universe and bank in another direction and *no,* he hadn't run to join them, though he remembered the joys of long-distance jogging before his knees, back, and the bullet remnants in his left shoulder all conspired against him.

Back then, he'd been passing through Washington as the

powers that governed this hydrogen-bomb-blessed country argued about blow jobs in the White House. When he jogged during that work trip, his aches & pains decoded as *no more running for fun & fitness*. He accepted that evolution.

But like he remembered blow jobs, he remembered how if you run fast and there's a littler kid near you, you've got a better chance because Beirut snipers prioritize wounding the littlest kids to tempt rescuers. *Run,* you can make it to that doorway if only that doorway were there instead of the intersection of Third Street, SE, and Independence Avenue where it's tonight, you don't have a bicycle, and there is no sheltering doorway or black-smoke stench of burning rubber tires at street barricades.

Focus: This is here. This is now. Washington, D.C. A chilly rainy evening.

Hold on to that.

You can hold on to that.

Sure.

There's a cover team on you.

If nothing else, have some pride. Make them work for it. Whatever *it* is.

Third Street, SE, is a one-way route from busy Pennsylvania Avenue, passes Independence Avenue that heads out of D.C. like an illusion of escape. Third Street means rows of parked cars on both its Adams side and across the road in front of town houses often harboring political action committees for Congressmen whose public offices are two blocks away, only a four-minute walk from their official duties to private property where they can make legal phone calls whoring money for elections. Any car—

Say a cover team's white car.

—any car parked facing the Adams Building on A Street, a block up from Independence Avenue, was stuck with a right-hand turn: the only legal choice. Parking where they had meant they couldn't pull out of their surveillance spot, turn, and drive down Third Street the wrong way against traffic, the route he always walked home, so—

So the cover team knew his predictable route. So they were that kind of *they*: informed, *briefed*. Knew he wouldn't—*couldn't*—walk past them, put his shoes on the sidewalk of A Street, SE, that close to *where*. Once they knew he was out & on the move, on foot, going toward Independence Avenue, the white car would turn right with the one-way traffic flow as if they weren't covering him.

Then circle the block. Given rush-hour traffic, rainy weather, odds are they'd be at the intersection of Pennsylvania Avenue and Third Street, SE, in time to spot whether he diverted down to Pennsylvania's main street of bars & restaurants or continued on his normal route up Independence. Odds are, he'd be walking with the outbound traffic, so the white car could slowly drive behind him, leapfrog parking to keep him ahead of their windshield. Eyes on him the whole way home.

Just in case they'd put shoes on him, too, he didn't look back.

Instead, he scanned the bright lights of the restaurants and chain-store coffee shops and bars that served both Congressional staffers on beer-bottle budgets and lobbyists who made champagne flow. He cranked his head as far as he could toward the giant yellow-bulbed traffic sign that had been set up after 9/11, with its insistent arrow ordering all trucks to turn off Pennsylvania Avenue's route between the House of Representatives office buildings and the Congress's iconic Capitol building.

He saw the Congressional cop standing in the rain beside a cruiser parked next to the flashing detour sign. Wouldn't matter if the truck that disobeyed the detour warnings was a cargo of dead tree products driven by a lost fool or a suicide bomber's rental truck packed with fertilizer in a concoction powerful enough to devastate two city blocks, the cop knew he'd need to risk holding position in the kill zone and try to shoot out the truck's tires before it blasted America's core of government.

The silver-haired man peered past the cop outside his cruiser and the yellow detour arrow. Told himself that through the bare trees and over two blocks away, he could see the edge of the Capitol building; visualize its dome, white and slick in the rain.

Before and for a while after Watergate, the FBI maintained a covert station on Pennsylvania Avenue in the first block of private commercial buildings he saw as he turned back from staring at Congress's domain. That former FBI lair had been a flat-faced concrete building with an underground garage, always shut. He'd learned about the building back when *this life* began. That the three-story gray building belonged to the FBI was gossiped about by all sorts of people who worked on Capitol Hill, including many of Congress's members and staffs. If any of them had the guts and power to ask the Bureau about the building at the corner of Congress & the world, the official FBI response labeled the substation "a translation center."

Sure, he thought: *And how does that translate?*

He stood on the corner of the block where he now worked, obeying the traffic light, faced down Independence Avenue with his head turned in its blue hood just enough so his peripheral vision might pick up the appearance in traffic of, *say,* a white car.

The DON'T WALK traffic signal he faced glowed orange with a line slashed across the orange stick-figure image of a walker and counting-down flashes:

. . . 30 . . . 29 . . . 28 . . .

On the way to his rampage in 1998, a lone gunman from Montana who killed two Congressional cops while trying to shoot his way into the U.S. Capitol visited the for-decades town house headquarters of a fringe political group across the street from where the silver-haired man now stood. What the diagnosed paranoid schizophrenic gunman wanted from that political group is unknown, but he was drawn to them. The since-moved political group's revered but deceased founder kept a life-sized black metal statue of Adolf Hitler at the foot of his bed and the group openly but illegally sold the same phony cancer-curing drug that failed to save movie star Steve McQueen.

. . . 3 . . . 2 . . . 1 . . . WALK flashed in traffic-light white and freed a white stick figure.

Hope you get where you're going, telepathed the silver-haired man to the white stick figure in the signal light as he himself crossed the road for his eight-block journey with the traffic flowing along Independence Avenue.

He didn't flinch when his peripheral glimpse of the intersection showed the rain-slick black street reflecting a red light and an idling white car.

At the next corner, Fourth Street, he let the green light send him to the right, across the road. Didn't look behind him up that street to *where it happened back then.* Didn't look sideways to see the white car he hoped was blocked a few vehicles back, not at this crosswalk revving its engine to roar off the slick street, smash into his blue-hooded figure, hurtle him to his death or under crushing wheels.

Rundowns are tricky.

What's the Mission Risk Allotment for the cover team in the white car?

He made it to the curb. Didn't look back as he turned left, his usual route.

Don't let them know the weight of your eyes.

The rain stopped two blocks later as he slogged past the long low barn of Eastern Market where J. Edgar Hoover had worked as a grocery delivery boy before his left-wing subversive hunting days during the last century's Palmer Raids.

Cars whooshed by his lone man walking. Homeward-bound citizens.

Four blocks later, as he neared his corner of Eleventh Street, he spotted the white hat and dark blue sweater of a Navy officer leaving the neighborhood dry cleaner's that often served personnel stationed at the nearby Commandant of the Marine Corps. Flashed to cradling a Marine corporal shot in Afghanistan as that man, *that boy,* who'd saved his life flopped, gurgled, and died without ever knowing the truth about his fellow American or having it told to his family back in Oklahoma.

The Navy officer at the dry cleaner's that evening drove away in a minivan outfitted with an empty child's car seat.

The silver-haired man noted the red neon sign in the dry cleaner's barred window:

ALTERATIONS

If only.

He focused on an address just past the corner: 309, a two-story blue-brick town house, four black metal steps up to its turquoise door, walked one step after another until *finally,* as he slid his key into the lock, he looked behind him, checked his four to eight.

The white car cruised past him, made a languid U-turn into one of the parking spots across the street, tinted windshield facing where he stood on his front stoop.

The white car's engine turned off.

No one got out of the white car. Those tinted windows stayed closed.

He slid his key into the turquoise door, unlocked it, turned the doorknob. His eyes caught a downward flutter by his thigh, as low as he could reach without showing what he was doing every day when he put a stolen leaf in the crack of that door he pulled closed. Last summer, he'd worried his neighbors might notice their bushes being nibbled in this neighborhood that had yet to be invaded by the deer who bred madly in D.C.'s Rock Creek Park.

But no one mentioned that to him. Not even the wild-haired witch next door who often stood inside the low black iron fence around her front yard with her yippy filthy white dog to scream: *"This place ain't near nothing like North Carolina!"* She was wrong, but like everyone else, he never risked correcting her.

Today's torn leaf fluttered from the doorjamb.

But it could have been replaced.

Someone could still have opened that door. Be inside.

Fuck 'em.

Then he was in the house, his back pressed against the door he slammed shut. Sundown pinked his landlord's lair, the furniture she'd left when she had to rush move to her new GS insurance & pension federal job in Boston on seventeen days' notice in order to hold her place for computation in the next budget. The flat-screen TV his Settlement Specialist insisted on delivering to him hung over the fireplace in which he burned papers along with pine wood bought from pickups from West Virginia that cruised the city during the cold months. The green sofa belonged to the landlord, as did the brass bed upstairs in the front bedroom where he slept. The rest of the household contents—a couple chairs, a little of this and less of that, what was on the walls, a satellite radio with speakers, those things belonged to him.

No one attacked him in pink light streaming through the house's barred windows.

Yet.

This row house with common walls was six paces wide and twenty-one paces deep. That journey from the front door back to the kitchen took a jag around the bathroom under the stairs leading up to where he showered and slept. He walked toward the kitchen, glanced at the brown wooden stair eye level to him, and saw that the clear dental floss strand strung there had not been blown or pushed away by a passing shoe.

Or the strand had been replaced.

If they were that good, that compulsive, waiting upstairs in his bedroom or in the junk-filled back room, hiding in a closet, then *fuck it: call him already deleted.*

He checked the downstairs half bath: toilet seat up. Only his reflection haunted the mirror above the sink. He pushed the blue hood off his silvered head.

No one waited in the kitchen, the inside back door still shut and the outer iron-bars door locked in place. Beyond those black iron bars waited a wooden slab deck in a tiny fenced backyard with nothing but a waist-high Japanese maple tree rising from an engineered square opening in the deck. The hook & eye latch on the weathered gray back gate looked in place, but anyone who walked past that wooden fence in the alley knew such security was a joke.

They let him have knives.

For cooking.

The Settlement Specialist casually mentioned that need as she filled his shopping cart on their Household Establishment visit to the Fort Meade PX between D.C. and Baltimore where the National Security Agency keeps its official headquarters. He had a set of steak knives, plus a kitchen counter wooden slotted "display holder" with a knife sharpener, a rapier-strong fileting blade, a serrated-edge bread knife, a monstrous isosceles triangle–bladed *tres Francais* carver, and a butcher blade that reminded him of Jim Bowie and the Alamo.

He refused to clutch one of those knives, sit *waiting* like a doomed fool on the living room couch.

His blue shell mountaineering coat was soaked. He shivered with that chill. Took the coat off, started back toward the living room—

Stopped in the bathroom to urinate. Told himself that wasn't nerves.

Heard the flush shut off as he hung his wet coat up on the living room coatrack.

They were out there. *Of course they were out there!*

But they might not come tonight.

Or ever.

The cover team might be taggers on a Sit & See, or—

The turquoise front door boomed with a knock.

2

The ones we don't know we don't know.
—U.S. Secretary of Defense Donald Rumsfeld

Faye Dozier eased the front passenger door shut on the car they parked on Washington, D.C.'s Eleventh Street, SE, unbuttoned her mid-thigh black coat and kept her eyes on the blue brick town house with the turquoise door. She flexed her empty bare hands. That comfortable metal weight rode on her right hip.

Her partner, Peter, slammed his driver's door shut, didn't give a damn who heard it or looked through the evening light to see her walk around the car to him. He wore a tan raincoat with something bigger than a book bulging its inside pocket and carried a silver briefcase.

"Remember," he told Faye. "You're lead on this one."

"Why him?" she said as she stared at the house, calculated approach angles. "Why now? He's not on today's action list."

"After that thing we just did over across the D.C. line in P.G. County, the Taliban guy who was fucking worried about his son getting into college, this guy is between there and base, due to hit our screen, so . . .

"We got a shot," said Peter. "Might as well take it now."

Like two hawks dropping off the same tree branch, this man and woman stepped together across the street toward the blue brick house.

"Not like you've got anything better to do with your night, right?" he said.

Then laughed.

Like he knew, thought Faye, knowing he didn't, no one did, no one could.

Peter said: "Heads up on this one, rookie."

"When did I become a rookie?"

"Out here, with me, rookie is who you are. You're lead on this one because I say so. Because it's time for you to pop your cherry."

"You're such a charmer."

"So people keep saying."

They reached the side of the street of the blue brick house with the turquoise door.

"Listen," he said to this *Okay, so she wasn't a rookie* partner he'd never asked for, never wanted. "Take your time. Do it smart, do it thorough, do it right.

"And then," he added as they reached the four black iron steps leading up to that narrow row house on the edge of Capitol Hill, "do the same for the report."

"*Wait*: What are you going to be doing while I'm doing that?"

"My report, my identifier, *your* work, my seniority time off-line, because, like you said, you got nothing better to do with the rest of your night." He smiled.

"I didn't say." She held the palm of her left hand low where anyone but another professional like him might have missed the *hang back* signal.

Peter retreated from the black iron steps. Stood where optics let him catch *movement* in the windows on both floors of the blue brick town house, where his sight line included her on the black iron stoop:

As she knocked on the turquoise door.

3

Runaway American dream.

—Bruce Springsteen, "Born to Run"

This is how you live or die.

Answer the knock on your front door.

That turquoise slab swung open to the rush of the world and *they* filled his vision.

Woman standing on front stoop.

Man posting on the minuscule front yard made of dirt and stone inside the black metal fence.

She's the shooter if this is a Buzz & Bang.

But she just stands there on the front porch, green eyes reflecting him.

Call her thirty, maybe older. Black coat unbuttoned. Pretty, but you might not spot her in a crowd. Brown hair long enough for *styled,* not so long it's an easy grab. An oval face from the stirred ethnicity of modern America. A nose that looked like it had been reset above unpainted lips. She carried her shoulders like a soldier. Her hands hung open by her side, her right strobed *gun hand*. No rings. Dark slacks. Sensible black shoes for running or a snap kick.

She waited in this sundown that smelled like rain on city streets.

The hardest thing.

Waiting.

For the right moment. The right move. For the target to appear.

Her backup man cleared his throat. *Familiar, he seems* . . . Older than her, say fifty, a bald white guy. Muscle in the mass under his tan raincoat. Silver metal briefcase in his left hand, right hand open by his side. He posted backup, a line of sight past her to whoever opened the turquoise door or moved in the front windows, yet the way he cleared his throat marked him as a boss, or maybe—

Standing on the black iron front stoop, she said: "How are you?"

Tell her the truth: "I don't know."

"Can we come in?"

Her backup man added: "You can't say no."

"I could, but what good would that do?" Walk backwards into the living room.

They follow. The man in the tan coat shut the door to the rest of the world.

Her smile lied: *"Damn,* I hope we got the right guy! Your name is . . . ?"

"I always hated my born-with-it name: *Ronald.* For a while, I think I was *Joe.* Sometimes I think I'm other names like *Raul, Nick, Jacques,* and oddly, *Xin Shou.*"

The bald man said: "Call him—"

Peter! The bald backup man's name is Peter!

"—Condor."

There it is.

The silver-haired man said: "That's a fluke."

"Why?" she asked.

"Because the Agency rotates code names. An earlier Condor was Frank Sturgis, a Watergate burglar. Then me. With a code name back then, I felt like two people. One was regular *me,* one was like the movie version of your life where you're better-looking and smarter and get the right girl. While I was locked up, the code name rotated. Something happened to that guy, they won't tell me what. But they redesignated me Condor."

"Right here, right now," she asked: "What's your work name?"

"Vin."

"Why Vin?"

"*The Magnificent Seven.* Steve McQueen played him. As long as I'm a lie, I might as well be a cool one."

"My name is Faye Dozier. What do you want me to call you? Condor or Vin?"

"Your choice."

Bald Peter set his silver briefcase on the floor, pulled an iPad out of his tan raincoat. "Remember the drill?"

"You made the first home evaluation visit after my Re-introduction Settlement."

Faye said: "Was he a charmer back then, too?"

"He had more hair."

"I was as bald then as—*never mind.*"

Faye caught the flicker of Condor/Vin's *gotcha* smile.

Peter told the silver-haired man: "Kick off your shoes, go stand with your heels and head pressed against that bit of bare wall next to your fancy radio."

Your black stocking feet press the wooden floor. Don't get caught flexing your knees or bending your hips to sink your weight but make yourself smaller, the option *no shoes* gave you. The wall of bricks grinds against your skull.

Bald Peter raised the iPad to scan the man with his back against the wall.

"Hold it," said Peter. "Calculations for metrics and . . ."

The iPad snapped that picture with a FLASH!

"Turn to your right," said Peter. "Face your radio setup."

Faye asked: "So you like radio? NPR, the news networks?"

FLASH!

"I'm lucky. I can afford a radio that pulls in more than that from satellites."

"Tell her about *clongs*." Disdain filled the voice of the bald man with the iPad. "Messages from outer space. And turn with your other shoulder to the wall."

"She knows."

"No I don't."

"Sure you do. You're somewhere doing something or thinking something. Maybe driving in a car. A song comes on and it's dead on target for whatever's happening, for who you are right then. The universe dialing in the exactly right soundtrack as everything epiphanies the message and feels perfect, feels . . . *yes!*"

FLASH!

"That's a *clong*. I don't like news on the radio. That's the invisibles telling me *what is*. No *clongs*. Songs coming out of the cosmos show me something, lining up *what could be,* something about me, us. Like poetry. A movie or a novel."

"But one kind of radio broadcast is about your real life," she argued.

"Yeah."

Peter muttered: "Instead of voices in his head, he gets *clongs*."

Condor said: "What helps you make sense of it all?"

"Me?" Peter held up his iPad. "I follow the program."

She asked Vin: "Any problems at work?"

"I show up. Do what's there. Come home."

"Just so you know," she told him, "there's no record of complaints."

"And yet, here you are." He smiled: "How do you like your job?"

"Better than some."

"Better than some people like their jobs, or better than some jobs you've had?"

"Yeah." She strolled toward the kitchen.

Bald Peter stared at the wall covered by taped-up newspaper articles and photographs, torn-out color bursts of magazine art, poems and paragraphs ripped from books destined for the furnace, scissored chunks of phonograph album covers and insert sleeves of lyrics from that all-but-dead medium. He raised the iPad.

FLASH! Working his way along the wall. FLASH!

Okay! It's okay, routine, just routine. The crazy's collage wall. Random weirdness. Textbook predictable. Nothing to see. Nothing to analyze.

Get your shoes on, go after her!

Faye stared into the kitchen's refrigerator.

"Milk, hope it's fresh. OJ, that's good. Styrofoam boxes of leftovers, butter. Vanilla yogurt: for the granola on the frig? Blueberries. Your bread looks dead. Mind if I throw out those single-serving boxes of white rice? You must eat a lot of Chinese."

"We all do."

She stared through the bars over the back door to the wooden deck.

Said: "You look like you're in good shape."

See the tile floor come rushing toward your face then you bounce up away from it again. Your arms burn. Set after set after set of pushups on prison time.

Then in the Dayroom where the murder has yet to happen, Victor comes over, says: "It's about your root, not your muscle. Your center, not your fist."

Faye, *if that's not just her work name,* Faye angled her head toward the fenced-in back deck beyond the bars, and with genuine curiosity said: "Is that where you do *t'ai chi*?"

"That's where I practice the form. I 'do' *t'ai chi* all I can."

"Like now?"

Give her the void of *no answer.*

She said: "Show me upstairs—*no*: after you."

They passed Peter on his way into the kitchen to make another FLASH!

"Do you always make your bed?" she asked after she'd glanced into his upstairs clutter room, moved to the room with the brass bed where dreams made him fly.

"Who would do it for me?" He shrugged. "It's a rule of lockup. A symptom."

She looked at his clothes hanging in the closet. Peter will photograph them, too.

Then she led him into the bathroom. Blue towel over the shower rod. The toilet seat up. She opened the mirrored door for the medicine cabinet above his sink.

"Holy shit."

On two shelves of the medicine cabinet stood lines of prescription pill bottles like squads of brave soldiers. Pill bottles labeled with words ending in "-*zines*" and "-*mine*." Drugs whose names contain an abundance of "*x*'s." The pills famous for clearing cholesterol-clogged arteries. Blue pills. White pills. Football-shaped pills. Gel tabs. Hard yellow circle pills. Green spheres.

She pointed to one prescription bottle: "The TV commercial shows that drug is for a man and a woman sitting naked in side-by-side bathtubs as the sun sets."

"The daily dose is also used for us guys with certain . . . *gotta go* issues."

"Really." She pushed him with her stare. "What's her name?"

"There is no *her*."

"Or he, I don't—"

"Romance is not as easy as just popping a pill."

"Tell me about it." She softened her eyes. "If there's nobody now, who was your last somebody?"

Ruby lips pucker: "Shhh."

"I'm not sure."

Faye said: "There are other medications for guys who need to go to the bathroom all the time. Maybe your doctors want the best you can be for you."

"Sure, that must be it."

She looked at him. Looked back at the army of pills. Her eyes scanned the chart taped to the inside of the medicine cabinet door. "Thirteen pills a day."

"*Everybody must get stoned.*" Looking at her, even as young as she was, she recognized that Bob Dylan quote.

"Is there anything they're not treating you for?"

"Cancer or similar assassins."

"You think a lot about assassins?"

"*Really?* That question? From you?"

Peter's heavy footsteps clumped up the stairs outside his bathroom.

She asked: "What's your diagnosis?"

"Post-Traumatic Stress Disorder. Paranoid Psychosis. Delusional. Alienation. Anxiety. Depression. Recurrent Temporal Dysfunctionality. Identity Integration Flux."

"That means . . . ?"

"Sometimes it's like I'm in a movie. I get lost in time. Can't handle remembering. The pills, the program, you: all to help me keep forgetting and move on."

"How's that working?"

"I get flashes. Dreams. Ghosts. But I'm functional. Mainstreamable."

They heard Peter enter the cluttered back room to upload its data with flashes.

"Names drift," Condor told her, Vin told her. "Like Kevin Powell. I can tell you how he died but who he was . . . *Beats me.* I remember Victor and four other friends locked up with me in the CIA's secret insane asylum but not my first boss in the Agency. I remember reading books for something called Section 9, Department 17, where something happened I can't think about it *don't make me think about it don't* . . .

"The big blur ends when I got out last year. What came before that . . . I remember the first woman who showed me herself naked, but not who I killed. Sometimes when I think about killing, I smell a men's room. I remember alleys in Beirut. Bars in Amsterdam. Airports in jungles. A Brooklyn diner. L.A. freeways. Getting shot. Shooting back. How to snap your neck. The Dewey Decimal System. The triggering event that made Dashiell Hammett a political lefty. Lying and laughing and creepy-crawlies on the back of my neck as I'm walking down some city street I can't remember the name of and that a 1911 Colt .45 automatic is my weapon of choice."

"Any changes lately?"

Lie. "All the time is all the same. Okay, as long as I keep taking the drugs."

"Medicines," she corrected.

"Aren't medicines supposed to make you better?"

She shrugged. But his question made her join him in a smile.

He said: "The diagnosis says what's best for me is not knowing what I don't know I don't know."

"But you know what real is."

"If you say so. I know I'm really here, or really at work. But sometimes . . .

"Sometimes I'm sitting on a park bench. Blue sky, trees. No sounds—or maybe whooshing. Smells like human sweat. I'm holding an iPad in my lap. In the tablet, I watch what a drone is seeing. Broadcasting. Wispy clouds. Clear air. My view drops from the sky. Buildings get distinct, bigger, then rushing closer in the center of the screen comes a park and benches and I know that if I can just keep sitting where I am, what I'll see any second now in the iPad screen is the drone's view of me."

She's staring at you, jaw dropped.

Bald Peter clunked his aluminum briefcase down outside the bathroom. Said: "Could you step out so I can get my data snaps."

In the hall, Faye pointed to the bedroom, then to the junk room. "I didn't spot any computer. Do you have one? A laptop? A tablet? A diary or dream journal or—"

"No, I comply with the conditions. And you know my cell phone is barely smart enough to call the Agent In Trouble line, plus you've got all its records."

From inside the bathroom came FLASH!

"Hey, Condor!" yelled Peter. "You know what's going to come out in the pee test, so tell us: you still buying pot from that anthropologist at the Smithsonian?"

FLASH!

"*Jah* provides."

The grin Peter carried out of the bathroom held no sympathy: "You get busted, you're busted and gone."

"Guess we all better be careful then."

Faye said: "What does the pot do for you?"

"I get stoned. On my own terms. Well, at least on the terms of my own drugs. I also drink a couple glasses of red wine now and then, but that's almost on doctor's orders. Clean out my All-American arteries and veins."

"Whatever," said Peter as he clicked open the silver

briefcase on the floor. "Drop your pants so I can be sure your business is your business, fill this plastic cup for me."

Peter's black marker pen wrote CONDOR on a specimen cup's white label.

"Sorry. I went right before I answered your knock on the door."

"Motherfucker!" said Peter.

"Are you talking to me?"

Faye freed the wisp of a smile.

Does she know that movie? Or is that just about you? Or is it all swirling data?

Peter shook the thirsty specimen cup at the man he'd come to see: "There's a glass pot of cold coffee on your kitchen stove, figure it's from this morning. I'm going to microwave a cup of it, you're going to drink it *pronto,* no matter how hot it comes out of the zap, then you're gonna fill this cup so we can go!"

"Milk."

"What?" said Peter.

"I like milk in my coffee. Won't take much longer to zap."

"Motherfucker." Peter clumped down the stairs.

Vin said: "*Motherfucker.* I wonder if I ever got to have kids."

He blinked. Stared at her. "You could have been my kid."

"You're nothing like my father."

"Why not?"

"You're here," she said. Too quickly looked away. "We should go with Peter."

"If I'd have asked, would your credentials have matched his?"

"What do you think?" she said.

"He's Homeland Security, has been for so long *before*

doesn't matter. You're . . . You're with the Firm. My old Firm. The CIA."

"We're both with Home Sec's National Resources Operations Division."

"By choice?"

"Let's go downstairs," said Faye.

"And speaking of *going*," she added as her inertia pulled him away from where he'd been: "Where's your car parked?"

"You know my release disallows having a car," he said at the top of the stairs. "My driver's license is just so I carry passable pocket litter. But I remember driving. The car skidding sideways on black ice."

"Me, too."

They clumped down the stairs.

"Lucky for you," she said as they stood alone in the living room, "the Metro has a subway stop nearby."

"It's a Blue Line."

"Yeah, but it connects to—"

"I don't like to ride the Blue Line."

BEEP! The microwave in the kitchen.

"So . . ."

"The Blue Line is blue. I like the Red Line."

She closed her eyes. Rubbed the bridge of her nose with a pinch of her fingers. No nail polish. She smelled of no perfume. Stretched her eyes open wide.

"Eyes tired?"

She shrugged.

"Glare off your white car even with the tinted glass?" asked Condor.

Faye said: "We didn't come here in a white car."

4

Zombie Jamboree
—The Kingston Trio

Faye swung open the turquoise door, stepped out to the twilight target zone.

The safest scenario put her walking down this side of the street, the line of cars slumbering along the curb putting at least some metal between her and the white car with tinted windows parked down the block and across the road.

She stepped off the black iron stairs. . . . Slid between two parked cars.

Thought she heard Peter shouting curses from where he was covering her—crouched behind the cold glass of the blue brick house's front upstairs bedroom window.

Figured he always took the safest scenario as she marched onto Eleventh Street to stride a direct diagonal intercept angle toward the white car, eleven, now nine vehicles away.

She heard a car engine start.

Keep both hands down! she ordered herself.

Power steering whined. Tires cried.

The white car snapped on a dragon's yellow eyes.

She froze like a deer caught by the headlights.

The white car whipped out of its opposite-curb parking,

swung through a U-turn, a 180-degree speed-away *gone,* red-eye taillights vanishing into the coming night.

Faye thumbed STOP on the iPhone she'd kept hidden in her low-hanging right hand and pointed toward the white car.

"You got nothing about nothing," Peter told her five minutes later in the kitchen that smelled like hot coffee as they watched the replay in her cell phone:

The waist-high wobble view of the sidewalk . . .

Parked cars she'd slid between . . .

This neighborhood's long line of cars slumbering across the street . . .

Two seconds of wild-shot bare trees and rooftops/jerk back to the parked cars—

Blinding yellow headlights, a blur of white, red taillights zooming away.

Condor said: "The white car is something. And turns out, real."

"Real?" said Peter. "You say a white car followed you home. We didn't see that. Then *gee,* what are the odds? A white car *really* was parked out front, but . . . went away."

Condor looked at her. "What do you think?"

"What I think is, I don't know," she answered.

"That's something."

"Oh yeah," said Peter. "Maybe actionable data will come to her in a *clong* on the way back to base. Me, I think you hit your herbal medication before we knocked on the door. Now take this cup, drop your drawers and give us the sample so we can go.

"And for the record," he added as Condor took the plastic cup: "Is there anything we representatives of a grateful nation need to do for you?"

Condor said: "You've already done me."

He told Faye: "I don't care, but you don't need to watch."

Unbuttoned his pants, let them fall to the kitchen floor.

She left the two men, walked back to the living room through the gauntlet of ripped newspapers, book pages, and torn trinkets taped or thumbtacked to the walls.

Maybe because of what she knew she had to do later, when those two men joined her, she let *Condor* shimmer into *Vin*. Saw him as a silver-haired man, blue eyes she figured the Agency fixed with laser surgery to increase his operational index. Strong cheekbones, clean jaw. *Fit* like she'd said, but showing six decades of wear & tear. Yet electricity crackled through him: *Is he more than just his diagnoses?*

"Vin," she said, "I put my Home Sec card on the mantel."

Peter packed up his silver briefcase: "He's got more Agent In Trouble and help-line numbers than he can use, plus shrink team monitors. Let's go."

"If you see that white car again," said Faye as Bald Peter's impatience pulled at her, "or anything else . . . *Call.*"

She left Vin with a real smile she lost as soon as she heard the turquoise door slam behind her, locked onto the tan raincoat back of Peter.

Faye stormed her partner: "What the hell! Why were you such a dick to him?"

Peter stopped in the middle of the street. Whirled to face her. His briefcase cut a silver streak in the night. "There are only two kinds of people—"

"Bullshit! There are as many kinds of people as there are people. Don't sell me some '*us and everybody else*' crap to justify you doing our job like a jerk to that guy!"

"What I was gonna say is, there are only two kinds of people who end up doing *our* job: *agents who fucked up* and *agents who don't give a fuck.*

"We're *so* fucking essential to national security. We check on old men who defected from the Soviet Union that has been gone almost as long as you've been alive. We make sure an al Qaeda guy who came over to us in Morocco six years ago is getting his checks while sitting on his ass with nothing to tell us now we don't already know. And now from what I saw back there with Condor, you give a fuck."

Peter shook his bald head. "That means they stuck me with a fuckup. Once a fuckup, always a fuckup, so woe the fuck is me.

"What did you do, huh?" he said. "Give a fuck about the wrong thing?"

"Maybe I shot my supervising agent."

"Like I care," he told her. "Like you could now. Hell, you're too busy wasting energy on a long-gone-to-crazy-town stoner like Condor."

"You saw that medicine cabinet. It's more like he's being stoned."

"Lucky him. He's got his legs, arms, his dick. He's together enough to bring in a paycheck plus *agent down* benefits. And teams of us check on him to see if he's all right."

He stabbed his forefinger at her: "Who's gonna check on me and you?"

"Maybe he deserves it. Earned it when he got fucked up on some mission."

"Or," said Bald Peter, "maybe we're just babysitting to keep Condor from fucking up. I don't give a fuck, so fuck him, I don't have to make nice to stoner fantasies."

He gave her his back and walked toward the car, whose keys he had.

"There are three kinds of people," Faye called out in the night: "*The living, the dead,* and *the turned-off.* Guess

which you are. It's this era's *big thing*. Movies, TV, political metaphors, fashion shows in New York. You're a *'don't
give a fuck'* zombie."

"Yeah," said Bald Peter. "And there are a lot of us. Get
in the car."

5

A candy-colored clown they call the sandman.
—Roy Orbison, "In Dreams"

Condor stared at his reflection trapped in the big-screen TV above the fireplace. That dark screen flowed with ghosts.

He looked at the business card left by the woman spy: Faye Dozier. *Is any of her data true?*

She and her bald partner had seen his walls. Uploaded flashing photos.

Flashings swirled Condor to a warehouse in some American nowhere.

Where one room held a sweat-stinking wrestling mat.

Where the schedule had him make gunshots *bang!* inside the baffled Shoot Room.

Where in the musty upstairs office amidst empty desks and silent typewriters stood a blurred man who had Saigon scars in his heart and a white Styrofoam cup of steaming coffee in his hand as he told twenty-something Condor: *"Learn to live your secrets in plain sight so when the bad Joes go looking, there's nothing to find."*

Then he tossed the scalding coffee in Condor's face.

On that rainy 2013 night in Washington, in his rented home, Condor flinched.

Scanned what he'd hidden amidst oddities taped to

his wall—newspaper photos, pages cut from books or magazines. So he'd remember, he poked tiny triangles into the "intelligence indicators." Other articles taped to his bricks also had holes, but only items patterned with three dots were clues hidden in plain sight on his seemingly mad wall.

If only he knew what the clues meant:

A *New York Times* photo of a black Predator drone flying in a blue sky with a silver full moon and a cutline that read: "Like our other less-lethal high-tech toys, unmanned crafts feed our addiction to instant gratification."

Cut from a book, a photo of a black-hooded British SAS commando peeking over the roof wall of the Iranian embassy in London during 1980's terrorist siege.

The 9/11 smoke-billowing World Trade Towers.

A 2013 newspaper photo showing Chinese citizens wearing white medical masks as they practice *t'ai chi* in a Beijing smog so thick people standing ten feet apart were barely visible to each other or the camera.

A movie review's black & white photo showing the black leather trench coat hero in a swirling sci-fi *kung fu* battle.

A *Washington Post* portrait of Bruce Springsteen that claimed "The Tao of Bruce" transcended the bitter battles of America's two ruling political parties.

A news service snapshot of a running man ablaze with orange flames from gas he poured over himself in the streets called Arab Spring.

Newspaper photos of paintings: Edward Hopper's lonesome American gas station, another artist's portrait of a woman, black hair tumbling around her shoulders, her face a pink blur.

The one *easy* triggering image: a newspaper photo of a soaring condor.

If only.

Call him *Vin* as he microwaved leftover Chinese food, ate a meal that tasted like cardboard and soy mush.

He carried a glass of water and a razor blade upstairs.

Strung a web of clear dental floss across the top of the stairs—a flimsy barricade, but it might startle an assassin, create noise of his arrival.

Vin used the razor blade to shave that night's prescribed pills, his gamble that a low but correct percentage of those drugs in the Home Sec/NROD urine test could pass as a testing, marijuana masked, or other aberration within Tasers & straitjackets–enforced limits. He swallowed his chop-shopped pills, flushed their shavings down his toilet with a pang of conscience for the fish swimming at the end of the sewer pipe in the Potomac River.

Condor raised his gaze from the bathroom sink.

Through his diminishing medication state saw the bathroom mirror reflecting a face that somehow had become his. He saw his eyes: impenetrable whites surrounding scarred blue orbs centered by zooming ever wider black pupils.

6

We deal in lead.
—Steve McQueen, *The Magnificent Seven*

Faye hid the flash drive in her closed fist as she navigated through a maze of cubicles in search of her target on the limbo level.

Or as it is officially known: the Situation Center for Task Force Umbrella of the Office of the Director of National Intelligence, the SC for TFU of ODNI, a vast spy factory that fills the fourth level of the ODNI Complex Zed building in Washington, D.C., not far from Wisconsin Avenue's "upper Georgetown" strip of stores and a private high school with an annual tuition that exceeded the cost of two years at the state university where Faye punched her ticket.

Call it the limbo level.

She always had, back when she was at the CIA.

Now I'm in limbo, she thought as she searched for her target in this windowless cavern's overhead lighting. Blue lightning bolts pulsated atop the walls of green cubicles. The blue lightning bolts zapped upward like Jacob's Ladders, only instead of being designed to inspire intellectual curiosity in hormone-frazzled teenagers, these blue lightning bolts block hostile rays beamed at the cubicles' computers. The limbo level hums and crackles like Dr.

Frankenstein's laboratory. Electrified ozone wafts through the cavern's smog of cubicle-caged office workers.

The limbo level houses units shuffled off the flow charts of America's sixteen officially admitted intelligence agencies, a catch-all centralization of crews whose duties drift across bureaucratic lines. A dozen desks are designated PITS—Personnel In Transition Stations, sometimes given to an agent, analyst, or exec on the way up some secret ladder, more often assigned as the pre-pension parking place for burnouts or screw-ups or rebels who were right but failed to cover their ass.

At least I dodged the PITS, thought Faye.

So far.

The hidden flash drive burned in her closed fist.

The National Resources Operations Division she'd been exiled to fills one corner of the limbo level's factory floor, looks like a Smithsonian museum diorama with plastic walls encasing a replica of a police detective squad consisting of twelve workstation desks shared by Faye and nineteen other field agents plus a plastic-walled "inner office" of command stations for the two executives in charge of monitoring defectors, PINSS (Persons In Need of Security Supervision) like Condor, and miscellaneous but unglamorous national security/intelligence tasks shoved by agencies like the CIA, ODNI, FBI, NSA, Secret Service, DIA, and DEA into the post–9/11 beast called Homeland Security.

She glanced at the time display on a workstation's computer: 7:22 P.M. outside in the real world of Washington, D.C.—ninety-eight minutes until 9 P.M.

You can make it. If you find Alex, you can still—

She spotted him inside a cubicle where the blue lightning bolts were turned off.

"You got a sec?" said Faye as she plopped down beside the thin redheaded man wearing a white shirt, striped tie, and khaki slacks.

"Barely," Alex said as he packed tools he'd used to install a hard drive in the cubicle's computer. "I got called off the bench!"

"Good for you."

"Hey, the Dumpster I backed into still works. I drove by and checked."

"Great, I'm kind of—"

"Anxious to tell me what you did to end up here?"

"No. What I can tell you is I need to cover my partner's ass to get out of here."

She handed the flash drive to her instructor, Alex, from a CIA Technical Services' training class whom she'd spotted wandering the limbo's floor the week before.

"That's cell-phone video. A white car flipping a U-turn, twilight. The headlights blur the license plate, but as it drives away, maybe between the taillights' red eyes . . ."

Took Alex four minutes, most of which was spent pulling software from the classified national security grid onto this cubicle computer's new hard drive.

"Virginia tag," he said as they stared at the screen's enhanced image. "I live in Virginia. You can tell me if you do, too. It's not like your real name or—"

A new window appeared on the computer screen: a completed government form.

"Weird," said Alex. "The DMV check says that plate belongs on a green Jeep Cherokee, not a white Nissan like you got here."

Faye suppressed the urge to grab her cell phone.

The white car knows we—somebody—was there. Drove away. If it comes back, it won't come back until it's sure it's safe, so time, I—we—Condor's got time.

He's a crazy old burnout who no opposition cares about, she told herself.

And if I bust protocol, go around my Supervising Agent Peter before officially filing the report I'm inputting in his name, trigger Alarm Status because of a license plate anomaly . . . *First*, given *my* status, nobody will do anything except cover their ass. *Second,* another strike on me, and I'll be lucky if I end up nailed to a PITS.

Plus she only had eighty-four minutes until *then*.

Took Faye twenty-three minutes to finish the F409 SIDER—Subject In Domicile Evaluation Report. She used the desktop her partner Peter favored, his sign-ins, prose style. Noted Condor's occasional irrationality yet lucidity and mainstream functionality, the log number for his urine sample, even their discussion of marijuana, and in Recommendations, after describing Condor's "possible paranoia" about the white car and its license plate anomaly, keyboarded: *"My partner Agent Faye Dozier strenuously urges immediate elevated security response and follow-up to potential hostile surveillance of subject as inferred by observation & verification of suspicious vehicle."* Clicks of the desktop mouse attached iPad shots of Condor and his house, plus the white car video and DMV files.

She read the electronic report one last time.

Saw nothing that would get her into trouble she couldn't handle.

Addressed it to the proper data submission points, cc'd it to her NROD agent e-mail account and her CIA agent account, plus her legendary CIA crew chief who, after her *horror show,* fought to be sure she *only* got detailed from the Agency to Home Sec's NROD and the limbo's floor. She cc'd Bald Peter's agent e-mail account, wondered whether he'd spin on whatever bar stool he'd snuck off to and check his phone when it *pinged!* with this report he'd

officially written. Whatever shit he'd give her because of
her recommendation would stay between them. Unless he
believed in payback. If so, that would come at her as if by
chance, without his fingerprints. But they'd both know.

She stared at the text on the glowing computer screen.

Made sure the F409 SIDER designation read CONDOR.

Clicked SEND.

The report shot into the cyber ether like a bullet into the
darkness.

She needed five minutes to log off duty, leave the limbo
level, ride the elevator down to the ground floor, get
through exit security screening and visibly *not hurry* out
the revolving door in the plexiglass walls that separate
Complex Zed from a stone plaza with its anti–truck bomber
cement planters and sentinel lights that hold back the
night.

Security cameras recorded her walk from the building
to her car in the bottom level of the employee garage. She
employed no obvious countersurveillance measures. Drove
her middle-American maroon Ford clear of the parking
garage.

Forty-nine minutes. I've got forty-nine minutes.

Faye lived in an apartment building on the edge of
the cupcake emporiums, art theater movie chain, and
yoga businesses district known as Bethesda-*landia*. That
"*landia*" slang suffix came to life early in the twenty-first
century when the middle-class but staid Maryland suburb
of Bethesda morphed into one of the ritziest inside-the-
Beltway 'hoods as Georgetown and upper northwest D.C.
became too crowded to house all the lawyers & lobbyists
& corporate & media stars who turned America's Martin
Luther King assassination riot–scarred capital into the big-
money burg it became beginning with *beat-an-assassin*
President Ronald Reagan.

She scanned her mirrors as she drove.

Jumped a red light. Careened through a quick left she didn't need to take, another right, another left, zoomed down an alley past green Dumpsters like the one tech guru Alex expensively backed an Agency car into after two too many beers at a Thai dinner with Army officers from that country who he was training and who the case officer masquerading as his assistant was scouting for recruitment.

Faye's mirrors revealed no yellow-eyed cover team beasts behind her.

Security cameras logged her driving into her apartment building's underground parking lot with thirty-eight minutes to go. She backed the Ford into her space on the second level, pushed the *wee-oo* lock button on her key fob as she marched through the gasoline-musty light of the concrete car barn to the elevator, rode it to the LOBBY. Found nothing in her snail mailbox, but it could have looked suspicious if she hadn't checked.

Faye guessed right: no one presided at the front desk. Night clerk Mr. Abdullah was probably sneaking onto the manager's computer, searching for news about his family in Somalia who were trapped amidst drought, famine, pirates, a United Arab Emirates funded anti-pirates army with its own Washington, D.C., law firm, fundamentalist Muslim revolutionaries, and twelve thousand blue-helmeted African Union peacekeeper troops trained by outsourced CIA contractors operating from a razor wire–surrounded complex at Mogadishu's airport that Somalis called "the pink house."

She spotted no one else in the lobby. Security cameras for the front door, the lobby, and the rear exit logged her as she walked past the elevators to the stairwell. A routine analysis might conclude she was an office worker who felt in need of exercise.

Stairwell security cameras only covered the first flight of concrete steps and the top-floor stairwell with its roof exit. She floated up two flights of stairs, her heart pounding hard but not from the climb—every day before work, she ran a paratrooper's six miles on a park trail and then home here to run up and down the building's nine flights of stairs.

Faye stopped at the cinder-block walls' switchback between the fourth and her fifth floor. Used her cell phone to link with the computer in her home, checked the log of her computer's camera she'd interfaced with motion detectors aimed at her unit's entrance and the sliding-glass-door balcony for her one-bedroom apartment's living room: NO ACTIVITY. The computer camera via her cell phone screen showed the inside of her locked apartment door and the shadowed living room *empty* of any intruder.

She went to her apartment. Slid inside. All was silent. Shadowed.

Faye stared out her balcony's closed sliding glass door to the purple night shotgunned with twinkles of city lights. Imagined that off in that darkness, she could see the glow of the Lincoln Memorial, the White House and Capitol she'd driven past earlier that day, the place where she'd once escaped termination.

A wall switch snapped on a lamp of here & now. The couch, the chairs, the coffee table from some garage sale. A chin-up bar filled the top of her bedroom door.

The clock read 8:31—twenty-nine minutes *until*.

Risk a shower.

She tossed her black coat over a chair, hurried to the dark bathroom, snapped the light on and shed her suitable-for-running-or-kicking shoes. The holstered .40 Glock on her right hip went on the back of the closed toilet, hilt toward the open shower. The cell phone and her credentials went on the sink. She unbuttoned her blouse.

The bathroom mirror captured her image. She wore a black bra. The thick pink scar slashed from her sternum to her right hip. Her slacks opened easily: a year after the last surgery, she still liked to wear them loose. They drifted to the floor. She laughed as she imagined insisting to some Boss In The Sky that *black bikini underwear is indeed professional attire suitable for the office* and less likely to bind if you throw a kick. Those black panties peeled off as she stood tall in the mirror. Black bra, arms like thick silk curtain sashes, smooth stomach. That scar.

She unhooked her black bra. Let it fall.

This is me.

Head of short hair. Green eyes special only in how they see, not how they look. Mouth special only for what it never will be allowed to say. *No wrinkles on my neck, not like Mom, not yet, and there'll be a "yet," there will be and . . .* Breasts some guys think are too small but only afterward. She felt her nipples pucker with the chill in the apartment.

Turned the shower on full blast, as hot as she dared, tried to lose what she had to do and an old man named *Condor* or *Vin* in the steam and the wet. She spun the shower handle. Icy water flooded her to *focused.*

Drying with a white towel, standing in the tub, tossing the towel over the shower rod, stepping out of the tub, pulling on her slacks, slipping into the blouse and buttoning the four buttons up to her neck. *Unfasten the top button.*

She shoved the black bra and panties into the hamper.

Tossed her shoes into the bedroom, heard them clunk against the wall, the floor.

Stared into the bathroom mirror.

Be you.

But a little lip gloss wouldn't be wrong.

The mirror watched her slide the gloss tube's smooth tip over her lips.

A snap off of the bathroom light and that reflection became only a black shape.

She took her credentials and gun with her, put them in the bedside night table drawer. Slid the drawer shut. All the way shut.

Don't think about the black pistol-grip shotgun in your closet. The Glock rigged under the other side of the bed. The snub-nose .38 revolver hidden for a quick grab in the kitchen, or the 9mm Beretta strapped under the couch. Or where the knives are.

You gotta do this with your own hands.

Nine minutes until nine o'clock.

What if he's late? What will that tell you? What will that mean?

What if you can't go through with it?

She was never supposed to need to do this.

Her left hand floated to her bedroom doorjamb like it was the dance studio bar across a mirror as she straightened her spine, rose to her full height in Third Position, let that motion float her right arm up to a graceful half-moon curve above her head, then sank straight down with her knees bending out and her bare heels rising off the bedroom carpet with *Le Grand Plié*. She held that deep crouch, felt her inner thigh muscles stretch and loosen and then *up* she came with a swoop of her hand as the ballet motion became grabbing & pulling the incoming punch of an invisible attacker while smashing her palm strike into his hyperextended elbow.

The digital clock on her night table read 8:53.

Seven minutes.

The lamp in the living room cast more shadows than light. Scant illumination came from the white bulb under the metal hood over her stove.

Faye unlocked her door to the world.

Stood far enough away not to get overwhelmed by a charge-in breach.

Stood in the flow of the indigo night beyond her walls of glass.

Stared at the unlocked wooden door. At the chain dangling from its mount.

You spend your life waiting for whoever walks through your door.

The tick-tock world fell away as she stood there. She made herself breathe from her belly. Made herself not look at any clock. Made herself *wait*.

The knock—*one two three,* soft but strong.

She stretched from her neck cords to her at-her-sides empty hands.

"Come in," she said.

The door swung open. There he stood, backlit by the yellow light in the hall.

He said: "How's my timing?"

"You're here now," said Faye.

BOLO (Be On Look Out *for*) data: male, Caucasian, early thirties, six foot two, 177 pounds. California-surfer prematurely thinning blond hair, face like a handsome eagle, glasses over blue eyes giving him a scholarly look, but muscled, graceful.

She faked a light tone: "Shut the door behind you. And lock it."

He even put the chain on.

The government-lawyer-like black shoes he wore were a workweek away from their last shine. His dark blue suit complemented his classic blue dress shirt and nicely offset his red cloth tie that dangled like a leash knotted around his neck.

The best move against a man wearing a tie is to charm your way in close, half your arm's length away. *Smile*. Slide the tie into your loose two-handed grip and lift it off the man's chest like you're admiring—

—grip the tie, whirl & duck so it's pulled across your shoulder as you slam your hips back into him and snap forward/down, jerking the tie toward the floor. Odds are, he'll flip over your back like judo's *Morote-seoi-nage* throw, crash at your feet as you go with inertia, drop your knees into his chest. Even if your knees don't explode his heart, his skeletal shock, vertigo, and blasted-away breath let you grip the tie's knot with one hand as your weight presses through that fist to his throat and your other hand pulls the slack end of the tie. His face turns purple, seventeen seconds to unconsciousness if the strangling tie cinches the right blood vessels as you choke off rescuing air.

Other options include *ring the bell,* the quick grab & jerk the tie to slam him bent over/*down,* but it's easy to miss the debilitating knee-to-face contact. The *garrote from behind* technique is more likely to fail and put you in position to get fucked up by his spinning counter than it is to be your clean kill.

Still, grab a man by his tie and you're halfway home.

He filled his eyes with Faye, said: "How was your Monday?"

"Same-old, same-old."

"I'll pretend that's good."

He watched her barefoot pad toward him, nine steps away, eight.

"Getting to see you," he said, six steps away, five, "that's not good, that's the best."

Faye slid her arms under his suit coat, along his *empty* belt until they met at his spine. Her face pressed against him. Her head reached the knot on his tie, his red cloth tie that smelled like wool and *smell,* she could smell him, his heat, his skin.

Arms wrapped around her—strong, eager.

She said: "Did anybody see you come here?"

"I hope the world."

When she said nothing, he told her: "I saw nobody who knew they saw me."

"Did you tell anybody?" she asked.

"I know your deal," he said.

Your: Subtle assertion through a possessive adjective.

Faye mimicked a TV game-show host: *"And the answer is . . . ?"*

He moved her just far enough away so they could see each other face-to-face.

Said: "We're our secret."

Then he kissed her. She felt his surprise—*joy*—as she opened her lips and flicked her tongue to his, led it into her mouth. Lifetimes later as she pulled her face away from his, her hands still holding his sides, their chests heaving, he brushed her cheek with his right hand, said: "So you said tonight has got to be special?"

He watched her nod as she said: "One time."

"Not just one-time special," he said. "We've got—"

She pursed her lips. *"Shhh."*

Her hands slid from his spine, under his suit coat, along the sides of his blue shirt.

"I have to know something," she said.

"What?"

Faye's fingers found his tie, his red cloth tie. Held it. Stroked it.

"If I can trust you."

"I've—"

Her fingers closed on the tie with a slight tug to snap short his sentence.

She said: "It's not you, it's me. I have to know I can allow myself to trust."

"What more—"

Her finger covered his lips as if now he were supposed to say *shhh*. She slid her fingers to his shirt collar. Watched his blue eyes dance behind his minimalist-frame glasses that would have been dorky on anyone else but on him . . .

Just right.

He blinked as he felt her undo the knot of his tie.

Pull it off his neck with a *snap!*

She turned and walked away from him, barefoot, red tie dangling from her hand.

As she walked toward the open-door bedroom where he, where they'd been before, yes and yes and even *yes,* but now . . .

She felt him pulled into her wake. Felt the burn of his eyes as she unbuttoned her blouse and let it fall, her back naked as she reached the bedroom. She unfastened her slacks, stepped out of them. Knew he was close behind her, his eyes on her bare ass, *like my whole world's globe* he'd said to her once as he ran his hand over its curve while she lay on her stomach hiding her smile, as his lips pressed against her flesh *there*.

The lamp on her night table glowed.

Naked, on her knees, she worked her way to the black iron headboard, heard his shoes hitting the floor, the zip of his pants as she lashed the thick end of the tie to the black iron. Kept her back to him as she knelt on her bed facing the wall where she'd mounted a framed poster-sized sepia art photograph, a wild horse plunging through a blizzard. She knotted the skinny end of his red tie around her wrists with loops she'd learned at E&E (Escape & Evasion Course). Her teeth tightened the last loop.

Trapped, unable to undo the tie alone, she turned, the short bond making her stretch out on her back, lie naked there in front of him.

He'd undressed. Put his glasses somewhere. Stared at her with wonder.

Said: "What—"

"Now be who you are," she said. "Do whatever you want, not what you think won't piss me off or will make me happy. Forget about me—fuck that, *fuck me.* I'm tied up because I have to know that I can't guide or stop you. I have to know that I've still got the ability to trust. To tie myself up without a chance, without a choice."

He climbed on the bed beside her, rose on her right side as she lay stretched out naked, her hands lashed up to the bed above her head.

And he kissed her *oh* and she kissed him back—

—nothing in her need said she couldn't take what she could get on the way to what she had to know—

—deep wet kisses, probing gnawing each other's mouths, faces, neck, *he's kissing my neck, down and oh yes, squeeze I'm not big yes yes I am squeeze oh!* he sucked her nipple into his mouth, his tongue rubbing it, lush and full and wet, she was so wet as his kisses marched down between her breasts, past the scar, not dwelling on it, not ignoring it *yes,* kissing down she saw his blond hair as he pushed her thighs wider—

Spun like by a strong wind, Faye felt and watched him pull her to the edge of the bed, stretch her out from her hands lashed above her head, turning her so she was straight, legs dangling over the edge of the bed where he knelt between them and *oh, oh yes, his mouth, his tongue and then his hands on me, liquid fire caressing my breasts heart going to explode his hands won't stop don't*—

She heard herself scream, a guttural animal cry as again and again—

Then he was up on the bed.

Pushing her.

Rolling her over.

Lashed wrists and she was on her stomach, facedown on the bed.

Then *oh,* rolling her on her right side: pressed against her, kissing her, *taste us, yes* her left leg up over his before his hand came down, pulled her leg higher guiding himself *in* and he cupped her ass pulled her so tight/deep to him and—

His pressed his left hand over her mouth.

So she couldn't scream.

Tied to the bed, I'm an idiot can't strike, deep in me, he's deep in me, pulling me closer, his hands pressing my hips wet hard to his, can't fight—

He said: "I love you."

Her world spun. She felt the push of one hand over her mouth, cupped like the perfect take-out of a sentry, pressing her against her spine so she couldn't look away, his other hand pulling her hips into him *oh* so she can't spin free, use her legs *oh* . . .

Can't turn away from his blue eyes: "*I love you.* You can't say anything back even if you want to or think you need to. Even if you're afraid, don't know what to say. Because you trusted me to take that away from you. You trusted me to do what I'm afraid you'll reject. But you can't reject a thing because no one can hear you scream.

"Whatever you want to say, you're not ready. Too soon. Too much. Too *not now.*

"So after I take my hand off your mouth, you got nothing to say. I'm gonna say it when I want to, when it bursts out of me because I'm all tied up in loving you. But you can't tell me you love me or you don't. Not now. Someday that's gotta come and now you know you can trust somebody—*me* because I love you, I love you!"

One hand pushed her smothered mouth back against her spine, one hand pulled her thrusting hips against his and he must have felt her come & come again as he cried out *I love you* like a mantra, faster and faster until he cried out beyond words as she screamed against his hand that cupped her mouth and muffled the sounds of her soul.

Done, frenzy slipping away, muscles relaxing, her leg heavy over him, his left hand now cupping her right cheek, the brush of his thumb against her swollen lips.

She had to coach him on how to free her hands.

That made them laugh and the laugh was everything, let them hold each other, slide down on the bed, let her lie across his chest, put her right cheek on his flesh where if she listened, she could hear every beat of his heart.

He kissed the top of her head, the coconut shampoo smell of her hair.

They held each other loosely. They held each other for forever.

His name is Chris Harvie.

"Don't worry," he said. "Love isn't lethal."

Faye said: "Sure it is."

7

Sure it is.
—Faye Dozier

"Now, it's now!" shouted ghosts to Condor as he woke the next morning.

He rolled out of bed.

Eased back the window's white curtains.

Dawn in Washington. Headlights still glowed on vehicles driving past his home. A seagull's shadow flickered across the morning's sunlit wall of town houses across the street. The dog next door barked at a passing jogger. A car horn honked.

Vin imagined he heard a bugle blowing reveille three blocks away at the redbrick-walled, block-sized barracks for the Commandant of the Marine Corps. The Marines host public parades there on summer Friday nights. Bands play rousing patriotic horn & snare drum anthems. Rows of brave & brilliant men and women in snappy white hats, tan shirts, and bright blue trousers march to the beat of political witches banging spoons against a low-bid government black pot boiling on the bonfire of time. What the witches see & sip from that brew helps decide if flag-draped coffins get shipped home to Beaver Crossing, Nebraska, and Truth or Consequences, New Mexico, and Shelby, Montana.

No white car lurked beyond the cool glass of the second-floor bedroom window.

Not seeing them means the Oppo has great street smarts.

Or they're not there, thought Condor. *Or something else happened.*

Today, it'll happen today.

Condor let the white curtain drop back over his window.

Didn't look in the mirror on the cabinet of stoned sanity as he used the bathroom.

No matter what's coming, when you gotta go, you gotta go.

He didn't look at the mirror as he washed his hands.

Left the bathroom with the gurgle of the flushing toilet.

Like a Marine on patrol, he descended the staircase. Turquoise door, still shut. No ninja crouched in the living room. Nothing seems disturbed on the wall of secrets. No vampire waited in the downstairs bathroom. *Do not look in the mirror!* Seen through the back door bars, the weathered gray wooden fence surrounding his blond pressure-treated wooden back deck contained no ambushers, only the lonely Japanese maple tree.

He flipped the wall switch. *A miracle*: light arrived. He filled the teakettle on the gas stove where he lit a blue flame with a *whump*. Vin ground his coffee. Threw out the leftover old brew, rigged the coffeepot to receive the new. Padded back upstairs in his bare feet to change. As the water boiled.

Wearing a torn black sweatshirt over a thermal top, gray sweatpants, white socks and black, hard-soled Chinese *gung fu* shoes, the silver-haired man had to be careful not to slip on the wooden stairs as he came back downstairs to rescue the whistling kettle.

Get your coffee cup later:

If your hands can't be strategically full, be sure they're operationally empty.

He flipped the locks and jerked open the turquoise door.

No one shot him.

No visible watchers hunched in the cars parked on both sides of the street, in the neighborhood windows, on the roofs. A Metro bus rumbled past: *Commuters. Citizens.*

On his front step waited thinly filled plastic sheaths of *The Washington Post* and *The New York Times*. He fetched them inside and locked the turquoise door. Put the newspapers on the breakfast bar in his kitchen. The refrigerator didn't explode when he opened the door to get his carton of milk from cows adulterated with antibiotics. He splashed milk into his cup, added coffee, set the cup on the breakfast bar. Shook *The Post* and *The Times* out of their condom sheaths. Turned on his satellite receiver and the radio blasted dead Warren Zevon singing "Lawyers, Guns and Money" and—

A civvies-clad Marine Recon Major clutches a stack of newspapers in some D.C. room. There's a not-so-secret war in Nicaragua. A murdered secret agent in L.A. The Marine doesn't know you exist, you're his shadow backup, and why, **why** are we reading the newspapers' horoscopes?

Hello! thought Vin to those new ghosts: *Who are you?*

But *like that,* like the steam coming from his coffee cup . . . Gone.

Must be the drugs not working.

Yes!

He read the news, *oh boy.* Didn't find his name in the reports of what's supposed to be real and who's supposed to be dead. Finished two cups of coffee. Knew he'd miss newspaper comics when they went extinct. Used the bath-room two more times (usual). And never looked in that downstairs mirror, not even a glance.

Outside on the back deck, he flowed through *t'ai chi*. Cool air surrounding him smelled like a city alley but so far D.C.'s stench is not the smog that strangles Beijing like in the three-dotted photo taped to Condor's brick wall. *T'ai chi* moving from his center snapped Condor's arms and hands up & out to *Ji*—press posture.

Victor in the asylum saying: "Power generates from your hips."

Hips thrusting Wendy's naked body astride him, he's on his back, Wendy says: "They lied to you. I was shot dead in the head." Her eyes close, she whispers: "You got it! You—"

Gone. Here, now, whenever: she was really gone.

But good to see her again. *Whoever she was.*

The *remember* caught Condor in his shower: *W.* The Marine Major was named *Wes. Wendy* and *Wes. Wendy* was long dead when Wes . . . when Wes . . .

Clouds of knowing vanished in the shower's pounding steam where it felt good to shave with hand soap and his own safety razor, not have to shave with a blue-handled disposable razor at one of the mirrored sinks in a commu-nal bathroom watched over by two orderlies who weren't as tough as they thought. Condor considered modifying the shave-off of his morning antipsychotics and anxiety meds—if that's what they were.

Naw. Too late to turn back now.

He razor-bladed his morning *stay-sane* doses down a full two-thirds.

Chose a blue shirt over a clean thermal undershirt. All his pants were black, kept him from getting lost in indecision or fashion indecency. Gray socks. Black shoes suitable for running or kicking.

Walk downstairs. Listen to the radio. Stare at the wall of secrets.

Nothing. Not a whisper. Not a *clong*.

"Well, that sucks," he told his empty home.

Yesterday the weather report said sunny and it rained. Today the report said rain and the sun shined. He thought about wearing the black leather sports jacket that his Settlement Specialist claimed was out of covert guidelines, too flashy, made him look like someone, made him look . . . intense.

"Yeah," he'd told her.

She'd decided not to push.

And that morning, he decided to wear the gray wool sports jacket instead: *You don't want to ring the wrong bells.*

Condor locked and left his house to walk to work. It was Tuesday, 7:42 A.M.

The crazy woman's dog barked at him as he walked to the corner of Eleventh Street and Independence Avenue, turned left and retraced his steps from the night before on sidewalks he'd tramped hundreds of—

Paris, Hartwell stalking you twenty meters back at your eight o'clock across the cobblestone road. Popped up smack where he wasn't supposed to be. Good that he's a bad brick man, you spot him, is he alone, what's he packing, and at the U.S. embassy where you can't go, can never go, they won't give you shelter, embassy walls draped red, white and Bicentennial blue and you're out here quickening through a swirl of French impressionism while behind you, with his every hungry step, with fanatic's fire blazing his eyes, Hartwell yells: "I know who you are, motherfucker!"

Now *here,* standing in the giant doorway of the Adams Building, a castle-like structure, the white-shirted Library of Congress cop wears a brass name tag: SCOTT BRADLEY.

The cop wears a holstered 9mm pistol you could grab. But don't.

"Hi, Vin," says Officer Scott Bradley.

Condor gave him a smile like this was just another day. Emptied his pockets. Passed through the metal & bomb detector archway without setting off a *beep.* Collected his personals and walked to the elevator bank, pushed the lone brass button for DOWN. Only then did he glance back at the open doorway's *noir* shaft of tall light where Officer Bradley stood as the first overt line of defense. Saw no ghosts.

As if Badge Bradley could stop them.

Call him *Condor,* call him *Vin*: he rode an elevator down alone.

His underground office waited behind a brown steel fireproof slab he opened by tapping a code into the digital lock that transmitted to the Library of Congress's central security computer linked to Homeland Security's NROD and its data flow to Bald Peter and Faye, the woman who wasn't his daughter.

His watch read 7:58 A.M.—more or less two hours *until.*

If I'm lucky.

Condor stood in his basement office's open doorway. Reached to an inside shelf for the rubber wedge he'd conned out of the carpenter's shop. Propped the door wide open to secure a view of the hall. Flipped on the lights for his domain.

Regular Library of Congress workers called it *the Grave Cave.*

Janitors had helped him move his scarred gray steel

desk so he sat behind a restricted-Internet computer on his left and two carts to his right, everything rigged so he could stare out to see anyone who passed by. Or tried to charge in. As he sat there.

Who cared if propping open his door created a firing lane to his heart.

Some ways we get shot are too sweet to forbid.

Eight in the morning. Underground at the Grave Cave. Two hours *until*.

Plain pine boxes made chest-high walls around his desk. On any given day, there'd be fifty boxes. Condor relished the smell of pine. Appreciated that the aroma of forests covered odors of must & dust & rot from the contents of the crates.

Books.

Blond white pine crates packed full of books.

Books from de-acquisitioning Air Force bases. Books from veterans' hospitals. Books from Army bases in Germany near where their Soviet Union counterparts no longer existed. Books from deactivated ICBM Minuteman silos dotting the northern prairies. Books from black site prisons that considered vetted knowledge about the outside world as acceptable torture more than rebellious escape. Books from classified CIA staging centers and duty stations. Obama-era books already cycling back from the under-construction, $3 billion-plus secret NSA spy data center in the same mountains of Utah that also shelter nine thousand members of the country's leading Mormon polygamous sect. Books snagged & bagged on commando raids of terrorist lairs. Books CIA *closers* retrieved from the rubble of dead spies.

But not just any books.

Novels. Short story collections. Scripts. Barely read books of poetry.

Volumes of what wasn't real—but was maybe, *just maybe,* true.

Histories, technical manuals, biographies, *how-to*s, TV-famous authors' declarations about *what I say really happened & what it means,* self-motivation manuals by parroting strangers, tomes of faith or brilliant insight and other nonfictions were vetted and disappeared further back up the chain of Review & Resolution.

What came to Condor in the one-room underground Grave Cave at the Library of Congress were stories swirled out of our ether by souls who couldn't stop screaming.

Mistakes were made, *sure*.

More than once Condor crowbarred open a crate and found stacks of what the previous century called *record albums,* cardboard-jacketed, flat black petroleum-based discs containing aural transmissions accessible only with technology most American homes no longer possessed. Sometimes he cried for what he found that he knew he knew but knew not from where. *Clongs* seized him. He'd scissor out an album jacket photo of a singer-songwriter or a scene that riveted his eyes. He hid such photos down the back of his pants and carefully walked home through the security detector arches to tape the stolen photos on his wall alongside newspaper salvages and prose or poetry lines also scissor-stolen from R&R crates.

Magazines sometimes survived R&R's usual toss straight to the trash. Condor tore out the *Spy vs. Spy* cartoon page of a satirical *Mad* magazine from 1968 when revolution fired the streets of Paris, of Prague, of Mexico City and Memphis, Tennessee. Two months out of the secret Ravens' asylum and into this job, Condor uncrated a stack of *Playboy* magazines—the publication starring a centerfold of women photographed nude with makeup & touched-up flesh. Many such photo fictions had already been torn from those magazines, but one surviving image nailed his eyes: a quarter-page color snap of a 1970s beauty "revisited" a decade later, a photo of her leaning on a brass bed, the mirror behind her reflecting a tumble of mature honey hair, a black garter belt above her moon of curved hips, black stockings on dancer-long legs in ridiculously decorative black stiletto heels, breasts heavy & low & full maroon *there,* her smile wide as her eyes look to see who's looking at her.

Condor taped that garter-belted photo to his brick wall a respectable distance from his newspaper art portrait of a lone woman with black hair tumbling to her simple blue sleeveless blouse and a pink surreal featureless swirl for her face.

One image reveals so much, one image reveals so little. The space between is enough to drive you mad.

Still, he stole and poked them both with the secret three holes: *Pay attention!*

But that wasn't his job.

What *they*'d told Condor to do was glance at each book, each discard of vision, and in as few possible heartbeats, decide which cart claimed the work.

Cart A went to Permanent Storage.

Cart B carried its captives to the pulp machine.

Condor once convinced a transport team to take him along to Cart B's disposal site, a thirty-seven-minute drive in the cramped truck's front seat with two men who argued about professional football and how fucked up the Navy had been and wasn't that the best time and when could they smoke with this *what the hell* stranger sitting between them. Seagulls circled the packed earth landfill, a wasteland where putting a pulping plant probably made environmental sense. Condor watched books he'd tossed onto

Cart B get dumped into a green steel maw, heard them sprayed with chemicals and the whining gear clanging crunch as they became a gooey mass poured into vats on other trucks and taken away to be turned into . . . *What?*

Rules prohibited Condor from saving more than one Cart A of books a week.

He agonized over filling Cart B with doomed books. As ordered, flipped their pages. Looked for indications this volume had been the key to a book code. Scanned for spy notes cribbed in the pages or classified documents slid in there and forgotten. He pondered *security risk quotient* amidst coming-of-age novels, con artist swaggers, flesh peddles, *noir* sagas, soul-revealing classics, cop stories, alternative times fantasies or science fictions, heaving bosomed romances about the President's lost love. A book could earn Cart A salvation with its reputation for *getting it right,* for tradecraft revealed or created, secrets shared.

Every workday made Condor unpack crates.

"You're a reader," said the Settlement Specialist. "This is like your first spy job."

"You mean it's not something the CIA made up so they know where I am?"

She smiled.

Helped him keyboard cover lies to his Library of Congress employee file.

Now it's now!

No shit, he told the new ghosts that Tuesday morning as he sat at his desk framed by the open doorway of the Grave Cave. At 9:51 he tossed a novel about a gunfighter come home to a small town on Cart B, then stared out his open door.

Waiting.

Clicking heels came up the hallway on the other side of

his wall, to his left, his heart side. Footsteps coming louder, drawing closer to his view through the open door.

Here she comes.

You've been here before.

Here and now spy-you spend hours tracking her data. The more you know, the more you need to know. She's fifty-three. Born in the year of the dragon. Never married, no dependents. *That makes no sense.* Employed by the Library of Congress for eighteen years, plus a three-year loan-out to the Smithsonian. First employment line on her résumé: U.S. Senate staff for five years when she was young & smart & schooled and snapped her way over the sidewalks while taxi passengers gawked at her. She rents an apartment in a building not yet transitioned from rundown to hip. Two promotions during her years here at the Library.

She heel-clicks into view beyond your open door.

Curly blond hair with gray roots falls off a widow's peak to brush a sigh of breasts under her form-fitting business black dress. Navy blue trench coat slung through her shoulder purse strap. She's thicker round the waist than she can change, black-stockinged legs yoga-muscled past trim, metronome-swinging arms and black shoes. Her face is softly lean, rectangular, tan skin that pulls sunlight. Smile lines scar her wide, thick-lipped unpainted mouth. Her eyes stare straight ahead and not at you.

She marches past the open doorway. Out of sight.

Heels click on the hallway floor. The elevator whirs.

There you sit.

Again.

Still.

Find out or fail forever.

Vin whirled from behind his desk. Charged out of the

Grave Cave in time to see the elevator close. His fingers woodpeckered the brass call button. Magnets pulled his eyes above the elevator to its floor indicator bar: "G" lit up.

The parallel elevator whirred open.

Vin jumped into that cage, pushed the button labeled "G." Got—

There she is! Clearing security. Slipping into her navy blue trench coat.

Once Vin walked behind her and her coworkers as she said: *"I hate the cold."*

She's going out the tall shaft back door.

Condor made it outside to the cool spring air in time to watch her turn right at the end of the Adams Building's U-shaped driveway.

No white car parked across the street.

You don't see the Oppo because they're street smart.

She's walking toward Pennsylvania Avenue with its wall of cafes and bars.

Vin tried not to run, knew he was born to *this* no matter what he could remember.

Get closer behind her. She's got the light, the WALK sign with its white stick man flaunting his freedom and for you turning orange *fuck him* scurry across the street. Call it twenty, call it fifteen steps from the drift of curly blond hair on her navy blue coat as she crosses Pennsylvania Avenue, opens the dinging-bell door of a Starbucks.

Coffee, thought Vin. *She's going for coffee.*

The world flowed around him. A silver-haired man standing still on the sidewalk as tourists and troopers used their time to walk past him. He made a perfect target.

Opened the tinkling-bell door of the Starbucks.

Ten o'clock, coffee hour, but it's only her standing in the line at the counter.

Sapphire blue eyes lightning-bolted him.

She said: "Sometimes you go crazy if you don't get outside the walls."

"Screaming doesn't help," said Vin.

"You've been hawking me for five months and that's the best you've got?"

The espresso steamer hissed.

He said: "You give what you can."

"And get what you get." Her smile seemed sad. "Not bad."

"What do you see in those old movies you catalog for the Library?"

Words whispered through her thick, soft lips: "It's what you don't see."

Walking toward them on the other side of the counter with a green apron over her white blouse came the young barista whose parents had fled El Salvador's right-wing death squads. Their daughter dreaded the refugee-spawned, international MS 13 gang that now ruled her family's suburban turf five miles away from this Capitol Hill Starbucks. The gang used its Web sites and Facebook tattoos to stalk for victims and volunteers and you never knew *until*. The barista told the *gringa* who spent drugstore dollars to stay blond: "Here's your cappuccino, ma'am."

The "*ma'am*" brought a different smile to the blond woman. She took the steaming white paper cup from the barista, walked to the Starbucks door.

Turned back, looked at the man watching her go, said: "So who are you?"

"How 'bout Vin?"

"How about Vin."

He shrugged. "I wasn't . . . all the way right with what I said before."

"Confessions don't impress me anymore," she told him.

"It's not about impressing you. It's about being true."

He met her sapphire stare.

Said: "Sometimes screaming lets you know you're there."

Sapphire eyes blinked.

She said: "Vin. *Huh*."

Turned and left the cafe with the tinkle of the bell above her exit.

"Can I help you, sir?" The barista stayed a patient professional.

"I'll take whatever she had." Vin did not chase the blonde who watched movies.

Some foggy instinct told him too bold *now* might generate *never*.

Plus if his cover team were active, he'd paint her with cross hairs.

Standing outside the Starbucks window, shrouded in black Giselle presses her hands and face against the glass and screams.

Waves of *I don't know what or why but I'm sorry!* washed Vin back to work.

The barista returned to the counter with a steaming white cup in her hand and before she realized she didn't see him there said: "Here's your coffee, sir."

All she ever knew about that and what came after was the strange man's *gone*.

All his empty sidewalks led him from the Starbucks back to the Grave Cave. He ate lunch in the library's cafeteria hoping to spot her at her usual table but knowing he wouldn't and being right. He sat in his office and stared at the open doorway. Come five o'clock, he stepped out onto the Adams Building stoop.

No white car.

No new ghosts.

His gray wool sports jacket kept the cool of the evening away from his bones. Concrete pushed his black shoes toward the home he'd been allowed. Cars rushed past him on Independence Avenue, their headlights turning on to probe the coming dark. The air smelled like spring. No cover team, no brick boys on his tail, no snipers on the rooftops, *no white car,* there was no white car now but there was one yesterday.

Of course there was. Sure there was.

A green leaf fell from its protective wedge when he opened his turquoise door.

As it should.

As it would—if everything is safe.

Condor stepped into his living room. Shut the door behind him. Thought he was merely hallucinating again as he saw the limits of safe.

Bald secret agent Peter sat slumped on the floor in front of the fireplace.

His arms spread wide across that place where Condor would burn wood.

His hands nailed to the fireplace, blood flowing from his palms pierced and nailed to the mantel by knives from Condor's kitchen carving set.

Blood soaked the dead agent's white shirt inside his sports jacket and tan raincoat.

Probably *before* the killer nailed Bald Peter to the fireplace, he cut the man's throat along that crimson gash above the knot of a dampened dark necktie.

Probably the assassin gouged out Peter's eyes *after* the crucifixion.

Call him *Vin,* call him *Condor,* a man who came home

from work on an ordinary Tuesday to find a blood-soaked American agent nailed to a fireplace with knives.

Vin saw a crucified man, the corpse's gaping mouth, his cheeks slickened red, eyes gouged to gory black holes.

Condor saw the *trickling* of freshly freed crimson tears.

8

The slow parade of fears.
—Jackson Browne, "Doctor My Eyes"

What a glorious Tuesday spring morning it was for Faye
as she walked across the plaza toward Complex Zed. She
didn't know Condor was right then offering his heart in a
Starbucks, but she knew she was going to rock the limbo's
floor and—

Walking across the plaza toward her: a stocky, tan-
skinned, black-haired man.

"What are you doing here?" said Faye.

They both knew that only Zed's security cameras kept
her from hugging him.

"Good to see you, Faye," said Sami. He gave her a
fatherly smile. "I don't want to hold you up, make you late."

"Don't worry," she said. "I'll say my run took longer
than usual."

"Did it?"

"No." A forgivable lie of omission. She hadn't run that
morning.

"You can tell them we ran into each other. It's natural,
and you're cleared."

"Am I getting off the limbo level? Coming back online?"

"There's cleared and there's *cleared*," he said.

"So you're not here about me?"

"Wish I was." He looked around the midmorning-lit plaza. Looked for who was there. Who wasn't. "Remember RTDs?"

"Real-Time Drills."

"Necessary risk even before Boston. A random day. Flash alert. Race to some game scenario site designed to see how you can do better. By noon, every crisis-clear East Coast headhunter worth his bullets will be in your building. But one real bomb go BOOM! under the right conference room table, and it's a great day for the bad guys."

Sami sighed. "Oh well, at least I got to run into my most charming colleague. She's kind of okay on the bricks, too."

"If it weren't for the cameras," smiled Faye, "I'd drop you."

"*A B C*," grinned Sami. "*A*lways *B*e *C*overed."

Risk it, she thought as they walked toward work. Told the man beside her: "You've been around a long time."

"You wouldn't have gotten odds on that back when I was a kid in Beirut."

"Rumors, legends, whispers: you're who knows."

Sami stopped an arm's length away from a security door in the wall of black glass that reflected the images of him and a younger woman with short hair, slacks, Op shoes.

He said: "Only three types of people are susceptible to flattery: *men, women*—"

"And *children*," finished Faye. "I don't want to talk to a child."

She said: "There are rumors about an agent who got caught in the shit in denied territory and called in a drone strike on himself."

"We're spies, Faye. Starting rumors is one of the *what*s we do."

"Come on, Sami. It's me asking."

"No matter what you heard," said her friend and former boss, "something like that happens, guy like that . . . Forget about him getting one of the no-name stars on the wall out at Langley. He'd be Congressional Medal of Honor material.

"Or completely nuts," added Sami. Smiled as he said: "And dead."

The breath of spring morning that Sami took seemed completely natural. He let his hand touch her arm. A mentor-to-protégé touch. A soft, sensitive touch. Innocent.

He looked straight into her green eyes. "Have you got some reason for asking?"

"I don't know what I got," said Faye. "If it is something, I'll play it straight."

"Never a doubt in my mind," said Sami as he held the door open for her.

Like he held the door for her that day eight months before *when* they didn't pillory her in the soundproofed, plexiglass "fishbowl" conference room of the Senate Intelligence Committee. That *when* morning, Sami looked away from the two Senators sitting across the table from him and Deputy Directors from both the CIA and the ODNI, looked at Faye in her chair, told her: "Would you step outside, please?"

Then he got up and held that door for her.

As if her wound might require special care and attention.

Sami loved subtle.

She left that fishbowl deep in the windowless office complex for the Senate Select Committee on Intelligence. Perhaps a dozen cubicles and other executive offices waited between where she stood outside the fishbowl and the Committee entrance. CIA task forces on paper clips have more personnel than this Congressional oversight force charged with keeping track of America's war status intelligence community.

Faye glanced back into the fishbowl. *Sami with four strangers wearing business suits, deciding what they're going to do to me, with me.*

She looked left, saw *him* standing by the coffee bar holding a white Styrofoam cup.

She'd seen him before—one of five Senate staffers in that morning's meeting with Sami, the two spy agency execs, and a Senator from each political party. And her. For the CONFIDENTIAL-level briefing about Paris. Then he'd been sent out with the other Senate staffers, with Faye and Sami still in there as the quorum of two Senators got briefed on America's spies' TOP-SECRET version of blood on *le rue de cobblestones.*

Et moi, thought Faye.

She looked at that Senate staffer. Just a guy, tall, blond, gray suit. Her age.

Fuck him, fuck the doctors, I need coffee.

He didn't retreat when she put a dollar bill in the Styrofoam cup by the coffeepot, filled her own Styrofoam cup. Indeed, he came closer, and *fuck trusting the Committee's metal detectors,* she eyeballed him for a hidden weapon, saw his cup contained only water.

Over the burn of long-heated coffee she had to admit he smelled good. She was drenched in nervous sweat, hoped the perfume she seldom wore covered that with a scent of lilacs. He sent a bespectacled nod to the Senators and spy execs in the fishbowl.

"So," he said, "after I left, what did you guys talk about in there?"

"Seriously?"

"I know you're CIA so I had to say something that would shock a real response," he told her. "Because if talking about what's really going on is out, we have to resort to some kind of disembodied chatter where I start out asking you safe things, like which camp were your parents, Rolling Stones or Beatles."

"That's your chatter?"

"I was hoping for *our* chatter, but *yeah*. What else can I say to you?"

"Are you hitting on me?"

"If I tried to hit on you, you'd break my arm in like six places."

"Probably only two."

"Thanks for your restraint." He shrugged both hands into the air and smiled with his blue eyes. "And while I'm not hitting on you, per se, the intent is clearly growing."

"Per se?"

"Sorry, I talk like that sometimes when I'm nervous."

"I make you nervous?"

"Since the moment I saw you."

"This oughta be good."

"It's the way you stood—*stand*. You're here. Stepping right up and taking it. And true to that. Whatever it is." He waved his gray-suited hand. "Blew me away."

"So you decided to recruit me."

"There's an idea. Do you play Ultimate?"

"What?"

"Ultimate Frisbee. Like soccer. Only with plastic discs. A stoner sport."

Faye said: "So you're a stoner? And think I am?"

"I'm a randomly drug-tested federal employee. Yesterday is gone if not forgotten.

"It's a simple game," he said. "You toss, you catch, you run. No contact."

"Rules," she said.

"Honor code," he replied.

"Sounds like a pastime for sophomores."

He nodded to the fishbowl where Senators frowned to show they were serious. "I spend all day up on this hill chasing back and forth after whatever gets thrown into the air by them, so getting to catch and toss something real while running in what passes for clean air . . . *Yeah,* that feels pretty good. And I'm a long way from being a sophomore."

"Which way?" *Don't stare at the fishbowl!*

And he laughed. Just . . . *did it.* Laughed. Out loud and in the open.

Said: "Some days that's open to debate.

"You should come," he said.

"What?"

"More or less seven o'clock tomorrow night unless we get a freak September storm. Down on the Mall, the grass alongside the east wing of the National Gallery."

"You want me to play?"

"I want you to give you the chance."

"You're all heart." She gulped the bitter coffee. Tossed the white cup in the trash, couldn't pretend anymore to ignore what was going on in the fishbowl.

"I'm Chris," he said. "Chris Harvie."

She walked away.

As he said: "Can I ask your name?"

Faye refused to turn around. Watched the fishbowl that trapped her tomorrows.

Traps my today, she thought that Tuesday seven months later as *après* Starbucks Condor walked back to work over empty sidewalks and she walked across the cubicle-crowded, blue-lightning-bolts limbo level and into NROD's clear-walls corral.

"Where's Peter?" she said to her half-dozen men and women colleagues.

"Did you lose your partner?" said Harris with a snide look that lied and said he knew more than he did.

He's not worth the bullet. Faye claimed an empty desktop computer, checked the online agent duty roster. Frowned. Saw one of the two bosses in NROD's inner office.

Stuck her head in, said: "Why is my partner detailed to Admin this morning?"

The section co-commander who insisted you call her *Pam* checked the computer at her desk, shrugged. "Probably some data-processing glitch."

"Is it about me?" asked Faye.

"Why, did you do something wrong?"

Faye returned Pam's shrug, said: "*Naw.* You know me, boss."

As she walked away, Faye heard Boss Pam say: "No, I don't."

No, Faye hadn't planned on going to that Ultimate Frisbee game the night after Sami worked a miracle, covered everyone's ass with the Senate oversight committee and cut some deals that eventually sent her to Home Sec's NROD in Complex Zed, but that next day she couldn't, she just *couldn't* stay in her new Bethesda apartment staring out at the autumn leaves of the political metropolis she'd need to get used to again.

She went for a late run like she often did, but that evening she and her backpack cleared any brick surveillance, only ran as far as the Bethesda Metro before she caught a train, transferred to the Blue Line, spotted Frisbee players on the grassy Mall, walked to them and watched him watch her (and miss a catch) as she took something from under her sweatshirt, put it in her knapsack that she secured to a tree with a bicycle lock.

He called out: "She's with us!"

But he cut her no slack when players switched around so they were on opposite sides. Between the post-surgery push-ups, pull-ups, and running, she was in better shape, but he never hesitated to play as hard against her as he could.

Standing beside him as he caught his breath, she said: "So this is what people do?"

"What people?" he gasped.

"People our age. Normal people."

"Nobody's normal," he said. "You know that."

Somebody yelled *Go!* They ran to and fro on the green grass under Washington's evening sky. The ivory Capitol dome rose a few blocks beyond one side of their playing field, while a quarter mile from the other sideline rose the Washington Monument topped by blinking red lights.

Faye had her cover story ready, a driver's license from Ohio, but no one hit her with Washington's ubiquitous defining question of *"What do you do?"*

She thought: *They've carved out this time from their imposed reality.*

Still, she deduced that many players were Congressional aides, that one handsome guy with curly hair worked for a telecommunications giant, a woman was a waitress waiting to hear about law school, two other women already were beginning associates in some D.C. legal factory where they'd go back to their desks and work toward midnight.

After the last game, Faye caught a ride with strangers to the chosen burgers & beers bar, watched him smoothly cut her out of the crowd to end up sitting with her and their third-round beers at the far end of the jukebox bar where no one could hear them.

"Nicely maneuvered," she told him. Told Chris. Chris Harvie.

"I am working my hardest here," he said.

"Not gonna get you anywhere."

"You mean besides where we already are." He shrugged. "So I might as well give you the worst of it."

Which was his father walked into a San Francisco fog one kindergarten night and never came back until another family sent high school junior Chris, his sister, and their mother his obituary for *their* husband-father. Which was exceeding law school rules on how much outside employment he could take driving pre-dawn bakery delivery trucks while going to Stanford. Which was a car wreck he shouldn't have walked away from, a few "bonehead" accidents on the summer-job California state highway crew that helped fill his undergraduate scholarship gap at Brown University, some unspecified "loutish" behavior with women. Which was breaking into an apartment a heartbeat ahead of a police raid to flush his buddy's LSD stash after the buddy's vindictive ex-girlfriend lied and ratted him out to the police as a dealer on her cell phone right in front of Chris.

"Oh, and I was a virgin until I was twenty-one," he told Faye.

Shrugged: "I wanted to get it right."

"What happened to her?"

"Better things." He drained what he'd said would be his last beer. "And the rest, well, you probably already ran a background check."

"That's the kind of thing you'd have a colleague who owes you do off the books."

"You sure don't need a lawyer."

"No, I don't." She got off the stool, slung her backpack weighted with her holstered gun she hadn't slipped back on under her sweatshirt.

Said: "My name is Faye Dozier."

"For real?"

Left him with her smile as she entered that night alone.

Faye worked alone all that Tuesday morning after the night she met Condor—"morning" being relative, given that NROD agents work staggered shifts and hers started at 10 A.M. She wrote an impassioned report on why Immigration should admit the neighbors of a young man who'd spent three years as an interpreter for U.S. soldiers in Afghanistan, not one betrayal, several acts of heroism, and all he wanted was to marry the girl next door and be free in Kansas.

At 1:23 P.M., she checked the online duty roster.

Peter was still "Detailed Admin."

Plus now he was NU/UC—No Unauthorized/Unnecessary Contact.

As per regs, he'd texted his Status Confirm every two hours.

One of the nicer and newer NROD agents, a sharp ex–Brooklyn cop named David, said: "I hope his Admin deal isn't Internal Affairs calling him out for drinking."

"We don't call it Internal Affairs," said Faye as they stared at the computer monitor screen. "We call it the Office of Professional Responsibility."

"Oh. Is that what '*we*' call it?"

"I'm a spy," she told David. "Not a rat."

The first Monday night after that Frisbee game, Chris Harvie came home from work to his U Street rented apartment—a neighborhood that went Obama-era *tres chic* after being Jimmy Carter–era *tres noir*—and found *My name is Faye Dozier* standing in his living room.

"I picked your locks," she said before he could speak. "I could have searched your place, but I didn't, I won't. I'll tell you nothing rather than lie. I expect the same from you."

September chilled that week. She wore ugly jeans. A ratty old sweater and a green nylon flight jacket with zero patches that she'd got in Kandahar. She unfastened the waistband holster heavy with her newly issued Glock, put it on top of a stack of novels on his sofa's cheap end table.

"That comes with me," she said.

She struggled out of her wool sweater.

Faye'd worn her ugliest, most unflattering white exercise bra.

That night her scar still puckered pink and angry.

"This is me, too. I might never tell you about it, but it's big, you can see, it's big, and no matter that I'm a hundred percent medically, I fucked up and it fucked me up."

She watched his blue eyes that hadn't looked away.

His mouth that hadn't said a thing.

Faye said: "I can walk out that door. No regrets. No blowback. No tears. Just gone. Or I can stay and we can see what we can see."

He crossed his room to her. Cupped her face in his hands.

Said: "Stay. You already beat my locks."

Never gonna forget that, Faye was thinking at 5:28 on the evening after the night Chris cupped her mouth & then . . . She blinked back into focus, into her computer monitor at a desk, scrolled down all field agents' mandated daily review of America's on-average 270+ Actions/Alerts.

"A/A is like a cop shop's daily lineup of who got popped the night before," ex–Brooklyn detective David had described it.

"Only it's all digital, all online, all the time," Faye'd replied.

At 5:29 P.M. that Tuesday, Faye read the classified A/A report from Los Angeles on how starving sea lion pups who were washing up on Southern California beaches at more than five times the usual frequency had cleared terrorist-linked toxicology analysis and therefore this Event Syndrome's TSR—Threat Spectrum Rating—had dropped from six to one out of one hundred possible data-rated TSR levels.

"Dozier!" yelled the deputy commander named Ralph from the doorway of his box within a box of NROD's dioramic squad room. "Get in here! David—"

He yelled to the ex–Brooklyn cop.

"—Harris," yelled the commander to the snide asshole. "You, too."

Faye beat the other agents to the huddle with their boss Ralph.

"Nineteen minutes ago," said the boss, "our boy Peter missed his two-hour window for routine Status Confirm. His detail contact to Admin gave him fifteen minutes' grace and had the decency to call me before they upload into the system. We all know that Peter sometimes . . . His bald head can be lax about things."

Harris started a snide drinking remark—ex-cop David elbowed him silent.

"Fuck Peter's '*I'm a star*' with a new NU/UC status," said his boss. "I called him. Straight to voice mail. The GPS ping on his phone . . ."

The boss focused on Faye: ". . . puts him on Capitol Hill at the address of a PINSS you two interviewed yesterday."

"*Condor*," whispered Faye. *Off work half an hour ago. Probably walked home.*

The boss said: "Fuck if I know why Peter's doing follow-up, but that's what I just found logged into the system. He's out there, dinging the grid, and we've got . . ."

The boss looked at the nearest row of digital clocks on the wall outside his office.

"We've got to cover his ass and beat some rat squad

react team there. Since I ordered a car brought out front *now,* technically we're already primary on this before the routine look-see goes out. Our team picks up its own shit— *hey!*"

Faye was out the boss's door before he ordered David and Harris to go with her.

They caught up with her at the elevator that let them all out at the ground-floor main lobby where they quick-marched past a group of out-of-complex colleagues standing in a friendly cluster to jive about where to go for dinner.

Sami stood on the fringe of that group of headhunters.

Saw Faye emerge from the elevator, and he started to smile . . .

Saw the look on her face.

Saw her see him.

Saw her clench her right fist by her belt buckle: *Running hot.*

Sami watched her gunners' trio stalk outside to a waiting sedan that screamed *badges,* said to his colleagues: "Let's go to the closest place.

"And guys," he added to this mixed-gender group who hung on his every word, "I'm thinking no beers yet."

"I thought the alert game was over!" said one of the headhunters, who felt the heat from his colleagues for his error of opposing the guru even as those words left his mouth.

Sami said: "You never know."

At 5:33, the Home Sec/NROD sedan peeled away from the curb—Faye drove, ex-cop David rode shotgun, Harris strapped himself into the backseat.

"It's rush hour!" yelled Harris. "Can't take Rock Creek Parkway!"

David snapped his cell phone into the cradle, on speaker to DISPATCH plus GPS.

At 5:41, they pushed the red light at Connecticut Avenue and Nebraska and sped by the last best independent bookstore in America.

Their boss's voice over the phone: "Team, be advised, a classified protocol activated automatically when the system posted a possible trouble alert under your destination coordinates and the Condor identifier. Nearest hard-duty unit was protocol triggered. A unit launched that should be on scene before you."

"Order them as backup!" yelled Faye. "No action until I—we get there!"

"Understood, but . . . I'm not sure I've got that authority."

Faye hit the switch for the red emergency lights in the grille and the siren. David pulled out the magnetic light-spinning cherry, slapped it on the roof of the car.

"What the fuck is going on?" yelled Harris from the backseat as they raced through siren-blasted gaps in the steel river of traffic stretching through affluent D.C. toward Capitol Hill.

"I don't know!" yelled Faye. "Heads up for a white car, tinted windows!"

Washington rush-hour traffic devours high-speed responses. Any other time of day, red lights & siren, they'd have made it from that last phone call to the Eleventh Street, SE, destination in eleven minutes. Took them seventeen minutes, even with Faye taking every possible risk and Harris screaming: *"Look out! Look out!"*

Their squad car slammed to a stop outside the turquoise door at 6:01 P.M. Faye'd killed the siren four blocks away, but their flashing red lights beat rhythms on the evening sunlit row of town houses.

"Harris—alley out back, gray wood fence. Post up where you can cover it, don't pass anybody I mean *anybody* but me or David. *GO!* Run, we'll give you thirty!"

Yippy dog barking—fenced in next door front yard.

Dirty white yippy dog.

Gun out and so is David, must have *been there before,* too, *fuckup like me not a don't give a fuck,* two-handed combat grip the Glock out front—no citizens, lucky break. Eyes on the turquoise door, white curtains drawn over the two stories of front windows.

"Yip! Yip yip!"

Nod to the sidewalk: David moves to that post, eyes on the windows, knowing—

"Freeze!" yells the ex–Brooklyn cop.

Faye whirls—

Male, white, late twenties, *gun, he's got a gun,* black automatic *zeroed on me!*

"I'm Home Sec!" yells the strange man in blue jeans, a blue nylon Windbreaker. "Yellow initials on my jacket back! You're Faye! Agent Dozier! I'm protocol!"

Seeing him over her gun barrel. Seeing his gun bore zero her face.

"Yip! Yip!"

Protocol is tall and lean. Wears a scruffy brass goatee, chopped-short hair, a poorly groomed surfer look.

He whirls. Aims his gun at the turquoise door.

Keep your gun on him.

Why? thinks Faye. But obeys her instincts.

Protocol says: "That's the place, right?"

Says: "My partner's posting our red-lights unit in the alley, block and secure."

Pauses, listens: wireless earpiece.

Protocol says: "Our two guys have hooked up."

Harris's voice in David's belt-packed, speaker-on phone confirms.

Faye swung her Glock toward Condor's home.

Protocol said: "You or me?"

Faye followed the flow of her gun sights to the turquoise door.

9

What rough beast.

—William Butler Yeats, "The Second Coming"

A throat-cut American spy slumps crucified by *your* knives over *your* fireplace.

Dark tears trickle from his empty eye sockets: *Fresh. Recent. Run!*

Across town in Complex Zed, Faye Dozier scanned Action/Alerts. Learned the Threat Spectrum Rating for starving sea lions washing up on Southern California beaches.

In the twilight outside a D.C. house with a turquoise door, the neighbor's dirty white dog yipped once more in triumph, strutted under "her" front porch, the human who'd dared come near her turf successfully *skedaddled* into its next-door cave.

Shh!

Silence. No one alive in here but you. No one in the kitchen. No one upstairs.

What kind of cover team is outside watching?

Condor shook his head.

Impeccable timing. T.O.D. (Time Of Death) matches my known schedule.

Peter, the corpse was Peter. Bald, and that pissed him off. Lots pissed him off.

No blood spray high on the walls, so not a slashing samurai.

Picture it:

Peter knocked out. Killer drags him to the fireplace. Probably finishes him first, *then* crucifies him. Situational genius even if the killer was following some Op script.

If you're going to frame a crazy, build a crazy frame.

A freshly butchered body smells like steamy ham. Feels like a warm beach ball that's lost a breath of inflation. Condor slid his hands around the dead man's waist.

Holster—*empty.*

So officially, you've taken his gun.

Are now obviously armed and dangerous. A trained and crazed murderer.

There'll be a fast behavioral science profile of the fugitive—*you*: "Crucifying the victim indicates a severe psychotic break. Gouging out the eyes means our subject doesn't want to be seen. And will attack anyone who seems to be stalking him."

Shoot on sight won't be the Operational Order.

But it will be the street-smart move.

What did the wet-work artist do with the murdered man's eyes?

Mumbo jumbo mind mappers will say: "Call them trophies or what he didn't know to discard, like a kid saving his graded exam paper."

If they find the eyes on you or linked to you . . .

So the artist assassin is still active. With a pocketful of eyeballs to plant on you after somebody—*anybody*—takes you off or shoots you down, which means . . .

He's inside the machine.

That's how he got Bald Peter here.

How much time do you have before they nail you?

Across town on the limbo floor of the Office of National Intelligence's Complex Zed, an NROD deputy commander stood in his glass-walled office door and yelled: "Dozier! Get in here. David, Harris: you, too."

Condor made himself check the rest of the crucified corpse.

No ankle-holster backup gun to take and be the actual threat you officially are. Forget about the dead man's phone, his IDs maybe imbedded with GPS chips, his credit card, his cash: That'll look like you panicked, didn't scavenge resources.

A bald, gouged-out-eyes, throat-cut agent of America slumps crucified with your knives over your fireplace.

You are so fucked.

On your way to Killed While Resisting.

Or BAM! Extraordinary rendition. No trial, locked forever in some asylum box.

Across town in the lobby of Complex Zed, a headhunter guru named Sami sees one of his protégés scrambling with a team toward a car waiting in the street beyond the glass walls. She spots Sami, clenches her right fist by her belt buckle: *Running hot.*

Condor ran to the kitchen, grabbed a canvas shopping bag from between the refrigerator and the counter, ran back toward the living room—

Stopped. Stared at his collage wall. At his triangle-marked images.

Tell me what I'm trying to say!

Nothing. He heard nothing.

No creaking boards.

No yipping from the dog next door.

No *ghosts.* No *clongs.* Only the *whoosh* of time outside in the evening street.

Vin grabbed his blue hooded raincoat off the wall hook in the living room, noticed dark splatters of *not rain* on it as he bounded upstairs, ignored whether the dental floss strand had been snapped. *The killers are gone and on their way.*

Three cardboard boxes stacked in his bedroom closet held Vin's junk. Most of it came from who knew where, who knew why, but the middle box . . .

Weighed about forty pounds. Inside were books he could conceivably care about. And a black leather zip-up bomber jacket wrapped around something heavy the size of a loaf of bread. He unwrapped the jacket to reveal a black plaster statue of the Maltese Falcon. But who cared about that bird: he freed his scruffy black leather jacket, the secret he'd been hiding by making it look like mere padding around a fragile treasure.

Or so he hoped any squirrels who black-bagged & tossed his home had thought.

No iPad photos of this jacket, of Vin in it. No data for a BOLO alert.

Condor stuffed the black leather bomber jacket in his shopping bag. Restacked the boxes. Grabbed thermal underwear top and bottoms from a drawer. Clean socks.

Look at your reflection in the bathroom mirror.

Running scared.

Again.

"Yeah," Condor told his image, told the ghosts. "But I was young then."

Grab the pill bottle of pee medicine, pain tablets, beta blockers and baby aspirin for your hyper heart, multivitamins. Drop them and the low-dose Valium into your shopping bag: you'll need to sleep if you live long enough. Take your toothbrush.

Rows of antipsychotic sedations stared at Condor.

Make them kill the real you.

Vin slammed the medicine cabinet door shut.

Grabbed yellow rubber gloves from under the bathroom sink.

Remembered to pocket his Maglite, a black metal flashlight the size of a fat tube of lipstick, perfectly acceptable and prudent for any PINSS-resettled home.

Condor pushed a stepstool against the blank white wall at the top of the stairs where he'd often been tempted to violate *Operational Readiness* and hang a picture or a movie poster of, *say,* Magnum-toting Lee Marvin and *noir* blonde Angie Dickinson in *Point Blank,* or maybe an art print like the ones tourists buy in the Smithsonian gift shop, Sargent's *Girl in the Street of Venice*, a black-shawled, white-dressed brunette walking past two men, one of them raises his head to—

Focus!

Vin snatched the cloth belt off the black & red checked bathrobe hanging in the bathroom, the seemingly innocent robe he bought for this cloth belt, and *it will work.*

He threaded his leather belt through the canvas handles of the shopping bag so it now both carried the shopping bag and held up his pants.

Vin took off, then tied his laces together to dangle his shoes around his neck.

Tied one end of the bathrobe belt through a slat on the stool, left as much slack as possible when he tied the other end of the robe belt around his left ankle.

Almost forgot!

Condor tossed his cell phone clattering down the hall to the floor of his bedroom.

Pulled on the yellow rubber gloves.

"Yip! Yip yip yip!"

Outside—the neighbor's yippy white dog: *Barking at who?*

Condor climbed on the stool next to the bare *oh so clean* white wall, reached up—

Yellow-rubber-gloved hands left no smudge marks on the white ceiling panel they pushed open to the crawl space between Condor's hallway and his roof.

"Yip! Yip yip!"

Vin grabbed the lip of that portal, stood on his left foot, bathrobe-belt-lashed and with the bag behind him, put his stockinged right foot on the bare white wall, took a deep breath—

Propelled himself up into the crawl space, his elbows held his weight on the frame of the passageway, his left leg stretched below him lashed to the stool launchpad.

In the trapdoor's maw, Condor dangled above the house floor tied to a stool.

"Yip yip!"

Outside the turquoise front door, something or someone was driving the yippy white dog mad. Condor shoved open the trapdoor to the roof.

Cool air tumbled over his sweaty face.

He scrambled out to the city sky. Pulled the stool lashed to his ankle up behind him. Slid the square white ceiling panel back in place, unsmudged.

Wood-splintering crash—someone kicked in his downstairs front door.

Condor quietly closed the trapdoor.

"Yipyipyipyip yip!"

Peel off the yellow gloves. Shove them in the shopping bag unlashed from your pants. Untie the bathrobe belt from your left ankle. Put on your shoes.

Cop car red lights spun in the alley below and off to his right: *Go left.*

Washington is a horizontal city defined more by what's inside its Beltway's circling eight lanes of whizzing cars, trucks, and bus traffic than by the borders of various legal jurisdictions like the District of Columbia, Maryland, and Virginia. Any of the city's twenty-first-century vertical growth higher than the white marble Washington Monument *by law* begins in outlying neighborhoods that are no longer distinct suburbs.

Condor ran across the top of the city.

Off to the right of that stumbling runner rose a horizon of the Capitol dome. Like most of the central city, wall-to-wall town houses filled his neighborhood. He stumbled over firewalls, past chimneys, toward the edge at end-of-the-block.

The last house on the block. The owner had chopped this three-story-plus-basement property into apartments, rigged a steel fire escape down the back of the top two units. The fire escape zigzagged down toward a minuscule backyard patio inside a tall wooden fence. Other buildings sticking farther into the alley blocked Condor's view back toward his home and where the alley pulsated with cops' red lights.

You can't see them, they can't see you.

The fire escape trembled, but he made it down the top two flights.

A silver-haired man wearing a gray sports jacket with a shopping bag looped on his shoulder dangled by his hands from the fire escape's bottom steel rung.

Let go.

Fall through cool spring air.

Crash to a heap on a postage stamp of lawn.

Everything hurt. Shoulders from climbing and dangling.

Sore arms. Legs—*right knee, oh man!* The jarring drop rattled his bones, his teeth. His heart pounded *no no no* against his ribs. He wanted to lie there. Vin stumbled to his feet.

A distant siren wailed.

Steel bars protected the door into the apartment from this backyard. The other exit was the gate through the man-high wood fence. He could run out to the alley . . .

Into whose gun sights from back where the red lights spun?

Condor shoved a lawn chair to the street side of the fence.

One more climb. One more fall.

Sirens screamed closer as he thumped onto the sidewalk screened from the view of his front stoop and back alley by the block of town houses he'd run over. Crossed the street, didn't look to his right down the alley.

Don't pull them with your eyes.

Nobody shot him. Nobody yelled stop. No sounds of running footsteps.

Get out of the cordon zone.

Don't go there.

Condor ducked into the garden-level alcove of a town house, unpacked his black leather jacket, revealed its satiny tan inner lining repaired with an L of gray duct tape. Ripped the tape free, stuck his hand between the inner lining and the outer black leather.

Found the money: four flat packs of bills sorted by denomination from $1s to $20s. Almost a year's worth of hoarding. Never so much his bank accounts plus expenses might alarm his minders' probable audit projections. Dollars short-changed out of waiters' tips. Five-dollar portraits of Abe Lincoln skimmed out of un-receipted sacks of homegrown tomatoes and fresh peaches and white corn and rainbow trout from the fish counter at the Eastern Market four blocks from Vin's house. Twenty-dollar bills palmed from what cover teams could have seen him stuffing in the pots of Christmas bell-ringing Salvation Army warriors. Vin had drawn the line at stealing for his cache: *You are the line you stand on.* Wouldn't dip his hand into an unknown Library of Congress staffer's open purse to snatch a loose twenty he saw in there as she rode beside him in the elevator. Standing in the alcove that night, he knew that if squirrels searching his place hadn't stolen any of his secret funds, he was stuffing $327 into his black jeans.

Enough operational cash to last, what: twenty-four hours in a major American city?

Condor shook his head. *How long did I last that first time?*

Inside the lining, he found the SmarTrip credit card to ride D.C.'s public buses and subways. The SmarTrip was a tradecraft coup: he'd bought it at a drugstore when the clerk was overwhelmed by a distraught mom holding a crying baby. They were the only people in that bright-lights store, no cover team to see what thirty dollars cash got him.

Drugstore, thought Condor as he put the SmarTrip in a cash-stuffed pants pocket.

Marra Drugs Superstore sprawls over the north-side block on Ninth and Pennsylvania, SE, welcomed Condor that Tuesday evening with a SPRING MADNESS SALE! banner over its double glass doors. He kept his face down for security cameras as he slid into a smog of deodorizers. Soulless instrumental music poured from the ceiling.

Don't notice me. His grip on the red plastic shopping cart let him control trembling while he rolled down the aisles. His shopping bag gaped open for any security inspection as he dropped items into his cart. *Don't stop me as a shoplifter.*

From the Close Out & Seasonal Goods aisle:

- A WASHINGTON REDSKINS logoed maroon & gold baseball cap.
- An XXL unlined maroon nylon REDSKINS jacket.
- A knapsack-like Kangaroo Love baby carrier designed to let the wee one ride strapped below Mommy or Daddy's beating heart.

From the Medical Devices aisle:

- Three pairs of Athlete's Foot & Odor Eater cushioned shoe inserts.
- The last pair of giant black plastic, square-framed, no-UV-protection sunglasses that at best evoked *the late, great* rock warbler Roy Orbison.
- A turquoise plastic travel-pack box of "lemon-fresh hypoallergenic" baby wipes.

From the Groceries & Sundries aisle:

- The lightest, cheapest, plastic bottle of water.
- Four "protein" bars.
- The thinnest roll of "stretch & cling tight" plastic wrap.
- The smallest spool of "magic" invisible tape.

From the Beauty Products aisle:

- A twelve-pack of silver-dollar-sized coated cotton makeup swabs.

- A dainty cuticle scissors, the only blades he'd seen in the store.
- Three—*no,* two $3.98 palm-sized bottles of HipGirlz liquid cover-up makeup in *Our Darkest Tone Yet!*

Condor rolled his shopping cart toward the cashier line. A white-haired woman shuffled toward the same register. She used a black cane with one hand and clutched a box of microwave popcorn in the other. Wore hearing aids.

The hitch & hide.

"Here," he said to the woman with a cane as he pushed his cart ahead of her in the checkout line and plucked the popcorn from her hand, "let me get that for you."

"What?" said that white-haired woman.

But Condor had already dropped her popcorn on the checkout conveyer belt, stacked his own purchases behind it, whispered to the cashier: "My wife loves popcorn."

"Un-huh," said the cashier, her eyes on her work.

And not seeing us, thought Condor. Because we're over fifty and thus invisible.

Now "solo fugitive you" were never here, are the silver-haired husband of a white-haired woman with a black cane and bad hearing who joneses for popcorn.

Condor gave the clerk cash, got change. Grabbed the store's giant white plastic bag stuffed with purchases, pushed his cart tòward the front door.

Called out to the white-haired cane lady behind him: "Come on, dear."

Please, please, please . . .

He heard the *tap tap tap* of her cane following behind him through sliding glass doors to sundown. Heard her not bust him.

"Whoever you are," said the white-haired woman standing on the sidewalk with him. "Even back in the day, took more'n popcorn to get me to go."

Condor gave her the popcorn.

"I could use a Scotch," she said. "How about you?"

She was maybe ten years older than him. Came of age before rock 'n' roll. Left fear in some footprints far behind her. Lived alone calmly waiting for *when*.

"I've got to run," he told her. "But you're spectacular."

He hurried up Pennsylvania Avenue toward the Capitol dome. Turned right on Eighth Street before Capitol Hill's commercial blocks where bank ATMs used constantly recording security cameras. With a shopping bag in each hand, walked past a mother with a baby in the car seat of the SUV she was parking. *Don't snatch them for her ride.*

The sky reddened. He spotted a passageway between two brick town houses, slid into that gap. *Peed,* a *call-the-cops* offense for any witness, but he stood with his back to the brick passageway's opening, a stream of his life gurgling into a circular storm drain.

When you gotta go.

Don't go there.

He ripped store tags off the REDSKINS cap, pulled it on. Wore the huge maroon nylon Windbreaker over his gray sports jacket. Calculated that the oversized Roy Orbison sunglasses would attract too much attention in this evening hour.

Everything ached. His head throbbed. His feet hurt. He felt his pulse slow to only 50 percent too fast. Popped a pain pill with a swallow from the drugstore water bottle. The passageway he stood in stank of his own urine, of wet cement, bricks.

Can't stay here.

Don't. Go. There.

Vin closed his ears to the ghosts, and with a shopping

bag weighing down each hand, left the passage, a sports fan shuffling north on Eighth Street. Crossed Independence Avenue and the route he'd taken home from work less than two hours earlier.

These are the streets of your life. Not your hometown but the town you made into someplace you could call home. When they let you. When you weren't on the run.

Washington, D.C., under a bloodred sky.

He marched toward the Adams Building five blocks away at Third and A, SE.

The white car had been parked at that corner *way back when*.

Vin hadn't been able to step on A Street back then when he'd been officially *safe*.

Now he walked *there*.

A white stucco three-story town house filled the corner of A and Fourth Street, SE. The building had long since blended into this neighborhood of town houses, unmemorable except for its size and the brass plaque mounted on the white wall beside the black iron stairs leading to the black wooden main door on the second floor. Blinds covered all the windows. Clearly not a personal home, the building looked like no one ever went in or came out. A low black iron fence surrounded this building the color of Moby Dick.

Vin stood on the corner across the street from the white town house.

Felt time fall away. Heard wind inside his head. Smelled . . .

Gunpowder. Sweat. Blood. Perfume from a pretty woman named . . .

What was her name? What were all their names, the names of the dead?

That was when you became Condor.

So long ago. Yesterday. This morning.

He stared at the brass plaque mounted on the town house white wall. What it said there now didn't matter, wasn't real, *was a lie*.

What it read once and forever was AMERICAN LITERARY HISTORICAL SOCIETY.

And that, too, was a lie.

Gone behind him in time like his shadow he could never shake.

Bags in hand, he marched up Fourth Street, crossed East Capitol. Glanced left at the looming Capitol building, bathed in crimson—then in the wink of his street crossing, darkness fell, freed electric illumination so the Capitol glowed like an ivory skull.

Walk through this chilling Tuesday night.

Walk far away from Union Station with its trains out of town, its subways underground, its buses to New York City, its restaurants and food court and chairs to rest in and its swiveling-high-on-the-marble-walls security cameras to capture your picture.

Darkness covered streets where he slouched past town houses with lit windows that showed him young lovers struggling to figure out what they felt behind their smiles. First-time parents coaxing spoons of food into a pint-sized person who mortgaged them to the future. Office warriors pacing in their living rooms pressed to the cell phones chaining them to careers of political conscience, power, status, and payouts. Group houses with five onetime strangers assuring each other that these days when they could only get paid to serve high-priced coffee weren't their to-morrows.

Real life, thought Condor. *Should have tried it.*

But he was years past blaming anyone for the sum of his choices.

There's something wrong with the car headlights at the end of this block.

Condor stopped by two reeking gray rubber Dumpsters. Headlights filled the town house city canyon ahead of him as a car *crept* not *sped* closer, closer.

One whirl stacked his bags next to the two gray rubber Dumpsters, let him dive and curl up behind them.

Yellow eyes eased down the street toward where two rubber Dumpsters sat in front of an ordinary town house. The purr of a car engine grew to a grumble.

They're nobody, Condor told himself. *Looking for a parking place or a lost dog.*

The view from the creeping-past car showed no one shuffling in the street. No one running away or looking back. Not even a rat on top of the stuffed gray Dumpsters.

Dark sedan. Two shadowed shapes hulking in the front seat.

Don't move. Don't breathe. Don't let your eyes weigh on them so they'll pass by.

Red taillights going . . . going . . . turning the corner . . . Gone.

You'll never know if that was the right move.

Walking on, he heard no sirens for a dozen blocks. Saw no spinning red lights. No roadblocks on New York Avenue he crossed before the neon glows of a McDonald's, a Burger King and kitty-corner gas stations franchised from the surviving multinational oil companies. And as he neared North Capitol Street, the pulsing north-south four-lane artery connecting the skull Capitol dome with the rest of the world, Vin needed fuel.

Risk it: Dark night, two miles from the Op epicenter, wearing sports camouflage, you can shuffle up North Capitol's bright-lights commercial zone and not get tagged.

Vin walked past a rehabbed check cashing store, glanced

through the front picture window, saw the new space sparsely filled with surplus government metal desks, tables that could have come from a church bankruptcy sale, two desktop computers where no one sat and a college-vintage laptop that lit the face of a woman in her mid-twenties with light brown hair. Working late. The white letters over the swirling blue wall poster behind her had a logo for The Public Trust Project and the words:

Today we're losing the fish, tomorrow . . . ?

Condor walked on from the sight of a young woman trying to save the world.

Left, left, left right left . . .

Ah, fuck.

We're back!

Vin focused on the yellow glow from a carryout restaurant on the next corner. The red neon sign above the picture windows read:

FULL DRAGON YUM

You step into that Chinese food carryout, into its yellow spotlight box. The L-shaped walls of picture windows make you visible to any cruising-past cars. There's a sense of steam, warmth beyond the humid cool outside, smells of sweat and grease and soy sauce and maybe something from the trash can against one wall. That trash can shows its black plastic bag. Above the trash can hang fourteen faded color pictures of food with labels like Foo Yung and Lo Mein. You face the bulletproof plexiglass separating customers from stoves covered by pots and pans and coolers stacked with soft drink bottles no shoplifter can reach. The white-clad cook wears some kind of hair net, keeps his back to the plexiglass and you, leaves the lookout for the taut tan face of the counterwoman wearing a flower-print blouse who eats you with her ebony eyes.

Watches you watch the black fly buzzing on your side of the bulletproof partition.

The black fly walked across the wall's color photo of Beef With Broccoli.

Vin stepped to the slatted speaker slot. Ordered the beef with broccoli, felt his stomach rumble and added a beef fried rice. Felt the cash dwindling in his black jeans pocket but still asked for a plastic bottle that advertised it contained REAL ORANGE JUICE! and thus, *perhaps,* a dash of Vitamin C and other actual nutrients.

The Chinese woman barked his order back to him, got his nod, yelled something in what Vin thought might be Mandarin to the white-clad cook.

If you can't shoot them through the plexiglass, they can't shoot you either.

There are no stools or chairs or tables for customers to sit down and stay awhile.

Outside, cars whiz through the city.

"Hai!" The ebony-eyed woman stands on the other side of the plexiglass. The brown paper sacks on the Lazy Susan pass-through in the partition need only a spin from her steady hand to come clear of the smudged plexiglass.

Vin put the exact change for the price she barked at him in the pay slot.

Wait.

He held up an extra dollar bill, pointed to the trash can against the wall: "I want to buy . . . say five of those black plastic trash can liners, the big thirty-gallon ones."

Her brow wrinkled. She stood on her tiptoes. Pushed herself up farther with her hands pressing down on the counter, a demonstration of strength Condor feared he barely still had in him. She saw two bags on the floor beside where the man waited, wearing a jacket over a jacket and a smile she didn't believe for a heartbeat.

She told him: "You *san jia quan*."

Turned and disappeared behind the cooler.

Came back into view clutching a wad of black plastic in one hand, put those bundled-up garbage bags beside the brown paper sack on the Lazy Susan and spun the lot through the bulletproof partition to Vin's waiting hands.

"You keep dollar," she said. "Sometime everybody is *trouble-lost dog*."

He knew better than to force the dollar or a tip on her. But gave her a smile that this time she believed. Her face stayed fixed. Her ebony eyes rode him out the door.

He tramped north like his favorite fictional character— mouse Stuart Little. Shuffled over residential sidewalks. Two foreclosed houses he passed were nailed shut too securely to repurpose. A birthday party pinwheel stuck in a postage-stamp front lawn spun slowly with this cool spring night and fried-rice-smelling air.

Down a street sloping to his right rose a brick high school with a cop car parked out front, its engine idling on watch, just like there'd be armed cops waiting inside the metal detectors of the front door come tomorrow morning.

Streetlights silhouetted trees clustered at the crest of the hill, turf surrounded by a black iron fence. Metal letters arcing over the chained entry gate bars read:

EVERWOOD CEMETERY

A sign on the gate read: WE PROSECUTE ALL TRES-PASSERS.

This garden of the dead covered a dozen square blocks of the city looming above North Capitol Street. Commuters to Congress drove past it every day. So did the bus to a Veterans Center where briefly Condor'd been sent to get his drugs—his medicines.

If only I was still as strong as that Chinese woman.

Condor shoved his two bags through the bars of the gate—tossing them over would have dumped everything on the entrance road asphalt.

Got no choice now. Dinner's on the other side of the bars. With your gear.

He jumped, grabbed as high as he could on the bars, flopped to the other side.

Again he dangled above the earth. Again he let go. This fall only jarred him.

Vin adjusted his cap. Took his two bags in one hand, filled his other with the Maglite that sent a pale white cone of light to illuminate the darkness.

Fog: Pale wisps snake through the flashlight beam.

Feel: Wet on your face.

Smell: Wet grass. Stones and pavement. A whiff of cooling fried rice.

Hear: Faraway, city traffic. Rustles of trees. Silence from stone angels on pedestals blowing horns, spreading their wings, beckoning.

Walk behind your flashlight beam over paved paths wide enough for a black hearse. Walk a random path past family plots, marble slabs. MOTHER. LOVING HUSBAND. PRECIOUS DAUGHTER. VETERAN. Amidst stone crosses and angels atop gravestones Vin spotted dozens of ten-foot-tall stone obelisks, miniatures of the Washington Monument rising hundreds of feet into the sky on the not-too-distant Mall.

No moon beamed down on him. No stars dotted the sky. Fog enveloped him. Now and then he glimpsed muted streetlights far off beyond the invisible black iron fence.

He mostly saw only as far as his Maglite shone. Didn't worry that some sniper waited off in the darkness, drawing a bead on the wink of the light in his hand.

His shoes crunched pebbles on the looping black pavement path.

Toolsheds he came upon all had locked doors. He discovered an artificial hill with crypts built into its face, but those stone shelters had steel doors and bars and chains with solid padlocks to foil their prisoners' escape.

Out of the fog and darkness loomed an Asian pavilion. Open walls around a handball-court-sized circle topped two pancaked layers of roof, the smaller one above the larger with a gap in between that come morning would let in the sun. Pavement for a floor and on the down slope, a pebbled Zen garden with a plaque that read:

FREEDOM'S GARDEN OF SCATTERED MEMORIES

This is where they give the wind the ashes of the cremated.

Like a burnt spy.

On the pavilion floor, Vin sat atop his bundled-up blue raincoat. His Maglite created a cone of visibility as he used a plastic fork to eat cold beef with broccoli and fried rice. He drank all the orange juice. *Ration the water.* The flashlight led him to the edge of the pavilion so he could relieve himself on the shadowed sea of grass.

He made his bed beneath the pavilion roof. Stretched two plastic trash bags lengthwise on the pavement, atop them put the blue blood-splattered raincoat from Peter's iPad pictures and the gray sports jacket he'd worn to work that day.

Cold. Spring, sure, but out here tonight: cold.

Vin stripped in the glow of the Maglite until he wore only his socks.

Ghosts mocked a burlesque striptease: "Wha-wha wa, wha-wha-wha wha..."

Condor pulled on thermal underwear, redressed in his shirt and black jeans, shoes. Used one swallow of the bottled water to take his need-to-pee pill, his heart-soother pill, a keep-calm Valium and a pain pill for aches and soreness that made him want to moan. Zipped into his black leather flight jacket and snapped the maroon nylon football jacket on over that, laid on his wilderness bed with his cloth shopping bag and the Kangaroo Love baby carrier for a pillow. Stuck his feet and legs into one black plastic shopping bag, patted another trash bag over his torso, pulled on the yellow rubber gloves.

Condor thumbed out the Maglite.

Snugged on the maroon cap, lay on his back with its bill sticking straight up.

Bet my target silhouette looks like a duck lying on its back in the darkness.

Vin heard it first.

Pattering on the metal roofs above him.

Pattering becoming drumming like thousands of bullets strafed from the stars.

Then wind that spun down a monster tornado in faraway Oklahoma came through the open walls on all sides of him. Wind cool, cold, *then wet* blown across *and on him* as the dark opened with torrents of rain.

"You've gotta be fucking kidding me!" yelled Condor, yelled Vin to whatever heaven was out there this stormy night. "Couldn't you pick another time to cry?"

10

Gonna fall.
—Bob Dylan, "A Hard Rain's A-Gonna Fall"

Faye leaned against the white wall opposite the brick fireplace where Peter, Bald Peter, her partner—a jerk, sure, *but her partner*—hung crucified by kitchen knives, his throat cut so he could not speak, his eyes stolen from their stare.

My fault. How much of this is my fault?

From outside came the incessant barks of the dog next door: *"Yip yip! Yip!"*

Lean against this wall. Not gonna fall. Just lean against the wall. Breathe.

She dropped her gaze to her watch: 6:42. Still light outside.

Emergency lights on top of unmarked cars beat blasts of red against the house.

"Yip!"

White flashes. Another of the gun-toters crowded in here, taking cell phone pictures of the murdered man nailed over a fireplace by *fucking* kitchen knives.

One of us.

Faye's instincts told her not to stare at the horror that had redefined her life, to focus instead on the whispering cluster of three men and one woman who wore suits that could have come from the same tailor. Through the shifting crowd, Faye kept her eyes on that quartet of bosses who thought they had the power to decide her fate.

"Yip yip!"

Sami.

Walking through the turquoise door with three men and two women, all wearing street clothes not unlike his shopping-mall slacks and tan Windbreaker. He gave a concerned glance to where Faye leaned against the wall even as he stepped past her, marched to close quarters with the command cluster.

"Yip yip!"

Sami demanded: *"Yes* or *no?"*

The black executive who played college ball glared at Sami: "Excuse me?"

"The question you gotta decide right now," said Sami. *"Yes or no? Yes,* I and my people are the umbrella covering this scene, in charge of everything, or not—*No."*

The chewed-lipstick frown on the cluster's lone woman curved like a scimitar as she told Sami: "Do you know who you're talking to?"

"Yeah. You're a Deputy Director of my CIA who jumped on this rollout because you know this bites our Agency—speaking of which . . . *Harlan!"*

Faye'd worked with the lanky man in Sami's cadre who replied: "Yo?"

"You got your silencer?" Sami kept his eyes on the command quartet.

"Sure," said Harlan.

"Shoot that fucking yippy dog."

Harlan stepped toward the door, one hand suddenly full of steel, the other reaching into his jacket pocket.

"What!" chorused the quartet of commanders.

"Cancel, Harlan," said Sami. "They're right, not my

show. If they weren't smart enough to neutralize a dog attracting a whole lot of public attention, that's on them.

"So," said Sami to the glaring bosses, "I know who you all are. You're the dead man's CO from NROD in Home Sec, *sorry,* I know what it's like to lose a man. Standing next to you, we got Supervising Special Agent Bechtel of the FBI, nice to see you again, Rich. I've never met you, Deputy Director Martinez, but the whispers are you seem to know how to navigate the ODNI mess you got.

"But our question is: *Are you putting me in charge of this or not?*

"Our luck means I got nineteen of the best headhunters ever carried a sanction posting up right here in the Action Area, coincidental training gig for a shit storm like this. What I see here and now, you're already behind on the ABCs."

Deputy Director Martinez from the Office of the Director of National Intelligence who only knew the legends about Sami said to him: "What alphabet?"

"*A,*" said Sami. "*Action.* This isn't one of our Ops, so any Action we do is part of somebody else's chain of cause and effect. Look at their Action: our guy nailed to the wall in the home listed to a High-Alert disabled vet of ours who's gone nobody knows where. Whatever our Action is, it needs to break free of the other guys' chains to do any good, so it's gotta be big and fast and hard all the way up to extreme prejudice.

"*B,*" said Sami. "*Bounce.* How's this thing gonna bounce around, how are we going to control everybody's everything so nothing more gets broken than it has to.

"But what you're most worried about is *C,*" said Sami. "*Cover.* How are we going to put a cover over all this so it doesn't hurt U.S. national security *or* hurt the *U* and *S* that spells *us.*

"You want to start?" said Sami. "Get half these people outta here. There's a school parking lot to reconvene at somewhere near here . . ."

A blond woman agent in his cadre shouted out the school name and address.

"Get most everybody gone before the crowd of citizens outside gets any bigger," said Sami. "And call an ambulance."

ODNI DD Martinez said: "He's—"

"Dead," said Sami. "Let's get him down from there, show some respect."

"Crime Scene Investigators haven't gotten here."

"If they're en route, wave them off. We're not cops. Unless Rich here is claiming this for the FBI, does anybody really think any of this is going to go to lawyers and rules of evidence some public fucking *trial*?"

ODNI DD Martinez blinked.

Ordered an ambulance called. Ordered "all nonessentials" out.

"Hold up." Sami looked at Faye. "Who rolled on this with you?"

"That would be me," said David, the ex–Brooklyn cop.

Asshole Harris pleaded with both hands raised: "I just got logged onto their ride."

Sami told him: "Now you're logged on for CPR."

"What?" said Harris.

"Ambulance gets here," said Sami, "bundles up our boy, you get on top of him, on top of the stretcher, ride it all the way into the ambulance, kneel on each side of our *man down* and make big show of giving him CPR chest compressions."

Ex-cop David *got it,* volunteered: "I'll work squeezing the breathing bag."

No one—not Faye, not Harris or the ex–Brooklyn cop

David, not any of the four national security executives—no one contradicted Sami.

Who said: "Everybody else except for my team and Faye, drift out of here. Hang around outside. You're concerned. Upset. Responded to one of those commercially available panic alarms for help from a disabled vet, a— ex-FBI, explains the badges, guns, the too fucking many red lights. What was our guy's work name?"

"UNN!" grunted one of the suits as he pulled the knife out of dead Peter's left hand. The bald man's body slumped toward the floor.

His pale former Home Sec NROD boss said: "The knifed agent is—was—"

"Not him," said Sami. "What was Condor's work name?"

Faye called out: "Vin."

Frowned. Asked Sami: "Do you know him?"

"Vin," Sami told the agents inside the murder house. "Every TV watcher knows every badge rolls on any *'officer down'* call. That's why so many of you came here, kicked in the door. Found our guy *Vin,* our colleague, your buddy, *lying on the floor.* No knives. Heart attack. Still alive. Now it's *Vin* going out of here on the stretcher to the ER. Old guys, heart attacks: ordinary news. Be like the cell phone cameras out there, watch them take a' old guy getting CPR away in an ambulance, listen for any dangerous leaks or rumbles gossiping in the bystanders, follow it up soft but certain. Let it be heard out there how the cops' association is asking for volunteer badges—who are gonna be us—to sit on *Vin*'s stuff because of the busted door. *Go!*"

Without waiting for confirmation from the official executives, the herd of America's security and intelligence agents did as Sami said.

That ex-Marine who'd thrived as a teenager in the sniper streets of Beirut turned to the quartet of his fellow Americans who all outranked him, said: "So?"

Four intelligence commanders looked at the legend in front of them.

Knew there was no more time for phone calls.

Knew they were on the line.

Knew how to hand off to a fall guy.

Martinez of the umbrella agency ODNI got the nods. Told Sami: "Green light."

"Full sanction." Not a question from Sami, but his stare demanded confirmation.

"Yes," said Martinez.

Within two minutes Sami'd made sure everyone on-scene had the phone number of a command center he'd set up but not activated at Complex Zed before he'd raced from there to here with carloads of his cadre.

"I've got two-man teams already working a wheel-out from here," said Sami. "They're driving in circles, progressively working their way out from the house. They got the iPad photos from yesterday's home visit report, the data on Condor."

He sent teams to Union Station to cover the tracks, its subway entrance, food courts and upper parking lots where buses left for Baltimore, New York, Boston. Made sure TSA at area airports had photos of Condor on their cell phones and alert screens. Made sure Condor's photos got Priority Match status with Facial Recognition Software programs on the grid of federal, state, and local Big Brother cameras.

"Circle a perimeter five blocks out so it won't hit the *looky-loos* who are here," said Sami. "Get the D.C. cops to help FBI guys, flash badges, describe Condor, see if him being around tonight hits with any witnesses *without* polluting their timeline credibility of having seen him around before. If we get a hit, confirm with pictures.

"Get our people to the homeless shelters," he told one of his cadre who was coordinating his commands. "One inside, backup outside. Stay the night. Gonna be cold out there. Gonna rain. He's not going to hide under bridges because he knows cops drive past with the spotlights on, and make sure they do. Hospitals, museums, any place that's been open since Condor got off work. Come back every four hours. Agents who officially approach gatekeepers should use a . . . a Department of Social Services rap, a lost Alzheimer tourist—*maybe*: say we don't want to create a false press report in case it's just an old guy sneaking off from visiting his grandkids to get laid."

The cadre's Harlan asked: "What Intensity Level?"

The room held its breath.

Sami said: "One of our guys got cut down. We lose no more people. We let no bad guys get away. Locate, cover, call in a collection team and back up. We got *zero* solid that Condor is a killer, though no doubt he cruises Crazytown. He's a person of extreme interest. We want him. Want to talk to him. But don't let him get away."

Sami pointed to a woman in his cadre. "I skimmed the visitation report from yesterday by our dead guy on the way here. A white car, stolen license plate. Go with uniformed cops from that jurisdiction, Virginia suburbs. A low-key investigation, but brace everybody associated with that license plate about a white car, smell out who they really are. If you don't get anything, smile, say thank you, just routine, drive away. But no matter what, full-spectrum geographic and behavior profiles, full cover teams on them."

He designated three agents to sit on this house, a fourth who was ex–murder police from Baltimore to "run the janitors, suck up the scene," bag any physical evidence beyond the bloody knives pulled from Peter's crucified palms.

Walked to where Faye leaned against the wall, said: "How are you doing?"

"Wasn't him," said Faye. "He's crazy, but he's more clever than this."

"Easy to buy either way, given his record."

"What record?" she said.

"What you know now is what's important. We'll go over that back at your HQ building. You're in quarantine. There's an ambush team already in your apartment."

And a squirrel team, she thought. Knew there was nothing there they'd find she couldn't live with. *Nothing in there about Chris.*

Faye said: "I want the streets."

"After we debrief," he said.

She said: "Do you know Condor?"

"What you don't know won't get in your way," he told her. "I want you running free and hard and full-on after you tell me what you can tell me."

Faye said: "Besides my two guys you put on the ambulance CPR scam, there were two Homeland Security hard guys who breached this place with me. The guy with the scraggy blond goatee, the other guy—"

"Can they tell me anything about Condor?"

"I don't see why."

"Then let's keep them on the streets. We want every gun looking."

"You mean every badge."

"We'll talk when I get back to the Task Force command center."

Sami walked away, past the ambulance crew muscling a butchered body onto a waist-high wheeled stretcher.

Harlan came to her and she knew to pass him the car

keys before he held out his hand. Faye waited with Harlan inside the bloody living room while the ambulance crew and Brooklyn cop David and asshole Harris kneeling on the stretcher played out the CPR farce on a corpse, roared off in the siren-screaming ambulance.

She left Sami staring at Condor's mad collage wall.

Heard him whisper: "What are you trying to say?"

11

Secret heart of lonely. (what Condor always
wrongly thought the song says)
—The Yardbirds, "Heart Full of Soul"

Screaming someone's screaming! Wet blood on—
Condor realized: *It's me screaming.*

Bolted upright wrapped in wet plastic bags & jackets.
Wearing a cap. Butt on the concrete of a cemetery in the
gray of false dawn. Fists in yellow rubber gloves.

Every joint, every muscle, everything ached. *Won't survive another night outside.*

Morning light bathed gravestones in the cemetery. He
smelled wet grass.

You're where you're going to end up. Stay.

Your canvas shopping bag holds drugstore scissors.

These are your wrists.

Right here, right now, cut yourself free from the
handcuffs of whoever *they* are.

Condor stood with his ghosts amidst a garden of gravestones in a city of marble dreams where so many somebodies wanted him dead or silent or a servant to what they
said was sensible. Wind stirred the trees and the sky was
blue and he could not fly away.

The only way you're not a lie is to fight to be true.

You're not going to choose to fucking lose.

Ghosts watched Vin eat leftover Chinese food, take *be healthy not cured* pills.

The scissors trimmed the three pairs of footpad inserts but only two sets fit under his feet in his black sneaker-like shoes. He felt taller, no worse balance.

Stones from the Zen garden let him break the dark lenses out of the Roy Orbison sunglasses. Condor taped plastic cling wrap into taut transparencies over the lens holes. Search metrics account for sunglasses or empty frames as disguises. The "lenses" he made registered on camera scans as existing, let him see—though with distorted translucence. The huge black frames dominated his face, changed his profile.

Condor kept his thermal underwear on under his blue shirt and black jeans, put his blue raincoat in a garbage bag. They have photos of that coat from that Faye and the murdered man's Monday visit two days ago. Yesterday's surveillance footage from the Library of Congress office building would show his gray sports jacket. He dropped the sports jacket into the trash bag. By now, squirrel teams would have cataloged his closets. Two missing jackets/coats doubled the data they had to BOLO.

Condor strapped himself into the Kangaroo Love baby carrier. Stuffed his black leather jacket into the baby pouch over his stomach. Hid that under his maroon nylon jacket.

Maybe discerning eyeballs will notice the jacket isn't really covering too many beers and fast-food hamburgers, but Facial Recognition Software in security cameras around town will register my fat guy as 0 not 1, signal NO MATCH to the grid.

He pulled on the baseball cap: amateur, but every bit of bad data helps.

Bottles of makeup clinked in his jacket pockets as he

policed the pavilion. His pill bottles bulged in his shirt pockets. Everything not in the Kangaroo Love or his pockets went into a trash bag he ditched behind a tree. *Keep your hands free.*

Condor shuffled over roads paved through this cemetery in the heart of the city. Found the locked office building. Its windows mirrored this empire of the dead. A stranger emerged in those windows' reflection as he rubbed Hip-Girlz cover-up over his face, his hands. Turned his skin some disgusting color of mud.

You look marvelous!

And then they laughed.

At 8:02 on the other side of the building, steel gates creaked open, let in workers.

Only ghosts saw Condor walk out of the cemetery.

One formula made sense.

Fuck with them.

Find some chance in the chaos.

Figure out what you can't remember or don't know, who and why.

Fix it. Or at least go down fighting.

He spotted an orange-plastic-wrapped *Washington Post* tossed in front of a house like it was still the twentieth century. Nobody'd come outside to claim this delivered reality while water boiled on the stove for morning coffee. *I would kill for a cup of coffee,* so stealing someone's newspaper seemed like an acceptable moral stretch.

When he started this life, it would have taken Condor twenty minutes to skim *The Post.* That morning, he scanned the newspaper in less time than it took to walk a block.

War in Afghanistan that was officially almost over. Car bombings in Iraq that weren't officially war. Slaughters in Syria that started as hopeful Arab Spring. Strong moves by the strong man in Russia. North Korea ranted. Europeans raged in the streets. Sound bytes shouted on the Senate floor. Hong Kong had coughing chickens, we all had whacky weather. Wall Street wages were up for the thirty-first straight year. A factory closed in Indiana. Traffic sucked. Divorcing Hollywood stars vowed to remain friends.

Nowhere in the newspaper did Condor spy a story about a crucified federal agent or a manhunt for a missing Library of Congress employee.

A handmade sign hung taped to the screen door of a corner grocery:

COFFEE.

The grizzled black man behind the store counter blinked at the entering freak.

"'Need coffee," said Condor.

The counterman filled a cup from the urn. "Take this one on me and walk on."

Vin shuffled down an access street parallel to North Capitol, here a used furniture store, there a nail salon he could imagine no one frequenting except "beauty students" scamming a few cents out of cash-strapped federal job-training programs.

A Hispanic man wearing a tool belt glanced at the weird gringo sipping coffee beside him while they waited for the traffic light, then watched his fellow crew members on scaffolding across the street. The light turned green. The workman hurried toward the scaffolding. Didn't feel Condor steal the cell phone out of his tool belt pouch.

A pickup truck hauling debris from a house gut idled at the red light.

Padding jiggled under his maroon nylon jacket as

Condor hurried toward the idling pickup while tapping the secret CIA Agent In Trouble digits into the stolen cell phone.

The traffic light's changing—

Made it, behind the pickup, in front of a car that honked at his jaywalking as he thumbed SEND on the cell phone he tossed into the pickup's cargo box.

The Panic Line Center at Langley won't recognize the caller ID. Won't hear a voice on the call. Will activate a GPS track. Divert headhunters off Condor. Maybe find the cell phone still *on,* maybe find fingerprints on it, maybe chase *maybes* all morning.

First time you called the panic line was from a pay phone.

Condor blinked. Cooling black coffee trembled in the paper cup he clutched.

Remembering, you're remembering.

Up ahead a man stepped outside of a glass-fronted store: CYBER WEB D.C. A poster read CYBER CAFE. Orange calligraphy on the store's glass read:

NEW AND USED COMPUTERS! LAPTOPS & COMPUTERS & CELL PHONES REPAIRED HERE! DISPOSABLE CELL PHONES! *SE HABLA ESPANOL!*

A man stood outside his store, smoked a cigarette, licked the street with his eyes.

Chicago. California Street, a Friday-night table in a dive bar, sitting with ebony-hued Ethelbert. He wears a perfect suit, Cary Grant confidence. Watches you sip the second shot of Scotch that he insisted you drink as he says:

"Do you think I care about any of that bicentennial happy 1976 going on out there in the good old U.S. of A.? I'm working the deal, two years of schooling you amateurs on short cons, then I'm out of a go-to-jail jacket."

"I'm a couple tough Ops past being an amateur."

That's you. That's Condor.

"Yet you just blew your cover to show me you've got a big dick." Ethelbert finished his Scotch. "But you also got some savvy. Didn't freak when I walked you in here, only white face around, and **yes,** maybe those days are over, but this has never been about white or black, it's about where you belong, whether you're an insider or an outsider. These are hard-line folks. They been put on it, they walk it and expect you to do the same. You spotted those two bad motherfuckers who are considering clobbering your ass **just because.** They're gonna clobber somebody tonight, might as well make it easy on themselves and clobber the outsider.

"You've got no money," said Ethelbert. "No guns. No knives. Not a two-way wrist-radio the comics keep promising we're going to have someday. You don't have a dime in your pocket for a pay phone, can't pay the tab for our top-shelf Scotch that I'm walking out of here leaving you holding.

"You want to learn, you got to do. You can't do, I can't teach you, so then tell our boss you're quitting the **knock-knock who's there** school. NOC, **'Non-Official Cover'—** Hell: everything is official out here in the street.

"Now con your way safe downtown by midnight.

"Remember, if you're an outsider, try working The Sideways Slide."

Wednesday morning in Washington, D.C., when we have *"two-way wrist-radios."*

The man outside this cyber store lets the smoke drift from his cigarette.

Condor walked up to him. "I been robbed."

"What do you want me to do about it?"

"You sell used cell phones," said Condor. "Good chance one of them is mine."

"We aren't that kind of store. We sell disposables. Burners."

"Whatever I buy, you're giving me my money's worth after what been stole."

The man laughed. Dropped his cigarette. Made a show of grinding it out.

Flicked *gonna fuck-you-up* eyes onto this freak.

Condor strobed back: *So what?*

Said: "I'm gonna buy a phone from you, twenty bucks fair, but what I'd really like to buy is what else they stole."

That Sideways Slide sank the hook into Cigarette Man.

So it was he who said: "What else you looking for?"

"My gun."

"What'd you lose?"

Like that matters. "An Army .45. Brought it AWOL back from 'Nam."

"Sentimental guy?"

"Practical," said the man with the weird dark skin in the Redskins cap and fucked-up glasses and some soft gut under his maroon jacket. "What works, works."

"If we did sell guns, we'd do it in the law. We don't do it here."

"But you might know somebody, and if they kick back to you, who cares."

Cigarette Man shrugged.

"Here's that twenty. I'm gonna tap on your keyboards in there, and the phone you sell me's gonna work."

Cigarette Man took Condor's twenty-dollar bill, gestured for him to enter.

Condor swept his hand toward the visibly empty cyber store: *After you*.

Cigarette Man added such caution to whoever he thought this freak was, went into the store's back room, out of sight.

Gonna happen how it's gonna happen.

Condor picked the computer workstation that let him watch the back room. Like he guessed, the desktop machine needed no password: such a legitimate feature created a record for income tax, money laundering, or fraud audits.

His first search engine result dropped him onto the "Ask Us!" page for the city government's Advisory Neighborhood Commission covering Capitol Hill, a window on the computer screen into which he typed: *"What happened with that murder in his house on Thirteenth Street, SE, of a Homeland Security agent last night?"*

The second search zapped him to the Web site for the Senate Select Committee on Intelligence where he skipped the thirty-second Hollywood-level movie highlighting the Committee as a streetwise defender of every American voter and found the "Contact the Committee" click: *"Why is the CIA overstepping its jurisdiction and investigating the murder of a Homeland Security agent on Capitol Hill last night?"*

Nine clicks in the third search revealed a "conspiracy center" Web site that ranked high on popular search results *and* had a flowing "HAPPENING NOW!" message board system where each posted "citizen's report" had a click for comments that spun into rants and cross-links to other Web entries. Condor typed: *"Who's running the cover-up of the murder of a Homeland Security agent in*

D.C. on Capitol Hill last night that the CIA is somehow involved in, too?"

His next two searches led him to phone numbers Condor wrote on scrap paper.

Cigarette Man came out of the back room waving a cell phone. "Cheapest one is thirty dollars. Say . . . four hours of use. The strip of white tape on the back shows its number."

"Say exactly four hours." Condor cleared his search history, exchanged another of his few bills for the cell phone. "Say I'll be pissed off if it doesn't. And on that other thing, say I'll be back around four this afternoon to see what's what and who's here."

"You will or you won't."

Condor left the store. *You will or you won't. What more is there to say?*

Ten minutes later, he stood in a bus stop, its three plexiglass walls filled by public service posters in Spanish. Condor understood the top banner of a poster that exhorted readers to call 911 in case of emergency, but didn't know that the *Jamas tendras que pagar!* line meant: "You never have to pay!"

He stared down the street to the entrance of a Metro station—D.C.'s subway.

Sure, there'd be security cameras. He'd done what he could about that.

Washington's subway doesn't run twenty-four hours. Last night, cover teams would have ridden the last train, swept the locking-up stations with Metro cops. Spy shop headhunters probably swept the system again when it opened before dawn. But now it's morning rush hour, deep into double shifts for spook agency headhunters, day shift for straight cops who'd be working only off a "regular" high-alert BOLO.

No uniformed cops stood scanning the commuters swiping their fare cards through the orange turnstiles. No men or women with *soft clothes & hard eyes* lingered by the escalators up to the platform. Could be patrols, cover teams he didn't see, but could be the hunt for him now focused on Facial Recognition and other search programs across Big Brother's grid.

A bus braked at the stop sheltering Condor. Bus doors freed morning commuters to flock toward the Metro subway stop. Condor slid into that pack of professionals carrying backpacks, a muscled man carrying a hard hat, a white-haired guy who wore a blue blazer and the gaze of someone who sits behind a downtown lobby desk with no hope of a pension.

Condor kept his head down, his cap obscuring his face as he swiped his way into the station, as he rode the UP escalator. His arms swung up from his sides whenever it seemed like someone might brush against his belly-bulging maroon jacket.

Back-to-back security cameras hung from the cement awning over the train platform. Condor stood directly under the cameras, hoped it was a blind spot.

A hundred bodies waited on those red tiles with him. The crowd formed two groups, each facing one of the two sets of tracks and beyond them, the open spaces looking out over low buildings, trees, into block-away high-rise office windows.

But no one else waiting on the subway platform was really there.

They read smartphones held in one hand. Tablets colored their faces with rivers of broadcasting TV or movies or YouTube clips of bacon-loving dogs. Earbuds closed and glazed eyes. A dozen people talked on cell phones Condor could see, a dozen more babbled into cell phones he couldn't spot, seemingly solo chatter as though they, too, experienced ghosts. Dozens of people used thumbs and fingers to text messages. All his fellow travelers existed in data flows they thought they controlled.

Condor cupped his empty left palm toward his face to look like everyone else.

He tapped his left palm with his right finger, with each tap thought: *This is me.*

A silver *whoosh* knifed through the sunlight above the tracks.

This is a train of now. A *whoosh,* a hum, a whine like an electric current, not the *clackety-clack* rhythm of Woody Guthrie, not the clatter on steel rails of bluesmen from Mississippi or settlers headed West to prairie won from the Cheyenne or soldiers coming home from guarding the Berlin Wall. The train of now slides in and out of stations with a whoosh, a whir, a rumble through this new world.

Bells chime. Train doors jump open. The brown-skinned man in the baseball cap and ridiculous glasses and maroon nylon jacket snapped over his big belly got on board.

Condor found a seat facing the direction the train was going. Even though commuters stood in the aisles, no one chose to sit beside him.

The robotic woman's voice over the loudspeaker called out: "DOORS CLOSING." Electronic bells chimed. Sliding doors sealed everyone inside. Condor felt himself sucked against his orange padded seat as the train accelerated.

Be more than a moving target.

Condor turned on his new cell phone. Called the *Washington Post* phone number he'd gotten at the *transa* store. Key-tapped through a voice menu of instructions.

The train slowed for a platform of waiting riders.

Could be wet boys waiting to get on board—HURRY!

The robotic woman's voice echoing through Condor's car announced "DOORS OPENING!" just as the robotic woman's voice speaking for *The Washington Post* in Condor's cell phone said: "Leave a message or news tip at the beep."

"Yeah, are you going to cover how the Capitol Hill ANC is getting the runaround from the cops about a murder of some Federal agent on Thirteenth Street last night?"

"DOORS CLOSING!"

No one shot him and the train whooshed from that station.

Travelers filled the subway car. Nannies with their charges. Parents who'd left their kids with nannies. Men and women of no fame who worked in buildings identified by initials like EPA and NIH, who did their best for places like the Justice Department, who roamed with the excited herd of twenty-somethings who staff Capitol Hill to sweat out laws and loopholes and to lance attacks approved by American voters via the smiling faces they send to this city from available big-dollar-approved selections. A soldier in green fatigues held on to an overhead bar as he rode standing in the aisle, the double bars of a captain on the rank patch on his chest. Here and there rode students, street dudes.

I hope some of them overheard me. Are e-mailing, maybe tweeting or Facebooking: "Anbdy know bout murdered cop on Hill lst nite?"

Condor dialed the second phone number.

Another robot answered: "You have reached *The New York Times.*"

They know you.

How? Who? Why?

No answers came to him as the train whooshed through its dark tunnel.

Again he worked his way through an automated phone menu: *"Why are your buddies at* The Washington Post *ignoring a story about a Federal agent getting killed last night on Capitol Hill and there's something about a Congressman, too. Fox News has some woman nosing around."*

The train roared into an underground station stop.

Bells chimed. Robot Woman alerted. Doors popped open, clunked closed. People shuffled on and off the train and still no one shot him.

So it went through the morning, Condor changing from one train to another at random underground stations, moving with crowds. Never riding one train long, always facing forward, trying to get the train window with the best view of arriving stations.

There! Two casual-clothes headhunters lurking on the coming platform!

Condor bent over in his subway car seat to tie his shoe.

"DOORS CLOSING!"

The train surged.

He sat straight up in his seat.

Those two headhunters hadn't gotten on this car. *If that's who they were.*

He rode this train to the end of its line, a park & ride plaza with blockish stone buildings for county bureaucracies beyond the border for the District of Columbia yet still inside the Beltway. Few people rode to this last stop at eleven in the morning.

Another elevated subway platform, red tiles, blue sky under the awning gaining warmth with the midday sun. He left the train, hit the smell of pine-scented ammonia.

A Metro janitor in his green jumpsuit mopped the red tiles near the escalators.

Two steps from the DOWN escalator, Condor spotted two uniformed Metro cops getting onto the adjoining UP escalator.

"DOORS CLOSING!" The empty train he'd left roared away without him.

Jumping off the sides of the subway platform meant the tracks, the killer third rail, and after it, a chain-link fence. Then a thirty-foot fall to concrete.

The Metro cops were halfway up their escalator ride.

Condor turned to the mopping janitor, smiled: "Hey man, you okay?"

The janitor blinked. "Ah . . . yeah, I'm fine."

"Your family still doing good?"

Radios crackled on the belts of two Metro cops stepping off the escalator, walking behind the freaky fat man in the baseball cap and Redskins maroon nylon jacket—*obviously* a friend of the janitor who was telling him: "Yeah, the family's okay."

"Good," said the fat guy as the cops walked past.

The cops were five steps past the janitor when he whispered to the friendly stranger: "What's wrong with your face? Looks streaky, like you been crying or—"

"The burns," ad-libbed Condor.

"Shit, man—I'm sorry."

The last those cops saw of the fat man was as he shook hands with the janitor.

Outside the subway station, Condor crossed the street to a franchise restaurant named after a Rolling Stones song. Condor's face horrified the hostess. She gave him a booth in the back. Launched a white shirt/black-tied server—*"Get him in, get him out!"* Condor yearned for the soup and salad bar, couldn't stand that kind of exposure, ordered the biggest cheeseburger he could afford and milk, waddled to the MEN's room.

Shoot him! Shoot him! This is where you shoot him!

Condor blinked into the bathroom mirror. The ghosts vanished. Left him staring at a browned face streaked by teardrops or terror from his sweat. He recolored his image with the last of the makeup.

Sometimes being less of a freak is all you can do.

He wanted to linger over his cheeseburger until the lunch crowd left him behind with only the serious drinkers at the bar who would sit there for hours pretending they were only playing hooky from success. But he couldn't risk staff coming around with *we need that booth*. He paid, slid outside to the midday sun, went next door to a Starbucks.

She's not going to be in here waiting for you. That's so yesterday!

Condor bought a small coffee to justify taking a chair not far from the picture window where he could see across the street to the Metro station.

Steam still floated out of the coffee cup when he spotted them.

An American sedan slid to the drop-off sidewalk near the subway station entrance. The car's rear doors sent a man and a woman into the Metro. They wore open jackets, kept their right hands on their sides as they walked, as their heads swiveled.

The sedan stayed parked out front of the station in a NO PARKING zone. Didn't bother to put on its flashers. Two watchers filled the front seat.

So they got badges to show.

Thirty-seven minutes later, after the third train had come and gone, a zebra team—a white guy and a black guy—stalked out of the station to the sedan.

Cover teams traveling both ways between Metro stops.

And now leaving their scheduled train patrols for the next Op maneuver.

But the white headhunter marched from the parked sedan toward the Starbucks.

Take your cup, DON'T RUN toward the back of the—

"Excuse me!" The barista pointed to the end of the counter.

Condor scooped up one of two keys there. Hurried down the hall to the back of the store. Slipped into the WOMEN's room as he heard the store entrance bell tinkle.

Hid in a bathroom's shiny stall.

That's where you shot Maronick! Blasted bullets through the metal walls of his stall without even looking him in the eyes.

Water flushed in the other bathroom: *Go when you can is a cover team creed.*

Condor waited five minutes. Left the bathroom, eased down the hall . . .

Saw only the barista.

Who said: "I thought you were gone."

"Me, too." Condor looked out the front window.

No cover team's sedan parked outside the Metro station across the street.

No uniformed cops patrolling inside the station.

He rode the next train out of there.

Maronick turns around in the seat in front of you. Smiles despite the bullet hole in his right cheek. "We know right where you are."

Riding tracks and tunnels through the city. Blue pinstripe suits means K Street. Tourist shoes in tight groups mean Smithsonian, Capitol Hill and White House stations that lead Americans out of the underground passageways to see How Things Really Work. The Dupont Circle stop near where CIA-funded D.C. cops burgled anti–Vietnam War think tanks and tear-gassed protesters now feeds the train bright-eyed young women with yoga mats and tattoos of Asian calligraphy. Condor rode one train sharing a seat with a double-shift nurse in blue scrubs.

On one run out of Union Station through the reddening evening light, Condor's train slid past a long tube-like concrete building deserted and scarred with graffiti: the Washington Coliseum where The Beatles exploded America with their first U.S. concert.

Wearing black suits, white shirts and jiving by the train car's middle doors:

Bullet-holed Maronick. Bald Peter and Kevin Powell, throats cut above their black ties. The young Marine who'd saved Condor's life.

Singing:

"Kill, kill you do,
You know they'll kill you.
Their aim is true,
So ple—ee—ee—ease . . . kill you do."

The train *whooshed* on.

Toward a Snatch & Stash.

The only play Condor had left.

You've done it before.

Find your mark. Figure a woman. A frail man. Alone. No wedding ring. In the darkening night. Few passengers on the train, on the platform. The end of the line, suburbs of strangers who mind their own business. Exit the station as a shadow. First chance, punch the base of the mark's spine—shocks them forward, knocks the breath out so they can't scream. Grab them, sell: "I've got a gun." *Should have risked going back to the transa store*. Let the snatched citizen stash you in his or her home.

Kill the chump.

No! That's not who—

The train he rode roared out of a dark tunnel into the gray light of a concrete cavern.

And through the windows . . . On the stop's red-tiled platform . . . Waiting for him . . .

Condor saw how he would die.

12

Trouble-Lost Dog
—Chinese Triad slang, *san jia quan*

Faye told Sami: "You didn't need to drug me."

They sat across a card table from each other on gray metal folding chairs in a soundproof glass booth on the vast warehouse floor of Complex Zed.

Sami sat there with his black curly hair, rolled-up sleeves on a rumpled white shirt and shopping-mall khaki slacks.

He shrugged and Faye pictured him as the middle-aged Beirut businessman he could have grown up to be, if not for the pickup trucks full of militiamen who'd driven into his sunny Lebanese neighborhood when he was nine and passed out free AK-47s to all the eagerly waving hands of the young boys who crowded around their coming.

"After we debriefed last night," Sami told her, "you spent six hours running the streets. Way past midnight, you got frantic, didn't trust the cover teams at his apartment, at his work. That's when I knew you were on adrenaline burn. I need you clear of your own smoke—mentally and physically."

"So you stood beside my cot and made me take a sleeping pill."

"Then I went to my cot and took one, too."

Faye said: "Is that all my pill was, Sami? A knockout?"

"I'm not the kind for date rape."

"But you are such the pro. Divert me with that horror so I don't ask the obvious."

"What's the obvious?"

"Interrogation drug."

Sami cocked his head. "You got me, Faye. I'm that devious. Evidently, so are you. Which is why I need you. But come on: *Really?* Truth serum?

"If the pill was anything extra," said Sami, "call it a test of trust. I give you a pill. Tell you it's mission critical that you take it. You got needed rest because you trusted me and I get confirmed trust that you'll do what it takes to nail the mission."

"I didn't dream. All I had to deal with, I should have."

"Dreamland isn't our turf, Faye. We live in the *gotta do* world."

"What do I *gotta do* now, *Boss*?"

"I know everything about what's happening and nothing about what's going on."

Sami looked at his wristwatch, a black metal chronometer with irradiated dials that glowed green in any darkness.

"It's coming up on six o'clock Wednesday evening," he told her. "And now we got a new problem. Seventh-Floor Langley called. There's buzz."

"Buzz?"

"Gossip, phone calls, Web traffic, weird alerts, whispers in halls, maybe some reporter from what's left of the mainstream media, I don't know: *buzz*.

"We're sticking with the cover of an ex–FBI agent named Vin had a heart attack last night, critical at undisclosed hospital, sorry for any confusion. So now we're welded to that story. One contradiction gets believed, becomes a meme on the Web, we're lying motherfuckers in a cover-up and facts become irrelevant to fury."

"I don't understand."

"Sure you do, but neither of us understands why your partner went back to Condor's place to get killed. There's a text message from his cell phone logged into NROD's system about follow-up on the report you say you wrote under his name."

"That's not Peter. He was a *don't give a fuck* guy."

"But there he was. And logged to Admin, not your unit."

Sami shook his head. "Oh, Condor."

Faye said: "You know him."

Faye let black-haired Sami who held her life in his hands fill her eyes.

Let the luminous second hand sweep a circle around his watch.

Let him fill the silence in their glass booth with what he thought he dared to say.

"We will never have talked about this."

"I've got to know if I'm going to help us, help you."

"Trust, right?" Sami smiled. "Was a time, no one I trusted more than Condor."

"He was your partner. Or your case officer."

"More than that. He was . . . the legend inside the legend."

Sami spoke a man's name.

Faye said: "Wait, I—"

"Under that name," said Sami, "he was a CIA whistle-blower back in the days of truth, justice and the American way after Watergate."

"He was the one who—"

"Went to *The New York Times*. I don't know the real details. Neither did the newspaper. Something about her-oin. Something about Middle East operations. Or the CIA lying about a reason to invade someplace with oil. Something about a bunch of people getting murdered in some undercover facility somewhere.

"The paper printed a bare-bones story. Used that citizen name of Condor's.

"*But nobody cared!* It slid into the deluge of stories about the Agency using the Mafia for assassinations, black-bagging citizens, secret LSD tests, overthrowing governments. Condor became a bit player, didn't get called to testify at the Church Committee Senate Hearings or mentioned in their final report. You'd think that whatever the reality was about Condor, it would have been a big deal, but if enough of the right people don't say *boo,* reality disappears into what's official. Or at least it did before the Web made alternate realities easier."

Faye shook her head. "The Agency would never forget. Maybe they decided not to prosecute Condor for violating any secrecy laws or oaths, but he would have been . . ."

She saw it.

Whispered: *"Holy shit."*

"Just like Phil Agee who published a book and blew the covers of a hundred of our people, everybody in our bad-guy streets knew Condor by that civilian name, knew he was on the CIA enemies list. The enemy of my enemy . . ."

"It was all cover Op to plant him out there!"

"No," said Sami. "Whatever bloody Op gone wrong triggered him, that was real. He started out some first-job-out-of-college guy in the right place at the right time.

"After-Action Evaluation was he'd tried to be on the side of the angels. The Agency rerecruited him. He had the perfect cover: a verifiable enemy of the CIA.

"Nobody knows all he's done. At least two stateside counter-spy Ops, one I think involved China. Mixed with American expat draft dodgers in Europe targeting Soviet agents and terrorists who tried to co-opt the antiwar GIs and draft resisters. Life isn't Hollywood, terrorist or rule-the-world megalomaniac organizations with chrome sky-scraper headquarters and pension plans, but I think he ran with Marxist-tinged groups in the seventies. Red Brigade types. Japanese Red Army. And neo-Nazis like the National Front, he told me about one night on the docks of London. Maybe even some IRA *boyos,* something about Paris. Locked onto the drug cartels early, they're more important politically than most countries. He was the perfect flytrap. They'd come to him. His truth became his cover."

"But he's been *Vin* for . . ."

"Since he got out of the CIA's secret insane asylum in Maine."

Faye's frown asked her question.

"No, he really was crazy. Or went crazy. Evidently, still is crazy.

"Your drone rumor," Sami told her. "That Op was one of the big ones he thought up after 9/11. That's what he was best at—the wild idea.

"Bottom line, *yeah,* he got cornered in the shit, used one of the first iPads to call in a drone strike on himself. Some al Qaeda wannabes decided he was who he really was, a CIA plant. The bad guys were racing to torture and/or kill him, we couldn't exfilt and evac his ass, he couldn't go under, so he waited until they were right on top of him . . .

"The drone killed bad guys and proved they were wrong: the CIA'd sent a drone to kill Condor, so he must have been their enemy, and the Op he'd created stayed safe."

"Why didn't he die?"

"Suicide is a hard shot when you've been taught to take out the other guy."

Sami leaned across the table and his gravity pulled Faye closer to him.

We're whispering in a soundproofed glass box, she thought.

Somehow, that doesn't seem crazy.

"That part of the world," said Sami, "when it does rain, it pours. Lot of runoff goes down the gutters into city parks, so cities like that, they got big storm drainage slits.

"The argument around the Seventh Floor is: Did he plan for the slit being there when he called in the drone, or did he call in the drone *then* suddenly see the slit and change his mind about being a kamikaze?"

"What do you think?" said Faye.

"Doesn't matter," answered Sami. "Whatever he decided, he got it done.

"Figure this: Hard as it might have been calling in the drone strike, after he exploded his world, when he was down there in that storm sewer, dust everywhere, a slit of sunlight, the sound of rescuers racing to find survivors . . .

"To be trapped there and *not* shout for rescue because that will reveal your truth . . . That buys him a hell of *get out of jail forever* card from me.

"Night comes, he can't claw his way out, crashes down and tumbles through the storm drains, into the city sewers. We figure fourteen hours he was down there. Saw the sunshine of another storm drain, crawled out with the rats. Had to mess some woman up to steal her cell phone, call the panic line, hide while he was soaked and stinking of shit."

Sami stared out the glass walls.

Drilled his eyes into Faye.

"When we got him back, he seemed damaged but doable. Had to stay officially dead, of course. Even had some surgery on his face—repair the drone attack damage away from *had been* to *what could be*. Getting older had changed his looks anyway.

"That was when I knew him best. That was back when private contractors were all the rage—Blackwater, a dozen others you know, a dozen more you've never heard of. Contractors still account for about one in four U.S. spooks, but their clout is dropping. Condor set me up in an out-sourced Op. If you don't trust who's in charge or how their show might go, stick in a player you rely on. I did what I did, it cost what it cost, never mind now. By the time I got clear of all that—got my head on straight, got back inside Uncle Sam—Condor'd officially gone crazy."

Sami said, "They didn't even let me know he'd gotten better."

"Maybe he hasn't," said Faye. "What's going on?"

"That's what I want to know."

"You're the boss."

"Really?" Sami smiled. "What about the buzz? What about 'the record' we keep rewriting with our ABCs? What about Seventh-Floor Langley or the West Wing of the White House? What about every hustler looking for anything that gets TV? What about our people out there hunting a fugitive who they think is as good a killer as they are?"

"They're going to shoot first."

"In their shoes," said Sami, "so would you."

Sami looked at her. "You're the last known contact with Condor I can trust."

"You want me to find him."

"Oh, he'll be found. Forget about the overt global BO-LOs, we got great shadow headhunters out there after him. He's not that good, not for long.

"But before that happens, before he gets grabbed up or

gunned down, either way out of my control, I want *you* to get found by *him*."

Faye blinked. "What makes you think he's looking for me?"

"Crazy as he's supposed to be, he might not be—*not looking for you,* I mean. But if he spots you . . . You're the last known official contact for him, too. If he's looking to escape the sewers, you're someone who might know a way out. Which is me."

"I have no idea what to do."

"Hit the bricks. Follow whatever it is that makes you duck before your mind tells you there's a bullet coming your way."

"There's a million miles of nowhere out there."

"Yeah." Sami didn't blink. "We can't give you a cover team. He spots that, he'll know and go, blood bath or back into hiding. Then the percentages suck for me, for us."

Sami leaned back in his chair. "You've got my phone number, I've got yours. I don't want to be the one who calls to say Condor's been got."

"He was your friend. You like him. Trusted him. You want him alive, right?"

"I want to know what I want to know, and I want this all to go down right."

Faye stood. "What about Peter? You would have turned his life inside out."

"The saddest thing about his dying is he left nothing behind him worth knowing. You ask me, Peter was the wrong guy in the wrong place at somebody's wrong time."

"What about Condor?"

"Yeah."

She put her hand on the handle of the glass door.

Looked back at him: "What, no parting ABCs?"

"*Always Be Careful.*" He shrugged. "If not: *Accept Being Crucified.*"

She walked through Complex Zed's warehouse, full of portable workstations and data screening posts and folded-up tables in front of giant steel trunks full of hardware and that glowing soundproof glass booth.

Thought: *Act Beyond Crazy.*

She wore post-shower clothes from her GO! bag she kept by her desk. Dark slacks, gray blouse, a business-acceptable blazer to cover the Glock .40 on her belt and carry the folders of official IDs and badge. Faye marched to the locker room and her locker searched by squirrels who were professionally respectful enough to leave it untidy so they wouldn't insult her by pretending not to have been there. She knew everything they found. Unless something had been planted there, in which case, *not knowing* had a better chance of being believed on a polygraph test or with whatever confession drugs the priests used in their interrogations.

Like maybe whatever drug they gave me last night.

Not a problem, she knew. She had nothing mission critical to hide.

So far.

But if they got me to offer up Chris . . .

Some things we don't like to think about.

She snapped the pouch with two ammo magazines on the left side of her belt under the jacket. Her dull metal spring-bladed jackknife had a belt clip on one of its flat handle's sides, rode on her belt over her spine—*tolerable* if she sat in a chair.

Smart tradecraft would have been to unpack the hip, suede leather backpack-like purse *thoughtfully,* put its contents on the locker shelves *in* and *with* some kind of order, a tidy display that implied she believed she was coming back, a trustable clue for profilers and squirrels who'd open her locker after she was gone.

She dumped her backpack purse into her locker, put back in only the pouch of mission toiletries, grabbed her short black raincoat she'd worn when she interviewed Condor, slammed the locker shut.

A handmade poster above the camp made from portable storage and delivery trunks read: EQUIPMENT DISBURSEMENT DETAIL. Two M4 carbine-slung SWAT guards paced near the bulletproof vest over his white shirt & tie Santa sitting behind EDD's unfolded table that would have fit in at a church social.

Faye confirmed her ID through Santa's portable retina scanner, established her Access/Action Level logging her identifier and Op code word into the laptop on the table, negotiated what she wanted out of what Santa said he had and could release.

Two credit cards with a phony female name came from him without a blink.

Cash was no problem, $2,500 in twenties and fifties, two tens, two fives.

Faye unbuttoned her blouse.

Santa stared at the list they'd typed into his iPad.

Said: "You going to war, Agent?"

"I know what I'm doing," lied Faye.

Before he disappeared in canyons of locked storage trunks, Santa gave her the advice every good government spymaster bestows on their secret agents: "Get receipts."

She laid her blouse on the table and stood there in her black bra.

Santa brought her a charger for her cell phone and spare battery, a forgettable light blue nylon jacket a size too big for her and a ballistic (bulletproof) vest.

"Seven pounds," he said as she strapped it on. Faye told

herself the vest fabric that would show above her blouse's open collar could pass for a hip T-shirt. "No plates, but rated for most combat pistols. Never had any complaints."

"If they had to, they couldn't."

His shrug conceded the point. He returned to the canyon of gear trunks for what he could get. Came back and helped her arrange that weight in her backpack purse.

"You were lucky we got these." Santa shrugged. "I'm a sentimentalist."

"I'm a satisfied shopper," lied Faye as she walked toward the elevators.

She knew it was useless to divert to the WOMEN's room. Rub her hands over her body. Use the spring-bladed jack-knife to check behind the badge in her folder. Smell the soles of her black sneaker-like shoes for the scent of fresh glue. Sami or her bosses at NROD or Home Sec or the CIA didn't need to plant a tracking bug on her. They and probably the whole world were pinging on the GPS in her cell phone.

Doesn't matter that they know where you are if they can't touch you there.

The elevator let her out at the main lobby.

Our world waited beyond those walls of glass.

Faye pushed her way through the revolving door, walked across the plaza to the sidewalk curb and raised her hand for a taxi.

He's presumed to be on foot, so I should be, too.

A taxi slid to a stop, she got in, told the driver where she wanted to go, didn't recognize him as one of Sami's soldiers—but he'd have used a face unknown to her.

After all, she wasn't *supposed* to have a cover team.

The backpack purse rode heavy on the seat beside her.

Cuts your speed and stamina. That weight better he worth it.

"Rush hour," said the cabby, a black guy with an accent of where: *Nigeria?* "Always rush hour where you got to get to, to get where you got to go."

"Yeah." She turned so he saw her face in the rearview mirror point toward the sidewalks they whizzed past and no more conversation. Let her eyes scan his side mirror.

The route he chose took them all the way down Wisconsin Avenue to the tricky left-hand turn onto Massachusetts Avenue by the fenced grounds of the Naval Observatory and the vice president's official residence.

Mass Avenue below the vice president's house is Embassy Row, the sprawling brick estate with Winston Churchill's V-fingered bronze statue out front for the Brits, the black glass castle-sized box of Brazil that had seemed *ultra modern* before Faye'd been born, gray stone mansions for European powers, the Islamic Center seized and held bloody hostage along with the headquarters for B'nai Brith and a D.C. government building by radical Hanafi Muslims in 1977.

A few blocks later, her taxi flowed with traffic around Sheridan Circle where in America's bicentennial, the year before the Hanafi siege, a wet squad including a former CIA agent from Waterloo, Iowa, remote-control bombed a car during the rush-hour commute in order to murder a former Chilean diplomat, also killing one American and wounding her husband as part of Operation Condor, the secret spy collaboration between six right-wing South American nations.

Faye had the taxi drop her at the corner of Third Street & Pennsylvania Avenue, SE. The Capitol waited behind her, Condor's Library of Congress office loomed a block-plus off to her left. Pennsylvania Avenue stretched away from the Congress's turf with blocks of cafes and bars and restaurants, there a Starbucks, there a two-story brick building with a street door listing offices for three different groups, all with public policy–sounding names that guaranteed nothing about what they really did.

This was your turf, Condor.

Faye corrected herself: Is *your turf.*

See me, she wished as she stood there, the last cars of rush hour whizzing past her, the crowd of Congressional staffers who'd headed somewhere after work now thinning.

Besides Starbucks, whose interior she cleared with a quick scan through its picture windows, the "social business" that appeared most in Condor's credit card bills waited down the block near Fourth Street.

The Tune Inn. A flat-fronted beer & burgers saloon sunk like a shaft into the block's wall of coat & tie–friendly restaurants and bars.

Two steps into The Tune and Faye knew why Condor came here.

Three steps into the saloon and she spotted Pulaski sitting at the bar to her left as she walked toward the back end of booths before the bathrooms and kitchen. Pulaski was pure Special Ops, a scraggy beard that would have let him drop from this stakeout cover team mission to the streets of Kabul without much more than a minor wardrobe adjustment from his dirty blue jeans and soiled cloth Windbreaker Faye was sure covered two pistols in shoulder-holster rigs. He kept his eyes on his bottle of Miller beer.

Three stools away from Pulaski sat Georgia, an ex-cop from Alabama, dressed like a hard-luck drinker who didn't take her eyes off the half-full glass of white wine in front of her and kept her hands resting lightly on the scarred bar beside her cell phone.

Sami wouldn't have called off the dogs of Standard Operating Procedure just because he'd sicced her solo into the streets. Beyond headhunter patrols, there'd be cover teams at Condor's house, at his work, at—*say*—the top five places he'd been known to frequent. Faye wondered who she hadn't spotted in the Starbucks, but maybe that cover team coded in the Op plan as an exterior post surveillance, maybe a van parked where the watchers could cover the Starbucks doors and also scan more of the target's turf.

She walked past her colleagues without a sign of recognition amongst them.

Knew one of them would text Control that she was onsite. As if the bosses didn't already know from pinging her cell phone.

"You want a booth, hon?" asked the strong but slumping sixtyish waitress with rusted hair and a face that as a teenager slowed all the pickup truck traffic in whichever small Maryland town she'd gotten this far from. "Wherever you want."

This is what Condor sought, thought Faye as she took an empty, black-cushioned booth. The Tune's brown-paneled walls were hung with stuffed animal heads and a rifle rack of guns that clearly wouldn't work, pictures and plaques and beer signs from truck stops along the highways of Out There, America. She smelled beer, cooking grease from the kitchen beyond a half-door, the scent of evening drifting in from the city street.

This was a bar an American could call home. A place that felt like those post–World War II days when everything still seemed possible. You could wear a torn T-shirt or a tux here, and probably both came in during the course of any business week. A sign said the bar had been here longer than any other alcohol stop on Capitol Hill. Faye believed it. Most of the other stools at the bars where Pulaski and

Georgia sat held people who'd not gotten where they were on easy roads.

One booth held two facing-fifty women whose blond dye jobs and white mohair sweaters and strings of pearls cost a lot of alimony, while their college-age sons, trying not to look bored or embarrassed, were clearly being shown where it used to be happening *back when*. Try as they might to maintain their aloof, Faye knew those college boys were tracking three scattered groups of Congressional aides who couldn't be more than a few years older than them, "men" and "women" who'd beaten the odds, gotten jobs, maybe'd gone to Harvard on Daddy's rep & billions or worked their way through heartland state universities on student loans they'd be repaying for decades, *but whatever,* they'd made it, they were here, "on the Hill."

In a bar that felt like the America they all wanted to believe was in their blood.

Faye didn't need to listen to the music above the bar chatter or check the jukebox to know Condor'd come here hoping for his *clongs* amidst sounds of Hank Williams and Dusty Springfield, Bruce Springsteen and a handful of country & western songbirds flying the same skies as Loretta Lynn and other icons Faye recognized only by name.

"What can I get you, hon?" The rust-haired waitress leaned on the back of Faye's booth and gave the customer a real smile—what the hell, we're stuck here, might as well go for the happy we can get.

Faye ordered a hamburger and a Coke. Protein and caffeine. Fuel and fire.

"Not Diet, right? Good for you, hon." The rust-haired waitress yelled the food order back to the kitchen, swayed toward the bar to get Faye's drink.

Let me count the ways I'm trapped, thought Faye as the jukebox played.

Don't know where I'm going, don't know how to do what I've got to do, don't know how to get found by a killer—the right killer, anyway. Don't know how I ended up here—well, ended up here like this.

Don't know how I can warn off the man who loves me.

Years ago, there'd have been a pay phone in this bar. If there was now, Faye still couldn't use it. The cover team would catch that, zap the pay phone coordinates to the command center, and NSA's MAINWAY computers would flash *who* or *where* Faye called. Same reason she couldn't use her cell phone to call Chris, leave a message for him at work or get him on his cell. Faye considered stealing a phone from one of the Congressional staffers who were one beer away from being more than a little drunk, but every complication on a mission increases risk and the risk of a stolen cell phone scenario equaled why she wanted to steal a phone: keeping Chris clear of all this, of her.

Or so she told herself.

Had nothing to do with wanting to reach out and touch him, know he was safe, know he was there, know he still cared.

Last thing I need, she told herself sitting in that black upholstered bar booth, sipping a Coke as the jukebox played some Sarah Lee Guthrie & Johnny Irion song, *is to worry about him worrying about me.*

Sunset pinked the front windows at the end of the bar as she forced herself to finish the hamburger she couldn't taste, the Coke that didn't quench her thirst.

Her stomach gurgled. She told herself it wasn't nerves, had to be the bar food, maybe the drug she'd swallowed the night before.

She took the heavy purse/backpack with her through the scruffed & scarred brown wooden door labeled WOMEN.

The hook & eye lock would stop a polite customer's pull but not much more.

If only it would be Condor jerking on that door!

But it won't be. And if it were, her two colleagues at the bar would claim him. Not her. Not just her and Sami and what the two of them needed.

She didn't shut the door on the metal stall when she did what she had to do in there: if someone burst into the bathroom, she wanted a chance for a clear shot.

Washing her hands in the white sink, she raised her eyes to the mirror.

Saw the face called hers staring back.

Saw the chance.

Stupid, sure. *Crazy,* sure. *Corny,* sure. *Risky.* With all that, still her best shot.

She found her mission toiletries in the backpack purse, the gold tube of cheap bright red lipstick, the kind Faye as herself would never wear, the kind of *notice me* lip paint that dominates a witness's perception, cheap tradecraft she'd never used.

She turned the dial so the glossy red tip slid up and out of its gold sheath.

On the glass of the mirror she made appear in bright smear cherry-red letters:

> Call Chris 202 555 4097
> Tell him better roads r
> around this bend. Tnx F

Then surrounded her lipstick plea with the outline of a red heart.

Slashed a long bloodred line under her heart on that mirror and—

Saw her second shot.

Do. Not. Run.

Walk out of the bathroom.

Go back to your booth.

She let her eyes sweep over her *sisters* who were in this bar, who were yet to come there tonight, would use the bathroom before the janitor mopped up with his ammonia cleaner and tired eyes. Surely some woman would come to that mirror who had a romantic soul, the courage of her curiosity. And a cell phone.

She counted out the cost of her dinner plus a great tip.

Showed she wasn't hurrying by standing there, dipping a last French fry into the plop of ketchup on her plate. She put the straw between her lips for a last sip of Coke.

Sure, that's all anyone sitting at the bar would see.

And she walked out without showing or saying a thing worth reporting.

Gray twilight muted by streetlamps swallowed her as she stepped onto the sidewalk. Could have turned to the right, but the formula of her epiphany mandated Condor being a sentimental guy, so she turned left as she cell-phoned Control.

Sami's voice in the cell phone pressed to her ear: "What have you got?"

"A hunch." Faye quickened her pace past a lucky mother who was her age and pushing a laughing baby boy in a stroller from *Me-ma*. "Give me room to play it."

"How?"

"Have cover teams pull back if they spot me come into surveillance Op zones."

"I'll do what I can, give you as much slack as is Op safe. Tell me—"

"Whatever you know, you'll try to plan ahead of, and that might mess me up."

"Then don't miss." Sami hung up.

Faye muttered *"ABC to you, motherfucker"* as she returned her cell phone to the shirt pocket above her bulletproof vest, but she meant it in the nicest possible way.

The white-icing dome of the Capitol slid past her heart side as she marched to Union Station where she thought she saw a homeless woman rolling her shopping cart of rags and remnants away with more purpose than prayer. Could have been a headhunter pulling back as ordered, could have been just another nobody in the night, Faye couldn't let herself care. Rode Union Station's exterior escalator down to the subway platform and stood in front of the poster-sized stations-and-routes map for Metro's subway, the names of the stops in black letters, the subway lines drawn between them in thick colored connectors of orange and blue and green and yellow. And red.

Red like blood.

Red like lipstick.

"I like the Red Line." She'd chalked that up to Condor sounding crazy.

Now hoped he'd told the truth.

Faye saw a man with a Metro patch on the shoulder of his blue sweater giving directions to two tourist-clad senior citizens—*older even than Condor,* thought Faye, buying that both the tourists and the Metro worker were true to those identities. The Metro worker finished with the grateful tourists and Faye caught his eye.

"Can I help you?" he said.

"I'm visiting my father," she said, and even though she rode the Metro at least three times a week, asked: "He said there's one stop on the Red Line that after rush hour gets deserted on the platform and that I should ride to the next one. Is there a Red Line stop where, like he said, not many people are on the platform after now?"

The Metro worker blinked. "Really?"

She gave him her friendliest *What can you do?* shrug.

"Could be . . . I don't know. This one, or this one . . . Maybe that one."

And Faye pictured *that one*: an underground platform. One set of escalators, the upper entry level with turnstiles visible from the red-tiled platform between the two sets of train tracks, a gray cement cavern with dark tunnels for the trains at either end.

She thanked him.

Rode the first train there.

"DOORS OPENING."

One person got off the train at that stop with Faye, a businesswoman who barely looked up from answering the endless stream of e-mails in her smartphone as she rode the escalator up, out through the turnstiles, gone.

This is the picture.

A woman standing alone on the red-tile platform in the gray concrete tunnel.

Me.

Wearing the black raincoat I had on when we met. Coat unbuttoned, Condor'd expect that, believe that. Could see me as any train he rode slowed into the station.

Faye calculated it made more sense to set the backpack purse on the red tiles in front of her shoes. *Sure,* not as in her control, but also, one more thing for his eyes to process. One more thing for her to worry about, but the weight of it during her waiting and the energy that would cost seemed worth avoiding.

*What if*s raced infinitely down each set of tracks. *What if she was wrong and he hadn't chosen to be a moving target on the line he liked? What if a Metro patrol scooped*

him up? Why hadn't they? What if he didn't see her wait-
ing on the platform or did and rode on anyway or jumped
out of the Metro car blazing away with Peter's stolen gun?

She let all that go.

Waited to deal with what the steel rails brought her.

A train rumbled roared *whooshed* into the station, rectangular windows of light dotting the long silver snake like
scales as it slid past her facing eyes, stopped.

"DOORS OPENING!"

No one got off.

None of the three people she looked at through the train
windows looked back.

"DOORS CLOSING!"

The train whooshed away.

She refused to look at her watch.

Or count the number of times trains whooshed into the
station, stopped, let one or two or three or mostly no one
off to ride the escalators up and out into the night.

A rumble roar whoosh, silver train sliding to a stop.

"DOORS OPENING!"

No one getting off, no one—

Standing in the subway car's open doorway twenty
paces from her.

A baseball-capped, fatboy freak in brown skin, hands
by his sides, *empty, are they empty?*

The freak stepped off the train.

13

A man and a woman stand alone on a red-tiled subway platform.

He's stepped out of the silver train on the track behind him.

She's keeping her stance soft and still, facing a maroon-jacketed, big-bellied apparition with a baseball cap, absurd eyeglasses, brown skin. He knows *she knows.*

"DOORS CLOSING!"

Rubber-edged doors *ca-thunk* shut behind him.

The silver train streaks from the station.

She said: "If I wanted you dead, you would be."

Her hands stay at her sides, fingers splayed open to show *empty.* The thirty feet of red tiles between them represent the optimal kill zone for a handgun.

What's that bag on the tiles near her feet? Remote-detonated flash-bang? Gas?

"How are you, Vin?"

"Call me Condor. That's why we're here."

"Do you remember who I am?"

"Your work ID is Faye something."

"Faye Dozier. And it's more than a work name, a cover."

"Who are you right now?"

"Your rescue. Your chaperone. Your minder to bring you in. Get you safe."

"I think I remember I've been told that before."

Take a step toward her.

She didn't move. Reposition. Shift her weight. Draw her gun.

Take another step closer. Close the gap.

She said: "My partner got whacked at your place. I need to know all about that."

"And you think I know."

"The white car," she said as he was three steps from being able to hit her. "That makes me think you don't know *enough*. So we're stuck on the same bull's-eye."

He stopped two paces from her. She was out of his striking zone. But close. If she moved to draw a weapon, *theoretically,* at least now he had a chance.

Condor said: "What's in the bag?"

"Proof you can trust me."

An electronic marquee on a hollow brown metal column listed glowing lines of train schedules. Rush hour was over, the next train was due in nineteen minutes, the one on the opposite track due three minutes after that. Empty escalators whirred up from and down to this platform where only the two of them stood.

He imagined she heard the slamming thunder of his heart beneath his maroon nylon jacket. Imagined he heard her muffled thunder, too. Inside her black coat that no doubt covered at least one pistol, under her blouse, he saw the thickness of a bulletproof vest.

Where they stood was the lowest level of the subway station. The closed orange doors of the "Handicap Accessible" elevator leading up to the street waited near the escalators that connected this passengers' platform to an entrance level twenty feet above the top of their heads, an apron of red tiles inside orange turnstiles that *whumped* open & closed. Beyond those turnstiles were fare card machines, and mere steps beyond them, a forty-one-second-long escalator ride connecting our world to these underground arteries. Condor couldn't see much past the top of the escalator up to the entrance level, couldn't see the orange turnstiles, certainly couldn't see the main escalators up to the night.

Faye said: "How long are we going to just stare at each other?"

"My chaperone." *What does she think of me: the dark skin, the baseball cap and big glasses, the fat-man jacket?* "I liked slow dances in high school."

"This isn't high school, Condor," she said.

She's worried I'm losing it.

Next train: eighteen minutes.

Concrete columns five times as thick as Condor's fat-man suit rose from the red tiles to the curved gray ceiling. He remembered two FBI agents and two bank robbers in . . . *Miami*, who'd chased each other around a parked car, all four of them blasting away with semiautomatic pistols, two of them reloading on the run, all the bullets missing flesh. The two columns on this subway platform needed fewer steps to race around than a parked car. And down in this tunnel, the perils of ricochets canceled out any advantage the concrete gave over bullet-porous car metal.

"Hey, chaperone," said Condor: "Slow dance."

He took two steps back.

Faye took two steps forward to preserve the distance he'd chosen between them.

Her shoes stopped beside the backpack purse on the red tiles.

Condor said: "Pick it up. Both hands."

Oh so slowly, she did.

No BOOM! No *flash-bang* stunning light. No eruption of tear gas or smoke.

"See?" she said. "So far, so good."

Green eyes, he thought. Her eyes are green.

"Don't see only what's in front of you."

Who taught me that? Let that go. Let that ghost dissolve.

Faye said: "What now?"

"Unzip it. Make sure the opening is toward your face, not mine."

The zipper *zuzzed* a slow opening of the backpack purse.

Condor said: "Show me—*easy.*"

She tilted the backpack so he could peek into the bag. "Take what you want."

He flicked his eyes up from the bag to meet hers.

"I was right," he said. "One way or another, you're how I'm going to die."

"Not now," she said. "Not with me. Not if I can help it."

"And this is your help?"

She shrugged. "And my bona fides."

He took the last step to be close enough to her.

Slid his right hand into the backpack. She didn't close it. Trap him. Try for some aikido or judo throw, she just . . . let him do it.

Feel cool steel, textured wood, the terrible weight of choice.

Condor filled his right fist in the bag with a snub-nosed .38 revolver.

He pulled out the hand-sized pistol. Let its death hole drift aimlessly and casually from side to side, but showing him the gold glint of brass cartridges in the wheel cylinder that implied the gun held ammunition that worked.

Faye said: "I thought you'd go for the .45 in there. The updated 1911, but still like you said you—"

Thunk! The cold steel bore of the snub-nosed revolver dug into her forehead.

"—prefer," she finished.

Her green eyes blinked.

But she didn't back away. Whirl/sweep her arm up to beat a bullet to her brain.

A man and a woman stand alone on a red-tiled subway platform.

His arm extended to press a gun's death bore against her third eye.

"I prefer to be murdered with my partner Peter's weapon," she said.

"Sorry, I don't have it."

"Then you'd be stupid to shoot me."

"Stupid comes easy."

"Here I thought you were a hard guy. If you don't have my partner's gun, then you didn't kill him and somebody took it to package you as armed and dangerous."

"Great minds," he said. "Theirs. Yours."

Slowly the steel barrel backed off her skull.

Still she didn't counterattack.

Condor put the revolver in his jacket pocket.

Smiled.

Lifted the holstered .45 semiautomatic out of the backpack. That gun came with a pouch of two spare ammunition magazines. He awkwardly shifted the bulk under his jacket to clip both the ammo pouch and the holstered .45 to his belt.

She shook her head. "You look ridiculous."

The marquee read fourteen minutes until the next train arrived.

"Moving," she told him. "Getting my phone."

She used her left thumb and forefinger in an overly

formal pincer grip to lift her cell from the blouse pocket over her heart.

Told Condor, "I'll put it on speaker."

Empty escalators whirred to and from this red-tiled station platform.

The cell phone buzzed once. Buzzed twice.

Condor heard faint background noise coming from the phone.

Faye told the device in her hand: "Someone's here to talk with you."

"Who?" said a man.

That voice! Here! D.C. National Airport. A little girl—Amy. A bomb.

Be sure: "Tell me something."

Eagerness came through the man's voice in the phone: *"Always Be Cool!* Condor, it's Sami!"

The question ripped from Condor's bones: *"Where have you been?"*

"Trying to bring you home. Where are you—both of you?"

Condor thrust his hand to block Faye's reply. "*Here*. Where's *there*? Langley?"

"No, our friend Faye, she knows where I am. Doesn't matter. GPS says our exfilt team will be to you in fourteen minutes."

"We'll be gone. See you."

Condor lifted the phone from the woman's hand and she let him, but her eyes flashed questions as he thumbed the phone here, there . . .

As Sami's voice in the phone said: "Faye, come—"

. . . Condor killed the call. Gave her back the phone.

"Turn off the power," he said.

She did.

"We've got to go now."

"Sami is—"

"Not here. We are."

Condor took a backward step away from her, his eyes on her as an image, his hand near his maroon nylon jacket's pocket, sagging with the weight of the gun.

Saw her green eyes decide before she gave him a nod.

"Okay, Condor. You're the star."

The marquee told them twelve minutes before the next train.

"You got a car?" he said as he gave her his back . . .

. . . and she didn't shoot him as he hurried toward the UP escalator.

"No," said Faye.

He climbed the escalator steps as they carried him up.

Heard her footsteps right behind him.

They hurried across the entrance level toward the orange turnstiles. Condor and Faye slapped their electronic SmarTrip cards over the data-reading strip in side-by-side turnstiles. The turnstiles jumped open to set them free.

Alone in the station, the man and woman quick-walked to the bottom of the three basketball-court-length, forty-one-second-ride UP escalators stretched through a slanting giant straw of concrete to D.C.'s neon blue night sky.

Condor hesitated. Stepped on the rising metal stair . . . and stayed there.

Sighed: "I wish I was in better shape."

"Or younger," he added as Faye climbed to ride up on the step below him. He felt energy coursing through her, her strobing urge to run up the stairs, move on, DO IT!

"We're on our way," she assured her quarry, her *protectee,* her de facto partner, as Condor looked back down the stairs toward her and the sliding-away tunnel of where they'd been, saw the thought light her face: *Not going to lose another one!*

He turned forward.

Looked up the long stairs carrying them toward the neon-blue night.

Said: "Too late."

14

Gonna shoot you right down.
—John Lee Hooker, "Boom Boom"

Faye spotted them at the top of the escalator carrying Condor and her ever upward toward the blue night: Four, *no,* six backlit silhouettes.

Two shapes moved with military grace at the top of the tunnel onto the DOWN escalator that ran past Faye's left. A man and a woman. *Like us,* thought Faye.

Faye whispered: "Be cool!"

Nothing! Condor's not answering! Did he hear me? What does he hear?

His right hand slid into the pocket of his maroon nylon jacket.

No! Had to make him trust me! He's not rogue! Or crazy!

Trapped bchind Condor on stairs carrying her up toward four *unknowns.*

As sliding down the escalator next to her, *toward her,* came two more strangers.

They could all be innocents. Six total. Six bullets in a revolver.

The escalator trembled Faye with its upward glide. Cooler outside air flowed over her face. The escalator smelled like oiled steel, the black rubber handrails.

Drawing nearer on the DOWN *escalator: Black man, white woman behind him.*

Twenty feet and a few seconds apart, fifteen, ten—

The black man wore a brown leather hip-length coat over weightlifter muscles.

The white woman, hair colored Midwestern brown and—

Whirled her hands up weapon pointing at Condor WUNK!

Taser! Two wire-leashed probes shot out—

Hit the giant belly of Condor's maroon nylon jacket, the *Gotcha!* frenzy on the Midwestern-haired woman's face turning to puzzlement as she squeezed the Taser's control handle to send fifty thousand volts of electricity coursing into . . .

Into nonconductive padding under Condor's maroon nylon jacket.

Condor fired the snub-nose .38 from inside his pocket.

The tunnel boomed with the gunshot roar. The bullet slammed into the Midwestern woman's chest, knocked her off balance on the sliding-down escalator stairs.

No blood spray! Ballistic vest, she's wearing armor!

The Midwestern woman crashed toward her black partner as he cross-drew—

Gun! Silenced pistol! His partner tumbles into him and he falls as he aims—

Faye heard *cough,* a bullet whine past her face.

Found the Glock in her hand, fired twice at the falling man, blood spraying from hits on unarmored flesh, then he was tumbling out of sight on the descending escalator.

BANG! Condor firing up the mouth of the tunnel.

Faye whirled—saw four human shapes dive out of sight of her escalator-up view.

Condor fired again. His bullet smacked into metal at the top of the escalators, whined off into the night *God don't let its ricochet hit some kid!*

"Stop!" she yelled. "Cease—"

Gun! Poked into the escalator shaft, wink of flame/bullet whines past Faye. She popped two shots into the metal at the top of these stairs. Gun pulled back.

"Condor!" she yelled. "Roll across to the other escalator, the DOWN stairs!"

Faye spotted motion near the street-level mouth of the escalator. Crashed a bullet into the metal escalator shaft up by where the steel stairs folded into the machine.

Condor lunged across the metal border separating the UP and the DOWN escalators, missed grabbing the moving rubber handrail, flopped into the shaft of the DOWN escalator. His baseball cap flew off, his fake glasses spun away, the Taser probes ripped free from him. A steel stair edge chopped his right arm. He yelled in pain as he somersaulted down the sliding stairs.

The snub-nose .38 flew from Condor's hand, bounced down the moving steel stairs, over the prone & gasping woman whose bulletproof vest had just proven its worth.

Condor tumbled into that Midwestern woman, rolled over her, past her, his feet pointing down on those sliding-into-the-earth steel stairs. He skidded, stopped.

Looked up the steel shaft passage to the receding half-moon of blue night.

Whine over Condor's head clangs into metal.

From the escalator beside him Faye's gun roared.

As she ran *backwards* down the steps of the moving UP escalator.

The Midwestern woman jackknifed up in front of Condor. Sat on the stairs, blocked his view up the tunnel as she gripped a black pistol, its bore zeroed on Condor.

Crimson spray flowered in the shiny steel–lit darkness behind her head.

She snapped forward, her ballistic vest springing her back so she sat upright on the descending escalator stairs between Condor and the shooters. A spritz of red mist glistened in her small-town-escapee hair. She rode those downward stairs sitting with dangling low arms at her sides like a "*come unto me*" Madonna.

Another bullet meant for Condor *thunked* into the dead woman, hit her vest-covered spine, not the back of her skull.

The gun she dropped filled his hand. He fired up at the night.

Condor ran down the DOWN escalator.

Chased by the skull-shot Madonna slumped on the stairs.

On the escalator stairs ahead of Condor lay a black man in a brown leather coat with a dark-stained left shoulder. Ooze covered the black man's left ear. He kicked as Condor staggered past him. Condor stomped his face. The black man slumped. Condor ran off the end of the moving-down stairs to the floor of the subway's entry platform where seconds later, the escalator dumped the unconscious black man.

Condor yelled up to Faye: "Covering you!"

Fired two rounds from the dead woman's Glock.

Faye vaulted onto the metal border between the escalators. Fist-sized knobs are built into that metal border to discourage the sliding Faye tried, so she improvised a scrambling charge and leapt off the escalator to the red tiles beyond Condor.

They ran deeper into the underground subway station.

She vaulted orange turnstiles, whirled to cover their retreat where descending stairs dumped a slumped Madonna on top of an unconscious black man.

"Move!" she yelled to Condor.

No vaulting over orange turnstiles for him. He used the emergency gate.

"Go!" she yelled, backing toward the escalators down to the subway platform.

He ran ahead of her. *Galumped* down the escalator to the red tiles. Staggered to the center of the platform so he could aim back up toward the turnstiles, yelled: "Now you!"

Faye ran down the last escalator.

Saw the subway schedule marquee:

Next train in five minutes.

Opposite-direction train arriving three minutes later.

A man and a woman stood alone on a red-tiled subway platform.

Both of them aiming guns up to the entrance level toward orange turnstiles they could barely see. They sidestepped apart to not cluster in one easily targetable group.

"Four left, minimum," said Faye. "Maybe they broke off."

"You wouldn't," said Condor.

The marquee above them displayed four minutes to the next train, but they didn't take their eyes off where shooters might appear.

Your train comes when it comes.

Up on the entrance level: two shapes vaulting the turnstiles.

Faye fired before Condor, then they flowed forward for new defensive positions.

Soaring through the concrete cavern air:

A black stone tossed from that upper entrance level on

a soared curving arc to the red-tiled platform where Faye and Condor crouched.

"Flash-bang!" Faye leapt alongside the solid sheltering wall of the escalators.

Condor jumped behind the thick concrete pillar.

Both turned their backs toward the grenades. Scrunched their eyes closed. Covered their ears. Opened mouths to ease explosive pressure, dropped low as—

White nova FLASHING seared their closed eyelids.

Ear-stabbing BANG! rocked their equilibrium.

Faye forced her eyes open.

The subway platform shimmered into view.

A giant invisible vacuum cleaner whined in her ears.

Gunpowder smoke tinged this concrete cavern.

Your back's pressed against the solid metal side of the escalators, and—

Condor: beside the concrete column aiming up toward the next level. His gun spits two flashes. He jumped behind the concrete pillar where POP! white dust flowers:

Someone's returning fire!

Charging feet pound down the escalator.

First attacker down the stairs, *a man,* running, squeezing rhythmic shots at the concrete pillar, keeping Condor pinned on the other side, killer closing to there as—

Second attacker, *young guy,* lunges over the escalator, thrusts his gun to shoot—

Faye grabbed her assailant. He toppled over the side of the escalator, crashed into her and they collapsed on the red tiles.

Don't let his gun point at you! He's grabbed your right wrist doing the same!

Faye drove her knee into the man on top of her.

He gasped, flung himself off her, their hands gripping them together like jitterbug dancers from her grandmother's era as he muscled their inertia, jerked her onto her feet.

She spins the man she grips in an airborne half circle.

They fly off the edge of the subway platform.

Crash onto the train tracks.

Third rail! Third rail! Where the fuck is the third—

Won't let go of each other, scramble to stand.

What's that noise . . .

She stomps her foot out to dragon kick his stomach.

He gets knocked back, trips over a rail—

—just a regular steel rail—

—his back hits the concrete edge of the platform.

Bouncing him off with a body slam that rockets her off her feet, barely catching her balance with her shoes on the grille covering the white lights along the tunnel's far wall as she sees her foe drop into a combat shooter's stance and swing his pistol—

Train slams into her attacker, whining stopping only after the silver snake scarfs his body under its steel snout and blood spray trickles down the engineer's window.

Train pins Faye with her back pressed against the curved gray concrete wall, her arms straight out to her sides. *Like I'm crucified.*

See the glow of train windows smack in front of her.

Smell the hot steel brakes.

Smell wet ham.

"DOORS OPENING!"

Bullet hole punched out the train window above her.

Two more shots, holes punched through the plastic windows. Cosmically, she knew the engineer heard *gunshots,* so *get out of here!*

"DOORS CLOSING!"

Faye pressed against the concrete wall as the train roared past her.

Going to suck me off my feet toss me bounce me crushed dead and—

Whump, she saw the butt of the train, red light vanishing down the tunnel *gone,* her feet settling on the steel grille over the tunnel wall floor lights.

From the track bed where she stood Faye stared across the waist-high red-tiled platform at a warrior edging his way around the concrete pillar to gun down Condor.

Faye shot the warrior in the head. Shot him dead.

Condor left the pillar's shelter as Faye hoisted herself out of the track bed.

"Four down!" she gasped to Condor.

The handicap-access elevator by the escalator DINGED!

Metro elevators ease down shafts from the sidewalk to the subway platform. Their metal walls create a closed box big enough to hold four wheelchair travelers. Blurry steel creates mirrors on the inside; on the outside, the elevator's doors are orange.

Take the harder shot, thought Faye, told Condor: "I got our backs!"

Faye aimed up to the main entrance.

Orange elevator doors slid open.

Faye felt Condor hustle toward that cube that could be their escape route.

Slow dance. She walked backwards in his wake, never wavering her aim.

Quick glance showed her *he's at the elevator, gun barrel moving toward the open doors* and as she swung back to scan the darkness beyond her gun sights.

Condor eased his left foot onto the crack between the elevator and the subway platform's red tiles so that the cage door's rubber guard closed on/bounced off his shoe as he flowed forward and swung the barrel of his gun up to—

The sky fell on Condor.

Dropped from spread-eagled across the top of the elevator cage, Monkey Man, long, whip lean and strong, missing a perfect ambush onto the old guy in the maroon nylon jacket but still grabbing his gun arm BANG!

Faye whirled—

Got knocked off her feet by Monkey Man shoving Condor into her, holding on to Condor, charging past him with a pivoting aikido throw that flung the Glock out of Condor's hand even as the throw also flipped Condor off his feet and onto the red tiles.

Monkey Man spun out of his pivot with a crescent kick that slammed his shoe into Faye's extended gun arm—the kick clattered her gun away on the tiles.

But the crescent kick required heartbeats and space for Monkey Man to settle, balance, recover—and only *then* be able to attack.

Whoosh of silver streaks into the subway station.

Time slows down if you survive enough fights, boxing or martial arts encounters. Doctors claim that's merely the relaxation/suppression of fear instincts and the startle impulse allowing you to be aware of, process and react to the accelerated flood of data generating from the person in front of you trying to rip your head off. Science favors the experienced who know about leverage and coverage and counters, who possess strength and speed and stamina. From the moment Monkey Man touched her, Faye knew she'd need more than science to survive on that subway platform. As she swooped her guard up, she prayed for the deliverance of poetry, of art.

She launched a snap kick, mostly feint, and Monkey Man didn't buy it, flowed back to suck her charge in further and then launched forward to blast through her guard with one of his long-ass punching arms but she dodged sideways, changed her angle of attack, came at him with a three-punch/one-kick combination—

"DOORS OPENING!"

Felt herself flipped over Monkey Man, aikido or judo *who cared* as he powered her head straight down to the red tiles, but she twisted tucked curled landed on the soles of her shoes. Shocked, still held by him, her counter-leveraging his arm only *kind of* worked as she dropped onto her butt. He staggered backward, got his balance—

BANG!

Monkey Man bounced back toward the subway train behind him.

Backlit by that silver snake with its yellow glow of empty windows, Faye saw Monkey Man staggering on his shoes, hand raising to his chest *no blood* and she saw his short-cropped dirty blond hair and scraggy goatee—*Special Ops guys stay bearded in case*—saw him in her mind's eye over her gun sights as he wears a blue nylon Homeland Security jacket and claims *protocol*.

BANG!

Condor, sprawled on the red tiles firing another round from the 1911 .45 created to stop fanatic Muslim Moro warriors from overwhelming American soldiers with a screaming sword-swinging charge.

Monkey Man staggered spun backwards hit in his ballistic-vested chest—

And hurtles through the open doors of the subway train, falls to the orange carpet.

"DOORS CLOSING!"

BANG! Condor blasted a third .45 slug through the train's closed metal doors toward the bottom of fallen Monkey Man's feet.

Whoosh and that train rocketed out of the station.

A man and a woman sprawled alone on a red-tiled subway platform.

Faye got to her feet first. Drew her second gun, scanned the upper platform—*No visible threats!*—quick-stepped over to help Condor stand.

Said: "I hope your last shot tore him a new asshole."

"Elevator," gasped Condor.

She saw those doors had slid closed, pushed the button. The orange doors slid open.

Condor said: "Sometimes all you can choose is where you're trapped."

Faye helped him into the cage.

Pressed the button labeled STREET.

Zeroed her pistol out the cage's entrance until that gray cavernous void disappeared beyond sliding-closed doors, orange on the outside, but in here, in the cage, steel walls of smudged silver mirrors showing Faye's crazed reflection, showing Condor's panting grotesqueness.

Lurch, and the elevator lifted them up.

"At least one more hostile posted by top of the escalators," said Faye, her gun at her side, her heart slamming against the ballistic vest.

"You think nobody called the cavalry?" said Condor.

"Whose cavalry?" muttered Faye.

Lurch. Bounce. Stopped.

Faye posted to one side of the elevator doors.

Condor to the other.

Second date in the cool blue D.C. night, Heather and Marcus as savvy as all twenty-four-year-olds stand on the street near a Metro stop, by the elevator that's sixty feet from the escalators, a perfect site for D.C.'s eco-friendly Bike Share program, lock-up racks all over the city with stand-up-handles orange bicycles to rent & ride & return, Marcus's idea that Heather hoped he, *like,* hadn't needed to get from some magazine or a Perfect Dates *dot com,* meet at the bike stand between their starter jobs downtown, work clothes but *never mind,* they're young and thus in enough shape to not sweat out the ride to the Potomac waterfront, let him buy her a fish sandwich off one of the boat/restaurants floating tied up to the wooden wharf, shame that soft-shell crabs aren't in season, white bread and tartar sauce and *so good,* sitting on benches watching moored yachts rock back and forth in the wide gray river as the sun sets, seagulls screeing, and *hey,* Marcus listens to everything Heather prattles on about and only says one or two not-smart things, then they pedal back close to where she lives and now they're standing there, *awkward,* each trying to figure out the next move because even though it's only the second date, *well, you know,* except they don't have much in common even if they're in each other's cute zone, so instead of locking the bikes into the steel rack, they're dawdling, watching something weird going on over by the top of the escalators where maybe two dozen people stand talking about *like* going down or not going down, *what's that* near the bottom of the escalator stairs and *did you see those flashes, did you hear bangs,* people have their cell phones out filming, *like,* nothing Heather and Marcus can see, check out that especially agitated bearded guy in a trench coat by the escalators and—

DING!

Orange metal doors on the Metro elevator beside Heather and Marcus . . .

. . . slide open.

Out of the elevator darts, *like,* somebody's kind of cool, way-intense older sister.

And *OMG!* right after her stumbles some Friday-night slasher-movie monster all silver-haired and shit-brown-smeared-faced with a weird body and maroon nylon jacket.

The older sister spots the bearded guy over by the subway escalators.

But the bearded guy stares down the tunnel toward *whatever,* doesn't see her see him.

Older sister zooms right up to Heather and Marcus and *OMG!* that's *like a fucking real gun* as she says: "Give us the bikes, hold hands, keep your other ones where we can see them and walk *don't run* down the street that way."

Sister Gun nods in the opposite direction of the subway entrance.

"Don't scream, don't cell phone, don't do anything but hold hands *fucking move!*"

Heather and Marcus remember that second date for, *like,* the rest of their lives.

Faye swung onto the orange bike, turned to see Condor struggling onto his bike.

Darted her eyes back toward the subway escalators, through the gathered crowd—

The bearded guy in a trench coat met her stare.

"Go!" she yelled to Condor, gambling that the posted rear guard gunner wouldn't cut loose on a city street for a *less than sure* shot through this small crowd.

Faye powered the bicycle into the street. *No cars* as she pedaled away from the subway, glanced back and saw the weird image that was Condor trying to keep up.

Lumbering across and down the street from Faye comes a Metro bus.

She glanced over her shoulder to check on Condor . . .

Saw a dark sedan skid around the corner behind them.

The sedan fishtailed, locked its headlights on the two bicyclists like a yellow-eyed dragon on rabbits. The sedan gunned its engine.

Faye whipped around, saw the giant Metro bus looming now *four* car lengths away, *three,* and yelled: "Condor!"

The woman biker zoomed straight into the path of the rushing-closer bus.

Whoosh and she's across that traffic lane, standing hard on the pedals, cranking the steering handles to the left—
Bike's wobbling skidding gonna spill!

But she bounced off a parked car, pedaled back the way she came.

Condor wheeled his bike behind the bus as a dragon-eyed sedan shuddered past him, brake lights burning the night red. Condor pumped pedals to follow Faye.

Car horns blared behind them as the sedan almost slammed into oncoming traffic while trying to make a U-turn to chase the bicycles.

Spinning red & blue lights on city cop cars, an ambulance, and a fire truck illuminated the entrance to the subway. Faye biked away from that chaos, powered down an alley, heard gravel crunch and Condor curse as he biked after her.

Yellow dragon eyes and a growling engine filled the alley a block behind them.

Two cyclists shot out of the alley and across the side street then into the opposite alley half a block ahead of a yellow-eyed monster roaring in their wake.

There! Off to the right: yellow glowing open door!

A Hispanic man in a kitchen worker's white uniform spotted two bikers charging toward where he stood in an open doorway. His eyes went wide, his jaw dropped. Black plastic trash bags jumped out of his hands as he leapt out of the way. Two bikers shot past him through the open back door under the blue neon back door sign:

Nine Nirvana Noodles

The *Washington Post* review called Nine Nirvana Noodles "a twenty-first-century culinary revelation" with its menu of peanut sauce *Pad Thai*, Lasagna, *Lo Mein*, Macaroni & Cheese, *Udon,* plus three daily specials, but the restaurant critic had no clue about who really owned this *fabbed-up* former hole-in-the-wall destined for hipness.

Faye ducked her head/braked her bike as she blew into the shiny metal kitchen.

Veer around that chopping table—knife worker leaping out of the way!

The wobbling woman biker pushed her foot off the grill.

Black rubber smoke from the scorched sole of her shoe polluted food aromas.

A redheaded waitress dropped her tray of steaming yellow noodles.

BAM! Faye's front tire banged open twin doors to the dining room, a long box of white-clothed tables below wall-mounted computer monitors that streamed Facebook and YouTube mixed with muted clips from old TV shows, the moon landing, presidential addresses, movies like *Blade Runner* and *Casablanca, Dr. Strangelove.*

A waiter jumped out of Faye's way/fell onto a table of divorced daters.

Exploding dropped plates. Screams from splashed hot tea. Behind her, Faye heard Condor's bike crash into this dining room.

A waiter and a customer crouched to grab the crazy biker woman.

"Police emergency!" Faye threw her GPS-hacked cell phone at the two citizens.

"Open the fucking doors to the hospital!" Faye yelled to the hostess in the white blouse and black leather skirt, hoping "hospital" would inspire the clearing of an exit.

Whatever worked, *worked*: the front door opened.

Faye shot through it, skidded to a stop outside the restaurant, looked back for—

Crashing tables busting glass screams—*"Don't touch him he's sick!"*

Condor pushed his bike out the restaurant's front door, swung onto it, yelled: "One's chasing us on foot!"

They sped away from Nirvana, pedaled two more blocks, a zig, a zag, an alley.

Faye heard Condor's bike skid, stop.

Turned in time to see him wave his hand at her, slouch, wheezing, *spent*.

Two bikers staggered in the garbage can alley behind slouching houses where American citizens lived. Near Faye, a gate on a peeling wooden fence as high as her shoulder hung broken in its frame. She swung off her bike, eased inside the gate . . .

Somebody's backyard. What started its existence as a modest middle-class 1950s house was now sixty-some years later probably worth more money than it and all its companions on this block sold for when new. A watch light glowed over the back door, and through rear windows, she saw that a lamp shone deeper into the first floor. No lights on the second floor. Nothing that made her believe anyone was home.

She dropped her bike on the lawn, went back to the alley, muscled Condor and his bike into the backyard, dumped them on the night's spring grass.

Still wearing my backpack!

Faye dropped that gear bag on the lawn.

Stared at the nylon-jacketed mess sprawled in front of her.

A garden hose snake lay in the grass near Condor. She unscrewed its sprinkler, walked to the faucet and turned it on. The hose in her hand gushed cool water.

Faye drank hose water, drank again. Splashed cool wet on her face.

Water tumbled from the hose as she shuffled toward the man sprawled on his back on the grass. Faye sprayed his face: "Get up! You don't get to die yet."

Choking, gasping, flopping . . . *Sitting,* Condor sitting on the grass.

She turned the hose away from him.

He said: "I'm too old for this shit."

"Shit doesn't care how old you are."

Pale light from nearby houses and streetlights let them see each other.

He said: "How much makeup is still on my face?"

"You're a disgusting smear."

"Squirt it all off."

And she did as he sat there, raising his hands to clean them, too.

"Enough," she said.

He rolled onto his hands and knees, pushed and staggered to his feet.

Like Faye, drank and drank again.

She turned off the hose.

Came back to him as he took off the maroon nylon jacket, the baby carrier. From the infant pouch came a black leather jacket, drier than his black jeans or blue shirt.

The .45 rode holstered on his right side, the ammo pouch on his left.

Condor checked his vials of pills, muttered that it felt like they were all there.

Looked at her.

Faye whispered: "Who did we just kill?"

"Who's trying to kill us?" answered Condor.

"Now?" she said. "Everybody."

15

The way I always do.
—Warren Zevon, "Lawyers, Guns and Money"

Taxi, you're in the backseat of a yellow taxi.

Smells like burnt coffee and pine-scented ammonia and passengers' sweat.

Your sweat.

A cool breeze through the driver's open window bathes your sticky face.

Look out your rolled-up window.

The street-lit night streams surreal images. Sidewalks. Stores. Bar lovers hurrying into their neon cathedrals. The window catches your blurred reflection sitting beside someone you barely know. The glass vibrates from your pounding heart.

Condor and Faye stumbled through blocks of alleys toward a 7-Eleven, caught a break when Faye waved down a long-way-from-home taxi.

Condor lied to the cabby about where they were going.

The cabby lied about the shortest way to get there.

Drove through Georgetown.

The yellow taxi glided through that zone of boutiques, bars and restaurants, clothing franchises just like in most malls *back home,* sidewalks where charm mattered less than cash. Houses off these commercial roads sold for millions and still held graying survivors who'd pioneered Georgetown for Camelot's glory of JFK, but the streets now belonged to franchisers with factories in Hong Kong and Hanoi.

The cabby turned up his radio—loud, brassy music not born in the U.S.A.

Condor stared out the taxi window.

Saw him holding a red flower amidst unseeing strangers on the sidewalk.

"Rose men," whispered Condor.

"What?" Faye's eyes darted from sidewalk to sidewalk to side mirror to side mirror to the rearview mirror to the taxi's windshield and back again.

"Jimmy Carter was President. Middle Eastern guys popping into Georgetown restaurants, table to table, selling single roses for a dollar. They were spies. Savak, Iranian secret police brick boys working for the Shah, tracking dissidents, exiles, allies."

"Way before my time," said Faye. "I'm a Reagan baby."

"So who are the rose men now?"

"You tell me."

The taxi rumbled through dark residential streets. Blocks of apartment buildings lined main avenues. Town houses and cramped GI Bill homes filled the side roads.

They drove two blocks past their true destination.

Condor and Faye scanned cars parked along the curbs. Looked for vans. Looked for hulks in the bushes, lingering inside alleys or stairwells to basements. Looked for security cameras. Tracked rooflines for silhouettes under the dark sky.

The cabby stopped at the intersection Condor'd requested.

Said: "You sure this where you want to go?"

"Sure," said the old man in the black leather jacket as

the woman who could be his daughter paid the fare they all knew was bogus. "This is where she grew up."

"Feels familiar." *True* & *False* intertwined from this woman who slipped into her backpack as the cabby hesitated so the change from the corrupt fee became his tip.

Condor and Faye watched the cab drive away into the night.

Stepped back out of the cone of light from the corner streetlamp.

Faye scanned the surrounding darkness. "You sure this where we should go?"

"Everything about you will be lit up in crosshairs," he said. "You told me nothing about this is in my target packet for Sami's headhunters."

"Do you think this is the right thing to do?"

"It's the only *do* I got left," he told her. "Don't ask me any more than that. Or come up with a better idea and come up with it fast. I'm dead on my feet."

"Not yet," she said. "Not on my watch."

Then she let him lead her where he'd never been before, where he'd dreamed, where he already felt falling into déjà vu.

"Nothing's ever like it used to be," he muttered as they walked through the dark.

He heard concern in her voice as she said: "Concentrate on here and now."

This residential neighborhood smelled of bushes and grass and sidewalks damp from the previous night's rain. Freshly budded trees lined the boulevards, spread their thickening branches like nets poised over where Faye and Condor walked.

TV clatter floated from an open window as someone surfed their remote—sitcom laughter, crime drama sirens, dialog from fictional characters viewers could trust.

Coming toward them across the street: a woman in a yellow rain slicker muttering encouragement to the rescue mutt scampering on the end of her leash: *"Come on now, you can do it, yes you can."*

Out of the apartment building next to their destination came a clean-shaven man zipping up a leather jacket that was brown instead of Condor's black. He didn't notice they slowed their pace until he drove away in a car with tail-lights like red eyes.

"You sure this is the right address?" asked Faye when they stood outside the glass lobby door to a seven-story apartment building built during the Korean War. Through the glass entrance, they saw no one in the lobby, no one waiting for the elevator.

Condor pointed to the label beside the buzzer for Apartment 513:

M. Mardigian

Because you never know, Faye pulled on this main glass door: locked.

She tapped the "M. Mardigian" label. "If we buzz and get a *no,* we're fucked."

They looked behind them to the night street.

"We can't stand out here exposed, waiting for a chance to try a hitch-in," she said.

Condor pushed his thumbs down two columns of buzzer buttons for the seventh floor.

The door lock buzzed as a man's voice in the intercom said: *"Yeah?"*

Faye jerked open the heavy glass door, told the intercom: "Like, thanks, but never mind, I found my key!"

Condor and Faye hurried into the lobby.

"You'd think people would have learned the spy tricks by now," said Faye.

"If they did, we'd be stuck out in the cold."

Steel silver elevator doors slid open.

He hesitated. Felt her do the same.

Then she said: "Come on. We've got nowhere to go but up."

They got in, pushed the button for five.

Steel doors slid closed. This silver cage rose toward heaven.

Make it work, you can make this work. And nobody will get hurt, it'll be okay.

Faye watched him with skeptical eyes.

Inertia surged their skulls as the elevator stopped. Silver doors slid open.

A lime green hallway. Black doors, brass apartment numbers over peepholes. Dark green indoor-outdoor industrial carpet that smelled long overdue for replacement.

Apartment 513. No name label, no door decorations, nothing to set it apart from other slabs of entry into strangers' lives in this long green hall. The round plastic peephole stared at them, a translucent Cyclops eye beneath brass numbers.

This is where I want to be never wanted this shouldn't do this déjà vu.

Poetry. *Clong.*

Condor whispered to Faye: "Try to look like just a woman."

Faced the slab of black.

Raised his fist . . .

Knocked.

16

Survival is a discipline.

—United States Marine Corps manual

Let us in.

Faye watched the black door swing open & away from her in this musty green hall. Smiled as she secretly coiled to charge or draw & shoot or . . . *Or.*

Let us in!

But the woman who opened the door just stood there—blocking entry.

M. Mardigian.

She looks younger than fifty-three. *Condor mining her data isn't creepy, you've done that.* M. Mardigian's hair is gray highlighted blond, and unlike most women in Washington, she wears it curling past her shoulder blades. She looks like the part-time yoga instructor Condor says she is, a slow flow, subtle but stocky, strong. Her face is a pleasant rectangle, big nose, unpainted slash of lush lips. Her eyes are set too wide. She lets the two visitors standing in her hall tumble into their slitted blue gaze.

"*Wow,*" she deadpanned. "You never know who's gonna knock on your door."

Faye felt the disturbing force of her and Condor in this empty hallway.

Felt peepholes on the other apartment doors staring at them.

LET US IN!

The yoga woman scanned Faye, then her blue gaze settled on Condor, a wrinkle crossing her brow as she said: "You show up here with your daughter?"

"We're not that lucky," said Condor.

"Who's '*we*'?"

Faye flashed one of her three sets of credentials. "Homeland Security. Let's step inside, Ms. Mardigian. You're not in any kind of trouble."

"If you're here, we all know that's some kind of not true."

Condor asked the graying blonde blocking the door: "Can I call you *Merle*?"

She stared at him.

Said: "Word around work is that you're some kind of spook."

Bust in, push in, bowl her over in ten, nine, eight—

Call her Merle stepped back out of the doorway and pulled Condor in her wake.

Faye edged between Merle and the black door, wrapped her fist around the lock-button knob, closed that black slab to block out the world. Faye glanced away from their hostess only long enough to shoot the deadbolt home, fasten the door's chain.

Merle's husky voice said: "Somehow that doesn't make me feel safe."

"Sorry," said Condor. "You're not."

"Thanks to you?"

"Guilty. At least, in the personal sense."

"This is personal?" She sent her eyes to Faye. "So what do you want with me?"

Already got it, got in here, thought Faye. *Just need to stay in control.*

"Would you do me a favor, please, Ms. Mardigian? Sit over there on the couch."

Yoga woman wore a gold pullover and dark blue jeans. Was barefoot. She settled on her couch. Faye saw the woman force herself to relax, to sit back from poised on the edge of the black leather sofa, to act as if nothing was too wrong.

Faye followed Condor's lead. "Thanks. Mind if I call you Merle?"

"You've got the credentials to do a whole lot no matter what I mind."

Condor claimed one of two swivel chairs across the glass coffee table from Merle.

Good, thought Faye. The chair closest to the door. He could probably grab Merle if she made a break for it, definitely catch her before she could defeat the locks and chain.

"Con—*Vin* will keep you company while I follow procedure. Take a quick look through your apartment. To be sure we're alone. To be sure we're safe."

"Does *safe* come with a warrant?"

"You don't need to worry about that," said Faye.

Her eyes swept the kitchen: no visible knives, a landline phone on the wall.

The fifth-floor windows showed the night—Jesus, it's only ten o'clock! *Call her Merle* had a balcony big enough to stand on. Or jump from. A wet team could rappel down from the roof, swing *crash* bust through the glass with blazing machine guns.

Faye walked to the bedroom as Merle asked Condor: *"What do you know about me?"*

Faye kept the white bedroom door open so she heard him answer: *"Not enough."*

In the bedroom. Windows with another suicide-sized balcony. A queen-sized bed. Dressers. Clothes hanging in a closet where a dozen pairs of shoes lined the floor, tidy couples waiting to be wanted.

Voices drifted in as Faye quietly slid open bureau drawers.

Merle asked again: *"What do you want from me?"*

Condor replied: *"That's . . . complicated."*

Underwear, leotards, sweaters. Jeans, yoga-type tops and pants. No gun.

"Complicated is never the answer you want."

"Let's wait until Faye—"

"So she's the boss? Who I should pay attention to?"

Framed photographs on the bedroom bureaus: Mother. Father. A middle-class house somewhere beyond the Beltway. A 1960s little girl jumping rope. A near-thirty Merle, fierce and glowing as she marches down the steps of the Capitol building. A cell-phone shot of this-age her stretching into a yoga pose while the class watches.

"You should pay attention to what's smart."

"Who gets to decide 'smart'? You?"

No wedding picture. No pictures of children. No pictures of men. Or women. No group photos from an office party. No snapshots of friends' kids, nephews or nieces.

Thumbtacks held picture postcards above the bedside table where a cell phone rested in its charger beside a land-line extension. A piazza in some Italian city. The theater district of London at night. The gargoyles on Notre Dame in Paris.

Faye's stomach scar burned when she saw the postcard of Paris. America's trained spy lifted the edge of the Paris postcard, then each of the others: no stamps on the backs, no written notes or Merle's address. Had she gone there, gotten them for herself?

"Please, trust us."

"Gosh, nobody's ever said that before."

The bedside table that held the phones had two books—fictions, *Beautiful Ruins* by Jess Walter, a woman named Maile Meloy writing *Both Ways Is The Only Way I Want It*. The bedside table's bottom drawer rattled with tubes of this and jars of that, moisturizers, Vitamin E oil. Bottles of headache meds, over-the-counter sleep aids.

"Doesn't matter if I trust you."

"Matters to me."

Faye found a white cardboard box from a dress shop under the bed.

Pulled it out—filled with photos, letters, a menu from a long-gone cafe.

Closed the lid on that coffin of memories, pushed it back under the bed.

Found nothing under the pillows.

"What happened to your face? It looks . . . smeared."

"That's left over from trying not to be me."

"How'd that work out?"

"I ended up here."

On the other side of the bed by the closet, a bedstand held a laptop computer. Faye clicked onto the e-mail—messages about yoga classes from the head teacher at some studio where Merle subbed and taught the "Sunday seniors seminar." No Facebook or other social media accounts. Faye didn't bother to snoop for financial records, pushed the POWER button until the whisper whine of the laptop turned off.

"Who are you now?"

"Better."

Faye slid open that bedstand table's bottom drawer. Odds and ends, an art deco glass pipe plus a plastic baggy with, *say,* a quarter cup of green marijuana.

She closed the drawer. Thought: *Good, Merle chooses to live like an outlaw.*

"And all this is your 'better' plan?"

"None of this was any plan until an hour ago."

The closet felt . . . culled. Gaps between the hangers with skirts and dresses, blouses, slacks, jackets. Empty spaces on the top shelf. Empty floorboards between the pairs of shoes, mostly office wear, but there, in the back, three pair of out-of-fashion high-heeled shoes, the kind of rhinestone footwear that once carried a little black dress from one big-dollar event to another to a not-so-quiet end of the night.

"So if I wasn't part of your plan, why have you been hawking me?"

"I was trying to work up the guts to do more than dream."

Faye knew she couldn't do a squirrel team full toss of the bedroom. Didn't think she needed to. Her eyes roamed over shelves of books. When she'd been recovering in the private hospital room, Faye'd avoided the TV mounted above her post-surgery bed for the controllable magic of books. Novels, not tomes of facts she knew were hollow of the hidden world where she lived and had just almost died. Now she stared at dozens of books on Merle's walls, knew all but a few were fictions, thought: *So she's looking for visions that make you feel something true, not data about other people trapped with you in a version called history. Looking for escape. Looking for . . .*

Whatever. Maybe Merle just liked the thrill of a good story.

"This is no dream. This is the edge of a nightmare."

"This is all I got."

Faye dropped Merle's cell phone into her black coat's pocket. Closed the laptop, carried it and the receiver for the landline phone in her left hand.

Bathroom, through the door beside the closet. A shower tub. Faye's free right hand opened the mirrored medicine cabinet: Nail scissors, lethal but only if you got lucky and knew what you were doing. More tubes and lotions. A half-full bottle of prescription pills she recognized from Condor's inventory as a generic antidepressant.

Voices in the living room came only as murmurs in this blue bathroom.

Faye toed open the cabinet under the sink. Toilet paper, other junk. Shelves held towels. A white bathrobe hung from a hook on the back of the bathroom door.

She walked back to the living room where Condor sat across from this woman they'd trapped who more and more scored like an innocent bystander.

Merle spotted her electronics under Faye's arm. "Did you get what you need?"

Faye left the electronics on the glass coffee table.

Opened two closed doors in the living room: a big closet, coats for all seasons, boots, a pillow and blankets on the top shelf; second door, a small bathroom.

Faye took off her backpack purse and her black coat, put their weight over their reluctant hostess's phone and laptop. Felt Merle's eyes drawn to the gun on her belt, the magazine pouch. Felt the ambushed woman's eyes follow her.

Faye sat in the other chair, said: "You have to understand our situation."

"No I don't," said Merle. "I just have to survive it."

Condor said: "Go for more than just that."

Take over. Faye said: "I'm a Federal agent, CIA detailed

to Homeland Security. Con—*Vin* . . . He's one of us, though how is not what you need to know. Someone penetrated the system, fit Vin for a frame. Now probably just wants him dead. Me, too."

"Call for help, backup. Rescue. This is America, these are our streets."

"If we call or e-mail, we're in the system. We won't know who will hear and find us first. This might be America, but the streets belong to whoever makes us run."

"*Run?* What if I get off the couch here and walk right out—"

"Merle, I'm sorry," said Faye. "That's not going to happen."

Faye bored her hunter's gaze through the older woman sitting on the black couch.

"Oh," whispered Merle. "Okay. I get it."

Merle blinked. "Why do you keep calling him *Con*?"

Give trust to get trust. "That's his classified code name. Condor."

"Is anybody ever who they say they are?" said Merle.

"He is," said Faye. "Except . . ."

Condor beat her to it: "I'm kind of crazy. Sometimes I space out. See ghosts. I'm officially not supposed to remember so that's what I'm trying to do."

"Remember what?" said Merle.

"Yeah," said Condor.

Get her to focus, thought Faye, *get her to what she needs to get over.*

Faye said: "We're sorry for the truth, which is you're stuck with us now. We need a place to hide. Every other place is compromised. We need to figure out what to do, rest. We've hijacked your life—not because of anything you've done but because you're just who we came up with. And sorry, but we're going to keep doing that until we can leave. We're asking you to cooperate. Don't try to call any-one, e-mail, whatever."

"Got it, but really, I can just go to a hotel and—"

Faye said: "We can't take that risk. You, out there, alone."

"What risk did you just pin on me?"

"I won't lie to you. There's been . . . combat. Some deaths."

"Some deaths?"

Condor said: "Nothing we wanted, nothing we could avoid."

Merle shook her head. *"Deaths. Combat.* Now you've signed me up for a . . . a *civilian casualty,* as *collateral damage."*

"No," said Faye. "Nobody knows we're here. Nobody will know about you until we get back in with the good guys."

"Your promise went from *nobody* to *somebody* in a blink." Merle gave the younger woman a brokenhearted smile. "It's good to know where I stand."

"You don't know," said Faye. "Neither do we. But we know we're here, we know you're covered when you're with us, we know we'll die to keep you that way."

"That's a hell of a promise for a first date." Merle blinked. Let her gaze address both of the strangers in her house. "Is that all you want?"

"Truthfully," said Faye, "we want all we can get."

"Oh."

Merle looked around where she called home. Shud-dered. Seemed to shrink.

Then Faye saw her inhale this new reality.

Merle whispered: "What do we do now?"

"Not much," said Faye. "Hunker down. We're safe, but we're both wiped out."

"Are you hungry?" Merle shrugged. "I buy giant frozen lasagnas, bake and cut it up and refreeze cooked portions for . . ."

She shrugged. "For my old ordinary everyday life."

"That's not where we are now," said Faye. "But we're still hungry."

"Then let's deal with that," said Merle. "Can I . . . ?"

Faye nodded permission for the older woman to get off the couch, walk into her own kitchen, open her refrigerator and pull out an aluminum baking tub three-quarters full of tomato & meat sauce and pasta, put it on the counter—

Merle froze.

Whispered: *"Jesus!"*

Here it comes, thought Faye.

"You people show up and people are dead and you've got guns and I'm just . . ."

Faye said: "Breathe. Just breathe. You can do this."

"All my life, that's what I keep hearing." Merle's eyes drifted to somewhere other than this kitchen, this apartment, this time of strangers and guns. "You *can* do this. *You* can do this. *'You wanna do this'* doesn't . . . But you can do *this*."

"You're doing great," said Faye, braced for Merle to go off, *full hysterics,* throw the aluminum tub of lasagna through the trapped air of this white-walled kitchen, charge the front door, scream for neighbors, for help, for anyone but who was here to hear her.

The husky-voiced woman muttered: "If I'm doing great, why am I here?"

Condor walked to two steps from Merle in the kitchen. Silver-haired, still wearing his black leather jacket, staring at this woman he'd stalked, told her: "You're here because of me. The last thing I ever wanted was for you to be here like this. But you're all I've got, all I know, my only chance. You're who matters."

Merle whispered: "I shouldn't have gone for coffee yesterday."

"Who knows where our *shouldn't-haves* start?" said Condor. "All we've got is what we do."

Merle stood in her white-walled kitchen, breathing hard. Condor *not* touching her.

And here I am, thought Faye. *Two strangers to save while not getting whacked.*

Merle said: "There's leftover salad."

Five microwave beeps, clattering dishes, stools scraping across chessboard-sized white square kitchen tiles to the island counter, and there they were, Merle perched on a stool between the stoves and the counter, Condor sitting across from her with his plate of lasagna and leafy green salad and glass of water, the same nourishment in front of Faye, who perched on the stool closest to the door with her back to it but her eyes able to see the older couple on stools in the open kitchen of this apartment.

Where we are all trapped.

Faye and her comrade fugitive were almost done with the food that another time might have had some taste when Merle said: "What happened?"

Condor said: "The less you know, the better it will be for you."

"Really? Ignorance equals safety?" Merle shook her head. "Forget about trying to sell me that, not while I can't walk out my own front door."

Faye saw Condor's eyes—tired, drooping, yet following the sway of the captive woman's hair as she shook her head *no*.

"What happened?" whispered Merle.

Faye sighed. "Again, what we can tell you about this—"

"No," interrupted Merle. "That's not what I'm talking about now.

"What happened?" she said. "Do you ever think about that? Here you are. With only who you've been. What you've done. What you thought was going to happen and never did. What little you can still do. Chunks of time fallen backwards away from you, and here you are locked in some landlord's mouse hole . . ."

She shook her head. Stared at the counter and the glass of water she had yet to drink.

"You're walking," said Condor. "See a store window that reflects cars, other people, but you don't see yourself in that mirror. Then you do, a face you barely recognize."

Merle said: "What kind of crazy are you?"

"Older."

The two of them laughed.

Faye noted how Condor slumped on the stool. Remembered their captor's medicine cabinet. Asked her silver-haired colleague: "Do you have any of your meds?"

"None that will make me go back to not seeing," he said.

From his shirt pockets, from his black leather jacket in the living room, Condor fetched pill bottles he lined out on the counter by his red sauce–smeared dinner plate.

Faye watched Merle scan the bottle labels. Watched Merle read the label for Condor's bladder control pills that also increased his ability to . . . Saw that knowledge flash through Merle but couldn't tell what it meant to the older woman.

Faye said: "You work at the Library of Congress?"

"Wow," said Merle. "Gun on your hip, door locked against *whoever,* you still ask the inescapable Washington question: *'What do you do?'*

"Funny," said Merle. "No one picked me as a library type twenty years ago. Now I could retire. Sit locked in here with what little is left of my little life."

She shook her head. "Sorry, I don't usually let myself get that way, but . . .

"Yes, I work at the Library of Congress. The Motion Picture Archives. I watch old black-and-white movies. Catalog them, rank them in the line of movies waiting to be digitalized for whatever survives the apocalypse, artistic worth plus print quality plus . . .

"You don't care." Merle shrugged. "I spend my days watching other people's ideas play out on a small white screen in a dark room. I watch what I'm not."

Condor said: "Like most of us."

Merle looked at him.

Turned to Faye. "So how are you going to negotiate your way out of here and into where you'll get what you want? Or at least not dead."

"Not a lot of negotiation happening," said Faye.

"Bullshit," said Merle, as shocked as her captors by her own force, her candor. "This town is all one interlocked negotiation. You do what you gotta do to convince whoever's got the power to let you get what you can."

"More to it than that," said Condor.

"Don't tell me about more," said Merle. "I spent twelve years on the Hill, Congressman's office, Senator's office manager. Come to find out, it's all about power and what you can get from the power that is."

"We're not there yet," said Faye.

Merle nodded toward the silver-haired man slumped on a stool in her kitchen. "You think he's going to get you somewhere?"

"*He*," said Condor, "might surprise you."

"So far," said Merle, "*yes*.

"But I'm going to call you Vin," she added. "Not Condor."

Faye saw him smile, but with effort, exhaustion.

"Man, do you need to clean up!" Merle told Vin, who reeked of sweat, of gunpowder, who had sticky smears of brown on his face, his wrist.

"We need to sleep more than anything," said Faye. "So do you."

Merle gave her back to the spies as she put their dirty dishes in her sink.

Faye told their captive's back: "Here are the options."

Options: such muted honesty.

"Best one," said Faye, "toss him in the shower, pop him full of pills he's got—"

"Right here," said Condor. "I'm still right here."

"And we want you to stay," said Faye. "But if you don't get real sleep . . .

"The bed is our option," continued Faye. "Best is him in it like it is designed. Next best is us making up the mattress for him out here on the floor. I'll take the couch, not big enough for him to stretch comfortably and if he cramps . . ."

Merle turned: "What about me?"

"You're in your bedroom," said Faye. "Don't want to deprive you of that."

"Plus I'll be another door away from getting out."

"Safer."

"Oh. Sure." Merle shrugged. "Keep the bed like it is for him. I can sleep on the floor or . . . Or beside him."

"I'll be out, I'll never know," said Condor.

"Okay, whatever," said Faye. "Condor—*Vin*: leave your gun out here with me."

"Just in case?" said Merle. "In case of what? Or who? Me?"

Faye helped Condor unclip the holstered .45 from his belt. Merle watched Faye ask him what pills he should take after his shower, put them in a cup she handed to him, put the glass of water in his other hand.

"Do you have something he can sleep in?" Faye asked.

Merle shrugged. "Something."

Condor said: "Have we said *thank you* yet?"

Before Merle could answer, he shook his head: "*Thank you*'s not enough."

Condor shuffled into the bedroom.

Faye stopped Merle from following him with a touch on her arm.

She didn't jump, didn't resist, but . . .

Waiting, sensing, not trained, just . . . smart.

Faye said: "Somehow he's the key to our way out of here. *All* of our way. So we need to keep him going as best as he can be. I'm asking you to keep an eye on him. If he fades more, if he starts to decompensate—"

"*De*compensate? What is he compensating for?"

"You do what you can, make sure I know what's going on with him."

"And don't touch his gun, right?" Merle smiled. "Oh, that's right: you took it."

Faye saw the fierceness caught by the photo of her on the steps of the Capitol flash in those blue eyes, if only for a moment, if only like a memory of what used to be.

Merle walked into the bedroom, pulled the white door closed behind her, *clunk*.

Before Faye went to *call it sleep* on the black couch positioned so she'd bolt awake facing the front door, her Glock and Condor's .45 a grab away on the glass coffee table, she used the living room's half bath, and from its medicine cabinet took dental floss, tied a taut line between the knob of the closed bedroom door and a tall drinking glass on the kitchen counter. Faye pushed one of the living room's black swivel chairs against the front door, knew it would only slow a SWAT breach by a second, maybe two.

But a second, maybe two . . .

In the second, maybe two after she snapped the kitchen into darkness but before she flipped off the light switch in the living room, she stared at the bedroom's white door, that closed white door.

17

Be my pillow.
—Jesse Colin Young, "Darkness, Darkness"

This is how her bedroom smells. Warm cotton sheets whiffed with musk. Vanilla wisps. Or maybe not vanilla. Some other bath & beautify lotion. Plus cirrus clouds of Ben-Gay or another sore-muscles liniment, something practical. But her. Here.

Night spinning tired everything aches skin so yuck clammy!

Behind him, Merle said: "Are you seeing ghosts?"

She's standing there. You turned around and there she was. Looking at you.

Saying again: "Ghosts? Are you seeing ghosts?"

Tell her: "No. Yes."

She blinked, blushed. "Let's pretend you're a poet and not a killer, a crazy."

"I'll be who you need."

"What about *want*?"

"Can't promise that."

"Who can." She frowned.

Took the cup of pills from his hand.

"You're holding on by your fingernails," she told him. "Gotta hurt."

"You can't ever make the hurt stop."

"Maybe, but you can back it off, get some peace. Like it or not, that's your best choice now. You can pass out where you stand, or if you got enough left in you, you can take a shower—and man, do I recommend that. Then your pills, then bed.

"The bed's just for sleep." Her blue eyes burned. "You don't have a gun."

"I couldn't use it like that. I wouldn't."

Nodding, agreeing with him to convince herself.

"Take off your shirt," she said.

And he did.

Gave its blue wrinkle to her.

She tossed it on a chair by the door, the closed white door.

He didn't wait to be told what she wanted.

Kicked off his shoes.

Took off his black jeans.

She held those pants out from her. Felt the weight of whatever was in his pockets, of the ammo mags in their pouch on his belt. Tossed the black jeans onto the chair.

"What are you wearing?" she said, staring at his revealed second skin.

"Thermal underwear," he said. "I didn't know how cold it would be out there."

A slow-motion movie walked her to a brown cardboard box in the far corner of the room. All of her moved when any of her changed. Her blond & gray hair undulated in soft waves on her shoulder, her strong back. Her arms floated with purpose. The roundness of her hips, taut for any age in her blue jeans, rolled from step to step, then he saw them rise out as she bent over, pulled things from that brown cardboard box.

She carried a ragged black sweatshirt and thin gray sweatpants to him.

"Here," she said.

Could have thrown the sweats, but she chose to hand them to you.

"At the Fifty Plus class I teach, people leave gear and clothes, books, water. I wash the clothes, take the Lost & Found box to class, but if nobody claims them . . . Every few weeks, there's some charity pickup."

He held up the black sweatshirt to read its gold logo: LUX ET VERITAS. Whatever that meant, what meant a universe more was what else he read emblazoned gold on black.

"*Montana*," he said. "How did you know?"

She shook her head. "It's just a sweatshirt I found."

"Nothing cosmic. Not a *clong*."

"A what? Why? Is that where you're from? Montana?"

"That's where I found out I was me."

"You're a spy," she said. "A killer. Not a poet."

"Yeah."

"Go shower," she said. "There's a blue towel on the shelf. You're not a conditioner kind of guy, but one of the bottles in the tub is shampoo. And on a shelf under the sink, there's an unopened toothbrush: the big-box store makes you buy five."

"I have my own. I think. Out there," he said, pointing to the closed white door.

"We're here, don't go drifting back or we'll never get you where you're going."

She pointed to the bathroom.

In there, slump, your back pressing against the door, your socks gripping tiny white tiles, close your eyes, she's not there, she can't see you, you can let go, let go.

Like inhales shift to exhales, his mind billowed back and forth between clarity and confusion. What kept him conscious in that bright bathroom was the scent of where he was, the pine ammonia of cleanliness, the vanillas of rejuvenation, the damp metal and porcelain hardness of *here* and *now* and *real*.

Fighting off the thermal top was almost more than he could do. He worked it up his chest, both hands inside it as he pulled the shirt over his face—*Stuck!*—staggered around the bathroom, bumped his right shin on the toilet, suffocating, arms pinned crossed over his head inside the clinging—

Off, face clear, dropping the top onto the floor, staring down at his minor victory.

Take what you can get.

He peeled down the long underwear pants, worked them and his socks off. Collapsed more than sat on the toilet, did what he had to do and didn't let his eyes close.

Next thing he knew, he's in the shower, hot water pounding down on him as he reaches back to pull the plastic shower curtain closed—

Psycho, *Alfred Hitchcock movie, Janet Leigh showering behind a plastic curtain, not seeing Anthony Perkins come into her bathroom with a butcher knife.*

Maronick jerks from bullets you shot into his bathroom stall.

Condor left the shower curtain open.

The water, *oh the water* pounding down on his skull, his face, his closed eyes, steam opening his sinuses, his pores. Ribbons of brown swirled down the drain. He found the shampoo bottle, a bar of soap, used both two or three times, lost count.

His arms burned as he used the blue softness and toweled himself dry, pulled on the gray sweatpants—way too big, barely held up by the frayed drawstring. He struggled into the black sweatshirt. LUX ET VERITAS pointed toward the steamed-over mirror. The sleeve he wore wiped the wet fog off that glass.

There you are. Here you are.

"Wow," whispered Condor.

The toothbrush he found under her sink was red. Her toothpaste was minty fresh.

Merle stood up from sitting on the bed as he opened the bathroom door.

She wore tightly tied green yoga pants. A bulky blue sweatshirt. With no buttons up its front. The woman held the cup of his pills out to him.

Said: "I put in an extra painkiller. Generic. Over the counter. Works."

Handed him an aluminum drinking bottle, its top screwed off.

"I make up a bunch of these for class use," she said. "With paper cups, or that would defeat the purpose. Store-bought low-cal lemonade with concentrated Vitamin C I dissolve in it. Stopping colds in my class helps me as much as them."

Lemonade. Cool, tangy.

He swallowed the pills. She took the cup, the now-empty aluminum bottle.

"You should sleep on the side of the bed near the bath-room. Get in, I'll be back."

She went into the bathroom. Closed that door.

He heard her brushing her teeth. The flush of the toilet. Sink water.

Then she's out, leaving the bathroom door open, snap-ping off that light.

Condor sank under covers into warmth he hadn't felt in what seemed like forever.

She circled around the foot of the bed.

Watch the ceiling, look up, look at heaven not her.

The bed sagged, the covers fluttered. He felt the heat of her in there with him.

"Forgot," said Merle.

Condor turned his head to the right.

Saw her blue-sweatshirt-with-no-buttons form bent over her side of the bed.

Sitting up straight, she put an aluminum bottle on her bedstand, turned toward him, a second aluminum bottle in her hand and she's reaching, *leaning* across . . .

Over me.

He lay beneath her as her blue sweatshirt blocked out the lamplit white ceiling. He saw only that blue sweatshirt. Believed in the sway, *the sway* of her breasts.

Clunk went the metal bottle on the bedstand beside him, for him.

She turned out his lamp.

Pulled herself back across him—

Gone, she's gone, pressure heat smell still—

Merle snapped out her lamp, dropped them, this room, this bed, into darkness.

He felt her stretch under the covers. Close enough to reach out and touch.

Falling through soreness and pain . . .

Not yet! Not yet!

Merle whispered: "Why me?

"You said I wasn't in your plan," she told the man lying beside her. "You said '*personal.*' You've been . . . eyeing me for months. To 'work up your guts.' Why me?"

Nothing left but true: "You're gravity I can't escape."

His sore heart labored beats in the darkness.

"What am I supposed to do with that?" she said.

"What you can," he said. "What you want."

She whispered his last name.

Said: "You're the only *Vin* on the Library of Congress's Web site of staff passes."

Said: "The photo's not that good."

Warm, so warm under here.

Merle let the word come out again: "Vin."

Then whispered: "Condor."

Swirling warm blackness going g—

18

Say your life broke down.
—Richard Hugo, "Degrees of Gray in Philipsburg"

What have I done?

Faye lay on the black sofa in someone else's dark apartment. She lay absolutely still, as if that would stop time, as if her stillness could make the last two days disappear.

Lay still and do not, DO NOT tremble or shake or vomit or cry.

Or cry.

A drinking glass stood sentry on the kitchen counter. The door's peephole was an eye of distorted light above the chair pushed against that locked portal to buy a second, maybe two for her to not get killed, not get machine-gunned as she tried to rise from this black leather couch of darkness.

Pulitzer Prize–winning reporter David Wood later that year would report that the most common medical trauma immediately suffered by American troops who survived combat in Iraq and Afghanistan translated into plain English as "deep sorrow."

What did I do? What did we do?

Hostiles. The Opposition. A wet team targeting her and Condor.

That's who they were in the subway battle.

Not our guys doing their job, my job, doing their duty, their righteous duty.

Playback:

Nobody shouts "Police!" or "Federal agents!" or "Freeze!" *Ambush or oversight?*

The woman on the escalator shot Condor first—but with a Taser, nonlethal.

Not a classic hit. A snatch move? The first-choice neutralization?

Condor shoots her, and I . . .

The black man draws, shoots at me . . . with a silencer-rigged pistol.

You don't use a silencer to take prisoners.

Shot him dropped him he didn't die. *Not from me.*

The team at the top of the escalator stairs threw bullets at us, not selecting who they hit, friendly fire killing their own team member. They didn't care about containing and covering everything as an Eyes Only secret. Taking us out had—*has*—a higher priority than the cost of any casualties or chaos.

The gunner the train hit.

The man I shot on the red-tile platform.

Monkey Man blasted back into a subway car, roared away dead or alive.

Sami said he'd pull our people—*No*: said he'd do what he could. He's the man, the guru, the go-to guy, so if he could, he would, he trusts—*trusted* me that much.

So if not Sami . . . It's them. Whoever they are.

And *if then* it was or *if now* it's become Sami . . . We are so fucked. Dead.

What happened to my life, when did the fall-apart start: Paris?

Or with Chris?

When you let yourself have something to lose, you do.

Faye stared at the bedroom holding Condor and Merle behind a closed door.

Bring him in safe, *yes,* call it an objective, but the mission, *her* mission was to nail who killed her partner, who was trying to kill her, who made her kill.

What's worth all this?

My life. What I pledge it to by what I do.

A deep breath flowed into her, pushed her breasts against the bulletproof vest and suddenly she felt like an anaconda was squeezing her ribs, the giant snake crushing her and *breathe, just breathe, got to*—

Faye stopped her hyperventilating.

Fall apart when you're finished. If you fall apart now you are finished.

Not me. Not now. Not yet.

Fuck them. Fuck that.

Oh, but *oh* she was so tired. So heavy with the vest, with the weight of two guns waiting on the glass coffee table beside where she lay on this black leather couch, with the weight of a man crucified over a fireplace, a man getting smashed by a train, a man crumpling to the red tiles of a subway platform beyond the smoke from her pistol.

She imagined floating up from the couch, the ballistic vest falling away from her. And the exhaustion and pain and soreness and seared memories . . . floated away, gone.

Faye saw herself naked.

The scar erased from her stomach.

Standing in this apartment. Facing the curtains drawn open from the floor-to-ceiling sliding windows. Standing there naked with no *must*s, no *should*s, no *can*s, no *who will die* consequences, no Mission no Op no Duty. With dreams she could believe. Standing in front of a transparent plane as she spreads her arms wide, her chest and heart uncovered as she smiles at the glass that won't shatter from a sniper's bullet.

Or if it does, it won't be her finger on the killing trigger.

Won't be a squeezed betrayal from her *us*.

She stands there, arms spread wide, naked in front of the night.

Waiting for the sound of busting glass.

19

The time to hesitate.
—The Doors, "Light My Fire"

From beside you in the dark bed, she says: "You're awake."

Condor exhaled the sigh he'd been holding back. She was already awake. His disturbing motion wouldn't matter now.

He told her: "Yes, but you can go back to sleep."

"It's almost dawn. You got up in the night—bathroom, I know, it's all right. Sometimes it's nice to hear you're not alone. Are you okay?"

"Are you kidding?"

The bed trembled with their quiet laughter.

"You have to go again." Not a question from her. Matter of fact.

He slid from the sheets without looking back. Inside the bathroom, door closed, light blasted on, he did what he did, washed his hands.

Looked in the mirror.

You're here. This is real.

Snapped out the light.

Opened the bathroom door to find she'd snapped on a nightlight.

"You look better than before," she told him.

"Better than before isn't much. He shrugged. "Six hours' sleep in a real bed."

What should you do?

He got back in bed. Under the covers. Lay on his right side. Facing her.

She'd propped herself up on two pillows, lay on her left side, facing him. Her shoulders in the blue sweatshirt were out from under the sheet.

"This could be my last good sleep," she said. "Today all your *this* could kill me."

"Today can always kill you."

She tossed her head to get strands of long hair off her face. "Are you scared?"

"Oh yeah."

"Of dying?"

"Sure, but . . . I'm more scared of you dying. Of not doing what I can right."

"How's '*doing what you can*' working for you so far?"

"Evidently not so good, I ended up here—I mean: putting you here."

"So I noticed." Her smile lacked joy. "Though I get some of the blame."

"Why blame?"

"What I *coulda shoulda* to not be here. Where I could have ended up."

"Where's that?"

"Not stuck in all this alone, waiting for trouble to knock on my door."

"Why are you alone?"

She stared at him.

"That was one thing I couldn't figure when . . ."

"When you were stalking me."

"No malice, but . . . okay, I hacked your employment

cover sheet. You checked SINGLE. No children. Not married, widowed, divorced. I don't understand why."

"Why what?"

"No woman as . . . great—"

She laughed.

". . . like you should be single."

"I know a dozen women my age and younger who are smarter and more accomplished and way *way* prettier and believe me: far, *far* nicer, but who are walking around with only their shadows. Like me."

"But why you?"

"You want to know," she said. Not a question.

"You want to tell me," he said. Not a question.

"Maybe I don't want to ruin my image in your eyes," she said. "Could be risky."

"I want to see the real you."

"Your real is crazy."

Oh so slightly came a smile to his lips.

"I'm a member of the jilted mistresses club," said Merle.

"Do you want to know *who*?" she said.

Condor shrugged. "If he's gone, who cares."

"Who he is makes the story."

And he guessed. Said: "You mean *what* he is."

"Oh, he's an asshole, but made for this town.

"I was twenty-four, nowhere near as smart as I thought. I was born when JFK got elected, thought that was somehow . . . magical. I got here in 1984 when Reagan ruled and things were going to be right, based on principles, an America for everybody.

"He was a freshman Republican Congressman from one state over. Young enough to be cool, old enough to feel like he was more substantive than me. I knew his district, parlayed an internship with my own Senator into working for—for David."

She told Condor—told *Vin*—the man's last name.

Meant little to Condor, to *Vin*: another cosmetic face on TV.

"His daddy had medium money, the country-club set. David mastered the sincere look, rumpled Ivy League polish. Knew where to stand to catch the light. Great hair. Could make you feel like you were the one in the crowded room he was talking to.

"In college, he knocked up a hometown princess. Her folks had money, too, so they had a white wedding extravagance, a merger, a kid, big fish in a small city, but he . . .

"He didn't have a spy war, an operation, a mission, a *whatever* you're stuck in. He had big ideas. Or so I thought. Nobody knows how to work a sound byte better than David, whether he's talking to TV cameras or across a pillow."

Vin's cheek burned on the pillow that held him.

"He was crusading, that was why he couldn't leave his wife. A divorce would wreck his reelection. He couldn't jeopardize his chance to serve. How dare I be selfish. Then it was the first Senate race. Then the second Senate race, the one that would set him up to *really* do what had to be done even if by then I wondered what that meant. But I hung in there—*Yeah*, don't tell me: apt image. On camera, he was a no-divorce religion, no abortion, though he didn't blink when it came to paying cash for . . ."

She looked away.

"I'd go to movies alone to be not waiting by the phone or the clock.

"He had great timing," she said. "I'd finally admitted he was one of the herd who come here to *be* rather than *do,* that he only followed the big bucks and floodlights and *the right kind of people*. But for '*us*,' I was going to give him one more chance, one . . .

"One day. That's all it took to end thirteen years. One conversation in a fucking underground parking garage where nobody could see if I made a scene. *'These things happen.'* And by the way, best *for me* if I left his Senate staff, left Congressional staffing, the only work I knew. *'You like movies, right?'* He'd engineered an archivist post in the Library of Congress. Where I could even earn a pension. As long as he protected my job at the budget table. He made that sound like kindness.

"Two months later, suddenly divorce became okay. Weeks after his, he married a divorcee. They'd been fucking long before either his first wife or I were gone. The bitch's first husband was an Internet genius from the defense contractors' sprawl out by Dulles Airport who thought life's reward for his hard work was a willowy model nine years younger than me. She walked with his millions all the way to queen for the now-distinguished white-haired Senator I'd paid my youth to."

She sighed. "Still think I'm worth looking at?"

"You're worth a lot of seeing."

Condor swore she blushed in the soft light as she said: "What about your exes?"

Flashes.

"Whoever they were, they got me here."

"In trouble. On the run."

She closed, then opened her eyes. "Can I get out of this okay?"

"If we're all lucky."

"You just got to find the best deal—right?"

"We're meat on some table. I don't know if there's any deal."

"This is Washington," she said. "There's always a deal. If you've got clout."

"Me, Faye out there: What you see is what we've got."

"Then maybe you don't know how to look. Or who you have on your side."

"Besides her?" said Condor.

"Guess that's where we start."

"We?"

"You don't give a girl much choice."

He said: "Why did you stay in D.C.? You had experience, education—probably a little clout you could have leveraged from *David*. You could have gone to . . ."

Condor blinked. "I think I always wanted to live in San Francisco."

"L.A.," she said. "Warm. No fog. You drive away from what goes wrong. And in L.A., people are honest about pretending to be somebody else."

"Why didn't you go?"

"The falling-apart years," she said.

"I know about them," said Condor.

Merle gave him a smile. "So you said.

"Me," she continued, "I might not have been wicked smart, but I was savvy functional when I was with David. Afterwards . . . Depression. Self-pity. Feeling stupid. If you cop to that, you're guilty of it. Inertia and kind bosses kept me in paychecks.

"Just as I was coming out of my cage of mirrors, Mom got everything that steals your last years. All she had was social security and what I could send back to Pennsylvania. I would go up and see her whimpering in a county nursing home that was all we could afford. Red Jell-O and the sound of scampering rats.

"The echo of dirt hitting her coffin was still in the air when I got lucky cancer."

"There's no such thing as—"

"Yeah there is. It's the kind you survive without too much damage and only a small mountain of medical bills, thanks to health insurance from the job you gotta keep to keep the insurance. Nothing special, only about ten million of us like that.

"So," she said straight into his stare, "here I am. With all my reasons *why*. No magic. No second chances. Men look past me for younger women. Women who didn't lose their chance to have babies. But I have a job I don't hate, a life I'm doing. All on my own. And until last night, all I had to fear was the real world."

"Then I showed up."

"Knock-knock," she said.

Sheets rustled. He felt her legs shift somewhere in the bed.

"Let's say you win," said Merle. "Then what?"

"Then I'm done being a target getting shot at by whoever, however, why-ever. Then maybe my life gets a new freedom. Depending on what I remember."

"And what you forget."

She sat up in the bed. The sheets fell to her lap. Merle turned so he saw the tumble of her gray-and blond hair on the back of her blue sweatshirt. When she faced him again, she was unscrewing an aluminum water bottle. Held the lid in one hand while she drank, lowered the hard bottle from her lips, her now wet lips, handed a drink to him.

He drank without thought: fortified lemonade.

Passed the hard bottle back to her. Watched her drink again.

"Now we taste the same," said Merle as she screwed the top back on.

She put the shiny metal bottle back on the bedstand, turned so she sat facing him. Her crossed yoga pants legs were mostly out of the bedcovers.

"If you lose, I'm fucked, right?" she said. "You made our interests coincide.

"But if you win and get out of this," she said, "then what about me?"

"Then I'll do everything I can for you."

" 'Everything' is a whole lot of ransom for a first kidnapping."

He felt himself smile with her. Felt his heart pounding his ribs. Felt . . .

Merle said: "Was I *really* the only place you could go?"

"Yes."

"Truth?"

"Yes, but . . . You were the only place I wanted to go."

"I've never been somebody's only."

Breathe. Just breathe.

The dark night outside her bedroom window faded toward morning gray.

Last time I saw that, I was in the garden of the dead.

Like a beautiful Buddha, Merle sat cross-legged and tangled up in the sheets on the bed in front of him. The ends of the drawstring securing her yoga pants dangled to her lap below the edge of her blue sweatshirt that covered trembling roundness he made his eyes leave, look up, see her tousled thick morning gray-and-sunshine hair. Her lemonade lips parted for soft, shallow breaths. He saw her face full on toward his as he sat across the bed from her, only an arm's length away, only that far from his touch. He felt all of him weighed by her cobalt blue eyes.

Her arms crossed and pulled off the blue sweatshirt, let it butterfly away.

She shook her head to settle her long hair. "You want to see the rest of my real."

A truth, a question, a dare, a plea, an offer, *everything*.

Her breasts were tears full with time and gravity *oh yes* swollen top-hatted pink.

She whispered: "Good thing we've got all the right drugs."

Like a laugh as she unfolded toward him, yoga graceful, sitting again but now right in front of him, between his accommodating open legs, her arm holding her weight through her palm splayed on the bed a breath away from his aching groin as she took his right hand in her heartside fingers, floated it to her warm breast to fill his grasp.

The lemonade fire of that first real kiss.

20

Maybe together we can get somewhere.
—Tracy Chapman, "Fast Car"

Knocking.

On the bedroom door.

Faye turned off the faucets on the sink in the bathroom across from the bedroom. She'd kept that bathroom door open. Refused to be trapped blind in there. Morning light filled this commandeered apartment. Condor's .45 lay on the bathroom sink. Her Glock rode in its holster on her hip. She wore the ballistic vest and pants from yesterday.

Yesterday, that was only yesterday.

She dried her palms on her pant legs.

Tucked Condor's pistol into the belt over her spine.

Stepped out of the bathroom without looking in its mirror so she could better ignore the best chance for Condor and her to escape, survive, and perhaps even triumph.

Knocking.

"Just a minute."

Faye stepped to the kitchen counter where a water glass stood tethered to the bedroom door. Lifted the glass free of its tether, a strand of dental floss that then fell like a fishing line to the kitchen floor and along the bedroom's white door.

"Okay." Faye stood back to avoid a charge-out. Her gun hand hung empty.

The bedroom door eased open and out came Merle wearing a clean blue blouse and fresh jeans. Her curly blond-gray hair looked damp, her arms cradled . . .

"Those are Condor's clothes," said Faye.

"Yes."

Merle pulled the bedroom door shut before Faye could see much in that room. Her eyes dodged Faye's. The older woman walked with nervous courage to the stainless-steel washer-dryer unit built into her kitchen island. She kept her back to Faye as she loaded the washer-dryer—a tub Faye had already checked for stashed weapons.

"Who told you to knock?" said Faye.

"We thought it would be smart. A good idea."

We, noted Faye.

"And now you're washing his clothes."

"They needed it. I can do yours next. I'm making coffee. Want some?"

"What's he doing in there?" Faye nodded to the closed bedroom door while her hostage poured coffee beans into a grinder, found a brown paper filter for a drip glass pot.

The grinder whined for thirty seconds. Anyone would have known better than to try to speak above that noise. Faye watched Merle's face brew answers for thirty seconds.

Merle shook the ground coffee into the filter-lined, cone-shaped dripper on top of the empty glass coffeepot and thus logically kept her eyes on what she was doing as she answered Faye: "You told me to see if I had clothes for him."

Merle watched herself fill a white teakettle with water from the steel sink faucet.

"What else did you see?" asked the woman with the gun.

Merle swung the teakettle from the shut-off sink to the stove, set the white kettle on a black burner, turned its stove knob to birth a *whump* of blue flame.

Merle met the younger woman's eyes. "What do you want to ask?"

"I heard him cry out in there. Twice."

"And yet you didn't come running to save your partner." The older woman's shrug raised her lips in a smile. "Twice, huh. Maybe he's having a good day."

"*Twice* is two truths that you better remember," said Faye. "His day will be a hell of a long way from good. And your day is going to be no better than his."

"Or yours."

"We're in this together," said Faye.

"Can we sit while the water boils? You look almost as bad as I feel."

Faye let the older woman choose her chair in the living room. Sat on the couch where she could watch the nervous archivist, the apartment entrance, and that white, *still closed* bedroom door.

The woman old enough to be Faye's mother said: "Did you get any sleep?"

"Enough," lied Faye.

Damp blond-and-gray hair nodded toward the closed bedroom door. "He got six hours. He could use six days."

"Couldn't we all."

Faye said: "When I was a kid, they told me it took six days to make this world."

"Do you have that kind of faith?"

"I want that kind of hope."

"Hope and perseverance and doing exactly what you're

supposed to do when you're supposed to do it is our—
your—best chance to make it in this world."

"And you're in charge of *supposed to*."

Faye nodded.

"I wouldn't want your job."

Let's hope not, thought Faye.

"I knew a woman cop—police officer. We were friends
for a few years. She was mostly plainclothes on the Capitol Hill police force—Congress's force, security guards
mostly, one of the *what,* twenty-some kinds of badges like
yours out there in this city. We used to go out for dinner
sometimes. Drinks. Check in with each other."

"Who is she?"

"For nine years she's been Mrs. Her Boss Finally Retired
And Divorced and they moved to Ohio where he's from."

"Does she still check on you?"

"Nobody checks on me." A sad smile signaled some
greater truth in the older woman's words. "Look, I'm
scared and nervous and trying to get to know you and this
thing . . . It's all up to you."

"Yeah, but it's all about him."

"What about him?" said the woman who'd emerged
from that bedroom.

"You can probably tell me as much about the man as I
can tell you," said Faye. Kept her tone neutral when she
added: "More."

The teakettle whistled.

"What I can tell you won't matter to what you gotta do,"
said Merle, her yoga grace overriding her years and fears
and unfolding her from her chair to walk into the kitchen,
turn the fire out under the white teakettle.

Bullshit, thought Faye: *You've built a bond with him and
you're banking on it.*

Her mind's eye blinked. *I hope some of fucking him was for real*.

She knew Condor hoped so, too, even knowing what they all knew.

Merle poured steaming water over the coffee beans in the cone atop the glass pot.

Water trickling over ground coffee seemed to cue the older woman. She whirled, stared at Faye standing there wearing a ballistic vest and sidearm, said: "Does your mother know what you do?"

"Does yours," said Faye.

"Never did." Merle sighed. "And now I'm never going to get that chance."

She blinked. Asked Faye: "How crazy is he?"

"Too much," answered Faye.

"Or not enough." The aroma of brewing coffee filled the apartment. "He thinks this is all happening because he was starting to lose the crazy that makes him forget."

"Maybe, but that's the kind of intel development that only he would know."

"Or maybe somebody inferred the possibility," said Merle. "And sometimes, the possibility of what might happen is enough to motivate somebody to act, strike first."

"I thought you were a mild-mannered librarian," said Faye as she watched the woman in the kitchen take one, take two, take three cups from the cabinet.

"I watch a lot of movies," said Merle. "And I worked for a movie called Congress."

"They need a better script."

The women shared a smile.

"Speaking of work," said Faye. "What about your job?"

Merle looked at the practical watch on her wrist. "I can call in sick or—*No*."

"No?"

"Better," said the older woman who'd survived decades in Washington, D.C. "I can call my boss and say I want to save my sick days but take some time off now, and offer to let him count it as me being in that whole 'sequester' budget-cutting mess the boys and girls in Congress forced on us. Him furloughing me for a few days will give him an out when the orders come down from our budget director, and they're gonna come, we're all just waiting to see if the cuts are going to make us personally bleed. I get credit for taking one for the team and nobody will come asking or looking for me."

She shrugged. "As if they would anyway."

Merle lifted the cone filled with dripped-through ground beans off the glass pot now filled with brown liquid she poured into two cups before setting down that pot of scalding brew she could have thrown at Faye's eyes, asked: "Milk? Sugar?"

"Black," answered Faye.

"Straight," said Merle as she passed the cup to her captor. She opened the refrigerator, topped off her own cup from a carton of milk she left on the counter.

Merle took a sip of her coffee, held the innocent cup in both her hands, said: "What else can I do to help?"

"So now you're on our team?"

"Looks like you two brought back the draft."

"And you trust us? Believe us?"

"You mean how do I know you are who you say you are?" Merle shrugged. "How do you know anybody is who they say they are?"

She shook her head. "We lie to ourselves about who we see, we lie to ourselves about who we are. Then we buy our own lies and try to spend them as our lives."

Merle gave Faye a smile both of them knew came from irony not amusement, said: "Guns are the ultimate reality check. You've got them, not me. But even without them, the odds of you two both being this particular crazy add up to unlikely, so who you are is probably who you say you are. Mostly."

"You play the odds?" asked Faye.

"I play what I get," answered Merle. "Now what else can I do?"

"Let's talk about that after he joins us." Faye nodded to the closed bedroom door.

The older woman with damp gray-blond hair smiled as she raised the cup of milk-colored coffee and before she sipped from it said: "Are you sure he's coming out?"

21

If I could hide, 'neath the wings.
—John Stewart, "Daydream Believer"

Close your eyes.

Lie on this bed.

Pretend you belong here.

That you deserve this.

That no one wants to kill you.

Alone & naked & flat on his back, Condor felt soft sheets on the mussed bed where he'd collapsed, his ankles dangling above the floor that led out of this room, this wonderful room smelling of sea and musk, out to the rest of the apartment where she'd gone, where Faye and the guns were, and from there down the green hall to the elevator or stairs, a street of residential Washington, roads that led to the monuments and Capitol and White House and Complex Zed and a mortuary in suburban Virginia with a crematorium that created ashes no one would ever scatter in some garden of the known dead.

Stay here in this sunlit bedroom.

Afterward, both of them naked under the sheets, his head on her pillow, his heart her pillow, a cloud of the lilac shampoo scent from her gray-blond hair floating with the musk of some past perfume and the scent, that scent, that warm sea scent.

Merle'd said: "Was it like you imagined?"

"Better. I was too worried about getting shot to be too nervous."

"Funny, I was worried about getting shot, too."

He felt her smile and she said: "*Bang.*"

The bed trembled with their soft chuckle.

Merle whispered: "What else should I be worried about?"

"Getting shot tops the list. Then everything else until it's all back to normal."

"Maybe I'm worried about that, too." He felt her fingers move on his chest. "Maybe it's lucky that my normal changed."

She whispered: "Should I be worried about you?"

"Getting shot?"

"You know what I mean," she said.

He didn't, wondered, said: "Whoever I am, it's too late to change."

Condor turned on his side so she could see his face even if he knew *she knew* better than to trust his expression, said: "But none of me wants you hurt. Hurt any way."

Her eyes dropped from his. Her lips softly kissed his bare chest.

She didn't look up, said: "What should I do?"

"Grasp your true reality," said Condor. "Course, that doesn't mean you can do anything about it, but then at least you've got a chance at taking your shot."

"Are you saying it all depends on your perspective?"

"Bullets don't care about your perspective. They only care where you stand."

He felt the mattress rise and fall with his four breaths.

She said: "So we better stand up."

Merle swung away from him, a swirl of long gray-blond hair and round flesh and bare feet kissing the floor, her nude spine to him, the yoga-conditioned swell of her hips curving before his eyes and then her hand reached back.

"Come on," she said. "We need a shower."

She put Condor under the nozzle spraying hot water into the white porcelain shower-tub, stepped in with him, closed the shower curtain—a gray plastic sheet colored by artwork, a translucent reproduced painting of nineteenth-century Parisians from a moneyed class walking in the park where everything seemed safely controlled.

He soaped and shampooed so as not to bump her, white suds of lather washing down her water-slick chest, sliding over her low-slung full breasts, her slight paunch that age won from exercise, down her loins, her legs that were just the right length of long. He stepped back to let water spray her face, rinse away the lather and scents of yesterday.

Then she stood as far away from him in the shower-tub as the porcelain and walls and plastic shower curtain allowed. Water beat down him, propelled drops flying around his blocking bulk to hit the edges of her naked front as her blue eyes pushed him.

She said: "I know one thing you're worried about."

Condor felt his breath deepen, his pulse race.

"*Yes*," she said: "You made me have to be here with you."

Oh so slowly took one barefooted step on the wet porcelain tub toward him, took another until only a breath separated their naked fronts as water beat down.

Merle said: "But I choose to be here like this."

She wrapped her arms around him and held her bare flesh to his.

How many breaths they'd stayed there, he didn't know, didn't count, didn't think.

Then her hands moved behind him, faucets cranked off and the spray of the water fell to nothing but drips from the showerhead, then silence.

Metal loops screeched on the shower rod as she jerked open the plastic art curtain.

"I'll get us towels."

She left him standing there, naked and wet in her white tub.

Pulled three towels off bathroom shelves. Wrapped her hair up in one so the towel became a turban. Wrapped a second towel around her chest so the downy soft white cloth covered her from the top of her breasts to mid-thigh. Tossed the third towel to him and smiled as he surprised himself and caught it.

"We need to do laundry." She walked back to the bedroom.

Condor stepped from the tub, drying off as he hurried to be with her.

Found her in the bedroom, stacking his clothes on the chair, a pile on the nearby table from his black jeans pockets of the money and stray receipts and his handkerchief.

Merle rambled: "I don't know about your thermal underwear, but I'll wash them, too. Supposed to be like a real April spring for the next couple days. I don't have men's shirts, but your blue shirt should wash out okay enough, brown stains on the collar, weird, but we'll see. I'm not much for ironing, but if it's too wrinkled, there's a ratty black sweater in the Lost & Found box that might fit you or over it and . . ."

She realized he was standing there.

Staring at her.

Or at least . . . toward her.

"What?" she said. Smiled.

Frowned: "Vin? Are you . . . here? Are you okay?"

"You don't have to do my laundry. Our laundry. You're not . . ."

"I'm not going to make it if they can smell you coming," she said.

"Whoever they are," he told her.

"That's your end."

She turned from the laundry pile in the chair and faced Condor. Unwound the towel turban, rubbed her gray-blond wet hair dry, squeezed its long locks with the towel she then dropped onto the laundry pile.

Merle closed her eyes. Shook her head from side to side, her long wet locks whipping out this way & that way flinging water drops from her hair like commanded rain. Her spinning loosed the towel around her body so it fell, a revelation of swaying breasts and belly and water-wet lap. She caught the towel with her right hand. Stopped shaking her head. Her eyes opened and saw her nakedness fill his stare.

As he stood there.

Towel over his shoulder.

By the edge of the bed *where*.

Her smile came long and slow and sweet as she saw what she saw of him.

"Well," she said. "That's a surprise."

can't talk can't move can't think can I can I . . .

She let the towel she held fall to the floor. Shook her head. Brushed damp hair off her face and over her shoulders to hang down her naked back as she smiled at him. As she stepped across the room toward him, saying: "But we've already showered."

Her arms circled his neck like snakes.

The wet warmth of her flesh pressed to him.

The crown of her damp head came to his chin and he kissed her there, smelled her blond-gray lilac shampoo tangle as his hands trembled and ached to move from his bare sides, to touch her. He kissed the side of her head, tried to turn her lips up to his with the gentle push of his cheek but her face burrowed against his chest.

She whispered: "We don't have time."

Then turned her face up to their kiss.

And his hands cupped the round surrender of her hips as he pulled her closer.

Her arms tightened around his neck as his hands slid up her sides and filled with the stiffening weight of her breasts.

She broke their kiss, nuzzled his chest, pressed her lips to his neck. Her hands cupped his hips as she kissed his heart, as she bent into him, her own hips brushed the edge of the bed and she said: "Make time."

Kissing him, pulling him closer as she sat on the bed and he stood there, saw her, felt and saw what she did, what she was doing and oh, *oh* when that moment came he could not kill his scream.

Again afterward, she lay with him on the bed, but only for a few moments. Left him there for the bathroom. He heard her brushing her teeth. She came back, crawled onto the bed, said: "Use my razor on the edge of the tub. And your toothbrush."

Smiled. "When you're ready."

She dressed in a blur, wore a black bra and matching panties under her loose jeans and blue shirt. Toweled her hair again though it still hung damp. Picked the laundry out of the chair. Told him: "I'm going to make coffee."

"Knock before you touch the doorknob."

"But it's my apartment."

"Not anymore."

Merle said: "What's a girl gotta do to have her own life?"

But smiled.

Shifted the laundry in her arms and knocked on her own bedroom door.

Waited, knocked again.

Through that closed door, Merle and Condor heard Faye say: *"Just a minute."*

Less than a minute, judged Condor, then Faye called out: *"Okay."*

Merle opened the door, stepped outside the bedroom and closed the door behind her exit all without Condor seeing his de facto mission partner.

The blue disposable razor was well past its prime as he scraped his soaped face smooth in the bathroom sink's mirror. Her toothpaste gave his mouth a minty-fresh taste.

He walked into the bedroom looking for the lost & found scavenged clothes—

Felt himself falling, plopping his butt on the bed, collapsing flat on his back with his eyes full of the solid ceiling pressing down on where he lay.

Stay here. John Stewart's song. Calculations of what he had to do and couldn't do. Dreams of staying *right here, right now* then *maybe . . .*

"Maybes drive you mad."

He didn't turn his eyes from the ceiling to see the *who* or *what* of that ghost.

Said: "Too late, I'm there now."

"Make time."

Those words, thought Condor: *She's not dead. She's just in the other room.*

"Are you sure?"

"I'm sure I want what I now know I can have."

"Grasp your true reality."

"Fuck you," Condor told the parroting ghost.

But without conviction.

And the ghost knew that.

I can't let her get killed.

Killed too, he added before the ghosts could get to him.

Merle's smile. The curving open of her lips. The perfect words she found. What he thought she knew. The way she let him hold her. How she'd held him back. That was enough, or almost enough, or at least far better than he had a right to expect. *Is she my last her?* He let that thought go as . . . unworthy.

Get Merle to her new normal, safe, alive.

Everything else . . .

"You already know everything else."

But *he* said that. Not some ghost.

Condor sat up, naked, his feet flat on the floor and his mind saved from illusions that he could hide.

He said out loud: "Are you satisfied now?"

Got no answer.

No answer from any ghosts.

Odd.

Aromas of coffee beckoned him.

He got off the bed. Dressed. Walked to the door he had.

22

The bedroom door opened.

Faye blinked when she saw who stepped out to join her and Merle in the kitchen.

Said: "You look . . ."

"Nowhere near as good as any of us want."

The man whose life Faye protected with her own wore gray sweatpants that were too small and a black college sweatshirt that was too big, bare feet, and a wry smile.

"Don't worry," he said, "I fake it better after coffee. Besides, it's barely nine A.M."

Merle said: "If you want me to make that call, this is when it should happen."

Faye chose the landline for Merle's call, put the exchange between the gray-blond archivist and her Library of Congress boss on speaker. Watched Condor *get it* as the telephone transaction played out like Merle'd predicted.

Like she'd promised.

"So we got cover," said Condor.

"We've maybe got a roof," answered Faye.

Condor smiled at the woman he'd helped Faye hijack.

Or did I help him get her?

He asked Merle: "Do you get the paper?"

Faye said: "We'll go online for—"

"Old school," said Condor: "We don't want to leave the newspaper out to raise questions."

"I get *The Post,*" said Merle. "Off the stack they deliver downstairs in the lobby."

Condor looked at Faye.

She reached behind her back. Passed the .45 to him. Grabbed her coat to cover the gun on her hip and obscure her body armor, took what Merle said were her apartment keys and left the two of them alone.

Low risk, right?

Leaving them alone. Armed. Phones.

The proper option for partners. Giving Condor his best chance *in case.*

Faye eased down five flights of stairs. Opened the LOBBY door a crack.

Saw no one, nothing amiss.

No one shot her as she stepped into the apartment building's front entryway.

No corridor security cameras caught her lifting a newspaper off a rack across from the elevator she marched to, tapping the call button and not showing the relief she felt when the doors jumped open and gave her an empty cage to ride. She pushed the button for the floor above Merle's, got out, walked down the fire stairs and knocked on 513's door, her right hand empty by her side.

Condor let her in, took the newspaper from her as she relocked the door.

He held up the newspaper: "My bet is a full-block blackout."

"No," said Faye. "Too much street action. Veil."

Condor shrugged. "With spin."

From her living room chair, Merle said: "What are you two talking about?"

"All the news that's fit to print," said Condor, riffing off the motto of *The Washington Post*'s then last remaining serious rival as a dead-trees newspaper.

Page one of *The Post*'s Metro section.

A boxed story the size of Faye's hand, probably shoved into print at the last possible second the night before: A drug deal gone bad on a subway platform left one innocent bystander stray-bullet dead, woman, identity withheld pending notification of next of kin, one street thug killed by police, one undercover officer shot in serious condition, one cop with minor injuries, no delays expected in morning rush-hour traffic.

"The bodies don't add up," said Condor.

"Depends on who sees what to count," said Faye.

"The Red Line," said Condor. "Janitors commandeer the next train for covert cleanup and removal."

"This cost," said Faye.

"The price on our heads keeps going up," said Condor.

Faye used their hostess's laptop. Found nothing about the D.C. Metro gunfight on the *New York Times* Web site. Read online editions of all Washington news outlets, checked local TV and radio stations' Web sites, many of which carried variations on the original *Post* story or "updates" that implied progress but offered no new details, though a couple sites had cell-phone photos of ambulance and cop cars parked at the subway entrance, their emergency lights spinning red & blue blasts into the night. She found a neighborhood Listserv report about "vandals" racing their bikes through a restaurant "breaking a lot of plates." The Listserv posted an eleven-second cell-phone video of clattering crockery & unintelligible shouts, showed the back of a man in a red jacket wobbling his bike toward the front of a cafe past stunned diners. One Listserv comment "linked" this "hooliganism" to an increase in graffiti spray-painted on neighborhood walls, while another noted that "incident shows America must have evolved because this not racial 'cause one biker /white one / blk," then the online discussion veered into rants about restaurants attracting rats.

"So nobody knows what's going on," said Merle.

"Including us," said Condor.

"Knowledge comes in levels," said Faye.

"Next comes a data blizzard," said Condor. "A shotgun blast of controlled misdirections, all 'factual,' all riding a big secret in plain sight."

"So what do we do now?" said Merle.

Faye looked at her, looked at Condor.

Condor looked at Faye, looked at Merle, looked back to Faye.

Shrugged.

Merle said: "No."

23

Too much cunning strategy . . . and strange
things start to happen.
—*Tao Te Ching / The Tao of Power,*
trans. by R. L. Wing

"I'm not going to let you two decide *what's next* without me," said Merle.

Smart, thought Condor. *Bold.* He told himself to cloak the pride in her he felt.

Faye said: "We don't want to get into an issue of what choice you have."

"We're there," countered Merle. "We always are. Right here, right now, I'm either your prisoner or something more."

"Like what?" said Faye.

"I don't think this has a name. I'm a woman you hijacked who wants out of your trouble. I'll do what I gotta do. You want me as part of your solution, not your problem."

"You could be a one-bullet problem."

Condor tensed.

Merle said: "We're all a one-bullet problem."

The Capitol Hill worker put her empty coffee cup on the glass table. Told the spies in her living room: "You don't know who your opponents are, or what's at the core of them wanting you . . . like dead. And now what happens to you, happens to me."

Acceptance and challenge shaped Merle's smile, but *she*

calls me Vin wished he knew all that the curve of her lips contained as she added: "I'm the only ally you know you've got."

"*Ally* is a strong word for a draftee," said Faye.

"Whatever," said Merle. "You've got to figure out how to get us safe, like into some kind of witness protection program."

Faye and Condor laughed.

"Been there," he said. "Got me here."

"So find a better program," snapped Merle. "You—*we* can't just wait on whatever it is your *they* do next. Not if they're as powerful as you say, as they seem."

Condor said: "You're trying to take us somewhere."

"You've found an agenda," said Faye.

"We've all got agendas so what the fuck difference does that make," said Merle. "What I, what *we* gotta do is figure the best way to stay alive. Politics is about what you do and Washington works on who you can convince to help you."

Merle put her eyes on Condor as she said: "I got a one-time I've never played with a Senator. Call it a favor, call it quid pro quo for what he'll be afraid I could do if he says *no,* call it his guilt, *whatever*: I've got one *ask*. He's got power. Do the math."

"You'd do that?" said Condor.

"It's the choice I've got."

"Senators are button-pushers, not *get you home alive* guys."

"He can make calls, get—"

Faye said: "Let's say he only calls the right guy. Whoever he calls has to figure out the politics and law of what they can do and what they will do. Even if he jumps when you snap your fingers, he's gotta politic others into getting airborne with him."

Condor said: "His power is in the suites, not the streets."

"But keep him in mind for when we're inside," Faye told the older woman.

"Inside where?"

"Inside our system with a shitload of angels or at least neutral gunners so we can get the good guys to move us off the bull's-eye and hunt what's really going on."

"You got a better way than me to do that?" Merle asked Faye.

Condor looked at his partner, his fellow pro, the government spook who said she wanted to save, the young woman with a Glock on her hip.

Saw Faye's face tremble with her silent scream *YES*.

24

Wheels turnin' round and round.
—Steely Dan, "Do It Again"

Faye hunkered down in the backseat of a car parked a block beyond Merle's apartment building. Cool air flowed over Faye from the curbside front window she'd punched out as quietly as possible seventeen minutes after they'd sent Merle on a run.

Merle on her own. Solo. In her car. Out of their control.

Time elapsed since Merle's launch: two hours, forty-three minutes, and a quarter-circle sweep of the second hand around the watch dial on Faye's wrist.

Time of day in D.C.'s real world: 11:23 A.M. on an ordinary April Thursday.

Crisp blue sky. Smells of spring green. Parking spaces along the curbs of this residential neighborhood materialized when its luckier residents went to work. Faye'd spotted uncrushed brown leaves banked at both undersides of this car's tires, its windshield dusted with green powder pollen, figured the vehicle belonged to someone who commuted via more economical public transportation where no delays were expected from last night's *incident* on the Red Line.

She's got seventeen minutes left before we pull the trigger, thought Faye.

They'd kept Merle's cell phone when they launched her.

"But what if something goes wrong?" she'd asked.

Condor'd said: "It's already wrong. This is your shot at making it right."

"No," said Merle, "what I mean is—"

"We know what you meant," said Faye. "Stick to the plan."

"Stick to what should happen, what we need to happen," added Condor.

Merle stared at both of them, then focused on him, said: "I'll do my best."

They gave her a thousand dollars in cash.

Faye'd expected the hug and kiss she watched Merle give Condor. Was surprised when the older woman wrapped her arms around her until Faye hugged her back.

"See you," said Merle.

She left the apartment, the door closing behind her with a *click*.

One heartbeat.

Two.

Faye slid Merle's laptop into the purse-backpack, dropped in Merle's cell phone along with batteries from the landline phones: that number still worked, took messages, but without the batteries no one could use the twentieth-century-style communicators to make a call, connect with 911, with anyone who would listen to anything Merle had to say.

Condor wore his black leather jacket, black jeans and wrinkled blue shirt. Faye saw his thermal underwear top under the blue shirt, black sneaker-like shoes tied with the hard-to-slip knots favored by mountain climbers and Special Ops teams. The .45 rode holstered on the right side of his belt along with a clip-on spring knife while the belt's left side held three stacked & packed spare magazines in a pouch. As long as he kept the jacket unzipped, he didn't *print*—show the outline of *concealed weapon*.

Faye'd strapped on her Glock and two spare magazines. *You had to shoot the gunners at the subway. You had to kill them.* Faye had two of Delta Force's new palm-sized nonpublic flash-bang grenades in her backpack, a silencer for her pistol, a sleek black flashlight, a cigar-sized aluminum tube containing lock picks and tension bars. She left the bullet-heavy speed loader for the lost .38 revolver on the glass coffee table.

They went out to the world.

Hunkered down in the broken-into car, Faye checked her watch: fifteen minutes left.

She stared over the car's front seat, past the sidewalk leading to Merle's building, uphill past the intersection to trees on a playground where chained swings hung empty and still. Condor hid in those trees. He'd have some phony cover alibi in case a nanny showed up with young charges and spotted an older man who could be accused of creepy loitering. But so far this morning, Faye'd seen no children on the sidewalks. Maybe the swings and playground were relics of what had been or totems to what could be.

Don't think about that. They're just empty swings.

Her watch said fourteen minutes to go.

Her eyes flicked to the rearview mirror she'd adjusted to capture the view behind the parked car—oncoming traffic plus a glimpse of anyone on the sidewalks who wasn't sneaking forward in a combat crouch and shielded by the parked cars. The passenger side mirror helped her surveillance of that sidewalk. As for across the street, even if she went beyond using the driver's side mirror and turned to look, what she saw was parked cars.

You never have perfect optics.

From his hide on the hill's playground, Condor could

cover traffic coming the other way or turning onto this road from either direction on the intersecting street.

Eleven minutes to go.

Ten.

Nine minutes and a red Ford parked in front of the apartment building with a flash of brake lights in the midday air. The driver's door opened. Out climbed Merle.

Alone.

Acting normal. Acting as if she always got out of her car like a refugee. Looking back the way she'd come, then looking the other way down the street toward where she didn't know Faye was hiding, so *not* acting like she was expecting someone. *Good.*

Why two sacks in her hands?

Merle walked from her parked car, followed the sidewalk to her apartment building. Ungraceful gait: *Nerves, natural, that's natural.* Entered the front door.

The elevator ride to her fifth floor will take Merle two minutes. Faye scanned the streets, sidewalks, hunting for anyone who'd followed Merle.

She'll find her apartment empty. Find us gone. And do what?

Give her seven more minutes. To see if she stays. To see if she runs outside, flees, tries to signal someone. To see if some cover team she'd summoned had given her a cell phone and would come charging when she called to report *targets lost.*

Give her seven minutes alone in her home.

That was Faye's plan with Condor.

He couldn't wait.

Or told time differently.

Two minutes early, Faye saw him leave the playground, growing bigger and more identifiable with each step he took toward the apartment building. A rebel but still a pro, not looking in Faye's direction—and not *not* looking her way.

No cars roared out of the high-noon sun to drop a snatch team on him.

No bullet cut Condor down as he entered Merle's building.

Give him five minutes.

When she'd waited and watched and no Op team appeared, Faye eased out of the car she'd vandalized, joined Condor and Merle in the apartment.

The older woman glared at Faye: "You didn't trust me."

"We don't trust our situation," said Faye.

"Like I told you," added Condor, "you could have been grabbed—"

"Or called someone *just* to betray you," snapped Merle. "That's what you think."

"That's how we have to think," said Faye.

Condor said: "It's all about the smart move. That was the smart move for us."

"Guess I should have thought of a smart move for me," said Merle. "For us."

"Sure," said Faye. "And you—"

"Got lunch." Merle lifted one of the sacks on the kitchen counter.

Faye focused on the four disposable phones from the other sack.

"I got more cash, too," said Merle. "From my ATM."

Faye frowned. "That's—"

"Not a risk until she's IDed as with us," said Condor. "Smart. Now or never."

"Yeah!" Merle told Faye with a defiant look.

Fay programmed the three expensive phones' CONTACTS with initials: C, F, M.

"Do you want to see the receipts?" asked Merle. "Like

you said, I bought them as separate cash transactions. Got the cheap phone in another store. Wore my baseball cap and sunglasses. You can check the receipts against your change. I paid for lunch."

"You were worried about us doing an audit?" said Faye.

Merle smiled. Met Faye's probing eyes. Said: "Be prepared."

They ate carryout plates of deli bar food from an upscale grocery store.

Faye knew the cold noodles she ate were sesame, knew the broccoli still had its crunch. Watched the older couple share bites off each other's plate. Faye stuffed lunch trash and the cell phones' wrappings into a sack, carried it, her backpack purse and the credit card she sneaked out of Merle's purse to the bedroom, said: "I'm going to check our gear and trash for the burn bag, grab a shower."

"I'm on watch," said Condor.

Then like he and Merle expected, Faye shut herself behind that white door.

Took Faye eleven minutes to log on to the Web site she'd found while sitting Charlie Sugar—counter-surveillance— in the burgled car outside the apartment building, use the credit card stolen from Merle, do what she did and hope that it worked. She crammed trash into the sack, forced herself to take a real shower, and for a moment, *for just a few moments* as the hot water beat down on her face, freed sobs of tears to wash her cheeks, ease the pressure in her spine, the weight gripping her heart.

Composed herself, her gear, her backpack, rejoined her comrades.

She sent Merle into the bedroom to pack an overnight bag.

When the older woman was out of sight, put the credit card back in Merle's purse.

Condor gave Faye a frown. Said nothing.

A rebel but a pro.

The three of them walked out of the apartment seven minutes later.

An ordinary April Thursday, 2:17 P.M.

Beautiful Rock Creek Parkway curves through Washington, D.C., alongside the Potomac River from the Navy Yard with its former espionage centers, past memorial gardens for FDR and the broken souls of the Depression who resurrected themselves through the horrors & heroism of WWII, around marble monuments for murder victims Martin Luther King and Abraham Lincoln, flows a rifle shot from the Vietnam Memorial's mirror black wall of names and statues of American soldiers from the Korean War who march through the riverside trees like ghosts. The Parkway passes under the multiauditorium albino complex named after one of our assassinated presidents and past what was an apartment/hotel/office complex called Watergate and the rehabbed former hotel where button men of that scandal staged one of their covert operations. As it flows toward Maryland suburbs, the Parkway passes Georgetown streets haunted by Rose Men, then comes the zoo where at dawn you can hear lions roar while off to the right rises the now gentrified neighborhood of Mt. Pleasant where brown-skinned Latinos rioted against mostly black-skinned D.C. cops in the last days of the twentieth century. The Parkway then widens from a tree-lined road to an urban canyon, a green valley with paths for bikers and joggers, tabled picnic sites and grassy stretches for volleyball games, shadowed glades that cloak dump sites for homicide victims both functionally famous and forever forgotten. Before the Parkway crosses the District line, roads lead out of its valley to neighborhoods of million-dollar homes, embassies surrounded by black steel fences and invisible electronic curtains, a public golf course nestled in the forest between the Parkway and Sixteenth Street that creates a straight drive south to the White House and north to Maryland past the legendary tree-lined grounds of Walter Reed Army Medical Center that on this day was slated to end its hundred-year reign as America's most famous military hospital for "commercial redevelopment" Faye believed was prompted not so much by facility obsolescence or tax-saving economics as it was to move wounded warriors out of the city so urban-dwelling policymakers need no longer routinely see wheelchair-captured and amputee and burn victim veterans of their decisions wandering the glorious capital city streets.

Merle drove her red Ford north on Rock Creek Parkway.

Condor rode shotgun.

Faye lay across the backseat.

A quick glance profiled this car as two aging, innocent civilians out for a drive.

The red Ford turned off the Parkway and onto the golf course road.

Faye heard Condor call *"Clear!"* and felt Merle brake the car to a crawl.

The red Ford was almost stopped when Faye leapt out of the backseat.

The Ford sped up, drove away, left her alone on the road.

Two minutes later, she'd walked out of the Parkway at the intersection of the golf course road and Sixteenth Street. She turned right, put the 209-meters-away specter of Walter Reed and its security cameras behind her, walked toward the 50-blocks-distant White House past blocks of apartment buildings where *maybe* no fish-eye lens recorded her passing. Two hundred paces in that direction and she jaywalked across the busy divided city street, walked back the way she'd come—but now on the other side of the road, headed north for any cell tower tracking analysis.

She used the cheap disposable cell phone. Kept walking as she dialed the cell phone number she'd memorized less than forty-eight hours before.

Second buzz and her call got answered with unresponsive silence.

Into her phone as she walked, Faye said: "Say it ain't you, Sami."

"Where are you?" said his voice. "Are you okay? What are you—"

"Why'd you sic a wet team on me, Sami?"

"Not our people! They beat us there. Do you have Condor? Are you—"

"Who were they?"

"Unknown."

"Bullshit! You're in the belly of the beast—*you are* the beast. They were trained, equipped, targeted and briefed pros and *the fuck* you don't know!"

"Never seen anything like it. One guy, sure, maybe two. But we've got four bodies we can't find in the system. Any system, including NATO and Interpol. No prints. No facial recognition. No forensics. No intercepted chatter about MIAs. Sterile gear, no consistency. All we got are ghosts."

"What's going on, Sami?"

"You tell me and we'll both know, kid. It's all we can do here to keep the world from flying apart, the cover from exploding."

In the street, somewhere far off to her right, Faye heard a distant police siren wail.

Nothing, it's nothing, routine, too soon to be connected and targeted to me.

And one siren in Washington's District of Crime

wouldn't be enough to give any listeners on Sami's call a quick bead on her.

"There's at least two more opposition gunners out there, Sami."

"How do you know?"

"How do you *not* know?"

"Condor: is he okay, is he functional, what's his state of mind, where—"

"And here I thought you cared about me."

"We care about the same things, Faye. You know that. Know me."

She didn't respond.

Sami said: "Think, Faye. I told you something was off, wrong, screwy. That's why I sent you out there on your own. And I was right!"

"Congratulations."

"How are we going to—"

"What 'we,' Sami? It was just you and me and then *we* included that wet team."

"I don't know how we got compromised. I don't know that we were. Maybe the opposition got lucky. Maybe you got . . ."

"Give me something I don't know, Sami. ABC: All Bullshit Considered."

"Whoever they are, why-ever they are . . . I got the tingles, the creeps that I can't promise you I'm not compromised in ways I can't see. So you tell me: what do we do?"

"I'm coming in."

"Yes! Where? How? With Condor, right? What should I—"

Faye hung up. Pulled the battery from that phone, tossed its parts into a trash can, crossed the street, walked back down the road to the golf course and Parkway.

The red Ford rolled back onto that same road when she was twenty steps into the trees, slowed to let her climb in, then sped off.

"Got nothing but denials," she told Condor as she lay on the backseat. "He's lying or telling the truth, maybe compromised, maybe not, but at least he and whoever he trusts now have to assume I—*we*—are coming in. They'll swarm the streets, *sure,* track the call to that neighborhood, but they'll concentrate on the two locations I'm most likely to exploit: Complex Zed and CIA HQ at Langley. The good guys will make perimeters to get us inside, the bad guys will stake those sites out to snipe us when we show."

Merle whispered: "*We* means . . ."

"I don't think they know about you."

"So I could just . . ."

Faye and Condor finished her thought with their silence.

"I can just drive," said Merle. "Where you tell me to."

They found an underground parking garage with rates by the hour, day or month two blocks from the target. Faye paid a vacant-eyed attendant for three days in advance.

The underground concrete cavern echoed with the closing of the car doors from the red Ford they parked in its designated yellow-striped slot. They stood in flickering artificial light. Smelled burnt gas, oil, cold metal from a dozen other vehicles crouched on this level. Shadows obscured the distant cement walls.

"Never liked these places," whispered Merle.

Faye said: "At least you can't get spotted by drones."

"Unless they've already cross-haired the building above us," said Condor. "Rubble buries anything."

"You're such cheerful people," said Merle.

The best Op formation called for Merle walking on the street side of the sidewalk, Faye between her and Condor, the collar turned up on his black leather jacket, not enough to obscure his face for later identification via any security camera they passed, but odds were, no lens in any of the storefronts or flat faces of the modern buildings they passed on this classy Washington street had cameras linked to the NSA grid.

Two blocks. They had to cover two blocks and not get spotted, caught, shot.

Midafternoon foot traffic was light, but they weren't alone enough to stand out. They reached their target address and caught a break: no security guard was on day duty at the building's front desk, no one was lurking in the lobby, no postman spotted them.

"The mailman," said Condor.

"What?" said Merle.

"Never mind," he said.

Faye herded them into the elevator, punched the floor button.

"Tool up," she told Condor.

Merle's eyes widened as the man she'd embraced filled his hand with the .45.

Condor kept the pistol pressed low along his right leg.

Faye heard the *click* as he thumbed off the safety.

The elevator stopped.

Those cage doors slid open.

Faye rolled out first and fast, checked both ways as Condor whirled behind her, his eyes probing the opposite direction as hers until she whispered: "Clear!"

Merle nervously stepped off the elevator.

"Stay between us," Faye told her as they hurried down a corridor of closed doors.

Stay closed stay closed stay closed!

At the target door, Condor gestured for Merle to stand against the opposite wall of the corridor, rooted himself

near the target portal, held his gun in front of him, ready
to whirl whichever way they'd need to send death.

Faye worked on the lock with her picks and tension bar
for thirty seconds before the first *click*. The second lock
took half that time, then she pushed the door open, stepped
in, whispered for the others, Merle coming in fast and Condor bringing up rear guard. Faye eased the door shut, had
to disturb the corridor's silence with the relocking *click*.

But they were in.

Merle whispered: "That was fast."

Faye said: "I've done this before."

25

Put yourself.

—Citizen Cope, "A Bullet and a Target"

Condor aimed his .45 at the blond man's face, said: "You're not who I expected."

Blue eyes blinked behind the blond man's glasses as he stood there in his own apartment, his eyes locked on the gun held by a stranger who'd surprised him, pushed the door closed behind his after-work entrance and zeroed him with what the suit & tie blond man would forever after think of as *"the biggest black hole in the fucking universe."*

Condor saw the blond man blink again, then say: "I didn't expect you either."

Across the room, Faye said: "You're both the right guy."

From off to his right, Condor heard Merle whisper: *"Don't shoot him."*

"Whoever you are, lady," said the blond man, "I'm with you."

Then he told Faye: "Actually, I came for you."

And Condor grinned.

"Chris Harvie," said Faye, "meet . . . Call him Condor. And this is Merle."

"Could he . . . I don't know, lower the gun now?"

Yeah, he's cool.

Condor holstered the .45 and claimed the younger, taller man's hand for a shake.

Why is Faye hanging back? Like she's . . . Embarrassed. Ashamed. Scared.

"Just like you said in your text," Chris told the green-eyed Glock-packing woman who trembled near him. "I came straight home after work."

"Told no one?" whispered Faye.

He shook his head *no.*

And she ran to him, into his arms, buried her face against his chest and said so everyone in their known universe could hear: "I'm sorry!"

Chris kissed the top of her head, then again, said: "Whatever, it's okay."

He'd previously only glimpsed the Faye who now stood back and stared at him, said: "No it's not."

I've been you, thought Condor.

The four of them sat on secondhand recycled office chairs in front of the wall made by Chris's sophisticated and expensive sound & cyber system.

Faye said: "I'm sorry, but this best choice puts you at terrible risk, your life, your career—I'm serious!"

"The big gun convinced me of that," said Chris.

"We can't laugh about this!" argued Faye, fighting a smile.

"We have to laugh about this."

Faye said: "You're a lawyer and there are laws and security codes we're probably breaking on top of all that, but . . . you have to know enough to know *why.*"

Then she revealed a framework of truth, disclosing Condor just enough, justifying and exonerating Merle, taking the blame and the blood all on her.

"And now we need you," she told Chris.

Condor interrupted: "Tomorrow, it's got to be tomorrow."

"What—" Chris held up a hand against both Faye and the man called Condor.

Who he frowned at, asked: "What did you mean, I'm not who you expected? This is my apartment, my home, she's my . . . my *I'm hers*."

Condor said: "The way she talked, I thought you'd be taller."

A smile twitched Chris's lips, he blushed, stared at the floor.

Faye's eyes searched that plane, too.

Let them have the moment.

Let it touch you.

Chris looked up, his motion pulling all others' eyes to him as he said: "I get it. Look, I don't do what I do because it's a job, and I didn't take this job to punch my ticket to some '*better*' gig, and if I'm not here to matter, I don't belong here at all."

Faye said: "I . . . *You know*."

"Yeah," said Chris, "*I know*. But now what matters is this . . . *thing* we're in."

He looked at Condor, said: "Besides the obvious cosmic reality, why does what we do next have to be tomorrow?"

"Because it's Friday," answered Condor.

Faye told the blond man who'd loosed the tic around his neck *why, what, how.*

"Yeah," said Chris, "it's gotta be tomorrow."

Merle said: "What about tonight?"

Tonight was frozen pizzas, a refrigerator six-pack of cold microbrewery beer, speculation and nervous silences, things said and not said, glances, eyes full of questions and words full of hope. They used Chris's computer to map out their moves, Google street view and satellite images to scan what they'd see in the future.

As the small one-bedroom apartment filled with the aromas of baking pizza crust and simmering tomato sauce, cheese bubbling and coins of pepperoni and sausage curling their circles in toward their centers, Condor inventoried this other place where he didn't want to die.

A particular bachelor's home. "Particular," *yes*, as in *this one*, but "particular" *more* in what was chosen and cherished.

Almost like me.

Or who you could have been *if*.

A wall of electronics. Great speakers, a dollar-devouring computer and music system, racks of CDs arranged in categories of subtle distinction. A few photos of a mom, a dad, a brother and two sisters, one older, one younger. Among the framed photos on the walls hung original art by a creator with a flair for purple and red crayons and dinosaurs, a display that screamed *nephew* to Condor. One frame held the iconic *New Yorker* magazine cover after 9/11, an all-black skyline enveloping even blacker silhouettes of twin towers. Another frame showed a rare indigo night aerial shot of the glowing U.S. Capitol dome that Condor and Chris saw from the sidewalks of every ordinary workday. Stacks of books lined walls, a couple volumes of Camus, law tomes and histories, novels. Titles Condor spotted included Dos Passos's *USA* trilogy, *East of Eden, Neuromancer, The Nature of the Game, Crimegate*. The TV was small, a few DVDs stacked beside it. A cable hookup. The quick search & secure stalk through the apartment he'd done with Faye after she broke them in had shown Condor the lone bedroom, a closet with half a dozen suits plus sports jackets, ties, plastic bagged from the dry cleaner's shirts and lots of running shoes—*"Ultimate,"*

Faye'd whispered, a comment he didn't understand but let pass as strategically irrelevant. Their good luck meant frozen pizzas in the otherwise bleakly sparse refrigerator unit.

You could live like this.

Almost.

But the madness you bring with you would crash this sophisticated order.

Condor looked across the five remaining slices of pizza to the floor space where Chris sat beside Faye, asked him: "Has anybody been watching you?"

"Ah . . . No."

"No odd looks at work? Strangers suddenly around? Familiar faces appearing when you didn't expect them?"

"You mean other than you?" Chris shook his head. "Nobody's watching me."

"Somebody's always watching you. What matters is who's looking and why and what do they see."

"Chris," said Faye, "if we—if *I* wasn't here, is this how it would be?"

"You mean am I maintaining a normal profile and not breaking my known patterns in a way that would alert whoever is crazy enough to care?"

"I care," said Condor.

Chris cocked his head and with an exaggerated expression of affirmation, said: "Exactly. But no, this—what's happening on the floor of my apartment on a Thursday evening, pizza with friends, not my usual after work, not a bite out or a game or a . . ."

He smiled at Faye. "But I've been spending more time like this lately. Waiting."

Condor said: "What's different between now and like then?"

"Noise," said Chris. "NPR, music or even a game. Something would be on."

"Make that happen," said Condor.

Chris's quick keying of commands into the sound system created a random playlist of songs heavy on alternative country/folk/rock songwriters shotgunned with jazz like Miles Davis and once fabulously famous but now tastefully forgotten moments of music.

Was one of those pop songs, a studio syncopation of electric guitars and violins and commercially soulful male voices wailing words that triggered memories in anyone who'd heard this tune more than thrice, a song with juvenile lyrics that meant nothing akin or ironic to this moment, nowhere near a *clong,* just a catchy three-minute musical chorus in rock 'n' roll slow-beat time.

Condor—

—*old man grunting, straining, but quickly*—

—got to his feet, his hand reaching down and finding Merle's instinctively reaching-up hand to be grasped.

"Dance with me," he said.

Unfolding, yoga graceful, wide eyes scanning him, saying: *"What?"*

"This is the chance we get. Dance with me."

Wet filled her blue eyes but she had no strength to resist him taking her in his arms, holding her right hand with his heart-side grasp, his gun hand pressed on her blouse, on her bra strap, on her spine as he swayed them into *step-step-slide, step-step-slide* and the music played and she pressed her face against his blue shirt to dot it with her tears, as he felt the push of her breasts, the smell of her gray-blond hair and *this moment,* this moment of dancing to cheesy music he would never have picked, music that meant only this dance, this dance in an apartment where a couple who could be their children sat on the floor with beer bottles and bad pizza and watched them sway through time.

"I was afraid you wouldn't come back," he whispered so only she could hear.

Her head shook *no* against his chest.

"We're here," he said.

"I'm trying," she whispered. "My best. My best."

She held him and she danced and they danced.

The song ended. Songs do.

He stopped, she stopped, they stopped, stood in a home that wasn't theirs.

Condor saw Faye sitting on the floor, fighting sinking into slumber.

Said: "Now there's something we need to risk."

"What?" whispered Merle standing *oh so close* to him.

"School," said Condor as he watched Faye stir herself back to the killing edge.

Chris echoed Merle: "What?"

"You never know what you'll need to know," said Condor.

So for thirty-seven minutes, he and Faye risked not being on a National Rifle Association (NRA)—Occupational Safety and Health Administration (OSHA)–approved range, and first with Condor's .45, then with Faye's Glock, made Chris and Merle practice aiming, firing, chambering rounds and (on Condor's pistol) learning the safety to click off. Spies made citizens learn how to load ammunition magazines even though almost no scenario envisioned that necessity, but the exercise helped demystify weapons neither Merle nor Chris knew before that night. They learned the three-point aim, breathe & squeeze, the Weaver stance, the OSS pioneered from-the-belt quick-fire move. Though such things are not advisable for long-term weapons preservation, long term for this crew projected as high noon tomorrow, so Chris and Merle practiced dry firing the pistols. *Click! Click!*

After Condor and Faye reholstered their fully operational pistols, Condor again led them all through tomorrow's best-case choreography.

Then made Chris and Merle talk through the plan backwards.

Condor quizzed them on *what-if*s he answered as soon as their faces showed him they understood the scenario he'd spelled out.

He saw Faye's concentration fade.

Lied and said: "We're ready."

Chris and Merle cleared a space on the main room's floor for a self-inflating air mattress left over from his sister and brother-in-law's visit. Merle used extra sheets, a fuzzy blue oversized blanket and two pillows to make a bed for her and Condor.

The apartment's one bathroom was in the hall.

Chris used the bathroom first, then Faye.

Faye motioned for Merle to take her turn. The older woman did.

Condor nodded toward the bedroom where Chris waited.

Told Faye: "You've done all you can do. Get what you can in there."

The bedroom door closed behind her.

Merle came out of the bathroom, walked past Condor with a tired, tearful smile. He heard her undressing, getting onto the bed held by this floor.

Behind the closed door of the bathroom, Condor used the toilet.

Washed his hands, brushed his teeth, rinsed his mouth and spit.

Counted out the nighttime pills he chose to take—his heart, his bladder, his pains, his edgy insomnia—swallowed them with water from the sink faucet he cupped in his hand.

Noted that no one living or dead was in the bathroom with him, that he was alone.

Condor stared at the man in the mirror.

Said: "There you are."

26

The essence of love is betrayal.
—Chris Harvie

Not here, not now, thought Faye as she entered Chris Harvie's bedroom.

But she knew that was a futile lie.

And as that door closed behind her, as *he* closed the exit behind *them,* Faye scanned this room lit by a lamp on the scarred wooden table holding the book he was reading, checked to be sure the shade was pulled down over the waiting-to-shatter glass window between her and the street-lit killing night.

She turned toward his comforting reach, said: "I'm sorry!"

He cupped her face, smiled at her tears: "What else could you do?"

"Not have gotten involved with you. At all. In the first place."

"In the first place, I love you. After that, it's just how our luck got us here."

She slid into his arms, whispered as loudly as she dared: "I love you."

"I know." He kissed her forehead, her wet cheeks, her dry lips.

"Come on, get in bed, go to sleep," he said. "You're dead on your fee—

"Bad choice of metaphors," he blurted.

"Wrong," she said. "Dead on."

Faye pulled the blue blouse out of her black pants, flew her hands up its line of white buttons until they were all undone. Opened the blouse. Touched the puckered white scar slashed up from her groin across her taut white stomach.

"You deserve to know how you got here," she told Chris. Her fingertips brushed the scar lined on her stomach like a lonesome road: "You deserve to know about this."

Tell him.

Paris. Call it last year. And you're doing everything right.

The Seine, stone bridges across its rolling gray ribbon between beautiful walls of apartments rising over streets that traffic in the best that humans can be. Museums. Sidewalk cafes. All the women are beautiful because they've found one thing in how they look to believe in as *magnifique*. All the men are taut with the intensity of caring. No one looks stupid except for an occasional tourist who brought his mirrors to the city of lights instead of his sunglasses. He's not like most of the millions of lucky souls who visit this *cosmopolis* where crosses of salvation rise in the same stone castle that's home to flesh-eating gargoyles. Marching past street stalls of North African leather goods comes a well-suited woman carrying a Hermès briefcase and closing a billion-euros financial package with curt orders into her cell phone. Profitable movie theaters play François Truffaut and John Ford movies older than 90 percent of their patrons. And though you can buy heroin at the plaza called Stalingrad, the retail market point for multinational cartels & syndicates, Parisian dealers never guarantee happiness.

But your Paris is narrow broken pavement streets, cramped apartment buildings violating housing codes in hundreds of *who cares* ways, smells of cooking goat and North African staples, water, *Mon Dieu* you'd kill for a glass of water and you could, *you can,* you're packing a Glock in a holster taped handle-down to your smooth stomach under the Moroccan blouse above the black slacks and flat shoes for running or kicking. Nobody you pass on the narrow sidewalks looks at anybody, or else it's some man who glares X-ray vision at everyone. You wear brown contact lenses because green eyes are a reveal. Thank God you're not pretty, so nobody's going to go out of their way to notice you except for people who hate the headscarf wrapped around your face and covering your dyed hair that passes for the Algerian-French blend you and your ID papers claim.

Six weeks' language prep at Langley sandpapering your textbook French.

Seventeen days of Immersion Familiarization with an NOC team in Algiers.

Boats, trains, buses and walking to a Paris address you only knew from videos.

Your Op name is Djamila.

The real Djamila has been Tagged & Targeted in another Op from some other CIA crew, or maybe they were Pentagon. The Agency scooped her up during a "family" trip to Yemen, found the explosives in her battered suitcase.

The al Qaeda affiliate barely trusted any woman, so her explosives' customized detonator with perhaps traceable components, that clue-carrying detonator went to Paris by UATT (Unknown At This Time)—pronounced "*you-at*"—means & methods.

The bad guys are obsessed with Op Security. Got great tradecraft.

Took four weeks, but our best wringers sweated enough lies and evasions and slips from Djamila to piece together much of what she knew, then bluffed her out of what she had left by letting her think we had it all anyway, but would turn her over to Malaysians or Israelis or somebody who scared her more than we did if she didn't tell us everything and if it didn't match what she thought we already knew.

Wonder whatever happened to Djamila.

But you can't think about that.

Not in your Op.

Not when she reveals the target is America in Paris.

Not when you're doing everything right.

Your Op plan is classic: You become Djamila. Cool it in Paris until she gets a mobile phone call to a rendezvous. A Montprix—a French franchise store. In the cosmetics aisle. You meet a man named Neuf—that's right: Nine, a number that implies a sizable Op cell, and that's an intel bonus or it's batshit, depending on how you play it, but so far you're doing everything right. Textbook. Streetwise.

Neuf's never seen Djamila. You only know he's got a scar on his wrist that can't be seen from street-pole surveillance cameras. He gives her—*you*—the attack's *when*:

Tomorrow.

Remember, you're in an NOC Op. No notice to the Agency Chief of Station in the embassy, no liaison to the DGSE (*Direction Générale de la Sécurité Extérieure*) or DCRI (*Direction Centrale du Renseignement Intérieur*), or to DRM (*Direction du Renseignement Militaire*) or DPSD (*Direction de la Protection et de la Sécurité de la Défense*), or even to their off-the-books group—*won't tell you that name.* You and your team are alone. All you know is the target is American or maybe NATO with a long shot of it being French, because chatter NSA monitored off suspects sweated out of the real Djamila indicate that the bad guys think they have some inside track about French intel and security moves and are about to make the French pissed off at their allies.

The analytical conclusion that the bad guys want to divide and conquer us with some America-targeted bomb attack in Paris with even a hint of our allies being compromised or penetrated made Langley nervous with its complexity. So they made Sami run this Op simple: totally in the black, no allies' involvement.

In that Paris drugstore aisle. Cheesy French music playing over the loudspeaker, Neuf says tomorrow he'll be "another person," which you figure means in disguise. The plan is for you *Djamila* to go to a safe house and deliver the explosives for him to check—which is why the Op couldn't switch phony material for real explosives. We knew they'd check, and if they found bogus bomb material, they'd go in the wind and come back at us some way we didn't have penetrated.

After he checks your delivery, only then will he phone someone called Sept—Seven—to bring the trigger device. They'll make the bomb operational. And off the three of you will go to the then-disclosed target. You're supposed to provide cover surveillance and film the whole thing with your cell phone, then wait to get the right call to e-mail it to the number you'll be given and maybe from there to YouTube.

What Neuf doesn't know is you're wired and geo-tracked and hooked in to a Black Ops cover team who, when you confirm the target, will charge while you shoot the guy holding the bomb—disable preferred, but do what you gotta do. Even if that means you taking on both Sept and Neuf, the cover team rescuers are close.

But they've got to hang back. The bad guys are Op savvy. Ready to rabbit. So it's up to you to wait until your team can grab the optimal *get* of the bomb, the trigger and Op soldiers.

And so far, you're doing everything right.

Come rendezvous, you know Uncle Sam has your back, though from a distance.

Neuf shows, wears a suit and tie, clean shaven. He's carrying the gym bag favored by stockbrokers, plus an attaché case—either one of them good for the bomb. He walks you to an apartment in the 18th arrondissement, bare white walls, no furniture.

And while you're waiting, he says when he gets to paradise, he hopes you'll be one of the blessed virgins waiting for him.

I mean, what can you, what can Djamila, what can anybody say to that? The bomber on his way to martyrdom has a crush on you.

You should have paid attention to the timing of his dream.

Sept shows up. A big guy, Western-looking. Like Neuf, he's suit & tie city.

But you wait. You tell yourself you gotta wait. No way could the cover team advance to a close and quick-enough breach of the apartment for a clean takedown. Get out in the street, after Neuf reveals the target, then speak the Go Code.

Neuf marries your explosives to the timer Sept brought. The bomb's in the attaché case. Neuf needs five seconds to unsnap the catches, open it, flip the bomb trigger. Plenty of time to shoot him first, shoot Sept if the Black Ops boys haven't dropped him because *first* you'll give the Go and they'll be running. You can grab the case. No explosion that will kill you, too. No intel scandal. The good guys win again.

What could go wrong when you're doing everything right?

You mutter something about sixty seconds, not the Go Code, but your throat mike broadcasts it as a "get ready," and knowing how your cover team works, you figure they'll be moving closer, ready—

Neuf shoves the attaché case into Sept's arms, whirls toward you—

Knife! Where'd he get that fucking knife stabbing—

He's multitasking. Making his virgin reward *and* obeying orders you'd never expected. Djamila was supposed to die in this apartment. She was an easy sacrifice for security, an expendable liability. Make her transport what you want into place. If she's caught, she's expendable, no great loss. If she completes her mission, then terminate her. Don't call it betraying her, call it Op security or serving the greater cause.

But Djamila's not Djamila, it's you.

Training. Hours of practice. One night in Buenos Aires. You grab the lunging knife wrist and jerk, palm heel smash Neuf's elbow. You hear the knife hit the floor.

Neuf gets off a punch, knocks enough wind out of you so all the throat mike transmits is a grunt. You finger slash Neuf's eyes, nail a snap kick into his hip . . .

Behind you, Sept punches for your spine. But he was smart enough to set down the bomb before swinging into a fight, and that *smart* delay gives you time to whirl, turn his off-balance strike through a hip throw and crash him to the floor.

Where he scoops up the knife, bounces up with a stab that cuts you . . .

Cuts me . . .

Cuts you groin to guts. Like a rip in time. You fall back.

Grabbing your gushing blood, grabbing your gun, years of training and BAM! BAM!

Sept flips ass over teakettle, drops the knife.

Neuf grabs the attaché case, runs out the door. You shoot. Hit the wall.

Burning fire in your guts as you swing your Glock to zero Sept who's flopping around on the floor and he screams at you.

Screams at you *in English*, in *British*: "Fockin' bitch!"

Both of you lie on the floor in that unfurnished Paris apartment. You realize he's some kind of London spook, SAS it turns out, all set to take down Neuf's Op they penetrated from their end. But now the man with the bomb has run out the door. Later we learn from two cell guys SAS sweeps up, Neuf's headed for a nearby apartment building where CIA has an NOC Op you and your team know nothing about. That secret CIA base being blown up would not only piss the French off because we made a target for killers in Paris, but we put spooks on their soil without telling them. Plus people will get slaughtered, damaged, public mess.

As the gun slides from your hands—BOOM!

Your cover team closed in on Neuf, but he's on the sidewalk, narrow street, running with his hand on the bomb in the case and when he spots *gonna get me* . . .

BOOM! He's a martyr. BOOM! A garbage truck and two parked cars. BOOM! Fragment wounds on three cover team gunners. BOOM! A seventy-three-year-old Parisian woman in a black coat, walking her yippy little dog . . . *Boom.*

Yeah, could have been a whole lot worse. Could have been so much better. One dead and your backups have wounded and you're lying in a puddle of your own blood hearing those classic French sirens *Wee-ooo! Wee-ooo!*

Then you black out.

And so now I'm officially a traitor. Told secrets to an unauthorized person.

Faye sat beside Chris on his bed.

Said: "I didn't die. Everybody's pissed off. The press cover story stinks. The French, the British, execs all over the CIA looking to point the finger of blame. The Agency had to—Sami had to—go up and tell the Hill a version of the truth, get lucky and get some kind of pass for fucking up. I earned some blame for not tumbling to *what was what* sooner, for shooting a British agent, for not dropping Neuf and the bomb. The French deny they were compromised by the bad guys and all we got saying otherwise is chatter we don't want to disclose how we got. But Sami pled my case. I got to start working my way back to being on the inside, being the *who who matters, who knows, who does.* Sami opened the door on the soundproof glass room inside your Committee offices and I walked out and got a cup of coffee."

"And me," said Chris.

"And you. You trusted me. Freed dreams. Let me fall for you. Let me believe. And now I've betrayed you. Put you here. And I'm sorry, I'm so sorry!"

"This is where I live." Chris wiped a tear off her cheek as they sat on the bed. He grinned. "You know how hard it is to find a great apartment in this town?"

Call it an upside-down grin and she leaned into him.

Faye said: "I got an innocent civilian killed in Paris. I can't do that again. I can't do that here. I can't, *I will not* do that to you."

"You forget," said Chris. "I'm no civilian and I'm not innocent."

"Liar," she whispered with all the love in her heart.

Let go, just let go.

"I got your message from the mirror in the Tune Inn," Chris told the spy in his arms. "The woman who found it called me from the bathroom. She read it to me three times. Didn't ask a single question. Promised to wash it off before she walked back out to the bar. Didn't let me thank her—thanked me for letting her be part of us, our story. For letting her believe someday she'd write on a bathroom mirror with her lipstick. She told me I was so lucky. I told her yes, I am."

As he laid Faye down to sleep, Chris switched off the bedroom light.

27

Better roads.
—Lipstick graffiti on a bathroom mirror

You're driving the car.

Spring morning. Friday. Washington, D.C.

A cocked & locked .45 as heavy as a heart attack rides in the inside left pocket of your unzipped black leather jacket for a *while-driving* grab.

City streets. Rush hour. Gliding with the flow of Metro buses and dark SUVs. Minivans, family sedans. Taxis. Kamikaze bicyclists wear swooping plastic helmets and cubicle clothes. Through your open windows come car honks, street shouts, amped-up music. You smell exhaust, city pavement, the sweat of fear.

Merle rides behind you. Her hands are empty. Nothing under her jacket but hope. Says she can work as left spotter. She's not schooled in what to see.

In the backseat next to Merle, Faye rides shotgun/right-side spotter. Holds her Glock, has the optimal post to shoot any shark cars.

Chris Harvie sits on the front passenger cushion of this vehicle he owns. He knows the way. Might be the face that needs to smile at some man with a badge & gun.

Call it a one-point-seven-mile drive from where the car

is parked in the underground garage of an apartment building rising out of streets once walked by Duke Ellington.

Call it a nineteen-minute trip.

You're gripping the black padded steering wheel.

The traffic light ahead turns RED.

"Watch your zones!" Faye, *tense*.

Standing on the corner beyond your driver's side window: Faded black baseball cap atop snowy hair. Scraggly white beard. Filthy green hoodie, worn blue jeans. Crinkled crimson skin, vacant blue eyes, dirty hands that hold a white sign black-marker scrawled: HOMELESS.

Condor knew the man on the corner was really there.

Thought: *Nobody's hunting him.*

Earlier that morning.

Chris's apartment.

Gearing up, and Faye says: "We don't *think* they know about this *us*. Don't *think* they've figured our play. The good guys are expecting Condor and me to make a move. We don't know the bad guys. Their only agenda we care about is they want us dead."

Merle said: "You mean you and Vin."

"Who's Vin?" said Chris.

"Now I'm me," said Condor.

Chris *got it,* asked Condor: "Any words of wisdom?"

"Everybody needs a way to die," said Condor.

"You're a horrible leader," said the man who worked for the U.S. Senate.

Condor said: "We also all need a way to live.

"And this," said Condor, his smile cupping them all, "this is our best shot."

Faye said: "Let's go."

"Wait!" Merle blushed. "Sorry, I . . . I need to use the bathroom again."

Nerves.

Five minutes later they're all riding down in the cage of Chris's elevator.

A slammed door boomed through the concrete cavern of his underground garage.

Roofs of parked cars. Empty parking slots. Flickering fluorescent lights wave shadows on concrete walls. Oil stains. Invisible rancid garbage.

Call the slamming door *nothing*. Call it *normal*. Get in the car's assigned seats, boom your doors shut. Lock them. Your job is to grind the engine into life, *GO*.

Now in traffic on the street, the overhead signal light flashes GREEN.

Drive Massachusetts Avenue east to Capitol Hill.

Check your mirrors. No cars change lanes with you. No smoke-glassed SUVs surge into your wake. No motorcycles zip alongside for a *confirm* look. Or a quick shot.

Mass Ave led to North Capitol Street, curved around the front of the giant Union Station center for trains and subways, Metro buses, double-decker tourist movers.

But Condor turned their car right onto North Capitol, past an Irish pub that caters to Congressional staffers, lobbyists, policy wonks and other white-collar workers who fill the flat-faced, mirror-windowed, multiple-storied office buildings rising off to the right of this moving car. Half a football field later, he turned left on Third Street . . .

Cranked a quick right turn through the unguarded vehicle entrance for a man-high black chain-link fence:

LOT 11
SAA AUTHORIZED PERMITS ONLY
U.S. Senate Sergeant At Arms
Unauthorized Vehicles Will Be Towed

As Condor followed Chris's directions to an empty parking slot, Faye said: "Congress has its own army-sized police force. Why no cops on this gate?"

Chris shrugged. "This is a staff lot. Mostly, the police guard the buildings."

"And the Members of Congress," said Merle in the backseat. "The Senators."

In the parking slot, front bumper almost kissing the black chain metal fence, Condor said: "Windows up. Look normal."

All four of them got out of Chris's car.

Across the parking lot by the open pedestrian gate stood a second wood kiosk—empty, no white-shirted cop or even a civilian political appointee with a steady if mind-numbing job checking IDs. Near that gate was a steel-boxed phone topped by a blue light. Bold blue letters down the side of the phone box read: EMERGENCY.

"Cameras?" said Faye.

Chris casually looked around. "Probably."

"Officially," said Faye, "BOSS [Biometric Optical Surveillance System] won't be on line for two more years, but we all know what *officially* means. Even without BOSS zapping real-time facial recognition scan results into the grid, if they know we're coming here and are up on or hacked this zone's cameras . . . They'll spot us first."

"Then they're already on us," said Condor. "We are who we are."

"A three-minute walk?" Faye asked Chris as they stood by his parked car.

"At most. You saw the map, the Google street view."

"The real terrain always surprises you," said Faye.

Condor said: "Let's go."

They stepped into the formation they planned at dawn.

Chris took *point.* Wore a suit, his Senate Staff ID dangling around his neck.

Faye walked two paces behind and to Chris's right: *forward fire position.*

Unarmed Merle walked behind the younger woman, and to her left.

Condor took *drag,* hands dangling alongside his unzipped black leather jacket. Two spare ammo magazines filled the back left pocket of his black jeans, their empty pouch and the .45's holster clipped to Faye's crowded belt under her black coat.

Don't let my pistol pop out of my belt.

Plan is, slip the .45 and ammo to badge-packing Faye before the metal detectors.

Don't let me need my gun until then.

"Two choices for our on-foot," Chris explained that morning when they were still safely in his apartment studying his computer screen. "Well, two *logical* choices.

"Out of Lot Eleven's pedestrian entrance on the diagonal Louisiana Avenue, maybe twenty steps to D Street. Go left two blocks. Right a short block. Walk up the white marble steps and we're at the Russell Senate Office Building. Most everybody takes that route.

"Or, detour through the park alongside D Street. From where we come out of Lot Eleven, cut through the park on crisscross diagonal sidewalks. Could be other pedestrians. Tourists. Union Station commuters. Staffers. Joggers. Bikers. Now and then you see a homeless person sleeping or slouched in the grass."

"Security cameras?" asked Faye.

"I doubt it. No place in the park to mount them, no pre–9/11 existing poles or structures. Every inch of land up there is historic preservation." He shrugged. "D Street is wide. Major sidewalks. Quicker, straight shot. You can scope out the cars driving past. See the first police checkpoint two-plus blocks away. See somebody coming."

"We're four somebodies," said Faye. "We'll stand out. Easier to spot, ID."

"Okay," said Chris, "one block through the park, zigzag sidewalks, then we gotta step out to D Street, but by then, we'll be right under the eyes of the police checkpoint."

"A walk in the park," said Merle. "To Hart's main entrance, right?"

"Yeah, the staff and public entrance," said Chris that morning in his apartment as he finished his cup of coffee. "We should time it so we get there after rush hour's long lines at the security check, white-shirted cops and metal detector arches. Sometimes they have a dog. We should show up between nine twenty and nine thirty."

Now it's nine fifteen on a beautiful spring Friday morning.

Carillon bells chimed atop the one-hundred-foot tall, thirty-foot wide white cement Robert A. Taft Memorial a few blocks from where they stood in the parking lot.

"Who's he?" said Condor after Chris named the source of the bells.

"Who cares?" said Faye.

They marched out of Lot Eleven to cut through a manicured urban oasis. A circular garden filled the center of that park with spring flowers and holly bushes whose emerald leaves cut like razors. Bushes and trees flanked their path, tunnel walls of intermittent foliage that dappled all views of Condor and Faye and Merle and Chris marching on that tan sidewalk toward the known necessity of a head shot.

Condor walked *drag,* the cowboy term for the last rider behind the herd.

Who says post–9/11 America has forgotten its heritage.

Merle marched two paces ahead of him. He knew the tactical folly of watching the rolling sway of round hips in her blue jeans, but *damn*. Walking ahead and off to Merle's left, out of line to increase the odds that one bullet won't drop two members of the patrol, came Faye in her black coat under her backpack purse, scanning the vacant path they're following, the path that runs past where Chris walks point.

Not as good as those Marines in the 'Stan, but they get the idea, thought Condor.

A bicyclist whipped around the cement circle surrounding the garden in the center of the park. Pedaled toward them on a ten-speed steed. Even at forty meters, thirty-nine, thirty-eight, Condor noticed the biker's a man, not wearing a safety helmet, has only the hood of his black sweatshirt pulled over his bent-down skull.

Call it thirty-two meters and like a show-off seventh grader, the whizzing-closer biker . . . sits up to ride with no hands.

Condor and Faye heard cinema archivist Merle who walked between them mutter: *"I've seen this movie."*

See the biker sitting tall twenty-nine meters & closing, riding with no hands—his hands coming together out in front of him holding—

"Gun!" yelled Condor.

Faye'd been looking back to Merle, whirled forward to face—

Great shot.

Black hoodie male, *no-hands*, balancing on a bike. Sitting tall. Racing twenty-seven, twenty-six meters toward Primary Threat/Priority 2 Target who's broken her expected motion to look away/whirl back and it's a silencer-handicapped 9 mm pistol two-handed shot, *propelled shooter* to *evading target* profiled as wearing a ballistic vest, a *phutt*-whine.

The bullet ripped across the right side of Faye's skull.

Her cry turned Chris around to see her staggering as double-tap follow-on rounds punched into her chest, her ballistic vest.

Chris charged their attacker: *"No!"*

The biker snapped a *phutt* shot that whined a bullet past Condor's right ear, then that black hoodie gunman needed to zero the suit & tie charging his bike.

Phutt! Phutt! Phutt! Silenced slugs punched red holes in Chris's center mass.

He crumpled on the sidewalk to become an island birthing its own maroon lake.

Biker one-hand grabbed his handlebars as he flew past the fallen man. The first target he shot is staggering. He scans to acquire Priority 1 Target, a guy in a black leather jacket who's crashed through a bush, off the path but not hidden and certainly not bulletproofed by foliage and—

Merle shoved the biker blowing past her.

Forward momentum plus inertia plus trained athleticism. They're not enough. The black hoodie killer somersaults over the handlebars of the bike as it flips into the air. He breaks his fall with a forward judo roll, but the sidewalk knocks the gun from his hand as he crashes into a bush opposite the foliage wall where Condor dived.

Faye staggers to a shaky combat crouch, claws her Glock into her right fist—

Spots Chris in a scarlet lake.

Condor's on his feet, .45 in fist, booms a shot toward a black shape scurrying on the ground beyond two mulched bushes.

Faye blasts a round toward their attacker, her shot even

more wild than Condor's. As Merle runs into their field of fire.

Condor swung the black barrel of his .45 from Merle to *where's the black hoodie biker*? Condor glanced left, behind him: Faye's wobbling toward where Chris is . . .

Is dead.

No doubt.

Faye's got a crimson smear matting the hair on the right side of her head, dazed eyes, she's trying to aim, shoot. *She'll kill us with wild fire!*

Condor pulled Merle behind him as he kept his gun zeroed to the last place he'd seen the assassin biker.

No other fire! No other shooters! Where are they? Where are they?

"Grab Faye!" he yelled to Merle.

Merle yanks Faye away from the sticky red lake surrounding Chris.

Condor backpedals across the park, pulls the two women with him.

Faye lunges toward where the killer should be. Fires two blasts from her Glock, bullets crashing through brush, the booms echoing off the marble of Union Station blocks behind them, the sound fading against the marble buildings of Congress.

Condor thrust the .45 in his belt, grabbed the Glock from Faye, and with Merle muscled and ran the sobbing, blood-matted-haired younger woman from the park.

Nobody's shooting at us! Still nobody shooting at us!

Sirens cut the air.

Their shoes scraped the pavement of Lot Eleven: Chris's car. Condor has the keys. Wet boys should be right behind them, a combat team in *move-shelter-shoot* attack mode. Condor shoved Merle and Faye into the backseat of Chris's

car, dove behind the steering wheel, keyed the engine to
life.

Any second! The bad guys will start shooting from be-
hind us any second!

He slammed the gearshift into REVERSE, punched the
gas/stomped on the brake. The car shot backwards out of
the yellow-striped parking spot—squealed shuddered
stopped. Condor jerked the gearshift to DRIVE, smashed
his foot on the accelerator.

The car rocketed back into its parking spot.

Crashed through the black chain-link fence.

Flew out of Lot Eleven. Tires bounce on the sidewalk,
steel scrapes concrete, the car lurches into the road. Cars
coming at it from both sides hit their horns and brakes.

Condor and his surviving crew careened toward downtown D.C., their engine-clattering getaway car spewing hot
metal & oil-stench black fumes.

28

No more forever.
—Chief Joseph

. . . head my head dead, he's dead why not me, him not him, head . . .

Faye's right hand blurred into focus as it dropped from her head and like an echo came her realization: *"Blood on my hand."*

Waking from nowhere, Faye felt herself thrown with inertia—

Caught, held, stopped, cradled in the arms of *woman, some woman* Merle.

Backseat, thought Faye. We're sitting, *riding* in the backseat of a car.

And . . .

Burning bright sunlight glaring blue and white flashes in all the windows.

And . . .

Sound, no sound, why is there no sound?

Condor is driving.

Like a bat out of hell, went through her mind, then: *Not bat, he's Condor.*

A swerving right-hand turn sucked Faye into a whirlpool of sound: *Car horns/shouts/crying tires/whooshing wind past the open windows*, and hot, sweating . . .

"Shot him," Faye heard herself mutter. "They shot him."

"Faye!" Condor yelled as he cranked the car around a corner. "Can you focus?"

Merle loosened her grip around the wounded woman. Said: "Are you okay?"

"They shot me in the head," whispered Faye.

She stared at her blood-smeared palm.

Merle kept her from touching her throbbing/burning skull.

"You're okay," Merle lied. "The bullet just cut along the side of . . . Gash in your hair, blood yeah, but . . . It didn't break the bone, go in your head!"

Condor yelled from the driver's seat: "Concussion!"

Merle locked her gaze on Faye's green eyes with their mushrooming black pupils.

"Yeah," said the older woman who had gray-blond hair that wasn't matted with her own fucking red gore. "Maybe."

Engine valves clattered. The hurtling car jerked, spasmed.

Faye said: "Stinks, oil, what's burning, what's . . ."

The car felt like a fighter plane, veered out, traffic 'n' Condor's swerved the car into empty space at the curb, but . . .

Bus stop. We're parked in a bus stop.

Car door opened as Condor disappeared between her eyes and the windshield.

Faye said: "Chris is dead."

The curbside door beside her flew open.

Condor helped Merle guide Faye from the backseat to the sidewalk. "Yeah, he's dead. We will be, too, if we don't move. You've gotta move, Faye. Come on!"

But no.

Faye felt herself zoom back as if she could see them standing on that sidewalk:

Condor in his black leather jacket, fretting beside her like a trapped raptor.

Merle looking older, terrified.

And her, *me,* a smear of dark red goo mat on my cracked head.

We're in Chinatown.

A grand three-pagodas-topped arch rose over the city street, a faux portal with fake gilt and green friezes of gold-painted calligraphy that could mean anything or nothing. Past the arch, Faye spotted a mammoth red-brick church with a rusted spire stabbing heaven. This early in the morning, this early in spring, this early in tourist season, vendors had yet to crowd the sidewalks in front of Asian restaurants and stores where you could buy plastic Buddhas (standing laughing or *zazen* somber), satin jackets emblazoned with dragons, black *gung fu* slippers, electronic gizmos for every credit card, herbs & spices and bins of red, white & blue souvenirs, postcards for if you still believed in Ben Franklin's snail mail, umbrellas—whatever the shopkeepers could make your heart desire.

"Come on!" said Condor.

But he left it for Merle to take Faye's arm, to help the wounded woman.

Keeping his hands open and dangling by his sides for the *gun,* realized Faye.

"Shooters!" muttered Faye as they made her stumble along H Street's sidewalk.

She pawed her belt where . . . *No gun! Where's my gun!*

"Wet boys, the Oppos, where are they, where . . . where . . ."

"They're out here." Condor led the way across H Street,

down toward the massive indoor amphitheater for Bruce Springsteen concerts and hockey games. "Gotta be."

She saw him scanning the air above other sidewalk shufflers.

What, what's he looking for? What— Cameras, closed-circuit surveillance.

Who's in that closed circuit?

Condor stepped into the doorway of an abandoned store with whitewashed windows bearing a sign: COMING SOON!

But what, thought Faye as Condor pulled her into the doorway that was the size of coffin standing on its end: *What soon comes?*

"Turn your bloody side away from the street," he said. "Act like you're crying."

Faye heard him tell Merle: "That drugstore. Get baby wipes, disinfectant ones. And there, the store next door, whichever, buy a hoodie sweatshirt for her—a big on her!"

All Faye could do was stand in that coffin-sized doorway.

Head throbbing, oh God fire on the right side of my brain!

Breathe. In. Out. Say: "Why haven't they killed us yet?"

"I don't know," said Condor.

The only time Faye knew was *now,* but there must have been more, because now Merle was here carrying store sacks that had not been before. Faye felt stinging dabs on the right side of her head, pats and *Oww!* pulls of her hair, smelled . . . *Lemons,* the wipes Merle's using smell of lemons and alcohol and . . . and . . .

"Watch out!" Condor pulled Merle away from the woman hidden in the doorway.

Faye jackknifed forward, vomited.

Staggered—stabilized standing in her own shoes by Merle's grip.

Another swirl of nausea, then Faye felt lighter, clearer.

Felt Merle wiping her face, her lips, a swab inside her mouth. The flutter of a wipe falling into the vomit-smelling concrete doorway *fuck littering*. Faye heard Condor tell the older woman: *"Stand beside me facing out, screen us, watch for scanners or shooters."* Faye felt him take off her backpack. Make sure the pockets of her black coat were empty. He eased that wrap off her. Tossed the coat over the puddle of what had been in her guts. Condor took the holster and ammo pouch for his .45 off her belt.

Then, *oh then,* that weight she'd carried for years rode holstered on her right hip. Energy flowed into her arms, her hands flexed. She helped more than hindered as Condor slid her into the soft sleeves of something, reached around to pull up a zipper, his hand brushing her breasts *Chris kisses no No NO* and then hands on her shoulders turned her around to face the street, see Condor's face, *blink,* and she's *here, now.*

Merle washed Faye's face with lemon wipes, tossed them into the rancid doorway, white squares fluttering down to another lifetime's black coat.

She gave a bottle of water to Faye.

Faye filled her mouth, swished it around, spit out what was to the sidewalk.

"Eww!" Two teenage girls pranced past toward the rest of their lives.

"Okay," said Faye. She started to nod *yes,* but that hurt far too much.

Condor covered her wounded head with the hood on the sweatshirt she now wore.

Pink. I'm wearing a candy-pink hoodie.

Condor slid his aviator mirror-lensed sunglasses over Faye's eyes.

Waved down a taxi and beckoned for Merle to climb in, help as he guided Faye in. His eyes scanned the street and he jumped in the taxi, told the cabby: "Go!"

Rolling, the taxi's driving us through downtown D.C.

Condor told the taxi driver to take them to the National Zoo.

Faye whispered: "We're going to see the animals."

No one in the cab knew if that was a question or a statement.

Didn't matter. After five minutes of Condor checking mirrors and side streets as the taxi drove, just past the hotel where a well-off white boy who'd failed as a Nazi and a rock musician tried—*and failed*—to murder President Ronald Reagan in order to impress a movie star, Condor said: "Pull over. Beautiful day, we'll walk from here."

The three of them stood on the curb near the first communist Chinese embassy.

Condor waited until he knew they'd vanished from the driving-off taxi's mirrors.

"Come on," he said. "We gotta get over the bridge."

Head-throbbing, but clearly, I can see clearly through his sunglasses.

Faye said: "You've got to be fucking kidding me. I've been . . . he's dead and . . ."

"*We're,*" he said. "Focus on that: *we are.* All the blood and shit, but *we still are.*

"And now, we are getting our asses across that bridge."

"Paris's great bridges," muttered part of Faye not yet back under her control.

But this was not Paris.

This was Washington, D.C.

Call it the Connecticut Avenue Bridge. Call it the William Howard Taft Bridge. *Who was he to the man whose name Chris taught us for the Capitol Hill tower with ringing bells?* Call it a long-ass way Faye wasn't sure she could walk.

Merle whispered: "What if they can see us?"

Maybe they could, but Faye could only shuffle one step in front of where she'd been, follow the sidewalk of this billion-mile-long bridge through the heart of Washington, D.C. Far on the other side, she saw two-story stores and cafes near the Woodley–National Zoo subway stop, knew she couldn't actually see the colorful high wall mural portrait of a white-blond wondrous Marilyn Monroe— *M.M., Merle is M.M., too, but gray-blond and Condor's something and holding my arm.*

Giant bronze statues of lions guard each corner of that bridge.

Faye glanced up at the lion they walked past: "He's got his eyes closed."

Halfway across this stone bridge supported by concrete arches a hundred feet above the treetops of Rock Creek Parkway, Faye looked over the corroded green railing—

Swooned with vertigo, swayed inside Merle's grip, closed her eyes behind Condor's sunglasses until the universe stopped spinning.

Let herself look.

Traffic whizzed past on the other side of the railing, its *whoosh* as unbalancing as looking down to the treetops and the long fall.

Faye glanced up to the blue sky.

Green lampposts topped by green metal eagles, their wings spread wide.

But they can never fly away.

There! The other side of the bridge, we made it, we're . . .
Still in killers' gun sights.

What a sight we make.

A sliver-haired, craggy man wearing a backpack purse over a black leather jacket.

A gray-blond *used to be a beauty* who could still move but had nowhere to go.

A slumping shuffling loser *bitch* hiding inside a candy-pink hoodie and aviator sunglasses with matted hair and stinking of vomit.

Condor led them away from the street corner with its subway entrance and outdoor cafe tables, down the slope of Calvert Street toward the access road for Rock Creek Parkway. Farther in that direction loomed the sprawling complex of a hotel that catered to conventions and tour groups and expense accounts and neighborhood residents who in the coming summer would scam their way in to use the outdoor pool. He led Faye and Merle to a grassy apron between the Parkway entrance/exit road and the hotel's fence of metal bars. Led them to shadows on the grassy slope made by three close-together trees. Led them to the other side of those tall living sentinels where they could sit, collapse, not so easily be seen.

Merle passed the last water bottle she'd bought in Chinatown.

Condor took a swig. Held the bottle to Faye: "Replenish."

She drank half of what was left, saved the rest for Merle.

Who took three swallows and clearly yearned for more as she screwed the cap back on the water bottle, saving some *just in case.*

Condor said: "Why was there only one shooter?"

"What the fuck!" exclaimed Merle. *"How many does it take!"*

Faye said: "Sami has an army."

"And our Uncle Sam sure does."

"If it's not any uncle Sami," said Faye, "then who?"

"Maybe it is us," said Condor, "and maybe it isn't."

More *all back* every second, Faye said: "What the fuck are you talking about?"

Condor whispered: *"The Vs."*

29

A walk in the park.
—The 1972 across the street from the White House
presidential aides' huddle on covert ops, including
the (*unsuccessful*) murder of muckraker journalist
Jack Anderson

What a rush.

The clarity of a blue sky spring morning.

Sitting on a grassy knoll.

"What are you talking about?" Faye said to Condor.

Merle glared at them: *"Who are you people?* She's been shot, Chris is dead, we're . . . You almost got us killed! I did everything I could and it didn't work. Now we're worse off and he's dead, and I can't . . ."

Her rant ran out, she took a breath, whispered: "Who are *we*?"

"No," said Faye, looking right at him, right at Condor: "Who are *Vs*?"

They sat there on a city park–smelling grassy knoll that April morning, Condor and two women he'd never even talked to the week before.

And he asked: *"What would you do?"*

"New York City is two towers of smoke. The Pentagon's wall is crashed in. Corpses cover a field in Pennsylvania. And except for a few novelists and one ex-spook living outside the Beltway, all our tomorrow people, the ones who are supposed to be looking ahead and seeing what's coming, their eyes didn't see or their mouths went unheard or their hands couldn't stop the horror.

"So a lot got done that we now can hardly believe. Forget about torture, renditions, secret prisons, us invading a country that had nothing to do with 9/11. That's old news and this is about what's new.

"How would you create a new spy service? We created Homeland Security and the Director of National Intelligence and got puzzle boxes on top of puzzle boxes."

Faye pressed: "The Vs?"

"Vapors. It's all vapors. No name, no headquarters, no gear, no IDs, no Web site or e-mail address, no data chains, no flow chart because there is no organization, no budget, no mention nowhere. No box. No credit. No blame. No existence, no personnel. Maybe seven policy czars know about it, maybe by now V is all automated.

"Because it's vapors. Software. The logical transitional constellation of a quintillion data points. Dark web. Deep web. Hidden web. Vapors running through it all. A regular Agency good guy enters a bad guy on a 'threat ladder' or watch lists. Threat identified. The software starts to work on him, or the group, or the money-laundering bank, or . . . whatever, whoever, he's targeted in the machine."

Merle said: "Machines don't shoot people."

"That's rather definitional. Armies and librarians are all part of some machine that sends pension credits and drones with missiles.

"The software computes that a guy named Seba Pezzani is a growing threat, but he isn't fitting into a doable profile for our '*real world*' spy or security agencies. So a plane ticket vanishes from some billion-dollar federal contract. An ATM activates. A pistol gets delivered from an Air Force base to a cafe in Rome and an action unit V with whatever credentials or authority and knowledge he needs.

Who knows where our orders come from, who's really in charge, how all our needs actually got created. It's not *'need to know,'* it's knowing *only* what *seems* to be needed.

"The V uses people and systems to get things done and they never realize it. Soldiers or cops or office managers or guys on the street never know who put them there. They do the job they're supposed to do. No extra pay, no full knowledge, no big picture the V doesn't control. The best puppets don't know they have strings.

"Maybe a Level-One Action Operative knows he's a V, but he never knows the whole system. Maybe he thinks he's detached from Delta for sanctioned Special Ops. Maybe he's an ex–Navy SEAL who works as a personal trainer at a Missouri YMCA until he gets a text. A CIA brick agent whose Case Officer isn't really in charge of her. A retired FBI agent, a homicide cop who gets an extra thousand bucks a month from a CIA black account that records as part of the regular bribe to a Mexican general and it's all covered by IRS's computers, though Level-One Vs don't do this for the money. They believe.

"And what gets done, gets done. Only extreme cases. Only high necessities."

"Targeted killings," said Faye. "Illegal assassinations. Other . . . neutralizations. Like throwing troublesome people into insane asylums, frame jobs."

"Beautiful system," said Condor. "An evolution from how the Intelligence Support Activity got its start, though the V will never become a Pentagon office."

Merle said: "It would never work."

"Facebook knows what ads to show you. Marketers profile what you'll want. Facial recognition systems plus behavior analysis, reconfiguring police reports and maintenance schedules on an airliner . . . *You get it*: if you link the vapors, you can see what needs to be done and you can do . . . amazing things. Not often, but when you do, nobody knows it was you, nobody knows it *was* done. You rewrite the record as you change it. Reality becomes what the data says it is."

"Case officer," said Faye. "The Green Light. The decider. There has to be—"

"A dead man's switch? A heart amidst the brains of the machines? The human touch?" Condor nodded. "There wouldn't *have* to be, but we still made one. But just one. One human entity as a fail-safe Level-Zero *control* with full knowledge programmed and final-say. Paychecks not on any audit. A quiet life with an intuitive desktop in an ordinary house in an American hometown. It's the twenty-first-century model. You work from home. The neighbor everybody waves to and nobody knows."

"Who did this?" whispered Merle.

Condor said: "I think it was me."

The woman he . . . he . . . call it *whatever,* Merle stared at him.

The woman warrior who sacrificed her life for his stared at him.

"Street years," he said, "the week before 9/11 and I was ready to walk away, not old, but there're only so many scars you can carry. Then *boom*. And as I recovered from . . . from one rough Op, I had a great idea, a reputation and clout, some access to a place where everybody wanted answers."

"But you went crazy," said Faye.

"Well . . . *yeah,*" said Condor. "The sheer rush of it, the knowing of what you could do and had to do and *did*."

"So why do they want you dead now?" asked Faye. "Jesus, back on Tuesday, they would have settled for you getting locked back up forever as a crazy murderer."

Condor shrugged. "Maybe somebody's pulling the plug on the whole system."

"Or the whole system is trying to be sure nobody pulls the plug on it," said Faye. "And you, fighting their *forget-it* meds . . . Your data metric would register high risk.

"But," she said, asking the investigator's ultimate question: "How do you know?"

"The lone shooter on a bike," said Condor. "Like a *clong* only no music. Seeing him made me *realize*. Realize it wasn't Sami or Uncle Sam Ops. Because they only sent one shooter. Had to be a system short on personnel. A small Op, small team—

"And *that* flashed me on remembering the V. We dropped four out of six at the subway. No replacements, especially if the V is getting shut down. All that fit with my cover team having made the first move. The V originally brought in every *street meat* unit they had for my neutralization. Pre-position every Level-One Action V to be ready, to be ahead of you and Sami and the real guys, to be in them but not of them."

Faye said: "The Homeland Security guy who showed up at your house, the guy I almost shot! He was the gunner on the subway platform who got away! *The biker!*"

"Got your partner working on orders V created, killed him, waited. Knew I'd be home from work. Knew you or a team would come. I'd get taken out by the good guys."

"But this morning," said Faye. "How did they know our play this morning? We're off all grids, no data for them to hijack, but even with only one guy—"

"Probably two guys," said Condor. "Six at the subway attack, two left. A spotter somewhere, plus the shooter on the bike. But somehow knowing we were coming, knowing Chris was taking us to the Senate Intelligence Committee offices where there'd be too many plugged-in people to hijack or control so then we couldn't be hit and we'd have gotten to Sami safe. And maybe figured all this out."

"Two guys," said Faye. "How?"

Merle whispered: *"Me."*

Faye and Condor chorused: "What?"

"Oh God, I'm sorry! *Me me me!*"

Merle said: "You people with your guns and your secrets, your claims that what I know isn't the real world, wasn't my world. Not after you came. Even if I . . . even if we . . .

"I'm smart. Savvy. In politics, in life, always cover your ass. I believed you, wanted to be with you, but I bought myself a protection policy. An outside alliance. You had me buy *four* phones, I went to my ATM and got money and bought *five*.

"I played my one *ask,*" she said. "The smart thing to do, not just meekly obey my way into some shit storm. I did what would have worked and would have made our chances better and maybe covered me if you . . . If I got dumped or duped or set up."

Condor said: "You called him."

"Who?" said Faye.

"The Senator who owes me," said Merle. "Called him yesterday. Told him to be ready, that he was going to help me with a whistleblower from the CIA, a guy I met at the Library of Congress, that maybe this would make the Senator a hero but if it didn't, it would cover his ass."

"And you said—"

"And I said *Condor.* I spoke the word. I should have guessed what he must have done. He covered *his* ass. Probably made a call, generated a query, created a *Condor* data link so that by last night . . . Your V trolling the grid knew he was linked."

"They just didn't know how," said Condor.

"Just before we left Chris's apartment this morning, I went to the bathroom, cell phone hidden in my panties . . . Sent the Senator a text. Told him hell or high water, hearings or constituent or fund-raiser meetings be damned, he had to show up at nine fifteen at the main entrance to Hart and wait to escort me and mine to the Intelligence Committee offices. Safety in numbers, right? Especially when one number is a U.S. Senator. That's what was so smart. Hiding behind him."

"Your phone!" Condor told Merle. "They were tracking that as soon as you texted the Senator. GPS knew where we were, the parking lot, knew we were coming on foot. One spotter on a laptop relaying data, the other . . . How he got a bike . . ."

Merle flowed to her feet before Condor or Faye could stop her.

"Oh God, they're on us now!" said Merle.

"The phone! Get it out, pull it—"

"No," she said.

"No," she whispered.

Her eyes focused far away as Merle said, "Me being smart got Chris killed. Me being smart might let you stay alive."

Merle's cheeks glistened.

Condor stepped to comfort her, took his hands in hers, she cupped his face—

Merle kneed him in the groin.

Condor collapsed to his knees on the grassy knoll.

Blinding pain gagging gasping . . .

Hearing Merle: "I wish I could be who you want me to be!"

His eyes opened to a teary blur of Faye in a pink hoodie struggling to stand.

As up the slope from the grassy knoll ran Merle, up to the busy D.C. street . . .

Gone.

She's gone.

"Come on." Faye pulled Condor to his feet, the wounded helping the lame. "You can't catch her. She did what she did. Now she's trying to make up for it. She knows they're on the phone she's got, they'll track her, so she's running until . . ."

Faye caught her breath. "She got Chris killed. And she bought us our *until.*"

She and Condor pulled the batteries of the cell phones Merle'd bought them, tossed the debris into the woods. Late-morning sun warmed them as they shuffled off a grassy knoll, the wounded leaning on the old & lame.

"I want to shoot her," confessed Faye as each step made her lean more on him.

"I want to shoot me," said Condor as a greater ache replaced the one in his groin.

They kept their guns holstered out of sight as Condor helped Faye toward the hotel's taxi & shuttle bus–crowded horseshoe driveway. He adjusted the pink hoodie to cover the mess on her head, didn't need to tell her to keep her face down because she could barely hold it up, barely keep walking beside him.

Nervous families everywhere, thought Condor as he shuffled toward the hotel's sliding glass doors, a female form in a pink hoodie wrapped in his left arm, his right hand pressed against his black leather jacket. *Dads. Moms.*

Half a dozen suits & ties fretted in the airplane-ride-dressed crowd of . . . *More than tourists.* Condor dodged an overstacked luggage cart, pushed through loud families.

College kids, he thought, then, *No: soon-to-be college kids.*

School visits. Lots of universities, colleges in D.C. Everybody should see Washington. Bring the whole family, make a vacation of it and *no,* we won't embarrass you, we deserve to see the place we'll mortgage our future to so you can learn how the world works and get a recognized passport to a tomorrow of paychecks and promises.

Someone's nine-year-old little brother in blue jeans and booger stains dashed through the crowd. A school-colors lanyard & plastic name-tagged ID flew off the boy, but he never looked back. Never saw Condor rescue the ID from being trampled by shoes hurrying across the vast hotel front lobby floor.

The lanyard's name tag read: VISITOR.

Aren't we all.

Deep in the lobby lounged couches and padded chairs, end tables to hold cocktails from the hotel bar. As eleven A.M. checkout ticked closer, most chairs were filled by suitcase-guarding spouses or (*less often*) solo high-schoolers thinking that back home wasn't so bad after all. Last-minute discards cluttered the end tables— brochures, visitor packets, other relics from the era of dead trees.

An older woman used a black cane to leverage herself from a lobby chair.

Condor lowered Faye into that vacated seat. Adjusted her slump so the hood covered most of her pained face. He shrugged out of her backpack purse he'd been wearing since Chinatown, set the clunking backpack in Faye's lap.

Whispered: "Don't let people see your face. Try to look young."

The lanyard draped around his neck.

I am who I say I am.

He floated here. He floated there. Cruised through the crowd. Past the lobby cart with the barista selling chocolate and coffee confections, pastries. Past the front desk where black-suited clerks dealt with a crush of airport-bound guests.

A packet from the same university as his VISITOR name tag drifted to his hands.

Elevator doors slid open. Out hurried a haggard dad with a sullen ten-year-old daughter whose hand was grabbed by a mom with an unmistakable *had it up to here* look. A nearby college-age daughter slouched in another world even though she could have reached out and touched the woman who gave birth to her. Mom yelled at the man who'd given these two daughters to her: "Come on, the Stevenses are parked out front to drive us to the airport!"

Already four steps behind his fleeing family, the father slapped an electronic key card on an unmanned counter with a slot on its front wall that read: KEY DEPOSIT. His face showed *good enough* as he hurried out of the hotel after his family.

No one saw Condor palm the key card off the counter.

The clock above the crowded front desk read 10:57.

No one destined for the Stevenses' airport ride came back through the hotel's sliding glass doors. Out there, in the horseshoe driveway, amidst the thinning herd of taxis and shuttle buses, Condor saw no anxiously parked & packed private vehicle.

A confident woman in her mid-thirties wearing a black-skirted business suit settled at the concierge's desk across the lobby, clicked on the desktop computer.

Condor and a posh woman clutching an iPhone reached the concierge's desk at the same time, but with a grandiose sweep of his arm, he signaled Ms. iPhone to go first.

Of course she said: "Thank you."

Sat down and started talking to the concierge, who met her words with a smile and only a fraction-of-a-second look at the silver-haired gentleman who'd kindly stepped aside and now waited with his hands crossed over his black leather jacket and a look that said he appreciated the concierge's appreciation.

At 11:04, the posh woman climbed into a taxi outside in the hotel's horseshoe driveway and the nice gentleman who'd waited took the seat across from the concierge.

Any hospitality professional could see he looked terrible.

The man wearing the lanyard used by parents visiting a D.C. university set the packet they'd given him on the desk, sighed. "I'm sorry, we didn't expect this trouble."

"What can I do to help, sir?"

"Got a time machine for guests? Or maybe a daughter exchange—bad joke, I love her, we wouldn't trade her for the world, but . . . They all say this is the difficult year."

The concierge's polite smile offered encouragement. Understanding.

"And I know, it's late, but the crowd at the front desk, and I didn't spot you here until . . ." *Now let her off the hook.* ". . . until that woman needed to go first, and yesterday, orientation, how were we to know? Sure, why not let the older girl spend the night with her new roommate and her parents, and this morning she's here waiting for us in the lobby like she was supposed to, but—*Don't look, but over there? In the pink hoodie?*"

The flick of the concierge's eyes confirmed: pink hoodie, female, slumped in a chair trying not to be seen, not to be here. Verified data.

"We come down to go with the Stevenses to their place in Virginia before we catch the plane out of Dulles to-morrow and *Oh shit,* she's sitting there trying to hide the scabbiest, yuckiest bloodiest bruise on her head, saying she won't go with the Stevenses, won't go to school here, just wants to go home, and *no* she won't talk to her mother and the little one's got . . . let's just call it 'a condition,' needs her mom to go with her, not be the one to stay here with Callie and get to the bottom of *what's going on*."

The concierge gave him a lipstick frown: "Sir, does your daughter need medical attention?"

"No, I was a medic— No way could you have even been alive during Vietnam. Bottom line, we split things up, my wife and I, so I didn't pay attention if she pre-checked out or at the desk, but here's the thing: Deb and my wife are going with the Stevenses, I'm going to stay here and let Callie come around to telling me what the hell's going on, and tomorrow we'll meet up at Dulles, but . . ."

The silver-haired father passed his key card to the concierge.

A hard piece of evidence, of reality, of truth.

"The waiting to get to you made me miss the check-out time, automatic or whatever my wife did at the front desk, but here's my key."

The concierge swiped the volunteered electronic key card through the reader slot on her desk, said: "Yes, Mr. Cordingley, we show an automatic checkout."

"You're right, and that's the problem. I've got a teenage girl trying not to burst out crying at any moment, answers to get before we get on the plane home tomorrow, and I needed to roll our checkout to then before eleven, but you weren't here until now and the wait . . ."

"You want to extend your reservation?"

"You're right, please, just like it is, or if we need to take another room . . ."

They did, smaller room, twin beds, 729 West, on the same credit card?

Of course.

The quiet of a hotel room.

Condor lay on one freshly made bed.

Faye lay on the other bed.

She started to cry.

Me, too.

Gone, then *whoosh*: back. Maybe he slept, maybe he didn't. Afternoon light filled the hotel room windows. His watch shows four o'clock.

And he heard Faye say: "Wait."

Condor sat on his bed to face her sitting up, feet on the floor to face him.

She said: "You've got the backpack, the laptop computer from Merle?"

He got the laptop, handed it to her.

"Confession," she said. "When I was alone, I downloaded a 'Protect Your Kids' program. Cost Merle's credit card a couple hundred dollars. I programmed our disposable phones with a GPS tracker parents buy to snoop on their teenagers, set up the system in this laptop. A full analysis of her phone at the Agency would spot it, but it's designed to hide itself from savvy teenagers, so . . ."

"So the Vs tracked her secret phone she hid from us, *but* because of what you hid from me and Merle, you and I can secretly track her other phone?"

Faye shrugged.

"Can it back trace? Can the V—"

"Maybe," said Faye. "But only if somebody's looking to do that."

"And if they've . . . got Merle, clearly it's a throwaway burner, they'll pull our pre-programmed numbers but we ditched those phones, no batteries, no signals, so . . ."

Three minutes and they were staring at the laptop screen's street map of a neighborhood just outside the Beltway in the urban sprawl that is America's capital.

A blue dot pulsed on the screen's map. The address displayed.

"She's there," whispered Condor.

"The *phone* is there." Faye worked the laptop. "Been there since 2:07. Before that—look, the map tracks her route, one stop near here at . . ."

"The zoo," said Condor. "She ran to the zoo. Found someplace to sit, the bear pit, watched animals until . . . They came and got her. They didn't just kill her there, or—"

He grabbed the laptop. Clicked onto the *Washington Post* Web site.

"Senate aide shot on Capitol Hill. Car stolen." He read the story by reporter Claudia Sandlin, a half-dozen paragraphs, Congressional police force, FBI, suspects including a woman, stolen car found oil pan burned-out in downtown D.C. Unknown if a strong-arm theft of a bicycle from a commuting EPA worker who was knocked unconscious six blocks away earlier in the morning was related.

Condor whispered: "They've lost control."

"Who?"

"Everybody. Sami and the Agency and the V. Too much, too fast, too public."

He clicked to fill the laptop screen with the map and its pulsing blue dot.

Tell Faye the truth.

"This much chaos," he said, "the V's down this much . . . Good chance we could Panic Line or other way go in, get to Sami, an official if . . . banged-up exfiltration. Get in alive and give it all up to the good guys, to the system, to what's supposed to work."

She stared at him with her green eyes where the pupils now looked normal.

But she's not seeing me.

The blue dot pulsed.

Condor said: "They either killed her or got her, but they got her phone. Either way, that's where I'm going."

"If we go in to the Agency—"

"What will be their priority?" said Condor. "Whoever they are. Whoever we can trust. Sami? The V still running on a hijacked official record? The moment we show up, we get logged in by somebody, and you know some innocent rule-follower will do that, then that blue dot . . . Then there's only one smart option for the V with that blue dot."

He picked his .45 off the bed. Looked around for his black leather jacket.

"It's about more than Merle's blue dot," he said. "She'd be enough, but . . . *Truth*?"

Faye nodded.

"If I go in without finishing this, I'm just part of the program," said Condor.

"You're only one beat-up old man." She wobbled to her feet. "Odds are, two of them minimum. And they're good. They could probably put us down in their sleep. You know that, I can see it in your face. Hell, even if I was at my best . . ."

"You've got a concussion."

"Pro football players get back in the game with concussions."

"They die young."

"It's not about dying anymore. This is about what I've got to live with."

She took a step—

Fell back to sitting on the bed, bumped into Condor, knocked him to his bed.

They stared at what they couldn't avoid seeing.

She said: "You can't take them on without me, and I can't make it. Not now."

The blue dot pulsed.

Faye said: "Whatever the worst of it is for Merle, it's already happening or happened or never gonna happen because they're holding her, maybe no extreme measures or . . . monster mayhem. Even if we could walk out that door now, quickest we could get there is forty minutes. Like this. Like who we are now. No prep, no Google street view recons, no nothing but two fucked-up, off-the-rez guns. You like those odds?"

Don't tell her that she's right.

She said: "If it's only a phone waiting for us, something some citizen found, if we go now, we'll get dropped like this and odds are, only our going down to show for it."

"When?" he said.

"When we see what more chaos breaks loose. When we see more whatever *they* does. When we got a chance. When you and I are who the fuck we can be."

"When?" he repeated.

"You know when," she said.

And when they'd showered, when they'd room serviced and when she'd eaten without throwing up, when they'd watched & read news and when they'd computer re-conned and strategized and when he'd gone out & come back, when he'd shared pills to fight pain & coax sleep and when they lay under the covers of their separate beds, when the turned-off laptop was set on the shelf near the black-screen TV . . .

What he knew, what he felt, what he saw and heard in his waking and his dreams and his nightmares was a blue dot pulsing like a lone human heart.

30

Everybody needs a way to die.
—Condor

Saturday-morning suburbia and Faye sits in a stolen car—
fuck it, fuck them.

Fuck me.

Outside the windshield is a cul-de-sac. Seven low brick
houses spun out around a traffic circle, a road spoke leading downhill to the dead-end street that got you here, *now,*
eleven A.M., checkout time back at the hotel for lies you
left at dawn, *sayonara suckers.*

Call here Silver Spring, Merry-land, just a kiss outside
the Beltway but still *D*eath *C*ity, America, a suburban human terrain of wage earners. The lucky households are
home to two of them. Too many households get too few or
too tiny paychecks in this neighborhood where *getting by*
is a step above *getting gone.*

Lots of April-green trees.

A wall of trees, then a high wooden fence on the Target
Zone's rear perimeter, a couple low bushes, sidewalk leading to the front porch, black steel railings, five painted-red
concrete steps, then the aluminum storm door with its top-
half window and behind it, a solid white door. Could just
be wood, could be reinforced metal, but if so, call that a

landlord's paranoia because V doesn't profile with permanently secured safe houses.

Call the TZ a Crash House.

No fucking shit.

Got a back door, but getting to it means vaulting the backyard fence. *No way* can Condor get over that wooden wall in great shape & good speed for a breach.

All the windows are rolled down on Faye's stolen car crouched at a curb outside the cul-de-sac circle where two of the six non-target houses still have cars parked near them instead of cars gone grocery shopping or to kids' soccer games or whatever real people with real families do on cool green April Saturday mornings. Gray-black clouds roll over the cul-de-sac, but when did a little rain kill anybody, whereas some days staying inside means you're home when trouble comes calling, even if trouble only means to hit the house next door, those guys who you never knew, who just moved in.

How many guys?

Two guys, got to be no more, maybe less.

Plus one.

Please: plus one.

And *please*: Don't let rain wash these streets. Not yet.

House windows blocked by drawn white shades. White door. Five red steps.

Her rolled-down windows brought sounds Faye strained to hear, the scent of lilacs. She slouched behind the steering wheel, eyes staked out scanning, not locked on the TZ where *nothing* moved, where nobody could be home. Her gaze dropped to the front seat, a laptop screen and the steady pulsing of a blue dot, the words: RANGE 232 FEET.

And that address.

That house.

The TZ.

Her left thigh pressed down on the Glock .40 on the seat between her legs.

Come on, Condor! They'll make me if I keep posting here!

He'd left her alone in the hotel room for ninety-seven minutes last night.

Left her propped up in a chair with the Glock first-aid-kit white-taped in her hand in case she fell asleep or the concussion inspired a seizure at the wrong moment, the door getting kicked in while she's flopping around with no gun.

Took three taxis, two stops, he said.

Fuck cruising cover teams: We own these streets. Or die trying.

Code-knocked on the hotel room door, followed up with his *"It's you."*

Showed her what was in the store sacks.

Look what we've got now, he'd said. Look what we can do now.

Now, motherfucker! thought Faye as she sat in the stolen car. *Now.*

An engine whined behind her on this suburban street to the cul-de-sac.

Faye scrunched beneath the stolen car's dashboard.

Thumping behind her came from the duct-taped man locked in this car's trunk.

Collateral damage. Civilian casualties. The blood of innocents.

Nothing's ever easy. Nothing's ever free. Nobody is a saint.

We're all sinners.

We're all the duct-taped man locked in the trunk of a stolen car.

Still . . . *Sorry.*

A whining engine wave rolled like a wall over the stolen car. Faye saw a blur of brown metal, then it was gone and the screaming engine noise flowed with it.

Ease up. Just enough. Eyes above the dashboard, watch the cul-de-sac.

You've seen a thousand such brown delivery vans in the streets of America, of Europe, of China and India, too. A global delivery service beyond any one government system. Street meat sent via cyber. You want it, you pay, brown brings it to your door.

The oversized step van everybody knew whined to a stop in front of a house across the cul-de-sac from TZ, one of the homes with no cars parked nearby.

The brown van's engine cut off.

No! What if it doesn't start again? What if it can't move?

Don't worry, Faye told herself. *The driver's a professional.*

The brown van's driver stepped to the pavement of the cul-de-sac. Even from half a block away, Faye recognized the driver's expected brown uniform pants & shirt. She saw his bald head, cue-ball bald and pink, and that's what you noticed, plus he wore those dorky flip-up sunglasses clipped to black horn-rimmed hipster eyewear. And even at this distance with her eyes behind Condor's aviator sunglasses, Faye's attention got diverted by a weird black smear on the left side of the driver's neck but she couldn't identify it as what it was, a spider web tattoo.

The brown-clad driver rattled open the van's rear cargo door. She couldn't see what was in the back of the van where a SWAT team could have huddled, but houses in the cul-de-sac could. The driver pulled a padded shipping envelope from a respectable load of shipping bags, packages, and boxes. He hurried up the sidewalk to the house he'd parked in front of, pushed what looked to be a doorbell.

Waited no more than five seconds before he knocked on then unlatched the aluminum storm door, put the padded envelope on the narrow ledge between the two front doors and scurried to his waiting brown van, no time to waste.

The brown van roared its engine to life. Gears ground.

The brown step van pulled away from that delivery address.

Circled along the top of the cul-de-sac.

Drove just past Faye's visual lock on the TZ.

Fucking stopped.

Again the van's engine died.

The bald spider-webbed driver hopped out of the van.

Rattled open the rear cargo hold. Got a brown-paper-wrapped box the size of an attaché case. Gripped one box edge in his left hand as he hurried . . .

Up the sidewalk to the TZ. Up the five red cement steps. Up to the aluminum outer door. Pushed the doorbell. Again, no more than five seconds and he's knocking on the aluminum storm door, opening it wide, bending over to position the heavy box on its narrow edge, but when he eased the aluminum door closed, it wouldn't shut all the way, gaped open enough for a curious citizen or a cruising cop to notice. The bald driver didn't care, hurried back to his van, fired up the engine, drove out of the cul-de-sac, turned left and cruised past where Faye huddled behind the steering wheel of a stolen car.

The van engine whined back the way it came, out of sight of where it had been.

Faye kept her eyes locked on the TZ with the gaping-open aluminum door.

Saturday morning in a quiet suburban neighborhood.

Back on Wednesday—*Jesus, was it only Wednesday, three days ago?*—at Complex Zed, when Sami sent her out, turned her loose, and she'd gone to the EDD, the Equipment

Disbursement Detail, got Santa to give her cash and credit cards, give her ammo for her own gun and the ballistic vest she wore now, the .38 and .45 Condor used.

And Santa'd said: "You going to war, Agent?"

Faye'd lied and told him: "I know what I'm doing."

Wish I could go back, say something different.

Tell Santa: "Not going to war, going to finish one."

Now on a suburban Saturday morning, the backpack purse Santa'd helped her fill lay crumpled and flat on the backseat of the stolen car. One of Santa's two Delta Force compact flash-bang grenades was *gently* duct taped to the left side of the bulletproof ballistic vest she wore under her fucking pink hoodie.

Eyes on TZ.

The door—*the white door,* last door before in there—that door slowly opened.

Let her see a compact man, short brown hair, beard like Spec Ops, unbuttoned shirt. The man in TZ's now open entryway stood on the other side of the outer aluminum door propped open by a delivered package, scanning for shooters.

Saw nobody.

He picked up the brown van–delivered package.

White light BANG! as the Delta Force grenade IED duct taped to the bottom of the delivered box blew the bearded man backwards into the house.

Faye swung up behind the stolen car's steering wheel, keyed its engine to life and stomped on the gas, careened a hard right turn into the cul-de-sac braking to a stop in front of the TZ, jumping out of the car with a Glock .40 in her right hand, her left hand slapping a store-bought, magnetized emergency spinning light that spun red flashes of officialdom from the top of the stolen car that might—*might*—convince civilians in the cul-de-sac that there was no need to call 911 after that big boom and flash at the house where the *could-be-a-cop-car* car now parked, with a woman wearing a pink hoodie charging the glass-broken, aluminum-buckled outer door.

A bald man now wearing black jeans and a black leather jacket ran toward the stolen car with the spinning red light.

Faye cleared the five red concrete steps in two strides, shoved the buckled aluminum door aside, snapped her Glock up to zero—

Man on the empty living room floor! Uncurling from fetal position! Beard, brown hair, gasping, face burned making noise he can't hear and—

Gun, he's got a gun, fumbling a pistol with a silencer, hands turning it!

The blind, deaf, and burned man was a warrior who knew his weapon.

Knew how to push its silencer-sausaged barrel into his mouth, jab the cold black bore toward the top of his skull— *Phutt!*

Crimson gore sprayed the white wall by the kitchen door.

The man with the gun in his mouth lay crumpled like a gone-to-sleep child.

What lie did you buy?

What truth couldn't you face?

No time, gun up, Faye zeroed the hall to the right of the empty living room:

Two open doorways on the hall, right side. Probably bedrooms.

End of the hall, open door, medicine cabinet above a sink: bathroom.

Left side of the hall, open door, a glimpse of . . . washer spigots, dryer plug-in, machines gone. Laundry room, storage closet.

Condor, beside her, bald head from the electric clippers and razors he'd bought at the late-night drugstore, the same family emporium with a children's aisle full of close-outs from last Halloween, temporary tattoos made from and washed off by water like the rain that mercifully hadn't yet fallen today to smear the ink on his neck, the eye-trapping spider web. He had his .45 combat focused, obeyed her gesture to clear the kitchen.

As he moved to his fire zone, she eased down the hall toward the open bathroom.

The hallway seen over the barrel of her Glock:

First bedroom door.

Edge forward along the wall.

Faye dropped to her hands and knees—

Whirled/rolled flat on her back & stomach past the first open bedroom door, facing & gun aiming *in,* watching a spinning topsy-turvy turning view of . . .

Sleeping bag * open suitcase * dirty clothes * water bottle * closet open empty—

Nobody.

She pulled her legs under her as she sat with her back pressed against the wall, the second bedroom door open and to her right, better view of the laundry room *empty,* see most of the interior of the end of the hall bathroom *empty,* second bedroom *Gotta be!*

One grenade left *fuck it* lob it in the bedroom *close eyes cover ears open mouth*—

White light/BANG!

Faye's world burned and bonged for maybe fifteen seconds before she could see and stagger to her feet, combat charge into the room she'd blasted.

The man pushing himself to sitting against the empty white wall was a mess: scrapes on his goatee/scraggly-bearded face, Band-Aid on his forehead below short-cropped dirty brass hair. He wore a white scooped-neck T-shirt, gray sweatpants, and bare feet. A non-hospital-applied long white bandage striped from his left collar-bone down his sinewy muscled chest to well below his heart, like it covered a furrow from, say, a .45 bullet. He had a black eye, puffy lips that must have drawn stares when he stalked through the zoo the day before, but he'd made it then, and he made it to sitting up now, but his gun, some kind of prototype black automatic pistol with a silencer, his pistol he'd been a star with yesterday, that gun lay blown across the room.

Faye guessed his still-dazed eyes came from field-kit pain-fighting morphine.

He'd been the executioner who crucified her asshole partner with knives.

He'd been the *protocol* Homeland Security agent outside Condor's house.

He'd been the Monkey Man on the subway platform before Condor's shots dropped him into a rushing-out train.

He was the biker.

He pushed his bare heels on the carpeted floor—not to get away, but to sit straighter against the white wall.

As he stared into the bore of Faye's gun.

She let her vision expand to take in where he'd been living. Sleeping bag on the floor, camping lamp and other gear, a cheap suitcase with his clothes, two high-quality black cloth material bags she instinctively knew were full of combat gear.

A paperback book lay on the floor beside his camping pillow. Some novel.

The Vs squatting in this house were out-of-towners. Brought in from the black.

The battered V stared at the woman beyond the gun zeroed on his life.

Said: "So . . . *Hey.*"

"*Hey,*" said Faye.

Black gun barrel pointed straight at the man sitting against the white wall.

Who told her: "Your turn."

Faye didn't see her Glock flash or hear the roar as she shot him in the head.

Then: *There he is, shooting nobody no more with his bloody three eyes.*

She combat swept the empty kitchen where the only documents were eviction notices this team had torn off the white door when they moved in to squat.

Eased down the basement stairs.

Condor sat on the basement floor beside a support beam for the ceiling. Once upon a time, the basement's other room had been a home office, wired for computers and a big-screen TV, but now that carpeted room was empty, as was its adjoining bathroom. Out here, where Condor sat, was only *empty basement* with a clear plastic drop cloth unfolded over the home-owner-installed floor tiles. On that plastic drop cloth sat Condor.

With Merle.

She was naked. Slumped with her spine against the support beam, arms limp at her sides, wrists stuck to strips of white tape. Condor'd cut her free from the beam. Her cheeks were red from ripped-away white tape stuck over her mouth. Blond-gray hair hung matted and tangled to her slumped bare shoulders. Faye smelled that Merle sat in her own waste. Condor'd been whispering to Merle as Faye followed her gun down the stairs to the basement, but by the time she joined them, he'd stopped. Merle's eyes were open but whatever she was seeing wasn't there.

"Did they drug her or . . ." Faye found no more words.

"Doesn't matter," whispered the suddenly old-looking man. "She's gone."

Faye heard him strangle a sigh, or maybe it was a sob.

He told her: "Maybe Maine. The hospital. Maybe she'll come back there."

Then . . .

Oh then!

. . . he softly so softly pressed his lips to her forehead.

Clumped back up the stairs, the .45 dangling limp and impotent in his hand.

They found Merle's phone on the kitchen counter.

Faye never knew what made her open the refrigerator door.

But she did.

The only thing she found in that cool-air refrigerator waited on its top shelf:

A clear glass jar where two eyeballs floated in pink lemonade-like liquid.

She felt Condor come stand behind her.

He said: "Your partner. What they took to frame me after they crucified him."

Faye whispered: "Who are these people?"

Condor reached around her, closed the refrigerator, said: "They're us."

When she looked at him, he added: "Only let's hope we're better and luckier."

"This isn't who I wanted to be," said Faye.

"Me either. But here we are."

Faye said: "We've got to decide—"

Condor dropped to his hands and knees beside the suicide corpse, sniffed the curled-up body like . . . *Like a werewolf,* though Faye. *Or a . . . vulture.*

"Smells like gasoline."

He spotted the bulge in the dead man's front pocket, pulled out an iPhone.

"There's a GPS in it, right?" he asked the younger woman.

She showed him how to access the GPS and its search request. She went to the bedroom, to the other KIA enemy, got the cell phone from beside his bed and didn't look at him, at what she'd done, no she didn't. *Deserved is deserved and dead, Chris is dead.*

Faye got back to the living room as Condor headed toward the front door, car keys he'd scooped off the counter in one hand, the suicide man's iPhone in the other.

Is his .45 in the holster under his black leather jacket?

Siren: coming closer.

Neighbors.

Not such an ordinary suburban Saturday.

"Wait!" said Faye as Condor walked outside, as she chased after him.

He stood on the red concrete front porch. Pointed the car key's fob at the parked vehicles other than the stolen car he'd scouted the night before then gotten the tools for at the drugstore and broken into with Faye at dawn three peaceful neighborhood blocks away from the hotel. Condor pushed the LOCATE button on the fob.

Lights flashed on a new-model Japanese-designed car built in Tennessee to politically appease Americans. Faye heard its driver's door unlock with a *clunk*.

Faye asked Condor: "What about the delivery van driver we hijacked and taped up and stuck in the trunk of the car we stole?"

Bald Condor said: "Let him breathe."

Then he roared away in the car that had been the killers', the Vs'.

Siren: maybe five blocks away.

Faye held the HOMELAND SECURITY ID folder out and open in her left hand.

Used her right thumb to work the cell phone from the man she killed, *I killed him, I killed him,* call the number she knew.

After two buzzes—he's checking caller ID, launching trace—Sami answered.

Faye said: "Guess who."

A police car topped by a spinning red light sirened into the cul-de-sac.

31

Gonna take someone apart.
—Richard Thompson, "I Feel So Good"

You're driving a stolen car where it's supposed to go.

A robot woman talking out of a cell phone tells you so.

"In fifty feet . . . turn right."

Of the last seven locations this phone had mapped, five had been gas stations near on/off ramps for the Beltway.

The sixth address belonged to the Crash House where Condor'd stolen this car.

Where Merle.

Location seven had to be it.

Familiar streets.

He wasn't sure if he remembered where he was, and if so from *when,* or if he'd just driven so many American suburbs that the streets now all looked the same. Certainly nothing outside the windows of his car showed a geographic or cultural individuality, an unmistakable identity, an easy clue that this "town" claimed its turf alongside quick highways to CIA headquarters and the Pentagon. To the National Security Agency, FBI headquarters, Complex Zed.

Once upon a time, these streets hosted a satellite veterans' hospital for Walter Reed—rumor had it, the psych ward—but that facility had been shut down, as had the 1950-something faux castle complex where two buildings were still surrounded by a gray cement wall complete with parapets to look like a local hustler's version of what in that *way back when* had been a brand-new futuristic dollar magnet called Disneyland.

A railroad track slid by Condor's view outside the driver's window, steel rails that made him think he heard a lonesome whistle blow.

You're done with hallucinations.

Stuck in this *real*.

With the graveyard the robot woman guided him past.

Gardens of the dead are everywhere.

The stolen car he drove smelled like gas inside its passengers' compartment.

Figure that one out.

He drove past old houses, some sagging, some rehabbed by the latest hopeful generation of Moms & Dads with kids, so there was a playground, another set of empty swings. Front porches, a seedy apartment complex from some pale lime stucco-walled former motel. Lawns led back from the street. Lots of space between the houses. Hard to hear what was happening next door.

"Arriving at destination . . . On left, one hundred feet."

He parked the car at the curb across the street and half a block from *destination*.

Looked like a horror-movie country house this capital city grew up around and forgot. Two stories, probably three bedrooms upstairs, downstairs dining room, study, front parlor maybe, kitchen, bath. Probably a basement for a furnace. Or whatever.

Almost looked like a real home.

Until you settled it in your eyes *just so*.

Saw the black iron fence around the double-lot property was more than hip-high to discourage hoppers without encouraging stares. Saw that though the house's white peeling paint looked like it could use another coat, there was a sheen over the whole structure, a reflective lacquer you couldn't buy in any hardware store. And the first-floor windows: tinted isn't the right word, for though they shone a quiet blue in both sunshine and moon glow, those windows let in light but not sight, let out vision but not voltage. Their glass was thick, far beyond the muscle of any rock-throwing neighborhood hooligan. The two doors over the front portal looked no more formidable than the doors you drive past in any crime-conscious American neighborhood, but looks . . .

Well, looks are as looks see.

What else Condor saw from the parked stolen car let him know the robot woman hadn't erred in bringing him here. A shed twice the size of that brown van from this morning rose a prudent distance from the house. Though no thick black wires connected the shed to the house, Condor knew the windowless and lightning-grounded shed held an emergency generator and sat on a vast underground fuel tank, just like he knew the glass rectangles on the house's roof that he could barely see through strategically planted trees, those glass panels were solar converters, *just in case* or even *just because*. And there was no mistaking one—*no*: three satellite dishes amidst the gables pointing up from the top-story windows where bedrooms awaited sweet surrenders of *yes, yes, yes*.

A nine-year-old dented tan American sedan sat in the pebbled driveway.

The car looked like it seldom saw any extended roads.

Why leave when you're already there.

Here: Tier Zero.

Like a movie director, Condor whispered: "And . . . *action*."

Opened the stolen car's door and climbed out to the street.

Knew security cameras watched him walk toward the house.

Worried not so much: he could have been made dead when he drove up.

Bet every badge & Black Ops gun is now dispatched to stay away from here.

Still, after he unlatched the black iron fence gate and crunched over the pebbled path to the front porch, he filled his hand with the .45.

If you're not bringing flowers . . .

His left fingers brushed the handle on the aluminum storm door.

No blast of electricity.

No trapdoor sprang open under his shoes to swallow him into the long fall.

No sound of an alarm.

The aluminum door creaked when he opened it. He wrapped his gun-free left hand around the inner door's brass knob . . . *that turned,* opened the door.

A whiff of gasoline came out to the front porch.

Then—as fast & smoothly as a battered sixty-something shaved-bald man could—Condor charged into the house, into the long front hall, his back slamming the inner door shut, his .45 swooping left, right, aiming up the empty stairs leading to the second floor.

Hooks on the hall wall held a rain slicker, a parka retired by increasingly mild and snow-less winters, a faded brown (*not candy-pink*) hoodie and a New York designer hip-length brown coat of quality leather.

Some security camera's showing you crouched here, black leather jacket, gun.

Against one hall wall stood two red plastic five-gallon jugs labeled GASOLINE.

Combat stalk down the hall.

Scan your target environment over the barrel of your .45.

Brown hardwood floors, scuffed but kept dust free by an undercover janitorial crew from the NSA's complex at not-far-away Fort Meade who had no idea why they climbed into phony "Maid Machine" vans to drive nearly to D.C. and clean a private house. But they knew the penalty for talking about this job fell under provisions of the Espionage Act of 1917 with a *maybe they'd skip the trial* penalty of death.

The walls were painted a soothing shade of ivory.

Dead ahead, at the end of the ten-steps hallway and before stairs to the second floor, the walls opened up, ceiling arches that in a regular house would reveal, *say,* a formal dining room off to the right, while off to the left would be the sitting room, the living room, the family room: call it what you will, what it was here wasn't that.

Condor kept his back against the hall wall as he eased toward the open rooms.

What he saw in that room to his right: a twentieth-century whiteboard wiped clean, file cabinets, stacks of computer disks, CPUs or Internet servers.

Two Vietnam-era five-gallon metal gas cans squatted near those cyber slaves.

Condor cradled his heavy gun in the two-handed grip, elbows bent so the .45 that had served America for more than a hundred years pointed toward the ceiling. The cold black barrel rose past the centerline of his face, his eyes looked over the steel shaft's hole, the scent of gun oil & fired bullets, the hard tang of metal close enough for his lips to kiss as he double-gripped the thick butt and his finger curled on the curved trigger.

Now or never.

He leapt into what could have been a living room—zeroed the .45.

At her.

She sat cupped in the C-curve of a touchscreen desk.

That flat C-shaped desk surface tilted up to face her eyes and hands with vermillion fingernails, short for keyboarding. When, *like now,* the desktop's touchscreen was in sleep mode, rather than go dark, the desktop became translucent, so Condor could see her mostly bare desk held a double-edged dagger.

A letter opener on a desk without a single scrap of paper.

Her hair looked like rusted steel streaked with silver wires and curved on each side of her face but . . . but like it often wasn't brushed, not like today when it was glorious and red. Her skin was pale white. Call the dark blue outfit she wore a business dress, open at her neck, trim tailored waist, a comfortable skirt that knew how to cling and ride above her knees to reveal slim black-stockings-sheathed legs. From the room's open arched doorway where he stood aiming his gun at her, Condor couldn't tell if she still had freckles, though time would never have let her lose the laugh wrinkles on her face, high cheekbones, clean jaw, burning blue eyes. Her thin smile was a fresh lipstick slash of midnight crimson.

She dressed up for this.

For you.

Every great strategy begins with a diversion.

Her voice was a strong tenor.

"You could have been a rock 'n' roll star," he'd once told her. She'd smiled.

Here and now, the words from her smile said: "You always wanted a big gun."

"I've got what I've got."

"I hope that's enough."

Nothing on her desk but the dagger that's at least six inches from her hand. Scan the room, the walls: shelves, books displayed like antiques, objets d'art or were they mementos, *both, whatever,* guns: no visible guns.

Gas cans near that wall of wispy blue windows.

She said: "So this is how you look when you're old. I thought you'd keep your hair."

"Some things gotta go."

"Some things come back."

Swing left, swing right, swing full circle and the world swirls past your gun sights and then it's back to her, on her. She hasn't moved. Looks right at you.

Says: "It's just you and me, kid."

"Nobody's a kid anymore."

"Have you gone and gotten all responsible on me? All adult? All . . . sane?"

"More than I was before."

"Is that going to be a problem?"

"You think so," said Condor. "That's why you tried to kill me."

"Be fair: the Op was to put you back someplace where you'd be safe and taken care of and not stressed. The killing you only came after you fucked up the program.

"In all fairness," she continued, "haven't you ever made a mistake?"

Condor stared at her.

Lowered the .45 from a dead-center aim.

Holstered his weapon.

Felt his heart slamming against his ribs.

She said: "So you didn't come here to kill me."

"I didn't come here to die."

"Why did you come here?"

He took one breath, took two before he said: "You knew I was coming."

"Your data lit up cyberspace."

"You knew I was coming *before,*" he said. "So you topped out my target index."

"You showing up here like this, guess I was right."

"Self-fulfilling prophecy."

"If you can't fulfill yourself, who'll do it for you."

Condor frowned. "What I can't figure is, are you full of shit, stoned on power or did you go crazy, too, or did the program just swallow you into what it can do."

"What do you care."

"Once upon a time," he said.

"Once upon a time," she said.

"Confession," she said. "You looked good in the surveillance footage. I don't mind bald, but I like you the way you really are."

She gave him a crimson frown. "The woman Merle: is she my replacement?"

"She was never a *promoted colleague.* A *conflict.* A *co-whatever* all we were."

"Just a co-conspirator. A collaborator."

"She's a person who cared—"

"—and couldn't get out of the way of Condor. Is she dead? I haven't looked."

"There's nothing there for you to see."

"How about for you?" Oh, that smile that knows you well.

Knew you well.

Condor drifted to his left—her right, she's right-handed, the dagger or whatever weapon, she'll prefer to use her right hand that's lying flat and empty on the desktop.

"Why didn't you run?" he said. "Ten strokes on a keyboard

and you could have vanished into some wealthy widow sunbathing on the shores of a luxury sea."

"Why go be somewhere when right here I can be everywhere?"

"Time and space are more than an illusion."

"Depends on your data.

"Besides," she said, "maybe I was waiting for you."

"Why?"

"Everybody needs somebody to talk to. Life is call and response."

"And that's what you want from me. Now."

"I want what I can get. One way or the other, you're going to give it to me."

"What about . . ." He nodded at her desktop portal to the world.

"Whatever I—*we*—get will be a change they can be made fine with."

"Are people getting nervous? Squeamish about the V? Is that why I suddenly became an imminent threat, because me in that mix *getting sane* . . . ?"

"People are always nervous. That's why they've got me. And you."

"Together."

"Again." She shrugged. "Control was always too complex a job for just one person. We made it work. A new *us* could be fun. And of course, vital."

"What about all the cans of gas?"

"I'm a careful girl."

"And if you can't be in control, well then . . ."

"Why wish that on anybody else?"

"Except me."

She smiled. "Or us."

"Or maybe just us *for a while*. Keeping your options open. Ready to reboot."

"My life is purpose, is about what's crucial, what needs to be done."

"Having that agent crucified on my—"

"He was worse than an incompetent asshole and a drunk. He was selling *sources & methods* intel to a private contractor. Fool thought he was just cashing in on what the private sector was going to get in five years anyhow. Such a terrible agent he didn't realize his buyers were fronts leading back to a terrorist group."

"So you terminate him and use that to frame me, two birds with one crucifixion. But what about killing that guy Chris? Merle and crashing everything into Faye?"

"They're more than just names."

"Yeah," said Condor. "They're people."

"They're data points of cause and effect. Maybe threat matrix computations and outcomes got a little out of control, but whose fault is that?"

"Whoever made them into *ones* or *zeroes* choices." Condor shook his head. "Not me."

"Really? Or were they consequences of something you created, something you did?"

"You took over."

"When you malfunctioned, I was there. You put me there. Here.

"And what I do," she said, "what the V does, what you did, you know it's true: if we don't do it, we'll get it done to us. We stop the worst there is before it becomes real."

She's shifting in her chair, keeping her eyes on you as you move around her desk.

Like a child, she said: "I finally like doing that thing you liked me to do."

Gas cans, guns, dagger, hidden buttons: what weapon?

"And now you're here," she said. "But instead of being the *what-if* whacko we both know you are, you're acting like the data indicated and predicted you might. Only this time, looks like you really might have a chance to destroy and deactivate like you failed to last time, back when you went crazy. Are you crazy now?"

"Who knows," he said. "How about you?"

"Who cares," she told him. Sighed. "I am lonely.

"But you know about that, too," she said. "That was why you recruited me."

"No," he argued. "You were the best of the Girl Scouts. The best of all those women CIA analysts who got Bin Laden after you came to work with me."

"Maybe," she allowed. Nylons crackled as she crossed her legs, their indigo-sheathed slimness slipping out from her skirt *oh God she's wearing the black garter belt* and she said: "It was so . . . touching how hard you worked to not let my legs matter."

You're around the end of the desk now. Close enough to lunge. Grab her. Standing to her right side. Her eyes are pointed in front of her, but what she's watching, who she's seeing, is you.

The dagger lay on her plexiglass desktop. He let his fingers float out. Stroke the length of the shiny blade. Her hand resting beside the dagger trembled.

Perfume, she smells of opening flowers and magazine dreams.

"What about now?" he said, walking behind her chair.

Now you're behind her, the smell of her hair, dark roots she has to dye, *what good spy doesn't,* a thin gold strand lies on the V of soft white flesh below her bare throat, the necklace hangs down to where he can't see but you know it holds the amulet given her by a woman trapped & broken in a Darfur refugee camp.

She'd refused to cry when she told you that tale.

We are held together by the songs of our times.

"Now you're here," she told the man looming behind her.

She didn't look. Let him be where he was like it didn't matter, like that was good.

Condor raked his fingers along the back of the tall black leather chair she sat in at her curved touchscreen desk that was years from being seen by the citizens of the country who'd paid for it. He felt the leather give under his fingers' scratch, wondered if she felt their pressure cross her back, kneading her flesh near her bra strap. If she wore a bra.

Then he was on her heart side.

She glanced up, blue eyes and a soft smile invitation.

Saw him looking at the technological marvel of her desktop.

Knew he was talking about the touchscreen that made minding the universe so simple a sixth grader could do it: "Seems like we're always one upgrade behind."

"Think how I feel," she said.

And he did.

"After all," she said, "I've been around a little longer than you."

She turned her lean V face toward the man bent over her desk. Slowly—oh so slowly—raised her left hand to brush away the red hair falling across her sky eyes.

Said: "Being older is more interesting. I'm glad you never minded."

He raised his gun-empty right hand. Held it palm out toward the inclined desktop screen. Said: "Like this?"

He felt the *chi* in her change even as the screen in front of his right palm lit up from the heat of a human. Tension flowed from her as she stretched her head toward heaven to better see over his hand with its remembered stroke of her flesh.

Condor karate-chopped her throat.

Her crimson head bounced off the black leather executive chair.

Grab her skull and chin whirl & twist!

He heard the snap of her spine and let go, *let go,* staggered away from the chair.

And what he'd done. What he hadn't delegated. Done not because it was part of a program. What he had the honest humanity, the guts to choose.

What worked better.

Who but you.

Condor staggered backwards. Hit the wall with his hips, the holstered .45 clunked. His left leg bumped something that vibrated: a five-gallon can of gas.

All over the house. Ferried here in the car he'd parked outside by a warrior, some nameless *wannabe hero.* What was left of dead dinosaurs now waited in war-surplus metal gas cans and ultra-new red plastic jugs to be spilled and sloshed and dumped on this fusion of the smartest we can be.

A roaring fireball of orange flames and black smoke movie in his mind.

Somehow the .45 ended up in his hand.

He lifted it up to consider.

Heard: *Who's left to shoot?*

32

Into the vacuum of his eyes.
—Bob Dylan, "Like a Rolling Stone"

Faye sat on an American front porch.

She wore a pink hoodie though her sore, scabbed head was bare to the sinking sun.

Gone was the ballistic vest she'd worn for most of the last three days.

Stone-faced handlers had it now. They'd shown up seventeen minutes after cops who'd been radioed to obey *Agent On Scene* and stay out of the 911 *dispatched to* residence. Later, inside that house, a sweatsuit medic dressed her wound. Faye didn't bother to wait until he was gone before pulling the white bandage off, he didn't bother to tell her *no.* An innocent-looking moving van showed up, let neighbors watching from their front porches and windows see its crew dolly out a refrigerator box, a washer/dryer box.

Merle . . .

They took Merle out in a horizontal box labeled *mattress.*

Opened that cardboard as soon as they'd lifted it to hidden deep in the van.

Sure they did.

Faye didn't see the movers get rid of the glass jar of eyeballs in the refrigerator. She didn't want to know about that. She didn't want to be part of that.

But I do. And I am.

Faye listened while a bone-tired woman from Sami's team worked out the cover story to dribble to this cul-de-sac's *looky-loos* and *street ears* and *tattle tongues* and *cell phone snappers*. Faye became *pink hoodie woman* became *real estate agent* shown up to prep for movers, found *squatters,* maybe a meth head cooking, saw a flash of something as the squatters boomed out the back door, over the fence, *gone* who knows where, cops checked the woods. How much of that the neighbors got & bought didn't matter, there was nothing over police scanners to attract an actual journalist who could publish a story.

Faye told the handlers *no* when they asked for her weapon.

Told them *no* when they asked *what happened*.

Told them *no* when they said *okay, time to leave*.

No one told her refusals *no*.

And the 911 cops left.

And the moving van left.

And the stone-faced handlers left.

All except for the bone-tired woman who worked for Sami plus two janitors in blue jeans and T-shirts and medical masks who'd be a long time washing white walls with their sponges and buckets of water & bleach. Well, one janitor was washing walls. The other one seemed only to be watching the bone-tired woman watch Faye.

We've all got a duty.

Faye said: "I'll wait outside."

Walked out to April's cool afternoon air, sat on the top stoop of the red concrete front porch like a pink hoodie teenager yearning for that better place to go.

She knew a bone-tired woman or a blue-jeaned janitor watched her from inside the house.

Faye watched the neighbors quit their vigils for what

waited inside their homes, TV or computer screens or someone who loved you and you loved.

She watched the shadows of trees and utility poles lengthen across the gray pavement of the suburban cul-de-sac.

They took the car we stole.

And the man duct-taped in the trunk. No doubt he went someplace where it was worth his while never to have a story to tell, including to his bosses.

Someone came home across the cul-de-sac, frowned at a box he found left by a delivery service, but there was no brown van parked anywhere near he could take it to.

Evening's chill reached through the long sunlight of this Saturday afternoon.

Would be rough to sleep outside in a cemetery tonight.

The car driving into the cul-de-sac could have been any-body's mobility machine.

Silver paint, four or five years old, nothing special for a steady paycheck. Faye didn't bother scanning the license plates after the windshield showed her who sat behind the steering wheel, who was alone in that steel and glass. The silver car drove around the cul-de-sac, cranked hard left—braked to a stop facing the center of the cul-de-sac. If the car had a standard transmission, the driver was smooth: white backup lights joined the red brake lights without grinding gears. The car parked with its rear tires touching the curb in front of the house with five red cement steps where Faye sat wearing a pink hoodie.

The older man who drove the car got out and walked toward her.

Faye felt whoever was behind her in the house draw away from the windows, from being able to hear a thing said outside on the front porch. She waited until the man from the silver car reached the bottom of the steps.

Then said: "What took you so long?"

"We're here now." Sami gave her sad smile. "How are you, Faye?"

"Fan-*fucking*-tastic."

"Your Chris was a good man. Better. There are no words for our kind of sorry."

"*Our kind of sorry?* Is that all you've got? What took you so long to get here?"

"Twenty steps from the launch car, my cell phone goes crazy. Calls I gotta take. Then a place I gotta be." He shrugged. "Few places, actually."

Faye said: "Where's Condor?"

"That's what this is about," said Sami.

He wore a shopping-mall tan Windbreaker plausibly unzipped to the cooling air. His shirt and khakis could have come to him via the Internet and a brown van. Faye knew that under that banal Windbreaker, there'd be a belt and a holster on that belt for a pistol, *fuck it, fuck him*. He stood there, aged as more than an older brother, less than father, gray-flecked curly short hair, teenage-fled Lebanon fostered in Detroit raised by the Marine Corps. There'd be a gun in an ankle holster, too. Sincerity in his soft sad smile that could cut to your core. And might.

Sami said: "Who's Condor?"

"Don't fuck with me."

"Never," he said. "But I've got to give you a choice."

"Is he dead?"

"Let's say there is or was someone by that identifier. It's been used so much that both *yes* and *no* to your question are true."

"*What the* . . . To cover your ass or . . . or who knows why, you could do a maximum-cover drop on Condor, fog who he really was and what he really meant until all that was more like some novel or movie than real. But why bother, even if it's to keep cover on the scandal, '*runaway rogue spy whatever*,' call it V, but . . ."

Faye blinked.

Sami came back into focus.

"You're the verifier," she said. "That's why it's you here instead of him. So I would believe. So I would . . .

"He's gone back in," whispered Faye. "He took out the V and the community took him back in."

"Close," said Sami.

"There is no close," said Faye. "He beat *them* or *it*—"

"*Her*," interrupted Sami.

Faye felt her jaw drop.

Didn't stop: "He either took out the V and *her* or they took him out. And if you're here, he won, but is he fucking alive?"

"*Yeah*."

Sunset bled the sky a redder pink than the wrap she wore.

"What's important for you to realize," said Sami, "what matters for you, is that he's alive, and the person who recklessly green-lit the man you loved and risked, that person, that woman . . . *Dead*."

"So I owe him one."

"Good to hear you say that," said Sami.

Faye's stomach went cold.

"You owe yourself, too," he told her.

The woman in the pink hoodie sitting on an American porch listened to the man who'd come there to . . . *To what?*

"The V," said Sami. "Not one entry in our whole Intelligence Community. Yet it's everywhere—and that's saying something. Our IC budget is fifty billion a year.

"That could change." He shrugged. "Go down some, these things have a cycle. Are keyed to wars, crises. Or us getting caught wild in the streets like . . . Poor Chris."

"Whatever you're doing," said Faye, "don't use him. You owe me that much."

Recognition slid along their stare.

"We were talking about cycles," said Sami. "The V predicted it, which surprised the hell out of newspaper names I had to meet with instead of responding to your call. All it takes is a triggering event to send a cycle one way or the other. Condor could have been a trigger for the system having to deal with the V and what it is."

"What it does—*did*," said Faye. "All illegal."

"Illegal is a term of law decided by courts and presidential signatures," said Sami.

"You've got to be fucking kidding me with that."

"What, your '*moral authority*'? That seldom triumphs in a Beirut back alley."

"Targeting Condor and Chris was not a Beirut alley, that was the V not wanting to be accountable for how and why they whack people."

"High value, high risk, high impact, hostile targets."

"Everyone qualifies as that kind of homicide to somebody, sometime," said Faye. "There are laws, due process."

"Exactly," said Sami. "What the processes do.

"One of the triggers in the cycles, maybe tomorrow, maybe the next day, some scandal or leak will blow a window into the IC, say NSA sucking up every e-mail, every phone call, every Web site and traffic. Maybe there'll be a public uproar, though I think not so much. The public—that great *whoever*—they already think all this is happening, but they just don't think it's happening to them, so *who cares, what can you do.* And the V is just the logical progression, merging software and necessity and probabilities."

"Data isn't truth," said Faye.

"Right, but we're damned to knowing only data and damned to having to do something about it. Or have something about it done to us. The V, when has such a wondrous capability ever been discarded? Only practical, smart, to recognize that."

"You want to be Big Brother, Sami?"

"There is no Big Brother, only Big Us.

"And in that us, there's *u* and the *s,* and the *s* can mean *the system* or it can mean *the shit* not necessarily of how you get to live, but certainly of whether you get a chance to be somebody who is more than just counted, to be somebody who does the counting.

"Being just *u* sucks, my friend, my comrade in arms, my colleague. But being *u* connected to the *s,* being *us* . . . That's a life where you can do something worth doing."

"The V," whispered Faye. "Condor didn't beat it, didn't destroy it."

"He is it," said Sami. "Now. But only partially."

"Yeah," said Faye, "he's got you."

"You don't get it yet." Sami put one foot on the bottom red cement step and held on to the porch's black steel railing so he could lean closer and confide to Faye.

"The V didn't get out of hand," he told her, "the V got into the wrong hands, and that's been corrected. All the people who know what we know recognize that human error shouldn't cause us to ignore inevitable capability."

"There's always human error, Sami. Unless you turn it all over to the machines."

"What are we, nuts?"

He pushed his hand against her glare. "Don't give me yet another singularity scenario. What it comes down to is who's the heart and mind of *us,* of control. Someone should have that job who knows just how horribly wrong the whole thing can go."

"Condor," she whispered.

"And you," said Sami.

Call it sundown in a suburban Saturday cul-de-sac.

"What do you mean: *me*?"

"Who better to be the V than you who knows how bad it can be?"

"Condor . . . And you . . . ?"

"And you. Three of us. A triangle. The strongest shape."

"That's a sphere," said Faye.

"Fuck your metaphors and mind games," said Sami. "You know the system is there. You know it went wrong. You know it's never going to be scrapped. Forget the more than two hundred Top Secret offensive cyber-operations we do a year, things like worms turned loose in a rogue nation's nuclear bomb programs, TAOs, Tailored Access Programs like the Chinese hit us with all the time. The V is progression beyond that. We're going to be fighting whole wars like this. Living whole lives like this. We're all wired in together. Pretty soon it'll be more about *the wire* than it is about *the we*. Doesn't matter if you think that's not so smart. We're so smart we fight wars over burning gas made from dinosaurs that couldn't adapt and those ignitions cause pollution that's making the polar ice cap melt so chunks float off and you can watch it all happen with your cell phone, watch the chunk coming.

"You got a chance to do something right now," said Sami. "You can be part of the process so guys like Chris won't get shot. You can shape power or . . ."

"*Or what*, Sami?" The Glock weighed on her belt. "Or be deleted?"

"Never happen. Not on my watch. Not on Condor's.

"You're a hero, Faye. But you can't do shit about stopping the V or your biggest fans Condor and me. Who you going to tell, who's going to believe you, who's going to let you get away with being a traitor? You can go back to the

Agency. Get any posting you want in the real world. You'll be a star without us. You can take their combat buyout, go build sand castles on the shore. Get a lucky not-Chris, get some kids, get old and gray and never know where you might have gone or the good you might have done."

"Or?"

"Or find out." Sami smiled. "We want you and need you to be you with us."

"Why are you doing this?"

"I know some of the streets in this night and what should be done."

"Why him? Why Condor?"

"I think he discovered he's always been this kind of crazy."

Sami stood back and settled in his shoes, said: "But it's up to you. Isn't that great? That's what all our fighting and dying is for, so it can be up to you."

Feels like something is skimming the air above me, watching me.

The man who'd been sent to save her, get her, walked back and got in his silver car that was parked pointed out of this suburban cul-de-sac. Faye heard him key the engine, heard it rumble, purr. And in the gray light, she saw him lean across that car's front seat.

Heard the clunk, saw the slow swing of gaping metal create a choice for her.

A waiting engine rumbled in that gray light.

As she stared at the car's empty front passenger *shotgun seat*.

At that car's open door.

Keep reading for the explosive short-story prequel,

NEXT DAY OF THE CONDOR

by

JAMES GRADY

They led him out of the CIA's secret insane asylum as the sun set over autumn's forest there in Maine.

Brian and Doug walked on either side of him, Brian a half-step back on the right, the package's strong side, because even when there'll be no problem, it pays to be prepared beyond a government salary you can only collect if you're still alive.

Brian and Doug seemed pleasant. Younger, *of course*, with functional yet fashionable short hair. Doug sported stubble that tomorrow could let him blend into Kabul with little more than a *shemagh* head wrap and minor clothing adjustments from the American mall apparel he wore today. Brian and Doug introduced themselves to the package at the Maine castle's front security desk. He hoped their mission was to take him where they said he was supposed to go and not to some deserted ditch in the woods.

Two sets of footsteps walked behind him and his escorts, but in what passes for our reality, he could only hear the walker with the clunky shoes. The soundless steps made more powerful cosmic vibrations.

The clunky shoes belonged to Dr. Quinton, who'd

succeeded the murdered Dr. Friedman and mandated Performance Protocols to replace the patient-centric approach of his predecessor, policies that hadn't gotten that psychiatrist ice picked through his ear, but why not use that tragic opportunity to institute a new approach of accountability?

After all, you can't be wrong if you've got the right numbers.

The soundless steps are the scruffy-sneakers footfalls of blond nurse Vicki.

She wore electric-red lipstick.

And her wedding band linked to her high school sweetheart who like every day for the last eight years lay in a Bangor Veterans' Home bed tubed & cabled to beeping machines tracking the flatline of his brain waves and his heart that refused to surrender.

The beating of that heart haunts the soft steps of she who no one really knows.

Except for the silver-haired man walking ahead of her from this secret castle.

And he's nuts, so . . .

The dimming of the day activates sensors in the castle's walled parking lot where these five public servants emerge. Brian and Doug steer the parade toward a "van camper," gray metal and tinted-black glass side windows, small enough to parallel park, big enough for "road living" behind two cushioned chairs facing the sloped windshield. Utah license plates lied with their implication of *not a government ride*.

Doug said: "October used to be colder."

Brian eyed the package's scruffy black leather jacket. "Seems like a nice enough guy, moves better than his silver hair might make you think."

Doug slid open the van's side rear door with a whirring

rumble. Lights came on in the rear interior with built-in beds on each side of a narrow aisle.

Brian said: "How we going to do this?"

Dr. Quinton took a step—

Stopped by Nurse Vicki, who thrust one hand at the psychiatrist's chest and used her other to pluck the purse-like black medical case from his grasp.

"Protocols dictate—"

"This is still America," said Vicki. "No dictators."

Dr. Quinton blinked but she was beyond that, standing in front of the package with the cobalt blue eyes, looking straight at him as she said: "Are you ready?"

"Does that matter?"

Her ruby smile said *yes*, said *no*.

He spoke to both her and the two *soft clothes* soldiers: "Where do you want me?"

"Like she said," answered Doug, "it's a free country. Pick either bed."

The package chose the slab on the shotgun seat's side of the van because it was less likely to catch a bullet crashing through the windshield to take out the driver.

Nurse Vicki entered the van behind him.

Said: "You need to take your jacket off."

"Might be more comfortable to stay that way," called Brian as he climbed behind the steering wheel and slammed the driver's door shut.

The black leather jacket had been his *before*, but *now* the inner pocket over his heart held a laboratory-aged wallet with never-used IDs and credit cards. Felt sad to take off his old friend, the black leather jacket. Felt good to shed its weight of new lies.

He wore a long-sleeved, suitable-for-an-office blue shirt over black long-sleeved thermal underwear suitable for the autumn forest. Fumbled with the buttons on his shirt.

Sensed the nurse resisting helping him pull off the thermal underwear.

He sat on the bed. Naked from the waist up. Shivered, maybe from the evening chill, maybe from the proximity of a red-lipped younger woman.

Who couldn't help herself, cared about who she was and was a nurse, stared at his scars but there was nothing she could do for them now, for him, she was not that able.

Or free.

She unzipped the medical bag that opened like the jaws of a trap: one side held hypodermic needles, alcohol and swabs, the other side held pill bottles.

"You already took your final dose of meds back in the ward," she said.

"I took what they gave me. Hope that's not *final*."

Crimson lips curled in a smile. Tears shimmered in her green eyes.

He said: "I'm glad it's you giving me the needle."

"Had to be," she whispered.

Swabbed his bare left shoulder.

Slid the needle into his flesh.

Pushed the plunger.

Said: "Not long now."

He dressed, stood to tuck his shirts into his black jeans.

Nurse Vicki turned down the blanket on the rack he'd chosen.

"Might want to keep your shoes on," said Doug from outside the van.

The package stretched out on his back, pillow under his head.

"Just a tip," said Doug. "Straps *first* is more comfortable."

Vicki—*made it through night school working as a grocery checker and sitting vigil beside a hospital bed where the patient never stirred*—Vicki fastened safety straps across the prone man, tucked the blanket over him to his chin, knew he could have been her father, knew she could have made him one, knew that wasn't—*isn't*—what mattered or what decided what was never going to be more than stolen heartbeats of rebellion and escape, comfort and yearning, the fever of beasts.

Let it go. Let it go.

"Do you remember the new name you picked?" she asked him. "*Not* Condor."

"How can I not be who I am?"

"That's part of the deal to get you out of here. Back to the real world."

"So that's where I'm going." His smile was sly.

"So they tell me." Her smile was honest. "Who are you, Condor?"

"Vin."

"*V* for *Vicki*," she said, like it was nothing.

"Yes," he lied to let her have everything he could give.

She pressed her crimson lips to his mouth: *Last kiss.*

Floated out of the van, a blur of white, the night spinning as Doug whirred the side door closed, climbed into the shotgun seat, slammed his door *thunk.*

Condor, Vin, whoever he was dropped into a black hole.

Drugged sleep. Flashes of sight, of sound, dreams in a heartbeat rhythm.

. . . white stripes flick through a night road's headlights . . .

. . . Springsteen guitars "State Trooper" . . .

. . . beeping machines web a hollow Marine to a hospital bed . . .

. . . naked thighs straining *yes yes yes* . . .

. . . *snap-clack* of a chambering .45 . . .

. . . red lips . . .

. . . Arab Spring crowds: *"Lib-er-te! Lib-er-te!"* . . .

. . . footsteps behind you on Paris cobblestones . . .

. . . the mailman clings to his pouch . . .

. . . drone's view of a rushing closer city square . . .

. . . plopped on a closet toilet, no pants, some guy saying, *"Okay, here you go"* . . .

. . . walk into the alley, a friend waves you forward . . .

JOLT. Awake. He felt himself . . . awake. Sunlight through black glass windows.

Blink and you're flat on your back on a bed in a van. That's stopped.

Coffee, that wondrous rich aroma.

"Okay, man," said . . . *Doug*, his name is Doug. "Straps are off. Sit up, have a cup of the good stuff from inside."

Inside where? Where am I?

He sipped coffee cut with milk from a paper cup logoed: 'bucks!

"You gotta go again?" said Brian from the behind the wheel of the parked van. "We took you in the middle of the night, but . . . *Hey*, you're a guy that age and your med reports say—*score*, by the way! The daily use pill with the TV commercial of the man and woman sitting in side-by-side bathtubs."

"Let's get you together before we meet the world," said Doug.

The Special Ops guys let him cram himself into the closet bathroom.

"Remember," Doug said through the closed bathroom door: "Your name is Vin."

After he flushed the van toilet—*Such a weird concept!*—Doug met him in the cramped aisle between the beds. Passed him a paper cup of pills to help him forget what he wasn't supposed to remember, and act like he believed what other people saw.

A plastic bag labeled "For Our Forgetful Guests!" that had been repurposed from a Los Angeles hotel waited beside the metal sink. The bag held a disposable toothbrush and a tiny tube of toothpaste trademarked with a notorious TV cartoon squirrel.

"We figured," said Doug, "feel fresh for a fresh start."

Brian called out from behind the van's steering wheel: "Don't be impressed, he's had the whole ride here to think of that one."

Mouthful of minty toothpaste.

The sink faucet worked—*Amazing!* He rinsed, spit.

Raised his eyes to the metal plate polished to reflect like a mirror.

Saw a silver-haired, craggy & scarred faced, blue-eyed man staring back at him.

Whispered: "Your name is Vin."

Thought: *"Condor."*

Radio voice from the van's dashboard:

"—is it for this edition of *Rush Hour Rundown* on New Jersey Public Radio, but throughout the day, stories we'll be following include attempts to bring Occupy Wall Street movements to middle America, life after Gadhafi in war-torn Libya, the last days of that Ohio zookeeper who freed his wild animals and then killed himself, and the billionaire brothers who've bought a chunk of America's politics, plus the latest actor to play Superman talks about his divorce from the, *um*, generously proportioned socialite hired by reality TV to play someone like herself, and one of our only two surviving Beatles is getting married—again. Finally, *remember*: today we're supposed to be terrified. Go forth in fear."

WHAT?

"Coming up, the third in our six-part series on how climate change—"

Click, off went the radio as Brian turned: "Did you say something?"

Doug held out the black leather jacket to *Vin*, said: "You ready to go?"

Then slid open the van's rear compartment side door and with the nostalgia of a paratrooper, hopped out into the rush of cool gray sunshine.

The silver-haired man put on his black leather jacket.

Stepped out into the light.

I'm in a parking lot.

Low gray sky, cool sun glistening on rows of parked cars surrounding a tan cement crouched-dragon building. Waves of sound whooshing past.

Slouching from the dragon building came a trio of zombies.

"No fucking way!" muttered Vin, muttered Condor.

Zombies, but their makeup and costumes were so lame you could tell who they weren't.

"Happy Halloween," said Brian as he posted beside Vin.

The zombies climbed into a five-year-old car with New Jersey license plates.

Doug said: "Today everybody else is in costume."

His partner shook his head: "Don't be impressed. He's had the whole ride to think of that one, too."

"Go figure," said Doug. "It's fucking 2011 and everywhere you look, zombies."

"If we've got zombies," said Condor, said Vin, "do you got guns?"

Call it a pause in the cool morning air.

Then Doug answered: "We're fully sanctioned."

Condor shrugged. "As long as what you're full of is sanction."

The Escort Operatives stared at him with eyes that were stone canyons.

"You expecting trouble?" said Brian.

"Always. Never." Condor shook his head. "My meds are supposed to suffocate expectations."

"You just need some breakfast," said Brian. "Stand here a minute, get your land legs under you, get your breath, then we'll get something to eat."

"Want to do *t'ai chi*?" Doug gestured to a white gazebo in the corner of the parking lot. "Get your form on?"

"That's not low-profile," said Vin, said Condor. "Citizens might think I'm weird."

"Really," said Brian. "*That's* what would make you seem weird?"

"Remember, *Vin*," said Doug: "We can do anything we want as long as nobody ever knows who we are. You know that's the heart and hard of any Op, so play it cool. Low key. Absolutely normal."

"Normal has been a problem."

"You're past that now," said Brian. "Remember?"

"Meanwhile," said Doug, "welcome to the Nick Logar rest stop on the New Jersey Turnpike."

"Monday morning, Halloween, 2011," said Brian. "Zero-nine-three-three."

Doug frowned. "Who was Nick Logar?"

"Who cares?" said Brian.

Condor surprised them: "Poet. Black & white movies days, tough times, people working hard to just hold on, rich guys on top even after the stock market crash, bad guys savaging the world. Kind of quirky getting a rest stop named after Nick Logar. Rebel politics, road crazy. But nobody likes to talk about that, just his Congressional Medal of Honor and Pulitzer Prize for poetry no one reads, except for that famous one that doesn't flap the flag like— *God, it feels good to just talk!*"

"And look at you!" said Doug. "Got a lot to say and up on literature and shit."

"My first spy job was to know things like that."

Brian shrugged. "My first was a takeout in Tehran. We're not talking dinner."

"Let's talk breakfast," said Doug.

"Fuck talking," said Brian. "Let's eat."

The silver-haired man brushed his hands down the front of his black leather jacket, amateurishly revealing worry over not finding a gun hidden under there and thus implying that years of confinement had succeeded in making him not *Condor* but *Vin*.

"Chill," said Brian. "Everything's normal and Okay. Just look."

Condor didn't tell his Escort Operative that *normal* and *Okay* are not the same.

But he did *look*.

The parked gray van faced a chain-link fence that made the north boundary of the rest stop. Beyond the fence, a yellowed marsh filled the median between northbound and southbound lanes of the Turnpike. The van sat closer to the southbound lane, and that route's exit into the rest stop made a sloping hill behind the white gazebo.

The van's rear bumper faced four rows of cars parked in white-striped spaces on the side of the rest stop's crouching dragon "facility" building, tan cement walls and a New Mexico meets Hong Kong green roof. The facility sat on a raised knoll to stay above rainwater runoff. Glass doors front & centered the facility, a dragon's face where a protruding tongue of concrete steps led down to the pavement between a mustache of two sloped ramps. The glass doors reflected the nearly full front parking lot.

People. Lots and lots of people.

A squat bleached blond woman in a pink mohair

sweater rummaged in her car's open trunk with one hand while her other held a straining leash clipped to the collar of a yippy terrier. The dog's and the bleached blonde's pink sweaters matched.

A young guy wearing a padded black costume, hip or horror, Condor couldn't tell, carried a brown paper sack as he walked toward the facility's rear and waiting green Dumpsters below circling seagulls, plus the entrance to the northbound road, the direction a mouse named Stuart Little took looking for love and a life to call his own.

A smiling family of Japanese tourists clustered together in the parking lot for pictures one of them took with a cell phone.

Call him twenty-four looking nineteen, baseball cap on backwards, gray sweatshirt, low-slung blue jeans, sneakers shuffling toward the facility.

Two men in suits parked their dark-colored car.

A married couple who'd seen fifty in their rearview mirrors stepped out of their parked Chevy, slammed its doors, and sighed as they shuffled in to use the bathrooms.

My next is now, thought Condor.

Brian said: "Let's get something before."

"Before what?" said Condor as his escorts walked him toward the facility.

Doug said: "Before your transfer ride shows up. Should have been here already."

"What about you guys?"

"Places to go," said Brian, "people to see."

"Is this the time you're going to do more than just *see*?" said Doug.

"Shut the fuck up," said his partner. Lovingly.

Three soda machines selling bottles and cans of caffeine & sugar & chemical concoctions stood sentinel near the ramp Condor and his escorts took to the glass front doors, past a bench where three *probably* just graduated high school girls sat, two of them wearing *hijab* headdresses, all of them smoking cigarettes.

What struck Condor inside the rest-stop facility was its atmosphere of closeness, of containment. The densely packed air smelled of . . .

Of floor tiles. Crackling meat grease. Hot sugar. Lemon-scented ammonia.

Ahead gaped entrances for MEN'S and LADIES' rooms. The wall between the restrooms held a YOU ARE HERE map and a bronze plaque with lines of writing that travelers hurrying into the bathrooms only glanced at but Condor read:

> Drive, drive on. These are the highways of our lives.
>
> Dwell not on the sharp quiet madness of our collective soul.
>
> Call us all New Jersey. Call us all Americans, as on we go
>
> alone together.

Nick Logar

Off to Condor's left waited the gift shop, wall racks of celebrity magazines and candy, glass coolers with yet more cans of syrupy caffeine, displays of key chains dangling green plastic models of the Statue of Liberty, T-shirts and buttons that "hearted" New York, postcards that nobody mailed anymore.

He turned right, toward the food court, a long open corridor with garish neon signs above each stop where money could be exchanged for sustenance.

There was 'bucks, the coffee-centered franchise intent on conquering the world.

DANDY DONUTS! came next in line, sold coffee, too, essentially the same concoctions as 'bucks but somehow not as costly.

The red, white & green logo for SACCO'S ITALIA seen mostly in airports, train stations or rest stops centered the food stops wall.

Italian green gave way to broccoli green letters on a white background: NATURAL EATS & FRO YO, where display cases held plastic sealed salads and silver machines hummed behind the counter.

Last in the line of eateries came BURGER BONANZA, the third biggest chain of hamburger and fries and cola drive-ins of Condor's youth, still clinging to that national sales rank partially because a dozen years remained on the company's fifty-year exclusive lease for this state's Turnpike stops signed with an unindicted former governor.

"Come on," Brian told Condor.

Gray tables lined the red tiles between the wall of eateries and the not-quite-ceiling-to-floor windows. Travelers sat on hard-to-shoplift black metal chairs.

Brian took a chair facing those front windows. Condor sat where he could look down the food court to the main doors, or look left out to the front parking lot through the wall of windows, or look right and see Doug shuffling in service lines. Behind Condor, a door labeled OFFICE waited near a glass door under a red sign glowing FIRE EXIT.

"What time is it?" asked Condor.

"No worries," said Brian. "We're where we belong and when we should be."

Doug came to them balancing cardboard trays like a

man who'd worked his way through college as a waiter. The trays held 'bucks cups, plastic glasses of white yogurt and strawberry chunks, containers of raisins and granola, bananas, spoons, napkins, a white plastic knife almost useless for cutting someone's throat.

"And six donuts?" said Brian.

"The secret to life is knowing how to mix and match," said his partner. "Evens out healthwise with the yogurt. Gives us some bulk and energy for the ride back. Three classic chocolate donuts, three seasonal special pumpkin maple donuts. In good conscience, how could we pass those up?"

"You guys are driving back to Maine?" said Condor.

"Brooklyn," said Brian as he sliced a banana into his yogurt.

"Somebody's insisting on an overnight there," explained his partner.

Two kindergarten-aged boys ran past the table trailed by their harried mother.

"You wouldn't believe Brooklyn now," Brian told Condor.

"I didn't believe it then."

Doug said: "There's this ultra-hip coffee shop not far from—"

"Hey!" said his partner.

"Come on," Doug told his partner. "You can't just show up hoping she will."

The silver-haired man, who was old enough to be the two gunners' father, smiled.

Said: "We've all done that."

"What's the worst that could happen if you finally talked to her?" said Doug.

Condor shrugged. "You could watch your dreams die in her eyes."

"Me," said Doug, "I was gonna say *alimony*, but, troop, if you do not engage the enemy, you create no chance of success."

His partner whispered: "Who's the enemy?"

"Ourselves," said Condor.

Brian blinked at the silver-haired legend. "*My man*: Welcome back!"

Condor ate his pumpkin-maple donut as he stared out the window at travelers walking to and from their steel rides. Saw the guy dressed in padded black close the door on . . . *yes*, it *was* an old black hearse, walking away, carrying a gym bag toward the south end of the rest stop and the rows of gas pumps controlled by attendants whose jobs were protected by state law. A yellow rental truck drove through Condor's view.

Buzz went cell phones in his escorts' pockets.

Doug read the text message, said: "Link-up ETA twelve minutes."

Seven minutes later, these three men were at the facility's main doors, Doug going through first, Brian posting drag, and Condor—

Flash!

From a cell phone held by a curly-haired woman on the other side of a glass door from Condor: *blurry picture* at best, and *sure*, she appeared innocently overwhelmed by carrying her purse and a takeout tray with two coffees, probably just clumsy fingers on her device, plus she didn't seem to notice that Brian followed her to her car, cell phoned photos of her and her license plate and her driver who stereotyped *husband*, as they drove to the southbound exit just ahead of a rusty black hearse, while hundreds of miles away near Washington, D.C., their metrics became an I&M (Investigate & Monitor) upload.

Doug and Condor posted near the parked van.

Forty feet away, an easy (for him) pistol shot, Brian drifted amidst parked cars.

Zen. They were here. They were now. Not waiting: *being*, *doing*. Ready *for*.

The red car drove around the dragon facility from the northbound entrance. A Japanese brand built in Tennessee that glided ever closer to two men standing by a gray van near the white gazebo.

Where the red car parked.

She opened the driver's door. Let them see no one rode with her (*unless they were laying on the backseat floor or huddled in the trunk*). Kept her hands in sight as she walked toward them, and *yes*, it was only a cell phone in her left hand.

Statistically, most people shoot right handed.

"Hey," she said: "Aren't you friends of Gary Pettigrew?"

"Don't know the guy," answered Doug. Said *guy* and not *him* or *man*.

"So where you from?"

"Where we're going," answered Doug, sounding ordinary enough for any eavesdropper (none around) but not a likely response from a random stranger.

"Then I'm in the right place." She grinned. "Sorry I'm late. Traffic."

Her left hand showed them the package's picture in her cell phone.

"You must be Condor," she said, extending her right hand to shake his.

"*Vin*," corrected Doug. "But yeah."

She was young. Short black hair. Clean caramel complexion and bright ebony eyes. Dark slacks and a white blouse under an unbuttoned navy blue jacket.

Said: "Want to see my credentials?"

"If you're bogus and got the recognition code, you'll pack fake flash," said Doug.

"*Damn it!* I've been dying for a chance to whip out my ID: *Homeland Security, up against the wall!*"

"Rookie," said Doug.

"Who else would get stuck with a one-day road trip up to here and back to D.C.?"

Her voice stayed easy. "I'm Malati Chavali, and is that guy walking this way one of us?"

Doug smiled: "Yeah, *rook*, he's with us."

Brian drifted to her red car, glanced in the backseat, turned and said like it was the reason for his detour: "Where do you want his two bags?"

"What do you think?" she said to Doug—looked at Condor. "*I'm sorry!* I should ask *you*, it's not like you're . . ."

"Just a package?" said the man who could technically *maybe* be her grandfather.

"And you want me to call you *Vin*, right?"

He shrugged. "Mission requirements."

"Speaking of," said Brian. "We gotta hit the road."

"Brooklyn calls," joked his partner.

Condor's suitcases went in the red car's trunk.

He and its driver, Malati, watched the gray van pull out of its parking space and drive onto the northbound ramp . . . gone.

"Can I ask you a favor?" she said to the silver-haired man as they stood in the cool morning air. "I know you're probably anxious to get to your new apartment—row house, actually, on Capitol Hill—your Settlement Specialist will meet us there, we'll call her when we hit the Beltway and . . . The thing is, I'm dying for coffee."

"Wouldn't want you to die," said Condor. "How would I get where I'm going?"

"There is that," she said.

They walked toward the rest stop's facility.

"Before we get where there are ears," he said as they moved between parked cars lined in rows of shiny steel, "you're Home Sec, not CIA?"

"Actually, detailed to the National Resources Operations Division of the Office of the Director of National Intelligence—there's CIA on staff there, too, but me . . . Yeah, I'm in Home Sec. For now. Grad school at Georgetown—"

"Don't vomit your whole cover story first chance you get," said the silver-haired man as they neared the main doors. "Even if it's true. Maybe especially if it's true."

Laughing coworkers in Groucho Marx glasses strode past them.

Malati whispered: "Sorry."

He held the building door open for her. "Shit happens. So far, ours works."

She smiled *thank you* as she stepped past the older gentleman.

Heard him say: "Should you have let me behind you?"

A chill claimed her amidst the thick air inside the rest-stop facility.

She answered: "I don't know."

Condor shrugged. "Too late to think about it now.

"I'm going in there," he said, pointing to the MEN's room. "Get your coffee and we'll meet at a table."

"I thought I was in charge."

"Good," he said. Walked into the bathroom, left her standing there. Alone.

Five minutes later, he spotted her sitting at a table in the food court facing the restrooms, the gift shop and the main doors. Tactically acceptable. The wall of eateries waited to her right, the windows to the parking lot on her heartside. Her eyes locked on him as he walked toward where she sat with two cups from 'bucks on the table.

"Please," she said. "Sit. We've got time."

"You sure?"

"No. But we can make it work."

He settled on the black steel chair facing her.

"Look around," she said. "Most people are tuned out. Plugged into their cells or tablets. Not really here. Plus there's nobody behind me, right? Nobody behind you. Nobody close enough to hear even if we're not careful what we say."

He gave her a nod and the smile that wanted to come.

"I'd like to start over," she said. "The coffee's a peace offering."

"Okay. We're probably going to have to stop at least once before D.C. anyway."

"When you want, when we can." She took a sip from her cup, left no lipstick stain.

Don't think about red lipstick. Gone. That's the forever. This is now.

Malati said: "Somehow now I don't think you're just, *say*, a former asset or KGB defector who's been in a retirement program and needs routine relocation."

"What do you know?"

"The code name I'm now not supposed to use." Malati shrugged. "*Vin*. Weird first name, but *whatever*, Vin: I volunteered for this *nobody wanted it* gig. Extra duty. Trying to prove I'm competent, trustable, a team player with initiative."

"What do you want?" he said.

"To do more than earn a paycheck. Serve my country. Do some good."

"And under that essay answer?"

"I don't want to be somebody who doesn't know what's really going on."

"*Reality*," he said: "I've heard of that."

He sipped his coffee. She'd gotten black and a couple to-go creamers so he could decide. He popped the lid off the cup, poured in cream, thought: *Why not?*

"Yesterday our bosses decided I was no longer crazy.

"Or," he added, "at least not so crazy that I couldn't be released to a kind of free."

Though most people would have seen nothing, Condor sensed her tense up, but she sat there and *took it*.

Malati said: "Are you?"

"Not so crazy or *kind of free?"*

"It's your answer."

And *that* made him like her. Told him she might be worth it.

"Guess we'll see," he said. "You're my driver."

"Just for this road trip." She blurted: "I want to learn."

Motion outside pulled his eyes from her to look out the window.

A school bus: classic yellow, slowing down out front. The school bus seemed to wobble, stopped haphazardly near the rows of citizens' parked vehicles.

He nodded toward the school bus. "Did you ever ride one of those?"

"I'm not supposed to vomit my cover story. Even if it's true."

"Lesson one," he told her. "Give trust to get trust."

"That's not my first lesson from you." That acknowledgment made him like her even more as she added: "Yeah, I did bus time in Kansas City."

"We're not in Kansas anymore," he quoted.

"*Hey!*" she said. "We're talking Kansas City, *Missouri*. Whole different place."

They laughed together and as she relaxed into *this is*

where I'm from stories, he looked around at where they were.

Sitting at a table by himself was a fortyish man munching a morning cheeseburger, tie loosened over a cheap shirt already straining against too many such meals, a franchise manager who couldn't figure out why his boss hated him. Two tables away sat a thirtyish mom leaning her forehead into one hand while the other held the cell phone against her ear for the report from the school on her daughter who'd been the teenage pregnancy that ended in getting out of what was now, for both, their hometown. Two male medical techs in green scrubs munched on fried chicken, one was white, one was black, neither wanted to get back to the hospital where they could only give morphine and more bills to a cancer warrior. There sat a down-vest-over-a-white sweater blond beauty, *like*, OMG machine-gun texting her cell phone and being *super careful* to not say she was scared to death because she had *no clue* about what came after nineteen. The gray-haired couple barely older than Condor sat staring everywhere but at each other and seeing nowhere better they could go. The two-years-out-of-college man who worked the night shift at a factory job one level above the summer work he'd done to help him pay for school sat drinking Diet Coke against the yawns, dreading tomorrow with its first-of-the-month loan bills coming to the clapboard house where he lived in the basement below his working parents who loved him so much. Like Malati noted, many of the road-dazed travelers seemed hypnotized by screens.

We're all packages transporting from some there to another where.

And yet, thought Condor, we find the hope or the dreams or the responsibility, the dignity and courage to push ourselves away from the tables at this nowhere transit zone, get up, get up *again*, go outside, get in our cars and go, *go on*, get to where we can, tears *yes,* but laughter at it all and at ourselves, because if nothing else, this is the ride we got and we refuse to just surrender.

The Nick Logar rest stop.

These are the highways of our lives.

". . . so my parents wanted me to go into business, *but*," Malati shrugged, "profit doesn't turn me on as much as purpose."

Children. Chattering. Squealing. Half a dozen of them running through the main doors *TO THE BATHROOMS!* ahead of a woman teacher shouting: *"Stay together!"*

Condor and Malati looked out the window.

Saw a straggling line of second graders, marching across the parking lot from the school bus. Some kids wore Halloween glory—a witch, a fairy tale princess, a ghost, a cowboy, Saturday-morning-cartoon costumes. All the kids carried an orange "Trick or Treat!" plastic bucket in the shape of a pumpkin stenciled with black eyes, a toothy grin and a corporate logo from the chain drugstore that accidentally ordered too many of the buckets to sell but cleverly recouped a tax donation to their local elementary school. As the children marched, those pumpkin heads swung wildly on wire loop handles gripped in their tiny hands.

"Time for us to go," said Condor.

Didn't matter who was in charge, they both knew he was right.

At the main entrance, Condor—*no*: Vin, his name is Vin—*the package*, brushed her out of the way as he held a door for a man not much older than Malati, a guy in a wheelchair who was rolling himself up the ramp, a Philly vet named Warren Iverson who wore his Army jacket

from the Tenth Mountain Division and a smile on his boyish face.

Malati realized Vin didn't just notice the vet with wasted
legs, Vin *saw* him.

Said: "Better hurry, man. A stampede of short stuffs is
coming up behind you."

"Always." Warren rolled past the silver-haired man in
the black leather jacket.

Malati leaned close to Vin as they stepped outside *and*
aside to let the parade of costumed kids squeal their way
into this wondrous rest stop oasis.

She whispered: "You keep doing stuff like that, you'll
ruin your tough guy act."

"Be your cover," Vin told her. "Besides, looks like he's
one of the men and women who pay when we fuck up our
job. Or some politician fucks it up for us."

He shrugged.

"Do what should be done, nothing special about that,"
he told her sounding *so much* like her father.

But only he heard the *beep . . . beep . . . beep* of machines webbed to a hospital bed as he said: "Probably I
owe guys like him something beyond *coulda* and *shoulda*."

She understood what he said but not what he meant.

Just walk beside him. Figure out what you can.

"My car's still there," she said as they started down one
ramp to the parking lot.

The red Japanese motion machine, squatting *way over*
by the north border fence and the white gazebo where ex-
iting the Turnpike southbound came a black hearse.

The black hearse parked in a row of cars near Malati's
red ride. As the hearse glided to a stop, Condor envisioned
the YOU ARE HERE map mounted on the wall between
the bathrooms. Nick Logar was one of the few rest stops

on the New Jersey Turnpike that serviced traffic going both directions. The padded-black-clad driver got out of the hearse, opened its back door. If he'd forgotten something at this rest stop from when he left earlier behind the southbound suspect cell phone photo couple, Mr. Black Costume would have had to drive about ten miles before he could exit, get back on the Turnpike north, then drive here, *but* . . . But then he would have needed to drive *past* this place or through it, go further north to another exit turnaround, again maybe ten miles away in order to come back and exit southbound back into the rest stop, *into here.*

Why make that long circle drive?

What's that sound? thought Condor as he and Malati neared the bottom of the ramp to the parking lot where two burly men stood with unlit cigarettes dangling from their lips. The man wearing the COUNTY SCHOOLS windbreaker pulled a silver lighter from his left front shirt pocket, clicked it open and thumbed its wheel to summon a flame and ignite the white-papered cancer sticks, barely a pause as that bus driver said:

"Couldn't believe it, twenty minutes from the school if the traffic held, sure as shit ain't holding now, shut down and backed up behind me, so I got off lucky, *whump*, bus starts to shake, *what the fuck*, get it to this exit and wrestle it down over there, at least get the kids where they can pee, but my tires got four little black steel like . . . like stars or some other pointy things, and with three flats, we barely made it here."

Malati felt *Vin* drift her away from her waiting car, into the front parking lot.

"Listen!" he said. Made them stop and stand still, absolutely still.

"To what?"

"There's no whooshing."

He faced the unseen empty lanes of the expressway going south, turned to look past the hulk of the rest stop facility to the unseen empty expressway lanes going north.

Heard that silence.

Felt his own thundering heart.

From deep inside Malati came the whisper: *"We've got to go now."*

They looked across rows of parked vehicles toward her distant red car.

Saw ordinary human beings, everyday people strolling to and fro, the guy in black walking toward the facility from the hearse. A honeymoon couple laughed.

The new husband aimed his cell phone camera.

The happy bride raised her face to the open sky.

Like a red mist flowered her skull as she flipped to the parking lot pavement.

The husband almost dropped his cell phone before a crimson fountain from his spine burst out of his blue-shirted chest.

Time became a child's clear marble dropped into a swimming pool . . .

. . . to slowly sink.

Not seeing what I'm seeing! Malati's mind registered her package, her responsibility, her . . . Condor, *call him Vin*: he lunged before the second shot's *crack!*

What she saw over rows of parked cars at an ordinary New Jersey Turnpike rest stop on an ordinary autumn Halloween was the not-so-far-away guy in black.

What she saw was that ordinary American boy face behind an assault rifle.

A gorilla roared from where the bus driver and the salesman were smoking.

The gunman sprayed bullets at what he heard.

The salesman and bus driver dropped twitching, bleeding, moaning, dying near the concrete ramp to where the children were.

Condor pulled the young fed down between two parked cars.

Yelled: "Can you get a good shot?"

"I don't have a gun! I'm not that kind of spy! And you're a crazy old man!"

Machine gun fire. Screams.

"Fucking Brooklyn." Condor waved her between two cars, stayed low as he scrambled two more cars over, eased his head above the hood of steel shelter.

The shooter looked like the robot of death. Padding under his black shirt and pants: *Had to be ballistic armor.* Working the assault rifle, thumbing the release to drop the spent magazine to the parking lot pavement, reaching in a pouch to pull out an expanded capacity mag and slap it home: that movie-star reload let Condor see a combat pump shotgun strapped across the robot's chest.

The robot stalked toward where Condor and Malati hid.

Gotcha! whirled the other way to *rat-a-tat-tat* a line of bullet holes through the food court's wall of windows. Condor spotted a pistol SWAT-style strapped to the shooter's right leg, a combat knife sheathed on his left ankle, strapped-on pouches. *Is that a computer tablet dangling from his belt?*

Condor dropped between the cars.

Malati said: "What's he doing?"

"Killing people."

"Why?"

"Because he can."

The machine gun buzzed like a monster's vibrating tongue.

"Did you see his hearse?" said Condor.

Malati started to rise—

Got jerked down. "You don't know where he's looking! You got no diversion!"

She shuddered in his grasp.

Condor said: "Shiny metal where the coffin should ride. Think they're bins."

"Bins?"

"The bus driver pulled black steel stars out of his tires. Caltrops. Tactical steel road tire spikes. State troopers and Army ambushers scatter them on the highway."

Somewhere in the parking lot a woman screamed like a fleeing banshee.

Malati shook her head. "What does that have to do with bins and where would—"

The machine gun roared.

No more banshee screaming.

"Maybe he got the spikes on Amazon," said Condor. "Get lots, rig metal bins in the coffin space. Cut holes in the back of the hearse, driver-controllable lids on the bins. He drove every stretch of road every direction out of here, probably weaving lane to lane to cover all drivable asphalt, picking his release spots just past or just before the rest stop exits and entrances, dropping, *what*, couple thousand of those things. A few flat tires, cars crashing into each other, stopped, and it's the mother of all backups every way in or out of here, walls of steel. He's isolated his kill zone. Stalled any rescue or escape."

BOOM! The robot switched to his shotgun.

Malati waved her arm: "When he's shooting the other way we can make it across the parking lot toward the Turnpike! Short fence, hop it, run, hide—"

She saw where Condor was looking.

The empty school bus.

She said: "All those kids."

He said: "All us everybody."

Machine gun bullets cut a line over their heads like the contrail of a jet on its way across this cool blue sky.

Her spine tensed. Her mind pushed against her forehead.

He said: "Cell phone!"

Pressed against her ear. "911 is . . . *Due to a high volume*—"

"Half the people here. Unless he's got a jammer."

"You can buy those?"

"You tell me, you're the one from the real world."

Car windows shatter. Bullets whine.

Why now? Why here? Why me?

Why not.

Her eyes were welded wide. "Where is he? Is he coming— Wait!"

Malati swooped the screen of her cell phone. Eased her cell above the car.

Camera app, the phone like a periscope lens scanning the sounds of gunfire.

Like a movie.

"He's moving toward the main doors!"

Standing tall, *man*, striding toward the funnel for the fools—*Whoops*: fat guy in parking lot, *where'd he pop up from*, pulling at the passenger door on that green car *bullets burst* and he's dancing and spraying red and sliding down to *dead, motherfucker*.

The side fire door of the rest stop facility flies open.

Half a dozen people charge out.

Crying tires as a silver SUV lunges out of its parking lot space.

Malati's cell phone showed the shooter drop flat on the pavement.

He fumbled with the book-sized computer thing lashed to his belt.

Silver SUV slows for six people running to its—

FLASH! by the green Dumpsters *then* came the BOOM! of garage-mixed explosive gel shelled by ball bearings and old nails as the paper sack bomb exploded.

Take that, Columbine motherfuckers! The shooter keyboarded the tablet lashed to his waist so it was re-primed to send a wireless signal to any of his other planted bombs.

Windshield-blasted-glass slivers blinded the silver SUV's driver, an engaged office manager/volunteer at a Paterson, New Jersey, soup kitchen.

Bomb shrapnel hit three of the runners, bodies crashed to the pavement. The other three runners staggered—*arm*, the blast blew off the arm of a mother-of-two lawyer on her way to a deposition, she crumpled, bled out.

Like a cat person on TV, the shooter rocketed off the pavement.

Saw two targets staggering beside the drifting silver SUV.

Sprayed them with bullets. Nailed one, the other, *ah fuck him*, let him stagger away, maybe he's hit, certain he's damaged.

The shooter tossed something like a rock toward the FIRE EXIT side of the facility.

Pop! Purple-smoke grenade, *rescue me* surplus, that store off the interstate.

"The grenade's to scare us," said Condor. "Keep the people inside."

Death's robot faced the stairs and ramps up to the main doors.

Malati stared at the huddled-beside-her silver-haired man in the black jacket who knew, who had to know: "What are we going to do?"

"Be crazier."

"Easy for you to say."

The robot of death. At the bottom of the ramp where the bus driver sprawled over the other smoker's corpse.

Marching out of the main doors: Two women. Teachers. Marching down the ramp straight toward the shooter. Commanding: "Stop! Stop this!"

Behind them, running down the other concrete ramp:

Kids, scared, crying, stumbling down to the parking lot as the young man from Teach For America and some other citizen urge the twenty-one children forward, go, run, *run!*

The main doors whir open.

Out rolls Warren.

Wheelchair. Army jacket. *Fuck-you* face.

Ready to charge. Ready to be *diversion*. Ready to take it to you, motherfucker.

Keep going kids! Run, run!

The shooter's stopped. Standing still. Assault rifle hanging on its sling.

Two teachers close on him, the *maybe maybe* prayer on their faces.

The robot drew his handgun *Bam! Bam-Bam!*

Schoolteachers collapsed in a heap atop the bus driver.

Tidy you want me to be *tidy* you want *tidy* I give you *tidy*!

Warren yelled and spun himself *charge* onto the ramp.

Bam! A third eye blasted into Warren.

The shooter aimed two-handed toward the main doors where Teach For America and some other guy lined up in the V front sight of a fifteen-shot semiautomatic pistol.

Count five blasted rounds into those two bodies, dropped them in a pile, *tidy.*

Wheelchair, carrying dead Warren, obeying inertia, rolling down the ramp—

Stopped as the shooter slammed his gun bore on the ribs under the Army jacket.

Why waste a bullet on this Army jacket guy with a red mush forehead?

He shoved the wheelchair. His force sent it freewheeling up to the flat landing outside the main doors. The burdened wheelchair spun sideways, stopped.

As twenty-one children stampede amidst parked cars.

The assault-rifle-sprayed zinging lead toward them.

But kids are short.

Bullets crashed through cars' windows, punched into steel chassis.

The shooter dropped to the ground.

Stared under rows of parked cars. Undercarriages of mufflers and pipes. Tires propped the cars at least six inches off the pavement and made a slit of scenery.

There, few rows away: running children's legs and feet.

The assault rifle fired a long sweep of bullets under the cars.

Zing ripped out from under the metal that hid Condor and Malati, cut right between where they were crouched, right past the knocked-over 'bucks cup she'd *only*, *God knows why*, just let go of. Slugs slammed into another parked car, punched a hole in one door and out the other. A tire blew. Bullets ricocheted off parking lot asphalt.

Is that smell—

Two kids. Frozen in the lane between parked cars. Bullets zinged past their legs—one wore brown cords his mom picked out, one wore her favorite blue jeans.

The girl pushed her classmate away from the shooter: "Split up!"

She turned to run the other way than the boy so the bad guy couldn't—

Saw two crouching-down adults waving their hands.

Ran between the cars, into the arms of the Grampa guy.

"Got you!" he said as she burrowed her face into his leather jacket.

No wet no red she's not shot. Condor saw a Halloween pumpkin bucket looped through the belt on her blue jeans, a red jacket, white blouse. "*It's not a dorky costume!*" she'd insisted that morning as she did what she was 'posed to and ate her scrambled eggies: "*It's the idea of the flag and it's 'posed to make you think!*" But that glitter on her seven-year-old face? *That,* she said, "*that's me.*" Didn't notice her mother not cry.

Machine-gun roars sliced the air.

The second grader looked back to where she'd been.

Whispered: "Run, Johnny."

The shooter slapped fresh ammo into the assault rifle. *Seen it.* He'd seen running snot-nose kids scramble onto the shutdown school bus across the parking lot. *You can't hide from me.* He machine-gunned the bus. Bullets banged through the yellow metal.

Malati held her cell phone above their parked cars cover.

"He's turning toward—I think he's going to go into the building, the food court!"

Risk it: Condor peeked over the car. Saw the black robot at the facility's main doors. Saw the dead vet in his wheelchair. Saw bodies heaped at the bottom of the ramp: bus driver who smoked, women. Saw the food court's bullet-holed tinted dark windows.

He glared at the little girl with the big brown eyes. "What's your name?"

"Phyllis Azar seven years old live at—"

Create focus.

"You're here. Now. With us."

The seven-year-old girl nodded: The silver-haired guy sounded like a principal!

Empower your asset to gain their trust.

Condor said: "What do you want me to call you?"

Bam! Bam! Bam! Paced steady rhythm shots hit the building.

Suppression fire as the black-clad shooter neared the main doors.

"Daddy calls me *Punkin.*" She shrugged at the orange plastic pumpkin bucket she'd looped to herself with her belt *special* so *no way* would she lose it.

"Punkin, I'm—*Condor*, *Vin*, doesn't matter, she's *Malati.*"

A bullet ricocheted off a car roof.

Punkin said: "We going to be Okay?"

The big girl woman nodded *yes* as Mr. Silver Hair said: "We might get hurt."

"Might get *dead.*" Punkin shook her head. "That would suck."

Malati watched her cell phone: "He's standing at the main doors!"

In the canyon of car metal next row over: a side mirror of an SUV dangled upside down, its cracked glass captured the reflection of a trapped man, woman, child.

Malati inhaled that sight of yesterday, today, tomorrow.

"Condor!" yelled Malati: "Smell that *oh my God!* Why didn't it it's going to—"

Like a piano chord exploded the meds' weight on his mind.

A lightning flash of seeing.

He grabbed the belt around the little girl NEVER NO-BODY 'POSED TO and he's jerking it undone saying: "Fifty-fifty shot at next to no chance in hell and *Punkin!*"

She locked on him as he said: "We got one chance to save anybody!"

Punkin gave him a nod from her bones.

"But you gotta do one thing you're not 'posed to."

Punkin didn't blink.

Condor told her: "You have to say a bad word."

The shooter paused outside the main doors. To his left were a heap of bodies he'd dropped with his pistol—*good fucking shots*. Behind him near the top of the ramp was the listless wheelchair full of some dead older guy wearing an Army jacket.

Crucial question: *Which gun?*

Level up *cool*. Now it's your game.

Nothing like a shotgun for close-quarters tactical situations.

He let the black military-cool rifle dangle on its sling, wrapped his right hand around the pistol grip of the black steel and plastic Italian-made shotgun manufactured after America's 1994 assault weapons ban expired.

And just for a moment, felt regret.

While he loved the high-tech look of his semiautomatic 12 gauge that fed new shells into the chamber after each shot, the *ratchet-clack* of pumping a fresh shell into an old-school "regular" shotgun was *epic*. But besides slowing his rate of fire, a pump shotgun made him clumsy, so as much as he appreciated cool, he knew he'd been smart to go semi-auto, out with the old, in with the new. *Right tool, right job.*

Like he expected, he saw no one standing beyond the closed glass doors.

There's the wall with doors to the bathrooms. There's that stupid plaque.

Good as Bruce Lee, he stomped his discount store black sneaker out to his side, a kick that smacked the circular-steel door-opener pressure plate and like the yawn this place was—used to be, had been *until me*—the doors gaped open for him.

My turn.

He slid through the open doors like a ninja. Blasted buckshot into the gift shop where the old Korean lady behind the counter, *yeah*, she'd ducked somewhere already. *Stay down, honey, I'll be back*. Pirouetted a slo-mo circle until the food court filled his vision—BOOM! Buckshot tore through air that smelled like coffee and burnt hamburgers. Like in *Slaughter Soldier 2* for Xbox, he grabbed a grenade from the pouch on his hip, pulled the pin with his teeth and made a left-handed throw, landed it on the tiles by the health-food rip-off place—BOOM! Purple smoke mushroomed through the food court.

Hope it won't hide too much from security cameras mounted in the ceiling.

He combat jumped into the MEN's room—looked empty, closed aluminum stalls.

Can't fool me with that shit. He switched the shotgun for his pistol, punched two bullets through the wall of the nearest stall.

A man screamed and fell off the toilet where he'd been crouched.

WOMEN's room. Suburban mom sobbing and pleading, holding up her hands.

Mom got shot right through her palm in front of her *crybaby* face.

From the entrance to the food court he surveyed his kingdom of Hell.

Purple smoke thicker at the far end where red letters glowed EXIT and that was a lie, *nowhere to go, suckers*. BOOM he shot that cloud. Some guy charged him throwing coins, made the shooter flinch BOOM, cut down that coin-thrower with a shotgun blast that also shattered a window facing the front parking lot.

Crashing glass: he liked the sound so much he blasted out three more windows.

Cool air and sunlight streamed into the purple-smoked debris of the food court.

He wondered who'd discovered that he'd chained the rear doors shut.

Ringing: a smoke detector in BURGER BONANZA as the meat abandoned on the hot grill crackled out black smoke. Theme music as he surveyed the food court.

Moms draped over their kids. Travelers cowered behind metal tables. Dead guy on the floor—must be a bonus score from the first burst sent through the windows. Pools and dribbles of darkness on the red floor tiles, blood from some-body who'd crawled or been carried away, he'd find them in good time.

For a moment he thought about swinging up his wire-less tablet to set off the other bombs he'd planted by the roads in and out of this rest stop so he could watch the judging-eyes people in here scramble and scream and break cover trying to escape.

Naw, stick to the plan.

Save the bombs for the wanna-be heroes, cops and fire-men who figure a way around the traffic backups and road spikes for their red lights and sirens.

You gotta do the walk, man.

He switched from the could-be-empty shotgun—in all the excitement, he kind of lost count of his shots. Slapped a fresh magazine into the assault rifle.

Stepped out among them, knowing their desperate hopes that he was looking for someone in particular, specific, for somebody who was the *why*, for someone *not me*.

Everybody thinking: *I don't deserve this!*

Walk your purple-smoke-ringing glory and what do you see.

A cash flow corridor of factory food for cubicle fools awaiting coffins.

TVs by the ceiling show talking heads who never say your name.

A lotto screen displays winning numbers for luck you never get.

An ATM machine holds money it won't ever give you.

Two guys hide behind a condiments counter, not so *high school cool* now.

Bald guy, white shirt, tie, name tag, hands in the air, so who's the boss?

College girl, on the floor like a dog, *yeah*, what do you got to say now, bitch?

Black leather biker with a gut wound by the wall, who's scared today?

Somebody praying to the big empty that never cares.

So who gets to play this next round of—

"YOU'RE A BIG BOOGER-HEAD!"

He heard it above the smoke detector ringing.

From outside. Through the shot-out windows. The parking lot. A . . . a kid.

"YOU'RE A SCARED MEANIE!"

Some little girl. Off the bus. Out there hiding amidst the parked cars.

"NOBODY WANTS TO FUCK YOU!"

The shooter cocked his head.

"NOBODY KNOWS WHO YOU ARE!"

He faced that new whine in his skull.

"YOU'RE A TEENY TINY NOBODY!"

Nothing. Just nothing. Just a snotty kid little bitch girl doesn't know nothing.

"AND *YOU'RE* WHO DOESN'T KNOW WHAT FUCK IS!"

He squeezed a burst out the window toward that sound in the parking lot.

Food court fading echo of gunshots ringing smoke detector and STILL he heard:

"NA-NANA-NA-NA, YOU CAN'T SHOOT NOTH-ING!"

The shooter thumbed his assault rifle to Select Fire.

Squeezed three shots in a sweep over the visible car roofs.

"YOU CAN'T GET ME!"

Not from in here.

The black robot whirled left, whirled right.

Fifty-fifty choice.

Either the side EXIT on the left and out alongside the building with its purple-smoke cloud still so thick the scavenging seagulls floating overhead couldn't see what they smelled sprawled on the black pavement.

Or back through the main doors to the flat cement slab entryway that would give him a 180-degree-plus field of fire from the purple-smoked zone, up to the white gazebo, then the easy sweep all over the whole front parking lot, then toward the right to the distant gas pumps that were destined to be awesome pillars of fire.

Main doors.

He's there. Elbows the shiny steel-plate automatic door opener. Rifle up, alert position, gun butt by his shoulder. Just like SWAT guys on TV. Staring over the barrel. Focused. Sliding past the heap of dead men blocking his way down one ramp. Past the Army jacketed meat slumped in a wheelchair nearly blocking the stairs by the top of the second ramp where the shooter had pushed it.

Stairs are tricky while aiming over an assault rifle, so he SWAT glides down the second ramp to the heap of bodies, women on top *fucking bitches.*

"YOU CAN'T FUCK!"

Two quick shots at that *in the parking lot* sound.

The shooter lowered his rifle, the better to see.

Gunshots ringing in his ears, the ringing smoke detector back in the food court: he doesn't hear the whirr of rubber tires on cement as coming behind him, the wheelchair bearing Army-jacketed meat rolls, *rushes* down the ramp.

Splashing hits his left side and back, head, stings his eyes. That splash hit him from off the ground and the heap of dead women.

Stinks, what—

SMACKED in his face with an empty plastic orange bucket pumpkin.

Eyes burning, the blur of some woman swinging a pumpkin to hit him again/*feint*, he knew that was a feint, blocked her true attack kick with the assault rifle and knocked her down. *Why do I smell?* His gun barrel sought the *her* to kill.

In the shooter's new *behind him*:

Warren's blood smeared on his forehead.

Warren's Army jacket worn for Trick or Treat.

Condor launched himself from the rolling wheelchair.

Yelled so the shooter whirled.

Tossed the 'bucks cup full of *wet* into the shooter's face.

Tripped with inertia from his wheelchair leap.

Condor crashed to his knees, heard the *falling on concrete* of that cup.

That paper cup he'd stuck into the stream spewing out of the bullet-punctured steel tank under a car that sheltered him and Malati and a child who wanted to be called Punkin and nodded all the way down into her bones that she *could* she *would* she'd do what she had to do even if she wasn't 'posed to.

The 'bucks cup he'd used to bail that spewing stream into Punkin's pumpkin bucket. Bucket full, he filled the cup to carry with him. Crouched low so the robot shooting inside the rest-stop facility couldn't see him as like in some *don't spill* Fourth of July picnic contest, he frog-ran to the level concrete right outside the main doors. Purple smoke mushroomed inside the food court. Condor set the cup down. *Don't spill!* He pulled the Army jacket off Warren. Got his black leather jacket on the dead vet. Smeared blood from Warren's third eye on his own forehead. Grunted the body onto the heap of corpses blocking the other ramp. Plunked himself into the wheelchair.

Malati, careful not to spill the liquid from the pumpkin she carried, fumbled where Condor'd told her, the throat-shot bus driver's shirt pocket—*Got it!*

Tossed a tumbling glint of silver to the man in the wheelchair.

Malati draped herself over the murdered teachers.

Punkin yelled like she was 'posed to.

Death stalked down the ramp.

Got ambush doused with gasoline.

That stinking-wet killer jerked Condor off his knees.

Condor pushed the bus driver's open silver cigarette lighter against the shooter and thumbed the wheel.

WHUMP! A fountain of fire engulfed the man who'd come to kill and die BUT NOT LIKE THIS!

Screaming. A human torch blazed the morning.

Dropped between the burning man's wobbling feet, Condor jerked the combat knife from its ankle sheath—slammed the blade up into the crease of the shooter's groin.

Blood sprayed Condor, wiped on the Army jacket as he scrambled away.

The burning man staggered.

Collapsed in a flaming heap.

Sickening sweet stench of baking crackling flesh and gasoline.

Condor, hands and knees scrambling up the ramp past

the overturned wheelchair to where his black leather jacket clad the body of Warren.

Helicopters.

Chopping the air, racing in low, fast, and hard to kill or capture who's crazy.

Whoever's crazy.

"*Remember,*" the soldier who'd had a gun and was named Doug had said: "*We can do anything we want as long as nobody ever knows who we are.*"

From his knees, Condor yelled: "Punkin!"

Thrashed his way free of the bloody Army jacket.

"Punkin! All clear! FREE BIRD! FREE BIRD!"

There! Running toward the main entrance from between parked cars.

Her face *not gonna cry* and *gonna run, run, RUN!*

Condor—*Vin, my name is Vin*—wiped his face with Warren's jacket, saw the smear of blood, hoped he looked close to whatever survivor's normal was.

The seven-year-old girl with curly brown hair and red-white-and-blue clothes ran toward the silver-haired man who'd revolutionized her *'posed to*s.

Condor pulled his black leather jacket off Warren.

Maneuvered that dead vet's arms and body enough so Warren wore the gas-and-blood-stained Army jacket he'd died in.

Shrugged himself into his own black leather jacket with its weight of legends.

Collided with and swept a little girl into his arms.

Swooping *roar* over them as helicopters flew a draw-fire pass.

Malati stumbled toward them.

The package, her responsibility, his arms wrapped tight around the *don't you dare call her a little girl,* that silver-haired Condor told Malati: "You spy, you lie."

Then he held the seven-year-old so they stared into each other's eyes.

"Punkin, I'm so proud of you! You did it! You did everything right! You saved so many people and *us*, you saved you and me and Malati. You're so great! But, Punkin: there's one more giant big *'posed to*."

She nodded with all her heart.

"You can't tell the whole truth. The real truth. You gotta tell the good truth. The guy who you helped, the man who saved you, the guy who got the gas from the shot-up car, rolled over there and did it, the guy who burned and stabbed the bad guy . . ."

"It was him." Condor nodded to Warren's body. "The guy in the Army jacket. That's the most anybody else probably saw. That's all you say or tell anybody *ever*. He did it. Got the gas. Tossed it, lit the monster on fire. He rolled his wheelchair away to escape, that bad guy squeezed off a wild shot. Must have hit the Army jacket guy, you don't know. You only know you made it and you did what you were 'posed to."

Every good lie needs a *why*.

"Punkin," said the silver-haired man, "me, Malati, we're spies. No matter what, we've got to be a super secret that nobody but you ever knows. You can only say that we were here with you. Just people who ran and hid and didn't get shot. We're all telling the same story with the true part being what you did. But with the wheelchair guy. You, her, me: we're a *cross-our-hearts*-forever secret."

Punkin nodded her solemn vow.

Must stay secret spies in that rampage of her life made as much sense as anything else anyone ever told her.

She hurled herself back into Condor's arms. He got held tight.

This, he prayed to the meds: *Let me remember this, this.*

Helicopters vibrated the world.

Burnt-flesh stench. Shattered glass. Purple-smoke swirls. Megaphone commands.

When the three of them sprawled on the sidewalk in front of the shot-to-shit rest stop, before she cell phoned the panic line and like a pro triggered the *make-sure-it-holds* cover story of them as *random survivors* not identified in official police reports, named in newspapers or broadcast by television crews who showed up on their own helicopters, while flying ambulances were ferrying out the sobbing wounded, before all that, her face pressed against asphalt, Malati whispered to the silver-haired man lying beside her:

"Is it always like this?"

And he said *yes*.

for Harlan Ellison

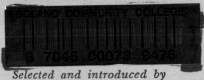
Selected and introduced by

HAROLD CLURMAN

FAMOUS
AMERICAN PLAYS
OF THE

1930s

THE LAUREL DRAMA SERIES

Published by Dell Publishing Co., Inc.
1 Dag Hammarskjold Plaza
New York, N.Y. 10017
Copyright © 1959 by Harold Clurman
Laurel ® TM 674623, Dell Publishing Co., Inc.

ISBN: 0-440-32478-5

First printing—January, 1968
Second printing—February, 1970
Third printing—August, 1970
Fourth printing—November, 1971
Fifth printing—August, 1972
Sixth printing—May, 1973
Seventh printing—October, 1974
Eighth printing—October, 1975
Ninth printing—July, 1976
Tenth printing—October, 1977
Eleventh printing—October, 1978
Twelfth printing—April 1980

Contents

Introduction

There is a tendency nowadays to downgrade the thirties. The reason for this is that the prevailing mood of the thirties was what used to be called "left of center." Beginning with the late forties—from the time the phrase about the "iron curtain" became part of the common vocabulary—our "intelligentsia" sounded the retreat. The Roosevelt administration, subjected to sharp criticism not infrequently close to slander, seemed to be in bad odor. "Left of center" might be construed as something worse than liberalism. To be "radical" implied that one might be tainted with some degree of "pink."

A good many of the writers, artists and theatre folk in the thirties were inclined to radicalism. (Had not the Roosevelt administration sponsored the Projects for writers, artists and theatre?) In the early forties the fervor of the thirties was gradually absorbed by the pressures of the war. Since Russia was one of our allies there was less strictly political feeling: everyone was chiefly concerned with victory and the return to peaceful prosperity.

Shortly after the peace conference suspicion of the Soviet Union increased. Radicalism of any sort might be interpreted as "softness" toward the potential enemy. Our artists and writers, including theatre people, had not only shown too much sympathy for social experiment but had also been too emphatic about the real or supposed shortcomings of their own country. At best the enthusiasm of the thirties was now considered a sign of juvenile simple-mindedness, at worst something close to treason.

Around the year 1953 this reaction to the thirties had come close to hysteria. Today there is certainly more calm but the notion that the thirties was a foolish period persists.

Presumably we are now far sounder in our thinking and work than we were then.

There is another aspect to the rather low esteem in which much of the dramatic work of the thirties is now held. The immediate past in the theatre always makes a poor impression. Writing about the twenties, which every student of our theatre history regards as a high point of the American theatre both in volume of activity and in achievement, Joseph Wood Krutch in the early thirties said that the record no longer seemed as bright as it once appeared. Very few of the best plays of that time would endure.

What most of us fail to note in this connection is that very few plays measured in the light of decades or generations have ever "endured." Shakespeare as we know Shakespeare is a nineteenth-century discovery! (He was neglected or disgracefully altered during the seventeenth and eighteenth centuries.) The number of plays which have come down to us from the Greeks of the fifth century B.C. and from the Elizabethan era are a paltry few compared to the number produced. How cavalier was the attitude of our drama critics toward Marlowe's *Tamburlaine* because he was not equal to Shakespeare!

We may explain this paradox through our own theatre-going experience. A play may be both enjoyable and important to us at the moment we see it, but when the circumstances of our lives have changed, it may well have lost its appeal. One of the most popular plays the American theatre has ever produced is the dramatization of *Uncle Tom's Cabin*. No one can deny its importance for its day even if we no longer have much regard for it as literature.

It is downright stupid to sneer at our erstwhile excitement over *Waiting for Lefty* because today a good many people (in Europe at any rate) are waiting for Godot. As theatre-goers we are very rarely able to estimate a play in the present as we shall view it twenty-five years hence. What appeared a very inconsiderable play to England's finest dramatic critic, Bernard Shaw, Oscar Wilde's *The Importance of Being Earnest,* has proved durable beyond anyone's belief when it was first presented.

I recall having seen Robert Sherwood's *The Petrified Forest* (1935) in the company of one of our country's most astute men of letters. He enjoyed it thoroughly. A few days later we spoke on the phone. He remarked that the theatre was a hoax: he had been "taken in" by the play as he watched it, he said, but on further reflection he realized the play's flaws in thought and plot. Most readers who are also playgoers are like that.

We enjoy the "show," but we *think* about the play. There is often a disparity of judgment between the two activities. For though we are intellectually aware that literature and theatre are not identical, we are prone to assume that the text of a play is equivalent to the texture of its production. But a play in the theatre communicates qualities beyond— sometimes, in a bad performance, less than—what we find on the printed page. Thus to evaluate the theatre of any period only with regard to its texts is a falsification.

The plays of the thirties sharpen certain tendencies that were already evident, and comparatively new, in the plays of the twenties. For the twenties, which may be said to represent America's second coming of age in literature (the first might be dated around 1850) and its true coming of age in the theatre, were marked by a rather harsh critical realism. What such men as Frank Norris and Theodore Dreiser had been saying about us in their novels began to be said somewhat more lyrically (though no less vehemently) in the plays of Eugene O'Neill. The theatre is ideologically almost always behind the times because it is a mass medium. It takes a while for people to acknowledge publicly what a few individuals may think and say privately.

It was the artistic pleasure of the twenties to deride, curse, bemoan the havoc, spiritual blindness and absurdity of America's materialistic functionalism with its concomitant acquisitiveness and worship of success.

Another marked feature of the theatrical twenties was the fact that plays which had previously satisfied audiences with the mere tracing of types (or stereotypes) began to strike them as increasingly hollow. Characters began to show their faces on the stage. Psychology was "introduced."

Men and women were no longer heroes or villains but "human," a mixture of contradictory traits. The standardized Puritanism typified by the old anti-vice societies became an object of scorn and ridicule.

The sentiment against war in *What Price Glory?* of the twenties was converted into the poignant and pointed satire of Paul Green's *Johnny Johnson* in the thirties. The sense of loneliness which informs O'Neill's pieces is rendered more acute and more general in Steinbeck's *Of Mice and Men* some ten years later. The plight of the colored people in the Heywards' *Porgy* or in Green's *In Abraham's Bosom* is intensified in John Wexley's *They Shall Not Die* in the thirties. The playful probing of Behrman's *The Second Man* in 1927 is given a social connotation in the same author's *Biography* and other of his later plays in the thirties. The laborer as a symbol of inner disharmony within the apparent health of the American commonwealth which we observe in O'Neill's *The Hairy Ape* (1922) becomes a leading theme on a more concrete basis in the thirties.

The most significant difference between the theatre of the twenties and that of the thirties is the emphasis in the later period on the social, economic and political background of the individual psychological case. The Wall Street crash of 1929, the Great Depression of the early thirties with its attendant scar of widespread unemployment, the hopeful attempt to remedy this bitter condition which ensued are the effective causes for the abrupt and drastic change.

The plays included in this volume are not all necessarily the "best" of the thirties, but all are representative. Space and other factors of publication permitting, I should certainly have included O'Neill's *Mourning Becomes Electra* (1931), an Irish play of Denis Johnston's, *The Moon in the Yellow River* (1932), Maxwell Anderson's *Winterset* (1935), Sidney Kingsley's *Dead End* (1935), Thornton Wilder's *Our Town* (1938), Robert Sherwood's *Abe Lincoln in Illinois* (1938), Lillian Hellman's *The Little Foxes* (1939).

Of the plays included one had to be the work of Clifford

Odets. Historically speaking he is the dramatist of the thirties *par excellence*. His immediate sources of inspiration, his point of view, his language, his import and perhaps some of his weaknesses are typical of the thirties.

I am not at all sure that *Awake and Sing!*, first presented by the Group Theatre on February 19, 1935, is the best of Odets' plays. The 1937 *Golden Boy* has a more striking story line and is more varied and personal in its meaning. But *Awake and Sing!* contains the "seed" themes of the Odets plays and indicates most unaffectedly the milieu and the quality of feeling in which his work is rooted. One might even go so far as to say that there is hardly another play of the thirties—except perhaps John Howard Lawson's *Success Story* (1932)— which so directly communicates the very "smell" of New York in the first years of the depression.

The keynotes of the period are struck in *Awake and Sing!* as never again with such warm intimacy. There is first of all the bafflement and all-pervading worry of lower middle-class poverty. This is conveyed in language based on common speech and local New York (including Jewish) idiom, but it is not precisely naturalistic speech, for Odets' writing is a personal creation, essentially lyric, in which vulgarity, tenderness, energy, humor and a headlong idealism are commingled.

What is Odets' basic impulse; what is his "program"? They are contained in Jacob's exhortation to his grandson, "Go out and fight so life shouldn't be printed on dollar bills," and in another reflection, "Life should have some dignity." It seems to me that not only is most of Odets expressed in these bare words but the greater part of the whole cry of the American "progressive" movement—its radicalism if you will—as the artists of the thirties sensed it, is summed up in these innocent mottoes.

The "biblical" fervor in *Awake and Sing!* impels a "revolutionary" conviction expressed in Jacob's comment, "It needs a new world," which leads his grandson to take heart and proclaim, "Fresh blood, arms. We've got 'em. We're glad we're living." This was the "wave" of the thirties. If that wave did not carry us on to the millennium, it is surely the height of folly to believe that it had no vital force and accomplished nothing of value in the arts as well as in our community life.

S. N. Behrman's *End of Summer,* produced by the Theatre Guild on February 17, 1936, gives us the depression period seen from another angle: that of the "privileged" classes. It is a comedy of manners which besides its merits in the way of urbane dialogue, etc., presents a central character who (apart from having a decided semblance to the play's author) is kin to most of the folk who buy the best seats in our metropolitan theatres. Leonie, says Behrman, "is repelled by the gross and the voluptuary: this is not hypocrisy. . . . In the world in which she moves hypocrisy is merely a social lubricant, but this very often springs from a congenital and temperamental inability to face anything but the pleasantest and most immediately appealing and the most flattering aspect of things, in life and in her own nature."

What *End of Summer* presents is the spectacle of such a person confronted by the unhappy phenomenon of mass unemployment, nascent radicalism, spectres of fascism and the ambiguities of the psychoanalysts. The treatment is characteristic of Behrman—joshing, debonair, slightly more lighthearted than the author actually feels.

The lady of the play for the first time meets "the young radicals our colleges are said to be full of nowadays." One such radical, a somewhat fictitious Irish Catholic young fellow, tells the lady, "The world is middle-aged and tired," at which the lady queries, "Can you refresh us?" The young man rejoins, "Refresh you! Leonie, we can rejuvenate you." That was another hope of the youth which during the thirties had reached the ages of twenty-five to thirty-five. It was not altogether a vain hope for, as I have already indicated and shall continue to indicate, there was a young and invigorating spirit that relieved the thirties of its blues and led to concrete benefits.

One of the faults easily spotted in *End of Summer* is also evident in Robert Sherwood's *Idiot's Delight,* produced by the Theatre Guild in the spring of 1936. Just as the young radicals of Behrman's play seem to be known by hearsay rather than by intimate acquaintance, so in *Idiot's Delight*

Sherwood's grasp of the European political situation is informed as it were by headlines rather than truly experienced. Thus he makes his French pacifist a Radical-Socialist who speaks of the workers' uprising and alludes to Lenin with reverence, whereas any knowledgeable foreign correspondent could have told Sherwood that the Radical-Socialists of France are the party of small business, abhor Lenin's doctrines and are neither radical nor socialist.

This slight error is worth mentioning because it is symptomatic of a not uncommon failing in American playwrights when they generalize or "intellectualize" on social or ethical themes. It is a species of dilettantism which consists of dealing with subjects in which one is certainly interested but not truly familiar.

More cogent than this flaw is the sentiment which inspired Sherwood to write *Idiot's Delight*. It echoes the American fear of and profound estrangement from the facts of European intrigue which led to war. One merit of Sherwood's play is that it gives us an inkling of the moral climate in our country shortly after the Italian-Ethiopian conflagration and at the outset of the Spanish civil conflict—two omens of the future scarcely understood by an average citizen. Sherwood's "solution" to the problem in his play is the idealistic injunction "You can refuse to fight."

This is significant because it shows that the attitude of our dramatists, generally speaking, was fundamentally moral rather than, as some are now inclined to believe, political. This explains why Sherwood, whose *Idiot's Delight* might indicate the opposition to war of the "conscientious objector," took a very different stand when Nazism threatened to engulf Europe and the world. The play also marks the transition from skepticism and pessimism in regard to modern life, suggested by several of Sherwood's earlier plays, to the willingness to be engaged in political struggle and an acceptance of war, exemplified by his *Abe Lincoln in Illinois*.

Sherwood was a shrewd showman: *Idiot's Delight* gives striking evidence of this. He himself is supposed to have said, "The trouble with me is that I start off with a big message and end with nothing but good entertainment." *Idiot's Delight* was good entertainment, particularly in the acting opportunities it afforded Alfred Lunt and Lynn Fontanne, just as Leonie in *End of Summer*, in itself a charming characterization, was given special fragrance by Ina Claire's delightful talent.

John Steinbeck's *Of Mice and Men*, produced by Sam H. Harris on November 23, 1937, is a parable of American loneliness and of our hunger for "brotherhood"—two feelings the depression greatly enhanced. This play, unlike most of the others we have cited, concentrates on the unemployed of the farm lands, the itinerants and ranch workers, while it alludes to the bus and truck drivers whose travels through the country permitted them to observe the state of the nation in its broad horizon.

The American theatre, centered in New York, is on the whole cut off from the rest of the country. The thirties was the time when the theatre, along with the other arts, rediscovered America. *Green Grow the Lilacs* (1931) is one of the several Lynn Riggs Oklahoma plays, Erskine Caldwell's *Tobacco Road* (1933), Osborn's *Morning's at Seven* (1939)—to mention only a few—are among the many which in one way or another perform a similar function. One of the reasons why Steinbeck's parable carries conviction on naturalistic grounds is that the author shares the background and the earthiness of his characters.

Steinbeck knows our longing for a home, not a mere feeding place. He has the same true sympathy for the lonesome devil whose sole companion is a mangy old dog as for the Negro cut off by his fellow workers because of his color. He suggests with something like an austere sorrow that America's "underprivileged" will never reach the home they crave till they arrive at greater consciousness.

Speaking of "austerity" I should point out that one of the ground tones of American art and theatre (particularly the latter) is sentimentality. This is also true of Steinbeck's play, though he tries to control his sentimentality. Now sentimentality is usually accounted a vice, because it bespeaks a propensity to express a greater degree of feeling than a specific situation warrants. But sentimentality need not be a vital flaw; it isn't in *Of Mice and Men*. It is often the characteristic of a young and vigorous people whose experience of life is, so to speak, still new and uncontaminated by too frequent disillusionment. In this sense our history makes us a sentimental people and it is only natural that our arts, particularly our folk arts, should reveal this quality.

This brings us to the last play of this volume: William Saroyan's *The Time of Your Life*, presented by the Theatre Guild in association with Eddie Dowling on October 25, 1939. This sentimental comedy is by way of being a little classic. It marks the deliquescence of the aggressive mood of the thirties. For though the moralistic and critical rationale of the thirties is still present in *The Time of Your Life*, it is there in a lyrically anarchistic manner, a sort of sweet (here and there mawkish) dream.

Another way, distinctly 1959, of describing this play is to call it pre-beatnik! "I believe dreams more than statistics," one character says. "Everybody is behind the eight ball," says another. Money appears as the root of most evil—anyway it is the filthiest thing that goes and "there's no foundation all the way down the. line," as the old man from the Orient mutters throughout the play.

In a way *The Time of Your Life* is a social fable: it turns its head away from and thumbs its nose at our monstrously efficient society which produces arrogance, cruelty, fear, headaches, constipation and the yammering of millions of humble folk, only to conclude that "all people are wonderful." Though this evinces more bewilderment than insight, it is nevertheless honestly American in its fundamental benevolence.

What saves this play, or rather what "makes" it, is its infectious humor, its anti-heroism (an oblique form of rebelliousness), its San Francisco colorfulness, its succulent dialogue, its wry hoboism and nonconformity. Though it is of another time, one still reads it with a sense of relief.

No account of the theatre of the thirties can convey any sense of its true nature and its contribution to our culture without emphasizing certain purely theatrical factors which played as decisive a role as the plays themselves.

The importance of the Group Theatre (1931–1941), whose origins may be traced back to the late twenties, can hardly be overestimated. (The first unofficial "group" meetings were held in 1928.) The Group Theatre was important not alone because it developed Odets from among its acting members, or even because it presented Sidney Kingsley's first play, *Men in White* (1933), Saroyan's first play, *My Heart's in the Highlands* (1939) as well as various plays by Paul Green, John Howard Lawson, Irwin Shaw and Robert Ardrey, but also because it organized its actors as a permanent company and trained them in a common craftsmanship which not only became emblematic for the era but which in many ways influenced the course of our theatre practice in the ensuing years.

Among the actors, directors, producers, designers, teachers trained or brought into prominence by the Group Theatre were: Stella Adler, Luther Adler, Boris Aronson, Harold Clurman, Lee Cobb, Cheryl Crawford, Morris Carnovsky, John Garfield, Elia Kazan, Mordecai Gorelik, Robert Lewis, Lee Strasberg, Franchot Tone.

The Group Theatre in certain respects continued a tradition established by such pioneer organizations as the Provincetown Players, the Theatre Guild, the Neighborhood Playhouse. In another way the Group served as a model for such organizations as the Theatre Union, the Theatre Collective, the Theatre of Action, which were "workers' theatres" with a more specifically political orientation. These were valuable organizations, particularly the Theatre Union, offering vivid productions of social plays. Our theatre needs more such organizations (there are none at present) which commit themselves to definite ideals or policies rather than wallowing in hit-or-miss show-shop opportunism.

Far more important than these special organizations was the Federal Theatre Project (1935–1939). Its rudest critics will not deny the interest of such productions as the "Living Newspaper," *One Third of a Nation*, the Negro *Macbeth*, Marlowe's *Dr. Faustus*, T. S. Eliot's *Murder in the Cathedral*, and the attempted production of Marc Blitzstein's momentous musical play, *The Cradle Will Rock*—ultimately presented under different auspices.

The Federal Theatre Project brought much excellent theatre fare to a national public at nominal prices, a public the greater part of which was barely acquainted with any form of "live" theatre. This was the first government-sponsored theatre in our history and it indicated how beneficial such an effort could be, even when circumstances were far from favorable.

Orson Welles was given his first opportunity as a director under the Federal Theatre Project. Because of his success there he was enabled to establish (with John Houseman) the short-lived but animated Mercury Theatre which produced a remarkably provocative *Julius Caesar* in the spirit of the times (1937).

Looking back from the vantage point of 1959 we may say that although admirable work still continues to be done on our constantly harassed and considerably shrunken stage, there are two virtues which may be claimed for the theatre of the thirties conspicuously lacking today. The theatre of the thirties attempted to make the stage an instrument of public enlightenment through a passionate involvement with the national scene. It made valiant and, to a remarkable degree, effective efforts to bring order and discipline into the helter-skelter of our theatre's artistic and financial organization.

An intelligent and successful Broadway producer of today recently said to me, "The theatre at present is twenty times more 'commercial' than it was in the thirties. For one thing, you could reach the hearts and souls of actors, playwrights, designers, etc., with good sense and considerations of sound craftsmanship. Today these people, whatever their personal dispositions, appear encircled by an iron ring forged by agents who protect their clients from all thought beyond income, percentages and publicity."

The lean days and hungry nights of the thirties were a brave time. Aren't we a little torpid now?

HAROLD CLURMAN

AWAKE AND SING!

by Clifford Odets

For my Father and Mother

From *Six Plays of Clifford Odets*.
Copyright 1935 by Clifford Odets.
Reprinted by permission of Random House, Inc.

*First production, February 19th, 1935,
at the Belasco Theatre, New York,
with the following cast from the
Group Theatre Acting Company:*

MYRON BERGER, *Art Smith*
BESSIE BERGER, *Stella Adler*
JACOB, *Morris Carnovsky*
HENNIE BERGER, *Phoebe Brand*
RALPH BERGER, *Jules Garfield*
SCHLOSSER, *Roman Bohnen*
MOE AXELROD, *Luther Adler*
UNCLE MORTY, *J. E. Bromberg*
SAM FEINSCHREIBER, *Sanford Meisner*

*The entire action takes place in an apartment
in the Bronx, New York City.*

The Characters of the Play

All of the characters in Awake and Sing!
share a fundamental activity:
a struggle for life amidst petty conditions.

BESSIE BERGER, *as she herself states, is not only the
mother in this home but also the father. She is constantly arranging and taking care of her family. She
loves life, likes to laugh, has great resourcefulness and
enjoys living from day to day. A high degree of energy
accounts for her quick exasperation at ineptitude. She
is a shrewd judge of realistic qualities in people in the
sense of being able to gauge quickly their effectiveness.
In her eyes all of the people in the house are equal.
She is naïve and quick in emotional response. She is
afraid of utter poverty. She is proper according to her
own standards, which are fairly close to those of most
middle-class families. She knows that when one lives in
the jungle one must look out for the wild life.*

MYRON, *her husband, is a born follower. He would like
to be a leader. He would like to make a million dollars. He is not sad or ever depressed. Life is an even
sweet event to him, but the "old days" were sweeter
yet. He has a dignified sense of himself. He likes people. He likes everything. But he is heartbroken without being aware of it.*

HENNIE *is a girl who has had few friends, male or female. She is proud of her body. She won't ask favors.
She travels alone. She is fatalistic about being trapped,
but will escape if possible. She is self-reliant in the best*

*sense. Till the day she dies she will be faithful to a
loved man. She inherits her mother's sense of humor
and energy.*

RALPH *is a boy with a clean spirit. He wants to know,
wants to learn. He is ardent, he is romantic, he is sensitive. He is naïve too. He is trying to find why so much
dirt must be cleared away before it is possible to "get
to first base."*

JACOB, *too, is trying to find a right path for himself
and the others. He is aware of justice, of dignity. He is
an observer of the others, compares their activities with
his real and ideal sense of life. This produces a reflective nature. In this home he is a constant boarder. He
is a sentimental idealist with no power to turn ideal to
action.*

*With physical facts—such as housework—he putters.
But as a barber he demonstrates the flair of an artist.
He is an old Jew with living eyes in his tired face.*

UNCLE MORTY *is a successful American business man
with five good senses. Something sinister comes out of
the fact that the lives of others seldom touch him
deeply. He holds to his own line of life. When he is
generous he wants others to be aware of it. He is
pleased by attention—a rich relative to the* BERGER *family. He is a shrewd judge of material values. He will die
unmarried. Two and two make four, never five with
him. He can blink in the sun for hours, a fat tomcat.
Tickle him, he laughs. He lives in a penthouse with a
real Japanese butler to serve him. He sleeps with dress
models, but not from his own showrooms. He plays
cards for hours on end. He smokes expensive cigars.
He sees every Mickey Mouse cartoon that appears. He*

is a 32-degree Mason. He is really deeply intolerant finally.

MOE AXELROD *lost a leg in the war. He seldom forgets that fact. He has killed two men in extra-martial activity. He is mordant, bitter. Life has taught him a disbelief in everything, but he will fight his way through. He seldom shows his feelings: fights against his own sensitivity. He has been everywhere and seen everything. All he wants is* HENNIE. *He is very proud. He scorns the inability of others to make their way in life, but he likes people for whatever good qualities they possess. His passionate outbursts come from a strong but contained emotional mechanism.*

SAM FEINSCHREIBER *wants to find a home. He is a lonely man, a foreigner in a strange land, hypersensitive about this fact, conditioned by the humiliation of not making his way alone. He has a sense of others laughing at him. At night he gets up and sits alone in the dark. He hears acutely all the small sounds of life. He might have been a poet in another time and place. He approaches his wife as if he were always offering her a delicate flower. Life is a high chill wind weaving itself around his head.*

SCHLOSSER, *the janitor, is an overworked German whose wife ran away with another man and left him with a young daughter who in turn ran away and joined a burlesque show as chorus girl. The man suffers rheumatic pains. He has lost his identity twenty years before.*

SCENE—*Exposed on the stage are the dining room and adjoining front room of the* BERGER *apartment. These two rooms are typically furnished. There is a curtain between them. A small door off the front room leads to* JACOB'S *room. When his door is open one sees a picture of Sacco and Vanzetti on the wall and several shelves of books. Stage left of this door presents the entrance to the foyer hall of the apartment. The two other bedrooms of the apartment are off this hall, but not necessarily shown.*

Stage left of the dining room presents a swinging door which opens on the kitchen.

Awake and sing, ye that dwell in dust:
ISAIAH—26:19

Act one

TIME. *The present; the family finishing supper.*
PLACE. *An apartment in the Bronx, New York City.*

RALPH. Where's advancement down the place? Work like crazy! Think they see it? You'd drop dead first.

MYRON. Never mind, son, merit never goes unrewarded. Teddy Roosevelt used to say—

HENNIE. It rewarded you—thirty years a haberdashery clerk!

[*Jacob laughs.*]

RALPH. All I want's a chance to get to first base!

HENNIE. That's all?

RALPH. Stuck down in that joint on Fourth Avenue — a stock clerk in a silk house! Just look at Eddie. I'm as good as he is—pulling in two-fifty a week for forty-eight minutes a day. A headliner, his name in all the papers.

JACOB. That's what you want, Ralphie? Your name in the paper?

RALPH. I wanna make up my own mind about things . . . be something! Didn't I want to take up tap dancing, too?

BESSIE. So take lessons. Who stopped you?

RALPH. On what?

BESSIE. On what? Save money.

RALPH. Sure, five dollars a week for expenses and the rest in the house. I can't save even for shoe laces.

BESSIE. You mean we shouldn't have food in the house, but you'll make a jig on the street corner?

RALPH. I mean something.

BESSIE. You also mean something when you studied on the drum, Mr. Smartie!

RALPH. I don't know. . . . Every other day to sit around with the blues and mud in your mouth.

MYRON. That's how it is—life is like that—a cake-walk.

RALPH. What's it get you?

HENNIE. A four-car funeral.

RALPH. What's it for?

JACOB. What's it for? If this life leads to a revolution it's a good life. Otherwise it's for nothing.

BESSIE. Never mind, Pop! Pass me the salt.

RALPH. It's crazy—all my life I want a pair of black and white shoes and can't get them. It's crazy!

BESSIE. In a minute I'll get up from the table. I can't take a bite in my mouth no more.

MYRON [restraining her]. Now, Mamma, just don't excite yourself—

BESSIE. I'm so nervous I can't hold a knife in my hand.

MYRON. Is that a way to talk, Ralphie? Don't Momma work hard enough all day?

[BESSIE allows herself to be reseated.]

BESSIE. On my feet twenty-four hours?

MYRON. On her feet—

RALPH [jumps up]. What do I do—go to night-clubs with Greta Garbo? Then when I come home can't even have my own room? Sleep on a day-bed in the front room! [Choked, he exits to front room.]

BESSIE. He's starting up that stuff again. [Shouts to him.] When Hennie here marries you'll have her room—I should only live to see the day.

HENNIE. Me, too. [They settle down to serious eating.]

MYRON. This morning the sink was full of ants. Where they come from I just don't know. I thought it was coffee grounds . . . and then they began moving.

BESSIE. You gave the dog eat?

JACOB. I gave the dog eat.

[HENNIE *drops a knife and picks it up again.*]

BESSIE. You got dropsy tonight.

HENNIE. Company's coming.

MYRON. You can buy a ticket for fifty cents and win fortunes. A man came in the store—it's the Irish Sweepstakes.

BESSIE. What?

MYRON. Like a raffle, only different. A man came in—

BESSIE. Who spends fifty-cent pieces for Irish raffles? They threw out a family on Dawson Street today. All the furniture on the sidewalk. A fine old woman with gray hair.

JACOB. Come eat, Ralph.

MYRON. A butcher on Beck Street won eighty thousand dollars.

BESSIE. Eighty thousand dollars! You'll excuse my expression, you're bughouse!

MYRON. I seen it in the paper—on one ticket—765 Beck Street.

BESSIE. Impossible!

MYRON. He did . . . yes he did. He says he'll take his old mother to Europe . . . an Austrian—

HENNIE. Europe . . .

MYRON. Six per cent on eighty thousand—forty-eight hundred a year.

BESSIE. I'll give you money. Buy a ticket in Hennie's name. Say, you can't tell—lightning never struck us yet. If they win on Beck Street we could win on Longwood Avenue.

JACOB [*ironically*]. If it rained pearls—who would work?

BESSIE. Another county heard from.

[RALPH *enters and silently seats himself.*]

MYRON. I forgot, Beauty—Sam Feinschreiber sent you a present. Since I brought him for supper he just can't stop talking about you.

HENNIE. What's that "mockie" bothering about? Who needs him?

MYRON. He's a very lonely boy.

HENNIE. So I'll sit down and bust out crying " 'cause he's lonely."

BESSIE [*opening candy*]. He'd marry you one two three.

HENNIE. Too bad about him.

BESSIE [*naïvely delighted*]. Chocolate peanuts.

HENNIE. Loft's week-end special, two for thirty-nine.

BESSIE. You could think about it. It wouldn't hurt.

HENNIE [*laughing*]. To quote Moe Axelrod, "Don't make me laugh."

BESSIE. Never mind laughing. It's time you already had in your head a serious thought. A girl twenty-six don't grow younger. When I was your age it was already a big family with responsibilities.

HENNIE [*laughing*]. Maybe that's what ails you, Mom.

BESSIE. Don't you feel well?

HENNIE. 'Cause I'm laughing? I feel fine. It's just funny —that poor guy sending me presents 'cause he loves me.

BESSIE. I think it's very, very nice.

HENNIE. Sure . . . swell!

BESSIE. Mrs. Marcus' Rose is engaged to a Brooklyn boy, a dentist. He came in his car today. A little dope should get such a boy.

[*Finished with the meal,* BESSIE, MYRON *and* JACOB *rise. Both* HENNIE *and* RALPH *sit silently at the table, he eating. Suddenly she rises.*]

HENNIE. Tell you what, Mom. I saved for a new dress, but I'll take you and Pop to the Franklin. Don't need a dress. From now on I'm planning to stay in nights. Hold everything!

BESSIE. What's the matter—a bedbug bit you suddenly?

HENNIE. It's a good bill—Belle Baker. Maybe she'll sing "Eli, Eli."

BESSIE. We was going to a movie.

HENNIE. Forget it. Let's go.

MYRON. I see in the papers [*as he picks his teeth*] Sophie Tucker took off twenty-six pounds. Fearful business with Japan.

HENNIE. Write a book, Pop! Come on, we'll go early for good seats.

MYRON. Moe said you had a date with him for tonight.

BESSIE. Axelrod?

HENNIE. I told him no, but he don't believe it. I'll tell him no for the next hundred years, too.

MYRON. Don't break appointments, Beauty, and hurt people's feelings.

[*Bessie exits.*]

HENNIE. His hands got free wheeling. [*She exits.*]

MYRON. I don't know . . . people ain't the same. N-O. The whole world's changing right under our eyes. Presto! No manners. Like the great Italian lover in the movies. What was his name? The Shiek. . . . No one remembers? [*Exits, shaking his head.*]

RALPH [*unmoving at the table*]. Jake . . .

JACOB. Noo?

RALPH. I can't stand it.

JACOB. There's an expression—"strong as iron you must be."

RALPH. It's a cock-eyed world.

JACOB. Boys like you could fix it some day. Look on the world, not on yourself so much. Every country with starving millions, no? In Germany and Poland a Jew couldn't walk in the street. Everybody hates, nobody loves.

RALPH. I don't get all that.

JACOB. For years, I watched you grow up. Wait! You'll graduate from my university.

[*The others enter, dressed.*]

MYRON [*lighting*]. Good cigars now for a nickel.

BESSIE [*to* JACOB]. After take Tootsie on the roof. [*To* RALPH.] What'll you do?

RALPH. Don't know.

BESSIE. You'll see the boys around the block?

RALPH. I'll stay home every night!

MYRON. Momma don't mean for you—

RALPH. I'm flying to Hollywood by plane, that's what I'm doing.

[*Doorbell rings.* MYRON *answers it.*]

BESSIE. I don't like my boy to be seen with those tramps on the corner.

MYRON [*without*]. Schlosser's here, Momma, with the garbage can.

BESSIE. Come in here, Schlosser. [*Sotto voce.*] Wait, I'll give him a piece of my mind. [MYRON *ushers in* SCHLOSSER *who carries a garbage can in each hand.*] What's the matter, the dumbwaiter's broken again?

SCHLOSSER. Mr. Wimmer sends new ropes next week. I got a sore arm.

BESSIE. He should live so long your Mr. Wimmer. For seven years already he's sending new ropes. No dumbwaiter, no hot water, no steam— In a respectable house, they don't allow such conditions.

SCHLOSSER. In a decent house dogs are not running to make dirty the hallway.

BESSIE. Tootsie's making dirty? Our Tootsie's making dirty in the hall?

SCHLOSSER [*to* JACOB]. I tell you yesterday again. You must not leave her—

BESSIE [*indignantly*]. Excuse me! Please don't yell on an old man. He's got more brains in his finger than you got—I don't know where. Did you ever see—he should talk to you an old man?

MYRON. Awful.

BESSIE. From now on we don't walk up the stairs no more. You keep it so clean we'll fly in the windows.

SCHLOSSER. I speak to Mr. Wimmer.

BESSIE. Speak! Speak. Tootsie walks behind me like a lady any time, any place. So good-bye . . . good-bye, Mr. Schlosser.

SCHLOSSER. I tell you dot—I verk verry hard here. My arms is . . . [*Exits in confusion.*]

BESSIE. Tootsie should lay all day in the kitchen maybe. Give him back if he yells on you. What's funny?

JACOB [*laughing*]. Nothing.

BESSIE. Come. [*Exits.*]

JACOB. Hennie, take care. . . .

HENNIE. Sure.

JACOB. Bye-bye.

[HENNIE *exits.* MYRON *pops head back in door.*]

MYRON. Valentino! That's the one! [*He exits.*]

RALPH. I never in my life even had a birthday party. Every time I went and cried in the toilet when my birthday came.

JACOB [*seeing* RALPH *remove his tie*]. You're going to bed?

RALPH. No, I'm putting on a clean shirt.

JACOB. Why?

RALPH. I got a girl. . . . Don't laugh!

JACOB. Who laughs? Since when?

RALPH. Three weeks. She lives in Yorkville with an aunt and uncle. A bunch of relatives, but no parents.

JACOB. An orphan girl—tch, tch.

RALPH. But she's got me! Boy, I'm telling you I could sing! Jake, she's like stars. She's so beautiful you look at her and cry! She's like French words! We went to the park the other night. Heard the last band concert.

JACOB. Music . . .

RALPH [*stuffing shirt in trousers*]. It got cold and I gave her my coat to wear. We just walked along like that, see, without a word, see. I never was so happy in all my life. It got late . . . we just sat there. She looked at me—you know what I mean, how a girl looks at you—right in the eyes? "I love you," she says, "Ralph." I took her home. . . . I wanted to cry. That's how I felt!

JACOB. It's a beautiful feeling.

RALPH. You said a mouthful!

JACOB. Her name is—

RALPH. Blanche.

JACOB. A fine name. Bring her sometimes here.

RALPH. She's scared to meet Mom.

JACOB. Why?

RALPH. You know Mom's not letting my sixteen bucks out of the house if she can help it. She'd take one look at Blanche and insult her in a minute—a kid who's got nothing.

JACOB. Boychick!

RALPH. What's the diff?

JACOB. It's no difference—a plain bourgeois prejudice— but when they find out a poor girl—it ain't so kosher.

RALPH. They don't have to know I've got a girl.

JACOB. What's in the end?

RALPH. Out I go! I don't mean maybe!

JACOB. And then what?

RALPH. Life begins.

JACOB. What life?

RALPH. Life with my girl. Boy, I could sing when I think about it! Her and me together—that's a new life!

JACOB. Don't make a mistake! A new death!

RALPH. What's the idea?

JACOB. Me, I'm the idea! Once I had in *my* heart a dream, a vision, but came marriage and then you forget. Children come and you forget because—

RALPH. Don't worry, Jake.

JACOB. Remember, a woman insults a man's soul like no other thing in the whole world!

RALPH. Why get so excited? No one—

JACOB. Boychick, wake up! Be something! Make your life something good. For the love of an old man who sees in your young days his new life, for such love take the world in your two hands and make it like new. Go out and fight so life shouldn't be printed on dollar bills. A woman waits.

RALPH. Say, I'm no fool!

JACOB. From my heart I hope not. In the meantime— [*Bell rings.*]

RALPH. See who it is, will you? [*Stands off.*] Don't want Mom to catch me with a clean shirt.

JACOB [*calls*]. Come in. [*Sotto voce.*] Moe Axelrod. [MOE *enters.*]

MOE. Hello girls, how's your whiskers? [*To* RALPH.] All dolled up. What's it, the weekly visit to the cat house?

RALPH. Please mind your business.

MOE. Okay, sweetheart.

RALPH [*taking a hidden dollar from a book*]. If Mom asks where I went—

JACOB. I know. Enjoy yourself.

RALPH. Bye-bye. [*He exits.*]

JACOB. Bye-bye.

MOE. Who's home?

JACOB. Me.

MOE. Good. I'll stick around a few minutes. Where's Hennie?

JACOB. She went with Bessie and Myron to a show.

MOE. She what?!

JACOB. You had a date?

MOE [*hiding his feelings*]. Here—I brought you some halavah.

JACOB. Halavah? Thanks. I'll eat a piece after.

MOE. So Ralph's got a dame? Hot stuff—a kid can't even play a card game.

JACOB. Moe, you're a no-good, a bum of the first water. To your dying day you won't change.

MOE. Where'd you get that stuff, a no-good?

JACOB. But I like you.

MOE. Didn't I go fight in France for democracy? Didn't I get my goddam leg shot off in that war the day before the armistice? Uncle Sam give me the Order of the Purple Heart, didn't he? What'd you mean, a no-good?

JACOB. Excuse me.

MOE. If you got an orange I'll eat an orange.

JACOB. No orange. An apple.

MOE. No oranges, huh?—what a dump!

JACOB. Bessie hears you once talking like this she'll knock your head off.

MOE. Hennie went with, huh? She wantsa see me squirm, only I don't squirm for dames.

JACOB. You came to see her?

MOE. What for? I got a present for our boy friend, Myron. He'll drop dead when I tell him his gentle horse galloped in fifteen to one. He'll die.

JACOB. It really won? The first time I remember.

MOE. Where'd they go?

JACOB. A vaudeville by the Franklin.

MOE. What's special tonight?

JACOB. Someone tells a few jokes . . . and they forget the street is filled with starving beggars.

MOE. What'll they do—start a war?

JACOB. I don't know.

MOE. You oughta know. What the hell you got all the books for?

JACOB. It needs a new world.

MOE. That's why they had the big war—to make a new world, they said—safe for democracy. Sure every big general laying up in a Paris hotel with a half dozen broads pinned on his mustache. Democracy! I learned a lesson.

JACOB. An imperial war. You know what this means?

MOE. Sure, I know everything!

JACOB. By money men the interests must be protected. Who gave you such a rotten haircut? Please [*fishing in his vest pocket*], give me for a cent a cigarette. I didn't have since yesterday—

MOE [*giving one*]. Don't make me laugh. [*A cent passes back and forth between them,* MOE *finally throwing it over his shoulder.*] Don't look so tired all the time. You're a wow—always sore about something.

JACOB. And you?

MOE. You got one thing—you can· play pinochle. I'll take you over in a game. Then you'll have something to be sore on.

JACOB. Who'll wash dishes?

[*Moe takes deck from buffet drawer.*]

MOE. Do 'em after. Ten cents a deal.

JACOB. Who's got ten cents?

MOE. I got ten cents. I'll lend it to you.

JACOB. Commence.

MOE [*shaking cards*]. The first time I had my hands on a pack in two days. Lemme shake up these cards. I'll make 'em talk.

[JACOB *goes to his room where he puts on a Caruso record.*]

JACOB. You should live so long.

MOE. Ever see oranges grow? I know a certain place—

One summer I laid under a tree and let them fall right in my mouth.

JACOB [*off, the music is playing; the card game begins*]. From "L'Africana" . . . a big explorer comes on a new land—"O Paradiso." From act four this piece. Caruso stands on the ship and looks on a Utopia. You hear? "Oh paradise! Oh paradise on earth! Oh blue sky, oh fragrant air—"

MOE. Ask him does he see any oranges?

[BESSIE, MYRON *and* HENNIE *enter.*]

JACOB. You came back so soon?

BESSIE. Hennie got sick on the way.

MYRON. Hello, Moe . . .

[MOE *puts cards back in pocket.*]

BESSIE. Take off the phonograph, Pop. [*To* HENNIE.] Lay down . . . I'll call the doctor. You should see how she got sick on Prospect Avenue. Two weeks already she don't feel right.

MYRON. Moe . . . ?

BESSIE. Go to bed, Hennie.

HENNIE. I'll sit here.

BESSIE. Such a girl I never saw! Now you'll be stubborn?

MYRON. It's for your own good, Beauty. Influenza—

HENNIE. I'll sit here.

BESSIE. You ever seen a girl should say no to everything. She can't stand on her feet, so—

HENNIE. Don't yell in my ears. I hear. Nothing's wrong. I ate tuna fish for lunch.

MYRON. Canned goods . . .

BESSIE. Last week you also ate tuna fish?

HENNIE. Yeah, I'm funny for tuna fish. Go to the show —have a good time.

BESSIE. I don't understand what I did to God He blessed me with such children. From the whole world—

MOE [*coming to aid of* HENNIE]. For Chris' sake, don't kibitz so much!

BESSIE. You don't like it?

MOE [*aping*]. No, I don't like it.

BESSIE. That's too bad, Axelrod. Maybe it's better by your cigar store friends. Here we're different people.

MOE. Don't gimme that cigar store line, Bessie. I walked up five flights—

BESSIE. To take out Hennie. But my daughter ain't in your class, Axelrod.

MOE. To see Myron.

MYRON. Did he, did he, Moe?

MOE. Did he what?

MYRON. "Sky Rocket"?

BESSIE. You bet on a horse!

MOE. Paid twelve and a half to one.

MYRON. There! You hear that, Momma? Our horse came in. You see, it happens, and twelve and a half to one. Just look at that!

MOE. What the hell, a sure thing. I told you.

BESSIE. If Moe said a sure thing, you couldn't bet a few dollars instead of fifty cents?

JACOB [*laughs*]. "Aie, aie, aie."

MOE [*at his wallet*]. I'm carrying six hundred "plunks" in big denominations.

BESSIE. A banker!

MOE. Uncle Sam sends me ninety a month.

BESSIE. So you save it?

MOE. Run it up. Run-it-up-Axelrod, that's me.

BESSIE. The police should know how.

MOE [*shutting her up*]. All right, all right— Change twenty, sweetheart.

MYRON. Can you make change?

BESSIE. Don't be crazy.

MOE. I'll meet a guy in Goldman's restaurant. I'll meet 'im and come back with change.

MYRON [*figuring on paper*]. You can give it to me to-morrow in the store.

BESSIE [*acquisitive*]. He'll come back, he'll come back!

MOE. Lucky I bet some bucks myself. [*In derision to* HENNIE.] Let's step out tomorrow night, Par-a-dise. [*Thumbs his nose at her, laughs mordantly and exits.*]

MYRON. Oh, that's big percentage. If I picked a winner every day . . .

BESSIE. Poppa, did you take Tootsie on the roof?

JACOB. All right.

MYRON. Just look at that—a cake-walk. We can make—

BESSIE. It's enough talk. I got a splitting headache. Hennie, go in bed. I'll call Dr. Cantor.

HENNIE. I'll sit here . . . and don't call that old Ignatz 'cause I won't see him.

MYRON. If you get sick Momma can't nurse you. You don't want to go to a hospital.

JACOB. She don't look sick, Bessie, it's a fact.

BESSIE. She's got fever. I see in her eyes, so he tells me no. Myron, call Dr. Cantor.

[MYRON *picks up phone, but* HENNIE *grabs it from him.*]

HENNIE. I don't want any doctor. I ain't sick. Leave me alone.

MYRON. Beauty, it's for your own sake.

HENNIE. Day in and day out pestering. Why are you always right and no one else can say a word?

BESSIE. When you have your own children—

HENNIE. I'm not sick! Hear what I say? I'm not sick! Nothing's the matter with me! I don't want a doctor.

[BESSIE *is watching her with slow progressive under-standing.*]

BESSIE. What's the matter?

HENNIE. Nothing, I told you!

BESSIE. You told me, but— [*A long pause of examination follows.*]

HENNIE. See much?

BESSIE. Myron, put down the . . . the . . . [*He slowly puts the phone down.*] Tell me what happened. . . .

HENNIE. Brooklyn Bridge fell down.

BESSIE [*approaching*]. I'm asking a question. . . .

MYRON. What's happened, Momma?

BESSIE. Listen to me!

HENNIE. What the hell are you talking?

BESSIE. Poppa—take Tootsie on the roof.

HENNIE [*holding* JACOB *back*]. If he wants he can stay here.

MYRON. What's wrong, Momma?

BESSIE [*her voice quivering slightly*]. Myron, your fine Beauty's in trouble. Our society lady . . .

MYRON. Trouble? I don't under—is it—?

BESSIE. Look in her face. [*He looks, understands and slowly sits in a chair, utterly crushed.*] Who's the man?

HENNIE. The Prince of Wales.

BESSIE. My gall is busting in me. In two seconds—

HENNIE [*in a violent outburst*]. Shut up! Shut up! I'll jump out the window in a minute! Shut up! [*Finally she gains control of herself, says in a low, hard voice:*] You don't know him.

JACOB. Bessie . . .

BESSIE. He's a Bronx boy?

HENNIE. From out of town.

BESSIE. What do you mean?

HENNIE. From out of town!!

BESSIE. A long time you know him? You were sleeping by a girl from the office Saturday nights? You slept good, my lovely lady. You'll go to him . . . he'll marry you.

HENNIE. That's what you say.

BESSIE. That's what I say! He'll do it, take *my* word he'll do it!

HENNIE. Where? [*To* JACOB.] Give her the letter. [JACOB *does so.*]

BESSIE. What? [*Reads.*] "Dear sir: In reply to your request of the 14th inst., we can state that no Mr. Ben Grossman has ever been connected with our organization . . ." You don't know where he is?

HENNIE. No.

BESSIE [*walks back and forth*]. Stop crying like a baby, Myron.

MYRON. It's like a play on the stage. . . .

BESSIE. To a mother you couldn't say something before. I'm old-fashioned—like your friends I'm not smart—I don't eat chop suey and run around Coney Island with tramps. [*She walks reflectively to buffet, picks up a box of candy, puts it down, says to* MYRON:] Tomorrow night bring Sam Feinschreiber for supper.

HENNIE. I won't do it.

BESSIE. You'll do it, my fine beauty, you'll do it!

HENNIE. I'm not marrying a poor foreigner like him. Can't even speak an English word. Not me! I'll go to my grave without a husband.

BESSIE. You don't say! We'll find for you somewhere a millionaire with a pleasure boat. He's going to night school, Sam. For a boy only three years in the country he speaks very nice. In three years he put enough in the bank, a good living.

JACOB. This is serious?

BESSIE. What then? I'm talking for my health? He'll come tomorrow night for supper. By Saturday they're engaged.

JACOB. Such a thing you can't do.

BESSIE. Who asked your advice?

JACOB. Such a thing—

BESSIE. Never mind!

JACOB. The lowest from the low!

BESSIE. Don't talk! I'm warning you! A man who don't believe in God—with crazy ideas—

JACOB. So bad I never imagined you could be.

BESSIE. Maybe if you didn't talk so much it wouldn't happen like this. You with your ideas—I'm a mother. I raise a family, they should have respect.

JACOB. Respect? [*Spits.*] Respect! For the neighbors' opinion! You insult me, Bessie!

BESSIE. Go in your room, Papa. Every job he ever had he lost because he's got a big mouth. He opens his mouth and the whole Bronx could fall in. Everybody said it—

MYRON. Momma, they'll hear you down the dumb-waiter.

BESSIE. A good barber not to hold a job a week. Maybe you never heard charity starts at home. You never heard it, Pop?

JACOB. All you know, I heard, and more yet. But Ralph you don't make like you. Before you do it I'll die first. He'll find a girl. He'll go in a fresh world with her. This is a house? Marx said it— abolish such families.

BESSIE. Go in your room, Papa.

JACOB. Ralph you don't make like you!

BESSIE. Go lay in your room with Caruso and the books together.

JACOB. All right!

BESSIE. Go in the room!

JACOB. Some day I'll come out, I'll— [*Unable to continue, he turns, looks at* HENNIE, *goes to his door and there says with an attempt at humor:*] Bessie, some day you'll talk to me so fresh . . . I'll leave the house for good! [*He exits.*]

BESSIE [*crying*]. You ever in your life seen it? He should dare! He should just dare say in the house another word. Your gall could bust from such a man. [*Bell rings,* MYRON *goes.*] Go to sleep now. It won't hurt.

HENNIE. Yeah?

[MOE *enters, a box in his hand.* MYRON *follows and sits down.*]

MOE [*looks around first—putting box on table*]. Cake. [*About to give* MYRON *the money, he turns instead to* BESSIE.] Six fifty, four bits change . . . come on, hand over half a buck. [*She does so. Of* MYRON.] Who bit him?

BESSIE. We're soon losing our Hennie, Moe.

MOE. Why? What's the matter?

BESSIE. She made her engagement.

MOE. Zat so?

BESSIE. Today it happened . . . he asked her.

MOE. Did he? Who? Who's the corpse?

BESSIE. It's a secret.

MOE. In the bag, huh?

HENNIE. Yeah . . .

BESSIE. When a mother gives away an only daughter it's no joke. Wait, when you'll get married you'll know. . . .

MOE [*bitterly*]. Don't make me laugh—when I get married! What I think a women? Take 'em all, cut 'em in little pieces like a herring in Greek salad. A guy in France had the right idea—dropped his wife in a bathtub fulla acid. [*Whistles.*] Sss, down the pipe! Pfft—not even a corset button left!

MYRON. Corsets don't have buttons.

MOE [*to* HENNIE]. What's the great idea? Gone big time, Paradise? Christ, it's suicide! Sure, kids you'll have, gold teeth, get fat, big in the tangerines—

HENNIE. Shut your face!

MOE. Who's it—some dope pullin' down twenty bucks a week? Cut your throat, sweetheart. Save time.

BESSIE. Never mind your two cents, Axelrod.

MOE. I say what I think—that's me!

HENNIE. That's you—a lousy fourflusher who'd steal the glasses off a blind man.

MOE. Get hot!

HENNIE. My God, do I need it—to listen to this mutt shoot his mouth off?

MYRON. Please. . . .

MOE. Now wait a minute, sweetheart, wait a minute. I don't have to take that from you.

BESSIE. Don't yell at her!

HENNIE. For two cents I'd spit in your eye.

MOE [*throwing coin to table*]. Here's two bits.

[HENNIE *looks at him and then starts across the room.*]

BESSIE. Where are you going?

HENNIE [*crying*]. For my beauty nap, Mussolini. Wake me up when it's apple blossom time in Normandy. [*Exits.*]

MOE. Pretty, pretty—a sweet gal, your Hennie. See the look in her eyes?

BESSIE. She don't feel well. . . .

MYRON. Canned goods . . .

BESSIE. So don't start with her.

MOE. Like a battleship she's got it. Not like other dames—shove 'em and they lay. Not her. I got a yen for her and I don't mean a Chinee coin.

BESSIE. Listen, Axelrod, in my house you don't talk this way. Either have respect or get out.

MOE. When I think about it . . . maybe I'd marry her myself.

BESSIE [*suddenly aware of* MOE]. You could— What do you mean, Moe?

MOE. You ain't sunburnt—you heard me.

BESSIE. Why don't you, Moe? An old friend of the

family like you. It would be a blessing on all of us.

MOE. You said she's engaged.

BESSIE. But maybe she don't know her own mind. Say, it's—

MOE. I need a wife like a hole in the head. . . . What's to know about women, I know. Even if I asked her. She won't do it! A guy with one leg—it gives her the heebie-jeebies. I know what she's looking for. An arrow-collar guy, a hero, but with a wad of jack. Only the two don't go together. But I got what it takes . . . plenty, and more where it comes from. . . . [*Breaks off, snorts and rubs his knee.*]

[*A pause. In his room* JACOB *puts on Caruso singing the lament from "The Pearl Fishers."*]

BESSIE. It's right—she wants a millionaire with a mansion on Riverside Drive. So go fight City Hall. Cake?

MOE. Cake.

BESSIE. I'll make tea. But one thing—she's got a fine boy with a business brain. Caruso! [*Exits into the front room and stands in the dark, at the window.*]

MOE. No wet smack . . . a fine girl. . . . She'll burn that guy out in a month. [MOE *retrieves the quarter and spins it on the table.*]

MYRON. I remember that song . . . beautiful. Nora Bayes sang it at the old Proctor's Twenty-third Street—"When It's Apple Blossom Time in Normandy." . . .

MOE. She wantsa see me crawl—my head on a plate she wants! A snowball in hell's got a better chance. [*Out of sheer fury he spins the quarter in his fingers.*]

MYRON [*as his eyes slowly fill with tears*]. Beautiful . . .

MOE. Match you for a quarter. Match you for any goddam thing you got. [*Spins the coin viciously.*] What the hell kind of house is this it ain't got an orange!!

SLOW—CURTAIN

Act two

*One year later, a Sunday afternoon. The front room.
JACOB is giving his son MORDECAI (UNCLE MORTY) a
haircut, newspapers spread around the base of the
chair. MOE is reading a newspaper, leg propped on a
chair. RALPH, in another chair, is spasmodically reading a paper. UNCLE MORTY reads colored jokes. Silence,
then BESSIE enters.*

BESSIE. Dinner's in half an hour, Morty.

MORTY [*still reading jokes*]. I got time.

BESSIE. A duck. Don't get hair on the rug, Pop. [*Goes
to window and pulls down shade.*] What's the matter the shade's up to the ceiling?

JACOB [*pulling it up again*]. Since when do I give a
haircut in the dark? [*He mimics her tone.*]

BESSIE. When you're finished, pull it down. I like my
house to look respectable. Ralphie, bring up two
bottles seltzer from Weiss.

RALPH. I'm reading the paper.

BESSIE. Uncle Morty takes a little seltzer.

RALPH. I'm expecting a phone call.

BESSIE. Noo, if it comes you'll be back. What's the matter? [*Gives him money from apron pocket.*] Take
down the old bottles.

RALPH [*to JACOB*]. Get that call if it comes. Say I'll
be right back.

[JACOB *nods assent.*]

MORTY [*giving change from vest*]. Get grandpa some
cigarettes.

RALPH. Okay. [*Exits.*]

JACOB. What's new in the paper, Moe?

MOE. Still jumping off the high buildings like flies—the big shots who lost all their cocoanuts. Pfft!

JACOB. Suicides?

MOE. Plenty can't take it—good in the break, but can't take the whip in the stretch.

MORTY [*without looking up*]. I saw it happen Monday in my building. My hair stood up how they shoveled him together—like a pancake—a bankrupt manufacturer.

MOE. No brains.

MORTY. Enough . . . all over the sidewalk.

JACOB. If someone said five-ten years ago I couldn't make for myself a living, I wouldn't believe—

MORTY. Duck for dinner?

BESSIE. The best Long Island duck.

MORTY. I like goose.

BESSIE. A duck is just like a goose, only better.

MORTY. I like a goose.

BESSIE. The next time you'll be for Sunday dinner I'll make a goose.

MORTY [*sniffs deeply*]. Smells good. I'm a great boy for smells.

BESSIE. Ain't you ashamed? Once in a blue moon he should come to an only sister's house.

MORTY. Bessie, leave me live.

BESSIE. You should be ashamed!

MORTY. Quack quack!

BESSIE. No, better to lay around Mecca Temple playing cards with the Masons.

MORTY [*with good nature*]. Bessie, don't you see Pop's giving me a haircut?

BESSIE. You don't need no haircut. Look, two hairs he took off.

MORTY. Pop likes to give me a haircut. If I said no he

don't forget for a year, do you, Pop? An old man's like that.

JACOB. I still do an A-1 job.

MORTY [*winking*]. Pop cuts hair to fit the face, don't you, Pop?

JACOB. For sure, Morty. To each face a different haircut. Custom built, no ready made. A round face needs special—

BESSIE [*cutting him short*]. A graduate from the B.M.T. [*Going.*] Don't forget the shade. [*The phone rings. She beats* JACOB *to it.*] Hello? Who is it, please? . . . Who is it, please? . . . Miss Hirsch? No, he ain't here. . . . No, I couldn't say when. [*Hangs up sharply.*]

JACOB. For Ralph?

BESSIE. A wrong number.

[JACOB *looks at her and goes back to his job.*]

JACOB. Excuse me!

BESSIE [*to* MORTY]. Ralphie took another cut down the place yesterday.

MORTY. Business is bad. I saw his boss Harry Glicksman Thursday. I bought some velvets . . . they're coming in again.

BESSIE. Do something for Ralphie down there.

MORTY. What can I do? I mentioned it to Glicksman. He told me they squeezed out half the people. . . .

[MYRON *enters dressed in apron.*]

BESSIE. What's gonna be the end? Myron's working only three days a week now.

MYRON. It's conditions.

BESSIE. Hennie's married with a baby . . . money just don't come in. I never saw conditions should be so bad.

MORTY. Times'll change.

MOE. The only thing'll change is my underwear.

MORTY. These last few years I got my share of gray hairs. [*Still reading jokes without having looked up once.*] Ha, ha, ha— Popeye the sailor ate spinach and knocked out four bums.

MYRON. I'll tell you the way I see it. The country needs a great man now—a regular Teddy Roosevelt.

MOE. What this country needs is a good five-cent earthquake.

JACOB. So long labor lives it should increase private gain—

BESSIE [*to* JACOB]. Listen, Poppa, go talk on the street corner. The government'll give you free board the rest of your life.

MORTY. I'm surprised. Don't I send a five-dollar check for Pop every week?

BESSIE. You could afford a couple more and not miss it.

MORTY. Tell me jokes. Business is so rotten I could just as soon lay all day in the Turkish bath.

MYRON. Why'd I come in here? [*Puzzled, he exits.*]

MORTY [*to* MOE]. I hear the bootleggers still do business, Moe.

MOE. Wake up! I kissed bootlegging bye-bye two years back.

MORTY. For a fact? What kind of racket is it now?

MOE. If I told you, you'd know something.

[HENNIE *comes from bedroom.*]

HENNIE. Where's Sam?

BESSIE. Sam? In the kitchen.

HENNIE [*calls*]. Sam. Come take the diaper.

MORTY. How's the Mickey Louse? Ha, ha, ha . . .

HENNIE. Sleeping.

MORTY. Ah, that's life to a baby. He sleeps—gets it in the mouth—sleeps some more. To raise a family nowadays you must be a damn fool.

BESSIE. Never mind, never mind, a woman who don't

raise a family—a girl—should jump overboard. What's she good for? [*To* MOE—*to change the subject.*] Your leg bothers you bad?

MOE. It's okay, sweetheart.

BESSIE [*to* MORTY]. It hurts him every time it's cold out. He's got four legs in the closet.

MORTY. Four wooden legs?

MOE. Three.

MORTY. What's the big idea?

MOE. Why not? Uncle Sam gives them out free.

MORTY. Say, maybe if Uncle Sam gave out less legs we could balance the budget.

JACOB. Or not have a war so they wouldn't have to give out legs.

MORTY. Shame on you, Pop. Everybody knows war is necessary.

MOE. Don't make me laugh. Ask me—the first time you pick up a dead one in the trench—then you learn war ain't so damn necessary.

MORTY. Say, you should kick. The rest of your life Uncle Sam pays you ninety a month. Look, not a worry in the world.

MOE. Don't make me laugh. Uncle Sam can take his *seventy* bucks and— [*Finishes with a gesture.*] Nothing good hurts. [*He rubs his stump.*]

HENNIE. Use a crutch, Axelrod. Give the stump a rest.

MOE. Mind your business, Feinschreiber.

BESSIE. It's a sensible idea.

MOE. Who asked you?

BESSIE. Look, he's ashamed.

MOE. So's your Aunt Fanny.

BESSIE [*naïvely*]. Who's got an Aunt Fanny? [*She cleans a rubber plant's leaves with her apron.*]

MORTY. It's a joke!

MOE. I don't want my paper creased before I read it. I want it fresh. Fifty times I said that.

BESSIE. Don't get so excited for a five-cent paper—our star boarder.

MOE. And I don't want no one using my razor either. Get it straight. I'm not buying ten blades a week for the Berger family. [*Furious, he limps out.*]

BESSIE. Maybe I'm using his razor too.

HENNIE. Proud!

BESSIE. You need luck with plants. I didn't clean off the leaves in a month.

MORTY. You keep the house like a pin and I like your cooking. Any time Myron fires you, come to me, Bessie. I'll let the butler go and you'll be my housekeeper. I don't like Japs so much—sneaky.

BESSIE. Say, you can't tell. Maybe any day I'm coming to stay.

[HENNIE *exits.*]

JACOB. Finished.

MORTY. How much, Ed. Pinaud? [*Disengages self from chair.*]

JACOB. Five cents.

MORTY. Still five cents for a haircut to fit the face?

JACOB. Prices don't change by me. [*Takes a dollar.*] I can't change—

MORTY. Keep it. Buy yourself a Packard. Ha, ha, ha.

JACOB [*taking large envelope from pocket*]. Please, you'll keep this for me. Put it away.

MORTY. What is it?

JACOB. My insurance policy. I don't like it should lay around where something could happen.

MORTY. What could happen?

JACOB. Who knows, robbers, fire . . . they took next door. Fifty dollars from O'Reilly.

MORTY. Say, lucky a Berger didn't lose it.

JACOB. Put it downtown in the safe. Bessie don't have to know.

MORTY. It's made out to Bessie?

JACOB. No, to Ralph.

MORTY. To Ralph?

JACOB. He don't know. Some day he'll get three thousand.

MORTY. You got good years ahead.

JACOB. Behind.

[RALPH *enters.*]

RALPH. Cigarettes. Did a call come?

JACOB. A few minutes. She don't let me answer it.

RALPH. Did Mom say I was coming back?

JACOB. No.

[MORTY *is back at new jokes.*]

RALPH. She starting that stuff again? [BESSIE *enters.*] A call come for me?

BESSIE [*waters pot from milk bottle*]. A wrong number.

JACOB. Don't say a lie, Bessie.

RALPH. Blanche said she'd call me at two—was it her?

BESSIE. I said a wrong number.

RALPH. Please, Mom, if it was her tell me.

BESSIE. You call me a liar next. You got no shame—to start a scene in front of Uncle Morty. Once in a blue moon he comes—

RALPH. What's the shame? If my girl calls I wanna know it.

BESSIE. You made enough mish mosh with her until now.

MORTY. I'm surprised, Bessie. For the love of Mike tell him yes or no.

BESSIE. I didn't tell him? No!

MORTY [*to* RALPH]. No!

[RALPH *goes to a window and looks out.*]

BESSIE. Morty, I didn't say before—he runs around steady with a girl.

MORTY. Terrible. Should he run around with a foxie-woxie?

BESSIE. A girl with no parents.

MORTY. An orphan?

BESSIE. I could die from shame. A year already he runs around with her. He brought her once for supper. Believe me, she didn't come again, no!

RALPH. Don't think I didn't ask her.

BESSIE. You hear? You raise them and what's in the end for all your trouble?

JACOB. When you'll lay in a grave, no more trouble. [*Exits.*]

MORTY. Quack quack!

BESSIE. A girl like that he wants to marry. A skinny consumptive-looking . . . six months already she's not working—taking charity from an aunt. You should see her. In a year she's dead on his hands.

RALPH. You'd cut her throat if you could.

BESSIE. That's right! Before she'd ruin a nice boy's life I would first go to prison. Miss Nobody should step in the picture and I'll stand by with my mouth shut.

RALPH. Miss Nobody! Who am I? Al Jolson?

BESSIE. Fix your tie!

RALPH. I'll take care of my own life.

BESSIE. You'll take care? Excuse my expression, you can't even wipe your nose yet! He'll take care!

MORTY [*to* BESSIE]. I'm surprised. Don't worry so much, Bessie. When it's time to settle down he won't marry a poor girl, will you? In the long run common sense is thicker than love. I'm a great boy for live and let live.

BESSIE. Sure, it's easy to say. In the meantime he eats out my heart. You know I'm not strong.

MORTY. I know . . . a pussy cat . . . ha, ha, ha.

BESSIE. You got money and money talks. But without the dollar who sleeps at night?

RALPH. I been working for years, bringing in money here—putting it in your hand like a kid. All right, I can't get my teeth fixed. All right, that a new suit's like trying to buy the Chrysler Building. You never in your life bought me a pair of skates even—things I died for when I was a kid. I don't care about that stuff, see. Only just remember I pay some of the bills around here, just a few . . . and if my girl calls me on the phone I'll talk to her any time I please. [*He exits.* HENNIE *applauds.*]

BESSIE. Don't be so smart, Miss America! [*To* MORTY.] He didn't have skates! But when he got sick, a twelve-year-old boy, who called a big specialist for the last $25 in the house? Skates!

JACOB [*just in. Adjusts window shade*]. It looks like snow today.

MORTY. It's about time—winter.

BESSIE. Poppa here could talk like Samuel Webster, too, but it's just talk. He should try to buy a two-cent pickle in the Burland Market without money.

MORTY. I'm getting an appetite.

BESSIE. Right away we'll eat. I made chopped liver for you.

MORTY. My specialty!

BESSIE. Ralph should only be a success like you, Morty. I should only live to see the day when he rides up to the door in a big car with a chauffeur and a radio. I could die happy, believe me.

MORTY. Success she says. She should see how we spend thousands of dollars making up a winter line and winter don't come—summer in January. Can you beat it?

JACOB. Don't live, just make success.

MORTY. Chopped liver—ha!

JACOB. Ha! [*Exits.*]

MORTY. When they start arguing, I don't hear. Suddenly I'm deaf. I'm a great boy for the practical side. [*He looks over to* HENNIE *who sits rubbing her hands with lotion.*]

HENNIE. Hands like a raw potato.

MORTY. What's the matter? You don't look so well . . . no pep.

HENNIE. I'm swell.

MORTY. You used to be such a pretty girl.

HENNIE. Maybe I got the blues. You can't tell.

MORTY. You could stand a new dress.

HENNIE. That's not all I could stand.

MORTY. Come down to the place tomorrow and pick out a couple from the "eleven-eighty" line. Only don't sing me the blues.

HENNIE. Thanks. I need some new clothes.

MORTY. I got two thousand pieces of merchandise waiting in the stock room for winter.

HENNIE. I never had anything from life. Sam don't help.

MORTY. He's crazy about the kid.

HENNIE. Crazy is right. Twenty-one a week he brings in—a nigger don't have it so hard. I wore my fingers off on an Underwood for six years. For what? Now I wash baby diapers. Sure, I'm crazy about the kid too. But half the night the kid's up. Try to sleep. You don't know how it is, Uncle Morty.

MORTY. No, I don't know. I was born yesterday. Ha, ha, ha. Some day I'll leave you a little nest egg. You like eggs? Ha?

HENNIE. When? When I'm dead and buried?

MORTY. No, when *I'm* dead and buried. Ha, ha, ha.

HENNIE. You should know what I'm thinking.

MORTY. Ha, ha, ha, I know.

[MYRON *enters.*]

MYRON. I never take a drink. I'm just surprised at myself, I—

MORTY. I got a pain. Maybe I'm hungry.

MYRON. Come inside, Morty. Bessie's got some schnapps.

MORTY. I'll take a drink. Yesterday I missed the Turkish bath.

MYRON. I get so bitter when I take a drink, it just surprises me.

MORTY. Look how fat. Say, you live once. . . . Quack, quack. [*Both exit.* MOE *stands silently in the doorway.*]

SAM [*entering*]. I'll make Leon's bottle now!

HENNIE. No, let him sleep, Sam. Take away the diaper. [*He does. Exits.*]

MOE [*advancing into the room*]. That your husband?

HENNIE. Don't you know?

MOE. Maybe he's a nurse you hired for the kid—it looks it—how he tends it. A guy comes howling to your old lady every time you look cock-eyed. Does he sleep with you?

HENNIE. Don't be so wise!

MOE [*indicating newspaper*]. Here's a dame strangled her hubby with wire. Claimed she didn't like him. Why don't you brain Sam with an axe some night?

HENNIE. Why don't you lay an egg, Axelrod?

MOE. I laid a few in my day, Feinschreiber. Hardboiled ones too.

HENNIE. Yeah?

MOE. Yeah. You wanna know what I see when I look in your eyes?

HENNIE. No.

MOE. Ted Lewis playing the clarinet—some of those high crazy notes! Christ, you coulda had a guy with some guts instead of a cluck stands around boilin' baby nipples.

HENNIE. Meaning you?

MOE. Meaning me, sweetheart.

HENNIE. Think you're pretty good.

MOE. You'd know if I slept with you again.

HENNIE. I'll smack your face in a minute.

MOE. You do and I'll break your arm. [*Holds up paper.*] Take a look. [*Reads.*] "Ten-day luxury cruise to Havana." That's the stuff you coulda had. Put up at ritzy hotels, frenchie soap, champagne. Now you're tied down to "Snake-Eye" here. What for? What's it get you? . . . a two by four flat on 108th Street . . . a pain in the bustle it gets you.

HENNIE. What's it to you?

MOE. I know you from the old days. How you like to spend it! What I mean! Lizard-skin shoes, perfume behind the ears. . . . You're in a mess, Paradise! Paradise—that's a hot one—yah, crazy to eat a knish at your own wedding.

HENNIE. I get it—you're jealous. You can't get me.

MOE. Don't make me laugh.

HENNIE. Kid Jailbird's been trying to make me for years. You'd give your other leg. I'm hooked? Maybe, but you're in the same boat. Only it's worse for you. I don't give a damn no more, but you gotta yen makes you—

MOE. Don't make me laugh.

HENNIE. Compared to you I'm sittin' on top of the world.

MOE. You're losing your looks. A dame don't stay young forever.

HENNIE. You're a liar. I'm only twenty-four.

MOE. When you comin' home to stay?

HENNIE. Wouldn't you like to know?

MOE. I'll get you again.

HENNIE. Think so?

MOE. Sure, whatever goes up comes down. You're easy —you remember—two for a nickel—a pushover! [*Suddenly she slaps him. They both seem stunned.*] What's the idea?

HENNIE. Go on . . . break my arm.

MOE [*as if saying "I love you"*]. Listen, lousy.

HENNIE. Go on, do something!

MOE. Listen—

HENNIE. You're so damn tough!

MOE. You like me. [*He takes her.*]

HENNIE. Take your hand off! [*Pushes him away.*] Come around when it's a flood again and they put you in the ark with the animals. Not even then—if you was the last man!

MOE. Baby, if you had a dog I'd love the dog.

HENNIE. Gorilla! [*Exits.* RALPH *enters.*]

RALPH. Were you here before?

MOE [*sits*]. What?

RALPH. When the call came for me?

MOE. What?

RALPH. The call came.

[JACOB *enters.*]

MOE [*rubbing his leg*]. No.

JACOB. Don't worry, Ralphie, she'll call back.

RALPH. Maybe not. I think somethin's the matter.

JACOB. What?

RALPH. I don't know. I took her home from the movie last night. She asked me what I'd think if she went away.

JACOB. Don't worry, she'll call again.

RALPH. Maybe not, if Mom insulted her. She gets it on both ends, the poor kid. Lived in an orphan asylum most of her life. They shove her around like an empty freight train.

JACOB. After dinner go see her.

RALPH. Twice they kicked me down the stairs.

JACOB. Life should have some dignity.

RALPH. Every time I go near the place I get heart failure. The uncle drives a bus. You oughta see him—like Babe Ruth.

MOE. Use your brains. Stop acting like a kid who still wets the bed. Hire a room somewhere—a club room for two members.

RALPH. Not that kind of proposition, Moe.

MOE. Don't be a bush leaguer all your life.

RALPH. Cut it out!

MOE [*on a sudden upsurge of emotion*]. Ever sleep with one? Look at 'im blush.

RALPH. You don't know her.

MOE. I seen her—the kind no one sees undressed till the undertaker works on her.

RALPH. Why give me the needles all the time? What'd I ever do to you?

MOE. Not a thing. You're a nice kid. But grow up! In life there's two kinds—the men that's sure of themselves and the ones who ain't! It's time you quit being a selling-plater and got in the first class.

JACOB. And you, Axelrod?

MOE [*to* JACOB]. Scratch your whiskers! [*To* RALPH.] Get independent. Get what-it-takes and be yourself. Do what you like.

RALPH. Got a suggestion?

[MORTY *enters, eating.*]

MOE. Sure, pick out a racket. Shake down the cocoanuts. See what that does.

MORTY. We know what it does—puts a pudding on your nose! Sing Sing! Easy money's against the law. Against the law don't win. A racket is illegitimate, no?

MOE. It's all a racket—from horse racing down. Marriage, politics, big business—everybody plays cops and robbers. You, you're a racketeer yourself.

MORTY. Who? Me? Personally I manufacture dresses.

MOE. Horse feathers!

MORTY [*seriously*]. Don't make such remarks to me

without proof. I'm a great one for proof. That's why
I made a success in business. Proof—put up or shut
up, like a game of cards. I heard this remark before
—a rich man's a crook who steals from the poor. Personally, I don't like it. It's a big lie!

MOE. If you don't like it, buy yourself a fife and drum
—and go fight your own war.

MORTY. Sweatshop talk. Every Jew and Wop in the
shop eats my bread and behind my back says, "a
sonofabitch." I started from a poor boy who worked
on an ice wagon for two dollars a week. Pop's right
here—he'll tell you. I made it honest. In the whole
industry nobody's got a better name.

JACOB. It's an exception, such success.

MORTY. Ralph can't do the same thing?

JACOB. No, Morty, I don't think. In a house like this
he don't realize even the possibilities of life. Economics comes down like a ton of coal on the head.

MOE. Red rover, red rover, let Jacob come over!

JACOB. In my day the propaganda was for God. Now
it's for success. A boy don't turn around without
having shoved in him he should make success.

MORTY. Pop, you're a comedian, a regular Charlie
Chaplin.

JACOB. He dreams all night of fortunes. Why not?
Don't it say in the movies he should have a personal
steamship, pyjamas for fifty dollars a pair and a toilet like a monument? But in the morning he wakes
up and for ten dollars he can't fix the teeth. And
millions more worse off in the mills of the South—
starvation wages. The blood from the worker's
heart. [MORTY *laughs loud and long.*] Laugh, laugh
. . . tomorrow not.

MORTY. A real, a real Boob McNutt you're getting to
be.

JACOB. Laugh, my son. . . .

MORTY. Here is the North, Pop.

JACOB. North, south, it's one country.

MORTY. The country's all right. A duck quacks in every pot!

JACOB. You never heard how they shoot down men and women which ask a better wage? Kentucky 1932?

MORTY. That's a pile of chopped liver, Pop.

[BESSIE *and others enter.*]

JACOB. Pittsburgh, Passaic, Illinois—slavery—it begins where success begins in a competitive system.

[MORTY *howls with delight.*]

MORTY. Oh, Pop, what are you bothering? Why? Tell me why? Ha ha ha. I bought you a phonograph . . . stick to Caruso.

BESSIE. He's starting up again.

MORTY. Don't bother with Kentucky. It's full of moonshiners.

JACOB. Sure, sure—

MORTY. You don't know practical affairs. Stay home and cut hair to fit the face.

JACOB. It says in the Bible how the Red Sea opened and the Egyptians went in and the sea rolled over them. [*Quotes two lines of Hebrew.*] In this boy's life a Red Sea will happen again. I see it!

MORTY. I'm getting sore, Pop, with all this sweatshop talk.

BESSIE. He don't stop a minute. The whole day, like a phonograph.

MORTY. I'm surprised. Without a rich man you don't have a roof over your head. You don't know it?

MYRON. Now you can't bite the hand that feeds you.

RALPH. Let him alone—he's right!

BESSIE. Another county heard from.

RALPH. It's the truth. It's—

MORTY. Keep quiet, snotnose!

JACOB. For sure, charity, a bone for an old dog. But in Russia an old man don't take charity so his eyes turn black in his head. In Russia they got Marx.

MORTY [*scoffingly*]. Who's Marx?

MOE. An outfielder for the Yanks.

[MORTY *howls with delight.*]

MORTY. Ha ha ha, it's better than the jokes. I'm telling you. This is Uncle Sam's country. Put it in your pipe and smoke it.

BESSIE. Russia, he says! Read the papers.

SAM. Here is opportunity.

MYRON. People can't believe in God in Russia. The papers tell the truth, they do.

JACOB. So you believe in God . . . you got something for it? You! You worked for all the capitalists. You harvested the fruit from your labor? You got God! But the past comforts you? The present smiles on you, yes? It promises you the future something? Did you found a piece of earth where you could live like a human being and die with the sun on your face? Tell me, yes, tell me. I would like to know myself. But on these questions, on this theme—the struggle for existence—you can't make an answer. The answer I see in your face . . . the answer is your mouth can't talk. In this dark corner you sit and you die. But abolish private property!

BESSIE [*settling the issue*]. Noo, go fight City Hall!

MORTY. He's drunk!

JACOB. I'm studying from books a whole lifetime.

MORTY. That's what it is—he's drunk. What the hell does all that mean?

JACOB. If you don't know, why should I tell you.

MORTY [*triumphant at last*]. You see? Hear him? Like all those nuts, don't know what they're saying.

JACOB. I know, I know.

MORTY. Like Boob McNutt you know! Don't go in the park, Pop—the squirrels'll get you. Ha, ha, ha . . .

BESSIE. Save your appetite, Morty. [*To* MYRON.] Don't drop the duck.

MYRON. We're ready to eat, Momma.

MORTY [*to* JACOB]. Shame on you. It's your second childhood.

[*Now they file out.* MYRON *first with the duck, the others behind him.*]

BESSIE. Come eat. We had enough for one day. [*Exits.*]

MORTY. Ha, ha, ha. Quack, quack. [*Exits.*]

[JACOB *sits there trembling and deeply humiliated.* MOE *approaches him and thumbs the old man's nose in the direction of the dining room.*]

MOE. Give 'em five. [*Takes his hand away.*] They got you pasted on the wall like a picture, Jake. [*He limps out to seat himself at the table in the next room.*]

JACOB. Go eat, boychick. [RALPH *comes to him.*] He gives me eat, so I'll climb in a needle. One time I saw an old horse in summer . . . he wore a straw hat . . . the ears stuck out on top. An old horse for hire. Give me back my young days . . . give me fresh blood . . . arms . . . give me—

[*The telephone rings. Quickly* RALPH *goes to it.* JACOB *pulls the curtains and stands there, a sentry on guard.*]

RALPH. Hello? . . . Yeah, I went to the store and came right back, right after you called. [*Looks at* JACOB.]

JACOB. Speak, speak. Don't be afraid they'll hear.

RALPH. I'm sorry if Mom said something. You know how excitable Mom is. . . . Sure! What? . . . Sure, I'm listening. . . . Put on the radio, Jake. [JACOB *does so. Music comes in and up, a tango, grating with an insistent nostalgic pulse. Under the cover of the music* RALPH *speaks more freely.*] Yes . . . yes . . . What's the matter? Why're you crying? What happened? [*To* JACOB.] She's putting her uncle on. Yes? . . . Listen, Mr. Hirsch, what're you trying to do? What's the big idea? Honest to God. I'm in no mood for joking! Lemme talk to her! Gimme Blanche! [*Waits.*] Blanche? What's this? Is this a joke? Is that true? I'm coming right down! I know, but— You wanna do that? . . . I know, but— I'm coming down . . . tonight! Nine o'clock . . . sure . . . sure . . . sure. . . . [*Hangs up.*]

JACOB. What happened?

MORTY [*enters*]. Listen, Pop. I'm surprised you didn't— [*He howls, shakes his head in mock despair, exits.*]

JACOB. Boychick, what?

RALPH. I don't get it straight. [*To* JACOB]. She's leaving. . . .

JACOB. Where?

RALPH. Out West— To Cleveland.

JACOB. Cleveland?

RALPH. . . . In a week or two. Can you picture it? It's a put-up job. But they can't get away with that.

JACOB. We'll find something.

RALPH. Sure, the angels of heaven'll come down on her uncle's cab and whisper in his ear.

JACOB. Come eat. . . . We'll find something.

RALPH. I'm meeting her tonight, but I know—

[BESSIE *throws open the curtain between the two rooms and enters.*]

BESSIE. Maybe we'll serve for you a special blue plate supper in the garden?

JACOB. All right, all right.

[BESSIE *goes over to the window, levels the shade and on her way out, clicks off the radio.*]

MORTY [*within*]. Leave the music, Bessie.

[*She clicks it on again, looks at them, exits.*]

RALPH. I know. . . .

JACOB. Don't cry, boychick. [*Goes over to* RALPH.] Why should you make like this? Tell me why you should cry, just tell me. . . . [JACOB *takes* RALPH *in his arms and both, trying to keep back the tears, trying fearfully not to be heard by the others in the dining room, begin crying.*] You mustn't cry. . . .

[*The tango twists on. Inside the clatter of dishes and the clash of cutlery sound.* MORTY *begins to howl with laughter.*]

CURTAIN

SCENE II

That night. The dark dining room.
AT RISE JACOB *is heard in his lighted room, reading from a sheet, declaiming aloud as if to an audience.*

JACOB. They are there to remind us of the horrors— under those crosses lie hundreds of thousands of workers and farmers who murdered each other in uniform for the greater glory of capitalism. [*Comes out of his room.*] The new imperialist war will send millions to their death, will bring prosperity to the pockets of the capitalist—aie, Morty—and will bring only greater hunger and misery to the masses of workers and farmers. The memories of the last world slaughter are still vivid in our minds. [*Hearing a noise he quickly retreats to his room.* RALPH *comes in from the street. He sits with hat and coat on.* JACOB *tentatively opens the door and asks:*] Ralphie?

RALPH. It's getting pretty cold out.

JACOB [*enters room fully, cleaning hair clippers*]. We should have steam till twelve instead of ten. Go complain to the Board of Health.

RALPH. It might snow.

JACOB. It don't hurt . . . extra work for men.

RALPH. When I was a kid I laid awake at nights and heard the sounds of trains . . . far-away lonesome sounds . . . boats going up and down the river. I used to think of all kinds of things I wanted to do. What was it, Jake? Just a bunch of noise in my head?

JACOB [*waiting for news of the girl*]. You wanted to make for yourself a certain kind of world.

RALPH. I guess I didn't. I'm feeling pretty, pretty low.

JACOB. You're a young boy and for you life is all in front like a big mountain. You got feet to climb.

RALPH. I don't know how.

JACOB. So you'll find out. Never a young man had such opportunity like today. He could make history.

RALPH. Ten p.m. and all is well. Where's everybody?

JACOB. They went.

RALPH. Uncle Morty too?

JACOB. Hennie and Sam he drove down.

RALPH. I saw her.

JACOB [*alert and eager*]. Yes, yes, tell me.

RALPH. I waited in Mount Morris Park till she came out. So cold I did a buck'n wing to keep warm. She's scared to death.

JACOB. They made her?

RALPH. Sure. She wants to go. They keep yelling at her—they want her to marry a millionaire, too.

JACOB. You told her you love her?

RALPH. Sure. "Marry me," I said. "Marry me tomorrow." On sixteen bucks a week. On top of that I had to admit Mom'd have Uncle Morty get me fired in a second. . . . Two can starve as cheap as one!

JACOB. So what happened?

RALPH. I made her promise to meet me tomorrow.

JACOB. Now she'll go in the West?

RALPH. I'd fight the whole goddam world with her, but not her. No guts. The hell with her. If she wantsa go—all right—I'll get along.

JACOB. For sure, there's more important things than girls. . . .

RALPH. You said a mouthful . . . and maybe I don't see it. She'll see what I can do. No one stops me when I get going. . . . [*Near to tears, he has to stop.* JACOB *examines his clippers very closely.*]

JACOB. Electric clippers never do a job like by hand.

RALPH. Why won't Mom let us live here?

JACOB. Why? Why? Because in a society like this today people don't love. Hate!

RALPH. Gee, I'm no bum who hangs around pool parlors. I got the stuff to go ahead. I don't know what to do.

JACOB. Look on me and learn what to do, boychick. Here sits an old man polishing tools. You think maybe I'll use them again! Look on this failure and see for seventy years he talked, with good ideas, but only in the head. It's enough for me now I should see your happiness. This is why I tell you—DO! Do what is in your heart and you carry in yourself a revolution. But you should act. Not like me. A man who had golden opportunities but drank instead a glass tea. No . . . [*A pause of silence.*]

RALPH [*listening*]. Hear it? The Boston air mail plane. Ten minutes late. I get a kick the way it cuts across the Bronx every night.

[*The bell rings:* SAM, *excited, disheveled, enters.*]

JACOB. You came back so soon?

SAM. Where's Mom?

JACOB. Mom? Look on the chandelier.

SAM. Nobody's home?

JACOB. Sit down. Right away they're coming. You went in the street without a tie?

SAM. Maybe it's a crime.

JACOB. Excuse me.

RALPH. You had a fight with Hennie again?

SAM. She'll fight once . . . some day. . . . [*Lapses into silence.*]

JACOB. In my day the daughter came home. Now comes the son-in-law.

SAM. Once too often she'll fight with me, Hennie. I mean it. I mean it like anything. I'm a person with a bad heart. I sit quiet, but inside I got a—

RALPH. What happened?

SAM. I'll talk to Mom. I'll see Mom.

JACOB. Take an apple.

SAM. Please . . . he tells me apples.

RALPH. Why hop around like a billiard ball?

SAM. Even in a joke she should dare say it.

JACOB. My grandchild said something?

SAM. To my father in the old country they did a joke . . . I'll tell you: One day in Odessa he talked to another Jew on the street. They didn't like it, they jumped on him like a wild wolf.

RALPH. Who?

SAM. Cossacks. They cut off his beard. A Jew without a beard! He came home—I remember like yesterday how he came home and went in bed for two days. He put like this the cover on his face. No one should see. The third morning he died.

RALPH. From what?

SAM. From a broken heart . . . Some people are like this. Me too. I could die like this from shame.

JACOB. Hennie told you something?

SAM. Straight out she said it—like a lightning from the sky. The baby ain't mine. She said it.

RALPH. Don't be a dope.

JACOB. For sure, a joke.

RALPH. She's kidding you.

SAM. She should kid a policeman, not Sam Feinschreiber. Please . . . you don't know her like me. I wake up in the nighttime and she sits watching me like I don't know what. I make a nice living from the store. But it's no use—she looks for a star in the sky. I'm afraid like anything. You could go crazy from less even. What I shall do I'll ask Mom.

JACOB. "Go home and sleep," she'll say. "It's a bad dream."

SAM. It don't satisfy me more, such remarks, when Hennie could kill in the bed. [JACOB *laughs*.] Don't laugh. I'm so nervous—look, two times I weighed myself on the subway station. [*Throws small cards to table.*]

JACOB [*examining one*]. One hundred and thirty-eight —also a fortune. [*Turns it and reads*.] "You are inclined to deep thinking, and have a high admiration for intellectual excellence and inclined to be very exclusive in the selection of friends." Correct! I think maybe you got mixed up in the wrong family, Sam.

[MYRON *and* BESSIE *now enter*.]

BESSIE. Look, a guest! What's the matter? Something wrong with the baby? [*Waits.*]

SAM. No.

BESSIE. Noo?

SAM [*in a burst*]. I wash my hands from everything.

BESSIE. Take off your coat and hat. Have a seat. Excitement don't help. Myron, make tea. You'll have a glass tea. We'll talk like civilized people. [MYRON *goes.*] What is it, Ralph, you're all dressed up for a party? [*He looks at her silently and exits. To* SAM.] We saw a very good movie, with Wallace Beery. He acts like life, very good.

MYRON [*within*]. Polly Moran too.

BESSIE. Polly Moran too—a woman with a nose from here to Hunts Point, but a fine player. Poppa, take away the tools and the books.

JACOB. All right. [*Exits to his room.*]

BESSIE. Noo, Sam, why do you look like a funeral?

SAM. I can't stand it. . . .

BESSIE. Wait. [*Yells.*] You took up Tootsie on the roof.

JACOB [*within*]. In a minute.

BESSIE. What can't you stand?

SAM. She said I'm a second fiddle in my own house.

BESSIE. Who?

SAM. Hennie. In the second place, it ain't my baby, she said.

BESSIE. What? What are you talking?

[MYRON *enters with dishes.*]

SAM. From her own mouth. It went like a knife in my heart.

BESSIE. Sam, what're you saying?

SAM. Please, I'm making a story? I fell in the chair like a dead.

BESSIE. Such a story you believe?

SAM. I don't know.

BESSIE. How you don't know?

SAM. She told me even the man.

BESSIE. Impossible!

SAM. I can't believe myself. But she said it. I'm a second fiddle, she said. She made such a yell everybody heard for ten miles.

BESSIE. Such a thing Hennie should say—impossible!

SAM. What should I do? With my bad heart such a remark kills.

MYRON. Hennie don't feel well, Sam. You see, she—

BESSIE. What then?—a sick girl. Believe me, a mother
knows. Nerves. Our Hennie's got a bad temper.
You'll let her she says anything. She takes after me
—nervous. [*To* MYRON.] You ever heard such a remark in all your life? She should make such a
statement! Bughouse.

MYRON. The little one's been sick all these months.
Hennie needs a rest. No doubt.

BESSIE. Sam don't think she means it—

MYRON. Oh, I know he don't, of course—

BESSIE. I'll say the truth, Sam. We didn't half the time
understand her ourselves. A girl with her own mind.
When she makes it up, wild horses wouldn't change
her.

SAM. She don't love me.

BESSIE. This is sensible, Sam?

SAM. Not for a nickel.

BESSIE. What do you think? She married you for your
money? For your looks? You ain't no John Barry-
more, Sam. No, she liked you.

SAM. Please, not for a nickel.

[JACOB *stands in the doorway*.]

BESSIE. We stood right here the first time she said it.
"Sam Feinschreiber's a nice boy," she said it, "a boy
he's got good common sense, with a business head."
Right here she said it, in this room. You sent her
two boxes of candy together, you remember?

MYRON. Loft's candy.

BESSIE. This is when she said it. What do you think?

MYRON. You were just the only boy she cared for.

BESSIE. So she married you. Such a world . . . plenty
of boy friends she had, believe me!

JACOB. A popular girl . . .

MYRON. Y-e-s.

BESSIE. I'll say it plain out—Moe Axelrod offered her plenty—a servant, a house . . . she don't have to pick up a hand.

MYRON. Oh, Moe? Just wild about her . . .

SAM. Moe Axelrod? He wanted to—

BESSIE. But she didn't care. A girl like Hennie you don't buy. I should never live to see another day if I'm telling a lie.

SAM. She was kidding me.

BESSIE. What then? You shouldn't be foolish.

SAM. The baby looks like my family. He's got Feinschreiber eyes.

BESSIE. A blind man could see it.

JACOB. Sure . . . sure. . . .

SAM. The baby looks like me. Yes . . .

BESSIE. You could believe me.

JACOB. Any day . . .

SAM. But she tells me the man. She made up his name too?

BESSIE. Sam, Sam, look in the phone book—a million names.

MYRON. Tom, Dick and Harry.

[JACOB *laughs quietly, soberly.*]

BESSIE. Don't stand around, Poppa. Take Tootsie on the roof. And you don't let her go under the water tank.

JACOB. Schmah Yisroeal. Behold! [*Quietly laughing he goes back into his room, closing the door behind him.*]

SAM. I won't stand he should make insults. A man eats out his—

BESSIE. No, no, he's an old man—a second childhood. Myron, bring in the tea. Open a jar of raspberry jelly.

[MYRON *exits.*]

SAM. Mom, you think—?

BESSIE. I'll talk to Hennie. It's all right.

SAM. Tomorrow, I'll take her by the doctor.

[RALPH *enters.*]

BESSIE. Stay for a little tea.

SAM. No, I'll go home. I'm tired. Already I caught a cold in such weather. [*Blows his nose.*]

MYRON [*entering with stuffs*]. Going home?

SAM. I'll go in bed. I caught a cold.

MYRON. Teddy Roosevelt used to say, "When you have a problem, sleep on it."

BESSIE. My Sam is no problem.

MYRON. I don't mean . . . I mean he said—

BESSIE. Call me tomorrow, Sam.

SAM. I'll phone supper time. Sometime I think there's something funny about me.

[MYRON *sees him out. In the following pause Caruso is heard singing within.*]

BESSIE. A bargain! Second fiddle. By me he don't even play in the orchestra—a man like a mouse. Maybe she'll lay down and die 'cause he makes a living?

RALPH. Can I talk to you about something?

BESSIE. What's the matter—I'm biting you?

RALPH. It's something about Blanche.

BESSIE. Don't tell me.

RALPH. Listen now—

BESSIE. I don't wanna know.

RALPH. She's got no place to go.

BESSIE. I don't want to know.

RALPH. Mom, I love this girl. . . .

BESSIE. So go knock your head against the wall.

RALPH. I want her to come here. Listen, Mom, I want you to let her live here for a while.

BESSIE. You got funny ideas, my son.

RALPH. I'm as good as anyone else. Don't I have some

rights in the world? Listen, Mom, if I don't do something, she's going away. Why don't you do it? Why don't you let her stay here for a few weeks? Things'll pick up. Then we can—

BESSIE. Sure, sure. I'll keep her fresh on ice for a wedding day. That's what you want?

RALPH. No, I mean you should—

BESSIE. Or maybe you'll sleep here in the same bed without marriage.

[JACOB *stands in his doorway, dressed.*]

RALPH. Don't say that, Mom. I only mean . . .

BESSIE. What you mean, I know . . . and what I mean I also know. Make up your mind. For your own good, Ralphie. If she dropped in the ocean I don't lift a finger.

RALPH. That's all, I suppose.

BESSIE. With me it's one thing—a boy should have respect for his own future. Go to sleep, you look tired. In the morning you'll forget.

JACOB. "Awake and sing, ye that dwell in dust, and the earth shall cast out the dead." It's cold out?

MYRON. Oh, yes.

JACOB. I'll take up Tootsie now.

MYRON [*eating bread and jam*]. He come on us like the wild man of Borneo, Sam. I don't think Hennie was fool enough to tell him the truth like that.

BESSIE. Myron!

[*A deep pause.*]

RALPH. What did he say?

BESSIE. Never mind.

RALPH. I heard him. I heard him. You don't needa tell me.

BESSIE. Never mind.

RALPH. You trapped that guy.

BESSIE. Don't say another word.

RALPH. Just have respect? That's the idea?

BESSIE. Don't say another word. I'm boiling over ten times inside.

RALPH. You won't let Blanche here, huh. I'm not sure I want her. You put one over on that little shrimp. The cat's whiskers, Mom?

BESSIE. I'm telling you something!

RALPH. I got the whole idea. I get it so quick my head's swimming. Boy, what a laugh! I suppose you know about this, Jake?

JACOB. Yes.

RALPH. Why didn't you do something?

JACOB. I'm an old man.

RALPH. What's that got to do with the price of bonds? Sits around and lets a thing like that happen! You make me sick too.

MYRON [*after a pause*]. Let me say something, son.

RALPH. Take your hand away! Sit in a corner and wag your tail. Keep on boasting you went to law school for two years.

MYRON. I want to tell you—

RALPH. You never in your life had a thing to tell me.

BESSIE [*bitterly*]. Don't say a word. Let him, let him run and tell Sam. Publish in the papers, give a broadcast on the radio. To him it don't matter nothing his family sits with tears pouring from the eyes. [*To* JACOB.] What are you waiting for? I didn't tell you twice already about the dog? You'll stand around with Caruso and make a bughouse. It ain't enough all day long. Fifty times I told you I'll break every record in the house. [*She brushes past him, breaks the records, comes out.*] The next time I say something you'll maybe believe it. Now maybe you learned a lesson.

[*Pause.*]

JACOB [*quietly*]. Bessie, new lessons . . . not for an old dog.

[MOE *enters*.]

MYRON. You didn't have to do it, Momma.

BESSIE. Talk better to your son, Mr. Berger! Me, I don't lay down and die for him and Poppa no more. I'll work like a nigger? For what? Wait, the day comes when you'll be punished. When it's too late you'll remember how you sucked away a mother's life. Talk to him, tell him how I don't sleep at night. [*Bursts into tears and exits*.]

MOE [*sings*]. "Good-bye to all your sorrows. You never hear them talk about the war, in the land of Yama Yama. . . ."

MYRON. Yes, Momma's a sick woman, Ralphie.

RALPH. Yeah?

MOE. We'll be out of the trenches by Christmas. Putt, putt, putt . . . here, stinker. . . . [*Picks up Tootsie, a small, white poodle that just then enters from the hall*.] If there's reincarnation in the next life I wanna be a dog and lay in a fat lady's lap. Barrage over? How 'bout a little pinochle, Pop?

JACOB. Nnno.

RALPH [*taking dog*]. I'll take her up. [*Conciliatory*.]

JACOB. No, I'll do it. [*Takes dog*.]

RALPH [*ashamed*]. It's cold out.

JACOB. I was cold before in my life. A man sixty-seven. . . . [*Strokes the dog*.] Tootsie is my favorite lady in the house. [*He slowly passes across the room and exits. A settling pause*.]

MYRON. She cried all last night—Tootsie—I heard her in the kitchen like a young girl.

MOE. Tonight I could do something. I got a yen . . . I don't know.

MYRON [*rubbing his head*]. My scalp is impoverished.

RALPH. Mom bust all his records.

MYRON. She didn't have to do it.

MOE. Tough tit! Now I can sleep in the morning. Who the hell wantsa hear a wop air his tonsils all day long!

RALPH [*handling the fragment of a record*]. "O Paradiso!"

MOE [*gets cards*]. It's snowing out, girls.

MYRON. There's no more big snows like in the old days. I think the whole world's changing. I see it, right under our very eyes. No one hardly remembers any more when we used to have gaslight and all the dishes had little fishes on them.

MOE. It's the system, girls.

MYRON. I was a little boy when it happened—the Great Blizzard. It snowed three days without a stop that time. Yes, and the horse cars stopped. A silence of death was on the city and little babies got no milk . . . they say a lot of people died that year.

MOE [*singing as he deals himself cards*].
    "Lights are blinking while you're drinking,
    That's the place where the good fellows go.
    Good-bye to all your sorrows,
    You never hear them talk about the war,
    In the land of Yama Yama.
    Funicalee, funicala, funicalo. . . ."

MYRON. What can I say to you, Big Boy?

RALPH. Not a damn word.

MOE [*goes "ta ra ta ra" throughout.*]

MYRON. I know how you feel about all those things, I know.

RALPH. Forget it.

MYRON. And your girl . . .

RALPH. Don't soft soap me all of a sudden.

MYRON. I'm not foreign born. I'm an American, and

yet I never got close to you. It's an American father's duty to be his son's friend.

RALPH. Who said that—Teddy R.?

MOE [*dealing cards*]. You're breaking his heart, "Litvak."

MYRON. It just happened the other day. The moment I began losing my hair I just knew I was destined to be a failure in life . . . and when I grew bald I was. Now isn't that funny, Big Boy?

MOE. It's a pisscutter!

MYRON. I believe in Destiny.

MOE. You get what-it-takes. Then they don't catch you with your pants down. [*Sings out.*] Eight of clubs. . . .

MYRON. I really don't know. I sold jewelry on the road before I married. It's one thing to— Now here's a thing the druggist gave me. [*Reads.*] "The Marvel Cosmetic Girl of Hollywood is going on the air. Give this charming little radio singer a name and win five thousand dollars. If you will send—"

MOE. Your old man still believes in Santy Claus.

MYRON. Someone's got to win. The government isn't gonna allow everything to be a fake.

MOE. It's a fake. There ain't no prizes. It's a fake.

MYRON. It says—

RALPH [*snatching it*]. For Christ's sake, Pop, forget it. Grow up. Jake's right—everybody's crazy. It's like a zoo in this house. I'm going to bed.

MOE. In the land of Yama Yama . . . [*Goes on with ta ra.*]

MYRON. Don't think life's easy with Momma. No, but she means for your good all the time. I tell you she does, she—

RALPH. Maybe, but I'm going to bed.

[*Downstairs doorbell rings violently.*]

MOE [*ring*]. Enemy barrage begins on sector eight seventy-five.

RALPH. That's downstairs.

MYRON. We ain't expecting anyone this hour of the night.

MOE. "Lights are blinking while you're drinking, that's the place where the good fellows go. Good-bye to ta ra tara ra," etc.

RALPH. I better see who it is.

MYRON. I'll tick the button. [*As he starts, the apartment doorbell begins ringing, followed by large knocking.* MYRON *goes out.*]

RALPH. Who's ever ringing means it.

[*A loud excited voice outside.*]

MOE. "In the land of Yama Yama, Funicalee, funicalo, funic—"

[MYRON *enters followed by* SCHLOSSER *the janitor.* BESSIE *cuts in from the other side.*]

BESSIE. Who's ringing like a lunatic?

RALPH. What's the matter?

MYRON. Momma . . .

BESSIE. Noo, what's the matter?

[*Downstairs bell continues.*]

RALPH. What's the matter?

BESSIE. Well, well . . . ?

MYRON. Poppa . . .

BESSIE. What happened?

SCHLOSSER. He shlipped maybe in de snow.

RALPH. Who?

SCHLOSSER [*to* BESSIE]. Your fadder fall off de roof. . . . Ja.

[*A dead pause.* RALPH *then runs out.*]

BESSIE [*dazed*]. Myron . . . Call Morty on the phone . . . call him. [MYRON *starts for phone.*] No. I'll do it myself. I'll . . . do it.

[MYRON *exits.*]

SCHLOSSER [*standing stupidly*]. Since I was in dis country . . . I was pudding out de ash can . . . The snow is vet. . . .

MOE [*to* SCHLOSSER]. Scram.

[SCHLOSSER *exits.*]

[BESSIE *goes blindly to the phone, fumbles and gets it.* MOE *sits quietly, slowly turning cards over, but watching her.*]

BESSIE. He slipped. . . .

MOE [*deeply moved*]. Slipped?

BESSIE. I can't see the numbers. Make it, Moe, make it. . . .

MOE. Make it yourself. [*He looks at her and slowly goes back to his game of cards with shaking hands.*]

BESSIE. Riverside 7— . . . [*Unable to talk she dials slowly. The dial whizzes on.*]

MOE. Don't . . . make me laugh. . . . [*He turns over cards.*]

CURTAIN

Act three

A week later in the dining room. MORTY, BESSIE *and* MYRON *eating. Sitting in the front room is* MOE *marking a "dope sheet," but really listening to the others.*

BESSIE. You're sure he'll come tonight—the insurance man?

MORTY. Why not? I shtupped him a ten-dollar bill. Everything's hot delicatessen.

BESSIE. Why must he come so soon?

MORTY. Because you had a big expense. You'll settle

once and for all. I'm a great boy for making hay while the sun shines.

BESSIE. Stay till he'll come, Morty. . . .

MORTY. No, I got a strike downtown. Business don't stop for personal life. Two times already in the past week those bastards threw stink bombs in the showroom. Wait! We'll give them strikes—in the kishkas we'll give them. . . .

BESSIE. I'm a woman. I don't know about policies. Stay till he comes.

MORTY. Bessie—sweetheart, leave me live.

BESSIE. I'm afraid, Morty.

MORTY. Be practical. They made an investigation. Everybody knows Pop had an accident. Now we'll collect.

MYRON. Ralphie don't know Papa left the insurance in his name.

MORTY. It's not his business. And I'll tell him.

BESSIE. The way he feels. [*Enter* RALPH *into front room.*] He'll do something crazy. He thinks Poppa jumped off the roof.

MORTY. Be practical, Bessie. Ralphie will sign when I tell him. Everything is peaches and cream.

BESSIE. Wait for a few minutes. . . .

MORTY. Look, I'll show you in black on white what the policy says. *For God's sake, leave me live!* [*Angrily exits to kitchen. In parlor,* MOE *speaks to* RALPH, *who is reading a letter.*]

MOE. What's the letter say?

RALPH. Blanche won't see me no more, she says. I couldn't care very much, she says. If I didn't come like I said. . . . She'll phone before she leaves.

MOE. She don't know about Pop?

RALPH. She won't ever forget me she says. Look what she sends me . . . a little locket on a chain . . . if she calls I'm out.

MOE. You mean it?

RALPH. For a week I'm trying to go in his room. I guess he'd like me to have it, but I can't. . . .

MOE. Wait a minute! [*Crosses over.*] They're trying to rook you—a freeze-out.

RALPH. Who?

MOE. That bunch stuffin' their gut with hot pastrami. Morty in particular. Jake left the insurance—three thousand dollars—for you.

RALPH. For me?

MOE. Now you got wings, kid. Pop figured you could use it. That's why . . .

RALPH. That's why what?

MOE. It ain't the only reason he done it.

RALPH. He done it?

MOE. You think a breeze blew him off?

[HENNIE *enters and sits.*]

RALPH. I'm not sure what I think.

MOE. The insurance guy's coming tonight. Morty "shtupped" him.

RALPH. Yeah?

MOE. I'll back you up. You're dead on your feet. Grab a sleep for yourself.

RALPH. No!

MOE. Go on! [*Pushes boy into room.*]

SAM [*whom* MORTY *has sent in for the paper*]. Morty wants the paper.

HENNIE. So?

SAM. You're sitting on it. [*Gets paper.*] We could go home now, Hennie! Leon is alone by Mrs. Strasberg a whole day.

HENNIE. Go on home if you're so anxious. A full tub of diapers is waiting.

SAM. Why should you act this way?

HENNIE. 'Cause there's no bones in ice cream. Don't touch me.

SAM. Please, what's the matter. . . .

MOE. She don't like you. Plain as the face on your nose . . .

SAM. To me, my friend, you talk a foreign language.

MOE. A quarter you're lousy. [SAM *exits.*] Gimme a buck, I'll run it up to ten.

HENNIE. Don't do me no favors.

MOE. Take a chance. [*Stopping her as she crosses to doorway.*]

HENNIE. I'm a pushover.

MOE. I say lotsa things. You don't know me.

HENNIE. I know you—when you knock 'em down you're through.

MOE [*sadly*]. You still don't know me.

HENNIE. I know what goes in your wise-guy head.

MOE. Don't run away. . . . I ain't got hydrophobia. Wait. I want to tell you. . . . I'm leaving.

HENNIE. Leaving?

MOE. Tonight. Already packed.

HENNIE. Where?

MORTY [*as he enters followed by the others*]. My car goes through snow like a dose of salts.

BESSIE. Hennie, go eat. . . .

MORTY. Where's Ralphie?

MOE. In his new room. [*Moves into dining room.*]

MORTY. I didn't have a piece of hot pastrami in my mouth for years.

BESSIE. Take a sandwich, Hennie. You didn't eat all day. . . . [*At window.*] A whole week it rained cats and dogs.

MYRON. Rain, rain, go away. Come again some other days. [*Puts shawl on her.*]

MORTY. Where's my gloves?

SAM [*sits on stool*]. I'm sorry the old man lays in the rain.

MORTY. Personally, Pop was a fine man. But I'm a great

boy for an honest opinion. He had enough crazy ideas for a regiment.

MYRON. Poppa never had a doctor in his whole life. . . . [*Enter* RALPH.]

MORTY. He had Caruso. Who's got more from life?

BESSIE. Who's got more? . . .

MYRON. And Marx he had.

[MYRON *and* BESSIE *sit on sofa.*]

MORTY. Marx! Some say Marx is the new God today. Maybe I'm wrong. Ha ha ha . . . Personally I counted my ten million last night. . . . I'm sixteen cents short. So tomorrow I'll go to Union Square and yell no equality in the country! Ah, it's a new generation.

RALPH. You said it!

MORTY. What's the matter, Ralphie? What are you looking funny?

RALPH. I hear I'm left insurance and the man's coming tonight.

MORTY. Poppa didn't leave no insurance for you.

RALPH. What?

MORTY. In your name he left it—but not for you.

RALPH. It's my name on the paper.

MORTY. Who said so?

RALPH [*to his mother*]. The insurance man's coming tonight?

MORTY. What's the matter?

RALPH. I'm not talking to you. [*To his mother.*] Why?

BESSIE. I don't know why.

RALPH. He don't come in this house tonight.

MORTY. That's what *you* say.

RALPH. I'm not talking to you, Uncle Morty, but I'll tell you, too, he don't come here tonight when there's still mud on a grave. [*To his mother.*] Couldn't you give the house a chance to cool off?

MORTY. Is this a way to talk to your mother?

RALPH. Was that a way to talk to your father?

MORTY. Don't be so smart with me, Mr. Ralph Berger!

RALPH. Don't be so smart with *me*.

MORTY. What'll you do? I say he's coming tonight. Who says no?

MOE [*suddenly, from the background*]. Me.

MORTY. Take a back seat, Axelrod. When you're in the family—

MOE. I got a little document here. [*Produces paper*.] I found it under his pillow that night. A guy who slips off a roof don't leave a note before he does it.

MORTY [*starting for* MOE *after a horrified silence*]. Let me see this note.

BESSIE. Morty, don't touch it!

MOE. Not if you crawled.

MORTY. It's a fake. Poppa wouldn't—

MOE. Get the insurance guy here and we'll see how— [*The bell rings*]. Speak of the devil . . . Answer it, see what happens.

[MORTY *starts for the ticker*.]

BESSIE. Morty, don't!

MORTY [*stopping*]. Be practical, Bessie.

MOE. Sometimes you don't collect on suicides if they know about it.

MORTY. You should let . . . You should let him. . . .

[*A pause in which* ALL *seem dazed. Bell rings insistently*.]

MOE. Well, we're waiting.

MORTY. Give me the note.

MOE. I'll give you the head off your shoulders.

MORTY. Bessie, you'll stand for this? [*Points to* RALPH.] Pull down his pants and give him with a strap.

RALPH [*as bell rings again*]. How about it?

BESSIE. Don't be crazy. It's not my fault. Morty said he should come tonight. It's not nice so soon. I didn't—

MORTY. I said it? Me?

BESSIE. Who then?

MORTY. You didn't sing a song in my ear a whole week to settle quick?

BESSIE. I'm surprised. Morty, you're a big liar.

MYRON. Momma's telling the truth, she is!

MORTY. Lissen. In two shakes of a lamb's tail, we'll start a real fight and then nobody won't like nobody. Where's my fur gloves? I'm going downtown. [*To* SAM.] You coming? I'll drive you down.

HENNIE [*to* SAM, *who looks questioningly at her*]. Don't look at me. Go home if you want.

SAM. If you're coming soon, I'll wait.

HENNIE. Don't do me any favors. Night and day he pesters me.

MORTY. You made a cushion—sleep!

SAM. I'll go home. I know . . . to my worst enemy I don't wish such a life—

HENNIE. Sam, keep quiet.

SAM [*quietly; sadly*]. No more free speech in America? [*Gets his hat and coat.*] I'm a lonely person. Nobody likes me.

MYRON. I like you, Sam.

HENNIE [*going to him gently; sensing the end*]. Please go home, Sam. I'll sleep here. . . . I'm tired and nervous. Tomorrow I'll come home. I love you. . . . I mean it. [*She kisses him with real feeling.*]

SAM. I would die for you. . . . [SAM *looks at her. Tries to say something, but his voice chokes up with a mingled feeling. He turns and leaves the room.*]

MORTY. A bird in the hand is worth two in the bush. Remember I said it. Good night. [*Exits after* SAM.]

[HENNIE *sits depressed.* BESSIE *goes up and looks at the picture calendar again.* MYRON *finally breaks the silence.*]

MYRON. Yesterday a man wanted to sell me a saxophone with pearl buttons. But I—

BESSIE. It's a beautiful picture. In this land, nobody works. . . . Nobody worries. . . . Come to bed, Myron. [*Stops at the door, and says to* RALPH.] Please don't have foolish ideas about the money.

RALPH. Let's call it a day.

BESSIE. It belongs for the whole family. You'll get your teeth fixed—

RALPH. And a pair of black and white shoes?

BESSIE. Hennie needs a vacation. She'll take two weeks in the mountains and I'll mind the baby.

RALPH. I'll take care of my own affairs.

BESSIE. A family needs for a rainy day. Times is getting worse. Prospect Avenue, Dawson, Beck Street— every day furniture's on the sidewalk.

RALPH. Forget it, Mom.

BESSIE. Ralphie, I worked too hard all my years to be treated like dirt. It's no law we should be stuck together like Siamese twins. Summer shoes you didn't have, skates you never had, but I bought a new dress every week. A lover I kept—Mr. Gigolo! Did I ever play a game of cards like Mrs. Marcus? Or was Bessie Berger's children always the cleanest on the block?! Here I'm not only the mother, but also the father. The first two years I worked in a stocking factory for six dollars while Myron Berger went to law school. If I didn't worry about the family who would? On the calendar it's a different place, but here without a dollar you don't look the world in the eye. Talk from now to next year—this is life in America.

RALPH. Then it's wrong. It don't make sense. If life made you this way, then it's wrong!

BESSIE. Maybe you wanted me to give up twenty years

ago. Where would you be now? You'll excuse my expression—a bum in the park!

RALPH. I'm not blaming you, Mom. Sink or swim—I see it. But it can't stay like this.

BESSIE. My foolish boy . . .

RALPH. No, I see every house lousy with lies and hate. He said it, Grandpa— Brooklyn hates the Bronx. Smacked on the nose twice a day. But boys and girls can get ahead like that, Mom. We don't want life printed on dollar bills, Mom!

BESSIE. So go out and change the world if you don't like it.

RALPH. I will! And why? 'Cause life's different in my head. Gimme the earth in two hands. I'm strong. There . . . hear him? The air mail off to Boston. Day or night, he flies away, a job to do. That's us and it's no time to die.

[*The airplane sound fades off as* MYRON *gives alarm clock to* BESSIE *which she begins to wind.*]

BESSIE. "Mom, what does she know? She's old-fashioned!" But I'll tell you a big secret: My whole life I wanted to go away too, but with children a woman stays home. A fire burned in *my* heart too, but now it's too late. I'm no spring chicken. The clock goes and Bessie goes. Only my machinery can't be fixed. [*She lifts a button: the alarm rings on the clock; she stops it, says "Good night" and exits.*]

MYRON. I guess I'm no prize bag. . . .

BESSIE [*from within*]. Come to bed, Myron.

MYRON [*tears page off calendar*]. Hmmm . . . [*Exits to her.*]

RALPH. Look at him, draggin' after her like an old shoe.

MOE. Punch drunk. [*Phone rings.*] That's for me. [*At*

phone.] Yeah? . . . Just a minute. [*To* RALPH.] Your girl . . .

RALPH. Jeez, I don't know what to say to her.

MOE. Hang up?

[RALPH *slowly takes phone*.]

RALPH. Hello. . . . Blanche, I wish. . . . I don't know what to say. . . . Yes . . . Hello? . . . [*Puts phone down*.] She hung up on me. . . .

MOE. Sorry?

RALPH. No girl means anything to me until . . .

MOE. Till when?

RALPH. Till I can take care of her. Till we don't look out on an airshaft. Till we can take the world in two hands and polish off the dirt.

MOE. That's a big order.

RALPH. Once upon a time I thought I'd drown to death in bolts of silk and velour. But I grew up these last few weeks. Jake said a lot.

MOE. Your memory's okay?

RALPH. But take a look at this. [*Brings armful of books from* JACOB'S *room—dumps them on table*.] His books, I got them too—the pages ain't cut in half of them.

MOE. Perfect.

RALPH. Does it prove something? Damn tootin'! A ten-cent nail-file cuts them. Uptown, downtown, I'll read them on the way. Get a big lamp over the bed. [*Picks up one*.] My eyes are good. [*Puts book in pocket*.] Sure, inventory tomorrow. Coletti to Driscoll to Berger—that's how we work. It's a team down the warehouse. Driscoll's a show-off, a wiseguy, and Joe talks pigeons day and night. But they're like me, looking for a chance to get to first base too. Joe razzed me about my girl. But he don't know why. I'll tell him. Hell, he might tell me something I don't know. Get teams together all over. Spit on your hands and get to work. And with enough teams together maybe we'll get steam in the warehouse so our fingers don't freeze off. Maybe we'll fix it so life won't be printed on dollar bills.

MOE. Graduation Day.

RALPH [*starts for door of his room, stops*]. Can I have . . . Grandpa's note?

MOE. Sure you want it?

RALPH. Please— [MOE *gives it.*] It's blank!

MOE [*taking note back and tearing it up*]. That's right.

RALPH. Thanks! [*Exits.*]

MOE. The kid's a fighter! [*To* HENNIE.] Why are you crying?

HENNIE. I never cried in my life. [*She is now.*]

MOE [*starts for door. Stops*]. You told Sam you love him. . . .

HENNIE. If I'm sore on life, why take it out on him?

MOE. You won't forget me to your dyin' day—I was the first guy. Part of your insides. You won't forget. I wrote my name on you—indelible ink!

HENNIE. One thing I won't forget—how you left me crying on the bed like I was two for a cent!

MOE. Listen, do you think—

HENNIE. Sure. Waits till the family goes to the open air movie. He brings me perfume. . . . He grabs my arms—

MOE. You won't forget me!

HENNIE. How you left the next week?

MOE. So I made a mistake. For Chris' sake, don't act like the Queen of Roumania!

HENNIE. Don't make me laugh!

MOE. What the hell do you want, my head on a plate? Was my life so happy? Chris', my old man was a bum. I supported the whole damn family—five kids and Mom. When they grew up they beat it the hell away like rabbits. Mom died. I went to the war; got clapped down like a bedbug; woke up in a room without a leg. What the hell do you think, anyone's got it better than you? I never had a home either. I'm lookin' too!

HENNIE. So what?

MOE. So you're it—you're home for me, a place to live! That's the whole parade, sickness, eating out your heart! Sometimes you meet a girl—she stops it— that's love. . . . So take a chance! Be with me, Paradise. What's to lose?

HENNIE. My pride!

MOE [*grabbing her*]. What do you want? Say the word —I'll tango on a dime. Don't gimme ice when your heart's on fire!

HENNIE. Let me go!

[*He stops her.*]

MOE. WHERE?!

HENNIE. What do you want, Moe, what do you want?

MOE. You!

HENNIE. You'll be sorry you ever started—

MOE. You!

HENNIE. Moe, lemme go— [*Trying to leave.*] I'm getting up early—lemme go.

MOE. No! . . . I got enough fever to blow the whole damn town to hell. [*He suddenly releases her and half stumbles backwards. Forces himself to quiet down.*] You wanna go back to him? Say the word. I'll know what to do. . . .

HENNIE [*helplessly*]. Moe, I don't know what to say.

MOE. Listen to me.

HENNIE. What?

MOE. Come away. A certain place where it's moonlight and roses. We'll lay down, count stars. Hear the big ocean making noise. You lay under the trees. Champagne flows like— [*Phone rings.* MOE *finally answers the telephone.*] Hello? . . . Just a minute. [*Looks at* HENNIE.]

HENNIE. Who is it?

MOE. Sam.

HENNIE [*starts for phone, but changes her mind*]. I'm sleeping. . . .

MOE [*in phone*]. She's sleeping. . . . [*Hangs up. Watches* HENNIE *who slowly sits.*] He wants you to know he got home O.K. . . . What's on your mind?

HENNIE. Nothing.

MOE. Sam?

HENNIE. They say it's a palace on those Havana boats.

MOE. What's on your mind?

HENNIE [*trying to escape*]. Moe, I don't care for Sam— I never loved him—

MOE. But your kid—?

HENNIE. All my life I waited for this minute.

MOE [*holding her*]. Me too. Made believe I was talkin' just bedroom golf, but you and me forever was what I meant! Christ, baby, there's one life to live! Live it!

HENNIE. Leave the baby?

MOE. Yeah!

HENNIE. I can't. . . .

MOE. You can!

HENNIE. No. . . .

MOE. But you're not sure!

HENNIE. I don't know.

MOE. Make a break or spend the rest of your life in a coffin.

HENNIE. Oh, God, I don't know where I stand.

MOE. Don't look up there. Paradise, you're on a big boat headed south. No more pins and needles in your heart, no snake juice squirted in your arm. The whole world's green grass and when you cry it's because you're happy.

HENNIE. Moe, I don't know. . . .

MOE. Nobody knows, but you do it and find out. When you're scared the answer's zero.

HENNIE. You're hurting my arm.

MOE. The doctor said it—cut off your leg to save your life! And they done it—one thing to get another.

[*Enter* RALPH.]

RALPH. I didn't hear a word, but do it, Hennie, do it!

MOE. Mom can mind the kid. She'll go on forever, Mom. We'll send money back, and Easter eggs.

RALPH. I'll be here.

MOE. Get your coat . . . get it.

HENNIE. Moe!

MOE. I know . . . but get your coat and hat and kiss the house good-bye.

HENNIE. The man I love. . . . [MYRON *entering.*] I left my coat in Mom's room. [*Exits.*]

MYRON. Don't wake her up, Beauty. Momma fell asleep as soon as her head hit the pillow. I can't sleep. It was a long day. Hmmm. [*Examines his tongue in a buffet mirror.*] I was reading the other day a person with a thick tongue is feebleminded. I can do anything with my tongue. Make it thick, flat. No fruit in the house lately. Just a lone apple. [*He gets apple and paring knife and starts paring.*] Must be something wrong with me—I say I won't eat but I eat. [HENNIE *enters dressed to go out.*] Where you going, little Red Riding Hood?

HENNIE. Nobody knows, Peter Rabbit.

MYRON. You're looking very pretty tonight. You were a beautiful baby too. 1910, that was the year you was born. The same year Teddy Roosevelt come back from Africa.

HENNIE. Gee, Pop; you're such a funny guy.

MYRON. He was a boisterous man, Teddy. Good night. [*He exits, paring apple.*]

RALPH. When I look at him, I'm sad. Let me die like a dog, if I can't get more from life.

HENNIE. Where?

RALPH. Right here in the house! My days won't be for nothing. Let Mom have the dough. I'm twenty-two and kickin'! I'll get along. Did Jake die for us to fight about nickels? No! "Awake and sing," he said. Right here he stood and said it. The night he died, I saw it like a thunderbolt! I saw he was dead and I was born! I swear to God, I'm one week old! I want the whole city to hear it—fresh blood, arms. We got 'em. We're glad we're living.

MOE. I wouldn't trade you for two pitchers and an out-fielder. Hold the fort!

RALPH. So long.

MOE. So long.

[*They go and* RALPH *stands full and strong in the doorway, seeing them off, as the curtain slowly falls.*]

CURTAIN

END OF SUMMER

by S. N. Behrman

For May and Harold Freedman

From *Four Plays by S. N. Behrman.*
Copyright 1936 by Samuel N. Behrman.
Reprinted by permission of Random House, Inc.

*First production, February 17, 1936,
at the Guild Theatre, New York,
with the following cast:*

WILL DEXTER, *Shepperd Strudwick*
MRS. WYLER, *Mildred Natwick*
PAULA FROTHINGHAM, *Doris Dudley*
ROBERT, *Kendall Clark*
LEONIE FROTHINGHAM, *Ina Claire*
SAM FROTHINGHAM, *Minor Watson*
DR. KENNETH RICE, *Osgood Perkins*
DENNIS MCCARTHY, *Van Heflin*
DR. DEXTER, *Herbert Yost*
BORIS, COUNT MIRSKY, *Tom Powers*

SCENE

*The action of the play takes place in the
living room of Bay Cottage, the Frothinghams'
summer place in Northern Maine.*

TIME—*The present.*

Act one

SCENE—*The verandah-living room of the Frothingham estate, Bay Cottage, in Northern Maine. It is a charmingly furnished room with beautiful old distinguished pieces. A chintz couch and chairs give the room an air of informality. Beyond the door back you see a spacious, more formal room. Through the series of glass windows over the curving window seat on the right wall you see the early budding lilac and sumach. Woodbine and Virginia creeper are sprawling over the fence of native stone. Silver birch and maple are beginning to put out their leaves. The tops of red pine and cedar are visible over the rocks which fall away to the sea.*

TIME. *The present. A lovely afternoon in May.*

AT RISE. MRS. WYLER, *a very old lady and* WILL DEXTER, *an attractive, serious boy, are engaged in conversation.* MRS. WYLER *is knitting.*

WILL. When you were a young girl in Cleveland, did you see much of Mr. Rockefeller?

MRS. WYLER. Not much. Of course my husband saw him every day at the office. But he never came to our house. We were young and worldly. He was strict and religious.

WILL. Did you suspect, in those days, how rich you were going to be?

MRS. WYLER. Mercy no! We debated a long time before we moved up to Cleveland from Oil City. My mother thought Oil City was no place to bring up a young girl. She finally persuaded my father to let us move up to Cleveland. But there was a lot of talk about the expense.

WILL. Was Oil City lively?

MRS. WYLER [*demurely*]. It was pretty rough! I remember the celebration when they ran the first pipe-line through to Pittsburgh. That was a celebration!

WILL. The oil just poured, didn't it? Gushed out of the ground in great jets, and the people swarmed from everywhere to scoop it up.

MRS. WYLER. I remember we had a gusher in our back-yard. We put a fence around it to keep the cows from lapping up the oil.

WILL. Were you excited?

MRS. WYLER. Not by the oil.

WILL. I should think you would have been!

MRS. WYLER [*dryly*]. We weren't. Oil was smelly. We wanted to get away from it. We discovered bath-salts.

WILL. You didn't know it was the true fountain of your —dynasty?

MRS. WYLER. We left it to the men—as I look back over my life the principal excitement came from houses— buying and building houses. The shack in Oil City to the mansion on Fifth Avenue. We had houses everywhere—houses in London, houses in Paris, Newport and this—and yet, it seemed to me, we were always checking in and out of hotels.

WILL. It seems strange to think—

MRS. WYLER. What?

WILL. This golden stream—that you stumbled on so accidentally—it's flowing still—quenchless—and you on it—all you dynastic families—floating along in it —in luxurious barges!

MRS. WYLER. When I read these books about the early days of oil—these debunking books, you call them— they make me smile.

WILL. Do they? Why? I'd like to know that.

MRS. WYLER. They're so far from the truth.

WILL. Are they?

MRS. WYLER. Of course they are!

WILL. Why?

MRS. WYLER. Because they're written from a foreign point of view—not *our* point of view. We did as well as anybody could have done according to our lights.

WILL. Yes, but what sort of lights were they?

MRS. WYLER [*tolerantly*]. There you are!

WILL. How lucky you were!

MRS. WYLER [*teasing him*]. Our young men didn't moon about. They made opportunities for themselves!

WILL. Or did the opportunities make them? All you had to do was pack your week-end bag and pioneer.

MRS. WYLER. Is the world quite exhausted then?

WILL. Possibly not, but our pioneering might take a form you would find—unpalatable.

MRS. WYLER. Yes yes. [*Benevolently.*] I suppose you're one of those young radicals our colleges are said to be full of nowadays. Tell me, what do you young radicals stand for?

WILL. I haven't decided exactly what I'm for, but I'm pretty certain what I'm against.

MRS. WYLER [*pumping him*]. Most young people are bored by the past. You're full of curiosity. Why is that?

WILL [*not committing himself*]. I'm interested.

MRS. WYLER. At my age to be permitted to talk of one's youth is an indulgence. Ask me anything you like. At my age also one has no reason for restraint. I have

had the bad judgment to survive most of my con-
temporaries.

WILL. I love talking to you, Mrs. Wyler. I think you're
very wise.

MRS. WYLER [*with a sigh*]. Go on thinking so—I'll try
not to disillusion you! [*A moment's pause.*] Are you
staying on here at Bay Cottage?

WILL. Oh, no, I have to go back to Amherst to get my
degree.

MRS. WYLER. And after that?

WILL [*humorously*]. The dole!

[*The old lady laughs.*]

MRS. WYLER. My daughter tells me she's invited your
father here.

WILL. Yes.

MRS. WYLER. I shall be so glad to meet him. He's an in-
ventor, isn't he?

WILL. He's a physicist. Specializes in—

MRS. WYLER. Don't tell me—in spite of my great wisdom
I can't keep up with science. Whenever anybody
makes a scientific explanation to me I find there are
two things I don't know instead of just one.

WILL [*cheerfully*]. Anyway, Dad's been fired.

MRS. WYLER. I am very sorry to hear that.

WILL. He's been working on a method for improving
high-speed steel.

MRS. WYLER. Did he fail?

WILL. He succeeded. [MRS. WYLER *is surprised.*] They
decided that his discovery, if perfected and mar-
keted, might increase the technological unemployment. They have decided therefore to call a halt on
scientific discovery—especially in those branches
where it might have practical results. That is one
of the differences, Mrs. Wyler, between my day—
and yours—in your day, you put a premium on in-
vention—we declare a moratorium on it.

[*The old lady gives him a shrewd look.*]

MRS. WYLER. Yes, yes. I am perfectly sure that you're in for a hard time, Will.

WILL [*lightly, shrugging his shoulders*]. As I have been elected by my class as the one most likely to succeed, I am not worrying, Mrs. Wyler. All I have to do is bide my time.

MRS. WYLER [*amused*]. I am perfectly certain you'll come out! Paula tells me you and your friend, Dennis McCarthy, want to start some kind of magazine.

WILL. Yes. A national magazine for undergraduate America. You see, Mrs. Wyler, before the rift in our so-called system, college men were supposed to live exclusively in a world of ukuleles, football slogans, and petting-parties—*College Humor* sort of thing. But it was never entirely true. Now it is less true than ever. This magazine—if we can get it going— would be a forum for intercollegiate thought. It would be the organ of critical youth as opposed—to the other.

MRS. WYLER. What other?

WILL. The R.O.T.C., the Vigilantes and the Fascists— the Youth Movement of guns and sabres—

MRS. WYLER. I see. Well, I wish you luck, Will.

WILL. Thank you.

[PAULA FROTHINGHAM *comes in, a lovely young girl in gay summer slacks.*]

PAULA [*to* WILL]. Aren't you swimming? Hello, Granny.

WILL. Your grandmother and I have been discussing life.

PAULA. With a capital L, I suppose?

WILL. Enormous! I've been getting data on the pioneer age. Your grandmother thinks the reason we're in the condition we're in is because we're lazy.

MRS. WYLER [*mildly*]. Lazy? Did I say that?

WILL. In a way.

MRS. WYLER. If I said it, it must be so. Everybody over seventy is infallible!

PAULA [*nestling to her*]. Darling.

MRS. WYLER. Survival is quite a knack. You children don't realize it.

WILL. Oh, don't we though! It's getting harder every day.

MRS. WYLER. Nonsense! At your age you can't help it.

WILL. In your stately opulence that's what you think, Mrs. Wyler. You just don't know!

MRS. WYLER. Nonsense! Do you think your generation has a monopoly on hard times?

WILL. Now please don't tell me we've had depressions before?

MRS. WYLER [*rising to go*]. Paula, your young man is impertinent. Don't have anything to do with him. [*She goes out.*]

PAULA. What a conquest you've made of Granny! Way and ahead of all my beaus!

WILL. That undistinguished mob! Who couldn't?

PAULA. As long as you admit there is a mob . . .

WILL. Why wouldn't there be? Everybody loves you for your money!

PAULA [*confidently*]. I know it! And of all the fortune-hunters I've had dangling after me you're easily the most . . .

WILL. Blatant!

PAULA. That's it! Blatant! Like my new slacks?

WILL. Love 'em.

PAULA. Love me?

WILL. Loathe you.

PAULA. Good! Kiss? [*They kiss quickly.*]

WILL. Funny thing about your grandmother . . .

PAULA. Now I won't have you criticizing Granny . . .

WILL. I'm crazy about her. You feel she's been through everything and that she understands everything. Not this though. Not the essential difference between her times and ours.

PAULA. Oh dear! Is it the end of the world then?

WILL. The end of this world.

PAULA [*goes to window seat right, with a sigh*]. Such a pretty world. [*She points through windows at the garden and sea beyond.*] Look at it! Too bad it has to go! Meantime before it quite dissolves let's go for a swim. [*She starts for door.*]

WILL [*abstracted*]. All right . . . [*Following her to window seat.*]

PAULA [*she turns back*]. What's on your mind?

WILL. Wanted to speak to you about something. . . .

PAULA. What?

WILL [*embarrassed slightly*]. Er—your mother. . . .

PAULA. What's Mother gone and done now? Out with it. Or is it you? My boy-friends are always in love with Mother. I've had to contend with that all my life. So if it's that you needn't even mention it . . . come on.

WILL. No, but really, Paula. . . .

PAULA. Well then, out with it! What is it!

WILL. This. [*He gives her note.*] Found it on my breakfast tray this morning in a sealed envelope marked "Confidential."

PAULA [*reading note aloud, rather bewildered*]. "To give my little girl a good time with. Leonie Frothingham."

WILL. And this! [*He hands her check.* PAULA *takes it and looks at it.*]

PAULA. A hundred dollars. Does Mother think her little girl can have a good time with *that*? She doesn't know her little girl!

WILL. But what'll I do with it? How'll I get it back to her?

PAULA. Over my dead body you'll get it back to her!

You'll spend it on Mother's little girl. Now come on swimming!

WILL. Does your mother put one of these on every breakfast tray?

PAULA. Argue it out with her.

WILL. I can't. It would seem ungracious. You must give it back to her for me.

PAULA. Catch me! Don't take it too seriously. She slips all the kids something every once in a while. She knows my friends are all stony. You overestimate the importance of money, Will—it's a convenience, that's all. You've got a complex on it.

WILL. I have! I've got to have. It's all right to be dainty about money when you've lots of it as you have. . . .

PAULA. Rotten with it is the expression, I believe. . . .

WILL. I repudiate that expression. It is genteel and moralistic. You can't be rotten with money—you can only be *alive* with it.

PAULA. You and the rest of our crowd make me feel it's bad taste to be rich. But what can I do? I didn't ask for it!

WILL. I know. But look here . . . I've got a brother out of college two years who's worked six weeks in that time and is broke and here I am in an atmosphere with hundred-dollar bills floating around!

PAULA [*with check*]. Send him that!

WILL. Misapplication of funds!

PAULA [*warmly*]. Mother would be only too . . .

WILL. I know she would—but that isn't the point. . . . You know, Paula—

PAULA. What?

WILL. Sometimes I think if we weren't in love with each other we should be irreconcilable enemies—

PAULA. Nothing but sex, eh?

WILL. That's all.

PAULA. In that case— [*They kiss.*]

WILL. That's forgiving. But seriously, Paula—

PAULA. Seriously what?

WILL. I can't help feeling I'm here on false pretenses. What am I doing with a millionaire family—with you? If your mother knew what I think, and what I've let you in for in college—she wouldn't touch me with a ten-foot pole. And you too—I'm troubled about the superficiality of your new opinions. Isn't your radicalism—acquired coloring?

PAULA. I hope not. But—so is all education.

WILL. I know but—!

PAULA. What are you bleating about? Didn't I join you on that expedition to Kentucky to be treated by that sovereign state as an offensive foreigner? My back aches yet when I remember that terrible bus ride. Didn't I get my name in the papers picketing? Didn't I give up my holiday to go with you to the Chicago Peace Congress? Didn't I?

WILL [*doubtfully*]. Yes, you did.

PAULA. But you're not convinced. Will darling, don't you realize that since knowing you and your friends, since I've, as you say, acquired your point of view about things, my life has had an excitement and a sense of reality it's never had before. I've simply come alive—that's all! Before then I was bored—terribly bored without knowing why. I wanted something more—fundamental—without knowing what. You've made me see. I'm terribly grateful to you, Will darling. I always shall be.

WILL. You are a dear, Paula, and I adore you—but—

PAULA. Still unconvinced?

WILL. This money of yours. What'll it do to us?

PAULA. I'll turn it over to you. Then you can give me an allowance—and save your pride.

WILL. I warn you, Paula—

PAULA. What?

WILL. If you turn it over to me, I'll use it in every way I can to make it impossible for anyone to have so much again.

PAULA. That's all right with me, Will.

WILL. Sometimes you make me feel I'm taking candy from babies.

PAULA. The candy is no good for the baby, anyway. Besides, let's cross that bridge when we come to it.

[ROBERT, *the butler, enters.*]

ROBERT. I beg your pardon, Miss Frothingham.

PAULA. Yes, Robert?

ROBERT. Telephone for you.

PAULA. Thank you, Robert. [*She crosses to table back of sofa for telephone. At phone.*] Yes—this is Paula— Dad!—Darling!—Where are you? . . . but how wonderful . . . I thought you were in New York . . . well, come right over this minute. . . . Will you stay the night? . . . Oh, too bad! . . . I'll wait right here for you. Hurry, darling! Bye! [*She hangs up.*] Imagine, Dad! He's motoring up to Selena Bryant's at Murray Bay—I'm dying to have you meet him. He's the lamb of the world.

WILL. Not staying long, is he?

PAULA. No. He wants to see Mother he says. I wonder . . . oh, dear!

WILL. What?

PAULA. I was so excited I forgot to tell him. . . .

WILL. What?

PAULA. That a new friend of Mother's is coming.

WILL. The Russian?

PAULA. The Russian's here. He dates from last winter. You're behind the times, Will.

WILL. Who's the new friend?

PAULA. I'm not sure about it all yet. Maybe Mother isn't either. But I've had some experience in watch-

ing them come and go and my instinct tells me Dr.
Rice is elected.

WILL. Who is Dr. Rice?

PAULA. Psychoanalyst from New York. [*Burlesquing
slightly.*] The last word, my dear—

[*At this point the object of* PAULA's *maternal impulse
comes in, running a little and breathless, like a
young girl.* LEONIE FROTHINGHAM, *as she has a daughter of nearly twenty, must be herself forty, but, at
this moment, she might be sixteen. She is slim, girlish, in a young and quivering ecstasy of living and
anticipation. For* LEONIE, *her daughter is an agreeable phenomenon whom she does not specially relate
to herself biologically—a lovely apparition who hovers intermittently in the wild garden of her life.
There is something, for all her gaiety, heartbreaking
about* LEONIE, *something childish and childlike—an
acceptance of people instantly and uncritically at the
best of their own valuation. She is impulsive and
warm-hearted and generous to a fault. Her own fragile and exquisite loveliness she offers to the world
half shyly, tentatively, bearing it like a cup containing a precious liquid of which not a drop must be
spilled. A spirituelle amoureuse, she is repelled by
the gross or the voluptuary; this is not hypocrisy—it
is, in* LEONIE, *a more serious defect than that. In the
world in which she moves hypocrisy is merely a social lubricant but this myopia—alas for* LEONIE!—
springs from a congenital and temperamental inability to face anything but the pleasantest and the
most immediately appealing and the most flattering
aspects of things—in life and in her own nature.
At this moment, though, she is the loveliest fabri-
cation of Nature, happy in the summer sun and
loving all the world.*]

LEONIE. My darlings, did you ever know such a day?

WILL [*he is a shy boy with her*]. It's nice!

LEONIE. Nice! It's . . . [*Her gesture conveys her utter inadequacy to express the beauties of the day.*] It's—radiant! It knows it's radiant! The world is pleased with herself today. Is the world a woman? Today she is—a lovely young girl in blue and white.

WILL. In green and white.

LEONIE [*agreeing—warmly*]. In green and white!—it depends where you look, doesn't it? I'm just off to the station to meet Dr. Rice. Will, you'll be fascinated by him.

PAULA [*cutting in—crisply*]. Sam telephoned.

LEONIE. Sam!

PAULA. Your husband. My father. Think back, Leonie.

LEONIE. Darling! Where is he?

PAULA. He's on his way here. He telephoned from Miller's Point.

LEONIE. Is he staying?

PAULA. No.

LEONIE. Why not?

PAULA. He's going on to Selena Bryant's.

LEONIE. What is this deep friendship between Sam and Selena Bryant?

PAULA. Now, Leonie, don't be prudish!

LEONIE [*appealing for protection to* WILL]. She's always teasing me. She's always teasing everybody about everything. Developed quite a vein. I must warn you, Paula—sarcasm isn't feminine. In their hearts men don't like it. Do you like it, Will? Do you really like it?

WILL. I hate it!

LEONIE [*in triumph to* PAULA]. There you see! He hates it!

PAULA [*tersely*]. He doesn't always hate it!

LEONIE [*her most winning smile on* WILL]. Does she

bully you, Will? Don't let her bully you. The sad thing is, Paula, you're so charming. Why aren't you content to be charming? Are you as serious as Paula, Will? I hope not.

WILL. Much more.

LEONIE. I'm sorry to hear that. Still, for a man, it's all right, I suppose. But why are the girls nowadays so determined not to be feminine? Why? It's coming back you know—I'm sure of it—femininity is due for a revival.

PAULA. So are Herbert Hoover and painting on china.

LEONIE. Well I read that even in Russia . . . the women . . . [*She turns again to* WILL *whom she feels sympathetic*.] It isn't as if women had done such marvels with their—masculinity! Have they? Are things better because women vote? Not that I can see. They're worse. As far as I can see the women simply reinforce the men in their—mistakes.

WILL [*to* PAULA]. She has you there!

LEONIE [*with this encouragement warming to her theme*]. When I was a girl the calamities of the world were on a much smaller scale. It's because the women, who, after all, are half of the human race, stayed at home and didn't bother. Now they do bother—and look at us!

PAULA. Well, that's as Victorian as anything I ever—

LEONIE. I'd love to have been a Victorian. They were much happier than we are, weren't they? Of course they were.

PAULA [*defending herself to* WILL]. It's only Mother that brings out the crusader in me—[*to* LEONIE.] When you're not around I'm not like that at all. Am I, Will?

[*But* WILL *is given no chance to answer because* LEONIE *is holding a sprig of lilac to his nostrils.*]

LEONIE. Smell. [WILL *smells.*] Isn't it delicious?

WILL. It's lovely.

LEONIE. Here . . . . [*She breaks off a sprig and pins it into his lapel. While she is doing it she broaches a delicate subject quite casually to* PAULA.] Oh, by the way, Paula . . .

PAULA. Yes, Mother?

LEONIE. Did you mention to Sam that—that Boris—

PAULA. I didn't, no. It slipped my mind.

LEONIE. It doesn't matter in the least.

PAULA. Father isn't staying anyway. . . .

LEONIE. Well, why shouldn't he? You must make him. I want him to meet Dr. Rice. He's really a most extraordinary man.

PAULA. Where'd you find *him?*

LEONIE. I met him at a party at Sissy Drake's. He *saved* Sissy.

PAULA. From what?

LEONIE. From that awful eye-condition.

PAULA. Is he an oculist too?

LEONIE [*to* WILL]. She went to every oculist in the world—she went to Baltimore and she went to Vienna. Nobody could do a thing for her—her eyes kept blinking—twitching really in the most unaccountable way. It was an ordeal to talk to her—and of course she must have undergone agonies of embarrassment. But Dr. Rice psychoanalyzed her and completely cured her. How do you suppose? Well, he found that the seat of the trouble lay in her unconscious. It was too simple. She blinked in that awful way because actually she couldn't bear to look at her husband. So she divorced Drake and since she's married to Bill Wilmerding she's as normal as you or me. Now I'll take you into a little secret. I'm having Dr. Rice up to see Boris. Of course Boris mustn't know it's for him.

PAULA. What's the matter with Boris?

LEONIE. I'm not sure. I think he's working too hard.

WILL. What's he working at?

LEONIE. Don't you know? Didn't you tell him, Paula? His father's memoirs. He's the son, you know, of the great Count Mirsky!

WILL. I know.

LEONIE. I must show you the photographs of his father —wonderful old man with a great white beard like a snow-storm—looks like Moses—a Russian Moses— and Boris is sitting on his knees—couldn't be over ten years old and wearing a fur cap and boots— boots!—and they drank tea out of tall glasses with raspberry jelly in—people came from all over the world, you know, to see his father . . . !

WILL. Isn't it strange that Count Mirsky's son should find himself in this strange house on this odd headland of Maine—Maine of all places!—writing his father's life? It's fantastic!

PAULA [*with some malice*]. Is Dr. Rice going to help you acclimate him?

LEONIE. I hope so. You and Paula will have to entertain him—you young intellectuals. Isn't it a pity I have no mind? [*She rises and crosses to table right to arrange lily-of-the-valley sprigs in a vase.*]

PAULA [*to* WILL]. She knows it's her greatest asset. Besides she's a fake.

WILL [*gallantly*]. I'm sure she is.

LEONIE. Thank you, my dears. It's gallant of you. [*She crosses to* PAULA—*embraces her from behind.*] But I'm not deceived. I know what Paula thinks of me— she looks down on me because I won't get interested in sociology. There never were any such things about when I was a girl. The trouble is one generation never has any perspective about another generation.

WILL. That's what your mother was saying to me just a little while ago.

LEONIE. Was she? [*She sits left of* WILL.] I'm sure though Mother and I are much closer—that is, we understand each other better than Paula and I. Don't you think so, Paula?

PAULA [*considering it*]. Yes. I do think so.

LEONIE. I knew you'd agree. Something's happened between my generation and Paula's. New concepts. I don't know what they are exactly but I'm very proud that Paula's got them.

PAULA [*laughing helplessly*]. Oh, Mother! You reduce everything to absurdity!

LEONIE [*innocently*]. Do I? I don't mean to. At any rate it's a heavenly day and I adore you and I don't care about anything so long as you're happy. I want you to be happy.

PAULA [*helplessly*]. Oh dear!

LEONIE. What's the matter?

PAULA. You're saying that!

LEONIE. Is that wrong? Will—did I say something wrong?

PAULA. You want me to be happy. It's like saying you want me to be eight feet tall and to sing like Lily Pons.

LEONIE. Is it like that? Why? Will . . .

WILL [*gravely feeling he must stand up for* PAULA, *but hating to*]. Paula means . . . [*Pause.*]

LEONIE. Yes . . . ?

WILL [*miserable*]. She means—suppose there isn't any happiness to be had? Suppose the supply's run out?

LEONIE. But, Will, really . . . ! On a day like this! Why don't you go swimming? [*Rises.*] Nothing like sea-water for—morbidity! Run out indeed! And to-day of all days! Really! [*Gets gloves.*] I'm disappointed in you, Will. I counted on you especially . . .

WILL [*abjectly*]. I was only fooling!

LEONIE. Of course he was. [*Sits on arm of sofa beside* WILL.] Will, I rely on you. Don't let Paula brood. Can't she drop the sociology in the summer? I think in the fall you're much better—braced—for things like that. Keep her happy, Will.

WILL. I'll do my best now that—thanks to you—I have the means.

LEONIE. Oh . . . [*Remembering.*] Oh, you didn't mind, did you? I hope you didn't mind.

WILL [*embarrassed*]. Very generous of you.

LEONIE. Generous! Please don't say that. After all— we who are in the embarrassing position nowadays of being rich must do something with our money, mustn't we? That's why I'm helping Boris to write this book. *Noblesse oblige.* Don't you think so, Will? Boris tells me that the Russians—the *present* Russians—

WILL. You mean the Bolsheviks?

LEONIE. Yes, I suppose I do. He says they don't like his father at all any more and won't read his works because in his novels he occasionally went on the assumption that rich people had souls and spirits too. You don't think like that too, do you, Will—that because I'm rich I'm just not worth bothering about at all— No, you couldn't! [*The appeal is tremulous.* WILL *succumbs entirely.*]

WILL [*bluntly*]. Mrs. Frothingham, I love you!

LEONIE [*rises from arm of sofa and sits in sofa beside* WILL. *To* PAULA]. Isn't he sweet? [*To* WILL.] And I love you, Will. Please call me Leonie. Do you know how Mother happened to name me Leonie? I was born in Paris, you know, and I was to be called Ruhama after my father's sister. But Mother said

no. No child of mine, she said, shall be called Ruhama. She shall have a French name. And where
do you think she got Leonie?

WILL. From the French version of one of those Gideon
Bibles.

LEONIE [*as breathless as if it happened yesterday*]. Not
at all. From a novel the nurse was reading. She asked
the nurse what she was reading and the nurse gave
her the paper book and Mother opened it and found
Leonie!

WILL. What was the book?

LEONIE. Everyone wants to know that . . . But I don't
know. Mother didn't know. She kept the book to
give to me when I grew up. But one day she met M.
Jusserand on a train—he was the French Ambassador
to Washington, you know—and he picked up the
book in Mother's compartment and he read a page
of it and threw it out of the window because it was
trash! You see what I've had to live down.

WILL. Heroic!

LEONIE. I hope you stay all summer, Will. I won't hear
of your going anywhere else.

WILL. Don't worry. I have nowhere else to go!

LEONIE. Tell me—that magazine you and Dennis want
to start—will it be gay?

WILL. Not exactly.

LEONIE. Oh, dear! I know. Columns and columns of
reading matter and no pictures. Tell me—your father
is coming to dine, isn't he? I am so looking forward
to meeting him. I love scientific men. They're usually so nice and understanding. Now, I've really got
to go. [*Rises and starts out.*]

PAULA. Dennis will be on that train.

LEONIE. Oh, good! I like Dennis. He makes me laugh
and I like people around who make me laugh, but I
do wish he'd dress better. Why can't radicals be

chic? I saw a picture of Karl Marx the other day and he looks like one of those advertisements before you take something. I'll look after Dennis, Will —save you going to the station— [*To* PAULA.] And Paula, tell Sam—

PAULA. Yes?

LEONIE [*forgetting the message to* SAM]. You know, I asked Dr. Rice if he would treat me professionally and he said I was uninteresting to him because I was quite normal. Isn't that discouraging? Really, I must cultivate something. Good-bye, darlings. [*She runs out.*]

WILL. But what was the message to Sam? [*He sits.*]

PAULA [*helplessly*]. I'll never know. Neither will she. [WILL *laughs.*] What can you do with her? She makes me feel like an opinionated old woman. And I worry about her.

WILL. Do you?

PAULA. Yes. She arouses my maternal impulse.

WILL [*who feels he can be casual about* LEONIE *now that she is gone*]. She relies rather too much on charm!

PAULA [*turning on him bitterly*]. Oh, she does, does she! [*Goes over to sofa and sits right of* WILL.] You renegade. You ruin all my discipline with Mother. You're like a blushing schoolboy in front of her . . .

WILL [*protesting sheepishly*]. Now, Paula, don't exaggerate!

PAULA. You are! I thought in another minute you were going to ask her to the frat dance. And where was all that wonderful indignation about her leaving you the check? Where was the insult to your pride? Where was your starving brother in Seattle? Where? Where?

WILL. I don't know but somehow you can't face your mother with things like that. It seems cruel to face her with realities. She seems outside of all that.

PAULA [*conceding that*]. Well, you're going to be no help to me in handling Mother, I can see that!

WILL [*changing subject—a bit sensitive about having yielded so flagrantly to* LEONIE]. This Russian—

PAULA. What about him?

WILL [*gauche*]. Platonic, do you suppose?

PAULA. Don't be naïve!

[*Enter* SAM FROTHINGHAM, PAULA's *father, a very pleasant-faced, attractive man between forty-five and fifty.*]

SAM. Oh, hello.

[WILL *rises.*]

PAULA [*flying to him*]. Darling!—

SAM [*they meet center and embrace*]. Hello, Paula. Delighted to see you.

PAULA. This is Will Dexter.

SAM [*shaking hands with* WILL]. How do you do?

WILL. I'm delighted to meet you.

PAULA [*to* WILL]. Wait for me at the beach, will you, Will?

WILL. No, I'll run down to the station and ride back with the others.

PAULA. Okay.

[SAM *nods to him.* WILL *goes out.*]

SAM [*crosses to front of sofa*]. Nice boy. [*Follows her.*]

PAULA. Like him?

SAM. Do you?

PAULA. I think so.

SAM. Special?

PAULA. Sort of.

SAM. Very special?

PAULA [*sits right end of sofa*]. Well—not sure.

SAM. Wait till you are. You've lots of time.

PAULA. Oh, he's not exactly impulsive.

SAM. Then he's just a fool.

PAULA. How are you, darling?

SAM. Uneasy.

PAULA. With me!

SAM. Especially.

PAULA. Darling, why?

SAM. I'll tell you. That's why I've come.

PAULA. Everything all right?

SAM. Oh, fine.

PAULA [*mystified*]. Then . . . ?

SAM [*switching off*]. How's Leonie?

PAULA. Fine. Delighted you were coming.

SAM. Was she?

PAULA. She really was. She's off to Ellsworth to meet a doctor.

SAM. Doctor?

PAULA. Psychoanalyst she's having up to massage her Russian's complexes.

SAM [*laughing*]. Oh— [*With a sigh.*] What's going to happen to Leonie?

PAULA. Why? She's on the crest!

SAM. She needs that elevation. Otherwise she sinks.

PAULA. Well—you know Mother . . .

SAM. Yes. [*A moment's pause.*] Paula?

PAULA. Yes, Dad.

SAM. The fact is—it's ridiculous I should feel so nervous about telling you—but the fact is . . .

PAULA. What?

SAM. I've fallen in love. I want to get married. There! Well, thank God that's out! [*He wipes his forehead, quite an ordeal.*] Romance at my age. It's absurd, isn't it?

PAULA. Selena Bryant?

SAM. Yes.

PAULA. She has a grown son.

SAM [*smiling at her*]. So have I—a grown daughter.

PAULA. You'll have to divorce Mother.

SAM. Yes.

PAULA. Poor Leonie!

SAM. Well, after all—Leonie—you know how we've lived for years.

PAULA. Has Leonie hurt you?

SAM. Not for a long time. If this with Selena hadn't happened we'd have gone on forever, I suppose. But it has.

PAULA. You know, I have a feeling that, in spite of everything, this is going to be a shock to Leonie.

SAM. Paula?

PAULA. Yes.

SAM. Do you feel I'm deserting you?

[*She turns her head away. She is very moved.*]

PAULA. No—you know how fond I am of you—I want you to be . . .

SAM [*deeply affected*]. Paula . . . !

PAULA. Happy. [*A silence. She is on the verge of tears.*]

SAM. I must make you see my side, Paula.

PAULA [*vehemently*]. I do!

SAM. It isn't only that—you're so young—but somehow —we decided very soon after you were born, Leonie and I, that our marriage could only continue on this sort of basis. For your sake we've kept it up. I thought I was content to be an—appendage—to Leonie's entourage. But I'm not—do you know what Selena—being with Selena and planning with Selena for ourselves has made me see—that I've never had a home. Does that sound mawkish?

PAULA. I thought you loved Bay Cottage.

SAM. Of our various ménages this is my favorite—it's the simplest. And I've had fun here with you— watching you grow up. But very soon after I married Leonie I found this out—that when you marry a very rich woman it's always *her* house you live in. [*A moment's pause.*]

PAULA. I'm awfully happy for you, Sam, really I am. You deserve everything but I can't help it, I . . .

SAM. I know. [*A pause.*] Paula . . .

PAULA. Yes, Dad?

SAM. You and I get on so well together—always have—Selena adores you and really—when you get to know her . . .

PAULA. I like Selena enormously. She's a dear. Couldn't be nicer.

SAM. I'm sure you and she would get on wonderfully together. Of course, Leonie will marry again. She's bound to. Why don't you come to live with us? When you want to . . .

PAULA. Want to!

SAM. All the time then. Leonie has such a busy life.

PAULA. It's awfully sweet of you.

SAM. Sweet of me! Paula!

PAULA. Where are you going to live?

SAM. New York. Selena has her job to do.

PAULA. She's terribly clever, isn't she?

SAM. She's good at her job.

PAULA. It must be wonderful to be independent. I hope I shall be. I hope I can make myself.

SAM. No reason you can't.

PAULA. It seems to take so much—

SAM. What sort of independence?

PAULA. Leonie's independent, but that independence doesn't mean anything somehow. She's always been able to do what she likes.

SAM. So will you be.

PAULA. That doesn't count somehow. It's independence in a vacuum. No, it doesn't count.

SAM. Maybe it isn't independence you want then?

PAULA. Yes, it is. I want to be able to stand on my own feet. I want to be—justified.

SAM [*understandingly*]. Ah! That's something else. [*A little amused.*] That's harder!

PAULA. I mean it, really I do— [*Pause.*] It's curious— how—adrift—this makes me feel. As if something vital, something fundamental had smashed. I wonder how Mother'll take it. I think—unconsciously— she depends on you much more than she realizes. You were a stabilizing force, Sam, in spite of everything and now . . .

SAM [*seriously*]. *You* are the stabilizing force, if you ask me, Paula. . . .

PAULA. I don't know.

SAM. What's worrying you, Paula? Is it this Russian?

PAULA. Oh, I think he's harmless really.

SAM. What then?

PAULA. That one of these days—

SAM. What?

PAULA. That one of these days—now that you're going —somebody will come along—who won't be harmless.—You know, I really love Leonie.

[LEONIE *comes running in just ahead of* DR. KENNETH RICE, DENNIS *and* WILL. LEONIE *is in the gayest spirits.* DR. RICE *is handsome, dark, magnetic, quiet, masterful. He is conscious of authority and gives one the sense of a strange, genius-like intuition.* DENNIS *is a flamboyant Irishman, a little older than* WILL, *gawky, black-haired, slovenly, infinitely brash.* SAM *and* PAULA *rise.* LEONIE *comes down to center with* KENNETH *at her left.* WILL *remains back of sofa.* DEN- NIS *follows down to right center.*]

LEONIE. Oh, Sam, how perfectly . . . This is Dr. Rice— my husband Sam Frothingham—and my daughter Paula! Sam, Dennis McCarthy.

DENNIS. How do you do?

[*No one pays any attention to him.* DR. RICE *shakes*

hands with SAM *and* PAULA. LEONIE *keeps bubbling,
her little laugh tinkling through her chatter.*]

LEONIE. It's courageous of me, don't you think, Dr.
Rice, to display such a daughter? Does she look like
me? I'll be very pleased if you tell me that she does.
Sit down, sit down, everybody.

DENNIS [*holding up his pipe*]. You don't mind if I—?

LEONIE. No, no, not at all— [*She sits center chair,*
PAULA *sits on right end sofa,* DENNIS *sinks into chair,
right, by table.*] Sam! How well you're looking! Are
you staying at Selena's? How is Selena?

SAM. She's very well.

LEONIE. Dr. Rice knows Selena.

KENNETH. Yes, indeed!

LEONIE. I envy Selena, you know, above all women. So
brilliant, so attractive and so self-sufficient. That is
what I envy in her most of all. I have no resources—
I depend so much on other people. [*Turns to* RICE.]
Do you think, Dr. Rice, you could make me self-
sufficient?

KENNETH. I think I could.

LEONIE. How perfectly marvelous!

KENNETH. But I shouldn't dream of doing it!

LEONIE. But if I beg you to?

KENNETH. Not even if you beg me to.

LEONIE. But why?

KENNETH. It would deprive your friends of their most
delightful avocation.

LEONIE. Now that's very grateful. You see, Sam, there
are men who still pay me compliments.

SAM. I can't believe it!

LEONIE. You must keep it up, Dr. Rice, please. So good
for my morale. [*To* PAULA.] Oh, my dear, we've been
having the most wonderful argument— [*To* DENNIS.]
Haven't we?

DENNIS. Yes.

LEONIE.. All the way in from Ellsworth— [*To* RICE.] Really, Doctor, it's given me new courage. . . .

PAULA. New courage for what?

LEONIE. I've always been afraid to say it for fear of being old-fashioned—but Dr. Rice isn't afraid.

KENNETH [*explaining to* SAM]. It takes great courage, Mr. Frothingham, to disagree with the younger generation.

SAM. It does indeed.

PAULA. Well, what is it about?

LEONIE. Yes—what *was* it about, Dennis?

DENNIS. Statistics and theology. Some metaphysics thrown in.

SAM. Good heavens! [*Sits.*]

DENNIS. Statistics as a symbol.

WILL. Dr. Rice still believes in the individual career.

KENNETH. I hang my head in shame!

DENNIS. He doesn't know that as a high officer of the National Student Federation, I have at my fingers' ends the statistics which rule our future, the statistics which constitute our horizon. Not your future, Paula, because you are living parasitically on the stored pioneerism of your ancestors.

PAULA. Forgive me, Reverend Father!

DENNIS. I represent, Doctor, the Unattached Youth of America—

KENNETH. Well, that's a career in itself!

[*They laugh.*]

DENNIS [*imperturbable*]. When we presently commit the folly of graduating from a benevolent institution at Amherst, Massachusetts, there will be in this Republic two million like us. Two million helots. [*Leaning over* LEONIE.] But Dr. Rice pooh-poohs statistics.

LEONIE [*arranging his tie*]. Does he Dennis?

DENNIS. He says the individual can surmount statistics, violate the graphs. Superman!

WILL. Evidently Dr. Rice got in just under the wire.

KENNETH. I'd never submit to statistics, Mr. Dexter— I'd submit to many things but not to statistics.

LEONIE. Such dull things to submit to—

DENNIS. You must be an atheist, Dr. Rice.

KENNETH. Because I don't believe in statistics?—the new God?

LEONIE. Well, *I'm* a Protestant and I don't believe in them either.

DENNIS. Well, Protestant is a loose synonym for atheist —and I, as an Irishman—and a—

KENNETH. Young man—

DENNIS. Yes?

KENNETH. Have you ever heard Bismarck's solution of the Irish problem?

DENNIS. No. What?

KENNETH. Oh, it's entirely irrelevant.

LEONIE. Please tell us. I adore irrelevancies.

KENNETH. Well, he thought the Irish and the Dutch should exchange countries. The Dutch, he thought, would very soon make a garden out of Ireland, and the Irish would forget to mend the dikes.

[*They laugh.*]

LEONIE. That's not irrelevant—

DENNIS. It is an irrelevance, but pardonable in an adversary losing an argument.

KENNETH [*to* PAULA]. Miss Frothingham, you seem very gracious. Will you get me out of this?

PAULA. No, I'm enjoying it.

LEONIE. Whatever you may say, Dennis, it's an exciting time to be alive.

DENNIS. That is because your abnormal situation renders you free of its major excitement.

LEONIE. And what's that, Dennis?

DENNIS. The race with malnutrition.

KENNETH. But that race, Mr.—?

DENNIS. McCarthy.

KENNETH. Is the eternal condition of mankind. Perhaps mankind won't survive the solution of that problem.

WILL [*with heat*]. It's easy to sit in this living room—and be smug about the survival of the fittest—especially when you're convinced you're one of the fittest. But there are millions who won't concede you that superiority, Dr. Rice. There are millions who are so outrageously demanding that they actually insist on the right to live! They may demand it one day at the cost of your complacency.

LEONIE. Will! We were just chatting.

WILL. I'm sorry! The next thing Dr. Rice'll be telling us is that war is necessary also—to keep us stimulated —blood-letting for the other fellow.

KENNETH. Well, as a matter of fact, there's something to be said for that too. If you haven't settled on a career yet, Mr. Dexter, may I suggest evangelism?

DENNIS. But Dr. Rice—!

KENNETH. And now, Mrs. Frothingham, before these young people heckle me too effectively, may I escape to my room?

LEONIE [*rising*]. Of course. Though I don't think you need be afraid of their heckling, Doctor. You say things which I've always believed but never dared say.

KENNETH [*as they walk out*]. Why not?

LEONIE. I don't know—somehow—I lacked the—the authority. I want to show you your rooms myself. [*Leaving the room, followed by* RICE.] I'll be right back, Sam—[RICE *nods to them and follows her out. As they go out she keeps talking to him.*] I am giving you my father's rooms—he built the wing especially so that when he wanted to work he'd be away from the rest of the house—you have the sea *and* the garden— [*They are off. A moment's pause.*]

PAULA. Well, that's a new type for Leonie!

DENNIS. There's something Rasputinish about him. What's he doing in Maine?

WILL. What, for the matter of that, are you and I doing in Maine? We should be in New York, jockeying for position on the bread-line. Let's go to the beach, Dennis. Pep us up for the struggle.

DENNIS. In that surf? It looks angry. I can't face life today.

PAULA. Swim'll do you good.

DENNIS [*starting for garden*]. It's not a swim I want exactly but a float—a vigorous float. Lead me to the pool, Adonais—

WILL. All right.

[*As he starts to follow* DENNIS, DR. DEXTER, WILL'S *father, comes in ushered by* ROBERT. *He is a dusty little man with a bleached yellow Panama hat. He keeps wiping his perspiring face with an old handkerchief. He doesn't hear very well.*]

DENNIS. Ah, the enemy—!

[PAULA *and* SAM *rise.*]

WILL. Hello, Dad. You remember Paula.

DEXTER. Yes . . . yes, I do.

WILL [*introducing* SAM]. My father—Mr. Frothingham.

SAM. Very glad to see you.

DEXTER [*shaking hands*]. Thank you.

DENNIS [*pointing dramatically at* DEXTER]. Nevertheless I repeat—the enemy!

PAULA. Dennis!

WILL. Oh, he's used to Dennis!

DEXTER [*wipes his forehead*]. Yes, and besides it was very dusty on the road.

PAULA. Won't you sit down?

[DEXTER *does so, in center chair. The others remain standing.*]

WILL. How long did it take you to drive over, Dad?

DEXTER. Let's see—left New Brunswick at two. . . .

WILL [*looks at watch*]. Three and one half hours—pretty good—the old tin Lizzie's got life in her yet.

DEXTER. You young folks having a good time, I suppose? [*He looks around him absent-mindedly.*]

PAULA. Dennis has been bullying us.

DEXTER. He still talking? [*Mildly.*] It's the Irish in him.

DENNIS [*nettled*]. You forgot to say shanty!

DEXTER [*surprised*]. Eh? Why should I say that?

WILL. Dennis is a snob. Wants all his titles.

DENNIS. You misguided children don't realize it—but here—in the guise of this dusty, innocent-seeming man—sits the enemy.

DEXTER [*turning as if stung by a fly—cupping his hand to his ear*]. What? What did he say?

DENNIS. The ultimate enemy, the true begetter of the fatal statistics—Science. You betray us, Paula, by having him in the house; *you* betray us, Will, by acknowledging him as a father.

DEXTER [*wiping his forehead*]. Gosh, it's hot!

SAM [*sensing a fight and urging it on—solemnly*]. Can all this be true, Dr. Dexter?

DEXTER. What be true?

SAM. Dennis's accusation.

DEXTER. I am slightly deaf and McCarthy's presence always fills me with gratitude for that affliction.

DENNIS. It's perfectly obvious. You've heard of technological unemployment. Well, here it sits, embodied in Will's father. Day and night with diabolical ingenuity and cunning he works out devices to unemploy us. All over the world, millions of us are being starved and broken on the altar of Science.

We Catholics understand that. We Catholics repudiate the new Moloch that has us by the throat.

WILL. Do you want us to sit in medieval taverns with
Chesterton and drink beer?

[DEXTER *turns to* DENNIS; *as if emerging suddenly from
an absent-minded daze, he speaks with great authority, casually but with clarity and precision.*]

DEXTER. The fact is, my voluble young friend, I am not
the Moloch who is destroying you but that you and
the hordes of the imprecise and the vaguely trained
—are destroying me! I have, you will probably be
pleased to learn, just lost my job. I have been interrupted in my work. And why? Because I am successful. Because I have found what, with infinite patience and concentration, I have been seeking to
discover. From the elusive and the indeterminate
and the invisible, I have crystallized a principle
which is visible and tangible and—predictable. From
the illimitable icebergs of the unknown I have
chipped off a fragment of knowledge, a truth which
so-called practical men may put to a use which will
make some of your numbers unnecessary in the
workaday world. Well—what of it, I say?—who de-
crees that you shall be supported? Of what importance are your lives and futures and your meander-
ing aspirations compared to the firmness and the
beauty and the cohesion of the principles I seek, the
truth I seek? None—none whatever! Whether you
prattle on an empty stomach or whether you prattle
on a full stomach can make no difference to anybody that I can see. [*To* PAULA *abruptly, rising.*]
And now, young woman, as I have been invited here
to spend the night, I'd like to see my room!

PAULA [*crossing to him*]. Certainly! Come with me. I'll
have Robert show you your room. [*They go to door*

back. She calls.] Robert! [ROBERT *enters.*] Will you take Dr. Dexter to his room?

[DEXTER *follows* ROBERT *out.*]

SAM. Gosh! I thought he was deaf!

WILL. He can hear when he wants to! [*To* DENNIS.] Now will you be good!

DENNIS. I'm sorry—I didn't know he'd lost his job or I wouldn't have . . .

WILL. Oh, that's all right. Well, Dennis, how does it feel to be superfluous?

DENNIS [*sourly*]. The man's childish! [*He goes out, door right through garden.*]

PAULA. Isn't he marvelous? Don't you love Will's father?

SAM. Crazy about him. He's swell.

WILL. He's a pretty good feller. He seems absent-minded but actually he's extremely present-minded. If you'll excuse me, I'm going out to soothe Dennis. [*He follows* DENNIS *out.*]

[*A pause.*]

SAM. That young man appears to have sound antecedents.

PAULA. Oh, yes—Will's all right, but—oh, Sam—!

SAM. What?

PAULA. With you gone—I'm terrified for Leonie. I really am! When I think of the foolish marriages Leonie would have made if not for you!

SAM. It's a useful function, but I'm afraid I'll have to give it up!

PAULA [*with new determination*]. Sam . . .

SAM. Yes, Paula.

PAULA. If Leonie goes Russian—

SAM. Well?

PAULA. Or if she goes Freudian—?

SAM. In any case you and this boy'll probably be getting married.

PAULA. That's far from settled yet.

SAM. Why?

PAULA. Will's scared.

SAM. Is he?

PAULA. Of getting caught in Leonie's silken web.

SAM. That's sensible of him.

[LEONIE *comes back, half running, breathless.*]

LEONIE. Well! Isn't Dr. Rice attractive?

SAM [*rising*]. Very.

PAULA [*rising*]. And so depressed about himself! [*She goes out—door right.*]

LEONIE. Isn't it extraordinary, Dr. Rice having achieved the position he has—at his age? He's amazing. And think of it, Sam—not yet forty.

SAM. Anybody under forty is young to me!

LEONIE. How old are you, Sam?

SAM. Forbidden ground, Leonie.

LEONIE. I should know, shouldn't I, but I don't. I know your birthday—I always remember your birthday. . . .

SAM. You do indeed!

LEONIE. It's June 14. But I don't know how old you are.

SAM. Knowledge in the right place—ignorance in the right place!

LEONIE [*meaning it*]. You're more attractive and charming than ever.

SAM. You're a great comfort.

LEONIE. It's so nice to see you!

SAM. And you too! [*He is not entirely comfortable—not as unself-conscious and natural as she is.*]

LEONIE. Sometimes I think Paula should see more of you. I think it would be very good for her. What do you think of her new friends?

SAM. They seem nice.

LEONIE. They're all poor and they're very radical. They

look on me—my dear, they have the most extraordinary opinion of me. . . .

SAM. What is that?

LEONIE. I'm fascinated by them. They think of me as a hopeless kind of spoiled Bourbon living away in a never-never land—a kind of Marie Antoinette. . . . [*She laughs.*] It's delicious!

SAM. Is Paula radical too?

LEONIE. I think she's trying to be. She's a strange child.

SAM. How do you mean?

LEONIE. Well, when I was a child I was brought up to care only if people were charming or attractive or . . .

SAM. Well-connected . . .

LEONIE. Yes . . . These kids don't care a hoot about that.

SAM. I think the difference between their generation and ours is that we were romantic and they're realistic.

LEONIE. Is that it?

SAM. I think so.

LEONIE. What makes that?

SAM. Changes in the world—the war—the depression . . .

LEONIE. What did people blame things on before—the war?

SAM [*smiling*]. Oh, on the tariff and on the Republicans—and on the Democrats! Leonie—

LEONIE. Yes, Sam.

SAM. I—I really have something to tell you.

LEONIE [*looks up at him curiously*]. What? [*Pause.*]

SAM. I am in love with Selena Bryant. We want to get married.

LEONIE [*pause—after a moment*]. Human nature is funny! Mine is!

SAM. Why?

LEONIE. I know I ought to be delighted to release you. Probably I should have spoken to you about it myself before long—separating. And yet—when you tell me—I feel—a pang. . . .

SAM. That's very sweet of you.

LEONIE. One's so possessive—one doesn't want to give up anything.

SAM. For so many years our marriage has been at its best—a friendship. Need that end?

LEONIE. No, Sam. It needn't. I hope truly that it won't.

SAM. What about Paula?

LEONIE. Did you tell Paula?

SAM. Yes . . .

LEONIE. Did she . . . ?

SAM [*rising*]. Leonie . . .

LEONIE [*pauses*]. Yes, Sam.

SAM. A little while ago you said—you thought Paula ought to see more of me.

LEONIE. Yes . . . I did. . . . [*She is quite agitated suddenly. The thought has crossed her mind that perhaps* PAULA *has told* SAM *that she would prefer to go with him. This hurts her deeply, not only for the loss of* PAULA *but because, from the bottom of her being, she cannot bear not to be loved.*]

SAM. Don't you think then . . . for a time at least . . .

LEONIE [*defeatist in a crisis*]. Paula doesn't like me! [*It is a sudden and completely accepted conviction.*]

SAM. Leonie!

LEONIE. She'd rather go with you!

SAM. Not at all—it's only that . . .

LEONIE. I know what Paula thinks of me. . . .

SAM. Paula adores you. It's only that . . .

LEONIE. It's only that what—

SAM. Well, for instance—if you should get married—

LEONIE. What if I did?

SAM [*coming to stand close to her left*]. It would mean

a considerable readjustment for Paula—wouldn't it? You can see that.

LEONIE [*rising*]. But it would too with you and Selena.

SAM [*taking step toward her*]. She knows Selena. She admires Selena.

LEONIE [*rising and walking down to front of sofa*]. What makes you think she wouldn't admire—whomever I married?

SAM [*after a moment, completely serious now*]. There's another aspect of it which I think for Paula's sake you should consider most carefully.

LEONIE. What aspect?

SAM [*coming down to her*]. Paula's serious. You know that yourself. She's interested in things. She's not content to be a Sunday-supplement heiress—floating along—she wants to do things. Selena's a working woman. Selena can help her.

LEONIE. I know. I'm useless.

SAM. I think you ought to be unselfish about this.

LEONIE. Paula can do what she likes, of course. If she doesn't love me . . .

SAM. Of course she loves you.

LEONIE. If she prefers to live with you and Selena I shan't stand in her way.

[*Her martyrish resignation irritates* SAM *profoundly. He feels that really* LEONIE *should not be allowed to get away with it.*]

SAM. You're so vain, Leonie.

LEONIE [*refusing to argue*]. I'm sorry.

[*This makes it worse.* SAM *goes deeper.*]

SAM. After all, you're Paula's mother. Can't you look at her problem—objectively?

LEONIE. Where my emotions are involved I'm afraid I never know what words like that mean.

[*He blunders in worse, farther than he really means to go.*]

SAM [*flatly*]. Well, this sort of thing isn't good for Paula.

LEONIE [*very cold, very hurt*]. What sort of thing? [*A moment's pause. He is annoyed with himself at the ineptitude of his approach.*] Be perfectly frank. You can be with me. What sort of thing?

SAM. Well—Leonie— [*With a kind of desperate bluntness.*] You've made a career of flirtation. Obviously Paula isn't going to. You know you and Paula belong to different worlds. [*With some heat.*] And the reason Paula is the way she is is because she lives in an atmosphere of perpetual conflict.

LEONIE. Conflict? Paula?

SAM. With herself. About you.

LEONIE [*rising*]. That's too subtle for me, I'm afraid.

SAM. Paula's unaware of it herself.

LEONIE. Where did you acquire this amazing psychological insight? You never used to have it. Of course! From Selena. Of course!

SAM. I've never discussed this with Selena.

LEONIE. No?

SAM. She's told me she'd be happy to have Paula but . . .

LEONIE. That's extremely generous of her—to offer without discussion. . . .

SAM [*she has him there; he loses his temper*]. It's impossible for you to consider anything without being personal.

LEONIE. I am afraid it is. I don't live on this wonderful rarefied, intellectual plane inhabited by Selena and yourself—and where you want to take Paula. I'm sorry if I've made Paula serious, I'm sorry she's in a perpetual conflict about me. I'm sorry I've let her in for—this sort of thing! I'm sorry! [*She is on the verge of tears. She runs out.*]

SAM. Leonie . . . ! [*He follows her to door back, call-*

ing.] Leonie! [*But it is too late. She is gone. He turns back into room.*] Damn!

[PAULA *comes in—from beach, door right.*]

PAULA. Where's Leonie?

SAM. She just went upstairs.

PAULA. I've been showing Dr. Rice our rock-bound coast.

SAM. What's he like?

PAULA. Hard to say. He's almost too sympathetic. At the same time—

SAM. What?

PAULA. At the same time—he is inscrutable! I can't tell whether I like him or dislike him. You say Selena knows him. What does she say about him?

SAM. Selena isn't crazy about him.

PAULA. Why not?

SAM. Brilliant charlatan, she says—also a charmer.

PAULA. I gather that, and I resent him. How'd you come out with Leonie?

SAM. I've made a mess of it. I'm a fool!

PAULA. My going with you, you mean?

SAM. Yes.

PAULA. Sam . . .

SAM. Yes?

PAULA. Will you mind very much . . .

SAM. What?

PAULA. If I don't go with Selena and you?

SAM. But I thought you said—and especially if she marries somebody—

PAULA [*slowly*]. That's just what I'm thinking of—

SAM. What's happened?

PAULA. There's no way out of it, Sam—I've got to stay.

SAM. But why?

PAULA [*simply, looking up at him*]. Somebody's got to look after Leonie. . . .

[KENNETH *enters.*].

KENNETH. My first glimpse of Maine. A masculine Riviera.

PAULA. It's mild now. If you want to see it really virile —come in the late fall.

KENNETH. You've only to crook your little finger. I'll be glad to look at more of Maine whenever you have the time. [*Sits, facing her.*]

PAULA. Of course. Tomorrow?

KENNETH. Yes. Tomorrow. [*To* SAM.] You know, from Mrs. Frothingham's description— [*Looking back at* PAULA, *intently.*] I never could have imagined her. Not remotely.

[ROBERT *enters.*]

SAM. What is it, Robert?

ROBERT. Mrs. Frothingham would like to see Dr. Rice in her study.

KENNETH [*rising*]. Oh, thank you. [*He walks to door back.*] Excuse me. [*He goes upstairs.*]

[PAULA *and* SAM *have continued looking front. As* KENNETH *starts upstairs they slowly turn and look at one another. The same thought has crossed both their minds—they both find themselves looking suddenly into a new and dubious vista.*]

CURTAIN

Act two

SCENE I

SCENE. *The same.*

TIME. *Midsummer—late afternoon.*

AT RISE: KENNETH *is at a bridge table working out a*

chess problem. He hears voices and footsteps approaching. Gets up, unhurried, and looks off into garden. Sees BORIS *and* LEONIE *approaching. As they come in he strolls off—they do not see him.* LEONIE's *arms are full of flowers. She is looking for* KENNETH. COUNT MIRSKY *follows her in.*

COUNT MIRSKY, *a Russian, is very good-looking, mongoloid about the eyes. His English is beautiful, with a slight and attractive accent. He is tense, jittery—a mass of jangled nerves—his fingers tremble as he lights one cigarette after another. He is very pale—his pallor accentuated by a dark scarf he wears around his neck.*

BORIS [*stopping center*]. It appears he is not here either.

LEONIE. He? Who? [*Crossing to table behind sofa to put some flowers in vase.*]

BORIS. When you're in the garden with me you think—perhaps he is in the house. When you are in the house you think perhaps he is in the garden.

LEONIE. Boris, darling, you have the odd habit of referring to mysterious characters without giving me any hint who they are. Is that Russian symbolism? There will be a long silence; then you will say: He would not approve, or they can't hear us. It's a bit mystifying.

BORIS [*crossing to stand near her*]. You know who I mean.

LEONIE [*going to table right to put flowers in vase*]. Really, you flatter me. I'm not a mystic, you know, Boris. I'm a simple extrovert. When you say "he," why can't it refer to someone definite—and if possible to someone I know.

BORIS [*crossing to back of table, facing her across it*]. You know him, all right.

LEONIE. There you go again! *Really, Boris!*

BORIS [*moving closer to her around table*]. You've been

divorced now for several weeks. You're free. We
were only waiting for you to be free—

LEONIE [*moving away, sitting in chair, right*]. Now that
I am free you want to coerce me. It's a bit unreasonable, don't you think?

[BORIS *walks to end of windowseat and sits. Enter* KEN-
NETH, *door back.*]

KENNETH [*strolling across stage toward* LEONIE]. Hello,
Leonie. Count Mirsky—

LEONIE. Kenneth—I haven't seen you all day.

KENNETH. I've been in my room slaving away at a scientific paper.

LEONIE. My house hums with creative activity. I love
it. It gives me a sense of vicarious importance.
What's your paper on?

KENNETH. Shadow-neurosis.

LEONIE. Shadow-neurosis. How marvelous! What does
it mean?

KENNETH [*looking at* BORIS]. It is a sensation of non-
existence.

LEONIE. Is it common?

KENNETH. Quite. The victim knows that he exists and
yet he feels that he does not!

LEONIE. In a curious way I can imagine a sensation
like that—do you know I actually can. Isn't it amusing?

BORIS. The doctor is so eloquent. Once he describes a
sensation it becomes very easy to feel it.

LEONIE. That's an entrancing gift. Why are you so an-
tagonistic to Kenneth? He wants to help you but
you won't let him. I asked him here to help you.

KENNETH [*to* BORIS]. Your skepticism about this particular disease is interesting, Count Mirsky, because,
as it happens, you suffer from it.

BORIS [*bearing down on* KENNETH]. Has it ever occurred
to you that you are a wasted novelist?

KENNETH. Though I have not mentioned you in my article I have described you.

LEONIE [*rising and crossing left to table behind sofa*]. You should be flattered, Boris.

BORIS. I am!

LEONIE. Another case history! I've been reading some of Kenneth's scientific textbooks. Most fascinating form of biography. Who was that wonderful fellow who did such odd things—Mr. X.? You'd never think you could get so interested in anonymous people. I'd have given anything to meet Mr. X.—though I must say I'd feel a bit nervous about having him in the house.

KENNETH. How is your book getting along, Count Mirsky?

BORIS. Very well. Oh—so—

KENNETH. Far along in it?

BORIS. Quite.

LEONIE. I'm crazy to see it. He's dedicating it to me but he hasn't let me see a word of it!

KENNETH. For a very good reason.

LEONIE. What do you mean?

KENNETH. Because there is no book. There never has been a book.

LEONIE [*she lets flowers drop*]. Kenneth!

KENNETH. Isn't that true, Count Mirsky?

BORIS. It is not!

KENNETH. Then why don't you let us see a bit of it?

LEONIE. Oh, do! At least the dedication page.

KENNETH. A chapter—

BORIS. Because it isn't finished yet.

LEONIE. Well, it doesn't have to be finished. We know the end, don't we? The end belongs to the world.

KENNETH. Let us see it, Count.

BORIS. I can't.

KENNETH. What are you calling the book?

BORIS. I haven't decided yet.

KENNETH. May I suggest a title to you—?

LEONIE. Oh, do! What shall we call it, Kenneth?

KENNETH. "The Memoirs of a Boy Who Wanted to Murder His Father."

LEONIE. What!

BORIS [*gripping arms of chair*]. I am not a hysterical woman, Doctor—and I'm not your patient!

LEONIE. But Kenneth—Boris worshipped his father.

KENNETH. No, he hated him. He hated him when he was alive and he hates him still. He grew up under the overwhelming shadow of this world-genius whom, in spite of an immense desire to emulate and even surpass—he felt he could never emulate and never surpass—nor even equal— Did you worship your father, Count Mirsky?

BORIS. It's true! I hated him!

LEONIE. Boris!

BORIS. I hated him!

KENNETH. Now you can let us see the book, can't you—now that we know the point of view—just a bit of it?

LEONIE. I'm more crazy than ever to see it now. I can tell you a little secret now, Boris. I was afraid—I was rather afraid—that your book would be a little like one of those statues of an ancestor in a frock-coat. Now it sounds really exciting. You hated him. But how perfectly marvelous! I can't wait to see it now. Do run up to your study and bring it down, Boris—do!

BORIS. No.

LEONIE. That's very unpleasant of you.

BORIS. You might as well know it then. There isn't any book. There never will be. Not by me.

LEONIE. But I don't understand—every day—in your room working—all these months!

BORIS [*facing her*]. One wants privacy! Possibly you can't realize that. You who always have to have a house full of people.

LEONIE [*goes back to flowers at table*]. Boris!

KENNETH [*rising*]. Why don't you write the book anyway, Count Mirsky? There is a vogue these days for vituperative biography.

BORIS. I am not interested in the vogue.

KENNETH. We are quite used nowadays to children who dislike their fathers. The public—

BORIS. To titillate the public would not compensate me for forcing myself to recall the atmosphere of saintly sadism in which my childhood was spent—I can still smell that living room, I can still smell those stinking, sexless pilgrims who used to come from all over the world to get my saintly father's blessing. I used to sit with my mother in a room no bigger than a closet to get away from the odor of that nauseating humanitarianism. There was no privacy in the Villa Mirskovitch. Oh, no—it was a Mecca—do you understand—a Mecca!

KENNETH. Yes, I think I understand.

BORIS. Well, I have been paying the haloed one back. I have been getting privacy at his expense at last.

LEONIE. Why have you never told me before that you felt this way about your father?

BORIS. I never said anything about him. It was you who did the talking. You always raved about the great man with that characteristic American enthusiasm for what you don't know.

LEONIE. Nevertheless, the world recognizes your father as a great man. The books are there to prove it. There they are. You can't write books like that without greatness—no matter what you say. You are a petulant child. Your father was a great man.

BORIS. It makes no difference how great he was—those pilgrims stank!

[LEONIE *turns away.*]

KENNETH. I suggest that to write that book, even if no one ever sees the manuscript but you, might amuse you—a kind of revenge which, when you were a boy, you were in no position to take.

BORIS. Are you trying to cure me, Doctor? Please don't trouble. I don't need your particular species of professionalism. I do not need any help from you. [*He goes to door back, turns to* LEONIE. LEONIE *looks bewilderedly at* KENNETH. BORIS *goes out.*]

LEONIE. How did you know? You're uncanny!

KENNETH. All in the day's work.

LEONIE. Why is it I always get myself involved with men weaker than myself? I certainly am no tower of strength.

KENNETH. Possibly not—but you are generous and impulsive. You have a tendency to accept people at the best of their own valuation.

LEONIE. I want to help them. I do help them. After they get used to my help, after they get to count on my help, I get impatient with them. Why, I ask myself, can't people help themselves?

KENNETH. And very natural.

LEONIE. I seem to attract people like that!

KENNETH. Leonie—you are the last woman on earth Count Mirsky should marry. He would only transfer his hatred of his father to you.

LEONIE. I don't think I understand you, Kenneth— really I don't—and I do so want to understand things.

KENNETH. Well—your charm, your gaiety, your position, your wealth, your beauty—these would oppress him. Again, he cannot be himself.—Or, if he is himself, it is to reveal his nonentity, his inferiority—again the secondary role—Leonie Frothingham's husband—the son of Count Mirsky—the husband of Leonie Frothingham. Again the shadow—again, eternally and always—non-existence. Poor fellow. [*Pause.*]

LEONIE. I'm so grateful to you, Kenneth.

KENNETH. Nonsense. You mustn't be grateful to me because I—exercise my profession.

LEONIE. I want to express my gratitude—in some tangible form. I've been thinking of nothing else lately. I can't sleep for thinking of it.

KENNETH. Well, if it gives you insomnia, you'd better tell me about it.

LEONIE. I want to make it possible for you to realize your ambition.

KENNETH. Ambition? What ambition?

LEONIE. Ah! You've forgotten, haven't you? But you let it slip out one day—you pump me professionally —but I do the same to you—non-professionally.

KENNETH. You terrify me!

LEONIE. That night last winter when we went to dinner in that little restaurant where you go with your doctor friends . . . you told me your dream.

KENNETH. My censor must have been napping.

LEONIE. He was. Or she was. What sex is your censor?

KENNETH. That's none of your business.

LEONIE. I'm sorry.

KENNETH. Which of my dreams was I so reckless as to reveal to you?

LEONIE. To have a sanatorium of your own one day—so you can carry out your own ideas of curing patients.

KENNETH. Oh, that! Out of the question.

LEONIE. Why?

KENNETH. To do it on the scale I visualize, would cost

more than I'm ever likely to save out of my practice.

LEONIE. I'll give you the sanatorium. I've never given anyone anything like that before. What fun!

KENNETH. Will I find it all wrapped up in silver foil on Christmas morning?

LEONIE. Yes. You will! You will! We'll have a suite in it for Mr. X.—for all your anonymous friends—we'll entertain the whole alphabet!

KENNETH. You see, Leonie!

LEONIE. What do you mean? I thought you'd be—

KENNETH. Of course, it's terribly generous of you. I'm deeply touched. But . . .

LEONIE. But . . . ?

KENNETH. I'm a stranger to you.

LEONIE. Kenneth!

KENNETH. Outside of my professional relation—such as I have with scores of patients—little more than that.

LEONIE. I thought—

KENNETH. And yet you are willing to back me in a venture that would cost a sizeable fortune—just on that. Leonie! Leonie!

LEONIE. It would be the best investment I've ever made. Paula's always telling me I have no social consciousness. Well, this would be.—It would keep me from feeling so useless. I do feel useless, Kenneth. Please!

KENNETH. I'm sorry. I couldn't hear of it. Of course, it's out of the question.

LEONIE. It isn't. I can afford it. Why shouldn't I? It would be helping so many people—you have no right to refuse. It's selfish of you to refuse.

KENNETH. I distrust impulsive altruism. You will forgive me, Leonie, but it may often do harm.

LEONIE. How do you mean, Kenneth?

KENNETH. I gather you are about to endow a radical magazine for the *boys*—

LEONIE. Will and Dennis! I thought it would be nice to give them something to do!

KENNETH. Yes. You are prepared to back them in a publication which; if it attained any influence, would undermine the system which makes you and your people like you possible.

LEONIE. But it never occurred to me anyone would read it.

KENNETH. There is a deplorably high literacy in this country. Unfortunately it is much easier to learn to read than it is to learn to think.

LEONIE. Well, if you don't think it's a good idea, Kenneth, I won't do it. But this sanatorium is different.

KENNETH. Why?

LEONIE. Because, if you must know it, it would be helping you—and that means everything in the world to me. There, I've said it. It's true! Kenneth —are you terrified?

KENNETH. You adorable child!

LEONIE. It's extraordinary, Kenneth—but you are the first strong man who's ever come into my life— [*Enter* PAULA, DENNIS, WILL, *door back.*] Oh, I'm very glad to see you! Will! Hullo, Dennis. You all know Dr. Rice. Mr. Dexter, Mr. McCarthy. Sit down, everybody. Well, children, how is New York?

[DENNIS *crosses down front of them to chair left by sofa and sits.*]

WILL. Stifling, thank you.

LEONIE. Any luck yet?

WILL. I am available, but New York is dead to its chief opportunity.

LEONIE. Then you can stay here for a bit. You can both stay here.

DENNIS. That was all right when we were in college, Mrs. Frothingham. Can't do it now.

LEONIE. Oh, you're working. I'm so glad!

DENNIS. I beg your pardon. Did you say working?

LEONIE. Well, then! I don't see why you can't stay here and take a holiday.

WILL. From what?

LEONIE. Since none of you are doing anything in town, you might as well stay here and do nothing and be comfortable.

DENNIS. Yes, but it's an ethical question. When we're in New York doing nothing, we belong to the most respectable vested group going! The unemployed. As such we have a status, position, authority. But if we stay here doing nothing—what are we? Low-down parasites.

KENNETH. No jobs about anywhere, eh?

WILL. Extinct commodity.

DENNIS. I did pretty well last week.

LEONIE. Really?

DENNIS. I was rejected by seven newspapers—including the *Bronx Home News* and the *Yonkers Herald*—six magazines and trade papers—a total of twenty-eight rejections in all, representing a net gain over the previous week of seven solid rejections. I submit to you, gentlemen, that's progress—pass the cigars, Will.

LEONIE. Couldn't you stay here and be rejected by mail?

DENNIS. Doesn't give you that same feeling somehow—that good, rich, dark-brown sensation of not being wanted!

LEONIE. You know, Kenneth, in a curious way, Dennis reminds me a bit of Mr. X.

DENNIS. And who's X.?

LEONIE. A sporting acquaintance.

DENNIS. There's one thing I'd like to ask Dr. Rice. . . . Do you mind?

KENNETH. At your service.

DENNIS [*turning chair and facing* KENNETH *upstage*]. In the psychoanalytic hierarchy Freud is the god, isn't he?

KENNETH. Of one sect, yes.

DENNIS. Well, the original sect—

KENNETH. Yes . . .

DENNIS. Now, every psychoanalyst has to have himself analyzed. That's true, isn't it, Doctor?

KENNETH. Generally speaking—yes.

DENNIS. As I understand it, the highest prices go to those nearest the Master himself.

KENNETH. This boy is irreverent . . .

DENNIS. I know whereof I speak. I prepared an article on the subject for *Fortune*.

WILL. Rejection number three hundred.

DENNIS. I am afraid, Will, that you are a success worshipper!

LEONIE. Dennis is an *enfant terrible,* and he exhausts himself keeping it up!

DENNIS. I have examined the racket with a microscopic patience and this I find to be true: at the top of the hierarchy is the Great Pan-Sexualist of Vienna. To be an orthodox and accepted Freudian, you must have been analyzed by another of the same. Now what I am burning to know is this: Who analyzed Sig Freud himself? Whom does he tell his repressions to? Why, the poor guy must be lonely as hell!

LEONIE. What would you do with him, Kenneth? He has no repressions whatever!

KENNETH. He needs some badly.

LEONIE. I wonder what Dennis would confess to his psychoanalyst that he isn't always shouting to the world?

DENNIS. I'd make the psychoanalyst talk. [*To* KENNETH. *Beckoning.*] Tell me, Doctor, what did you dream last night?

KENNETH [*behind his cupped hand*]. Not in public.

DENNIS [*rises and crosses straight right*]. You see—he's repressed! I tell you these psychoanalysts are repressed. They've got nobody to talk to! I'm going swimming. It's pathetic! [*He goes out.*]

LEONIE. I'm going too. He makes me laugh. How about you, Kenneth?

KENNETH. Oh, I'll watch.

LEONIE [*to others*]. Come along with us. There's plenty of time for a swim before dinner.

[KENNETH *starts out with* LEONIE, *stops on the way.*]

KENNETH. I suppose you and your Irish friend edited the comic paper at college?

WILL. No, we edited the serious paper.

KENNETH. Just the same it must have been very funny. [*He goes out after* LEONIE.]

WILL. Don't think that feller likes me much.

PAULA. You're psychic.

WILL. Well, for the matter of that I'm not crazy about him either.

PAULA. Don't bother about him. Concentrate on me!

WILL. How are you, darling?

PAULA. Missed you.

WILL [*pulls her to sofa and sits with her.* PAULA *left end sofa*]. And I you. Pretty lousy in town without you.

PAULA. Oh, poor darling!

WILL. Although my star is rising. I did some book-reviews for *The New York Times* and the *New Masses.*

PAULA. What a gamut!

WILL. I made, in fact, a total of eleven dollars. The student most likely to succeed in the first four months since graduation has made eleven dollars.

PAULA. Wonderful!

WILL. My classmates were certainly clairvoyant. As a matter of fact, I shouldn't have told you. Now I'll be tortured thinking you're after me for my money.

PAULA. You'll never know!

WILL [*putting arm around her shoulders and drawing her to him*]. What've you been doing?

PAULA. Lying in the sun mostly.

WILL. Poor little Ritz girl.

PAULA. Wondering what you do every night.

WILL. Forty-second Street Library mostly. Great fun! Voluptuary atmosphere!

PAULA. Is your life altogether so austere?

WILL. Well, frankly, no. Not altogether.

PAULA. Cad!

WILL. What do you expect?

PAULA. Loyalty.

WILL. I am loyal. But you go around all day job-hunting. You find you're not wanted. It's reassuring after that to find a shoulder to lean on, sort of haven where you *are* wanted. Even the public library closes at ten. You have to go somewhere. If I'm ever Mayor of New York, I'll have the public libraries kept open all night . . . the flop-houses of the intellectuals!

PAULA. Is it anyone special . . . ?

WILL. Just a generalized shoulder.

PAULA. Well, you're going to have a special one from now on—mine! You know, the way you're avoiding the issue is all nonsense.

WILL. You mean my gallant fight against you?

PAULA. I've decided that you are conventional and bourgeois. You're money-ridden.

WILL. Eleven dollars. They say a big income makes you conservative.

PAULA. I don't mean your money. I mean—my money. It's childish to let an artificial barrier like that stand between us. It's also childish to ignore it.

WILL [*rising*]. I don't ignore it. That's what worries me. I count on it. Already I find myself counting on it. I can't help it. Sitting and waiting in an office for some bigwig who won't see me or for some underling who won't see me I think: "Why the hell should I wait all day for this stuffed shirt?" I don't wait. Is it because of you I feel in a special category? Do I count on your money? Is that why I don't wait as long as the other fellow? There's one consolation: the other fellow doesn't get the job either. But the point is disquieting!

PAULA. What a Puritan you are!

WILL [*sitting beside her again*]. Will I become an appendage to you—like your mother's men?

PAULA. You're bound to—money or no money.

WILL [*taking her into his arms*]. I suppose I might as well go on the larger dole—

PAULA. What?

WILL. Once you are paid merely for existing—you are on the dole. I rather hoped, you know—

PAULA. What?

WILL. It's extraordinary the difference in one's thinking when you're in college and when you're out—

PAULA. How do you mean?

WILL. Well, when I was in college, my interest in the— "movement"—was really impersonal. I imagined myself giving my energies to the poor and the downtrodden in my spare time. I didn't really believe I'd

be one of the poor and down-trodden myself. In my
heart of hearts, I was sure I'd break through the iron
law of Dennis's statistics and land a job somewhere.
But I can't—and it's given a tremendous jolt to
my self-esteem.

PAULA. But you'll come through. I'm sure of it. I wish
you could learn to look at my money as a means
rather than an end.

WILL. I'd rather use my own.

PAULA. You're proud.

WILL. I am.

PAULA. It's humiliating but I'm afraid I've got to ask
you to marry me, Will.

WILL. It's humiliating but considering my feelings I
see no way out of accepting you.

PAULA. You submit?

WILL [*kissing her hand*]. I submit.

PAULA. After a hard campaign—victory!

WILL. You *are* a darling.

PAULA [*getting up and crossing to center*]. I can't tell
you what a relief it'll be to get away from this
house.

WILL. Why?

PAULA. I don't know. It's getting very complicated.

WILL. Leonie?

PAULA. *And* Boris. *And* Dr. Rice. Funny thing how
that man . . .

WILL. What?

PAULA. Makes you insecure somehow.

WILL. Supposed to do just the opposite.

PAULA. He answers every question—and yet he's se-
cretive. I've never met a man who—who—

WILL. Who what?

PAULA. Really, I can't stand Dr. Rice.

WILL. I believe he fascinates you.

PAULA. He does. I don't deny that. And I can't tell

you how I resent it. Isn't it silly? [*The old lady*
WYLER *in a wheel chair is propelled in by a nurse.
The old lady is much wasted since the preceding
summer; she is touched with mortality.*] Granny!

MRS. WYLER. Paula! How are you, my dear?

PAULA. I came up to see you before, but you were
asleep.

MRS. WYLER. Nurse told me.

[*Exit* NURSE, *door left.*]

PAULA. You remember Will?

WILL. How do you do, Mrs. Wyler?

MRS. WYLER. Of course. How do you do, young man?

PAULA. Well, this is quite an adventure for you, isn't
it, Granny?

MRS. WYLER. You're the boy who was always so curious
about my youth.

WILL. Yes.

MRS. WYLER. I've forgotten most of it. Now I just live
from day to day. The past is just this morning. [*A
moment's pause.*] And I don't always remember
that very well. Aren't there insects who live only
one day? The morning is their youth and the afternoon their middle age. . . .

PAULA. You don't seem yourself today. Not as cheerful
as usual.

MRS. WYLER. Can't I have my moods, Paula? I am
pleased to be reflective today. People are always
sending me funny books to read. I've been reading
one and it depressed me.

PAULA. Well, I'll tell you something to cheer you up,
Granny— Will and I are going to be married.

MRS. WYLER. Have you told your mother?

PAULA. Not yet. It's a secret.

[*Enter* KENNETH.]

KENNETH. Well, Mrs. Wyler! Wanderlust today?

MRS. WYLER. Yes! Wanderlust!

KENNETH. Paula, if you're not swimming, what about our walk, and our daily argument?

MRS. WYLER. What argument?

KENNETH. Paula is interested in my subject. She hovers between skepticism and fascination.

PAULA. No chance to hover today, Kenneth. Will's improving his tennis. Sorry.

KENNETH. So am I.

MRS. WYLER. I've a surprise for you, Paula.

PAULA. What?

MRS. WYLER. Your father's coming.

PAULA. No!

MRS. WYLER. Yes.

PAULA. But how—! How do you know?

MRS. WYLER. Because I've sent for him, and he wired me he's coming. He's driving from Blue Hill. He should be here now.

PAULA. That's too—! Oh, Granny, that's marvelous! Will, let's drive out to meet him, shall we? Does Mother know?

MRS. WYLER. I only had Sam's wire an hour ago.

PAULA. Granny, you're an angel.

MRS. WYLER. Not quite yet. Don't hurry me, child.

PAULA. Come on, Will. [*Exit* PAULA *and* WILL.]

MRS. WYLER. I can see you are interested in Paula. You are, aren't you, Dr. Rice?

KENNETH. Yes. She's an extraordinary child. Adores her father, doesn't she?

MRS. WYLER. How would you cure that, Doctor?

KENNETH. It's quite healthy.

MRS. WYLER. Really? I was hoping for something juicy in the way of interpretation.

KENNETH. Sorry!

MRS. WYLER. What an interesting profession yours is, Dr. Rice.

KENNETH. Why particularly?

MRS. WYLER. Your province is the soul. Strange region.

KENNETH. People's souls, I find are, on the whole, infinitely more interesting than their bodies. I have been a general practitioner and I know.

MRS. WYLER. These young people—don't they frighten you?

KENNETH. Frighten!

MRS. WYLER. They are so radical—prepared to throw everything overboard—every tradition—

KENNETH. Paula's friends have nothing to lose, any change would be—in the nature of velvet for them.

MRS. WYLER. What do you think of Will?

KENNETH. I'm afraid I've formed no strongly defined opinion on Will.

MRS. WYLER. Oh, I see— That is a comment in itself.

KENNETH. He's nondescript.

MRS. WYLER. Do you mean to point that out to Paula?

KENNETH. I don't think so. That won't be necessary.

MRS. WYLER. Why not?

KENNETH. Blood will tell.

MRS. WYLER. That's very gracious of you, Doctor. [*Pause.*] And what do you think of Leonie?

KENNETH. Very endearing—and very impulsive.

MRS. WYLER. For example—I mean of the latter—

KENNETH. She offered to build me a sanatorium—a fully equipped modern sanatorium.

MRS. WYLER. Did she? Convenient for you.

KENNETH. Except that I refused.

MRS. WYLER. Wasn't that quixotic?

KENNETH. Not necessarily.

[PAULA *and* SAM *enter, door-back.*]

PAULA. Here he is!

MRS. WYLER. Sam!

SAM. Louise!

PAULA. He wouldn't come if I'd ask him. He said so shamelessly. You know Dr. Rice?

SAM. Of course.

KENNETH. Excuse me. [KENNETH *goes out.*]

SAM. Well, Louise!

MRS. WYLER. Hello, Sam.

[SAM *kisses her.*]

SAM. How's she behaving?

PAULA. Incorrigible. Dr. Prentiss tells her to rest in her room. You see how she obeys him. She'll obey you though.

SAM. Well, I'll sneak her away from Dr. Prentiss and take her abroad.

MRS. WYLER. I want to go to Ethiopia. Run along, dear. I want to talk to Sam.

PAULA. Keep him here, Granny. Pretend you're not feeling well.

MRS. WYLER. I'll try. [*Exit* PAULA *door back.*] Well, Sam—

SAM. I got your wire last night. Here I am.

MRS. WYLER. It's nice of you.

SAM. Oh, now, Louise. You know you're the love of my life.

MRS. WYLER. Yes, Sam, I know—but how is Selena?

SAM. Flourishing.

MRS. WYLER. You're all right then?

SAM. Unbelievably.

MRS. WYLER. I knew you would be.

SAM. And you?

MRS. WYLER. I'm dying, Sam.

SAM. Not you—

MRS. WYLER. Don't contradict me. Besides, I'm rather looking forward to it.

SAM. Is Dr. Prentiss—?

MRS. WYLER. Dr. Prentiss soft-soaps me. I let him. It relieves his mind. But that's why I've sent for you.

SAM. You know, my dear—

MRS. WYLER. Yes, Sam. I know I can count on you. I'm

dying. And I'm dying alone. I have to talk to somebody. You're the only one.

SAM. Is anything worrying you?

MRS. WYLER. Plenty.

SAM. What, dear?

MRS. WYLER. The future. Not my own. That's fixed
or soon will be. But Leonie's—Paula's—

SAM. Aren't they all right?

MRS. WYLER. I am surrounded by aliens. The house is
full of strangers. That Russian upstairs; this doctor.

SAM. Rice? Are you worried about him?

MRS. WYLER. What is he after? What does he want? He
told me Leonie offered to build him a sanatorium—

SAM. Did he accept it?

MRS. WYLER. No. He refused. But something tells me
he will allow himself to be persuaded.

SAM. I don't think Rice is a bad feller really. Seems
pretty sensible. Are you worried about this boy—
Dexter, and Paula?

MRS. WYLER. Not in the same way. I like the boy. But
Paula—I'm worried about what the money'll do
to her. We know what it's done to Leonie. You
know, Sam, in spite of all her romantic dreams Leonie has a kind of integrity. But I often wonder
if she's ever been really happy.

SAM. Oh, now, Louise, this pessimism's unlike you—

MRS. WYLER. This money we've built our lives on—it
used to symbolize security—but there's no security
in it any more.

SAM. Paula'll be all right. I count on Paula.

MRS. WYLER. In the long run. But that may be too late.
One can't let go of everything, Sam. It isn't in nature. That's why I've asked you to come. I want
you to remain as executor under my will.

SAM. Well, I only resigned because—since I'm no
longer married to Leonie—

MRS. WYLER. What has that got to do with it?

SAM. All right.

MRS. WYLER. Promise?

SAM. Certainly.

MRS. WYLER. I feel something dark ahead, a terror—

SAM. Now, now, you've been brooding.

MRS. WYLER. Outside of you—Will is the soundest person I'll leave behind me, the healthiest—but in him too I feel a recklessness that's just kept in—I see a vista of the unknown—to us the unknown was the West, land—physical hardship—but he's hard and bitter underneath his jocularity—he isn't sure, he says, what he is— Once he is sure, what will he do?—I want you to watch him, Sam, for Paula's sake.

SAM. I will.

MRS. WYLER. They're all strange and dark. . . . And this doctor. A soul doctor. We didn't have such things—I am sure that behind all this is a profound and healing truth. But sometimes truths may be perverted, and this particular doctor—how are we to know where his knowledge ends and his pretension begins? Now that I am dying, for the first time in my life I know fear. Death seems easy and simple, Sam—a self-indulgence—but can I afford it? [*She smiles up at him. He squeezes her hand.*]

SAM. Everything will be all right. Trust me.

MRS. WYLER. I do. [*A pause.*] You'll stay the night?

SAM. Of course.

MRS. WYLER. Now I feel better.

SAM. That's right. [*Pause.*]

MRS. WYLER. I'd like to live till autumn.

SAM. Of course you will. Many autumns.

MRS. WYLER. Heaven forbid. But this autumn. The color—the leaves turn. [*Looking out window.* SAM *looks too.*] The expression seems strange. What do they turn to?

SAM [*softly, helping her mood*]. Their mother. The earth.

MRS. WYLER. I'm happy now. I'm at peace.

SAM [*puts arm around her and draws her to him*]. That's better.

MRS. WYLER [*smiling up at him*]. It's very clever of me to have sent for you, Sam. I'm pleased with myself. Now, Sam, let 'em do their worst—

SAM [*smiling back at her and patting her hands*]. Just let 'em . . . !

CURTAIN

SCENE II

SCENE. *The same.*

TIME. *A few hours later—before dinner.* LEONIE *is standing in doorway looking out.* BORIS *center; he is fatalistically quiet at first.*

BORIS. What it comes to is this then! You're through with me. You want me to go!

LEONIE. I'm no good to you! I can no longer help you.

BORIS. Frustrated altruist!

LEONIE. You hate me!

BORIS. That would be encouraging!

LEONIE. We have nothing more for each other.

BORIS. Less than we had in the beginning!

LEONIE. Less than I thought we had.

BORIS [*walking toward her*]. And the man of science?

LEONIE. What?

BORIS [*still bearing down on her*]. This intricate man of science. You fluctuate so, Leonie. [*Facing her.*]

LEONIE. Please, Boris. I've failed. Can't we part—beautifully?

BORIS. What do you want to do? Go out on the bay and say farewell before the villagers in a barge drawn by a flock of swans? Shall we have a little orchestra to play—with the strings sobbing—and the bassoon off key?

LEONIE. You are bitter and cruel. Why? I've tried to help you. Why are you bitter?

BORIS [*moving close to her*]. At least I'm honest. Can you say the same?

LEONIE [*breaking away from him*]. I don't know what you mean by that.

BORIS [*getting in front of her*]. Yes, you do.

LEONIE. You're eating yourself up. You're killing yourself. There's the great lovely world outside and you sit in your room hating—

BORIS. What do you recommend? Cold showers and Swedish massage? What does the man of science prescribe for me?

LEONIE. Why do you hate Kenneth so?

BORIS. I'm jealous, my dear!

LEONIE. Poor Boris. You're beyond a simple emotion like that, aren't you?

BORIS. I envy you, Leonie. All like you.

LEONIE. Do you?

BORIS. I envy all sentimental liars who gratify their desires on high principle. It makes all your diversions an exercise in piety. You're sick of me and want to sleep with the man of science. [LEONIE *turns away. He seizes her arms and turns her to him.*] Does this suffice for you? No. It must be that you can no longer help me. [*Little silent laugh.*] My sainted father was like that! God!

LEONIE. This is the end, Boris.

BORIS. Of course it is. I tell you this though: Beware of him, Leonie. Beware of him.

LEONIE. Your hatred of Kenneth—like all your hatreds

—they're unnatural, frightening. I'm frightened of you. [*Turning from him.*]

BORIS [*crossing before her, closing door so she can't escape*]. Much better to be frightened of him. You know what I think. What does he think? Does he tell you? Do you know?

LEONIE. Yes, I know.

BORIS. You know what he tells you. This clairvoyant who gets rich profoundly analyzing the transparent. [*Enter* KENNETH, *door back.*]

KENNETH. Your mother would like to see you, Leonie.

LEONIE. Is she all right?

[BORIS *goes upstage to small table. Gets cigarette.*]

KENNETH. Oh, very chipper, Mr. Frothingham is with her.

LEONIE. She sent for Sam, didn't she? I wonder why.

BORIS. Perhaps she felt the situation too complicated —even for *you*, Dr. Rice.

KENNETH. I don't think so.

BORIS. You are so Olympian, Dr. Rice. Would it be possible to anger you?

KENNETH. Symptoms, my dear Count, never anger me. I study them.

BORIS. Really, you are in a superb position. I quite envy you. One might cut oneself open in front of you—and it would be a symptom. Wouldn't it?

LEONIE. Boris, please—what's the good?

BORIS [*crossing slowly to* LEONIE]. You are quite right, my dear, no good—no good in the world. Give your mother this message for me. Tell her that under the circumstances I shall simplify the situation by withdrawing.

LEONIE. You make me very unhappy, Boris.

BORIS. How agreeable then that you have Dr. Rice here —to resolve your unhappiness. [*Crosses quickly to table behind sofa and puts out cigarette.*]

LEONIE [*following him*]. Where will you be in case I—in case you—Boris?

BORIS. Don't worry about me. A magazine syndicate has offered me a great deal for *sentimental* reminiscences of my father. Imagine that, sentimental! They have offered me—charming Americanism—a ghost-writer. It will be quaint—one ghost collaborating with another ghost. [*Raising hand like Greek priest.*] My blessings, Leonie. [*Kisses her hand.*] You have been charming. Dr. Rice— [*He bows formally. Exit* BORIS.]

LEONIE. Poor Boris— [*She sinks into a chair, overcome.*]

KENNETH. He's part of the past. You must forget him.

LEONIE. Poor Boris!

KENNETH. You will forget him.

LEONIE. I'll try.

KENNETH. Exorcised!

LEONIE. You know, Kenneth, I feel you are the only one in the world I can count on.

KENNETH. Not me.

LEONIE. Whom else?

KENNETH. Yourself!

LEONIE. Light reed! Fragile! Fragile!

KENNETH. Pliant but unbreakable.

LEONIE. No. Don't think much of myself, Kenneth. Really I don't. My judgment seems to be at fault somehow. Paula thinks so too. She's always lecturing me. [*Sits right end of sofa.*]

KENNETH. Paula can't abide me.

LEONIE. It's not true!

KENNETH. You know, Leonie, I have an instinct in these matters—so, also, has your daughter.

LEONIE. Don't you like Paula?

KENNETH. I love her. Everyone connected with you.

LEONIE. Kenneth! How dear of you! Of course Paula and I are poles apart. Look at her friends!

KENNETH. Raffish!

LEONIE [*a little taken aback by this*]. Oh, do you think so? All of them? Don't you like Will?

KENNETH. Nice enough. Clever in his way. With an eye to the main chance.

LEONIE. Really?

KENNETH. Naturally—penniless boy.

LEONIE. I've always encouraged Paula to be independent. I've never tried to impose my ideals or my standards on her. Have I done wrong to give her her own head this way? She's such a darling, really. She's killing, you know. So superior, so knowing. The other day—the other day, Kenneth . . . I took her to lunch in town and she criticized me—now what do you think about?

KENNETH [*sitting on arm of chair*]. For once my intuition fails me.

LEONIE. About my technique with men. She said it was lousy. Isn't it delicious?

KENNETH. Not more specific than simply lousy?

LEONIE. She said I threw myself at men instead of reversing the process.

KENNETH. But I should think she would have approved of that. She makes such a fetish of being candid!

LEONIE. That's just what I said—exactly. I said I couldn't pretend—that I couldn't descend to—technique. I said that when my feelings were involved I saw no point in not letting the other person see it. I reproached her for deviousness. Strange ideas that child has—strange!

KENNETH. I'm afraid her generation is theory-ridden! [*Pause.*]

LEONIE. Kenneth?

KENNETH. Yes, Leonie?

LEONIE. It's true of course.

KENNETH. What?

LEONIE. Paula's—criticism. I can't conceal my feelings. Least of all—from you. [*Slight pause.*]

KENNETH. Why should you?

LEONIE. Oh, Kenneth, I'm so useless! You know how useless I am!

KENNETH. I know only that you are gracious and lovely —and that you have the gift of innocence.

LEONIE. I hate my life. It's been so scattered—emotionally.

KENNETH. Whose isn't?

LEONIE. You are such a comfort. Really it's too much now to expect me to do without you. Kenneth?

KENNETH. Yes . . . Leonie.

LEONIE. Will you be a darling—and marry me?

KENNETH. Leonie?

LEONIE [*returning his gaze*]. Yes, Kenneth.

KENNETH. Have you thought this over?

LEONIE. It's the first time—the very first time—that I've ever been sure.

KENNETH. You are so impulsive, Leonie.

LEONIE. Kenneth, don't you think we'd have a chance —you and I—don't you think?

[*Enter* PAULA, *door back.*]

PAULA [*realizes she has interrupted a tête-à-tête*]. Oh, sorry—!

LEONIE. Paula dear, have you been with Mother?

PAULA. Yes. Granny wants to see you, as a matter of fact.

LEONIE. Oh, I forgot! Is she all right? Cheerful?

PAULA. Oh, very.

LEONIE. I'll be right there. Stay and talk to Kenneth, Paula. He thinks you don't like him. Prove to him it isn't true. Do you think you could be gracious, Paula? Or is that too old-fashioned? [*Exit* LEONIE *door back.*]

[*In the following scene* PAULA *determines to get rid of*

*the tantalizing and irritating mixed feelings she has
about* KENNETH, *her sense of distrusting, disliking
and simultaneously being fascinated by him—she
feels he has something up his sleeve; she is playing a
game to discover what it is and yet she becomes increasingly conscious that game is not unpleasant to
her because of her interest in her victim.*]

PAULA. Leonie's all a-flutter. What is it?

KENNETH. She was just telling me—she envies you your
poise.

PAULA. Your intentions are honorable, I hope.

KENNETH. Old hat, Paula.

PAULA. I beg your pardon.

KENNETH. Undergraduate audacity. Scott Fitzgerald.
Old hat.

PAULA. We don't like each other much, do we?

KENNETH. That's regrettable.

PAULA. And yet—I'm very curious about you.

KENNETH. What would you like to know?

PAULA. Your motive.

KENNETH. Ah!

PAULA. And yet even if you told me—

KENNETH. You wouldn't believe it?

PAULA [*facing him*]. No. Now why is that? Even when
you are perfectly frank, your frankness seems to me
—a device. Now why is that?

KENNETH. I'll tell you.

PAULA. Why?

KENNETH. Because you yourself are confused, muddled,
unsure, contradictory. I am simple and co-ordinated.
You resent that. You dislike it. You envy it. You
would like such simplicity for yourself. But, as you
are unlikely to achieve it, you soothe yourself by
distrusting me.

PAULA. You say I'm muddled. Why am I muddled?

KENNETH. You've accepted a set of premises without

examining them or thinking about them. You keep them like jewels in a box and dangle them. Then you put them back in the box, confident that they belong to you. But as they don't you feel an occasional twinge of insecurity—

PAULA. Do you mind dropping the parables—?

KENNETH. Not at all—

PAULA. Why am I muddled? For example—

KENNETH. You're a walking contradiction in terms—

PAULA. For example?

KENNETH. For example—for example—your radicalism. Your friends. Your point of view. Borrowed. Unexamined. Insincere.

PAULA. Go on.

KENNETH. You are rich and you are exquisite. Why are you rich and exquisite? [*Walking back to face her.*] Because your forebears were not moralistic but ruthless. Had they been moralistic, had they been concerned, as you pretend to be, with the "predatory system"—this awful terminology—you'd be working in a store somewhere wrapping packages or waiting on querulous housewives with bad skins or teaching school. Your own origins won't bear a moralistic investigation. You must know that. Your sociology and economics must teach you that.

PAULA. Suppose I repudiate my origins?

KENNETH. That takes more courage than you have.

PAULA. Don't be so sure.

KENNETH. But why should you? If you had a special talent or were a crusader there might be some sense in it. But you have no special talent and you are not a crusader. Much better to be decorative. Much better for a world starving for beauty. Instead of repudiating your origins you should exult in them and in that same predatory system that made you possible. [*Crossing to table behind sofa for cigarette.*]

[*Pause.*]

PAULA. What were your origins?

KENNETH [*lighting cigarette*]. Anonymous.

PAULA. What do you mean?

KENNETH. I was discovered on a doorstep.

PAULA. Really?

KENNETH. Like Moses.

PAULA. Where were you brought up?

KENNETH. In a foundling asylum in New England. The place lacked charm. This sounds like an unpromising beginning but actually it was more stimulating than you might imagine. I remember as a kid of twelve going to the library at Springfield and getting down the *Dictionary of National Biography* and hunting out the bastards. Surprising how many distinguished ones there were and are. I allied myself early with the brilliant and variegated company of the illegitimate.

PAULA. You don't know who your parents were?

KENNETH. No.

PAULA. Did you get yourself through college?

KENNETH. *And* medical school.

PAULA. Did you practice medicine?

KENNETH. For a bit. I devoted myself—when the victims would let me—to their noses and throats. It was a starveling occupation. But I gave up tonsillectomy for the soul. The poor have tonsils but only the rich have souls. My instinct was justified—as you see.

PAULA. You've gone pretty far.

KENNETH. Incredible journey!

PAULA. Having come from—from—

KENNETH. The mud—?

PAULA. Well—I should think you'd be more sympathetic to the under-dogs.

KENNETH. No, why should I? The herd bores me. It interests me only as an indication of the distance I've traveled.

PAULA. Will would say that you are a lucky individual who—

KENNETH. Yes, that is what Will would say. It always satisfies the mediocrity to call the exceptional individual lucky.

PAULA. You don't like Will?

KENNETH. I despise him.

PAULA. Why?

KENNETH. I detest these young firebrands whose incandescence will be extinguished by the first job! I detest radicals who lounge about in country-houses.

PAULA. You're unfair to Will.

KENNETH. I have no interest in being fair to him. We were discussing you.

PAULA. You are too persuasive. I don't believe you.

KENNETH. My advice to you is to find out what you want before you commit yourself to young Mr. Dexter.

PAULA. But I have committed myself.

KENNETH. Too bad.

PAULA. For him or for me?

KENNETH. For both of you; but for him particularly.

PAULA. Why?

KENNETH. I see precisely the effect your money will have on him. He will take it and the feeling will grow in him that in having given it you have destroyed what he calls his integrity. He will even come to believe that if not for this quenching of initiative he might have become a flaming leader of the people. At the same time he will be aware that both these comforting alibis are delusions—because he has no integrity to speak of nor any initiative to speak of. Knowing they are lies he will only proclaim them the louder, cling to them the harder. He will hate you as the thief of his character—petty larceny, I must say.

PAULA [*jumping up, taking several steps away from him*]. That's a lie.

KENNETH. Will is an American Puritan. A foreigner—Boris, for example—marries money, feeling that he gives value received. Very often he does. But young Dexter will never feel that—and maybe he'll be right.

PAULA. You hate Will.

KENNETH. You flatter him.

PAULA. How did you get to know so much about people? About what they feel and what they will do?

KENNETH. I began by knowing myself—but not lying to myself. [*A silence. He looks at her. He takes in her loveliness. He speaks her name, in a new voice, softly.*] Paula—

PAULA [*she looks at him fixedly*]. What?

KENNETH. Paula—

PAULA. What?

KENNETH. Do you know me any better now? Do you trust me any better now?

PAULA. I don't know.

[*Enter* WILL.]

KENNETH. Paula, Paula, Paula— [PAULA *starts toward door back.*] Don't go, Paula!

WILL. Oughtn't you to be changing for dinner? [PAULA *stops upstage.*] Hello, Doctor. What's the matter?

KENNETH. May I congratulate him?

WILL. What's he been saying?

KENNETH. Paula told me she is going to marry you.

PAULA. The doctor is a cynic.

KENNETH. We were discussing the European and American points of view toward money marriages—There's a great difference. The European fortune hunter, once he has landed the bag, has no more twinge of conscience than a big-game hunter when he has made his kill. The American—

WILL. Is that what you think I am, Doctor?

KENNETH [*to* PAULA *amiably*]. You see. He resents the mere phrase. But, my dear boy, that is no disgrace. We are all fortune hunters—

PAULA [*pointedly*]. Not all, Kenneth—!

KENNETH. But I see no difference at all between the man who makes a profession of being charming to rich ladies—or any other—specialist. The former is more arduous.

PAULA. Are you defending Will or yourself?

KENNETH. I am generalizing. [*To* WILL.] Congratulations! I admit that to scatter congratulations in this way is glib, but we live in a convention of glibness. Good God, we congratulate people when they marry and when they produce children—we skim lightly over these tremendous hazards— Excuse me. [*Exit* KENNETH.]

WILL. God damn that man!

PAULA. Will!

WILL. I can't stand him—not from the moment I saw him—because he's incapable of disinterestedness himself, he can't imagine it in others. He's the kind of cynical, sneering— He's a marauder. The adventurer with the cure-all. This is just the moment for him. And this is just the place!

PAULA. I've never seen you lose your temper before, Will.

WILL. You know why, don't you?

PAULA. Why?

WILL. Because he's right! While he was talking I felt like hitting him. At the same time a voice inside me said: Can you deny it? When I came in here he was saying your name. He was looking at you—it seems he hasn't quite decided, has he?

PAULA. I'm worried about him and Leonie—

WILL. He's got Leonie hook, line and sinker. That's obvious.

PAULA. She mustn't! Will, she mustn't!

WILL. You can't stop it—you can't do anything for Leonie. Nobody can do anything for anybody. Nobody should try.

PAULA. Will—you mustn't go back to New York. You must stay and help me.

WILL. Sorry. Nothing doing.

PAULA. Will!

WILL. I have a feeling you'll rather enjoy saving Leonie from the doctor.

PAULA. Will! That's not fair, Will!

WILL. It may not be fair but it is obvious. Also, it is obvious that the doctor won't mind being saved.

PAULA. It's lucky for both of us that one of us has some self-control.

WILL. No, I won't stay here. I hate the place, I hate Dr. Rice, I hate myself for being here!

PAULA. Don't let me down, Will—I need you terribly just now—

WILL [*at white heat*]. I haven't quite the technique of fortune hunting yet—in the European manner. Which of the two is he after—you or Leonie? Will he flip a coin?

PAULA. I hate you! I hate you!

WILL. Well, we know where we are at any rate.

PAULA. Yes. We do!

[LEONIE *comes running in. She wears an exquisite summer evening frock. She is breathless with happiness.*]

LEONIE. Paula! Why aren't you dressed? I want you to wear something especially lovely tonight! Do you like this? It's new. I haven't worn it before. [*She twirls for them.*] I've a surprise for you, Will. You'll know what it is in a minute. I was thinking of you and it popped into my mind. You know, Will, I'm very, very fond of you. And I think you are equally fond of me. I can't help liking people who like me. I suppose you think I'm horribly vain. But then, everybody's vain about something. [BUTLER *comes in with cocktails and sandwiches, to table right of fireplace.*] If they're not, they're vain about their lack of vanity. I believe that's a mot! Pretty good for a brainless— Here, Will, have a cocktail— [WILL *takes cocktail.*] Paula—what's your pet vanity? She thinks mine's my looks but it's not. If I had my way I shouldn't look at all the way I look.

[*Enter* DR. DEXTER, *door back. He wears a sea-green baggy dinner-suit; he looks as "hicky" and uncertain as ever.*]

DEXTER. Good evening, Mrs. Frothingham.

LEONIE. Dr. Dexter—how good of you to come. Delighted to see you.

DEXTER. Good evening. Hello, Will.

WILL. Dad!

DEXTER. Mrs. Frothingham invited me. Didn't you know?

LEONIE [*takes* DEXTER'S *arm and goes to* WILL]. You told me you had to leave tomorrow to visit your father in Brunswick so I just called him up in Brunswick—

DEXTER. She sent the car all the way for me. Nice car. Great springs.

LEONIE [*to* WILL]. Now you won't have to leave tomorrow. You can both spend the week-end here.

WILL [*walking away a little right*]. Awfully nice of you, Leonie.

LEONIE [*following him.* DEXTER *sits on sofa*]. You see, Will, I leave the big issues to the professional altruists. I just do what I can toward making those around me happy. And that's *my* vanity!

[*Enter* DENNIS, *door back*.]

DENNIS. Well! Well! Fancy that now, Hedda!

LEONIE. Oh, hello, Dennis, just in time for a cocktail. [LEONIE *leads him over to sofa.* WILL *is isolated down right center*.]

DENNIS [*to* DEXTER]. How are you?

DEXTER [*not friendly*]. I'm all right.

DENNIS. Complicated week-end! You and the Healer! Faraday and Cagliostro. That'll be something.

LEONIE [*takes* DENNIS's *arm*]. Everybody tells me to like you, Dennis. I'm in such a mood that I'm going to make the effort.

DENNIS. I've been waiting for this. I'm thrilled!

LEONIE [*strolling with him across stage front*]. Something tells me you could be very charming if you wanted to. Tell me, Dennis, have you ever tried being lovable and sweet?

DENNIS. For you, Mrs. Frothingham, I would willingly revive the age of chivalry!

LEONIE. But there's no need of that. I just want you to be nice. Here, have a cocktail. Give you courage.

DENNIS. Just watch me from now on, Mrs. Frothingham.

LEONIE. I will. Passionately. [*Hands him cocktail*.] I'll be doing nothing else.

[BUTLER *crosses back of sofa, offers* DEXTER *and* PAULA *cocktails.* DR. RICE *comes in*.]

DENNIS [*stage sigh*]. A-h-h! The doctor! Just in time to look at my tongue, Doctor.

KENNETH. That won't be necessary, young man. I can tell— It's excessive.

LEONIE [*crossing to* KENNETH]. Kenneth—you remember Will's father—Dr. Dexter.

KENNETH. How do you do?

[*They shake hands. A second* BUTLER *has come in and he and* ROBERT *are passing cocktails and hors d'oeuvres.* LEONIE *keeps circulating among her guests.* KENNETH *and* DEXTER *are in the center—*DENNIS, *obeying a malicious impulse, presides over them. Announces a theme on which he eggs them on to utter variations.*]

DENNIS. A significant moment, ladies and gentlemen— the magician of Science meets the magician of Sex— The floating libido bumps the absolute! What happens?

DEXTER [*cupping his hand to his ear*]. What?

[WILL *crosses to door and looks out moodily.*]

DENNIS. The absolute hasn't got a chance. Isn't that right, Dr. Rice?

KENNETH. I shouldn't venture to contradict a young intellectual. Especially a very young intellectual.

LEONIE [*crosses front of* KENNETH, *to* DENNIS]. There, you see, I'm afraid, after all, I'll have to give you up, Dennis. You can't be lovable. You can't be sweet.

DENNIS. But I didn't promise to be winsome to everybody, only to you.

LEONIE. You really must treat him, Kenneth. He has no censor at all.

DENNIS. My censor is the Catholic tradition. We Catholics anticipated both Marx and Freud by a little matter of nineteen centuries. Spiritually, we have a Communion in the Holy Ghost—Communion. As for Dr. Rice, he offers confession without absolution. He is inadequate.

[LEONIE *returns with tray of canapes.*]

LEONIE. It seems such bad taste to discuss religion at cocktail time. Try a stuffed olive.

DEXTER. By the time you get your beautiful new world, true science will have perished.

LEONIE. Aren't you too pessimistic, Dr. Dexter? Too

much science has made you gloomy. Kenneth, the depression hasn't stopped your work, has it? Depression or no depression—

[WILL *springs up.*]

WILL [*tensely*]. That's right, Leonie. [*Everyone faces* WILL.] Depression or no depression—war or peace—revolution or reaction—Kenneth will reign supreme!

[KENNETH *stares at him.* WILL *confronts him.*]

LEONIE. Will!

WILL. Yes, Leonie. His is the power and the glory!

LEONIE. Dennis, this is your influence—

WILL. I admire you unreservedly, Doctor. Of your kind you are the best. You are the essence.

KENNETH. You embarrass me.

WILL. Some men are born ahead of their time, some behind, but you are made pat for the instant. Now is the time for you—when people are unemployed and distrust their own capacities—when people suffer and may be tempted—when integrity yields to despair—now is the moment for you!

KENNETH [*strolling closer to him so they are face to face*]. When, may I ask, is the moment for you—when if ever?

WILL. After your victory. When you are stuffed and inert with everything you want, then will be the time for me. [*He goes out.*]

PAULA [*running after* WILL]. Will . . . Will . . .Will . . . [*She follows him out.*]

LEONIE [*devastated by this strange behavior*]. What is it? I don't like it when people stand in the middle of the floor and make speeches. What's the matter with him? Dennis, do you know?

DENNIS [*with a look at* KENNETH]. I can guess.

LEONIE. Has he quarreled with Paula? Paula is so inept. She doesn't know how to . . . At the same time, if he had a grievance, why couldn't he have kept it until after dinner?

[*Enter* ROBERT.]

ROBERT. Dinner is served. [*Exit* ROBERT.]

LEONIE. Well, we'll do what we can. Sam is dining with Mother in her room, Boris has a headache. Dennis, you and Dr. Dexter—

DENNIS. You've picked me, Dr. Dexter. I congratulate you.

DEXTER. Thank God, I can't hear a word you say. [*Exit* DEXTER, *door back*.]

DENNIS [*sadistically*]. Oh, yes, he can. And we'll fight it out on these lines if it takes all dinner. [*He follows* DEXTER *out*.]

LEONIE. What extraordinary behavior! What do you suppose, Kenneth—shall I go after them?

KENNETH. I wouldn't. It's their problem. Give them time.

LEONIE [*reassured*]. You are so wise, Kenneth. How did I ever get on without you? I have that secure feeling that you are going to be my last indiscretion. When I think how neatly I've captured you—I feel quite proud. I guess my technique isn't so lousy after all. [*She takes his arm and swings along beside him as they waltz in to dinner*.]

CURTAIN

Act three

SCENE. *The same.*

TIME. *Late that fall. The trees have turned. The sumach have put out the brilliant red flowers of autumn.*

AT RISE. WILL *and* DENNIS *have just arrived, and are
standing at fireplace, back.* LEONIE *comes in to greet
them.* SAM *strolls in with her.*

LEONIE. I'm so glad to see you! [*She shakes hands with
each of them warmly.*] Will! How are you? [*To* DEN-
NIS.] It's so good of you to come.
SAM [*shaking hands with* WILL]. Very glad to see you.
WILL. Thanks.
[SAM *shakes hands with* DENNIS.]
LEONIE. Sam drove over for a few hours from Blue Hill
to talk business to me. He hasn't had much luck so
far. It's simply wonderful having you boys here—
it's like old times. I didn't tell Paula. [*To* SAM.] I
did all this on my own. It's a surprise for Paula.
DENNIS. She'll be overcome when she sees me. Maybe
you should prepare her.
WILL. Where is Paula?
LEONIE. Isn't it provoking! She and Kenneth went for
a walk. They should have been back long before
this. [*Turning back to them.*] Paula hasn't been at
all herself, Will. I thought you would cheer her up.
DENNIS. I will be very glad to do what I can, of course.
Several very stubborn cases have yielded to my
charm.
LEONIE. I'm sure! Do sit down. [*She sits.*]
DENNIS [*taking out his pipe*]. Do you mind?
[WILL *sits.*]
LEONIE. Oh, please—I can't tell you how I appreciate
your coming—
DENNIS [*the harassed business man*]. Well, as a matter
of fact, Leonie, it wasn't easy to get away from the
office—
LEONIE. Are you in an office?
DENNIS. Sometimes as many as fifteen in a day. [LEONIE

laughs.] But when I got your appealing letter—*and the return tickets*—I'm chivalrous at heart, you know, Leonie—

LEONIE. I know you are!

SAM. How's town?

WILL. Very hot.

SAM. I'm just on my way down. Stopped by to go over several things with Leonie—

LEONIE. Poor Sam's been having an awful time with me. He keeps putting things in escrow. Where is escrow?

DENNIS. It's where squirrels put nuts in the wintertime.

LEONIE. I see! Dennis is much more lucid than you, Sam.

DENNIS. I have a knack for making the abstruse translucent. Especially in economics. Now, would you like to know why England went off gold?

LEONIE. No, I wouldn't.

DENNIS. I shall yield to your subconscious demand and tell you.

LEONIE [*to others*]. Help!

DENNIS. I see that there is no audience for my peculiar gift.

LEONIE. You know, Will, I've thought perhaps you were angry with us.

WILL. Why?

LEONIE. You haven't been here for so long. [*To* SAM.] Since Granny died—none of them have been here. Did Paula write you about Granny's funeral?

WILL. No. She didn't.

LEONIE. Of course I hate funerals—I can't bear them—but this was so—natural. Mother wanted to live till the fall and she did. It was a dreaming blue sky and there was that poignant haze over the hills and over the bay, and the smell of burning wood from somewhere. Burning wood never smells at any other time the way it does in Indian summer. And the colors that day! Did you ever, Sam, see such a day?

SAM. It was beautiful.

LEONIE. They say the colors of autumn are the colors of death, but I don't believe that. They were in such strength that day. I cried—but not on account of Mother—that kind of day always makes me cry a little bit anyway. You couldn't cry over consigning anyone you loved to an earth like that—on a day like that. I put some blazing leaves over her, but when I passed there the other day, they were withered and brown—

SAM [*chiding her*]. Now, Leonie—

LEONIE. Sam thinks I shouldn't talk about Mother. But I don't see why. She doesn't depress me. I think of her with joy. She had a wonderful life.

SAM. She was a wonderful woman.

LEONIE [*to* WILL]. Imagine, Will—when Sam was here last time—you were here that week-end—she *knew*. She asked Sam to be executor of her will.

SAM [*very annoyed at her for bringing this up*]. Leonie—

LEONIE. Why didn't you tell me, Sam, then?

SAM. Seemed no point.

LEONIE. She didn't want me to know, did she?

SAM. No. She didn't want to distress you. [*A moment's pause.*]

LEONIE. What can be keeping Paula? [*She glances out of the window.*] Sam, do you want to talk business to me some more?

SAM. I'd like to talk to Will a minute.

LEONIE. Oh—yes. Well, Dennis, wouldn't you like me to show you to your room? [*She rises, goes to door into hallway.* DENNIS *follows.*]

DENNIS. Thanks. I've got to answer a chain letter.

LEONIE. I've given you a room you've never had. The tower room.

DENNIS. Is it ivory? I won't be comfortable if it isn't ivory.

LEONIE. Well just this once you're going to be uncomfortable—and like it! [*She goes out.*]

DENNIS [*tragically*]. And for this I gave up a superb view of the gas-house on 149th Street. [*He goes out.*]

SAM [*rises and goes up toward fireplace*]. Will—

WILL. Yes, Mr. Frothingham.

SAM. Oh—call me Sam.

WILL. All right.

SAM. I'll have to be pushing off in an hour or so. I rather wanted to talk to you.

WILL. Yes—

SAM [*wipes his forehead*]. Gosh, Leonie's a difficult woman to talk business to. [*Sits.*]

WILL. I can imagine that. She's not interested in business.

SAM. *She—is—not!!!*

WILL. What do you want to speak to me about?

SAM. Paula.

WILL. What about Paula?

SAM. As I'm her father—I hope you won't think me—

WILL. Of course not—

SAM. It's not altogether easy—

WILL. Do you want me to help you?

SAM. Yes. I wish you would!

WILL. You're worried about Paula and me, aren't you? So was her grandmother. You think me irresponsible. Less responsible for example—[*as if making a random comparison*] than Dr. Rice?

SAM. Well, as a matter of fact, I've rather gotten to know Dr. Rice, and in many respects, he's a pretty sound feller. [*Rising and going to stand above*

WILL.] Hang it all, Will, I like you, and I don't like to preach to you, you know.

WILL. Go on.

SAM. Well, there are—from my point of view at least— a lot of nonsensical ideas knocking about. I'd like to point out just one thing to you. Your radicalism and all that— Well, the point is this—if you marry Paula —and I hope you do, because I like you—and, what is more important, Paula likes you—you'll have responsibilities. Paula will be rich. Very rich. Money means responsibility. Now, I shouldn't, for example, like you to start radical magazines with it. I shouldn't like you to let money drift through your fingers in all sorts of aimless, millennial directions that won't get anywhere.

WILL. Who told you that was my intention?

SAM. A little bird.

WILL. With a black moustache?

SAM. Does that matter?

WILL. No.

SAM [*putting hand on* WILL's *shoulder*]. As a matter of fact, I'm not worried about you at all. Money, I expect, will do to you what getting power does to radical opposition, once it gets office—

WILL. Emasculate me, you mean?

SAM. Well, hardly. Mature you. Once you're rich, I have no doubt you'll be—

WILL. Sound.

SAM. Yes. Sound. But your friends—this McCarthy boy—

WILL. Well, I can easily cut Dennis—all my poor and unsound friends—

SAM [*quietly*]. I'm sorry you're taking this tone with me, Will. I'm the last person in the world to ask you to drop anybody. I'd be ashamed of you if you did. Only—

WILL. Only?

SAM. I must tell you that I am in position—by virtue of the will left by Mrs. Wyler—to keep Paula's money from being used for any purpose that might be construed as—subversive.

WILL. From whose point of view?

SAM [*quietly*]. From mine.

WILL. I see.

SAM. Possibly you may not believe this—but I trust you, Will. Mrs. Wyler trusted you.

WILL. You needn't worry. Paula seems to have other interests apparently.

SAM. What do you mean?

WILL. Sounder interests—

[DENNIS *enters, through door back.*]

DENNIS. The tower room lets in light on four sides, but nothing to look at. Just the sea and the landscape.

SAM. What did you do with Leonie?

DENNIS. She's gone to her mother's room to potter around.

SAM. Maybe I can get her attention while she's pottering. Excuse me. [SAM *goes out.*]

DENNIS. Poor Leonie—she's the last of the lovely ladies. The inheritance taxes'll get 'em soon. You know we were by way of getting our magazine from Leonie when Dr. Rice spiked our guns. So I'm leaving. My time is too valuable. But the Healer won't last forever, and when he goes, I shall return. Take heart, my good man. I know you feel a little tender about this, but remember, my lad, it's the Cause that counts. Remember what Shaw says: "There is no money but the devil's money. It is all tainted and it might as well be used in the service of God." [*A moment—*WILL *is obviously thinking of something else.*] What's the matter?

WILL. Nothing.

DENNIS [*bringing down chair to sit left of* WILL, *he imitates* RICE'S *manner*]. Now you must speak, young man—how can I sublimate your subconscious troubles, if you won't speak? Are you unhappy about Paula, my lad? [*No answer.*] Tell me what's happened between you—relieve your soul, and, as a reward, I may make you co-editor of our magazine. [*No response. He rises and walks to opposite side of table.*] No? Assistant editor you remain. I may even fire you. Yes, I think I will fire you. [*Crossing in front of* WILL *to fireplace.*] Dexter—you're through. Go upstairs and get your check. [*Rubs his hands together in glee.*] God, it gives me a sense of power to fire a man—especially an old friend!

[PAULA *and* KENNETH *come in door right from the garden.*]

PAULA [*amazed to see them*]. Will! But how—! Dennis!

WILL [*rather coolly*]. Hello, Paula.

DENNIS. We came to surprise you. Now that we have surprised you, we can go home.

WILL. Leonie asked me to come.

PAULA. Oh. Well, it's very nice to see you.

WILL. Thanks.

PAULA. When I wired you to come a few weeks ago, you were too busy. It takes Leonie, doesn't it?

DENNIS. You should have tried me, Paula. Hello, Dr. Rice. How's business? Any suppressions today?

KENNETH [*significantly*]. Apparently not.

DENNIS. Well, come on up to my room, Doctor, and we'll play Twenty Questions. [*He goes out.*]

WILL. Hello, Dr. Rice.

KENNETH. How are you?

PAULA. Will—I'm awfully glad to see you. I was just going to write you to thank you for the sweet letter you sent me after Granny died.

KENNETH. I'm afraid it's my fault, Dexter. I do my best

to keep Paula so busy that she finds no time to write letters.

WILL. I was sure I could count on you, Doctor. [WILL *goes out.*]

PAULA. You enjoy hurting Will, don't you?

KENNETH. When there is an obstacle in my path, I do my best to remove it.

PAULA. What makes you think it is only Will that stands between us— That if left to myself I—

KENNETH. Because it is true. Were it not for the squids of idealistic drivel spouted around you by Will and his friends, there would be no issue at all between us. I resent even an imputed rivalry with someone I despise.

PAULA. Rivalry?

KENNETH. Paula— There's no reason any longer why I shouldn't tell you the truth.

PAULA. What is it, Kenneth?

KENNETH [*after a moment—slowly*]. Do you know what I feel like? I feel like a man on a great height, irresistibly tempted to jump over. Do you want the truth really? [*She says nothing. Somehow his words, his voice, his attitude make her feel that really now he may reveal something which before he wouldn't have revealed. He is in a trance-like state almost; she feels it; she is rather horribly fascinated—somehow, though she distrusts him utterly, some instinct tells her that at this moment actually he is tempted by a force, disruptive to himself, to tell her the truth.*] Don't you know it? Don't you feel it? [*Pause.*] Haven't you known it? Haven't you felt it? [*A moment's pause.*] I love you.

PAULA. What?

KENNETH. I love you.

[*A pause. She is too stupefied to speak. She too is under a spell. She is fascinated by him—by the enor-*

*mity of this. She rises, walks away from him to
stand by sofa.*]

PAULA. I suppose I should be afraid of you. I am not
afraid of you.

KENNETH. I am afraid of you. You tempt me to venture
the impossible. That is impractical. And I have always been eminently practical.

PAULA. I'm sure you have. [*She feels herself talking
automatically, as if out of a hypnotic state—at the
same time some vanity and shrewdness keeps pounding inside her: "See how far he will go—see how far
he will go!"*]

KENNETH. I have lived by a plan. The plan has ma-
tured. But I have yearned for a face that would give
me joy, for the voice that would soothe me. It is
your face. It is your voice.

[PAULA *is fighting not to scream; at the same time she
is caught in a nightmarish fascination.*]

PAULA [*very faintly*]. Don't you love Mother?

KENNETH. No. [*A moment's pause.*] You are the youth
I have never had, the security I have never had—you
are the home I have hungered for. [*Moves toward
her—stands over her and a little back.*] That I am
standing near you now, that I have achieved a share
in your life, that you are listening to me, that you
are thinking of me and of what I am, to the exclu-
sion of everything else in the whirling universe—
this is a miracle so devastating, that it makes any
future possible—Paula—

PAULA. What?

KENNETH. Paula?

PAULA. What *is* it?

KENNETH [*bending over her*]. Paula . . . [*It is as if he
got a sexual joy from saying her name.*] I love your
name. I love to say your name.

PAULA. I *am* afraid of you. I'm sorry for you.

KENNETH. Do you think me insane?

PAULA. Yes.

KENNETH. Because I am ambitious, because I am forth-right, because I deal scientifically with the human stuff around me—you think me insane. Because I am ruthless and romantic, you think me insane. This boy you think you love—who spends his time snivel-ing about a system he is not strong enough to dom-inate—is he sane?

PAULA. I don't expect you to—

KENNETH. When I hear the chatter of your friends, it makes me sick. While they and their kind prate of co-operative commonwealths, the strong man takes power, and rides over their backs—which is all their backs are fit for. Never has the opportunity for the individual career been so exalted, so infinite in its scope, so horizontal. House-painters and minor jour-nalists become dictators of great nations. [*With puckish humor—leaning on arm of her chair.*] Imag-ine what a really clever man could do? See what he has done! [*He smiles, makes a gesture of modest self-assertion, indicating the room as part of his con-quest. She laughs, rather choked and embarrassed. He goes on.*] And this I have done alone. From an impossible distance—I have come to you, so that when I speak, you can hear. What might we not do together, Paula—you and I—

[*To her surprise,* PAULA *finds herself arguing an incon-ceivable point. She loathes the strange fascination she feels in this man, and yet is aware that it might turn to her advantage.*]

PAULA. We don't want the same things.

KENNETH. You want what everyone wants who has vi-tality and imagination—new forms of power—new domains of knowledge—the ultimate sensations.

PAULA. You *are* romantic, aren't you?

KENNETH. Endlessly. And endlessly—realistic. [*Staring at her.*] What are you thinking?

PAULA [*shrewd against him—against herself*]. I keep thinking—what you want now—what you're after now?

KENNETH [*moving toward her*]. You don't believe then —that I love you?

PAULA [*leaning back in chair—not looking at him*]. You are a very strange man.

KENNETH. I am simple really. I want everything. That's all!

PAULA. And you don't care how you get it.

KENNETH. Don't be moralistic, Paula—I beg you. I am directly in the tradition of your own marauding ancestors. They pass now for pioneers—actually they fell on the true pioneers, and wrested what they had found away from them, by sheer brutal strength. I am doing the same thing—but more adroitly.

PAULA. Why are you so honest with me?

KENNETH [*with his most charming smile*]. Perhaps because I feel that, in your heart, you too are an adventurer.

[*A pause. During these half-spellbound instants a thought has been forming slowly in* PAULA'S *mind that crystallizes now. This man is the enemy. This man is infinitely cunning, infinitely resourceful. Perhaps—just the possibility—he really feels this passion for her. If so, why not use this weakness in an antagonist so ruthless? She will try.*]

PAULA. I shouldn't listen to you—

[*A moment. He senses her cunning. He looks at her.*]

KENNETH. You don't trust me?

PAULA. Have I reason to trust you?

KENNETH. What reason would you like? What proof would you like?

PAULA. Aren't you going to marry Mother?

KENNETH. Only as an alternative.

PAULA. Will you—tell her so? Will you give up the alternative?

KENNETH. And if I do?

PAULA. What shall I promise you?

KENNETH. Yourself.

PAULA [*looks at him—speaks*]. And if I do?

KENNETH. Then . . .

PAULA [*taking fire*]. You say you love me! If you feel it —really feel it— You haven't been very adventurous for all your talk! Taking in Mother and Sam! Give up those conquests. Tell her! Tell Mother! Then perhaps I will believe you.

KENNETH. And then?

PAULA. Take your chances!

KENNETH [*quietly*]. Very well.

PAULA. You will?

KENNETH. I will.

PAULA. You'll tell Mother—you love me?

KENNETH. Yes.

PAULA [*going to the foot of the stairs, calls*]. Mother! Mother!

LEONIE [*offstage*]. Yes, Paula. I'm coming right down! I've the most marvelous surprise for you! Wait and see!

[PAULA *walks to end of sofa—looking at* KENNETH. LEONIE *comes in. She is wearing an exquisite old-fashioned silk wedding-dress which billows around her in an immense shimmering circle. She is a vision of enchantment.*]

LEONIE [*in a great flurry of excitement*]. Children, look what I found! It's Mother's. It's the dress she was married in. I was poking around in Granny's room while Sam was talking to me about bonds, and I came upon it. Do you like it, Kenneth? Isn't it ador-

able? Have you ever . . . What's the matter? Don't
you like it?

PAULA. It's very pretty.

LEONIE [*overwhelmed by the inadequacy of this word*].
Pretty! Pretty! [*She hopes for more from* KENNETH.]
Kenneth . . . ?

KENNETH. It's exquisite.

LEONIE. Isn't it? [*She whirls around in the dress.*] Isn't
it? Yes. Exquisite. Can you imagine the scene? Can
you imagine Granny walking down the aisle—and
all the august spectators in mutton-chop whiskers
and Prince Alberts? We've lost something these days
—a good deal—oh, I don't miss the mutton-chops—
but in ceremony, I mean—in punctilio and grace. . . .

PAULA [*cutting ruthlessly through the nostalgia*].
Mother!

LEONIE. What is it, Paula?

PAULA. Kenneth has something to tell you.

LEONIE. Kenneth?

PAULA. Yes. He has something to tell you.

LEONIE. Have you, Kenneth?

KENNETH. Yes.

LEONIE. What is it?

KENNETH [*quietly*]. I love Paula. I want to marry
Paula.

[*A pause. Granny's wedding dress droops.*]

LEONIE. Do you mean that, Kenneth?

KENNETH. Yes.

LEONIE [*piteously*]. This isn't very nice of you, Paula.

PAULA. I had nothing to do with it. I loathe Kenneth.
But I wanted you to know him. Now you see him,
Mother, your precious Lothario—there he is! Look
at him!

LEONIE. These clothes are picturesque, but I think our
modern ones are more comfortable. I think—I feel
quite faint—isn't it ridiculous? [*She sways.*]

PAULA. I'm sorry, Mother. I had to. But I love you. I really do.

LEONIE [*very faint*]. Thank you, Paula.

PAULA. You'd better go up and lie down. I'll come to you in a moment.

LEONIE. Yes. I think I'd better. Yes. [*She begins to sob; she goes out, hiding her face in the lace folds of her dress.* PAULA, *having gone with her to the door, rings bell for* ROBERT, *turns to* KENNETH.]

PAULA. I suppose you're going to tell me this isn't cricket. Well, don't, because it will only make me laugh. To live up to a code with people like you is only to be weak and absurd.

KENNETH [*his voice is low and even but tense with hate*]. You, Miss Frothingham, are my *last* miscalculation. I might even say my first. Fortunately, not irreparable!

[ROBERT *enters.*]

PAULA. Robert.

ROBERT. Yes, Miss Frothingham.

PAULA [*still staring fixedly at* KENNETH]. Dr. Rice is leaving. Will you see that his bags are packed, please?

ROBERT. Yes, Miss. [*He goes out.*]

KENNETH. Forgive me—for having overestimated you. [*He goes out door right.*]

[PAULA *comes slowly down and sits on sofa. She gets a reaction herself now from all she has been through; this game hasn't been natural to her; she is trembling physically; she is on the verge of tears.* WILL *comes in.*]

PAULA. Will—Will darling— [*She clings to* WILL.]

WILL [*worried*]. Paula!

PAULA. Put your arms around me, Will—hold me close—

[WILL *obeys*.]

WILL. What's happened?

PAULA. I've tricked him. I made him say in front of Mother that he loved me, that he wanted to marry me. Poor Leonie! But it had to be done! And do you know, Will—at the end I felt—gosh, one has so many selves, Will. I must tell you—for the—well, for the completeness of the record—

WILL [*curious*]. What?

PAULA. At the end I felt I had to do it—not only to save Leonie—but to save myself. Can you understand that? I felt horribly drawn to him, and by the sordid thing I was doing— But it's over. Thank God it's over. Will, darling, these six weeks have been hell without you. When I got your letter about Granny, I sat down and cried. I wanted to go right to New York to be with you. And yet I couldn't. How could I? But now, Will—I don't want to wait for you any longer. I've done what I can. It's cost me almost— Will—I need you terribly—

WILL. And I you, Paula. But listen, darling—I've decided during the weeks I've been away from you— I can't marry you now— I can't face what I'd become—

PAULA. But, Will, I— [*Springing up*.] But, Will, I'll give up the money. I'll live with you anywhere.

WILL. I know that, Paula. But I mustn't. You mustn't let me. I've thought it all out. You say you'd live with me anywhere. But what would happen? Supposing I didn't get a job? Would we starve? We'd take fifty dollars a week from your grandmother's estate. It would be foolish not to. Taking fifty, why not seventy-five? Why not two hundred? I can't let myself in for it, Paula. [*A long pause*.] Paula, darling—do you hate me?

PAULA. No.

WILL. Supposing you weren't rich? Is it a world in which, but for this, I'd have to sink? If it is, I'm going to damn well do what I can to change it. I don't have to scrabble for the inheritance of dead men. That's for Kenneth—one robber baron—after the lapse of several generations—succeeding another. I don't want this damn fortune to give me an unfair advantage over people as good as I am who haven't got it. [*Torn with pity for her.*] Paula—my dearest—what can I do?

PAULA. I see that you can't do anything. I quite see. Still—

WILL. I love you, Paula, and I'll be longing for you terribly, but I can't marry you—not till there's somebody for you to marry. When I've struck my stride, I won't care about Sam, or the money, or anything, because I'll be on my own. If you feel the way I do, you'll wait.

PAULA [*very still voice*]. Of course, Will. I'll wait.

WILL [*overcome with gratitude and emotion—seizes her in his arms passionately*]. Darling—darling—

[LEONIE *comes in.* WILL, *overcome with emotion, goes out.*]

LEONIE. It's easy to say "lie down." But what happens then? Thoughts assail you. Thoughts . . .

PAULA. Mother . . .

LEONIE. Kenneth's going. He's leaving. I suppose you're happy. It's the end—the end of summer.

PAULA [*herself shaken with emotion*]. Mother— [*She wants to talk to* LEONIE, *to tell her what has happened, but* LEONIE *is lost in her own maze.*]

LEONIE. It's cold here. I hate this place. I'm going to sell it. [*She sits, in chair, right of fireplace.*] I've always wanted things around me to be gay and warm and happy. I've done my best. I must be wrong. Why do I find myself this way? With nothing. With nothing.

PAULA [*running to her mother and throwing herself on her knees beside her*]. Mother—Mother darling—

LEONIE [*not responding, reflectively*]. I suppose the thing about me that is wrong is that love is really all I care about. [*A moment's pause.*] I suppose I should have been interested in other things. Good works. Do they sustain you? But I couldn't somehow. I think when you're not in love—you're dead. Yes, that must be why I'm . . . [*Her voice trails off rather.* PAULA *drops her head in her mother's lap and begins to cry.*]

LEONIE [*surprised*]. Paula—what is it? What's the matter? Are you sorry? It's all right, child.

PAULA [*through her tears*]. It's Will—

LEONIE. Will?

PAULA. He's going away.

LEONIE. Why don't you go with him?

PAULA. He doesn't want me.

LEONIE. That's not true. It must be something else.

PAULA. The money.

LEONIE. Oh, the money. Yes, the money. The money won't do anything for you. It'll work against you. It's worked against me. It gives you the illusion of escape—but always you have to come back to yourself. At the end of every journey—you find yourself.

PAULA. What shall I do, Mother?

LEONIE. You and Will want the same things. In the end you will find them. But don't let him find them with someone else. Follow him. Be near him. When he is depressed and discouraged, let it be your hand that he touches, your face that he sees.

PAULA [*breathless*]. Mother—you're right—he told me

last summer—"you must have a shoulder to lean on"—

LEONIE. Let it be your shoulder, Paula; follow him. Be near him.

PAULA. Thank you, Mother.

LEONIE [*ruefully*]. I am telling you what *I* should do. It must be bad advice.

PAULA [*gratefully*]. Darling!

[DENNIS *and* WILL *come in.*]

DENNIS. Here you are! We're off to the boat! Thirty minutes! Why don't you and Paula come too? What do you say, Leonie?

LEONIE. You know, all these years I've been coming up here, and I've never been on the Bar Harbor boat.

DENNIS. It may be said, Mrs. Frothingham, if you have never been on the Bar Harbor boat, that you have not lived!

LEONIE. Really! I'd always heard it was poky.

DENNIS. Poky! The *Normandie* of the Kennebec poky! Mrs. Frothingham!

LEONIE. It's fun, is it? But doesn't it get into New York at some impossible hour?

DENNIS. At seven a.m.

LEONIE. Seven! [*She shudders.*]

DENNIS [*the brisk executive*]. Seven! Yes, sir! At my desk at nine! All refreshed and co-ordinated and ready to attack my South American correspondence.

LEONIE. I must learn not to believe him, mustn't I?

DENNIS. I am my own master, Leonie. All day for nine mortal hours I grind out escape fiction for the pulp magazines. But one day I shall become famous and emerge into the slicks and then I doubt very much whether I shall come here.

LEONIE. I shall miss you.

DENNIS. Then I'll come.

LEONIE. I hate to have you go, Dennis. You cheer me up. Why don't you stay?

DENNIS. Impossible, Leonie. I must go to New York to launch the magazine. But for the moment, good-bye, Leonie. As a reward for your hospitality I shall send you the original copy of one of my stories. Would you like to escape from something?

LEONIE [*smiling wanly*]. I would indeed!

DENNIS. Think no more about it. You're as good as free. The story is yours, typed personally on my Underwood. Those misplaced keys—those inaccuracies—how they will bemuse posterity! [*He goes out.*]

WILL [*awkwardly*]. Good-bye, Leonie.

LEONIE. Good-bye, Will. [*He goes out without looking at* PAULA. *In pantomime,* LEONIE *urges* PAULA *to go after him.* PAULA *kisses her quickly and runs after* WILL. *Left alone,* LEONIE *walks to the chair in which her mother sat so often—she looks through the glow-ing autumn at the darkening sea.* KENNETH *comes in. There is a pause.*]

KENNETH. Leonie—

LEONIE. Yes, Kenneth.

KENNETH. I don't expect you to understand this. I shall not try to make you understand it.

LEONIE. Perhaps I'd better not.

KENNETH. Really I am amused at myself—highly entertained. That I should have almost had to practice on myself what hitherto I have reserved for my patients—that I who have made such a fetish of discipline and restraint so nearly succumbed to an inconsistency. I must revise my notion of myself.

LEONIE. And I too.

KENNETH. Why? Why you?

LEONIE. I seem to be a survival—Paula's directness—and your calculations—they are beyond me.

KENNETH. Nevertheless, it's curious how you and Paula

are alike—no wonder that, for a moment at least, you seemed to me—interchangeable.

LEONIE. Did you know it from the beginning—that it was Paula?

KENNETH. I was attracted by her resemblance to you—for exercising this attraction I hated her. She felt it too—from the beginning and she must have hated me from the beginning. Between us there grew up this strange, unnatural antagonism—

LEONIE. What?

KENNETH. This fused emotion of love and hate. It had to be brought out into the open. It's a familiar psychosis—the unconscious desire of the daughter to triumph over the mother.

LEONIE. But I don't understand—

KENNETH. There is so much in these intricate relationships that the layman can't understand—

LEONIE. You mean that you—felt nothing for Paula?

KENNETH. No, I don't mean that at all. But I saw that what I felt for her was some twisted reflection of what I felt for you. And I saw there was only one way out of it—to let her triumph over you. I told her that I loved her. But this was not enough. I must repeat it in front of you. You must witness her triumph. I made it possible. I gave her her great moment. Well, you see what it's done. It freed her so beautifully that she was able to go to Will. They've gone away together. Perfect cure for her as well as for myself. [*A moment's pause.*]

LEONIE. It all sounds almost too perfect, Kenneth.

KENNETH. I said I didn't expect you to understand it—you have lived always on your emotions. You have never bothered to delve beneath them. You are afraid to, aren't you?

LEONIE. I know this, Kenneth. I heard you say that you loved Paula. I heard your voice. No, I can't accept

this, Kenneth! It's not good enough. I've never done
that before. I only think now that everything you
did, everything you said, was to cover what you
felt. And I'd end by telling myself that I believed
you. I'd end by taking second best from you. No, I
must guard myself from that. I felt this a month
ago—that's why I sent for Will.

KENNETH. Some day, Leonie, you will learn that feeling
is not enough.

LEONIE. But I trust my instinct, Kenneth.

KENNETH. That, Leonie, is your most adorable trait—

LEONIE. What?

KENNETH. That trust—that innocence. If it weren't for
that, you wouldn't be you—and everyone wouldn't
love you—

LEONIE. Oh, no, Kenneth—

[DENNIS *comes in.*]

DENNIS. Oh, excuse me. But I left my brief-case. Oh,
here it is. [*He picks it up.*] Without my brief-case I
am a man without a Destiny. With it I am—

KENNETH. A man with a brief-case.

LEONIE [*crossing rather desperately to* DENNIS—*this
straw in the current*]. What's in it—your stories?

DENNIS. Stories—no, that wouldn't matter. I am fertile;
I can spawn stories. But the plans for the magazine
are in here—the future of Young America is here—

LEONIE. Will you stay and have a whiskey and soda?

DENNIS. Thanks, but if I do, I shall miss the boat.

LEONIE. Suppose you do?

KENNETH. Leonie—that would delay the millenium one
day.

DENNIS. The doctor's right. That would be selfish.

LEONIE. Be selfish. Please stay.

DENNIS. No. Once you are enlisted in a cause, you can't
live a personal life. It is a dedication.

LEONIE. Kenneth is leaving. I shall be lonely, Dennis. I can't bear to be alone.

KENNETH. Your need for people is poignant, isn't it, Leonie?

LEONIE. Stay for dinner. After dinner we can talk about your magazine.

DENNIS. Oh, well—that makes it possible for me to stay. Thank you, Kenneth. [*He goes to sofa, sits, busying himself with brief-case.*]

[*She goes to console to make highball.*]

KENNETH. Send me your magazine, Dennis. I shall be honored to be the first subscriber.

DENNIS. I'll be glad to. Your patients can read it in the waiting-room instead of the *National Geographic*.

KENNETH. Your first subscriber—and very possibly your last. [*He crosses to door and turns back.*] Good-bye, Leonie. Good luck, Dennis. We who are about to re-tire—salute you. [*She does not look at him. He bows formally to* DENNIS's *back, makes a gesture of "good luck" and exits.*]

DENNIS. Trouble with that fellow is—he lives for him-self. No larger interest. That's what dignifies human beings, Leonie—a dedication to something greater than themselves.

LEONIE [*coming down to hand him his highball*]. Yes? Here's your whiskey and soda. I envy you, Dennis. I wish I could dedicate myself to something—something outside myself.

DENNIS [*rising to sit beside her*]. Well, here's your op-portunity, Leonie—it's providential. You couldn't do better than this magazine. It would give you a new interest—impersonal. It would emancipate you, Leo-nie. It would be a perpetual dedication to Youth— to the hope of the world. The world is middle-aged and tired. But we—

LEONIE [*wistfully*]. Can you refresh us, Dennis?

DENNIS. Refresh you? Leonie, we can rejuvenate you!

LEONIE [*grateful there is someone there—another human being she can laugh with*]. That's an awfully amusing idea. You make me laugh.

DENNIS [*eagerly selling the idea*]. In the youth of any country, there is an immense potentiality—

LEONIE. You're awfully serious about it, aren't you, Dennis?

DENNIS. Where the magazine is concerned, Leonie, I am a fanatic.

LEONIE. I suppose if it's really successful—it'll result in my losing everything I have—

DENNIS. It'll be taken from you anyway. You'll only be anticipating the inevitable.

LEONIE. Why—how clever of me!

DENNIS. Not only clever but grateful.

LEONIE. Will you leave me just a little to live on—?

DENNIS. Don't worry about that—come the Revolution —you'll have a friend in high office.

[LEONIE *accepts gratefully this earnest of security. They touch glasses in a toast as the curtain falls.*]

IDIOT'S DELIGHT

by Robert E. Sherwood

This play is lovingly dedicated to
Lynn Fontanne and Alfred Lunt

First production, March 9th, 1936,
at the National Theatre, Washington, D.C.,
with the following cast:

DUMPTSY, *George Meader*
ORCHESTRA LEADER, *Stephen Sandes*
DONALD NAVADEL, *Barry Thompson*
PITTALUGA, *S. Thomas Gomez*
AUGUSTE, *Edgar Barrier*
CAPTAIN LOCICERO, *Edward Raquello*
DR. WALDERSEE, *Sydney Greenstreet*
MR. CHERRY, *Bretaigne Windust*
MRS. CHERRY, *Jean Macintyre*
HARRY VAN, *Alfred Lunt*
SHIRLEY, *Jacqueline Paige*
BEULAH, *Connie Crowell*
BEBE, *Ruth Timmons*
FRANCINE, *Etna Ross*
ELAINE, *Marjorie Baglin*
EDNA, *Frances Foley*
MAJOR, *George Greenberg*
FIRST OFFICER, *Alan Hewitt*
SECOND OFFICER, *Winston Ross*
THIRD OFFICER, *Gilmore Bush*
FOURTH OFFICER, *Tomasso Tittoni*
QUILLERY, *Richard Whorf*
SIGNOR ROSSI, *Le Roi Operti*
SIGNORA ROSSI, *Ernestine de Becker*
MAID, *Una Val*
ACHILLE WEBER, *Francis Compton*
IRENE, *Lynn Fontanne*

The scene of the play is the cocktail lounge
of the Hotel Monte Gabriele, in the Italian Alps,
near the frontiers of Switzerland and Austria.

ACT I

Afternoon of a winter day in any imminent year.

ACT II

Scene 1. *Eight o'clock that evening.*

Scene 2. *Eleven o'clock that evening.*

Scene 3. *After midnight.*

ACT III

The following afternoon.

Act one

The cocktail lounge of the Hotel Monte Gabriele.

The hotel is a small one, which would like to consider itself a first-class resort. It was originally an Austrian sanatorium. Its Italian management has refurnished it and added this cocktail lounge and a few modern bedrooms with baths, in the hope that some day Monte Gabriele may become a rival for St. Moritz. So far, this is still a hope. Although the weather is fine, the supply of winter sports enthusiasts at Monte Gabriele is negligible, and the hotel is relying for its trade upon those itinerants who, because of the current political situation, are desirous of leaving Italy.

Near at hand are a railway line into Switzerland, highways into Switzerland and Austria, and an Italian army airport.

At the left, up-stage, is a large doorway, leading to the lobby, in which we can just see the Reception Desk.

At the upper right is a staircase. A few steps up is a landing, above which is a high window with a fine view of the Alpine scenery to the North and West. The panes are fringed with frost. From the landing, the stairs continue up to a gallery which leads to bedrooms off to the upper left.

Downstairs left is a swinging door marked with the word "BAR."

Over this bar entrance are crossed skis and the head of a mountain goat. On the wall at the right is a Fascist emblem with crossed Italian flags. About the Reception Desk, off to the left, are signs assuring the guest that this hotel has been approved by all the automobile associations of Europe and that Travelers' Cheques may be cashed here. Somewhere on the walls are pictures of the Coliseum and the S.S. "Conte de Savoia."

There are small tables and chairs about, with perhaps a couch or two. At the left is a piano, and when the first curtain rises a dismal little four-piece orchestra is playing "June in January."

Note a line in the dialogue along toward the end of Act One: there is something about this place that suggests "a vague kind of horror." This is nothing definite, or identifiable, or even, immediately, apparent. Just an intimation.

Behind the Reception Desk, PITTALUGA *is occasionally visible. He is the proprietor of the hotel—a fussy, worried little Italian in the conventional morning coat and striped pants.*

On the landing at the upper right, looking dolefully out the window, is DONALD NAVADEL, *a rather precious, youngish American, suitably costumed for winter sports by Saks Fifth Avenue. Experienced in the resort business, he was imported this year to organize sporting and social life at Monte Gabriele with a view to making it a Mecca for American tourists. He is not pleased with the way things have turned out.*

DUMPTSY *comes in from the left. He is an humble, gentle little bell-boy, aged about forty, born in this district when it was part of Austria, but now a subject of the Fascist Empire. He has come in to clean the ashtrays. He listens to the music.*

DUMPTSY. Come si chiama questa musica che suonate?

ORCHESTRA LEADER. Il pezzo si chiama: "Giugno in Gennaio."

DUMPTSY. Oh, com'e bello! Mi piace! [*To* DON.] It's good.

DON. Will you please for God's sake stop playing that same damned tiresome thing?

DUMPTSY. You don't like it, Mr. Navadel?

DON. I'm so sick of it, I could scream!

DUMPTSY. I like it. To me, it's good.

DON. Go on, and clean the ash-trays.

DUMPTSY. But they're not dirty, sir. Because there's nobody using them.

DON. There's no need to remind me of *that!* Do as you're told!

DUMPTSY. If you please, sir. [*He whistles the tune and goes out.*]

DON [*to the* LEADER]. You've played enough. Get out!

LEADER. But it is not yet three o'clock.

DON. Never mind what time it is. There's nobody here to listen to you, is there? You can just save the wear and tear on your harpsichord and go grab yourselves a smoke.

LEADER. Very good, Mr. Navadel. [*To the other* MUSICIANS.] E inutile continuare a suonare. La gente non ascolta più. Si potrà invece far quattro chiachiere e fumare una sigaretta.

[*They put away instruments and music and start to go out, as* PITTALUGA *appears bristling.*]

PITTALUGA [*to* LEADER]. Eh, professori? Perchè avete cessato di suonare? Non sono ancora le tre.

LEADER. Il Signor Navadel ci ha detta di andare a fumare egli ne ha avuto abbastanza della nostra musica.

[*The* MUSICIANS *have gone.*]

PITTALUGA [*going to* DON]. You told my orchestra it would stop?

DON [*untroubled*]. I did.

PITTALUGA. My orders to them are they play in here until three o'clock. Why do you take it to yourself to countermand my orders?

DON. Because their performance was just a little too macabre to be bearable.

PITTALUGA. So! You have made yourself the manager of this hotel, have you? You give orders to the musicians. Next you will be giving orders to me—and to the guests themselves, I have no doubt. . . .

DON. The guests! [*He laughs drily.*] That's really very funny. Consult your room chart, my dear Signor Pittaluga, and let me know how many guests there are that I can give orders to. The number when last I counted . . .

PITTALUGA. And you stop being insolent, you—animale fetente. I pay you my money, when I am plunging myself into bankruptcy. . . .

DON. Yes, yes, Signor—we know all about that. You pay me your money. And you have a right to know that I'm fed to the teeth with this little pension that you euphemistically call a high-grade resort hotel. Indeed, I'm fed to the teeth with you personally.

PITTALUGA [*in a much friendlier tone*]. Ah! So you wish to leave us! I'm very sorry, my dear Donald. We shall miss you.

DON. My contract expires on March the first. I shall bear it until then.

PITTALUGA. You insult me by saying you are fed with me, but you go on taking my money?

DON. Yes!

PITTALUGA. Pezzo mascalzone farabutto prepotente canaglia . . .

DON. And it will do you no good to call me names in

your native tongue. I've had a conspicuously successful career in this business, all the way from Santa Barbara to St. Moritz. And you lured me away from a superb job . . .

PITTALUGA [*as* DON *continues*]. Lazzaronè, briccone, bestione. Perdio.

DON. . . . with your glowing descriptions of this handsome place, and the crowds of sportlovers, gay, mad, desperately chic, who were flocking here from London, Paris, New York. . . .

PITTALUGA. Did *I* know what was going to happen? Am *I* the king of Europe?

DON. You are the proprietor of this obscure tavern. You're presumably responsible for the fact that it's a deadly, boring dump!

PITTALUGA. Yes! And I engaged you because I thought you had friends—rich friends—and they would come here after you instead of St. Moritz, and Muerren, and Chamonix. And where are your friends? What am I paying for you? To countermand my orders and tell me you are fed . . . [*Wails from warning sirens are heard from off-stage right.* PITTALUGA *stops short. Both listen.*] Che cosa succede?

DON. That's from down on the flying field.

PITTALUGA. It is the warning for the air raids!

[AUGUSTE, *the barman, is heard in bar off-stage, left.*]

AUGUSTE'S VOICE. Che cosa?

[PITTALUGA *and* DON *rush to the window.*]

PITTALUGA. Segnali d'incursione. La guerra e incominiciata e il nemico viene.

[*Airplane motors are heard off right.*]

DON [*looking through window*]. Look! The planes are taking off. They're the little ones—the combat planes.

[CAPTAIN LOCICERO *enters from the lobby. He is the officer in charge of the frontier station. He is tired, quiet, nice.* AUGUSTE *enters from the bar.* DUMPTSY *follows the* CAPTAIN.]

AUGUSTE. Signor Capitano!

CAPTAIN. Buona sera!

[AUGUSTE *helps him take off his coat.*]

DUMPTSY. Che cosa succede, Signor Capitano? È la guerra?

CAPTAIN. No—no—datemi cognac.

[DUMPTSY *puts coat on chair right of table and goes up and exits through arch center.* CAPTAIN *sits chair left of table.*]

AUGUSTE [*as he goes out*]. Si, Signor Capitano.

[*The* CAPTAIN *sits down at a table.* PITTALUGA *and* DON *cross to him.* DUMPTSY *goes.*]

PITTALUGA. Che cosa significano quei terribili segnali? È, forse, il nemico che arriva?

DON. What's happened, Captain? Is there an air raid? Has the war started?

CAPTAIN [*smiling*]. Who knows? But there is no raid. [*The porter's hand-bell in the lobby is heard.*] They're only testing the sirens, to see how fast the combat planes can go into action. You understand— it's like lifeboat drill on a ship.

[DUMPTSY *enters.*]

DUMPTSY. Scusi, padrone. Due Inglesi arrivati. [*He hurries out.*]

PITTALUGA. Scusi. Vengo subito. Presto, presto! [*He goes.*]

CAPTAIN. Have a drink, Mr. Navadel?

DON. Thank you very much—but some guests are actually arriving. I must go and be very affable. [*He goes.*]

[DR. WALDERSEE *appears on the gallery above and comes down the stairs as* AUGUSTE *enters from the bar and serves the* CAPTAIN *with brandy and soda.*

The DOCTOR *is an elderly, stout, crotchety, sad German.*]

CAPTAIN. Good afternoon, Doctor. Have a drink?

DOCTOR. Thank you very much—no. What is all that aeroplanes?

[AUGUSTE *goes.*]

CAPTAIN. This is a crucial spot, Dr. Waldersee. We must be prepared for visits from the enemy.

DOCTOR. Enemy, eh? And who is that?

CAPTAIN. I don't quite know, yet. The map of Europe supplies us with a wide choice of opponents. I suppose, in due time, our government will announce its selection—and we shall know just whom we are to shoot at.

DOCTOR. Nonsense! Obscene nonsense!

CAPTAIN. Yes—yes. But the taste for obscenity is incurable, isn't it?

DOCTOR. When will you let me go into Switzerland?

CAPTAIN. Again I am powerless to answer you. My orders are that no one for the time being shall cross the frontiers, either into Switzerland or Austria.

DOCTOR. And when will this "time being" end?

CAPTAIN. When Rome makes its decision between friend and foe.

DOCTOR. I am a German subject. I am not your foe.

CAPTAIN. I am sure of that, Dr. Waldersee. The two great Fascist states stand together, against the world.

DOCTOR [*passionately*]. Fascism has nothing to do with it! I am a scientist. I am a servant of the whole damn stupid human race. [*He crosses toward the* CAPTAIN.] If you delay me any longer here, my experiments will be ruined. Can't you appreciate that? I must get my rats at once to the laboratory in Zurich, or all my months and years of research will have gone for nothing.

[DON *enters, followed by* MR. *and* MRS. CHERRY—*a pleas-*

ant young English couple in the first flush of their honeymoon.]

DON. This is our cocktail lounge. There is the American bar. We have a *thé dansant* here every afternoon at 4:30—supper dancing in the evening.

CHERRY. Charming.

DON. All this part of the hotel is new. Your rooms are up there. [*He crosses to the window.*] I think you'll concede that the view from here is unparalleled. We can look into four countries. [*The* CHERRYS *follow him to the window.*] Here in the foreground, of course, is Italy. This was formerly Austrian territory, transferred by the treaty of Versailles. It's called Monte Gabriele in honor of D'Annunzio, Italian poet and patriot. Off there is Switzerland and there is Austria. And far off, you can just see the tip of a mountain peak that is in the Bavarian Tyrol. Rather gorgeous, isn't it?

CHERRY. Yes.

MRS. CHERRY. Darling—*look* at that sky!

CHERRY. I say, it *is* rather good.

DON. Do you go in for winter sports, Mrs. Cherry?

MRS. CHERRY. Oh, yes—I—we're very keen on them.

DON. Splendid! We have everything here.

CHERRY. I've usually gone to Kitzbuhel.

[PITTALUGA *and* DUMPTSY *appear up-stage and speak in Italian through the dialogue.*]

PITTALUGA. Dumptsy, il bagaglio è stato portato su?

DUMPTSY. Si, signore, è già sopra.

PITTALUGA. Sta bene, vattene.

DON. It's lovely there, too.

CHERRY. But I hear it has become much too crowded there now. I—my wife and I hoped it would be quieter here.

DON. Well—at the moment—it is rather quiet here.

PITTALUGA [*coming down*]. Your luggage has been sent

up, Signor. Would you care to see your room now?

CHERRY. Yes. Thank you.

PITTALUGA. If you will have the goodness to step this way. [*He goes up the stairs.*] 'Scuse me.

CHERRY [*pauses at the window on the way up*]. What's that big bare patch down there?

DON [*casually*]. Oh, that's the airport. [PITTALUGA *coughs discreetly.*] We have a great deal of flying here.

PITTALUGA. Right this way, please.

CHERRY. Oh—I see.

[*They continue on up, preceded by* PITTALUGA.]

DON. And do come down for *thé dansant.*

MRS. CHERRY. We should love to.

PITTALUGA. Right straight ahead, please. [*They exit through gallery.*]

DON [*standing on first step*]. Honeymooners.

CAPTAIN. Yes—poor creatures.

DON. They wanted quiet.

DOCTOR [*rises*]. Ach Gott! When will you know when I can cross into Switzerland?

CAPTAIN. The instant that word comes through from Rome. [*The hand-bell is heard.*] You understand that I am only an obscure frontier official. And here in Italy, as in your own Germany, authority is centralized.

DOCTOR. But you can send a telegram to Rome, explaining the urgency of my position.

[DUMPTSY *appears, greatly excited.*]

DUMPTSY. More guests from the bus, Mr. Navadel. Seven of them! [*He goes.*]

DON. *Good God!* [*He goes out.*]

DOCTOR. Ach, es gibt kein Ruhe hier.

CAPTAIN. I assure you, Dr. Waldersee, I shall do all in my power.

DOCTOR. They must be made to understand that time is of vital importance.

CAPTAIN. Yes, I know.

DOCTOR. I have no equipment here to examine them properly—no assistant for the constant observation that is essential if my experiments are to succeed . . .

CAPTAIN [*a trifle wearily*]. I'm so sorry . . .

DOCTOR. Yes! You say you are so sorry. But what do you *do?* You have no comprehension of what is at stake. You are a soldier and indifferent to death. You say you are sorry, but it is nothing to you that hundreds of thousands, *millions,* are dying from a disease that it is within my power to cure!

CAPTAIN. Again, I assure you, Dr. Waldersee, that I . . .

DON'S VOICE. Our Mr. Pittaluga will be down in a moment. In the meantime, perhaps you and the—the others . . . [*He comes in, followed by* HARRY VAN, *a wan, thoughtful, lonely American vaudevillian promoter, press agent, book-agent, crooner, hoofer, barker or shill, who has undertaken all sorts of jobs in his time, all of them capitalizing his powers of salesmanship, and none of them entirely honest. He wears a snappy, belted, polo coat and a brown felt hat with brim turned down on all sides*] . . . would care to sit here in the cocktail lounge. We have a *thé dansant* here at 4:30 . . . supper dancing in the evening. . . .

HARRY. Do you run this hotel?

DON. I'm the Social Manager.

HARRY. What?

DON. The Social Manager.

HARRY. Oh! American, aren't you?

DON. I am. Santa Barbara's my home, and Donald Navadel is my name.

HARRY. Happy to know you. My name's Harry Van [*They shake hands.*]

DON. Glad to have you here, Mr. Van. Are you—staying with us long?

DOCTOR [*rising*]. I shall myself send a telegram to Rome, to the German Embassy.

CAPTAIN. They might well be able to expedite matters. [*The* DOCTOR *goes.*]

HARRY. I've got to get over that border. When I came in on the train from Fiume, they told me the border is closed, and the train is stuck here for tonight and maybe longer. I asked them why, but they either didn't know or they refused to divulge their secrets to me. What seems to be the trouble?

DON. Perhaps Captain Locicero can help you. He's the commander of Italian Headquarters here. This is Mr. Van, Captain.

CAPTAIN [*rising*]. Mr. Van, my compliments.

HARRY. And mine to you, Captain. We're trying to get to Geneva.

CAPTAIN. You have an American passport?

HARRY. I have. Several of them. [*He reaches in his pocket and takes out seven passports, bound together with elastic. He fans them like a deck of cards and hands them to the* CAPTAIN.]

CAPTAIN. You have your family with you?

HARRY. Well—it isn't exactly a family. [*He goes to the right.*] Come in here, girls!

SHIRLEY [*from off-stage*]. Come on in, kids. Harry wants us.

[*Six blonde chorus girls come in. They are named:* SHIRLEY, BEULAH, BEBE, FRANCINE, EDNA *and* ELAINE. *Of these,* SHIRLEY *is the principal, a frank, knowing fan dancer.* BEULAH *is a bubble dancer, and therefore ethereal.* BEBE *is a hard, harsh little number who shimmies.* DON *doesn't know quite how to take this surprising troupe, but the* CAPTAIN *is impressed, favorably.*]

HARRY. Allow me to introduce the girls, Captain. We call them "Les Blondes." We've been playing the Balkan circuit—Budapest, Bucharest, Sofia, Belgrade, and Zagreb. [*He turns to* DON.] Back home, that would be the equivalent of "Pan Time." [*He laughs nervously, to indicate that the foregoing was a gag.*]

CAPTAIN [*bowing*]. How do you do?

HARRY. The Captain is head man, girls.

GIRLS. How do you do? . . . Pleased to meet you. . . . Etc.

HARRY. The situation in brief is this, Captain. We've got very attractive bookings at a night spot in Geneva. Undoubtedly they feel that the League of Nations needs us. [*Another laugh.*] It's important that we get there at once. So, Captain, I'll be grateful for prompt action.

CAPTAIN [*looking at the first passport*]. Miss Shirley Laughlin.

HARRY. Laughlin. This is Shirley. Step up, honey. [*Shirley steps forward.*]

CAPTAIN [*pleased with* SHIRLEY]. How do you do?

SHIRLEY. Pleased to meet you.

CAPTAIN. This photograph hardly does you justice.

SHIRLEY. I know. It's terrible, isn't it!

HARRY [*interrupting*]. Who's next, Captain?

CAPTAIN. Miss Beulah Tremoyne.

HARRY. Come on, Beulah. [*She comes forward in a wide sweep, as* SHIRLEY *goes up and joins the group.*] Beulah is our bubble dancer, a product of the aesthetic school, and therefore more of a dreamer.

CAPTAIN. Exquisite!

BEULAH. Thank you *ever* so much. [*She starts to sit down by the* CAPTAIN. *She is turning it on.*]

HARRY. That'll be all, Beulah.

CAPTAIN. Miss Elaine Messiger—

HARRY. Come on, babe.

CAPTAIN. Miss Francine Merle—

HARRY. No tricks, Francine. This is just identification.

CAPTAIN. Miss Edna Creesh—

HARRY. Turn it off, honey.

CAPTAIN. And Miss Bebe Gould.

HARRY. You'll find Bebe a very, very lovely girl.

BEBE [*remonstrating*]. Harry!

HARRY. A shimmy artiste, and incorrigibly unsophisticated.

CAPTAIN [*summing up*]. Very beautiful. Very, very beautiful. Mr. Van, I congratulate you.

HARRY. That's nice of you, Captain. Now, can we . . .

CAPTAIN. And I wish I, too, were going to Geneva. [*He hands back the passports to* HARRY.]

HARRY. Then it's O.K. for us to pass?

CAPTAIN. But won't you young ladies sit down?

SHIRLEY. Thanks, Captain.

BEULAH. We'd love to.

FRANCINE. He's cute.

EDNA. I'll say. [*They all sit.*]

HARRY. I don't want to seem oblivious of your courtesy, Captain, but the fact is we can't afford to hang around here any longer. That train may pull out and leave us.

CAPTAIN. I give you my word, that train will not move tonight, and maybe not tomorrow night, and maybe never. [*He bows deeply.*] It is a matter of the deepest personal regret to me, Mr. Van, but—

HARRY. Listen, pal. Could you stop being polite for just a moment, and tell us how do we get to Geneva?

CAPTAIN. That is not for me to say. I am as powerless as you are, Mr. Van. I, too, am a pawn. [*He picks up his coat and hat.*] But, speaking for myself, I shall not be sorry if you and your beautiful companions are forced to remain here indefinitely. [*He salutes the girls, smiles and goes out.*]

HARRY. Did you hear that? He says he's a pawn.

BEBE. He's a Wop.

BEULAH. But he's cute!

SHIRLEY. Personally, I'd just as soon stay here. I'm sick of the slats on those stinking day coaches.

HARRY. After the way we've been betrayed in the Balkans, we can't afford to stay any place. [*He turns to* DON.] What's the matter, anyway? Why can't decent respectable people be allowed to go about their legitimate business?

DON. Evidently you're not fully aware of the international situation.

HARRY. I'm fully aware that the international situation is always regrettable. But what's wrong now?

DON. Haven't you been reading the papers?

HARRY. In Bulgaria and Jugo-Slavia? [*He looks around at the girls, who laugh.*] No.

DON. It may be difficult for you to understand, Mr. Van, but we happen to be on the brink of a frightful calamity.

HARRY. What?

DON. We're on the verge of war.

SHIRLEY. War?

BEBE. What about?

HARRY. You mean—that business in Africa?

DON. Far more serious than that! *World* war! All of them!

HARRY. No lie! You mean—it'll be started by people like that? [*Points after the* CAPTAIN.] Italians?

DON. Yes. They've reached the breaking point.

HARRY. I don't believe it. I don't believe that people like that would take on the job of licking the world. They're too romantic. [PITTALUGA *steps forward.*]

PITTALUGA. You wish rooms, Signor?

HARRY. What have you got?

PITTALUGA. We can give you grande luxe accommodations, rooms with baths. . . .

HARRY. What's your scale of prices?

PITTALUGA. From fifty lira up.

DON. That's about five dollars a day.

HARRY [*wincing*]. What?

DON. Meals included.

HARRY. I take it there's the usual professional discount.

PITTALUGA [*to* DON]. Che cosa significa?

DON. Mr. Van and the young ladies are artists.

PITTALUGA. Ebbene?

DON [*scornfully*]. In America we give special rates to artists.

PITTALUGA [*grimly*]. Non posso, non posso.

[*The* CHERRYS *appear on the balcony above.*]

DON. I'm sure Mr. Pittaluga will take care of you nicely, Mr. Van. He will show you attractive rooms on the *other* side of the hotel. They're delightful.

HARRY. No doubt. But I want to see the accommodations.

PITTALUGA. Step this way, please.

HARRY. Come on, girls. Now—I want two girls to a room, and a single room for me adjoining. I promised their mothers I'd always be within earshot. Put on your shoes, Beulah. [*He goes out right, followed by the* GIRLS *and* DON.]

BEULAH [*as they go*]. Why's he kicking? I think this place is *attractive!*

SHIRLEY. Oh—you know Harry. He's always got to have something to worry about. [*They have gone.*]

MRS. CHERRY [*coming down*]. What an extraordinary gathering!

CHERRY. There's something I've never been able to understand—the tendency of Americans to travel en masse. [*They pause to admire the view and each other. He takes her in his arms and kisses her.*] Darling!

MRS. CHERRY. What?

CHERRY. Nothing. I just said, "Darling"! [*He kisses her again.*] My sweet. I love you.

MRS. CHERRY. That's right. [*She kisses him.*]

CHERRY. I think we're going to like it here, aren't we, darling?

MRS. CHERRY. Yes. You'll find a lot to paint.

CHERRY. No doubt. But I'm not going to waste any time painting.

MRS. CHERRY. Why not, Jimmy? You've got to work and—

CHERRY. Don't ask "why not" in that laboriously girlish tone! You know damned well why not!

MRS. CHERRY [*laughing*]. Now really darling. We don't have to be maudlin. We're old enough to be sensible about it, aren't we!

CHERRY. God forbid that we should spoil everything by being sensible! This is an occasion for pure and beautiful foolishness. So don't irritate me by any further mention of work.

MRS. CHERRY. Very well, darling. If you're going to be stinking about it . . . [*He kisses her again.*]

[*The* DOCTOR *comes in from the right and regards their love-making with scant enthusiasm. They look up and see him. They aren't embarrassed.*]

CHERRY. How do you do?

DOCTOR. Don't let me interrupt you. [*He rings a bell and sits down.*]

CHERRY. It's quite all right. We were just starting out for a walk.

MRS. CHERRY. The air is so marvelous up here, isn't it?

DOCTOR [*doubtfully*]. Yes.

[DUMPTSY *comes in from the right.*]

CHERRY. Yes—we think so. Come on, darling. [*They go out at the back.*]

DOCTOR. Mineral water.

DUMPTSY. Yes, sir.

[QUILLERY *comes in and sits at the left. He is small, dark, brooding and French—an extreme-radical-socialist, but still, French.*]

DOCTOR. Not iced—warm.

DUMPTSY. If you please, sir. [*He goes out, left.*]

[*A group of five Italian flying corps officers come in, talking gaily in Italian. They cross to the bar entrance and go out.*]

FIRST OFFICER. Sono Americane.

SECOND OFFICER. Sono belle, proprio da far strabiliare.

THIRD OFFICER. Forse sarrano stelle cinematografiche di Hollyvood.

SECOND OFFICER. E forse ora non ci rincrescerà che abbiano cancellato la nostra licenza. [*They go into the bar.*]

HARRY [*coming in*]. Good afternoon.

DOCTOR. Good afternoon.

HARRY. Have a drink?

DOCTOR. I am about to have one.

HARRY. Mind if I join you? [*He sits down near the* DOCTOR.]

DOCTOR. This is a public room.

HARRY [*whistles a snatch of a tune*]. It's a funny kind of situation, isn't it?

DOCTOR. To what situation do you refer?

HARRY. All this stopping of trains . . . [DUMPTSY *enters from the bar and serves the* DOCTOR *with a glass of mineral water.*] and orders from Rome and we are on the threshold of calamity.

DOCTOR. To me it is not funny. [*He rises with his mineral water.*]

HARRY. Get me a Scotch.

DUMPTSY. With soda, sir?

HARRY. Yes.

DUMPTSY. If you please, sir.

QUILLERY. I will have a beer.

DUMPTSY. We have native or imported, sir.

QUILLERY. Native will do.

DUMPTSY. If you please, sir. [*He goes out.*]

DOCTOR. I repeat—to me it is *not* funny! [*He bows.*] You will excuse me.

HARRY. Certainly. . . . See you later, pal. [*The* DOCTOR *goes.* HARRY *turns to* QUILLERY.] Friendly old bastard!

QUILLERY. Quite! But you were right. The situation *is* funny. There is always something essentially laughable in the thought of a lunatic asylum. Although, it may perhaps seem less funny when you are inside.

HARRY. I guess so. I guess it isn't easy for Germans to see the comical side of things these days. Do you mind if I join you? [*He rises and crosses to the left.*]

QUILLERY. I beg of you to do so, my comrade.

HARRY. I don't like to thrust myself forward—[*He sits down.*]—but, you see, I travel with a group of blondes, and it's always a relief to find somebody to talk to. Have you seen the girls?

QUILLERY. Oh, yes.

HARRY. Alluring, aren't they?

QUILLERY. Very alluring.

[DUMPTSY *comes in with the drinks and goes.* HARRY *takes out his chewing gum, wraps it in paper, places it in a silver snuff box, which he shows to* QUILLERY.]

HARRY. That's a genuine antique snuff box of the period of Louis Quinze.

QUILLERY. Very interesting.

HARRY. It's a museum piece. [*Puts the box in his pocket.*] You've got to hoard your gum here in Europe.

QUILLERY. You've traveled far?

HARRY. Yeah—I've been a long way with that gorgeous array of beautiful girls. I took 'em from New York to Monte Carlo. To say we were a sensation in Monte Carlo would be to state a simple incontrovertible fact. But then I made the mistake of accepting an offer from the manager of the Club Arizona in Budapest. I found that conditions in the South-East are not so good.

QUILLERY. I traveled on the train with you from Zagreb.

HARRY. Zagreb! A plague spot! What were you doing there?

QUILLERY. I was attending the Labor Congress.

HARRY. Yeah—I heard about that. The night club people thought that the congress would bring in a lot of business. They were wrong. But—excuse me— [*Rises.*] My name is Harry Van.

QUILLERY [*rises*]. Quillery is my name.

HARRY. Glad to know you, Mr.—?

QUILLERY. Quillery.

HARRY. Quillery. [*Sits.*] I'm an American. What's your nationality?

QUILLERY. I have no nationality. [*Sits.*] I drink to your good health.

HARRY. And to your lack of nationality, of which I approve. [*They drink.*]

[SIGNOR *and* SIGNORA ROSSI *come in and cross to the bar.* ROSSI *is a consumptive.*]

ROSSI. Abbiamo trascorso una bella giornata, Nina. Beviamo un po'?

SIGNORA ROSSI. Dopo tutto quell' esercizio ti farebbe male. Meglio che tu ti riposi per un'oretta.

ROSSI. Ma, no, mi sento proprio bene. Andiamo. Mi riposerò più tardi. [*They go into the bar.*]

HARRY. I get an awful kick hearing Italian. It's beautiful. Do you speak it?

QUILLERY. Only a little. I was born in France. And I love my home. Perhaps if I had raised pigs—like my father, and all his fathers, back to the time when Caesar's Roman legions came—perhaps, if I had done that, I should have been a Frenchman, as they were. But I went to work in a factory—and machinery is international.

HARRY. And I suppose pigs are exclusively French?

QUILLERY. My father's pigs are! [HARRY *laughs*.] The factory where I have worked made artificial limbs—an industry that has been prosperous the last twenty years. But sometimes—in the evening—after my work —I would go out into the fields and help my father. And then, for a little while, I would become again a Frenchman.

HARRY [*takes out his cigarette case*]. That's a nice thought, pal. [*Offers* QUILLERY *a cigarette*.] Have a smoke?

QUILLERY. No, thank you.

HARRY. I don't blame you. These Jugo-Slav cigarettes are not made of the same high-grade quality of manure to which I grew accustomed in Bulgaria.

QUILLERY. You know, my comrade—you seem to have a long view of things.

HARRY. So long that it gets very tiresome.

QUILLERY. The long view is not easy to sustain in this short-sighted world.

HARRY. You're right about that, pal.

QUILLERY. Let me give you an instance: There we were—gathered in Zagreb, representatives of the workers of all Europe. All brothers, collaborating harmoniously for the United Front! And now—we are rushing to our homes to prevent our people from plunging into mass murder—mass suicide!

HARRY. You're going to try to stop the war?

QUILLERY. Yes.

HARRY. Do you think you'll succeed?

QUILLERY. Unquestionably! This is not 1914, remember! Since then, some new voices have been heard in this world—loud voices. I need mention only one of them—Lenin—Nikolai Lenin!

[*A ferocious looking* MAJOR *of the Italian flying corps comes in and goes quickly to the bar. As he opens the door, he calls "Attention!" He goes into the bar, the door swinging to behind him.*]

HARRY. Yes—but what are you going to do about people like *that?*

QUILLERY. Expose them! That's all we have to do. Expose them—for what they are—atavistic children! Occupying their undeveloped minds playing with outmoded toys.

HARRY. Have you *seen* any of those toys?

QUILLERY. Yes! France is full of them. But there is a force more potent than all the bombing planes and submarines and tanks. And that is the mature intelligence of the workers of the world! There is one antidote for war—Revolution! And the cause of Revolution gains steadily in strength. Even here in Italy, despite all the repressive power of Fascism, sanity has survived, and it becomes more and more articulate. . . .

HARRY. Well, pal—you've got a fine point there. And I hope you stick to it.

QUILLERY. I'm afraid you think it is all futile idealism!

HARRY. No—I don't. And what if I did? I am an idealist myself.

QUILLERY. You too believe in the revolution?

HARRY. Not necessarily in *the* revolution. I'm just in favor of any revolution. Anything that will make people wake up, and get themselves some convictions. Have you ever taken cocaine?

QUILLERY. Why—I imagine that I have—at the dentist's.

HARRY. No—I mean, for pleasure. You know—a vice.

QUILLERY. No! I've never indulged in that folly.

HARRY. I have—during a stage of my career when luck was bad and confusion prevailed.

QUILLERY. Ah, yes. You needed delusions of grandeur.

HARRY. That's just what they were.

QUILLERY. It must have been an interesting experience.

HARRY. It was illuminating. It taught me what is the precise trouble with the world today. We have become a race of drug addicts—hopped up with false beliefs—false fears—false enthusiasms. . . .

[*The four* OFFICERS *emerge from the bar, talking excitedly.*]

SECOND OFFICER. Ma, è state fatta la dichiarazone di guerra attuale?

FIRST OFFICER. Caricheremo delle bombe esplosive?

THIRD OFFICER. Se la guerra è in cominciata, allora vuol dire che noi. . . .

FOURTH OFFICER. La guerra è in cominciata.

MAJOR. Silenzio! Solo il vostro commandante conosce gli ordini. Andiamo! [*All five go out hurriedly.*]

QUILLERY [*jumps up*]. Mother of God! Did you hear what they were saying?

HARRY [*rises*]. I heard, but I couldn't understand.

QUILLERY. It was about war. I know only a little Italian—but I thought they were saying that war has already been declared. [*He grabs his hat.*] I *must* go and demand that they let me cross the border! At once! [*He starts to go.*]

HARRY. That's right, pal. There's no time to lose.

QUILLERY. Wait— I haven't paid. . . . [*He is fumbling for money.*]

HARRY. No, no. This was my drink. You've got to hurry!

QUILLERY. Thank you, my comrade. [*He goes out quickly.*]

[*Airplane motors are heard, off at the right.* HARRY *crosses to the window.* DUMPTSY *comes in to remove the empty glasses.*]

DUMPTSY. Fine view, isn't it, sir?

HARRY. I've seen worse.

DUMPTSY. Nothing quite like it, sir. From here, we look into four nations. Where you see that little village, at the far end of the valley—that is Austria. Isn't that beautiful over there?

HARRY. Are you Italian?

DUMPTSY. Well, yes, sir. That is to say, I didn't used to be.

HARRY. What did you used to be?

DUMPTSY. Austrian. All this part was Austria, until after the big war, when they decided these mountains must go to Italy, and I went with them. In one day, I became a foreigner. So now, my children learn only Italian in school, and when I and my wife talk our own language they can't understand us. [*He gets* HARRY's *drink and brings it over to him.*] They changed the name of this mountain. Monte Gabriele—that's what it is now. They named it after an Italian who dropped poems on Vienna. Even my old father—he's dead—but all the writing on the gravestones was in German, so they rubbed it out and translated it. So now he's Italian, too. But they didn't get my sister. She married a Swiss. She lives over there, in Schleins.

HARRY. She's lucky.

DUMPTSY. Yes—those Swiss are smart.

HARRY. Yeah, they had sense enough to get over there in the first place.

DUMPTSY [*laughs*]. But it doesn't make much difference who your masters are. When you get used to
them, they're all the same.

[*The porter's bell rings.* PITTALUGA *appears.*]

PITTALUGA. Dumptsy! Dumptsy! Una gentildonna arriva. Prendi i suoi bagagli. Affretati!

DUMPTSY. Si, Signore. Vengo subito. [*He goes.*]

PITTALUGA [*claps his hands*]. Sciocco! Anna, Per Dio!
Dove sei stata, va sopra a preparare la stanza. [ANNA,
the maid, enters with towels.] Presto, presto!

[ANNA *runs up the steps, exits.* PITTALUGA *goes back
into the lobby.*]

IRENE'S VOICE. Vieni, Achille.

DON [*coming in*]. This is our cocktail lounge, madame.

[IRENE *enters. She is somewhere between thirty and
forty, beautiful, heavily and smartly furred in the
Russian manner. Her hair is blonde and quite
straight. She is a model of worldly wisdom, chic,
and carefully applied graciousness. Her name is
pronounced "*EAR-RAY-NA.*" . . . She surveys the
room with polite appreciation, glancing briefly at
HARRY.*]

DON. Your suite is up there, madame. All this part of
the hotel is quite new.

IRENE. How very nice!

DON. We have our best view from this side of the
hotel. [*He goes to the window.* IRENE *follows slowly.*]
You can see four countries—Italy, Switzerland, Austria and Bavaria.

IRENE. Magnificent!

DON. Yes—we're very proud of it.

IRENE. All those countries. And they all look so very
much alike, don't they!

DON. Yes—they do really—from this distance.

IRENE. All covered with the beautiful snow. I think
the whole world should be always covered with

snow. It would be so much more clean, wouldn't it?

DON. By all means!

IRENE. Like in my Russia. White Russia. [*Sighs, and goes up to the next landing.*] Oh, and—how exciting! A flying field. Look! They're bringing out the big bombers.

DON. Madame is interested in aviation?

IRENE. No, no. Just ordinary flying bores me. But there is no experience in life quite so thrilling as a parachute jump, is there!

DON. I've never had that thrill, I'm ashamed to say.

IRENE. Once I had to jump when I was flying over the jungle in Indo-China. It was indescribable. Drifting down, sinking into that great green sea of enchantment and hidden danger.

[DUMPTSY *comes in.*]

DON. And you weren't afraid?

IRENE. No—no—I was not afraid. In moments like that, one is given the sense of eternity.

HARRY [*viciously*]. Dumptsy! Get me another Scotch.

DUMPTSY. Yes, sir.

HARRY. And put ice in it, this time. If you haven't got any ice, go out and scoop up some snow.

DUMPTSY. If you please, sir. [*He goes into the bar.*]

IRENE [*her gaze wandering about the room*]. But your place is really charming.

DON. You're very kind.

IRENE. I must tell everyone in Paris about it. There's something about this design—it suggests a—an amusing kind of horror.

DON [*not knowing quite how to interpret that*]. Madame is a student of decoration?

IRENE. No, no. Only an amateur, my friend. An amateur, I'm afraid, in everything.

[*The siren sounds from off at the right.* IRENE, *near the top of the staircase, stops to listen.*]

IRENE. What is that?

DON. Oh—it's merely some kind of warning. They've been testing it.

IRENE. Warning? Warning against what?

DON. I believe it's for use in case of war.

IRENE. War? But there will be no war.

[PITTALUGA *enters from the lobby, escorting* ACHILLE WEBER—*which is pronounced* "VAY-BAIR." *He is a thin, keen executive, wearing a neat little mustache and excellent clothes. In his lapel is the rosette of the Legion of Honor. He carries a brief case.*]

PITTALUGA [*as they come in*]. Par ici, Monsieur Weber. Vous trouverez Madame ici . . .

IRENE [*leaning over the railing*]. Achille!

WEBER [*pausing and looking up*]. Yes, my dear?

IRENE. Achille—there will be no war, will there?

WEBER [*amused*]. No, no—Irene. There will be no war. They're all much too well prepared for it. [*He turns to* PITTALUGA.] Where are our rooms?

PITTALUGA. Votre suite est par ici, Monsieur. La plus belle de la maison! La vue est superbe!

IRENE [*to* DON]. There, you see! They will not fight. They are all much too much afraid of each other.

[WEBER *is going up the staircase, ignoring the view.* PITTALUGA *is following.*]

IRENE [*to* WEBER]. Achille—I am mad about this place! Je rafolle de cette place!

WEBER [*calmly*]. Yes, my dear.

IRENE. We must be sure to tell the Maharajah of Raj-pipla, Achille. Can't you imagine how dear little "Pip" would love this? [*They go out on the landing above.*]

HARRY. Who was that?

DON [*impressed*]. That was Achille Weber. One of the biggest men in France. I used to see him a lot at St. Moritz.

[*There is a sound of airplane motors off at the right.*]

HARRY. And the dame? Do you assume that is his wife?

DON [*curtly*]. Are you implying that she's not?

HARRY. No, no—I'm not implying a thing. [*He wanders to the piano.*] I'm just kind of—kind of baffled.

DON. Evidently. [*He goes out.*]

[HARRY *at the piano strikes a chord of the Russian song, "Kak Stranna." DUMPTSY enters from the bar and serves HARRY with Scotch. The off-stage noise increases as more planes take the air.*]

DUMPTSY [*at the window*]. Do you see them—those aeroplanes—flying up from the field down there?

HARRY [*glances toward window, without interest*]. Yes —I see them.

DUMPTSY. Those are the big ones. They're full of bombs, to drop on people. Look! They're going north. Maybe Berlin. Maybe Paris.

[*Harry strikes a few chords.*]

HARRY. Did you ever jump with a parachute?

DUMPTSY. Why, no—sir. [*He looks questioningly at* HARRY.]

HARRY. Well, I have—a couple of times. And it's nothing. But—I didn't land in any jungle. I landed where I was supposed to—in the Fair Grounds.

DUMPTSY [*seriously*]. That's interesting, sir.

[*The* ROSSIS *enter from the bar. He is holding a handkerchief to his mouth. She is supporting him as they cross.*]

SIGNORA ROSSI. Non t'ho detto che dovevi fare attenzione? Te l'ho detto, te l'ho detto che sarebbe accaduto ciò. Vedi, ora ti piglia un accesso di tosse.

ROSSI. 'Scusatemi, Mina. [*Another coughing fit.*]

SIGNORA ROSSI. Va a sdraiarti. Dovresti riposarti a lungo. E adopera il termometro. Scometto che t'è aumentata la temperatura. [*They go out.*]

DUMPTSY. That Signor Rossi—he has tuberculosis.

HARRY. Is he getting cured up here?

[*The* DOCTOR *appears on the landing above.*]

DUMPTSY. Ja. This used to be a sanatorium, in the old days. But the Fascisti—they don't like to admit that anyone can be sick! [*He starts to go.*]

DOCTOR. Dumptsy!

DUMPTSY. Herr Doctor.

DOCTOR [*coming down*]. Mineral water.

DUMPTSY. Ja wohl, Herr Doctor. [DUMPTSY *goes out, left.*]

[*The* DOCTOR *sits down.* HARRY *takes one more look toward the gallery, where* IRENE *had been. He then looks at the* DOCTOR, *and decides not to suggest joining him. He starts to play "Kak Stranna." The* DOCTOR *turns and looks at him, with some surprise. The uproar of planes is now terrific, but it starts to dwindle as the planes depart.*]

DOCTOR. What is that you are playing?

HARRY. A Russian song, entitled "Kak Stranna," meaning "how strange!" One of those morose ballads about how once we met, for one immortal moment, like ships that pass in the night. Or maybe like a couple of trucks, side-swiping each other. And now we meet again! How strange!

DOCTOR. You are a musician?

HARRY. Certainly. I used to play the piano in picture theatres—when that was the only kind of sound they had—except the peanuts.

[DUMPTSY *brings the mineral water and stops to listen, admiringly.*]

DOCTOR. Do you know Bach?

HARRY. With pleasure. [*He shifts into something or other by Bach.*]

DOCTOR [*after a moment*]. You have good appreciation, but not much skill.

HARRY. What do you mean, not much skill? Listen to

this. [*He goes into a trick arrangement of* "The Waters of the Minnetonka."] "The Waters of the Minnetonka"—Cadman. [*He goes on playing.*] Suitable for Scenics—Niagara Falls by moonlight. Or—if you play it this way—it goes fine with the scene where the young Indian chief turns out to be a Yale man, so it's O.K. for him to marry Lillian "Dimples" Walker. [*Starts playing* "Boola Boola."]

DOCTOR. Will you have a drink?

HARRY. Oh! So you want me to stop playing?

DOCTOR. No, no! I like your music very much.

HARRY. Then, in that case, I'd be delighted to drink with you. Another Scotch, Dumptsy.

DUMPTSY. If you please, sir. [*He goes out.*]

DOCTOR. I'm afraid I was rude to you.

HARRY. That's all right, pal. I've been rude to lots of people, and never regretted it. [*He plays on, shifting back into* "Kak Stranna."]

DOCTOR. The fact is, I am a man who is very gravely distressed.

HARRY. I can see that, Doctor. And I sympathize with you.

DOCTOR [*fiercely*]. You cannot sympathize with me, because you do not know!

HARRY. No—I guess I don't know—except in a general way.

DOCTOR. You are familiar with the writings of Thomas Mann. [*It is a challenge, rather than a question.*]

HARRY. I'm afraid not, pal.

[*The* DOCTOR *opens* "The Magic Mountain," *which he has been reading.*]

DOCTOR. "Backsliding"—he said—"spiritual backsliding to that dark and tortured age—that, believe me, is disease! A degradation of mankind—a degradation painful and offensive to conceive." True words, eh?

HARRY. Absolutely!

[DUMPTSY *comes in with the Scotch.* HARRY *gets up from the piano and crosses.* DUMPTSY *goes.* HARRY *sits down with the* DOCTOR.]

DOCTOR. Have you had any experience with cancer?

HARRY. Certainly. I once sold a remedy for it.

DOCTOR [*exploding*]. There *is* no remedy for it, so far!

HARRY. Well—this was kind of a remedy for everything.

DOCTOR. I am within *that* of finding the cure for cancer! You probably have not heard of Fibiger, I suppose?

HARRY. I may have. I'm not sure.

DOCTOR. He was a Dane—experimented with rats. He did good work, but he died before it could be completed. I carry it on. I have been working with Oriental rats, in Bologna. But because of this war scare, I must go to neutral territory. You see, nothing must be allowed to interfere with my experiments. Nothing!

HARRY. No. They're important.

DOCTOR. The laboratory of the University of Zurich has been placed at my disposal—and in Switzerland, I can work, undisturbed. I have twenty-eight rats with me, all in various carefully tabulated stages of the disease. It is the disease of civilization—and I can cure it. And now they say I must not cross the border.

HARRY. You know, Doctor, it *is* funny.

DOCTOR. What's funny? To you, everything is funny!

HARRY. No—it's just that you and I are in the same fix. Both trying to get across that line. You with rats—me with girls. Of course—I appreciate the fact that civilization at large won't suffer much if *we* get stuck in the war zone. Whereas with you, there's a lot at stake. . . .

DOCTOR. It is for me to win one of the greatest victories of all time. And the victory belongs to Germany.

HARRY. Sure it does!

DOCTOR. Unfortunately, just now the situation in Germany is not good for research. They are infected with the same virus as here. Chauvinistic nationalism! They expect all bacteriologists to work on germs to put in bombs to drop from airplanes. To fill people with death! When we've given our lives to *save* people. Oh—God in heaven—why don't they let me do what is good? Good for the whole world? Forgive me. I become excited.

HARRY. I know just how you feel, Doctor. Back in 1918, I was a shill with a carnival show, and I was doing fine. The boss thought very highly of me. He offered to give me a piece of the show, and I had a chance to get somewhere. And then what do you think happened? Along comes the United States Government and they drafted me! You're in the army now! They slapped me into a uniform and for three whole months before the Armistice, I was parading up and down guarding the Ashokan Reservoir. They were afraid your people might poison it. I've always figured that that little interruption ruined my career. But I've remained an optimist, Doctor.

DOCTOR. *You* can afford to.

HARRY. I've remained an optimist because I'm essentially a student of human nature. You dissect corpses and rats and similar unpleasant things. Well—it has been my job to dissect suckers! I've probed into the souls of some of the God-damnedest specimens. And what have I found? Now, don't sneer at me, Doctor—but above everything else I've found faith. Faith in peace on earth and good will to men—and faith that "Muma," "Muma" the three-legged girl, really has got three legs. All my life, Doctor, I've been selling phony goods to people of meager intelligence and great faith. You'd think that would make me contemptuous of the human race, wouldn't you? But—on the contrary—it has given *me* faith. It has made me sure that no matter how much the meek may be bulldozed or gypped they *will* eventually inherit the earth.

[SHIRLEY *and* BEBE *come in from the lobby.*]

SHIRLEY. Harry!

HARRY. What is it, honey?

[SHIRLEY *goes to* HARRY *and hands him a printed notice.*]

SHIRLEY [*excited*]. Did you see this?

HARRY. Doctor—let me introduce, Miss Shirley Laughlin and Miss Bebe Gould.

SHIRLEY. How do you do?

DOCTOR [*grunts*]. How do you do.

BEBE. Pleased to know you, Doctor.

[HARRY *looks at the notice.*]

SHIRLEY. They got one of those put up in every one of our rooms.

HARRY [*showing it to the* DOCTOR]. Look— "What to do in case of air raids"—in all languages.

DOCTOR. Ja—I saw that.

SHIRLEY. Give it back to me, Harry. I'm going to send it to Mama.

HARRY [*handing it to her*]. Souvenir of Europe.

SHIRLEY. It'll scare the hell out of her.

BEBE. What's the matter with these people over here? Are they all screwy?

HARRY. Bebe—you hit it right on the nose! [*Turns to the* DOCTOR.] I tell you, Doctor—these are very wonderful, profound girls. The mothers of tomorrow! [*He beams on them.* BEULAH *comes in.*]

SHIRLEY. Oh—shut up!

BEULAH. Say—Harry . . .

HARRY. What is it, honey?

BEULAH. Is it all right if I go out with Mr. Navadel and try to learn how to do this ski-ing?

[WEBER *comes out on the gallery and starts down.*]

HARRY. What? And risk those pretty legs? Emphatically—no!

BEULAH. But it's healthy.

HARRY. Not for me, dear. Those gams of yours are my bread and butter. [WEBER *crosses. They look at him. He glances briefly at them.*] Sit down, girls, and amuse yourselves with your own thoughts.

[*The* GIRLS *sit.* WEBER, *at the left, lights his cigar. The* CAPTAIN *comes in, quickly, obviously worried.*]

CAPTAIN. I have been trying to get through to headquarters, Monsieur Weber.

WEBER. And when can we leave?

CAPTAIN. Not before tomorrow, I regret to say.

[IRENE *appears on the gallery.*]

WEBER. Signor Lanza in Venice assured me there would be no delay.

CAPTAIN. There would be none, if only I could get into communication with the proper authorities. But—the wires are crowded. The whole nation is in a state of uproar.

WEBER. It's absurd lack of organization.

[*The* PIANIST *and* DRUMMER *come in from the lobby. The* VIOLINIST *and* SAXOPHONIST *follow.*]

CAPTAIN [*with tense solemnity*]. There is good excuse for the excitement now, Monsieur Weber. The report has just come to us that a state of war exists between Italy and France.

HARRY. What?

CAPTAIN. There is a rumor of war between Italy and France!

HARRY. Rumors—rumors—everything's rumors! When are we going to *know*?

CAPTAIN. Soon enough, my friend.

DOCTOR. And what of Germany?

CAPTAIN. Germany has mobilized. [IRENE *pauses to listen.*] But I don't know if any decision has been reached. Nor do I know anything of the situation anywhere else. But—God help us—it will be serious enough for everyone on this earth.

[IRENE *joins* WEBER, *who has sat down at the left.*]

IRENE [*to* WEBER, *and straight at him*]. But I thought they were all too well prepared, Achille. Has there been some mistake somewhere?

WEBER [*confidentially*]. We can only attribute it to spontaneous combustion of the dictatorial ego.

IRENE [*grimly*]. I can imagine how thrilling it must be in Paris at this moment. Just like 1914. All the lovely soldiers—singing—marching! We must go at once to Paris, Achille.

HARRY [*rises*]. What's the matter with the music, professor? Us young folks want to dance.

[ELAINE *and* FRANCINE *come in.*]

ELAINE. Can we have a drink now, Harry?

HARRY. Sure. Sit down.

[DON *enters, exuding gratification at the sight of this gay, chic throng. The* ORCHESTRA *starts to play "Valencia."*]

WEBER. Will you have a drink, Irene?

IRENE. No, thank you.

WEBER. Will you, Captain Locicero?

CAPTAIN. Thank you. Brandy and soda, Dumptsy.

DUMPTSY. Si, Signor.

BEBE [*yells*]. Edna! We're going to have a drink!

[EDNA *comes in.*]

WEBER. For me, Cinzano.

DUMPTSY. Oui, Monsieur. [*He goes into the bar.*]

DOCTOR. It is all incredible.

HARRY. Nevertheless, Doctor, I remain an optimist. [*He looks at* IRENE.] Let doubt prevail throughout this

night—with dawn will come again the light of truth!
[*He turns to* SHIRLEY.] Come on, honey—let's dance.
[*They dance.*]

[DON *dances with* BEULAH. *The* ORCHESTRA *continues with its spirited but frail performance of "Valencia." There are probably "border incidents" in Lorraine, the Riviera, Poland, Czecho-Slovakia and Mongolia.*]

CURTAIN

Act two

SCENE I

It is about 7:30 in the evening of the same day.
The CHERRYS *are seated, both of them dressed for dinner.* AUGUSTE *is serving them cocktails.*

CHERRY. Thank you.

AUGUSTE. Thank you, Signor.

CHERRY. Has any more news come through?

AUGUSTE. No, Signor. They permit the wireless to say nothing.

CHERRY. I suppose nothing really will happen.

AUGUSTE. Let us pray that is so, Signor. [AUGUSTE *goes into the bar.* CHERRY *leans over and kisses his wife.*]

CHERRY. My sweet . . . you're really very lovely.

MRS. CHERRY. Yes. [*He kisses her again, then lifts his glass.*]

CHERRY. Here's to us, darling.

MRS. CHERRY. And to hell with all the rest.

CHERRY. And to hell with all the rest. [*They drink, solemnly.*]

MRS. CHERRY. Jimmy—

CHERRY. What is it, darling?

MRS. CHERRY. Were you just saying that—or do you believe it?

CHERRY. That you're lovely? I can give you the most solemn assurance. . . .

MRS. CHERRY. No—that nothing is going to happen.

CHERRY. Oh.

MRS. CHERRY. Do you believe that?

CHERRY. I know this much: they can't start any real war without England. And no matter how stupid and blundering our government may be, our people simply won't stand for it.

MRS. CHERRY. But people can be such complete fools.

CHERRY. I know it, darling. Why can't they all be like us?

MRS. CHERRY. You mean—nice.

CHERRY. Yes—nice—and intelligent—and happy.

MRS. CHERRY. We're very conceited, aren't we?

CHERRY. Of course. And for good and sufficient reason.

MRS. CHERRY. I'm glad we're so superior, darling. It's comforting.

[HARRY *comes in from bar.*]

CHERRY. Oh—good evening, Mr. Van.

HARRY. Good evening. Pardon me— [*He starts to go.*]

CHERRY. Oh—don't run away, Mr. Van. Let's have some music.

MRS. CHERRY. Won't you have a drink with us?

HARRY. No, thanks, Mrs. Cherry—if you don't mind. [*Sits down at the piano.*] I'm afraid I put down too many Scotches this afternoon. As a result of which, I've just had to treat myself to a bicarbonate of soda. [*Starts playing* "Some of These Days."]

MRS. CHERRY. I love that.

HARRY. Thanks, pal—always grateful for applause from the discriminating. [*Finishes the chorus and stops.*]

CHERRY. Do play some more.

HARRY. No. The mood isn't right.

MRS. CHERRY. I can't tell you what a relief it is to have you here in this hotel.

HARRY. It's kind of you to say that, Mrs. Cherry. But I don't deserve your handsome tribute. Frequently, I can be an asset to any gathering—contributing humorous anecdotes and bits of homely philosophy. But here and now, I'm far from my best.

CHERRY. You're the only one here who seems to have retained any degree of sanity.

MRS. CHERRY. You and your young ladies.

HARRY. The girls are lucky. They don't know anything. And the trouble with me is that I just don't give a damn.

MRS. CHERRY. We've been trying hard not to know anything—or not to give a damn. But it isn't easy.

HARRY. You haven't been married very long, have you? I hope you don't mind my asking. . . .

CHERRY. We were married the day before yesterday.

HARRY. Let me offer my congratulations.

CHERRY. Thank you very much.

HARRY. It's my purely intuitive hunch that you two ought to get along fine.

CHERRY. That's our intention, Mr. Van.

MRS. CHERRY. And we'll do it, what's more. You see— we have one supreme thing in common:

HARRY. Yeah?

MRS. CHERRY. We're both independent.

CHERRY. We're like you Americans, in that respect.

HARRY. You flatter us.

MRS. CHERRY. Jimmy's a painter.

HARRY. You don't say!

MRS. CHERRY. He's been out in Australia, doing colossal murals for some government building. He won't show me the photographs of them, but I'm sure they're simply awful. [*She laughs fondly.*]

CHERRY. They're allegorical. [*He laughs, too.*]

HARRY. I'll bet they're good, at that. What do you do, Mrs. Cherry?

MRS. CHERRY. Oh, I work in the gift department at Fortnum's—

HARRY. Behind a counter, eh!

MRS. CHERRY. Yes—wearing a smock, and disgracing my family.

HARRY. Well, what d'ye know!

MRS. CHERRY. Both our families hoped we'd be married in some nice little church, and settle down in a nice little cottage, in a nice little state of decay. But when I heard Jimmy was on the way home I just dropped everything and rushed down here to meet him—and we were married, in Florence.

CHERRY. We hadn't seen each other for nearly a year —so, you can imagine, it was all rather exciting.

HARRY. I can imagine.

MRS. CHERRY. Florence is the most perfect place in the world to be married in.

HARRY. I guess that's true of any place.

CHERRY. We both happen to love Italy. And—I suppose—we're both rather on the romantic side.

HARRY. You stay on that side, no matter what happens.

MRS. CHERRY [*quickly*]. What do you think is going to happen?

HARRY. Me? I haven't the slightest idea.

CHERRY. We've looked forward so much to being here with no one bothering us, and plenty of winter sports. We're both keen on ski-ing. And now—we may have to go dashing back to England at any moment.

MRS. CHERRY. It's rotten luck, isn't it?

HARRY. Yes, Mrs. Cherry. That's what it is—it's rotten. [QUILLERY *enters from the bar, reading a newspaper.*] So they wouldn't let you cross?

QUILLERY. No!

HARRY. Is there any news?

QUILLERY [*glaring*]. News! Not in this patriotic journal. "Unconfirmed rumors"—from Vienna, London, Berlin, Moscow, Tokyo. And a lot of confirmed lies from Fascist headquarters in Rome. [*He slaps the paper down and sits.*] If you want to know what is really happening, ask *him*—up there! [*Indicates the rooms above.*]

CHERRY. Who?

QUILLERY. Weber! The great Monsieur Achille Weber, of the Comité des Forges! He can give you all the war news. Because he *made* it. You don't know who he is, eh? Or what he has been doing here in Italy? I'll tell you. [*He rises and comes close to them.*] He has been organizing the arms industry. Munitions. To kill French babies. And English babies. France and Italy are at war. England joins France. Germany joins Italy. And that will drag in the Soviet Union and the Japanese Empire and the United States. In every part of the world, the good desire of men for peace and decency is undermined by the dynamite of jingoism. And it needs only one spark, set off anywhere by one egomaniac, to send it all up in one final, fatal explosion. Then love becomes hatred, courage becomes terror, hope becomes despair. [*The DOCTOR appears on the gallery above.*] But—it will all be very nice for Achille Weber. Because he is a master of the one *real* League of Nations— [*The DOCTOR slowly comes down steps.*] The League of Schneider-Creusot, and Krupp, and Skoda, and Vickers and Dupont. The League of Death! And the workers of the world are expected to pay him for it, with their sweat, and their life's blood.

DOCTOR. Marxian nonsense!

QUILLERY. Ah! Who speaks?

DOCTOR. *I* speak.

QUILLERY. Yes! The eminent Dr. Hugo Waldersee. A wearer of the sacred swastika. Down with the Communists! Off with their heads! So that the world may be safe for the Nazi murderers.

DOCTOR. So that Germany may be safe from its oppressors! It is the same with all of you—Englishmen, Frenchmen, Marxists—you manage to forget that Germany, too, has a right to live! [*Rings handbell on the table.*]

QUILLERY. If you love Germany so much, why aren't you there, now—with your rats?

DOCTOR [*sitting*]. I am not concerned with politics. [AUGUSTE *enters from the bar.*] I am a scientist. [*To* AUGUSTE.] Mineral water!

[AUGUSTE *bows and exits into the bar.*]

QUILLERY. That's it, Herr Doctor! A scientist—a servant of humanity! And you know that if you were in your dear Fatherland, the Nazis would make you abandon your cure of cancer. It might benefit too many people outside of Germany—even maybe some Jews. They would force you to devote yourself to breeding malignant bacteria—millions of little germs, each one trained to give the Nazi salute and then go out and poison the enemy. You—a fighter against disease and death—you would become a Judas goat in a slaughter house.

[DON *has appeared during this.*]

CHERRY. I say, Quillery, old chap—do we have to have so much blood and sweat just before dinner?

QUILLERY [*turning on him*]. Just before dinner! And now we hear the voice of England! The great, well-fed, pious hypocrite! The grabber—the exploiter—the immaculate butcher! It was *you* forced this war, because miserable little Italy dared to drag its black shirt across your trail of Europe. What do *you* care if civilization goes to pieces—as long as you have your dinner—and your dinner jacket!

CHERRY [*rising*]. I'm sorry, Quillery—but I think we'd better conclude this discussion out on the terrace.

MRS. CHERRY. Don't be a damned fool, Jimmy. You'll prove nothing by thrashing him.

QUILLERY. It's the Anglo-Saxon method of proving everything! Very well—I am at your disposal.

DON. No! I beg of you, Mr. Cherry. We mustn't have any of that sort of thing. [*He turns to* QUILLERY.] I must ask you to leave. If you're unable to conduct yourself as a gentleman, then . . .

QUILLERY. Don't say any more. Evidently I cannot conduct myself properly! I offer my apologies, Mr. Cherry.

CHERRY. That's quite all right, old man. Have a drink. [*He extends his hand. They shake.*]

QUILLERY. No, thank you. And my apologies to you, Herr Doctor.

DOCTOR. There is no need for apologizing. I am accustomed to all that.

QUILLERY. If I let my speech run away with me, it is because I have hatred for certain things. And you should hate them, too. They are the things that make us blind—and ignorant—and—and dirty. [*He turns and goes out quickly.* DON *goes with him.*]

MRS. CHERRY. He's so right about everything.

CHERRY. I know, poor chap. Will you have another cocktail, darling?

MRS. CHERRY. I don't think so. Will you, Doctor? [*He shakes his head, indicates the mineral water. She rises.*] Let's dine.

CHERRY. It will be a bit difficult to summon up much relish. [*They go out, hand in hand.*]

HARRY. I find them very appealing, don't you, Doctor? [*The* DOCTOR *doesn't announce his findings.*] Did you know they were married only the day before yesterday? Yeah—they got themselves sealed in Florence—because they love Italy. And they came here hoping to spend their honeymoon on skis. . . . Kind of pathetic, isn't it?

DOCTOR. What did you say?

HARRY. Nothing, pal. [DON *comes in.*] Only making conversation.

DOCTOR [*rising*]. That Communist! Making me a criminal because I am a German!

DON. I'm dreadfully sorry, Dr. Waldersee. We never should have allowed the ill-bred little cad to come in here.

DOCTOR. Oh— It's no matter. I have heard too many hymns of hate before this. To be a German is to be used to insults, and injuries. [*He goes out.* DON *starts to go out left.*]

HARRY. Just a minute, Don.

DON. Well?

HARRY. Have you found out yet who that dame is?

DON. What "dame"?

HARRY. That Russian number with Weber.

DON. I have not inquired as to her identity.

HARRY. But did he register her as his wife?

DON. They registered separately! And if it's not too much to ask, might I suggest that you mind your own damned business?

HARRY. You might suggest just that. And I should still be troubled by one of the most tantalizing of questions—namely, "Where have I seen that face before?" Generally, it turns out to be someone who was in the second row one night, yawning.

DON. I'm sure that such is the case now. [*He starts again to go.*]

HARRY. One moment, Don. There's something else.

DON [*impatiently*]. What is it?

HARRY. I take it that your job here is something like that of a professional greeter.

DON. You're at liberty to call it that, if you choose.

HARRY. You're a sort of Y.M.C.A. secretary—who sees to it that all the guests get together and have a good time.

DON. Well?

HARRY. Well—do you think you're doing a very good job of it right now?

DON [*simply furious*]. Have you any suggestions for improving the performance of my duties?

HARRY. Yes, Don—I have.

DON. And I'd very much like to know just exactly who the hell do you think you are to be offering criticism of my work?

HARRY. Please, please! You needn't scream at me. I'm merely trying to be helpful. I'm making you an offer.

DON. What is it?

HARRY [*looking around*]. I see you've got a color wheel here. [*Referring to the light.*]

DON. We use it during the supper dance. But—if you don't mind, I—

HARRY. I see—well—how would it be if I and the girls put on part of our act here, tonight? For purposes of wholesome merriment and relieving the general tension?

DON. What kind of an act is it?

HARRY. And don't say, "What kind of an act," in that tone of voice. It's good enough for this place. Those girls have played before the King of Rumania. And if some of my suspicions are correct—but I won't pursue that subject. All that need concern you is that we can adjust ourselves to our audience, and tonight we'll omit the bubble dance and the number in which little Bebe does a shimmy in a costume composed of detachable gardenias, unless there's a special request for it.

DON. Do you expect to be paid for this?

HARRY. Certainly not. I'm making this offer out of the goodness of my heart. Of course, if you want to make any appropriate adjustment on our hotel bill . . .

DON. And you'll give me your guarantee that there'll be no vulgarity?

[IRENE *appears on the gallery and starts to come down. She is wearing a dinner dress.*]

HARRY. Now be careful, Don. One more word like that and the offer is withdrawn . . .

[DON *cautions him to silence.*]

DON. It's a splendid idea, Mr. Van. We'll all greatly appreciate your little entertainment, I'm sure. [*To* IRENE]. Good evening, madame.

IRENE [*with the utmost graciousness*]. Good evening, Mr. Navadel. [*She pauses at the window.*] It *is* a lovely view. It's like a landscape on the moon.

DON. Yes—yes. That's exactly what it's like.

[*She comes down.*]

HARRY. You understand, we'll have to rehearse with the orchestra.

DON. Oh, yes—Mr. Van. Our staff will be glad to co-operate in every way. . . . Do sit down, madame.

IRENE [*sitting*]. What became of those planes that flew off this afternoon? I haven't heard them come back. [*Takes out a cigarette.*]

DON. I imagine they were moving to some base farther from the frontier. I hope so. They always made the most appalling racket. [*Lights her cigarette for her.*]

HARRY. About eleven o'clock?

[WEBER *appears on the gallery.*]

DON. Yes, Mr. Van. Eleven will do nicely. You'll have a cocktail, madame?

[HARRY *goes into the lobby.*]

IRENE. No, no. Vodka, if you please.

DON. I shall have it sent right in. [*He goes off at the left into bar.*]

[IRENE *looks slowly off, after* HARRY. *She smiles slightly.* WEBER *comes down the stairs quickly. He is not in evening dress. He too pauses at the window.*]

WEBER. A perfectly cloudless night! They're very lucky. [*He comes on down.*]

IRENE. Did you get your call?

WEBER. Yes. I talked to Lanza.

IRENE. I gather the news is, as usual, good.

WEBER. It is extremely serious! You saw those bombers that left here this afternoon?

IRENE. Yes.

WEBER. They were headed for Paris. Italy is evidently in a great hurry to deliver the first blow.

IRENE. How soon may we leave here?

WEBER. None too soon, I can assure you. The French high command will know that the bombers come from this field. There will be reprisals—probably within the next twenty-four hours.

IRENE. That will be exciting to see.

WEBER. An air raid?

IRENE. Yes—with bombs bursting in the snow. Sending up great geysers of diamonds.

WEBER. Or perhaps great geysers of us.

IRENE [*after a moment*]. I suppose many people in Paris are being killed now.

WEBER. I'm afraid so. Unless the Italians bungle it.

IRENE. Perhaps your sister—Madame d'Hilaire—perhaps she and her darling little children are now dying.

WEBER [*sharply*]. My sister and her family are in Montbeliard.

IRENE. But you said the Italians might bungle it. They might drop their bombs on the wrong place.

WEBER. I appreciate your solicitude, my dear. But you can save your condolences until they are needed. [DUMPTSY *comes in from the bar and serves the vodka.* WEBER *rises.*] I must telegraph to Joseph to have the house ready. It will be rather cold in Biarritz now—but far healthier than Paris. You are going in to dinner now?

IRENE. Yes.

WEBER. I shall join you later. [*He goes out.*]

[DUMPTSY *picks up the* CHERRYS' *glasses.*]

DUMPTSY. We will have a great treat tonight, madame.

IRENE. Really?

DUMPTSY. That American impresario, that Mr. Harry Van—he will give us an entertainment with his dancing girls.

IRENE. Is he employed here regularly?

DUMPTSY. Oh, no, madame. He is just passing, like you. This is a special treat. It will be very fine.

IRENE. Let us hope so. [*She downs the vodka.*]

DUMPTSY. Madame is Russian, if I may say so.

IRENE [*pleased*]. How did you know that I am Russian? Just because I am having vodka?

DUMPTSY. No, madame. Many people try to drink vodka. But only true Russians can do it gracefully. You see—I was a prisoner with your people in the war. I liked them.

IRENE. You're very charming. What is your name?

DUMPTSY. I am called Dumptsy, madame.

IRENE. Are you going again to the war, Dumptsy?

DUMPTSY. If they tell me to, madame.

IRENE. You will enjoy being a soldier?

DUMPTSY. Yes—if I'm taken prisoner soon enough.

IRENE. And who do you think will win?

DUMPTSY. I can't think, madame. It is all very doubtful. But one thing I can tell you: whoever wins, it will be the same as last time—Austria will lose.

IRENE. They will all lose, Dumptsy. [*The* CHERRYS *come in. She greets them pleasantly.*] Good evening.

CHERRY. Good evening, madame. [*The* CHERRYS *start to sit, across from* IRENE.]

IRENE. Bring some more vodka, Dumptsy. Perhaps Mr. and Mrs. Cherry will have some, too.

CHERRY. Why, thank you—we . . .

MRS. CHERRY. I'd love to. I've never tasted vodka.

IRENE. Ah—then it's high time. Bring in the bottle, Dumptsy.

DUMPTSY. Yes, madame. [*He goes in to the bar.*]

IRENE. Come, sit down here. [*The* CHERRYS *sit by her.*] You will find vodka a perfect stimulant to the appetite. So much better than that hybrid atrocity, the American cocktail!

CHERRY. To tell you the truth, madame—we've already dined.

IRENE. It is no matter. It is just as good as a liqueur.

MRS. CHERRY. We didn't really dine at all. We merely looked at the minestrone and the Parmesan cheese—and we felt too depressed to eat anything.

IRENE. It's the altitude. After the first exhilaration there comes a depressive reaction, especially for you, who are accustomed to the heavy, Pigwiggian atmosphere of England.

CHERRY. Pigwiggian?

IRENE. Yes, Pigwig—Oliver Twist—you know, your Dickens?

[DUMPTSY *enters from bar with a bottle of vodka and*

two more glasses, which he places on the table. He returns to the bar.]

CHERRY. You know England, madame?

IRENE [*fondly*]. Of course I know England! My governess was a sweet old ogre from your north country—and when I was a little girl I used to visit often at Sandringham.

CHERRY [*impressed*]. Sandringham?

MRS. CHERRY. The palace?

IRENE. Yes. That was before your time. It was in the reign of dear, gay King Edward, and the beautiful Alexandra. [*She sighs a little for those days.*] I used to have such fun playing with my cousin David. He used to try to teach me to play cricket, and when I couldn't swing the bat properly, he said, "Oh, you Russians will never be civilized!" [*Laughs.*] When I went home to Petersburg I told my uncle, the Tsar, what David had said, and he was so amused! But now—you must drink your vodka. [*They rise, and lift their glasses.*] A toast! To his most gracious Majesty the King. [*They clink glasses.*] God bless him.

CHERRY. Thank you, madame. [*All three drink and* MRS. CHERRY *coughs violently.*]

IRENE [*to* MRS. CHERRY]. No—no! Drink it right down. Like this. [*She swallows it in a gulp.*] So! [*Refills the glasses from the bottle.*] The second glass will go more easily. [*They sit.*] I used to laugh so at your funny British Tommies in Archangel. They all hated vodka until one of them thought of mixing it with beer.

MRS. CHERRY. How loathsome!

IRENE. It was! But I shall be forever grateful to them—those Tommies. They saved my life when I escaped from the Soviets. For days and nights—I don't know how many—I was driving through the snow—snow—

snow—snow—in a little sleigh, with the body of my father beside me, and the wolves running along like an escort of dragoons. You know—you always think of wolves as howling constantly, don't you?

CHERRY. Why, yes—I suppose one does.

IRENE. Well, they don't. No, these wolves didn't howl! They were horribly, confidently silent. I think silence is much more terrifying, don't you?

CHERRY. You must have been dreadfully afraid.

IRENE. No, I was not afraid for myself. It was the thought of my father. . . .

MRS. CHERRY. Please! I know you don't want to talk about it any more.

IRENE. Oh, no—it is so far away now. I shall never forget the moment when I came through the haze of delirium, and saw the faces of those Tommies. Those simple, friendly faces. And the snow—and the wolves—and the terrible cold—they were all gone— and I was looking at Kew Gardens on a Sunday afternoon, and the sea of golden daffodils—"fluttering and dancing in the breezes."

[WEBER *has come in with the daffodils.*]

WEBER. Shall we go in to dinner now, Irene?

IRENE. Yes, yes, Achille. In a minute. I am coming. [WEBER *goes.* IRENE *rises.*] Now—we must finish our vodka. [CHERRY *rises.*] And you must make another try to eat something.

CHERRY. Thank you so much, madame. [*They drink.*]

IRENE. And later on, we must all be here for Mr. Van's entertainment—and we must all applaud vigorously.

MRS. CHERRY. We shall, madame.

CHERRY. He's such a nice chap, isn't he?

IRENE [*going*]. Yes—and a real artist, too.

CHERRY. Oh—you've seen him?

IRENE. Why—yes—I've seen him, in some *café chantant,* somewhere. I forget just where it was.

[*The three of them have gone out together. The light is dimmed to extinction. The curtain falls.*]

SCENE II

About two hours later.
  WEBER *is drinking brandy. The* CAPTAIN *is standing.*

CAPTAIN. I have been listening to the radio. Utter bedlam! Of course, every government has imposed the strictest censorship—but it is very frightening—like one of those films where ghostly hands suddenly reach in and switch off all the lights.

WEBER. Any suggestions of air raids?

CAPTAIN. None. But there is ominous quiet from Paris. Think of it—Paris—utterly silent! Only one station there is sending messages, and they are in code.

WEBER. Probably instructions to the frontier.

CAPTAIN. I heard a man in Prague saying something that sounded interesting, but him I could not understand. Then I turned to London, hopefully, and listened to a gentleman describing the disastrous effects of ivy upon that traditional institution, the oak.

WEBER. Well—we shall soon know. . . . There'll be no trouble about crossing the frontier tomorrow?

CAPTAIN. Oh, no. Except that I am still a little worried about madame's passport.

WEBER. We'll arrange about that. Have a cigar, Captain?

CAPTAIN. Thank you.

[*Irene comes in as the* CAPTAIN *starts to light the cigar.*]

IRENE. Do you hear the sound of airplanes?

[*All stop to listen, intently. The sound becomes audi-*

ble. *The* CAPTAIN *shakes out the match, throws the unlit cigar on the table, and dashes to the window and looks upward.*]

CAPTAIN. It is our bombers. One—two—three. Seven of them. Seven out of eighteen. You will excuse me? [*He salutes and dashes out.*]

WEBER. Seven out of eighteen! Not bad, for Italians.

[IRENE *has gone to the window to look out.*]

IRENE. I'm so happy for you, Achille.

WEBER. What was that, my dear?

IRENE. I said—I'm so happy for you.

WEBER. But—just why am I an object of congratulation?

IRENE. All this great, wonderful death and destruction, everywhere. And you promoted it!

WEBER. Don't give me too much credit, Irene.

IRENE. But I *know* what you've done.

WEBER. Yes, my dear. You know a great deal. But don't forget to do honor to Him—up there—who put fear into man. I am but the humble instrument of His divine will.

IRENE [*looking upward, sympathetically*]. Yes—that's quite true. We don't do half enough justice to Him. Poor, lonely old soul. Sitting up in heaven, with nothing to do, but play solitaire. Poor, dear God. Playing Idiot's Delight. The game that never means anything, and never ends.

WEBER. You have an engaging fancy, my dear.

IRENE. Yes.

WEBER. It's the quality in you that fascinates me most. Limitless imagination! It is what has made you such an admirable, brilliant liar. And so very helpful to me! Am I right?

IRENE. Of course you are right, Achille. Had I been bound by any stuffy respect for the truth, I should never have escaped from the Soviets.

WEBER. I'm sure of it.

IRENE. Did I ever tell you of my escape from the Soviets?

WEBER. You have told me about it at least eleven times. And each time it was different.

IRENE. Well, I made several escapes. I am always making escapes, Achille. When I am worrying about you, and your career, I have to run away from the terror of my own thoughts. So I amuse myself by studying the faces of the people I see. Just ordinary, casual, dull people. [*She is speaking in a tone that is sweetly sadistic.*] That young English couple, for instance. I was watching them during dinner, sitting there, close together, holding hands, and rubbing their knees together under the table. And I saw him in his nice, smart, British uniform, shooting a little pistol at a huge tank. And the tank rolls over him. And his fine strong body, that was so full of the capacity for ecstasy, is a mass of mashed flesh and bones—a smear of purple blood—like a stepped-on snail. But before the moment of death, he consoles himself by thinking, "Thank God *she* is safe! She is bearing the child I gave her, and he will live to see a better world." [*She walks behind* WEBER *and leans over his shoulder.*] But I know where she is. She is lying in a cellar that has been wrecked by an air raid, and her firm young breasts are all mixed up with the bowels of a dismembered policeman, and the embryo from her womb is splattered against the face of a dead bishop. That is the kind of thought with which I amuse myself, Achille. And it makes me so proud to think that I am so close to you—who make all this possible.

[WEBER *rises and walks about the room. At length he turns to her.*]

WEBER. Do you talk in this whimsical vein to many people?

IRENE. No. I betray my thoughts to no one but you. You know that I am shut off from the world. I am a contented prisoner in your ivory tower.

WEBER. I'm beginning to wonder about that.

IRENE. What? You think I could interest myself in someone else—?

WEBER. No—no, my dear. I am merely wondering whether the time has come for you to turn commonplace, like all the others?

IRENE. The others?

WEBER. All those who have shared my life. My former wife, for instance. She now boasts that she abandoned me because part of my income is derived from the sale of poison gas. Revolvers and rifles and bullets she didn't mind—because they are also used by sportsmen. Battleships too are permissible; they look so splendid in the news films. But she couldn't stomach poison gas. So now she is married to an anemic duke, and the large fortune that she obtained from me enables the duke to indulge his principal passion, which is the slaughtering of wild animals, like rabbits, and pigeons and rather small deer. My wife is presumably happy with him. I have always been glad you are not a fool as she was, Irene.

IRENE. No. I don't care even for battleships. And I shall not marry an anemic duke.

WEBER. But—there was something unpleasantly reminiscent in that gaudy picture you painted. I gather that this silly young couple has touched a tender spot, eh?

IRENE. Perhaps, Achille. Perhaps I am softening.

WEBER. Then apply your intelligence, my dear. Ask yourself: why shouldn't they die? And who are the greater criminals—those who sell the instruments of death, or those who buy them, and use them? You know there is no logical reply to that. But all these little people—like your new friends—all of them consider me an arch-villain because I furnish them with what they want, which is the illusion of power. That is what they vote for in their frightened governments—what they cheer for on their national holidays—what they glorify in their anthems, and their monuments, and their waving flags! Yes—they shout bravely about something they call "national honor." And what does it amount to? Mistrust of the motives of everyone else! Dog in the manger defense of what they've got, and greed for the other fellow's possessions! Honor among thieves! I assure you, Irene—for such little people the deadliest weapons are the most merciful.

[*The* CHERRYS *enter. He is whistling* "Minnie the Moocher."]

IRENE. Ah! Mr. and Mrs. Cherry!

CHERRY. Hello there. [*They come down.*]

IRENE. You have dined well!

MRS. CHERRY. Superbly!

CHERRY. We ate everything—up to and including the zabaglione.

IRENE. You can thank the vodka for that. Vodka never fails in an emergency.

CHERRY. And we can thank you, madame, and do so.

IRENE. But—permit me to introduce Monsieur Weber. [WEBER *rises.*] Mrs. Cherry—Mr. Cherry. [*They are exchanging greetings as* DON *comes in.*]

DON. We're going to have a little cabaret show for you now, madame.

WEBER. I don't think I shall wait for it, my dear.

IRENE. But you must—

WEBER. I really should look over Lanza's estimates—

IRENE. Please, Achille—Mr. Van is an artist. You will be so amused.

WEBER [*resuming seat*]. Very well, Irene.

DON [*his tone blandly confidential*]. Between ourselves, I don't vouch for the quality of it. But it may be unintentionally amusing.

IRENE. I shall love it.

CHERRY. This is the most marvelous idea, Mr. Navadel.

DON. Oh, thank you. We try to contrive some novelty each evening. If you'll be good enough to sit here— [DON *goes up to usher in the* ROSSIS *and direct them to their seats.*]

[*The* MUSICIANS *come in and take their places. The* DOCTOR *comes in.* DUMPTSY *is busily moving chairs about, clearing a space for the act.* IRENE *and the* CHERRYS *chat pleasantly.* ANNA, *the maid, appears on the gallery above to watch the entertainment.* HARRY *comes in. He is wearing a tight-fitting dinner jacket, and carries a cane and a straw hat.*]

HARRY. All set, Don?

DON. Quite ready, whenever you are.

HARRY. Okey-doke. Give us a fanfare, professor. [*He goes out. The* BAND *obliges with a fanfare.* HARRY *returns, all smiles.*] Before we start, folks, I just want to explain that we haven't had much chance to rehearse with my good friend, Signor Palota, and his talented little team here. [*He indicates the* ORCHESTRA *with a handsome gesture.*] So we must crave your indulgence and beg you to give us a break if the rhythm isn't all kosher. [*He waits for his laugh.*] All we ask of you, kind friends, is "The Christian pearl of charity," to quote our great American poet, John Greenleaf Whittier. We thank you. Take it away! [*He bows. All applaud. He then sings a song— The* GIRLS *come on in costume and dance.*]

[*During the latter part of the act, the* CAPTAIN, *the*

MAJOR, and four flying corps OFFICERS *come in. The latter are dirty and in a fever of heroically restrained excitement. They survey the scene with wonderment and then with delight, saying, in Italian, "What's all this?" and "What brought these blonde bambinos to Monte Gabriele?" etc.* HARRY *interrupts the act and orders the orchestra to play the Fascist anthem, "Giovinezza." The officers acknowledge this graceful gesture with the Fascist salute. The* GIRLS *wave back. The* CAPTAIN *gets the* OFFICERS *seated and then goes to order drinks.* HARRY *and the* GIRLS *resume.*]

[*At the end of the act, all applaud and the* OFFICERS *shout "Brava—Bravissima" and stamp their feet with enthusiasm. The* GIRLS *take several bows and go.* HARRY *returns for a solo bow, waving his straw hat. One of the* OFFICERS *shouts, in Italian, "We want the young ladies!"*]

CAPTAIN [*to* HARRY]. My friends wish to know respectfully if the young ladies will care to join them in a little drink?

HARRY. Certainly! Come back in, girls. Get over there and join the army! [*The* GIRLS *do so.*] Now, folks— with your kind permission—I shall give the girls an interlude of rest and refreshment and treat you to a little piano specialty of my own. Your strict attention is not obligatory. [*He starts his specialty, assisted by* SHIRLEY *and* EDNA. *The* OFFICERS *don't pay much attention. Bottles of champagne are brought for them and the* GIRLS.]

[WEBER *goes and speaks to the* CAPTAIN. *He beckons him up to the landing of the stairs where they converse in low tones, the* CAPTAIN *telling him about the air raid.*]

[HARRY'S *act is interrupted by the entrance of* QUILLERY.]

QUILLERY [*to* HARRY]. Do you know what has happened?

DON. I told you we didn't want you here.

PITTALUGA. We're having an entertainment here.

QUILLERY. Yes! An entertainment!

HARRY. If you'll just sit down, pal . . . [*He and the* GIRLS *continue with their singing.*]

QUILLERY. An entertainment—while Paris is in ruins!

CHERRY [*rises*]. What?

DOCTOR. What are you saying?

QUILLERY. They have bombed Paris! The Fascisti have bombed Paris!

DON. What? It can't be possible—

HARRY. Go on, Shirley. Keep on singing.

QUILLERY. I tell you—tonight their planes flew over and—

CHERRY. But how do you know this?

QUILLERY. It is on the wireless—everywhere. And I have just talked to one of their mechanics, who was on the flight, and saw, with his own eyes—

HARRY. Won't you please sit down, pal? We're trying to give you a little entertainment— [*Stops playing.*]

QUILLERY. For the love of God—listen to me! While you sit here eating and drinking, tonight, Italian planes dropped twenty thousand kilos of bombs on Paris. God knows how many they killed. God knows how much of life and beauty is forever destroyed! And you sit here, drinking, laughing, with *them*— the murderers. [*Points to the* FLYERS, *who ask each other, in Italian, what the hell is he talking about.*] They did it! It was their planes, from that field down there. Assassins!

[*The* OFFICERS *make a move toward* QUILLERY—*one of them arming himself with a champagne bottle.*]

HARRY [*comes down from the piano*]. We can't have any skull-cracking in this club. Hey, Captain, speak to your men before anything starts.

[*The* CAPTAIN *comes down to the* OFFICERS *and pacifies them.* CHERRY *comes down to stand by* QUILLERY.]

MRS. CHERRY. Jimmy! . . . You keep out of this!

MAJOR *and* FIRST *and* THIRD OFFICERS [*jump up*]. Assassini!

HARRY. Now listen, pal . . .

SHIRLEY. Harry! Don't get yourself mixed up in this mess!

QUILLERY. You see, we stand together! France—England—America! Allies!

HARRY. Shut up, France! It's O.K., Captain. We can handle this—

QUILLERY. They don't dare fight against the power of England and France! The free democracies against the Fascist tyranny!

HARRY. Now, for God's sake stop fluctuating!

QUILLERY. England and France are fighting for the hopes of mankind!

HARRY. A minute ago, England was a butcher in a dress suit. Now we're Allies!

QUILLERY. We stand together. We stand together forever. [*Turns to* OFFICERS.] I say God damn you. God damn the villains that sent you on this errand of death.

CAPTAIN [*takes a few steps toward* QUILLERY]. If you don't close your mouth, Frenchman, we shall be forced to arrest you.

QUILLERY. Go on, Fascisti! Commit national suicide. That's the last gesture left to you toy soldiers.

HARRY. It's all right, Captain. Mr. Quillery is for peace. He's going back to France to stop the war.

QUILLERY [*turns on* HARRY]. You're not authorized to speak for me. I am competent to say what I feel. And what I say is "Down with Fascism! Abbasso Fascismo!"

[*There is an uproar from the* OFFICERS.]

CAPTAIN [*ordinarily gentle, is now white hot with rage*]. Attenzione!

QUILLERY. Vive la France! Viv—

CAPTAIN. E agli arresti.

QUILLERY. Call out the firing squad! Shoot me dead! But do not think you can silence the truth that's in me.

CAPTAIN [*grabs* QUILLERY *from the left and calls the* FIRST OFFICER]. Molinari! [FIRST OFFICER *grabs* QUILLERY *from the right. They start to take him out.*]

QUILLERY [*as he is being led out*]. The Empire of the Fascisti will join the Empire of the Caesars in smoking ruins. Vive la France! Vive la France!

[WEBER *goes upstairs and exits. They have gone.*]

CHERRY [*to* HARRY]. You'd better carry on with your turn, old boy.

HARRY. No, pal. The act is cold. [*To the* ORCHESTRA LEADER.] Give us some music, Signor. [*The* ORCHESTRA *starts playing.*] Let dancing become general.

CHERRY. Let's dance, my sweet.

MRS. CHERRY. I can't bear to, Jimmy.

CHERRY. I think we should.

MRS. CHERRY. Very well, darling. [*They dance. The* OFFICERS *dance with the* GIRLS.]

HARRY [*goes over to* IRENE]. Would you care to dance?

IRENE. Why—why, thank you. [*She stands up, and they join the slowly moving mob.*]

[SHIRLEY *is singing as loud as she can. The color wheel turns so that the dancers are bathed in blue, then amber, then red.*]

CURTAIN

Later that night.

IRENE *and* HARRY *are alone. She is sitting, telling the story of her life. He is listening with fascination and doubt.*

IRENE. My father was old. The hardships of that terrible journey had broken his body. But his spirit was strong—the spirit that is Russia. He lay there, in that little boat, and he looked up at me. Never can I forget his face, so thin, so white, so beautiful, in the starlight. And he said to me, "Irene—little daughter," and then—he died. For four days I was alone, with his body, sailing through the storms of the Black Sea. I had no food—no water—I was in agony from the bayonet wounds of the Bolsheviki. I knew I must die. But then—an American cruiser rescued me. May God bless those good men! [*She sighs.*] I've talked too much about myself. What about you, my friend?

HARRY. Oh—I'm not very interesting. I'm just what I seem to be.

IRENE. C'est impossible!

HARRY. C'est possible! The facts of my case are eloquent. I'm a potential genius—reduced to piloting six blondes through the Balkans.

IRENE. But there is something that you hide from the world—even, I suspect, from yourself. Where did you acquire your superior education?

HARRY. I worked my way through college selling encyclopedias.

IRENE. I knew you had culture! What college was it?

HARRY. Oh—just any college. But my sales talk was so

good that I fell for it myself. I bought the God-
damned encyclopedia. And I read it all, traveling
around, in day coaches, and depot hotels, and Fox-
time dressing rooms. It was worth the money.

IRENE. And how much of all this have you retained?

HARRY [*significantly*]. I? I—never forget anything.

IRENE. How unfortunate for you! Does your encyclopedia help you in your dealings with the girls?

HARRY. Yes, Mrs. Weber. . . . I got considerable benefit
from studying the lives of the great courtesans, and
getting to understand their technique. . . .

IRENE. Forgive me for interrupting you—but that is
not my name.

HARRY. Oh—pardon me, I thought . . .

IRENE. I know what you thought. Monsieur Weber and
I are associated in a sort of business way.

HARRY. I see.

IRENE. He does me the honor to consult me in matters
of policy.

HARRY. That's quite an honor! Business is pretty good,
isn't it!

IRENE. I gather that you are one of those noble souls
who does not entirely approve of the munitions industry?

HARRY. Oh, no—I'm not noble. Your friend is just another salesman. And I make it a point never to criticize anybody else's racket.

IRENE. Monsieur Weber is a very distinguished man.
He has rendered very distinguished services to all
the governments of the world. He is decorated with
the Legion of Honor, the Order of the White Eagle,
the Order of St. James of the Sword, and the Military Order of Christ!

HARRY. The Military Order of Christ. I never heard of
that one.

IRENE. It is from Portugal. He has many orders.

HARRY. Have you ever been in America?

IRENE. Oh, yes—I've seen it all—New York, Washington, Palm Beach . . .

HARRY. I said America. Have you ever been in the West?

IRENE. Certainly I have. I flew across your continent. There are many White Russians in California.

HARRY. Did you ever happen to make any parachute landings in any places like Kansas, or Iowa, or Nebraska?

IRENE [*laughing*]. I have seen enough of your countrymen to know that you are typical.

HARRY. Me? I'm not typical of anything.

IRENE. Oh, yes, you are. You are just like all of them— an ingenuous, sentimental idealist. You believe in the goodness of human nature, don't you?

HARRY. And what if I do? I've known millions of people, intimately—and I never found more than one out of a hundred that I didn't like, once you got to know them.

IRENE. That is very charming—but it *is* naïve.

HARRY. Maybe so. But experience prevents me from working up much enthusiasm over anyone who considers the human race as just so many clay pigeons, even if he does belong to the Military Order of Christ.

IRENE. If you came from an older culture, you would realize that men like Monsieur Weber are necessary to civilization.

HARRY. You don't say.

IRENE. I mean, of course, the sort of civilization that we have got. [*She smiles upon him benevolently. It is as though she were explaining patiently but with secret enjoyment the facts of life to a backward nephew.*] Stupid people consider him an arch-villain because it is his duty to stir up a little trouble here and there to stimulate the sale of his products. Do you understand me, my friend?

HARRY. I shouldn't wonder.

IRENE. Monsieur Weber is a true man of the world. He is above petty nationalism; he can be a Frenchman in France—a German in Germany—a Greek—a Turk —whatever the occasion demands.

HARRY. Yes—that little Quillery was an Internationalist, too. He believed in brotherhood, but the moment he got a whiff of gunpowder he began to spout hate and revenge. And now those nice, polite Wops will probably have to shut him up with a firing squad.

IRENE [*takes out a cigarette from her case*]. It is a painful necessity.

HARRY. And it demonstrates the sort of little trouble that your friend stirs up. [*He takes out his lighter and lights her cigarette.*]

IRENE. Do you know that you can be extremely rude?

HARRY. I'm sorry if I've hurt your feelings about Mr. Weber, but he just happens to be a specimen of the one per cent that I *don't* like.

IRENE. I was not referring to that. Why do you stare at me so?

HARRY. Have I been staring?

IRENE. Steadily. Ever since we arrived here this afternoon. Why do you do it?

HARRY. I've been thinking I could notice a funny resemblance to someone I used to know.

IRENE. You should know better than to tell any woman that she resembles somebody else. We none of us like to think that our appearance is commonplace.

HARRY. The one you look like wasn't commonplace.

IRENE. Oh! She was someone near and dear to you?

HARRY. It was somebody that occupies a unique shrine in the temple of my memory.

IRENE. That *is* a glowing tribute. The temple of your memory must be so crowded! But I am keeping you from your duties.

HARRY. What duties?

IRENE. Shouldn't you be worrying about your young ladies?

HARRY. They're all right; they've gone to bed.

IRENE. Yes—but there are several Italian officers about. Aren't you supposed to be the chaperon?

HARRY. I leave the girls to their own resources, of which they have plenty. [*He stares hard at her.*] Have you always been a blonde?

IRENE. Yes—as far as I can remember.

HARRY. You don't mind my asking?

IRENE. Not at all. And now, may I ask you something?

HARRY. Please do so.

IRENE. Why do you waste yourself in this degraded work? Touring about with those obvious little harlots?

HARRY. You mean you think I'm fitted for something that requires a little more mentality?

IRENE. Yes.

HARRY. How do you know so much about me? [*It should be remembered that all through this scene* HARRY *is studying her, trying to fit together the pieces of the jigsaw puzzle of his memory.*]

IRENE. For one thing, I saw your performance tonight.

HARRY. You thought it was punk?

IRENE. I thought it was unworthy.

HARRY. It was unfortunately interrupted. You should have seen . . .

IRENE. I saw enough. You are a very bad dancer.

HARRY. The King of Rumania thought I was pretty good.

IRENE. He is entitled to his opinion—and I to mine.

HARRY. I'll admit that I've done better things in my

time. Would it surprise you to know that I was once with a mind-reading act?

IRENE. Really?

HARRY. Yeah.

IRENE. Now you're staring at me again.

HARRY. Have you ever been in Omaha?

IRENE. Omaha? Where is that? Persia?

HARRY. No. Nebraska. That's one of our states. I played there once with the greatest act of my career. I was a stooge for Zuleika, the Mind Reader. At least she called me her stooge. But I was the one who had to do all the brain work.

IRENE. And she read people's minds?

HARRY. I did it for her. I passed through the audience and fed her the cues. We were sensational, playing the finest picture houses in all the key cities. Zuleika sat up on the stage, blindfolded—and usually blind drunk.

IRENE. Oh, dear. And was *she* the one that I resemble?

HARRY. No! There was another act on the same bill. A troupe of Russians . . .

IRENE. Russians?

HARRY. Singers, mandolin players, and squat dancers. One of them was a red-headed girl. She was fascinated by our act, and she kept pestering me to teach her the code. She said she could do it better than Zuleika.

IRENE. Those poor Russians. There are so many of them all over the world. And so many of them completely counterfeit!

HARRY. This dame was counterfeit all right. In fact, she was the God-damnedest liar I ever saw. She lied just for the sheer artistry of it. She kept after me so much that I told her finally to come up to my hotel room one night, and we'd talk it over.

IRENE. I hope you didn't tell her the code.

HARRY. No. After the week in Omaha the bill split. The Russians went to Sioux Falls and we went on the Interstate Time. I played with Zuleika for another year and then the drink got her and she couldn't retain. So the act busted up. I've always hoped I'd catch up with that red-headed Russian again sometime. She might have been good. She had the voice for it, and a kind of overtone of mystery.

IRENE. It's a characteristic Gypsy quality. And you never saw her again?

HARRY. No.

IRENE. Perhaps it is just as well. She couldn't have been so clever—being duped so easily into going to your room.

HARRY. She wasn't being duped! She knew what she was doing. If there was any duping going on, she was the one that did it.

IRENE. She *did* make an impression!

HARRY [*looking straight at her*]. I was crazy about her. She was womanhood at its most desirable—and most unreliable.

IRENE. And you such a connoisseur. But—it's getting late.

HARRY [*rises*]. Do you know any Russian music? [*He crosses to the piano.*]

IRENE [*rises*]. Oh, yes. When I was a little girl my father used to engage Chaliapin to come often to our house. He taught me many songs.

HARRY. Chaliapin, eh? Your father spared no expense. [*He sits at the piano.*]

IRENE. That was in *old* Russia. [*He plays a few bars of* "Kak Stranna."] "Kak Stranna!"

HARRY. Yeah! How strange! [*He starts to play* "Prostchai."] Do you know this one? [IRENE *sings some of it in Russian.*] How do you spell that name—Irene?

IRENE. I-R-E-N-E. [HARRY *pounds the piano and jumps up.*] What's the matter?

HARRY. That's it! Irene! [*He pronounces it* I-REEN.]

IRENE. But what—?

HARRY. I knew it! You're the one!

IRENE. What one?

HARRY. That red-headed liar! Irene! I knew I could never be mistaken. . . .

IRENE. Irene is a very usual name in Russia. [*She laughs heartily.*]

HARRY. I don't care how usual it is. Everything fits together perfectly now. The name—the face—the voice —Chaliapin for a teacher! Certainly it's you! And it's no good shaking your head and looking amazed! No matter how much you may lie, you can't deny the fact that you slept with me in the Governor Bryan Hotel in Omaha in the fall of 1925. [IRENE *laughs heartily again.*] All right—go ahead and laugh. That blonde hair had me fooled for a while —but now I know it's just as phony as the bayonet wounds, and the parachute jumps into the jungle. . . .

IRENE [*still laughing*]. Oh—you amuse me.

HARRY. It's a pleasure to be entertaining. But you can't get away with it.

IRENE. You amuse me very much indeed. Here we are —on a mountain peak in Bedlam. Tonight, the Italians are bombing Paris. At this moment, the French may be bombing Rome, and the English bombing Germany—and the Soviets bombing Tokyo, and all you worry about is whether I am a girl you once met casually in Omaha.

HARRY. Did I say it was casual?

IRENE [*laughing*]. Oh—it *is* amusing!

HARRY [*angrily*]. I know you're amused. I admit it's all

very funny. I've admitted everything. I told you I was crazy about you. Now when are you going to give me a break and tell me—

IRENE. You! You are so troubled—so—so uncertain about everything.

HARRY. I'm not uncertain about it any more, babe. I had you tagged from the start. There was something about you that was indelible . . . something I couldn't forget all these years.

[WEBER *appears on the gallery, wearing his Sulka dressing gown.*]

WEBER. Forgive me for intruding, my dear. But I suggest that it's time for you to go to bed.

IRENE. Yes, Achille. At once. [WEBER *treats* HARRY *to a rather disparaging glance and exits.* IRENE *starts upstairs.*] Poor Achille! He suffers with the most dreadful insomnia—it is something on his mind. [*She goes up a few more steps.*] He is like Macbeth. Good night, my friend—my funny friend.

HARRY. Good night.

IRENE. And thank you for making me laugh so much—tonight.

HARRY. I could still teach you that code.

IRENE. Perhaps—we shall meet again in—what was the name of the hotel?

HARRY. It was the Governor Bryan.

IRENE. Oh, yes! The Governor Bryan! [*Laughing heartily, she exits.*]

[HARRY *goes to the piano, sits down and starts to play* "Kak Stranna." DUMPTSY *enters from the bar.*]

DUMPTSY. That was wonderful—that singing and dancing.

HARRY [*still playing*]. Thanks, pal. Glad you enjoyed it.

DUMPTSY. Oh, yes, Mr. Van—that was good.

HARRY [*bangs a chord*]. Chaliapin—for God's *sake!*

DUMPTSY. I beg your pardon, sir?

HARRY [*rises*]. It's nothing. Good night, Dumptsy. [*He goes out into the lobby.*]

DUMPTSY. Good night, sir. [*He starts for the bar.*]

CURTAIN

Act three

The following afternoon.

HARRY *is at the piano, idly playing the "Caprice Viennoise," or something similar. His thoughts are elsewhere.*

SHIRLEY *is darning some stockings and humming the tune.* BEBE *is plucking her eyebrows.*

BEULAH, ELAINE, FRANCINE *and* EDNA *are seated at a table.* BEULAH *is telling* ELAINE'S *fortune with cards. The others are watching. All are intensely serious, and all chewing gum.*

SHIRLEY. What's that number, Harry?

HARRY. The "Caprice Viennoise"—Kreisler.

SHIRLEY. It's pretty.

HARRY. You think so? [*He shifts to something jazzier.*]

BEULAH. You are going to marry.

ELAINE. Again?

BEULAH. The cards indicate dis*tinctly* two marriages, and maybe a third.

ELAINE [*chewing furiously*]. For *God's* sake!

SHIRLEY [*to* HARRY]. We certainly need some new stockings.

HARRY. We'll renovate the wardrobe in Geneva.

BEULAH. Now—let's see what the fates tell us next.

BEBE. Say, Harry—when do we lam it out of here?

HARRY. Ask Beulah. Maybe she can get it out of the cards.

BEBE. I hate this place. It's spooky.

BEULAH [*to* HARRY]. What'd you say, honey?

ELAINE. Ah—don't pay any attention to him. What else do they say about me?

BEULAH. Well . . . you'll enter upon a period of very poor health.

ELAINE. When?

BEULAH. Along about your thirty-seventh year.

SHIRLEY. That means any day now. [*She winks broadly at* BEBE, *who laughs.*]

HARRY [*vehemently*]. Listen to me, you nymphs! We can't be wasting our time with card tricks. We've got to do a little rehearsing.

SHIRLEY. Why, Harry—what are you mad about now?

HARRY. Who said I was mad about anything?

SHIRLEY. Well—every time you get yourself into a peeve, you take it out on us. You start in hollering, "Listen, girls—we got to rehearse."

HARRY. I am not peeved. Merely a little disgusted. The act needs brushing up.

BEBE. Honestly, Harry—don't you think we know the routine by now?

HARRY. I'm not saying you don't know it. I'm just saying that your performance last night grieved me and shocked me. You had your eyes on those officers and not on your work. That kind of attitude went big in Rumania, but now we're going to a town where artistry counts. Some day, I'll take the whole bunch of you to watch the Russian ballet, just to give you an idea of what dancing is.

[CAPTAIN LOCICERO *comes in.*]

CAPTAIN. Your pardon, Mr. Van.

HARRY. Ah, Captain. Good afternoon. . . . Rest, girls.

CAPTAIN [*to the* GIRLS]. Good afternoon.

GIRLS. Good afternoon, Captain.

HARRY. You bring us news?

CAPTAIN. Good news, I hope. May I have your passports?

HARRY. Certainly. [*He gets them out of his coat and hands them to the* CAPTAIN.]

CAPTAIN. Thank you. I hope to have definite word for you very shortly. [*He salutes and starts to go.*]

HARRY. What about Mr. Quillery, Captain? What's happened to him?

CAPTAIN. Mr. Quillery was very injudicious. Very injudicious. I am glad that you are so much more intelligent. [*He goes out.*]

SHIRLEY. I don't think they could have done anything cruel to him. They're awfully sweet boys, those Wops.

HARRY. So I observed. . . . Now listen to me, girls. Geneva's a key spot, and we've got to be good. Your audiences there won't be a lot of hunkies who don't care what you do as long as you don't wear practically any pants. These people are accustomed to the best. They're mains—big people, like prime ministers, and maharajahs and archbishops. If we click with them, we'll be set for London and Paris. We may even make enough money to get us home!

BEBE. Oh—don't speak of such a thing! Home!

EDNA. To get a real decent henna wash again!

HARRY. The trouble with all of you is, you're thinking too much about your own specialties. You're trying to steal the act, and wreck it. Remember what the late Knute Rockne said: "Somebody else can have the all-star, all-American aggregations. All *I* want is a team!" Now, you—Beulah. You've got plenty of chance to score individually in the bubble number. But when we're doing the chorus routine, you've got to submerge your genius in the mass.

BEULAH. What do I do wrong, honey?

HARRY. Your Maxie Ford is lackluster. Here—I'll show you. . . . [HARRY *gets up to demonstrate the Maxie Ford.*]

SHIRLEY [*laughs*]. If you do it that way, Beulah, you'll go flat on your face. Here—*I'll* show you.

HARRY. Just a minute, Miss Laughlin. Who's the director of this act, you or me?

SHIRLEY [*amiably*]. You are, you old poop. But you just don't know the steps.

ELAINE. Don't let her get fresh, Harry.

BEBE. Slap her down!

SHIRLEY. Give us the music, Harry.

BEULAH. Please, Harry. Shirley just wants to be helpful.

HARRY. I feel I should resent this—but— [*He returns to the piano.*] Go ahead, Miss Laughlin. Carry on. [*He plays.* SHIRLEY *demonstrates.* BEULAH *tries it.*]

BEULAH. Have I got it right?

SHIRLEY. Sure! He's just shooting his face off!

[*During this, the following conversation goes on.*]

ELAINE. You know that Wop that was giving me a play last night?

FRANCINE. You mean the one with the bent nose?

BEBE. I thought he was terrible. But that boy I had is a Count.

ELAINE. Well, look what he gave me.

EDNA. What is it?

BEBE. Let me see it.

ELAINE. I don't know what it is.

BEBE. Looks like money. What kind of money is that, Harry.

HARRY. It's an old Roman coin.

SHIRLEY. How much is it worth?

HARRY. I haven't looked up the latest rate of exchange on dinars. But I think, dear, you've been betrayed. Now, pay attention, girls. . . . As I said, we've got to improve the act, and with that in view, I'm going to retire from all the dance routine.

BEBE. What?

BEULAH. Why, *Harry*—we couldn't. . . .

SHIRLEY. Oh! I hurt you, didn't I! [*She rushes to him, coos over him.*] Yes, I did, you poor baby. I hurt his feelings—and I'm sorry—I'm very, very sorry.

HARRY. All right, Shirley. We can dispense with the regrets. Save your lipstick. [*He thrusts her away.*]

SHIRLEY. But why . . . ?

HARRY. I've decided that I'm a thinker, rather than a performer. From now on, I shall devote myself to the purely creative end of the act, and, of course, the negotiation of contracts.

BEULAH. But when did you make up your mind to this, honey?

HARRY. I've been considering it for a long time.

SHIRLEY. Say! What were you talking about to that Russian dame?

HARRY. We discussed world politics.

FRANCINE. Oh!

SHIRLEY. And how are politics these days?

BEBE. Did you get anywheres near to first base, Harry?

HARRY. I find it impossible to explain certain things to you girls. You're children of nature.

SHIRLEY. We're *what?*

BEULAH. He means we're natural.

HARRY. Never mind, sweetheart. You'll sing the number, Shirley.

SHIRLEY. Me?

BEBE. With that terrible voice?

HARRY. She handled it fine that time I had bronchitis in Belgrade. And with a little rehearsal, you'll have the whole League of Nations rooting for you. Now—let's have it. [*He plays,* SHIRLEY *sings,* BEBE *disapproves.*]

[DON *comes in, dressed for traveling.*]

DON. Captain Locicero has got the orders to let us through and the train is due to leave about four o'clock. What a relief to be out of this foul place!

HARRY. You going too, Don?

DON. Yes. There's nothing for me here. In fact, I'm sick and tired of Europe as a whole. I was in town this morning when they shot Quillery.

BEBE. Who?

SHIRLEY. It was that little guy that bawled out the Wops.

BEULAH. They *shot* him? Why did they have to do that?

DON. Of course, he asked for it. But even so, it's pretty sickening to see one of your fellow human beings crumpled up in horrible, violent death. Well—there'll be plenty more like him, and right here, too. The French know all about this air base, and they'll be over any minute with their bombs. So—it's California here I come!

HARRY. And run right into the Japs? Better stop off at Wichita.

DON. I'll see you all on the train. [*He goes up the stairs.*]

HARRY. You girls go get yourselves ready.

[*The* CHERRYS *appear on the gallery.* DON *speaks to them, then goes out. The* CHERRYS *come down.*]

ELAINE. O.K., Harry.

EDNA [*going*]. I'm surprised at those Wops. They seemed like such sweet boys.

BEBE. Sure—when they talk they sound like opera. But they're awful excitable.

[BEBE, ELAINE, EDNA *and* FRANCINE *have gone out.*]

BEULAH. But I can't understand—why did they have to shoot that poor boy?

HARRY. It's hard to explain, Beulah. But it seems

there's some kind of argument going on over here, and the only way they can settle it is by murdering a lot of people.

BEULAH. You don't need to tell *me* what it's like. I was in the Club Grotto the night the Purple Gang shot it out with the G's. And was that terrible! Blood all over everything!

[SHIRLEY *and* BEULAH *have gone out.*]

HARRY. You heard what they did to Quillery?

CHERRY. Yes. It seems that he died like a true patriot, shouting "Vive La France."

HARRY. Better if he died like a man—sticking to what he knew was right.

CHERRY. He was a nice little chap.

MRS. CHERRY. The Italians are swine!

[DON *reappears on the balcony and comes down.*]

CHERRY. Oh, they had a perfect right to do it.

MRS. CHERRY. But to kill a man for saying what he thinks!

CHERRY. Many people will be killed for less than that.

HARRY. I'll have to be saying good-bye pretty soon. Did you say the train goes at four, Don?

DON. Four o'clock. Correct! [*He goes.*]

HARRY. I hope all this unpleasantness won't spoil your winter sports.

CHERRY. Oh, that's all washed up. We're going, too—if they'll let us cross the border.

HARRY. So the honeymoon has ended already?

MRS. CHERRY. Yes—I suppose so.

CHERRY. England is coming into this business. We have to stand by France, of course. And so there's nothing for it but . . .

MRS. CHERRY. And so Jimmy will have to do his bit, manning the guns, for civilization. Perhaps he'll join in the bombardment of Florence, where we were married.

CHERRY. You know—after the ceremony we went into the Baptistery and prayed to the soul of Leonardo da Vinci that we might never fail in our devotion to that which is beautiful and true. I told you we were a bit on the romantic side. We forgot what Leonardo said about war. Bestial frenzy, he called it. And bestial frenzy it is.

MRS. CHERRY. But we mustn't think about that now. We have to stand by France. We have to make the world a decent place for heroes to live in. Oh, Christ! [*She starts to sob.* CHERRY *rushes to her.*]

CHERRY. Now, now, darling. We've got to make a pretense of being sporting about it. Please, darling. Don't cry.

HARRY. Let her cry, the poor kid. Let her sob her heart out—for all the God-damned good it will do her. You know what I often think? [*He is trying to be tactful.*] I often think we ought to get together and elect somebody else God. Me, for instance. I'll bet I'd do a much better job.

MRS. CHERRY. You'd be fine, Mr. Van.

HARRY. I believe I would. There'd be a lot of people who would object to my methods. That Mr. Weber, for instance. I'd certainly begin my administration by beating the can off him.

CHERRY. Let's start the campaign now! Vote for good old Harry Van, and his Six Angels!

[*The* CAPTAIN *comes in with a brief-case full of papers and passports. He takes these out and puts them on a table.*]

CAPTAIN. Good afternoon, Mrs. Cherry. Gentlemen.

HARRY. Do we get across?

CAPTAIN. Here is your passport, Mr. Van—and the young ladies', with my compliments. They have been duly stamped. [*He hands them over.*]

HARRY. Thanks, Captain. And how about Mr. Weber

and his—friend? Are they going, too?

CAPTAIN. I have their passports here. I advise you to make ready, Mr. Van. The train will leave in about forty-five minutes.

HARRY. O.K., Captain. See you later, Mr. and Mrs. Cherry. [*He goes.*]

CHERRY. O.K., Harry.

MRS. CHERRY. And what about us, Captain?

CAPTAIN. Due to a slight technicality, you will be permitted to cross the frontier. Here are your passports.

CHERRY. I can't tell you how grateful we are.

[WEBER *appears on the gallery.*]

CAPTAIN. You needn't be grateful to me, Mr. Cherry. The fact that you are allowed to pass is due to the superb centralization of authority in my country. The telegram authorizing your release was filed at 11:43 today, just seventeen minutes before a state of war was declared between Great Britain and Italy. I must obey the order of Rome, even though I know it's out of date. Is your luggage ready?

CHERRY. It's all out here in the hall. We're off now, Captain. Well, good-bye and good luck!

CAPTAIN. And good luck to you—both of you.

CHERRY. I need hardly say that I'm sorry about all this. It's really a damned rotten shame.

CAPTAIN. It is. All of that. Good-bye, my friend. [*He extends his hand and Cherry shakes it.*] Madame. . . . [*He extends his hand to* MRS. CHERRY.]

MRS. CHERRY. Don't call *me* your friend, because I say what Quillery said—damn you—damn your whole country of mad dogs for having started this horror.

CAPTAIN [*bows*]. It is not my fault, Mrs. Cherry.

CHERRY. It's utterly unfair to talk that way, darling. The Captain is doing his miserable duty as decently as he possibly can.

CAPTAIN [*tactfully*]. In this unhappy situation, we are

all in danger of losing our heads.

MRS. CHERRY. I know . . . I know. Forgive me for the outburst. [*She extends her hand to the* CAPTAIN *and they shake.*] I should have remembered that it's everybody's fault.

CHERRY. That's right, my sweet. Come along. [*They go out.*]

CAPTAIN [*to* WEBER]. Frankly, my heart bleeds for them.

WEBER. They're young. They'll live through it, and be happy.

CAPTAIN. Will they? I was their age, and in their situation, twenty years ago, when I was sent to the Isonzo front. And people said just that to me: "Never mind, you are young—and youth will survive and come to triumph." And I believed it. That is why I couldn't say such deceiving words to them now.

WEBER. The cultivation of hope never does any immediate harm. Is everything in order?

CAPTAIN [*rises*]. Quite, Monsieur Weber. Here it is. [*He hands over* WEBER'S *passport.*]

WEBER. And Madame's?

[*The* CAPTAIN *picks up a document on foolscap.*]

CAPTAIN. This is an unusual kind of passport. It has given us some worry.

WEBER. The League of Nations issues documents like that to those whose nationality is uncertain.

CAPTAIN. I understand—but the attitude of Italy toward the League of Nations is not at the moment cordial.

WEBER. Then you refuse to honor Madame's passport?

CAPTAIN. My instructions are to accord you every consideration, Monsieur Weber. In view of the fact that Madame is traveling with you, I shall be glad to approve her visa.

WEBER. Madame is not traveling with me. She has her own passport.

CAPTAIN. But it is understood that you vouch for her, and that is enough to satisfy the authorities.

WEBER [*with cold authority*]. Vouch for her? It is not necessary for anyone to vouch for Madame! She is entirely capable of taking care of herself. If her passport is not entirely in order, it is no affair of mine.

CAPTAIN [*genuinely distressed*]. But—I must tell you, Monsieur Weber—this is something I do not like. This places me in a most embarrassing position. I shall be forced to detain her.

WEBER. You are a soldier, my dear Captain, and you should be used to embarrassing positions. Undoubtedly you were embarrassed this morning, when you had to shoot that confused pacifist, Quillery. But this is war, and unpleasant responsibilities descend upon you and on me as well. However . . . [*He sees* HARRY, *who is coming in.*] I shall attend to my luggage. Thank you, Captain. [*He goes out.*]

CAPTAIN. Don't mention it. [*To* HARRY.] The young ladies are ready?

HARRY. Yes—they're ready. And some of your aviators are out there trying to talk them into staying here permanently.

CAPTAIN [*smiling*]. And I add my entreaties to theirs.

HARRY. We won't have any more trouble, will we?

[*The* DOCTOR *appears on the gallery with coat, hat, books done in a bundle, and umbrella. He comes downstairs.*]

CAPTAIN. Oh, no, Mr. Van. Geneva is a lovely spot. All of Switzerland is beautiful, these days. I envy you going there, in such charming company.

HARRY. Hi, Doctor. Have you got the rats all packed?

DOCTOR. Good afternoon. I am privileged to go now? [*He puts down all of his belongings and crosses.*]

CAPTAIN. Yes, Dr. Waldersee. Here is your passport.

DOCTOR. Thank you. [*He examines the passport carefully.*]

HARRY. I can tell you, Doctor—I'm going to be proud to have known you. When I read in the papers that you've wiped out cancer and won the Nobel prize, and you're the greatest hero on earth, I'll be able to say, "He's a personal friend of mine. He once admired my music."

DOCTOR [*solemnly*]. Thank you very much. [*To the* CAPTAIN.] This visa is good for crossing the Austrian border?

CAPTAIN. Certainly. But you are going to Zurich?

DOCTOR [*rises*]. I have changed my plans. I am going back into Germany. Germany is at war. Perhaps I am needed. [*He crosses to pick up his coat.*]

HARRY. Needed for what?

DOCTOR. I shall offer my services for what they are worth.

[HARRY *goes to help him on with his coat.*]

HARRY. But what about the rats?

DOCTOR [*fiercely*]. Why should I save people who don't want to be saved—so that they can go out and exterminate each other? Obscene maniacs! [*Starts to put on his gloves.*] Then I'll be a maniac, too. Only I'll be more dangerous than most of them. For I know all the tricks of death! And—as for my rats, maybe they'll be useful. Britain will put down the blockade again, and we shall be starving—and maybe I'll cut my rats into filets and eat them. [*He laughs, not pleasantly, and picks up his umbrella and books.*]

HARRY. Wait a minute, Doctor. You're doing this without thinking. . . .

DOCTOR. I'm thinking probably that remedy you sold is better than mine. Hasten to apply it. We are all diseased. . . .

HARRY. But you can't change around like this! Have you forgotten all the things you told me? All that about backsliding?

DOCTOR. No, I have not forgotten the degradation of mankind—that is painful and offensive to conceive. [*He is going out.*] I am sorry to disappoint you about the Nobel prize. [*He has gone.*]

HARRY. Good-bye, Doctor. [*He sits down, wearily.*] Why in the name of God can't somebody answer the question that everybody asks? Why? Why? Oh—I know the obvious answers, but they aren't good enough. Weber—and a million like him—they can't take credit for *all* of this! Who is it that did this dirty trick on a lot of decent people? And why do you let them get away with it? That's the thing that I'd like to know!

CAPTAIN. We have avalanches up here, my friend. They are disastrous. They start with a little crack in the ice, so tiny that one cannot see it, until, suddenly, it bursts wide open. And then it is too late.

HARRY. That's very effective, Captain. But it don't satisfy me, because this avalanche isn't made out of ice. It's made out of flesh and blood—and—and *brains*. . . . It's God-damned bad management—that's what it is! [*This last is half to himself.*]

[IRENE *has appeared on the gallery and started to come down.*]

IRENE. Still upset about the situation, Mr. Van? Ah—good afternoon, my dear Captain Locicero.

CAPTAIN. Good afternoon, madame.

IRENE. I have had the most superb rest here. The atmosphere is so calm, and impersonal, and soothing. I can't bear to think that we're going to Biarritz, with the dull, dismal old sea pounding in my ears.

[WEBER *comes in.*]

IRENE. We are leaving now, Achille?

WEBER. I believe that some difficulties have arisen. [*He looks toward the* CAPTAIN.]

IRENE. Difficulties?

CAPTAIN. I regret, madame, that there must be some further delay.

IRENE. Oh! Then the train is not going through, after all?

CAPTAIN. The train is going, madame. But this passport of yours presents problems which, under the circumstances—

IRENE. Monsieur Weber will settle the problems, whatever they are. Won't you, Achille?

WEBER. There is some question about your nationality, Irene.

CAPTAIN [*referring to the passport*]. It states here, madame, that your birthplace is uncertain, but assumed to be Armenia.

IRENE. That is a province of Russia!

CAPTAIN. You subsequently became a resident of England, then of the United States, and then of France.

IRENE [*angrily*]. Yes—it's all there—clearly stated. I have never before had the slightest difficulty about my passport. It was issued by the League of Nations.

WEBER. I'm afraid the standing of the League of Nations is not very high in Italy at this moment.

CAPTAIN. The fact is, madame, the very existence of the League is no longer recognized by our government. For that reason, we can not permit you to cross the frontier at this time. [*She looks at him and then at* WEBER. *The* CAPTAIN *hands her the passport.*] I'm sure you will appreciate the delicacy of my position. Perhaps we shall be able to adjust the matter tomorrow. [*He salutes and goes out, glad to escape.* HARRY *goes with him, asking,* "What's the trouble, Captain? Can't something be done about it?"]

WEBER. I should of course wait over, Irene. But you

know how dangerous it is for me to delay my return
to France by so much as one day. I have been in
touch with our agents. The premier is demanding
that production be doubled—trebled—at once.

IRENE. Of course.

WEBER. Here— [*He takes out an envelope containing
money.*] This will cover all possible expenses. [*He
gives her the envelope.*] There is a train for Venice
this evening. You must go there and see Lanza. I
have already sent him full instructions.

IRENE. Yes, Achille. And I thank you for having man-
aged this very, very tactfully.

WEBER [*smiles*]. You are a genuinely superior person,
my dear. It is a privilege to have known you.

IRENE. Thank you again, Achille. Good-bye.

WEBER. Good-bye, Irene. [*He kisses her hand.* HARRY
returns.] Coming, Mr. Van?

HARRY. In a minute. [WEBER *goes.* IRENE *puts the
money in her handbag.*] Tough luck, babe.

IRENE. It's no matter.

HARRY. I just talked to the Captain and he isn't going
to be as brutal as the Bolsheviks were. I mean, you
won't suffer any bayonet wounds. He'll fix it for
you to get through tomorrow.

IRENE. You want to be encouraging, my dear friend.
But it's no use. The Italian government has too
many reasons for wishing to detain me. They'll see
to it that I disappear—quietly—and completely.

HARRY. Yes—I know all about that.

IRENE. All about what?

HARRY. You're a person of tremendous significance.
You always were.

[SHIRLEY *appears at the left.*]

SHIRLEY. Hey, Harry! It's time for us to go.

HARRY. I'll be right out.

[SHIRLEY *goes.*]

IRENE. Go away—go away with your friends. If I am to die, it is no concern of yours!

HARRY. Listen, babe—I haven't any wish to . . .

IRENE [*flaming*]. And please don't call me *babe!* [*She stands up and walks away from him. He follows her.*]

HARRY. My apologies, madame. I just call everybody "babe."

IRENE. Perhaps that's why I do not like it!

HARRY. Even if I don't believe anything you say, I can see pretty plainly that you're in a tough spot. And considering what we were to each other in the old Governor Bryan Hotel—

IRENE. Must you always be in Omaha?

HARRY. I'd like to help you, Irene. Isn't there something I can do?

IRENE. I thank you, from my heart, I thank you, for that offer. But it's useless. . . .

HARRY. You don't have to thank me. Tell me—what can I do?

IRENE. You're very kind, and very gallant. But, unfortunately, you're no match for Achille Weber. He has decided that I shall remain here and his decision is final!

HARRY. Is he responsible for them stopping you?

IRENE. Of course he is. I knew it the moment I saw that ashamed look on Captain Locicero's face, when he refused to permit me . . .

HARRY. So Weber double-crossed you, did he! What has the son of a bitch got against you?

IRENE. He's afraid of me. I know too much about his methods of promoting his own business.

HARRY. Everybody knows about his methods. Little Quillery was talking about them last night. . . .

IRENE. Yes—and what happened to Quillery? That's what happens to everyone who dares to criticize him. Last night I did the one thing he could never forgive. I told him the truth! At last I told him just what I think. And now—you see how quickly he strikes back!

[SHIRLEY *and* BEBE *appear.*]

SHIRLEY. Harry! The bus is going to leave.

HARRY. All right—all right!

BEBE. But we got to go this *minute!*

HARRY. I'll be with you. Get out!

SHIRLEY [*as they go*]. Can you imagine? He stops everything to make another pass at that Russian. [*They have gone.*]

IRENE. Go ahead—go ahead! You can't help me! No one can! [*He picks up his coat and hat.*] But—if it will make you any happier in your future travels with Les Blondes, I'll tell you, yes—I did know you, slightly, in Omaha!

HARRY [*peering at her*]. Are you lying again?

IRENE. It was room 974. Does that convince you?

HARRY [*ferociously*]. How can I remember what room it was?

IRENE [*smiling*]. Well, then—you'll never be sure, Mr. Van.

BEBE'S VOICE. Harry!

SHIRLEY'S VOICE. For God's sake, Harry!

DON [*appearing*]. We can't wait another instant! [*DON goes.*]

SHIRLEY'S VOICE. Come *on!*

HARRY [*he turns and starts for the door, addressing the* GIRLS *en route*]. All right, God damn it! [*He goes out.*]

[IRENE *takes out her vanity case, and does something to her face. She takes off her hat and cloak.* DUMPTSY *comes in from the back. He is wearing the uniform of a private in the Italian army, with gas mask at the alert, and a full pack on his back.*]

DUMPTSY. Good afternoon, madame.

IRENE [*turning*]. Why, Dumptsy—what is that costume?

DUMPTSY. They called me up. Look! I'm an Italian soldier.

IRENE. You look splendid!

DUMPTSY. If you please, madame. But why didn't you go on that bus?

IRENE. I've decided to stay and enjoy the winter sports.

DUMPTSY. I don't think this is a good place any more, madame. They say the war is very big—bigger than last time.

IRENE. Yes—I hear that on all sides.

DUMPTSY. The French will be here to drop bombs on everybody.

IRENE. It will be thrilling for us if they do. Won't it, Dumptsy?

DUMPTSY. Maybe it will, madame. But—I came to say good-bye to Auguste, the barman, and Anna, the maid. They're both cousins of mine. They'll laugh when they see me in these clothes. [*He goes to the left.*] Can I get you anything, madame?

IRENE. Yes, Dumptsy. I'll have a bottle of champagne. Bring two glasses. We'll have a drink together.

DUMPTSY. If you please, madame. [DUMPTSY *goes into the bar.*]

[IRENE *lights a cigarette and goes up to the window to look out.* PITTALUGA *comes in.*]

PITTALUGA. Your luggage is in the hall, madame. Will you wish it taken to the same suite?

IRENE. No—I didn't really care much for those rooms. Have you anything smaller?

PITTALUGA [*in a less deferential tone*]. We have smaller rooms on the other side of the hotel.

IRENE. I'll have the smallest. It will be cozier.

PITTALUGA. You wish to go to it now?

IRENE. No. You can send up the luggage. I'll look at it later.

[PITTALUGA *bows and goes.* DUMPTSY *returns with the champagne.*]

DUMPTSY. I was right, madame. Auguste laughed very much.

IRENE [*coming down*]. What will happen to your wife and children, Dumptsy?

DUMPTSY. Oh—I suppose the Fascisti will feed them. They promised to feed all the families with a man who is out fighting for their country. [*He has filled her glass. She sits down.*]

IRENE. Go ahead and pour yourself one, Dumptsy.

DUMPTSY. Thank you so much, madame. I wasn't sure I heard correctly.

IRENE. Here's to you, Dumptsy—and to Austria.

DUMPTSY. And to you, madame, if you please.

IRENE. Thank you. [*They drink.*]

DUMPTSY. And may you soon be restored to your home in Petersburg.

IRENE. Petersburg?

DUMPTSY. Yes, madame. Your home.

IRENE [*with a slight smile*]. Ah, yes. My home! [*They drink again.*] And have no fear for the future, Dumptsy. Whatever happens—have no fear!

DUMPTSY. If you please, madame. [*He finishes his drink.*] And now I must go find Anna, if you will excuse me.

IRENE. Here, Dumptsy. [*She hands him a note of money.*] Good-bye, and God bless you.

DUMPTSY. Thank you so much, madame. [DUMPTSY *leans over and kisses her hand.*] Kiss die hand, madame.

[*The* CAPTAIN *and* MAJOR *come in from the lobby.* DUMPTSY *salutes, strenuously, and goes out. The* MA-

JOR *goes across and into the bar. The* CAPTAIN *is following him.*]

IRENE. Some champagne, Captain?

CAPTAIN. No, thank you very much.

IRENE. You needn't be anxious to avoid me, Captain. I know perfectly well that it wasn't your fault.

CAPTAIN. You are very understanding, madame.

IRENE. Yes—that's true. I am one of the most remarkably understanding people on earth. [*She swallows her drink.*] I understand so damned much that I am here, alone, on this cold mountain, and I have no one to turn to, nowhere to go. . . .

CAPTAIN. If I can be of service to you in any way . . .

IRENE. I know you'll be kind, Captain Locicero. And faultlessly polite.

CAPTAIN [*with genuine sympathy*]. I realize, madame, that politeness means nothing now. But—under these tragic circumstances—what else can I do?

IRENE [*deliberately*]. What else can you do? I'll tell you what else you can do in these tragic circumstances. You can refuse to fight! Have you ever thought of that possibility? You can refuse to use those weapons that they have sold you! But—you were going into the bar. Please don't let me detain you.

CAPTAIN. You will forgive me, madame?

IRENE. Fully, my dear Captain. . . . Fully.

CAPTAIN. Thank you. [*He salutes and goes into the bar.*]

[IRENE *pours herself another drink. Then she picks it up, goes to the piano, and starts to play a sketchy accompaniment for "Kak Stranna." She seems to be pretty close to tears. Perhaps she does cry a little, thoroughly enjoying the emotion.* HARRY *comes in wearing his snappy overcoat and his hat. He pays no attention to her, as he takes off his coat and hat and throws them down somewhere.*]

IRENE. Did you have some trouble?

HARRY. No. Whose is that champagne?

IRENE. Mine. Won't you have some?

HARRY. Thanks.

IRENE. Dumptsy used that glass.

HARRY. That's all right. [*He fills the glass and drinks.*]

IRENE. What happened? Didn't the train go?

HARRY. Yes—the train went. . . . I got the girls on board. Mr. and Mrs. Cherry promised to look out for them. They'll be O.K.

IRENE. And you came back—to me?

HARRY [*curtly*]. It seems fairly obvious that I did come back. [*He refills his glass.*]

IRENE. You meant it when you said that you wanted to help me.

HARRY. You said I'd never be sure. Well—I came back to tell you I *am* sure! I got thinking back, in the bus, and I came to the conclusion that it *was* Room 974 or close to it, anyway. And somehow or other, I couldn't help feeling rather flattered, and touched, to think that with all the sordid hotel rooms you've been in, you should have remembered that one. [*He has some more champagne.*]

IRENE [*after a moment*]. Bayard is not dead!

HARRY. Who?

IRENE. The Chevalier Bayard.

HARRY. Oh?

IRENE. Somewhere in that funny, music-hall soul of yours is the spirit of Leander, and Abelard, and Galahad. You give up everything—risk your life— walk unafraid into the valley of the shadow—to aid and comfort a damsel in distress. Isn't that the truth?

HARRY. Yes—it's the truth—plainly and simply put. [*He pours himself more champagne and drinks it quickly.*] Listen to me, babe—when are you going to break down and tell me who the hell are you?

IRENE. Does it matter so very much who I am?

HARRY. No.

IRENE. Give me some more champagne. [HARRY *goes to her and pours.*] My father was not one of the Romanoffs. But for many years, he was their guest—in Siberia. From him I learned that it is no use telling the truth to people whose whole life is a lie. But you —Harry—you are different. You are an honest man.

HARRY [*after a short pause*]. I am—am I? [*He crosses to the bar.*] Another bottle of champagne. . . . Hi, Captain.

CAPTAIN'S VOICE [*offstage in bar*]. What has happened, Mr. Van? Did you miss the train?

HARRY. No—just a God-damned fool. [*He closes the bar door.* IRENE *is gazing at him. He goes to her and kisses her.*]

IRENE. All these years—you've been surrounded by blondes—and you've loved only me!

HARRY. Now listen—we don't want to have any misunderstanding. If you're hooking up with me, it's only for professional reasons—see?

IRENE. Yes—I see.

HARRY. And what's more, I'm the manager. I'll fix it with the Captain for us to cross the border tomorrow, or the next day, or soon. We'll join up with the girls in Geneva—and that's as good a place as any to rehearse the code.

IRENE. The code! Of *course*—the code! I shall learn it easily.

HARRY. It's a very deep complicated scientific problem.

IRENE. You must tell it to me at once.

HARRY. At once! If you're unusually smart and apply yourself you'll have a fairly good idea of it after six months of study and rehearsal.

IRENE. A mind reader! Yes—you're quite right. I shall be able to do that very well!

[AUGUSTE *enters from the bar with a bottle of champagne. He refills their glasses, then refills* HARRY'S *glass, gives* HARRY *the bottle and goes back in to the bar.*]

HARRY. And, another thing, if you're going to qualify for this act with me, you've got to lay off liquor. I mean, after we finish this. It's a well-known fact that booze and science don't mix. [*He has another drink.* IRENE *is as one in a trance.*]

IRENE. I don't think I shall use my own name. No—Americans would mispronounce it horribly. No, I shall call myself—Namoura . . . Namoura the Great —assisted by Harry Van.

HARRY. You've got nice billing there.

IRENE. I shall wear a black velvet dress—very plain— My skin, ivory white. I must have something to hold. One white flower. No! A little white prayer book. That's it. A little white . . . [*The warning siren is heard.*] What's that?

HARRY. Sounds like a fire. [*The* CAPTAIN *and* MAJOR *burst out of the bar and rush to the big window, talking excitedly in Italian and pointing to the northwestern sky. The siren shrieks continue. The* MAJOR *then rushes out, the* CAPTAIN *about to follow him.*] What's up, Captain?

CAPTAIN. French aeroplanes. It is reprisal for last night. They are coming to destroy our base here.

HARRY. I see.

CAPTAIN. They have no reason to attack this hotel. But —there may easily be accidents. I advise the cellar.

[AUGUSTE *rushes in from the bar,* PITTALUGA *from the lobby. The latter orders* AUGUSTE *to lower the Venetian blinds.*]

IRENE. Oh, no, Captain. We must stay here and watch the spectacle.

CAPTAIN. I entreat you not to be reckless, madame. I have enough on my conscience now, without adding to it your innocent life!

IRENE. Don't worry, Captain. Death and I are old friends.

CAPTAIN. God be with you, madame. [*He goes out.*]

[HARRY *and* IRENE *empty their glasses.* HARRY *refills them. Airplane motors are heard, increasing. Then the sound of machine guns. Bombs are heard bursting at some distance.* AUGUSTE *and* PITTALUGA *go.*]

IRENE. Those are bombs.

HARRY. I guess so.

IRENE. We're in the war, Harry.

HARRY. What do you think we ought to do about it? Go out and say "Boo"?

IRENE. Let them be idiotic if they wish. We are sane. Why don't you try singing something?

HARRY. The voice don't feel appropriate. Too bad we haven't got Chaliapin here. [*She laughs.*] You know, babe—you look better blonde.

IRENE. Thank you.

[PITTALUGA *runs in.*]

PITTALUGA. The French beasts are bombing us! Everyone goes into the cellar.

HARRY. Thanks very much, Signor.

PITTALUGA. You have been warned! [*He rushes out.*]

IRENE. Ridiculous! Here we are, on top of the world— and he asks us to go down into the cellar. . . . Do you want to go into the cellar?

HARRY. Do you?

IRENE. No. If a bomb hits, it will be worse in the cellar. [*He holds her close to him. She kisses him.*] I love you, Harry.

HARRY. You do, eh!

IRENE. Ever since that night—in the Governor Bryan Hotel—I've loved you. Because I knew that you have a heart that I can trust. And that whatever I would say to you, I would never—*never* be misunderstood.

HARRY. That's right, babe. I told you I had you tagged, right from the beginning.

IRENE. And you adore me, don't you, darling?

HARRY. No! Now lay off—

IRENE. No—of course not—you mustn't admit it!

HARRY. Will you please stop pawing me? [*She laughs and lets go of him.*]

[HARRY *pours more champagne, as she crosses to the window, opens the slats of the blinds, and looks out. There is now great noise of planes, machine guns and bombs.*]

IRENE. Oh, you must see this! It's superb! [*He crosses to the window with his glass and looks out. The light on the stage is growing dimmer, but a weird light comes from the window. The scream of many gas bombs is heard.*] It's positively Wagnerian—isn't it?

HARRY. It looks to me exactly like "Hell's Angels." Did you ever see that picture, babe?

IRENE. No. I don't care for films.

HARRY. I *do*. I love 'em—every one of them. [*He is dragging her to the piano—a comparatively safe retreat.*] Did you know I used to play the piano in picture theatres? Oh, sure—I know all the music there is. [*They are now at the piano—*HARRY *sitting,* IRENE *standing close by him. She is looking toward the window. He starts to accompany the air raid with the* "Ride of the Valkyries." *There is a loud explosion.*]

IRENE. Harry . . .

HARRY. Yes, babe?

IRENE. Harry—do you realize that the whole world has gone to war? The *whole world!*

HARRY. I realize it. But don't ask me why. Because I've stopped trying to figure it out.

IRENE. I know why it is. It's just for the purpose of killing *us* . . . you and me. [*There is another loud explosion.* HARRY *stops playing.*] Because we are the little people—and for us the deadliest weapons are the most merciful. . . .

[*Another loud explosion.* HARRY *drinks.*]

HARRY. They're getting closer.

IRENE. Play some more. [*He resumes the* "Valkyrie."] Harry—do you know any hymns?

HARRY. What?

IRENE. Do you know any hymns?

HARRY. Certainly. [*He starts to play* "Onward, Christian Soldiers" *in furious jazz time, working in strains of* "Dixie." *There is another fearful crash, shattering the pane of the big window. He drags her down beside him at the piano.* HARRY *resumes* "Onward, Christian Soldiers" *in a slow, solemn tempo.*]

HARRY [*sings*]. Onward, Christian Soldiers—

[IRENE *joins the loud singing.*]

BOTH [*singing*].
>   Marching as to war—
>   With the Cross of Jesus
>   Going on before. . . .

[*The din is now terrific. Demolition-bombs, gas-bombs, airplanes, shrapnel, machine guns.*]

CURTAIN

OF MICE AND MEN

by John Steinbeck

SYNOPSIS OF SCENES

ACT I

Scene 1. *A Sandy bank of the Salinas River.*
         Thursday night.
Scene 2. *The interior of a bunkhouse. Late Friday*
         morning.

ACT II

Scene 1. *The same as Act I, Scene 2. About seven-thirty*
         Friday evening.
Scene 2. *The room of the stable buck, a lean-to.*
         Ten o'clock Saturday evening.

ACT III

Scene 1. *One end of a great barn. Mid-afternoon, Sunday.*
Scene 2. *Same as Act I, Scene 1.*

TIME: *The present.*
PLACE: *An agricultural valley in Southern California.*

Act one

Thursday night.

A sandy bank of the Salinas River sheltered with willows—one giant sycamore right, upstage.

The stage is covered with dry leaves. The feeling of the stage is sheltered and quiet.

Stage is lit by a setting sun.

Curtain rises on an empty stage. A sparrow is singing. There is a distant sound of ranch dogs barking aimlessly and one clear quail call. The quail call turns to a warning call and there is a beat of the flock's wings. Two figures are seen entering the stage in single file, with GEORGE, *the short man, coming in ahead of* LENNIE. *Both men are carrying blanket rolls. They approach the water. The small man throws down his blanket roll, the large man follows and then falls down and drinks from the river, snorting as he drinks.*

GEORGE [*irritably*]. Lennie, for God's sake, don't drink so much. [*Leans over and shakes* LENNIE.] Lennie, you hear me! You gonna be sick like you was last night.

LENNIE [*dips his whole head under, hat and all. As he sits upon the bank, his hat drips down the back*]. That's good. You drink some, George. You drink some too.

GEORGE [*kneeling and dipping his finger in the water*]. I ain't sure it's good water. Looks kinda scummy to me.

LENNIE [*imitates, dipping his finger also*]. Look at them wrinkles in the water, George. Look what I done.

GEORGE [*drinking from his cupped palm*]. Tastes all right. Don't seem to be runnin' much, though. Lennie, you oughtn' to drink water when it ain't running. [*Hopelessly.*] You'd drink water out of a gutter if you was thirsty. [*He throws a scoop of water into his face and rubs it around with his hand, pushes himself back and embraces his knees. LENNIE, after watching him, imitates him in every detail.*]

GEORGE [*beginning tiredly and growing angry as he speaks*]. God damn it, we could just as well of rode clear to the ranch. That bus driver didn't know what he was talkin' about. "Just a little stretch down the highway," he says. "Just a little stretch" —damn near four miles. I bet he didn't want to stop at the ranch gate. . . . I bet he's too damn lazy to pull up. Wonder he ain't too lazy to stop at Soledad at all! [*Mumbling.*] Just a little stretch down the road.

LENNIE [*timidly*]. George?

GEORGE. Yeh . . . what you want?

LENNIE. Where we goin', George?

GEORGE [*jerks down his hat furiously*]. So you forgot that already, did you? So I got to tell you again! Jeez, you're a crazy bastard!

LENNIE [*softly*]. I forgot. I tried not to forget, honest to God, I did!

GEORGE. Okay, okay, I'll tell you again. . . . [*With sarcasm.*] I ain't got nothin' to do. Might just as well spen' all my time tellin' you things. You forgit 'em and I tell you again.

LENNIE [*continuing on from his last speech*]. I tried

and tried, but it didn't do no good. I remember about the rabbits, George!

GEORGE. The hell with the rabbits! You can't remember nothing but them rabbits. You remember settin' in that gutter on Howard Street and watchin' that blackboard?

LENNIE [*delightedly*]. Oh, sure! I remember that . . . but . . . wha'd we do then? I remember some girls come by, and you says—

GEORGE. The hell with what I says! You remember about us goin' in Murray and Ready's and they give us work cards and bus tickets?

LENNIE [*confidently*]. Oh, sure, George . . . I remember that now. [*Puts his hand into his side coat-pocket; his confidence vanishes. Very gently.*] . . . George?

GEORGE. Huh?

LENNIE [*staring at the ground in despair*]. I ain't got mine. I musta lost it.

GEORGE. You never had none. I got both of 'em here. Think I'd let you carry your own work card?

LENNIE [*with tremendous relief*]. I thought I put it in my side pocket. [*Puts his hand in his pocket again.*]

GEORGE [*looking sharply at him; and as he looks, LENNIE brings his hand out of his pocket*]. Wha'd you take out of that pocket?

LENNIE [*cleverly*]. Ain't a thing in my pocket.

GEORGE. I know there ain't. You got it in your hand now. What you got in your hand?

LENNIE. I ain't got nothing, George! Honest!

GEORGE. Come on, give it here!

LENNIE [*holds his closed hand away from GEORGE*]. It's on'y a mouse!

GEORGE. A mouse? A live mouse?

LENNIE. No . . . just a dead mouse. [*Worriedly.*] I didn't kill it. Honest. I found it. I found it dead.

GEORGE. Give it here!

LENNIE. Leave me have it, George.

GEORGE [*sternly*]. Give it here! [LENNIE *reluctantly gives him the mouse.*] What do you want of a dead mouse, anyway?

LENNIE [*in a propositional tone*]. I was petting it with my thumb while we walked along.

GEORGE. Well, you ain't pettin' no mice while you walk with me. Now let's see if you can remember where we're going. [GEORGE *throws it across the water into the brush.*]

LENNIE [*looks startled and then in embarrassment hides his face against his knees*]. I forgot again.

GEORGE. Jesus Christ! [*Resignedly.*] Well, look, we are gonna work on a ranch like the one we come from up north.

LENNIE. Up north?

GEORGE. In Weed!

LENNIE. Oh, sure I remember—in Weed.

GEORGE [*still with exaggerated patience*]. That ranch we're goin' to is right down there about a quarter mile. We're gonna go in and see the boss.

LENNIE [*repeats as a lesson*]. And see the boss!

GEORGE. Now, look! I'll give him the work tickets, but you ain't gonna say a word. You're just gonna stand there and not say nothing.

LENNIE. Not say nothing!

GEORGE. If he finds out what a crazy bastard you are, we won't get no job. But if he sees you work before he hears you talk, we're set. You got that?

LENNIE. Sure, George . . . sure, I got that.

GEORGE. Okay. Now when we go in to see the boss, what you gonna do?

LENNIE [*concentrating*]. I . . . I . . . I ain't gonna say nothing . . . jus' gonna stand there.

GEORGE [*greatly relieved*]. Good boy, that's swell! Now

say that over two or three times so you sure won't forget it.

LENNIE [*drones softly under his breath*]. I ain't gonna say nothing . . . I ain't gonna say nothing. . . . [*Trails off into a whisper.*]

GEORGE. And you ain't gonna do no bad things like you done in Weed neither.

LENNIE [*puzzled*]. Like I done in Weed?

GEORGE. So you forgot that too, did you?

LENNIE [*triumphantly*]. They run us out of Weed!

GEORGE [*disgusted*]. Run us out, hell! We run! They was lookin' for us, but they didn't catch us.

LENNIE [*happily*]. I didn't forget that, you bet.

GEORGE [*lies back on the sand, crosses his hands under his head. And again* LENNIE *imitates him*]. God, you're a lot of trouble! I could get along so easy and nice, if I didn't have you on my tail. I could live so easy!

LENNIE [*hopefully*]. We gonna work on a ranch, George.

GEORGE. All right, you got that. But we're gonna sleep here tonight, because . . . I want to. I want to sleep out.

[*The light is going fast, dropping into evening. A little wind whirls into the clearing and blows leaves. A dog howls in the distance.*]

LENNIE. Why ain't we goin' on to the ranch to get some supper? They got supper at the ranch.

GEORGE. No reason at all. I just like it here. Tomorrow we'll be goin' to work. I seen thrashing machines on the way down; that means we'll be buckin' grain bags. Bustin' a gut liftin' up them bags. Tonight I'm gonna lay right here an' look up! Tonight there ain't a grain bag or a boss in the world.

Tonight, the drinks is on the . . . house. Nice house we got here, Lennie.

LENNIE [*gets up on his knees and looks down at* GEORGE, *plaintively*]. Ain't we gonna have no supper?

GEORGE. Sure we are. You gather up some dead willow sticks. I got three cans of beans in my bindle. I'll open 'em up while you get a fire ready. We'll eat 'em cold.

LENNIE [*companionably*]. I like beans with ketchup.

GEORGE. Well, we ain't got no ketchup. You go get the wood, and don't you fool around none. Be dark before long. [LENNIE *lumbers to his feet and disappears into the brush.* GEORGE *gets out the bean cans, opens two of them, suddenly turns his head and listens. A little sound of splashing comes from the direction that* LENNIE *has taken.* GEORGE *looks after him; shakes his head.* LENNIE *comes back carrying a few small willow sticks in his hand.*] All right, give me that mouse.

LENNIE [*with elaborate pantomime of innocence*]. What, George? I ain't got no mouse.

GEORGE [*holding out his hand*]. Come on! Give it to me! You ain't puttin' nothing over. [LENNIE *hesitates, backs away, turns and looks as if he were going to run. Coldly*]. You gonna give me that mouse or do I have to take a sock at you?

LENNIE. Give you what, George?

GEORGE. You know goddamn well, what! I want that mouse!

LENNIE [*almost in tears*]. I don't know why I can't keep it. It ain't nobody's mouse. I didn' steal it! I found it layin' right beside the road. [GEORGE *snaps his fingers sharply, and* LENNIE *lays the mouse in his hand.*] I wasn't doin' nothing bad with it. Just stroking it. That ain't bad.

GEORGE [*stands up and throws the mouse as far as he can into the brush, then he steps to the pool, and washes his hands*]. You crazy fool! Thought you could get away with it, didn't you? Don't you think I could see your feet was wet where you went in the water to get it? [LENNIE *whimpers like a puppy.*] Blubbering like a baby. Jesus Christ, a big guy like you! [LENNIE *tries to control himself, but his lips quiver and his face works with an effort.* GEORGE *puts his hand on* LENNIE's *shoulder for a moment.*] Aw, Lennie, I ain't takin' it away just for meanness. That mouse ain't fresh. Besides, you broke it pettin' it. You get a mouse that's fresh and I'll let you keep it a little while.

LENNIE. I don't know where there is no other mouse. I remember a lady used to give 'em to me. Ever' one she got she used to give it to me, but that lady ain't here no more.

GEORGE. Lady, huh! . . . Give me them sticks there. . . . Don't even remember who that lady was. That was your own Aunt Clara. She stopped givin' 'em to you. You always killed 'em.

LENNIE [*sadly and apologetically*]. They was so little. I'd pet 'em and pretty soon they bit my fingers and then I pinched their head a little bit and then they was dead . . . because they was so little. I wish we'd get the rabbits pretty soon, George. They ain't so little.

GEORGE. The hell with the rabbits! Come on, let's eat. [*The light has continued to go out of the scene so that when* GEORGE *lights the fire, it is the major light on the stage.* GEORGE *hands one of the open cans of beans to* LENNIE.] There's enough beans for four men.

LENNIE [*sitting on the other side of the fire, speaks patiently*]. I like 'em with ketchup.

GEORGE [*explodes*]. Well, we ain't got any. Whatever we ain't got, that's what you want. God Almighty, if I was alone, I could live so easy. I could go get a job of work and no trouble. No mess . . . and when the end of the month come, I could take my fifty bucks and go into town and get whatever I want. Why, I could stay in a cat-house all night. I could eat any place I want. Order any damn thing.

LENNIE [*plaintively, but softly*]. I didn't want no ketchup.

GEORGE [*continuing violently*]. I could do that every damn month. Get a gallon of whiskey or set in a pool room and play cards or shoot pool. [LENNIE *gets up to his knees and looks over the fire, with frightened face.*] And what have I got? [*Disgustedly.*] I got *you.* You can't keep a job and you lose me every job I get!

LENNIE [*in terror*]. I don't mean nothing, George.

GEORGE. Just keep me shovin' all over the country all the time. And that ain't the worst—you get in trouble. You do bad things and I got to get you out. It ain't bad people that raises hell. It's dumb ones. [*He shouts.*] You crazy son-of-a-bitch, you keep me in hot water all the time. [LENNIE *is trying to stop* GEORGE's *flow of words with his hands. Sarcastically.*] You just wanta feel that girl's dress. Just wanta pet it like it was a mouse. Well, how the hell'd she know you just wanta feel her dress? How'd she know you'd just hold onto it like it was a mouse?

LENNIE [*in panic*]. I didn't mean to, George!

GEORGE. Sure you didn't mean to. You didn't mean for her to yell bloody hell, either. You didn't mean for us to hide in the irrigation ditch all day with guys out lookin' for us with guns. Alla time it's something you didn't mean. God damn it, I wish I could put you in a cage with a million mice and let them pet *you.* [GEORGE's *anger leaves him suddenly. For the first time he seems to see the expression of terror on* LENNIE's *face. He looks down ashamedly at the fire, and maneuvers some beans onto the blade of his pocket-knife and puts them into his mouth.*]

LENNIE [*after a pause*]. George! [GEORGE *purposely does not answer him.*] George?

GEORGE. What do you want?

LENNIE. I was only foolin', George. I don't want no ketchup. I wouldn't eat no ketchup if it was right here beside me.

GEORGE [*with a sullenness of shame*]. If they was some here you could have it. And if I had a thousand bucks I'd buy ya a bunch of flowers.

LENNIE. I wouldn't eat no ketchup, George. I'd leave it all for you. You could cover your beans so deep with it, and I wouldn't touch none of it.

GEORGE [*refusing to give in from his sullenness, refusing to look at* LENNIE]. When I think of the swell time I could have without you, I go nuts. I never git no peace!

LENNIE. You want I should go away and leave you alone?

GEORGE. Where the hell could you go?

LENNIE. Well, I could . . . I could go off in the hills there. Some place I could find a cave.

GEORGE. Yeah, how'd ya eat? You ain't got sense enough to find nothing to eat.

LENNIE. I'd find things. I don't need no nice food with ketchup. I'd lay out in the sun and nobody would hurt me. And if I found a mouse—why, I could keep it. Wouldn't nobody take it away from me.

GEORGE [*at last he looks up*]. I been mean, ain't I?

LENNIE [*presses his triumph*]. If you don't want me, I can go right in them hills, and find a cave. I can go away any time.

GEORGE. No. Look! I was just foolin' ya. 'Course I want you to stay with me. Trouble with mice is you always kill 'em. [*He pauses.*] Tell you what I'll do, Lennie. First chance I get I'll find you a pup. Maybe you wouldn't kill it. That would be better than mice. You could pet it harder.

LENNIE [*still avoiding being drawn in*]. If you don't want me, you only gotta say so. I'll go right up on them hills and live by myself. And I won't get no mice stole from me.

GEORGE. I want you to stay with me. Jesus Christ, somebody'd shoot you for a coyote if you was by yourself. Stay with me. Your Aunt Clara wouldn't like your runnin' off by yourself, even if she is dead.

LENNIE. George?

GEORGE. Huh?

LENNIE [*craftily*]. Tell me—like you done before.

GEORGE. Tell you what?

LENNIE. About the rabbits.

GEORGE [*near to anger again*]. You ain't gonna put nothing over on me!

LENNIE [*pleading*]. Come on, George . . . tell me! Please! Like you done before.

GEORGE. You get a kick out of that, don't you? All right, I'll tell you. And then we'll lay out our beds and eat our dinner.

LENNIE. Go on, George. [*Unrolls his bed and lies on his side, supporting his head on one hand.* GEORGE *lays out his bed and sits cross-legged on it.* GEORGE *repeats the next speech rhythmically, as though he had said it many times before.*]

GEORGE. Guys like us that work on ranches is the loneliest guys in the world. They ain't got no family. They don't belong no place. They come to a ranch and work up a stake and then they go in to town and blow their stake. And then the first thing you know they're poundin' their tail on some other ranch. They ain't got nothin' to look ahead to.

LENNIE [*delightedly*]. That's it, that's it! Now tell how it is with us.

GEORGE [*still almost chanting*]. With us it ain't like that. We got a future. We got somebody to talk to that gives a damn about us. We don't have to sit in no barroom blowin' in our jack, just because we got no place else to go. If them other guys gets in jail, they can rot for all anybody gives a damn.

LENNIE [*who cannot restrain himself any longer. Bursts into speech.*] But not us! And why? Because . . . because I got you to look after me . . . and you got me to look after you . . . and that's why! [*He laughs.*] Go on, George!

GEORGE. You got it by heart. You can do it yourself.

LENNIE. No, no. I forget some of the stuff. Tell about how it's gonna be.

GEORGE. Some other time.

LENNIE. No, tell how it's gonna be!

GEORGE. Okay. Some day we're gonna get the jack together and we're gonna have a little house, and a couple of acres and a cow and some pigs and . . . .

LENNIE [*shouting*]. And live off the fat of the land! And have rabbits. Go on, George! Tell about what we're gonna have in the garden. And about the rabbits in the cages. Tell about the rain in the winter . . . and about the stove and how thick the cream is on the milk, you can hardly cut it. Tell about that, George!

GEORGE. Why don't you do it yourself—you know all of it!

LENNIE. It ain't the same if I tell it. Go on now. How I get to tend the rabbits.

GEORGE [*resignedly*]. Well, we'll have a big vegetable patch and a rabbit hutch and chickens. And when it rains in the winter we'll just say to hell with goin' to work. We'll build up a fire in the stove, and set around it and listen to the rain comin' down on the roof— Nuts! [*Begins to eat with his knife.*] I ain't got time for no more. [*He falls to eating.* LENNIE *imitates him, spilling a few beans from his mouth with every bite.* GEORGE, *gesturing with his knife.*] What you gonna say tomorrow when the boss asks you questions?

LENNIE [*stops chewing in the middle of a bite, swallows painfully. His face contorts with thought*]. I . . . I ain't gonna say a word.

GEORGE. Good boy. That's fine. Say, maybe you're gettin' better. I bet I can let you tend the rabbits . . . specially if you remember as good as that!

LENNIE [*choking with pride*]. I can remember, by God!

GEORGE [*as though remembering something, points his knife at* LENNIE's *chest*]. Lennie, I want you to look around here. Think you can remember this place? The ranch is 'bout a quarter mile up that way. Just follow the river and you can get here.

LENNIE [*looking around carefully*]. Sure, I can remember here. Didn't I remember 'bout not gonna say a word?

GEORGE. 'Course you did. Well, look, Lennie, if you just happen to get in trouble, I want you to come right here and hide in the brush.

LENNIE [*slowly*]. Hide in the brush.

GEORGE. Hide in the brush until I come for you. Think you can remember that?

LENNIE. Sure I can, George. Hide in the brush till you come for me!

GEORGE. But you ain't gonna get in no trouble. Because if you do I won't let you tend the rabbits.

LENNIE. I won't get in no trouble. I ain't gonna say a word.

GEORGE. You got it. Anyways, I hope so. [GEORGE *stretches out on his blankets. The light dies slowly out of the fire until only the faces of the two men can be seen.* GEORGE *is still eating from his can of beans.*] It's gonna be nice sleeping here. Lookin' up . . . and the leaves . . . Don't build no more fire. We'll let her die. Jesus, you feel free when you ain't got a job—if you ain't hungry.

[*They sit silently for a few moments. A night owl is heard far off. From across the river there comes the sound of a coyote howl and on the heels of the howl all the dogs in the country start to bark.*]

LENNIE [*from almost complete darkness*]. George?

GEORGE. What do you want?

LENNIE. Let's have different color rabbits, George.

GEORGE. Sure. Red rabbits and blue rabbits and green rabbits. Millions of 'em!

LENNIE. Furry ones, George. Like I seen at the fair in Sacramento.

GEORGE. Sure. Furry ones.

LENNIE. 'Cause I can jus' as well go away, George, and live in a cave.

GEORGE [*amiably*]. Aw, shut up.

LENNIE [*after a long pause*]. George?

GEORGE. What is it?

LENNIE. I'm shutting up, George.

[*A coyote howls again.*]

CURTAIN

SCENE II

Late Friday morning.
  The interior of a bunkhouse.

Walls, white-washed board and bat. Floors un-painted.

There is a heavy square table with upended boxes around it used for chairs. Over each bunk there is a box nailed to the wall which serves as two shelves on which are the private possessions of the working men.

On top of each bunk there is a large noisy alarm clock ticking madly.

The sun is streaking through the windows. Note: Articles in the boxes on wall are soap, talcum powder, razors, pulp magazines, medicine bottles, combs, and from nails on the sides of the boxes a few neckties.

There is a hanging light from the ceiling over the table, with a round dim reflector on it.

The curtain rises on an empty stage. Only the ticking of the many alarm clocks is heard.

CANDY, GEORGE *and* LENNIE *are first seen passing the open window of the bunkhouse.*

CANDY. This is the bunkhouse here. Door's around this side. [*The latch on the door rises and* CANDY *enters, a stoop-shouldered old man. He is dressed in blue jeans and a denim coat. He carries a big push broom in his left hand. His right hand is gone at the wrist. He grasps things with his right arm between arm and side. He walks into the room followed by* GEORGE *and* LENNIE. *Conversationally.*] The boss was expecting you last night. He was sore as hell when you wasn't here to go out this morning. [*Points with his handless arm.*] You can have them two beds there.

GEORGE. I'll take the top one . . . I don't want you falling down on me. [*Steps over to the bunk and throws his blankets down. He looks into the nearly empty box shelf over it, then picks up a small yellow can.*] Say, what the hell's this?

CANDY. I don't know.

GEORGE. Says "positively kills lice, roaches and other scourges." What the hell kinda beds you givin' us, anyway? We don't want no pants rabbits.

CANDY [*shifts his broom, holding it between his elbow and his side, takes the can in his left hand and studies the label carefully*]. Tell you what . . . last guy that had this bed was a blacksmith. Helluva nice fellow. Clean a guy as you'd want to meet. Used to wash his hands even *after* he et.

GEORGE [*with gathering anger*]. Then how come he got pillow-pigeons?

[LENNIE *puts his blankets on his bunk and sits down, watching* GEORGE *with his mouth slightly open*.]

CANDY. Tell you what. This here blacksmith, name of Whitey, was the kinda guy that would put that stuff around even if there wasn't no bugs. Tell you what he used to do. He'd peel *his* boiled potatoes and take out every little spot before he et it, and if there was a red splotch on an egg, he'd scrape it off. Finally quit about the food. That's the kind of guy Whitey was. Clean. Used to dress up Sundays even when he wasn't goin' no place. Put on a necktie even, and then set in the bunkhouse.

GEORGE [*skeptically*]. I ain't so sure. What da' ya say he quit for?

CANDY [*puts the can in his pocket, rubs his bristly white whiskers with his knuckles*]. Why . . . he just quit the way a guy will. Says it was the food. Didn't give no other reason. Just says "give me my time" one night, the way any guy would.

[GEORGE *lifts his bed tick and looks underneath, leans over and inspects the sacking carefully.* LENNIE *does the same with his bed.*]

GEORGE [*half satisfied*]. Well, if there's any gray-backs in this bed, you're gonna hear from me!

[*He unrolls his blankets and puts his razor and bar of soap and comb and bottle of pills, his liniment and leather wristband in the box.*]

CANDY. I guess the boss'll be out here in a minute to write your name in. He sure was burned when you wasn't here this morning. Come right in when we was eatin' breakfast and says, "Where the hell's them new men?" He give the stable buck hell, too. Stable buck's a nigger.

GEORGE. Nigger, huh!

CANDY. Yeah. [*Continues.*] Nice fellow too. Got a crooked back where a horse kicked him. Boss gives him hell when he's mad. But the stable buck don't give a damn about that.

GEORGE. What kinda guy is the boss?

CANDY. Well, he's a pretty nice fella for a boss. Gets mad sometimes. But he's pretty nice. Tell you what. Know what he done Christmas? Brung a gallon of whiskey right in here and says, "Drink hearty, boys, Christmas comes but once a year!"

GEORGE. The hell he did! A whole gallon?

CANDY. Yes, sir. Jesus, we had fun! They let the nigger come in that night. Well, sir, a little skinner named Smitty took after the nigger. Done pretty good too. The guys wouldn't let him use his feet so the nigger got him. If he could a used his feet Smitty says he would have killed the nigger. The guys says on account the nigger got a crooked back Smitty can't use his feet. [*He smiles in reverie at the memory.*]

GEORGE. Boss the owner?

CANDY. Naw! Superintendent. Big land company. . . . Yes, sir, that night . . . he comes right in here with a whole gallon . . . he set right over there and says, "Drink hearty, boys," . . . he says. . . . [*The door opens. Enter the* BOSS. *He is a stocky man, dressed in blue jean trousers, flannel shirt, a black unbuttoned vest and a black coat. He wears a soiled brown Stetson hat, a pair of high-heeled boots and spurs. Ordinarily he puts his thumbs in his belt.* CANDY, *shuffling towards the door, rubbing his whiskers with his knuckles as he goes.*] Them guys just come. [CANDY *exits and shuts the door behind him.*]

BOSS. I wrote Murray and Ready I wanted two men this morning. You got your work slips?

GEORGE [*digs in his pockets, produces two slips, and hands them to the* BOSS]. Here they are.

BOSS [*reading the slips*]. Well, I see it wasn't Murray and Ready's fault. It says right here on the slip, you was to be here for work this morning.

GEORGE. Bus driver give us a bum steer. We had to walk ten miles. That bus driver says we was here when we wasn't. We couldn't thumb no rides. [GEORGE *scowls meaningly at* LENNIE *and* LENNIE *nods to show that he understands.*]

BOSS. Well, I had to send out the grain teams short two buckers. It won't do any good to go out now until after dinner. You'd get lost. [*Pulls out his time book, opens it to where a pencil is stuck between the leaves. Licks his pencil carefully.*] What's your name?

GEORGE. George Milton.

BOSS. George Milton. [*Writing.*] And what's yours?

GEORGE. His name's Lennie Small.

BOSS. Lennie Small. [*Writing.*] Le's see, this is the twentieth. Noon the twentieth . . . [*Makes positive mark. Closes the book and puts it in his pocket.*] Where you boys been workin'?

GEORGE. Up around Weed.

BOSS [*to* LENNIE]. You too?

GEORGE. Yeah. Him too.

BOSS [*to* LENNIE]. Say, you're a big fellow, ain't you?

GEORGE. Yeah, he can work like hell, too.

BOSS. He ain't much of a talker, though, is he?

GEORGE. No, he ain't. But he's a hell of a good worker. Strong as a bull.

LENNIE [*smiling*]. I'm strong as a bull.

[GEORGE *scowls at him and* LENNIE *drops his head in shame at having forgotten.*]

BOSS [*sharply*]. You are, huh? What can you do?

GEORGE. He can do anything.

BOSS [*addressing* LENNIE]. What can you do?

[LENNIE, *looking at* GEORGE, *gives a high nervous chuckle.*]

GEORGE [*quickly*]. Anything you tell him. He's a good skinner. He can wrestle grain bags, drive a cultivator. He can do anything. Just give him a try.

BOSS [*turning to* GEORGE]. Then why don't you let *him* answer? [LENNIE *laughs.*] What's he laughing about?

GEORGE. He laughs when he gets excited.

BOSS. Yeah?

GEORGE [*loudly*]. But he's a goddamn good worker. I ain't saying he's bright, because he ain't. But he can put up a four hundred pound bale.

BOSS [*hooking his thumbs in his belt*]. Say, what you sellin'?

GEORGE. Huh?

BOSS. I said what stake you got in this guy? You takin' his pay away from him?

GEORGE. No. Of course I ain't!

BOSS. Hell, I never seen one guy take so much trouble for another guy. I just like to know what your percentage is.

GEORGE. He's my . . . cousin. I told his ole lady I'd take care of him. He got kicked in the head by a horse when he was a kid. He's all right. . . . Just ain't bright. But he can do anything you tell him.

BOSS [*turning half away*]. Well, God knows he don't need no brains to buck barley bags. [*He turns back.*]

But don't you try to put nothing over, Milton. I got my eye on you. Why'd you quit in Weed?

GEORGE [*promptly*]. Job was done.

BOSS. What kind of job?

GEORGE. Why . . . we was diggin' a cesspool.

BOSS [*after a pause*]. All right. But don't try to put nothing over 'cause you can't get away with nothing. I seen wise guys before. Go out with the grain teams after dinner. They're out pickin' up barley with the thrashin' machines. Go out with Slim's team.

GEORGE. Slim?

BOSS. Yeah. Big, tall skinner. You'll see him at dinner. [*Up to this time the* BOSS *has been full of business. He has been calm and suspicious. In the following lines he relaxes, but gradually, as though he wanted to talk but felt always the burden of his position. He turns toward the door, but hesitates and allows a little warmth into his manner.*] Been on the road long?

GEORGE [*obviously on guard*]. We was three days in 'Frisco lookin' at the boards.

BOSS [*with heavy jocularity*]. Didn't go to no night clubs, I 'spose?

GEORGE [*stiffly*]. We was lookin' for a job.

BOSS [*attempting to be friendly*]. That's a great town if you got a little jack, Frisco.

GEORGE [*refusing to be drawn in*]. We didn't have no jack for nothing like that.

BOSS [*realizes there is no contact to establish; grows rigid with his position again*]. Go out with the grain teams after dinner. When my hands work hard they get pie and when they loaf they bounce down the road on their can. You ask anybody about me. [*He turns and walks out of the bunkhouse.*]

GEORGE [*turns to* LENNIE]. So you wasn't gonna say a word! You was gonna leave your big flapper shut. I was gonna do the talkin'. . . . You goddamn near lost us the job!

LENNIE [*stares hopelessly at his hands*]. I forgot.

GEORGE. You forgot. You always forget. Now, he's got his eye on us. Now, we gotta be careful and not make no slips. You keep your big flapper shut after this.

LENNIE. He talked like a kinda nice guy towards the last.

GEORGE [*angrily*]. He's the boss, ain't he? Well, he's the boss first an' a nice guy afterwards. Don't you have nothin' to do with no boss, except do your work and draw your pay. You can't never tell whether you're talkin' to the nice guy or the boss. Just keep your goddamn mouth shut. Then you're all right.

LENNIE. George?

GEORGE. What you want now?

LENNIE. I wasn't kicked in the head with no horse, was I, George?

GEORGE. Be a damn good thing if you was. Save everybody a hell of a lot of trouble!

LENNIE [*flattered*]. You says I was your cousin.

GEORGE. Well, that was a goddamn lie. And I'm glad it was. Why, if I was a relative of yours— [*He stops and listens, then steps to the front door, and looks out.*] Say, what the hell you doin', listenin'?

CANDY [*comes slowly into the room. By a rope, he leads an ancient drag-footed, blind sheep dog. Guides it from running into a table leg, with the rope. Sits down on a box, and presses the hind quarters of the old dog down*]. Naw . . . I wasn't listenin'. . . . I was just standin' in the shade a minute, scratchin' my dog. I jest now finished swamping out the washhouse.

GEORGE. You was pokin' your big nose into our business! I don't like nosey guys.

CANDY [*looks uneasily from* GEORGE *to* LENNIE *and then back*]. I jest come there . . . I didn't hear nothing you guys was sayin'. I ain't interested in nothing you was sayin'. A guy on a ranch don't never listen. Nor he don't ast no questions.

GEORGE [*slightly mollified*]. Damn right he don't! Not if the guy wants to stay workin' long. [*His manner changes.*] That's a helluva ole dog.

CANDY. Yeah. I had him ever since he was a pup. God, he was a good sheep dog, when he was young. [*Rubs his cheek with his knuckles.*] How'd you like the boss?

GEORGE. Pretty good! Seemed all right.

CANDY. He's a nice fella. You got ta take him right, of course. He's runnin' this ranch. He don't take no nonsense.

GEORGE. What time do we eat? Eleven-thirty?

[CURLEY *enters. He is dressed in working clothes. He wears brown high-heeled boots and has a glove on his left hand.*]

CURLEY. Seen my ole man?

CANDY. He was here just a minute ago, Curley. Went over to the cookhouse, I think.

CURLEY. I'll try to catch him. [*Looking over at the new men, measuring them. Unconsciously bends his elbow and closes his hand and goes into a slight crouch. He walks gingerly close to* LENNIE.] You the new guys my ole man was waitin' for?

GEORGE. Yeah. We just come in.

CURLEY. How's it come you wasn't here this morning?

GEORGE. Got off the bus too soon.

CURLEY [*again addressing* LENNIE]. My ole man got to get the grain out. Ever bucked barley?

GEORGE [*quickly*]. Hell, yes. Done a lot of it.

CURLEY. I mean him. [*To* LENNIE.] Ever bucked barley?

GEORGE. Sure he has.

CURLEY [*irritatedly*]. Let the big guy talk!

GEORGE. 'Spose he don't want ta talk?

CURLEY [*pugnaciously*]. By Christ, he's gotta talk when he's spoke to. What the hell you shovin' into this for?

GEORGE [*stands up and speaks coldly*]. Him and me travel together.

CURLEY. Oh, so it's that way?

GEORGE [*tense and motionless*]. What way?

CURLEY [*letting the subject drop*]. And you won't let the big guy talk? Is that it?

GEORGE. He can talk if he wants to tell you anything. [*He nods slightly to* LENNIE.]

LENNIE [*in a frightened voice*]. We just come in.

CURLEY. Well, next time you answer when you're spoke to, then.

GEORGE. He didn't do nothing to you.

CURLEY [*measuring him*]. You drawin' cards this hand?

GEORGE [*quietly*]. I might.

CURLEY [*stares at him for a moment, his threat moving to the future*]. I'll see you get a chance to ante, anyway. [*He walks out of the room.*]

GEORGE [*after he has made his exit*]. Say, what the hell's he got on his shoulder? Lennie didn't say nothing to him.

CANDY [*looks cautiously at the door*]. That's the boss's son. Curley's pretty handy. He done quite a bit in the ring. The guys say he's pretty handy.

GEORGE. Well, let 'im be handy. He don't have to take after Lennie. Lennie didn't do nothing to him.

CANDY [*considering*]. Well . . . tell you what, Curley's like a lot a little guys. He hates big guys. He's alla time pickin' scraps with big guys. Kinda like he's mad at 'em because *he* ain't a big guy. You seen little guys like that, ain't you—always scrappy?

GEORGE. Sure, I seen plenty tough little guys. But this here Curley better not make no mistakes about Lennie. Lennie ain't handy, see, but this Curley punk's gonna get hurt if he messes around with Lennie.

CANDY [*skeptically*]. Well, Curley's pretty handy. You know, it never did seem right to me. 'Spose Curley jumps a big guy and licks him. Everybody says what a game guy Curley is. Well, 'spose he jumps 'im and gits licked, everybody says the big guy oughta pick somebody his own size. Seems like Curley ain't givin' nobody a chance.

GEORGE [*watching the door*]. Well, he better watch out for Lennie. Lennie ain't no fighter. But Lennie's strong and quick and Lennie don't know no rules. [*Walks to the square table, and sits down on one of the boxes. Picks up scattered cards and pulls them together and shuffles them.*]

CANDY. Don't tell Curley I said none of this. He'd slough me! He jus' don't give a damn. Won't ever get canned because his ole man's the boss!

GEORGE [*cuts the cards. Turns over and looks at each one as he throws it down*]. This guy Curley sounds like a son-of-a-bitch to me! I don't like mean little guys!

CANDY. Seems to me like he's worse lately. He got married a couple of weeks ago. Wife lives over in the boss's house. Seems like Curley's worse'n ever since he got married. Like he's settin' on a ant-hill an' a big red ant come up an' nipped 'im on the turnip. Just feels so goddamn miserable he'll strike at anything that moves. I'm kinda sorry for 'im.

GEORGE. Maybe he's showin' off for his wife.

CANDY. You seen that glove on his left hand?

GEORGE. Sure I seen it!

CANDY. Well, that glove's full of vaseline.

GEORGE. Vaseline? What the hell for?

CANDY. Curley says he's keepin' that hand soft for his wife.

GEORGE. That's a dirty kind of a thing to tell around.

CANDY. I ain't quite so sure. I seen such funny things a guy will do to try to be nice. I ain't sure. But you jus' wait till you see Curley's wife!

GEORGE [*begins to lay out a solitaire hand, speaks casually*]. Is she purty?

CANDY. Yeah. Purty, but—

GEORGE [*studying his cards*]. But what?

CANDY. Well, she got the eye.

GEORGE [*still playing at his solitaire hand*]. Yeah? Married two weeks an' got the eye? Maybe that's why Curley's pants is fulla ants.

CANDY. Yes, sir, I seen her give Slim the eye. Slim's a jerkline skinner. Hell of a nice fella. Well, I seen her give Slim the eye. Curley never seen it. And I seen her give a skinner named Carlson the eye.

GEORGE [*pretending a very mild interest*]. Looks like we was gonna have fun!

CANDY [*stands up*]. Know what I think? [*Waits for an answer.* GEORGE *doesn't answer.*] Well, I think Curley's married himself a tart.

GEORGE [*casually*]. He ain't the first. Black queen on a red king. Yes, sir . . . there's plenty done that!

CANDY [*moves towards the door, leading his dog out with him*]. I got to be settin' out the wash basins for the guys. The teams'll be in before long. You guys gonna buck barley?

GEORGE. Yeah.

CANDY. You won't tell Curley nothing I said?

GEORGE. Hell, no!

CANDY [*just before he goes out the door, he turns back*]. Well, you look her over, mister. You see if she ain't a tart! [*He exits.*]

GEORGE [*continuing to play out his solitaire. He turns to* LENNIE]. Look, Lennie, this here ain't no set-up. You gonna have trouble with that Curley guy. I seen that kind before. You know what he's doin'. He's kinda feelin' you out. He figures he's got you scared. And he's gonna take a sock at you, first chance he gets.

LENNIE [*frightened*]. I don't want no trouble. Don't let him sock me, George!

GEORGE. I hate them kind of bastards. I seen plenty of 'em. Like the ole guy says: "Curley don't take no chances. He always figures to win." [*Thinks for a moment.*] If he tangles with you, Lennie, we're goin' get the can. Don't make no mistake about that. He's the boss's kid. Look, you try to keep away from him, will you? Don't never speak to him. If he comes in here you move clear to the other side of the room. Will you remember that, Lennie?

LENNIE [*mourning*]. I don't want no trouble. I never done nothing to him!

GEORGE. Well, that won't do you no good, if Curley wants to set himself up for a fighter. Just don't have nothing to do with him. Will you remember?

LENNIE. Sure, George . . . I ain't gonna say a word. [*Sounds of the teams coming in from the fields, jingling of harness, croak of heavy laden axles, men talking to and cussing the horses. Crack of a whip and from a distance a voice calling.*]

SLIM'S VOICE. Stable buck! Hey! Stable buck!

GEORGE. Here come the guys. Just don't say nothing.

LENNIE [*timidly*]. You ain't mad, George?

GEORGE. I ain't mad at you. I'm mad at this here Curley bastard! I wanted we should get a little stake together. Maybe a hundred dollars. You keep away from Curley.

LENNIE. Sure I will. I won't say a word.

GEORGE [*hesitating*]. Don't let 'im pull you in—but— if the son-of-a-bitch socks you—let him have it!

LENNIE. Let him have what, George?

GEORGE. Never mind. . . . Look, if you get in any kind of trouble, you remember what I told you to do.

LENNIE. If I get in any trouble, you ain't gonna let me tend the rabbits?

GEORGE. That's not what I mean. You remember where we slept last night. Down by the river?

LENNIE. Oh, sure I remember. I go there and hide in the brush until you come for me.

GEORGE. That's it. Hide till I come for you. Don't let nobody see you. Hide in the brush by the river. Now say that over.

LENNIE. Hide in the brush by the river. Down in the brush by the river.

GEORGE. If you get in trouble.

LENNIE. If I get in trouble.

[*A brake screeches outside and a call: "Stable buck, oh, stable buck!" "Where the hell's that goddamn nigger?" Suddenly* CURLEY'S WIFE *is standing in the door. Full, heavily rouged lips. Wide-spaced, made-up eyes, her fingernails are bright red, her hair hangs in little rolled clusters like sausages. She wears a cotton house dress and red mules, on the insteps of which are little bouquets of red ostrich feathers.* GEORGE *and* LENNIE *look up at her.*]

CURLEY'S WIFE. I'm lookin' for Curley!

GEORGE [*looks away from her*]. He was in here a minute ago but he went along.

CURLEY'S WIFE [*puts her hands behind her back and leans against the door frame so that her body is thrown forward*]. You're the new fellas that just come, ain't you?

GEORGE [*sullenly*]. Yeah.

CURLEY'S WIFE [*bridles a little and inspects her fingernails*]. Sometimes Curley's in here.

GEORGE [*brusquely*]. Well, he ain't now!

CURLEY'S WIFE [*playfully*]. Well, if he ain't, I guess I'd better look some place else.

[LENNIE *watches her, fascinated.*]

GEORGE. If I see Curley I'll pass the word you was lookin' for him.

CURLEY'S WIFE. Nobody can't blame a person for lookin'.

GEORGE. That depends what she's lookin' for.

CURLEY'S WIFE [*a little wearily, dropping her coquetry*]. I'm jus' lookin' for somebody to talk to. Don't you never jus' want to talk to somebody?

SLIM [*offstage*]. Okay! Put that lead pair in the north stalls.

CURLEY'S WIFE [*to* SLIM, *offstage*]. Hi, Slim!

SLIM [*voice offstage*]. Hello.

CURLEY'S WIFE. I—I'm trying to find Curley.

SLIM'S VOICE [*offstage*]. Well, you ain't tryin' very hard. I seen him goin' in your house.

CURLEY'S WIFE. I—I'm tryin' to find Curley. I gotta be goin'! [*She exits hurriedly.*]

GEORGE [*looking around at* LENNIE]. Jesus, what a tramp! So, that's what Curley picks for a wife. God Almighty, did you smell that stink she's got on? I can still smell her. Don't have to see *her* to know she's around.

LENNIE. She's purty!

GEORGE. Yeah. And she's sure hidin' it. Curley's got his work ahead of him.

LENNIE [*still staring at the doorway where she was*]. Gosh, she's purty!

GEORGE [*turning furiously at him*]. Listen to me, you crazy bastard. Don't you even look at that bitch. I don't care what she says or what she does. I seen 'em poison before, but I ain't never seen no piece of jail bait worse than her. Don't you even smell near her!

LENNIE. I never smelled, George!

GEORGE. No, you never. But when she was standin' there showin' her legs, you wasn't lookin' the other way neither!

LENNIE. I never meant no bad things, George. Honest I never.

GEORGE. Well, you keep away from her. You let Curley take the rap. He let himself in for it. [*Disgustedly.*] Glove full of vaseline. I bet he's eatin' raw eggs and writin' to patent-medicine houses.

LENNIE [*cries out*]. I don't like this place. This ain't no good place. I don't like this place!

GEORGE. Listen—I don't like it here no better than you do. But we gotta keep it till we get a stake. We're flat. We gotta get a stake. [*Goes back to the table, thoughtfully.*] If we can get just a few dollars in the poke we'll shove off and go up to the American River and pan gold. Guy can make a couple dollars a day there.

LENNIE [*eagerly*]. Let's go, George. Let's get out of here. It's mean here.

GEORGE [*shortly*]. I tell you we gotta stay a little while. We gotta get a stake. [*The sounds of running water and rattle of basins are heard.*] Shut up now, the guys'll be comin' in! [*Pensively.*] Maybe we ought to wash up. . . . But hell, we ain't done nothin' to get dirty.

SLIM [*enters. He is a tall, dark man in blue jeans and a short denim jacket. He carries a crushed Stetson hat under his arm and combs his long dark damp hair straight back. He stands and moves with a kind of majesty. He finishes combing his hair. Smooths out his crushed hat, creases it in the middle and puts it on. In a gentle voice].* It's brighter'n a bitch outside. Can't hardly see nothing in here. You the new guys?

GEORGE. Just come.

SLIM. Goin' to buck barley?

GEORGE. That's what the boss says.

SLIM. Hope you get on my team.

GEORGE. Boss said we'd go with a jerk-line skinner named Slim.

SLIM. That's me.

GEORGE. You a jerk-line skinner?

SLIM [*in self-disparagement*]. I can snap 'em around a little.

GEORGE [*terribly impressed*]. That kinda makes you Jesus Christ on this ranch, don't it?

SLIM [*obviously pleased*]. Oh, nuts!

GEORGE [*chuckles*]. Like the man says, "The boss tells you what to do. But if you want to know how to do it, you got to ask the mule skinner." The man says any guy that can drive twelve Arizona jack rabbits with a jerk line can fall in a toilet and come up with a mince pie under each arm.

SLIM [*laughing*]. Well, I hope you get on my team. I got a pair a punks that don't know a barley bag from a blue ball. You guys ever bucked any barley?

GEORGE. Hell, yes. I ain't nothin' to scream about, but that big guy there can put up more grain alone than most pairs can.

SLIM [*looks approvingly at* GEORGE]. You guys travel around together?

GEORGE. Sure. We kinda look after each other. [*Points*

at LENNIE *with his thumb.*] He ain't bright. Hell of a good worker, though. Hell of a nice fella too. I've knowed him for a long time.

SLIM. Ain't many guys travel around together. I don't know why. Maybe everybody in the whole damn world is scared of each other.

GEORGE. It's a lot nicer to go 'round with a guy you know. You get used to it an' then it ain't no fun alone any more.

[*Enter* CARLSON. *Big-stomached, powerful man. His head still drips water from scrubbing and dousing.*]

CARLSON. Hello, Slim! [*He looks at* GEORGE *and* LENNIE.]

SLIM. These guys just come.

CARLSON. Glad to meet ya! My name's Carlson.

GEORGE. I'm George Milton. This here's Lennie Small.

CARLSON. Glad to meet you. He ain't very small. [*Chuckles at his own joke.*] He ain't small at all. Meant to ask you, Slim, how's your bitch? I seen she wasn't under your wagon this morning.

SLIM. She slang her pups last night. Nine of 'em. I drowned four of 'em right off. She couldn't feed that many.

CARLSON. Got five left, huh?

SLIM. Yeah. Five. I kep' the biggest.

CARLSON. What kinda dogs you think they gonna be?

SLIM. I don't know. Some kind of shepherd, I guess. That's the most kind I seen around here when she's in heat.

CARLSON [*laughs*]. I had an airedale an' a guy down the road got one of them little white floozy dogs, well, she was in heat and the guy locks her up. But my airedale, named Tom he was, he et a woodshed clear down to the roots to get to her. Guy come over one day, he's sore as hell, he says, "I wouldn't mind if my bitch had pups, but Christ Almighty, this

morning she slang a litter of Shetland ponies. . . ."
[*Takes off his hat and scratches his head.*] Got five
pups, huh! Gonna keep all of 'em?

SLIM. I don' know, gotta keep 'em awhile, so they can
drink Lulu's milk.

CARLSON [*thoughtfully*]. Well, looka here, Slim, I been
thinkin'. That dog of Candy's is so goddamn old he
can't hardly walk. Stinks like hell. Every time Candy
brings him in the bunkhouse, I can smell him two
or three days. Why don't you get Candy to shoot his
ol' dog, and give him one of them pups to raise up?
I can smell that dog a mile off. Got no teeth. Can't
eat. Candy feeds him milk. He can't chew nothing
else. And leadin' him around on a string so he don't
bump into things . . . [*The triangle outside begins
to ring wildly. Continues for a few moments, then
stops suddenly.*] There she goes!

[*Outside there is a burst of voices as a group of men
go by.*]

SLIM [*to* LENNIE *and* GEORGE]. You guys better come on
while they's still somethin' to eat. Won't be nothing left in a couple of minutes. [*Exit* SLIM *and* CARL-
SON, LENNIE *watches* GEORGE *excitedly.*]

LENNIE. George!

GEORGE [*rumpling his cards into a pile*]. Yeah, I heard
'im, Lennie . . . I'll ask 'im!

LENNIE [*excitedly*]. A brown and white one.

GEORGE. Come on, let's get dinner. I don't know
whether he's got a brown and white one.

LENNIE. You ask him, right away, George, so he won't
kill no more of 'em!

GEORGE. Sure! Come on now—le's go. [*They start for
the door.*]

CURLEY [*bounces in, angrily*]. You seen a girl around
here?

GEORGE [*coldly*]. 'Bout half an hour ago, mebbe.

CURLEY. Well, what the hell was she doin'?

GEORGE [*insultingly*]. She *said* she was lookin' for you.

CURLEY [*measures both men with his eyes for a moment*]. Which way did she go?

GEORGE. I don't know. I didn't watch her go. [CURLEY *scowls at him a moment and then turns and hurries out the door.*] You know, Lennie, I'm scared I'm gonna tangle with that bastard myself. I hate his guts! Jesus Christ, come on! They won't be a damn thing left to eat.

LENNIE. Will you ask him about a brown and white one? [*They exeunt.*]

CURTAIN

Act two

SCENE I

About seven-thirty Friday evening.

Same bunkhouse interior as in last scene.

The evening light is seen coming in through the window, but it is quite dark in the interior of the bunkhouse.

From outside comes the sound of a horseshoe game. Thuds on the dirt and occasional clangs as a shoe hits the peg. Now and then voices are raised in approval or derision: "That's a good one." . . . "Goddamn right it's a good one." . . . "Here goes for a ringer. I need a ringer." . . . "Goddamn near got it, too."

SLIM *and* GEORGE *come into the darkening bunk-house together.* SLIM *reaches up and turns on the tin-*

shaded electric light. Sits down on a box at the table.
GEORGE *takes his place opposite.*

SLIM. It wasn't nothing. I would of had to drown most of them pups anyway. No need to thank me about that.

GEORGE. Wasn't much to you, mebbe, but it was a hell of a lot to him. Jesus Christ, I don't know how we're gonna get him to sleep in here. He'll want to stay right out in the barn. We gonna have trouble keepin' him from gettin' right in the box with them pups.

SLIM. Say, you sure was right about him. Maybe he ain't bright—but I never seen such a worker. He damn near killed his partner buckin' barley. He'd take his end of that sack [*a gesture*], pretty near kill his partner. God Almighty, I never seen such a strong guy.

GEORGE [*proudly*]. You just tell Lennie what to do and he'll do it if it don't take no figuring.

[*Outside the sound of the horseshoe game goes on: "Son of a bitch if I can win a goddamn game."* . . . *"Me neither. You'd think them shoes was anvils."*]

SLIM. Funny how you and him string along together.

GEORGE. What's so funny about it?

SLIM. Oh, I don't know. Hardly none of the guys ever travels around together. I hardly never seen two guys travel together. You know how the hands are. They come in and get their bunk and work a month and then they quit and go on alone. Never seem to give a damn about nobody. Jest seems kinda funny. A cuckoo like him and a smart guy like you traveling together.

GEORGE. I ain't so bright neither or I wouldn't be buckin' barley for my fifty and found. If I was bright, if I was even a little bit smart, I'd have my own place and I'd be bringin' in my own crops 'stead of doin' all the work and not gettin' what comes up out of the ground. [*He falls silent for a moment.*]

SLIM. A guy'd like to do that. Sometimes I'd like to cuss a string of mules that was my own mules.

GEORGE. It ain't so funny, him and me goin' round together. Him and me was both born in Auburn. I knowed his aunt. She took him when he was a baby and raised him up. When his aunt died Lennie jus' come along with me, out workin'. Got kinda used to each other after a little while.

SLIM. Uh huh.

GEORGE. First I used to have a hell of a lot of fun with him. Used to play jokes on him because he was too dumb to take care of himself. But, hell, he was too dumb even to know when he had a joke played on him. [*Sarcastically.*] Hell, yes, I had fun! Made me seem goddamn smart alongside of him.

SLIM. I seen it that way.

GEORGE. Why, he'd do any damn thing I tole him. If I tole him to walk over a cliff, over he'd go. You know that wasn't so damn much fun after a while. He never got mad about it, neither. I've beat hell out of him and he could bust every bone in my body jest with his hands. But he never lifted a finger against me.

SLIM [*braiding a bull whip*]. Even if you socked him, wouldn't he?

GEORGE. No, by God! I tell you what made me stop playing jokes. One day a bunch of guys was standin' aroun' up on the Sacramento River. I was feelin' pretty smart. I turns to Lennie and I says, "Jump in."

SLIM. What happened?

GEORGE. He jumps. Couldn't swim a stroke. He damn

near drowned. And he was so nice to me for pullin' him out. Clean forgot I tole him to jump in. Well, I ain't done nothin' like that no more. Makes me kinda sick tellin' about it.

SLIM. He's a nice fella. A guy don't need no sense to be a nice fella. Seems to be sometimes it's jest the other way round. Take a real smart guy, he ain't hardly ever a nice fella.

GEORGE [*stacking the scattered cards and getting his solitaire game ready again*]. I ain't got no people. I seen guys that go round on the ranches alone. That ain't no good. They don't have no fun. After a while they get mean.

SLIM [*quietly*]. Yeah, I seen 'em get mean. I seen 'em get so they don't want to talk to nobody. Some ways they got to. You take a bunch of guys all livin' in one room an' by God they got to mind their own business. 'Bout the only private thing a guy's got is where he come from and where he's goin'.

GEORGE. 'Course Lennie's a goddamn nuisance most of the time. But you get used to goin' round with a guy and you can't get rid of him. I mean you get used to him an' you can't get rid of bein' used to him. I'm sure drippin' at the mouth. I ain't told nobody all this before.

SLIM. Do you want to get rid of him?

GEORGE. Well, he gets in trouble all the time. Because he's so goddamn dumb. Like what happened in Weed. [*He stops, alarmed at what he has said.*] You wouldn't tell nobody?

SLIM [*calmly*]. What did he do in Weed?

GEORGE. You wouldn't tell?—No, 'course you wouldn't.

SLIM. What did he do?

GEORGE. Well, he seen this girl in a red dress. Dumb bastard like he is he wants to touch everything he likes. Jest wants to feel of it. So he reaches out to feel this red dress. Girl let's out a squawk and that gets Lennie all mixed up. He holds on 'cause that's the only thing he can think to do.

SLIM. The hell!

GEORGE. Well, this girl squawks her head off. I'm right close and I hear all the yellin', so I comes a-running. By that time Lennie's scared to death. You know, I had to sock him over the head with a fence picket to make him let go.

SLIM. So what happens then?

GEORGE [*carefully building his solitaire hand*]. Well, she runs in and tells the law she's been raped. The guys in Weed start out to lynch Lennie. So there we sit in an irrigation ditch, under water all the rest of that day. Got only our heads stickin' out of water, up under the grass that grows out of the side of the ditch. That night we run outa there.

SLIM. Didn't hurt the girl none, huh?

GEORGE. Hell, no, he jes' scared her.

SLIM. He's a funny guy.

GEORGE. Funny! Why, one time, you know what that big baby done! He was walking along a road— [*Enter* LENNIE *through the door. He wears his coat over his shoulder like a cape and walks hunched over.*] Hi, Lennie. How do you like your pup?

LENNIE [*breathlessly*]. He's brown and white jus' like I wanted. [*Goes directly to his bunk and lies down. Face to the wall and knees drawn up.*]

GEORGE [*puts down his cards deliberately*]. Lennie!

LENNIE [*over his shoulder*]. Huh? What you want, George?

GEORGE [*sternly*]. I tole ya, ya couldn't bring that pup in here.

LENNIE. What pup, George? I ain't got no pup.

[GEORGE *goes quickly over to him, grabs him by the shoulder and rolls him over. He picks up a tiny puppie from where* LENNIE *has been concealing it against his stomach.*]

LENNIE [*quickly*]. Give him to me, George.

GEORGE. You get right up and take this pup to the nest. He's got to sleep with his mother. Ya want ta kill him? Jes' born last night and ya take him out of the nest. Ya take him back or I'll tell Slim not to let you have him.

LENNIE [*pleadingly*]. Give him to me, George. I'll take him back. I didn't mean no bad thing, George. Honest I didn't. I jus' want to pet him a little.

GEORGE [*giving the pup to him*]. All right, you get him back there quick. And don't you take him out no more.

[LENNIE *scuttles out of the room.*]

SLIM. Jesus, he's just like a kid, ain't he?

GEORGE. Sure he's like a kid. There ain't no more harm in him than a kid neither, except he's so strong. I bet he won't come in here to sleep tonight. He'll sleep right alongside that box in the barn. Well, let him. He ain't doin' no harm out there.

[*The light has faded out outside and it appears quite dark outside. Enter* CANDY *leading his old dog by a string.*]

CANDY. Hello, Slim. Hello, George. Didn't neither of you play horseshoes?

SLIM. I don't like to play every night.

CANDY [*goes to his bunk and sits down, presses the old blind dog to the floor beside him*]. Either you guys got a slug of whiskey? I got a gut ache.

SLIM. I ain't. I'd drink it myself if I had. And I ain't got no gut ache either.

CANDY. Goddamn cabbage give it to me. I knowed it was goin' to before I ever et it.

[*Enter* CARLSON *and* WHIT.]

CARLSON. Jesus, how that nigger can pitch shoes!

SLIM. He's plenty good.

WHIT. Damn right he is.

CARLSON. Yeah. He don't give nobody else a chance to win. [*Stops and sniffs the air. Looks around until he sees* CANDY's *dog.*] God Almighty, that dog stinks. Get him outa here, Candy. I don't know nothing that stinks as bad as ole dogs. You got to get him outa here.

CANDY [*lying down on his bunk, reaches over and pats the ancient dog, speaks softly*]. I been round him so much I never notice how he stinks.

CARLSON. Well, I can't stand him in here. That stink hangs round even after he's gone. [*Walks over and stands looking down at the dog.*] Got no teeth. All stiff with rheumatism. He ain't no good to you, Candy. Why don't you shoot him?

CANDY [*uncomfortably*]. Well, hell, I had him so long! Had him since he was a pup. I herded sheep with him. [*Proudly.*] You wouldn't think it to look at him now. He was the best damn sheep dog I ever seen.

GEORGE. I knowed a guy in Weed that had an airedale that could herd sheep. Learned it from the other dogs.

CARLSON [*sticking to his point*]. Lookit, Candy. This ole dog jus' suffers itself all the time. If you was to take him out and shoot him—right in the back of the head . . . [*Leans over and points.*] . . . right there, why he never'd know what hit him.

CANDY [*unhappily*]. No, I couldn't do that. I had him too long.

CARLSON [*insisting*]. He don't have no fun no more. He stinks like hell. Tell you what I'll do. I'll shoot him for you. Then it won't be you that done it.

CANDY [*sits up on the bunk, rubbing his whiskers*

nervously, speaks plaintively]. I had him from a pup.

WHIT. Let 'im alone, Carl. It ain't a guy's dog that matters. It's the way the guy feels about the dog. Hell, I had a mutt once I wouldn't a traded for a field trial pointer.

CARLSON [*being persuasive*]. Well, Candy ain't being nice to him, keeping him alive. Lookit, Slim's bitch got a litter right now. I bet you Slim would give ya one of them pups to raise up, wouldn't ya, Slim?

SLIM [*studying the dog*]. Yeah. You can have a pup if you want to.

CANDY [*helplessly*]. Mebbe it would hurt. [*After a moment's pause, positively.*] And I don't mind taking care of him.

CARLSON. Aw, he'd be better off dead. The way I'd shoot him he wouldn't feel nothin'. I'd put the gun right there. [*Points with his toe.*] Right back of the head.

WHIT. Aw, let 'im alone, Carl.

CARLSON. Why, hell, he wouldn't even quiver.

WHIT. Let 'im alone. [*He produces a magazine*]. Say, did you see this? Did you see this in the book here?

CARLSON. See what?

WHIT. Right there. Read that.

CARLSON. I don't want to read nothing. . . . It'd be all over in a minute, Candy. Come on.

WHIT. Did you see it, Slim? Go on, read it. Read it out loud.

SLIM. What is it?

WHIT. Read it.

SLIM [*reads slowly*]. "Dear Editor: I read your mag for six years and I think it is the best on the market. I like stories by Peter Rand. I think he is a whingding. Give us more like the Dark Rider. I don't write many letters. Just thought I would tell you I think your mag is the best dime's worth I ever spen'." [*Looks up questioningly.*] What you want me to read that for?

WHIT. Go on, read the name at the bottom.

SLIM [*reading*]. "Yours for Success, William Tenner." [*Looks up at* WHIT.] What ya want me to read that for?

CARLSON. Come on, Candy—what you say?

WHIT [*taking the magazine and closing it impressively. Talks to cover* CARLSON]. You don't remember Bill Tenner? Worked here about three months ago?

SLIM [*thinking*]. Little guy? Drove a cultivator?

WHIT. That's him. That's the guy.

CARLSON [*has refused to be drawn into this conversation*]. Look, Candy. If you want me to, I'll put the old devil outa his misery right now and get it over with. There ain't nothing left for him. Can't eat, can't see, can't hardly walk. Tomorrow you can pick one of Slim's pups.

SLIM. Sure . . . I got a lot of 'em.

CANDY [*hopefully*]. You ain't got no gun.

CARLSON. The hell, I ain't. Got a Luger. It won't hurt him none at all.

CANDY. Mebbe tomorrow. Let's wait till tomorrow.

CARLSON. I don't see no reason for it. [*Goes to his bunk, pulls a bag from underneath, takes a Luger pistol out.*] Let's get it over with. We can't sleep with him stinking around in here. [*He snaps a shell into the chamber, sets the safety and puts the pistol into his hip pocket.*]

SLIM [*as* CANDY *looks toward him for help*]. Better let him go, Candy.

CANDY [*looks at each person for some hope.* WHIT *makes a gesture of protest and then resigns himself.*

The others look away, to avoid responsibility. At last, very softly and hopelessly]. All right. Take him.
[*He doesn't look down at the dog at all. Lies back on his bunk and crosses his arms behind his head and stares at the ceiling.* CARLSON *picks up the string, helps the dog to its feet*].

CARSON. Come, boy. Come on, boy. [*To* CANDY, *apologetically.*] He won't even feel it. [CANDY *does not move nor answer him.*] Come on, boy. That's the stuff. Come on. [*He leads the dog toward the door.*]

SLIM. Carlson?

CARLSON. Yeah.

SLIM [*curtly*]. Take a shovel.

CARLSON. Oh, sure, I get you.

[*Exit* CARLSON *with the dog.* GEORGE *follows to the door, shuts it carefully and sets the latch.* CANDY *lies rigidly on his bunk. The next scene is one of silence and quick staccato speeches.*]

SLIM [*loudly*]. One of my lead mules got a bad hoof. Got to get some tar on it.

[*There is a silence.*]

GEORGE [*loudly*]. Anybody like to play a little euchre?

WHIT. I'll lay out a few with you.

[*They take places opposite each other at the table but* GEORGE *does not shuffle the cards. He ripples the edge of the deck. Everybody looks over at him. He stops. Silence again.*]

SLIM [*compassionately*]. Candy, you can have any of them pups you want.

[*There is no answer from* CANDY. *There is a little gnawing noise on the stage.*]

GEORGE. Sounds like there was a rat under there. We ought to set a trap there.

[*Deep silence again.*]

WHIT [*exasperated*]. What the hell is takin' him so

long? Lay out some cards, why don't you? We ain't
gonna get no euchre played this way.

[GEORGE *studies the backs of the cards. And after a
long silence there is a shot in the distance. All the
men start a bit, look quickly at* CANDY. *For a moment he continues to stare at the ceiling and then
rolls slowly over and faces the wall.* GEORGE *shuffles
the cards noisily and deals them.*]

GEORGE. Well, let's get to it.

WHIT [*still to cover the moment*]. Yeah . . . I guess you
guys really come here to work, huh?

GEORGE. How do you mean?

WHIT [*chuckles*]. Well, you come on a Friday. You got
two days to work till Sunday.

GEORGE. I don't see how you figure.

WHIT. You do if you been round these big ranches
much. A guy that wants to look over a ranch comes
in Saturday afternoon. He gets Saturday night supper, three meals on Sunday and he can quit Monday
morning after breakfast without turning a hand.
But you come to work on Friday noon. You got ta
put in a day and a half no matter how ya figure it.

GEORGE [*quietly*]. We're goin' stick around awhile. Me
and Lennie's gonna roll up a stake.

[*Door opens and the Negro* STABLE BUCK *puts in his
head. A lean-faced Negro with pained eyes.*]

CROOKS. Mr. Slim.

SLIM [*who has been watching* CANDY *the whole time*].
Huh? Oh, hello, Crooks, what's the matter?

CROOKS. You tole me to warm up tar for that mule's
foot. I got it warm now.

SLIM. Oh, sure, Crooks. I'll come right out and put it
on.

CROOKS. I can do it for you if you want, Mr. Slim.

SLIM [*standing up*]. Naw, I'll take care of my own
team.

CROOKS. Mr. Slim.

SLIM. Yeah.

CROOKS. That big new guy is messing round your pups in the barn.

SLIM. Well, he ain't doin' no harm. I give him one of them pups.

CROOKS. Just thought I'd tell ya. He's takin' 'em out of the nest and handling 'em. That won't do 'em no good.

SLIM. Oh, he won't hurt 'em.

GEORGE [*looks up from his cards*]. If that crazy bastard is foolin' round too much jus' kick him out.

[SLIM *follows the* STABLE BUCK *out.*]

WHIT [*examining his cards*]. Seen the new kid yet?

GEORGE. What kid?

WHIT. Why, Curley's new wife.

GEORGE [*cautiously*]. Yeah, I seen her.

WHIT. Well, ain't she a lulu?

GEORGE. I ain't seen that much of her.

WHIT. Well, you stick around and keep your eyes open. You'll see plenty of her. I never seen nobody like her. She's just workin' on everybody all the time. Seems like she's even workin' on the stable buck. I don't know what the hell she wants.

GEORGE [*casually*]. Been any trouble since she got here?

[*Obviously neither man is interested in the card game.* WHIT *lays down his hand and* GEORGE *gathers the cards in and lays out a solitaire hand.*]

WHIT. I see what you mean. No, they ain't been no trouble yet. She's only been here a couple of weeks. Curley's got yellow jackets in his drawers, but that's all so far. Every time the guys is around she shows up. She's lookin' for Curley. Or she thought she left somethin' layin' around and she's lookin' for that. Seems like she can't keep away from guys. And Curley's runnin' round like a cat lookin' for a dirt road. But they ain't been no trouble.

GEORGE. Ranch with a bunch of guys on it ain't no place for a girl. Specially like her.

WHIT. If she's give you any ideas you ought to come in town with us guys tomorrow night.

GEORGE. Why, what's doin'?

WHIT. Just the usual thing. We go in to old Susy's place. Hell of a nice place. Old Susy is a laugh. Always cracking jokes. Like she says when we come up on the front porch last Saturday night: Susy opens the door and she yells over her shoulder: "Get your coats on, girls, here comes the sheriff." She never talks dirty neither. Got five girls there.

GEORGE. What does it set you back?

WHIT. Two and a half. You can get a shot of whiskey for fifteen cents. Susy got nice chairs to set in too. If a guy don't want to flop, why he can just set in them chairs and have a couple or three shots and just pass the time of day. Susy don't give a damn. She ain't rushin' guys through, or kicking them out if they don't want to flop.

GEORGE. Might go in and look the joint over.

WHIT. Sure. Come along. It's a hell of a lot of fun—her crackin' jokes all the time. Like she says one time, she says: "I've knew people that if they got a rag rug on the floor and a kewpie doll lamp on the phonograph they think they're runnin' a parlor house." That's Gladys's house she's talkin' about. And Susy says: "I know what you boys want," she says: "My girls is clean," she says. "And there ain't no water in my whiskey," she says. "If any you guys want to look at a kewpie doll lamp and take your chance of gettin' burned, why, you know where to go." She says: "They's guys round here walkin' bowlegged because they liked to look at a kewpie doll lamp."

GEORGE. Gladys runs the other house, huh?

WHIT. Yeah.

[*Enter* CARLSON. CANDY *looks at him.*]

CARLSON. God, it's a dark night. [*Goes to his bunk; starts cleaning his pistol.*]

WHIT. We don't never go to Gladys's. Gladys gits three bucks, and two bits a shot and she don't crack no jokes. But Susy's place is clean and she got nice chairs. A guy can set in there like he lived there. Don't let no Manila Goo-Goos in, neither.

GEORGE. Aw, I don't know. Me and Lennie's rollin' up a stake. I might go in and set and have a shot, but I ain't puttin' out no two and a half.

WHIT. Well, a guy got to have some fun sometimes.

[*Enter* LENNIE. LENNIE *creeps to his bunk and sits down.*]

GEORGE. Didn't bring him back in, did you, Lennie?

LENNIE. No, George, honest I didn't. See?

WHIT. Say, how about this euchre game?

GEORGE. Okay. I didn't think you wanted to play.

[*Enter* CURLEY *excitedly.*]

CURLEY. Any you guys seen my wife?

WHIT. She ain't been here.

CURLEY [*looks threateningly about the room.*] Where the hell's Slim?

GEORGE. Went out in the barn. He was goin' put some tar on a split hoof.

CURLEY. How long ago did he go?

GEORGE. Oh, five, ten minutes.

[CURLEY *jumps out the door.*]

WHIT [*standing up*]. I guess maybe I'd like to see this. Curley must be spoilin' or he wouldn't start for Slim. Curley's handy, goddamn handy. But just the same he better leave Slim alone.

GEORGE. Thinks Slim's with his wife, don't he?

WHIT. Looks like it. 'Course Slim ain't. Least I don't

think Slim is. But I like to see the fuss if it comes
off. Come on, le's go.

GEORGE. I don't want to git mixed up in nothing. Me
and Lennie got to make a stake.

CARLSON [*finishes cleaning gun, puts it in his bag and
stands up*]. I'll look her over. Ain't seen a good fight
in a hell of a while. [WHIT *and* CARLSON *exeunt.*]

GEORGE. You see Slim out in the barn?

LENNIE. Sure. He tole me I better not pet that pup no
more, like I said.

GEORGE. Did you see that girl out there?

LENNIE. You mean Curley's girl?

GEORGE. Yeah. Did she come in the barn?

LENNIE [*cautiously*]. No—anyways I never seen her.

GEORGE. You never seen Slim talkin' to her?

LENNIE. Uh-uh. She ain't been in the barn.

GEORGE. Okay. I guess them guys ain't gonna see no
fight. If they's any fightin', Lennie, ya get out of the
way and stay out.

LENNIE. I don't want no fight. [GEORGE *lays out his solitaire hand.* LENNIE *picks up a face card and studies
it. Turns it over and studies it again.*] Both ends the
same. George, why is it both ends the same?

GEORGE. I don't know. That jus' the way they make
'em. What was Slim doin' in the barn when you
seen him?

LENNIE. Slim?

GEORGE. Sure, you seen him in the barn. He tole you
not to pet the pups so much.

LENNIE. Oh. Yeah. He had a can of tar and a paint
brush. I don't know what for.

GEORGE. You sure that girl didn't come in like she come
in here today?

LENNIE. No, she never come.

GEORGE [*sighs*]. You give me a good whorehouse every
time. A guy can go in and get drunk and get it over

all at once and no messes. And he knows how much it's goin' set him back. These tarts is jus' buckshot to a guy. [LENNIE *listens with admiration, moving his lips, and* GEORGE *continues.*] You remember Andy Cushman, Lennie? Went to grammar school same time as us?

LENNIE. The one that his ole lady used to make hot cakes for the kids?

GEORGE. Yeah. That's the one. You can remember if they's somepin to eat in it. [*Scores up some cards in his solitaire playing.*] Well, Andy's in San Quentin right now on account of a tart.

LENNIE. George?

GEORGE. Huh?

LENNIE. How long is it goin' be till we git that little place to live off the fat of the land?

GEORGE. I don't know. We gotta get a big stake together. I know a little place we can get cheap, but they ain't givin' it away.

[CANDY *turns over and watches* GEORGE.]

LENNIE. Tell about that place, George.

GEORGE. I jus' tole you. Jus' last night.

LENNIE. Go on, tell again.

GEORGE. Well, it's ten acres. Got a windmill. Got a little shack on it and a chicken run. Got a kitchen orchard. Cherries, apples, peaches, 'cots and nuts. Got a few berries. There's a place for alfalfa and plenty water to flood it. There's a pig pen. . . .

LENNIE [*breaking in*]. And rabbits, George?

GEORGE. I could easy build a few hutches. And you could feed alfalfa to them rabbits.

LENNIE. Damn right I could. [*Excitedly.*] You goddamn right I could.

GEORGE [*his voice growing warmer*]. And we could have a few pigs. I'd build a smokehouse. And when we kill a pig we could smoke the hams. When the salmon run up the river we can catch a hundred of 'em. Every Sunday we'd kill a chicken or rabbit. Mebbe we'll have a cow or a goat. And the cream is so goddamn thick you got to cut it off the pan with a knife.

LENNIE [*watching him with wide eyes, softly*]. We can live off the fat of the land.

GEORGE. Sure. All kinds of vegetables in the garden and if we want a little whiskey we can sell some eggs or somethin'. And we wouldn't sleep in no bunkhouse. Nobody could can us in the middle of a job.

LENNIE [*begging*]. Tell about the house, George.

GEORGE. Sure. We'd have a little house. And a room to ourselves. And it ain't enough land so we'd have to work too hard. Mebbe six, seven hours a day only. We wouldn't have to buck no barley eleven hours a day. And when we put in a crop, why we'd be there to take that crop up. We'd know what come of our planting.

LENNIE [*eagerly*]. And rabbits. And I'd take care of them. Tell how I'd do that, George.

GEORGE. Sure. You'd go out in the alfalfa patch and you'd have a sack. You'd fill up the sack and bring it in and put it in the rabbit cages.

LENNIE. They'd nibble and they'd nibble, the way they do. I seen 'em.

GEORGE. Every six weeks or so them does would throw a litter. So we'd have plenty rabbits to eat or sell. [*Pauses for inspiration.*] And we'd keep a few pigeons to go flying round and round the windmill, like they done when I was a kid. [*Seems entranced.*] And it'd be our own. And nobody could can us. If we don't like a guy we can say: "Get to hell out," and by God he's got to do it. And if a friend come along, why, we'd have an extra bunk. Know what we'd say? We'd say, "Why don't you spen' the night?" And by God he would. We'd have a setter dog and a couple of striped cats. [*Looks sharply at* LENNIE.] But you gotta watch out them cats don't get the little rabbits.

LENNIE [*breathing hard*]. You jus' let 'em try. I'll break their goddamn necks. I'll smash them cats flat with a stick. I'd smash 'em flat with a stick. That's what I'd do. [*They sit silently for a moment.*]

CANDY [*at the sound of his voice, both* LENNIE *and* GEORGE *jump as though caught in some secret.*] You know where's a place like that?

GEORGE [*solemnly*]. S'pose I do, what's that to you?

CANDY. You don't need to tell me where it's at. Might be any place.

GEORGE [*relieved*]. Sure. That's right, you couldn't find it in a hundred years.

CANDY [*excitedly*]. How much they want for a place like that?

GEORGE [*grudgingly*]. Well, I could get it for six hundred bucks. The ole people that owns it is flat bust. And the ole lady needs medicine. Say, what's it to you? You got nothing to do with us!

CANDY [*softly*]. I ain't much good with only one hand. I lost my hand right here on the ranch. That's why they didn't can me. They give me two hundred and fifty dollars 'cause I lost my hand. An' I got fifty more saved up right in the bank right now. That's three hundred. And I got forty more comin' the end of the month. Tell you what . . . [*He leans forward eagerly.*] S'pose I went in with you guys? That's three hundred and forty bucks I'd put in. I ain't much good, but I could cook and tend the chickens and hoe the garden some. How'd that be?

GEORGE [*his eyes half closed, uncertainly*]. I got to

think about that. We was always goin' to do it by
ourselves. Me an' Lennie. I never thought of nobody
else.

CANDY. I'd make a will. Leave my share to you guys in
case I kicked off. I ain't got no relations nor nothing. You fellas got any money? Maybe we could go
there right now.

GEORGE [*disgustedly*]. We got ten bucks between us.
[*He thinks.*] Say, look. If me and Lennie work a
month and don't spend nothing at all, we'll have a
hundred bucks. That would be four forty. I bet we
could swing her for that. Then you and Lennie
could go get her started and I'd get a job and make
up the rest. You could sell eggs and stuff like that.
[*They look at each other in amazement. Reverently.*]
Jesus Christ, I bet we could swing her. [*His voice is
full of wonder.*] I bet we could swing 'er.

CANDY [*scratches the stump of his wrist nervously*]. I
got hurt four years ago. They'll can me pretty soon.
Jest as soon as I can't swamp out no bunkhouses
they'll put me on the county. Maybe if I give you
guys my money, you'll let me hoe in the garden,
even when I ain't no good at it. And I'll wash dishes
and little chicken stuff like that. But hell, I'll be on
our own place. I'll be let to work on our own place.
[*Miserably.*] You seen what they done to my dog.
They says he wasn't no good to himself nor nobody
else. But when I'm that way nobody'll shoot me. I
wish somebody would. They won't do nothing like
that. I won't have no place to go and I can't get no
more jobs.

GEORGE [*stands up*]. We'll do 'er! God damn, we'll fix
up that little ole place and we'll go live there. [*Won-
deringly.*] S'pose they was a carnival, or a circus
come to town or a ball game or any damn thing.
[CANDY *nods in appreciation.*] We'd just go to her.

We wouldn't ask nobody if we could. Just say we'll go to her, by God, and we would. Just milk the cow and sling some grain to the chickens and go to her.

LENNIE. And put some grass to the rabbits. I wouldn't forget to feed them. When we gonna to do it, George?

GEORGE [*decisively*]. In one month. Right squack in one month. Know what I'm gonna do? I'm goin' write to them ole people that owns the place that we'll take 'er. And Candy'll send a hundred dollars to bind her.

CANDY [*happily*]. I sure will. They got a good stove there?

GEORGE. Sure, got a nice stove. Burns coal or wood.

LENNIE. I'm gonna take my pup. I bet by Christ he likes it there.

[*The window, center backstage, swings outward.* CURLEY'S WIFE *looks in. They do not see her.*]

GEORGE [*quickly*]. Now don't tell nobody about her. Jus' us three and nobody else. They'll liable to can us so we can't make no stake. We'll just go on like we was a bunch of punks. Like we was gonna buck barley the rest of our lives. And then all of a sudden, one day, bang! We get our pay and scram out of here.

CANDY. I can give you three hundred right now.

LENNIE. And not tell nobody. We won't tell nobody, George.

GEORGE. You're goddamn right we won't. [*There is a silence and then* GEORGE *speaks irritably.*] You know, seems to me I can almost smell that carnation stuff that goddamn tart dumps on herself.

CURLEY'S WIFE [*in the first part of the speech by* GEORGE *she starts to step out of sight but at the last words her face darkens with anger. At her first words everybody in the room looks around at her and remains rigid during the tirade*]. Who you callin' a tart! I come from a nice home. I was brung up by nice people. Nobody never got to me before I was married. I was straight. I tell you I was good. [*A little plaintively.*] I was. [*Angrily again.*] You know Curley. You know he wouldn't stay with me if he wasn't sure. I tell you Curley is sure. You got no right to call me a tart.

GEORGE [*sullenly*]. If you ain't a tart, what you always hangin' round guys for? You got a house an' you got a man. We don't want no trouble from you.

CURLEY'S WIFE [*pleadingly*]. Sure I got a man. He ain't never home. I got nobody to talk to. I got nobody to be with. Think I can just sit home and do nothin' but cook for Curley? I want to see somebody. Just see 'em an' talk to 'em. There ain't no women. I can't walk to town. And Curley don't take me to no dances now. I tell you I jus' want to talk to somebody.

GEORGE [*boldly*]. If you're just friendly what you givin' out the eye for an' floppin' your can around?

CURLEY'S WIFE [*sadly*]. I just wanta be nice.

[*The sound of approaching voices: "You don't have to get mad about it, do you?" . . . "I ain't mad, but I just don't want no more questions, that's all. I just don't want no more questions."*]

GEORGE. Get goin'. We don't want no trouble.

[CURLEY'S WIFE *looks from the window and closes it silently and disappears. Enter* SLIM, *followed by* CURLEY, CARLSON *and* WHIT. SLIM'S *hands are black with tar.* CURLEY *hangs close to his elbow.*]

CURLEY [*explaining*]. Well, I didn't mean nothing, Slim. I jus' ast you.

SLIM. Well, you been askin' too often. I'm gettin' god-damn sick of it. If you can't look after your own wife, what you expect me to do about it? You lay off of me.

CURLEY. I'm jus' tryin' to tell you I didn't mean nothing. I just thought you might of saw her.

CARLSON. Why don't you tell her to stay to hell home where she belongs? You let her hang around the bunkhouses and pretty soon you're goin' to have somethin' on your hands.

CURLEY [*whirls on* CARLSON]. You keep out of this 'less you want ta step outside.

CARLSON [*laughing*]. Why, you goddamn punk. You tried to throw a scare into Slim and you couldn't make it stick. Slim throwed a scare into you. You're yellow as a frog's belly. I don't care if you're the best boxer in the country, you come for me and I'll kick your goddamn head off.

WHIT [*joining in the attack*]. Glove full of vaseline!

CURLEY [*glares at him, then suddenly sniffs the air, like a hound*]. By God, she's been in *here*. I can smell— By God, she's been in here. [*To* GEORGE.] You was here. The other guys was outside. Now, God damn you—you talk.

GEORGE [*looks worried. He seems to make up his mind to face an inevitable situation. Slowly takes off his coat, and folds it almost daintily. Speaks in an unemotional monotone*]. Somebody got to beat the hell outa you. I guess I'm elected.

[LENNIE *has been watching, fascinated. He gives his high, nervous chuckle.*]

CURLEY [*whirls on him*]. What the hell you laughin' at?

LENNIE [*blankly*]. Huh?

CURLEY [*exploding with rage*]. Come on, you big bastard. Get up on your feet. No big son-of-a-bitch is gonna laugh at me. I'll show you who's yellow.

[LENNIE *looks helplessly at* GEORGE. *Gets up and tries*

to retreat upstage. CURLEY *follows slashing at him.*
The others mass themselves in front of the two con-
testants: "*That ain't no way, Curley—he ain't done*
nothing to you." . . . "*Lay off him, will you, Curley.*
He ain't no fighter." . . . "*Sock him back, big guy!*
Don't be afraid of him!" . . . "*Give him a chance,*
Curley. Give him a chance."

LENNIE [*crying with terror*]. George, make him leave
me alone, George.

GEORGE. Get him, Lennie. Get him! [*There is a sharp*
cry. The gathering of men opens and CURLEY *is*
flopping about, his hand lost in LENNIE's *hand.*] Let
go of him, Lennie. Let go! ["*He's got his hand!*" . . .
"*Look at that, will you?*" . . . "*Jesus, what a guy!*"
LENNIE *watches in terror the flopping man he holds.*
LENNIE's *face is covered with blood.* GEORGE *slaps*
LENNIE *in the face again and again.* CURLEY *is weak*
and shrunken.] Let go his hand, Lennie. Slim, come
help me, while this guy's got any hand left.

[*Suddenly* LENNIE *lets go. He cowers away from*
GEORGE.]

LENNIE. You told me to, George. I heard you tell me to.

[CURLEY *has dropped to the floor.* SLIM *and* CARLSON
bend over him and look at his hand. SLIM *looks*
over at LENNIE *with horror.*]

SLIM. We got to get him to a doctor. It looks to me
like every bone in his hand is busted.

LENNIE [*crying*]. I didn't wanta. I didn't wanta hurt
'im.

SLIM. Carlson, you get the candy wagon out. He'll have
to go into Soledad and get his hand fixed up. [*Turns*
to the whimpering LENNIE.] It ain't your fault. This
punk had it comin' to him. But Jesus—he ain't
hardly got no hand left.

GEORGE [*moving near*]. Slim, will we git canned now?
Will Curley's ole man can us now?

SLIM. I don't know. [*Kneels down beside* CURLEY.] You got your sense enough to listen? [CURLEY *nods.*] Well, then you listen. I think you got your hand caught in a machine. If you don't tell nobody what happened, we won't. But you jest tell and try to get this guy canned and we'll tell everybody. And then will you get the laugh! [*Helps* CURLEY *to his feet.*] Come on now. Carlson's goin' to take you in to a doctor. [*Starts for the door, turns back to* LENNIE.] Le's see your hands. [LENNIE *sticks out both hands.*] Christ Almighty!

GEORGE. Lennie was just scairt. He didn't know what to do. I tole you nobody ought never to fight him. No, I guess it was Candy I tole.

CANDY [*solemnly*]. That's just what you done. Right this morning when Curley first lit into him. You says he better not fool with Lennie if he knows what's good for him.

[*They all leave the stage except* GEORGE *and* LENNIE *and* CANDY.]

GEORGE [*to* LENNIE, *very gently*]. It ain't your fault. You don't need to be scairt no more. You done jus' what I tole you to. Maybe you better go in the washroom and clean your face. You look like hell.

LENNIE. I didn't want no trouble.

GEORGE. Come on—I'll go with you.

LENNIE. George?

GEORGE. What you want?

LENNIE. Can I still tend the rabbits, George?

[*They exeunt together, side by side, through the door of the bunkhouse.*]

CURTAIN

SCENE II

Ten o'clock Saturday evening.

The room of the stable buck, a lean-to off the barn. There is a plank door upstage center; a small square window center right. On one side of the door a leather working bench with tools racked behind it, and on the other racks with broken and partly mended harnesses, collars, hames, traces, etc. At the left upstage CROOKS' *bunk. Over it two shelves. On one a great number of medicines in cans and bottles. And on the other a number of tattered books and a big alarm clock. In the corner right upstage a single-barreled shotgun and on the floor beside it a pair of rubber boots. A large pair of gold spectacles hang on a nail over* CROOKS' *bunk.*

The entrance leads into the barn proper. From that direction and during the whole scene come the sounds of horses eating, stamping, jingling their halter chains and now and then whinnying.

Two empty nail kegs are in the room to be used as seats. Single unshaded small-candlepower carbon light hanging from its own cord.

As the curtain rises, we see CROOKS *sitting on his bunk rubbing his back with liniment. He reaches up under his shirt to do this. His face is lined with pain. As he rubs he flexes his muscles and shivers a little.*

LENNIE *appears in the open doorway, nearly filling the opening. Then* CROOKS, *sensing his presence, raises his eyes, stiffens and scowls.*

LENNIE *smiles in an attempt to make friends.*

CROOKS [*sharply*]. You got no right to come in my room. This here's my room. Nobody got any right in here but me.

LENNIE [*fawning*]. I ain't doin' nothing. Just come in the barn to look at my pup, and I seen your light.

CROOKS. Well, I got a right to have a light. You go on and get out of my room. I ain't wanted in the bunkhouse and you ain't wanted in my room.

LENNIE [*ingenuously*]. Why ain't you wanted?

CROOKS [*furiously*]. 'Cause I'm black. They play cards in there. But I can't play because I'm black. They say I stink. Well, I tell you all of you stink to me.

LENNIE [*helplessly*]. Everybody went into town. Slim and George and everybody. George says I got to stay here and not get into no trouble. I seen your light.

CROOKS. Well, what do you want?

LENNIE. Nothing . . . I seen your light. I thought I could jus' come in and set.

CROOKS [*stares at* LENNIE *for a moment, takes down his spectacles and adjusts them over his ears; says in a complaining tone*]. I don't know what you're doin' in the barn anyway. You ain't no skinner. There's no call for a bucker to come into the barn at all. You've got nothing to do with the horses and mules.

LENNIE [*patiently*]. The pup. I come to see my pup.

CROOKS. Well, God damn it, go and see your pup then. Don't go no place where you ain't wanted.

LENNIE [*advances a step into the room, remembers and backs to the door again*]. I looked at him a little. Slim says I ain't to pet him very much.

CROOKS [*the anger gradually going out of his voice*]. Well, you been taking him out of the nest all the time. I wonder the ole lady don't move him some place else.

LENNIE [*moving into the room*]. Oh, she don't care. She lets me.

CROOKS [*scowls and then gives up*]. Come on in and set awhile. Long as you won't get out and leave me alone, you might as well set down. [*A little more friendly.*] All the boys gone into town, huh?

LENNIE. All but old Candy. He jus' sets in the bunkhouse sharpening his pencils. And sharpening and figurin'.

CROOKS [*adjusting his glasses*]. Figurin'? What's Candy figurin' about?

LENNIE. 'Bout the land. 'Bout the little place.

CROOKS. You're nuts. You're crazy as a wedge. What land you talkin' about?

LENNIE. The land we're goin' to get. And a little house and pigeons.

CROOKS. Just nuts. I don't blame the guy you're traveling with for keeping you out of sight.

LENNIE [*quietly*]. It ain't no lie. We're gonna do it. Gonna get a little place and live off the fat of the land.

CROOKS [*settling himself comfortably on his bunk*]. Set down on that nail keg.

LENNIE [*hunches over on the little barrel*]. You think it's a lie. But it ain't no lie. Ever' word's the truth. You can ask George.

CROOKS [*puts his dark chin on his palm*]. You travel round with George, don't you?

LENNIE [*proudly*]. Sure, me and him goes ever' place together.

CROOKS [*after a pause, quietly*]. Sometimes he talks and you don't know what the hell he's talkin' about. Ain't that so? [*Leans forward.*] Ain't that so?

LENNIE. Yeah. Sometimes.

CROOKS. Just talks on. And you don't know what the hell it's all about.

LENNIE. How long you think it'll be before them pups will be old enough to pet?

CROOKS [*laughs again*]. A guy can talk to you and be sure you won't go blabbin'. A couple of weeks and them pups will be all right. [*Musing.*] George knows what he's about. Just talks and you don't understand nothing. [*Mood gradually changes to excitement.*] Well, this is just a nigger talkin' and a busted-back nigger. It don't mean nothing, see. You couldn't remember it anyway. I seen it over and over —a guy talking to another guy and it don't make no difference if he don't hear or understand. The thing is they're talkin'. [*He pounds his knee with his hand.*] George can tell you screwy things and it don't matter. It's just the talkin'. It's just bein' with another guy, that's all. [*His voice becomes soft and malicious.*] S'pose George don't come back no more? S'pose he took a powder and just ain't comin' back. What you do then?

LENNIE [*trying to follow* CROOKS]. What? What?

CROOKS. I said s'pose George went into town tonight and you never heard of him no more. [*Presses forward.*] Just s'pose that.

LENNIE [*sharply*]. He won't do it. George wouldn't do nothing like that. I been with George a long time. He'll come back tonight. . . . [*Doubt creeps into his voice.*] Don't you think he will?

CROOKS [*delighted with his torture*]. Nobody can tell what a guy will do. Let's say he wants to come back and can't. S'pose he gets killed or hurt so he can't come back.

LENNIE [*in terrible apprehension*]. I don't know. Say, what you doin' anyway? It ain't true. George ain't got hurt.

CROOKS [*cruelly*]. Want me to tell you what'll happen? They'll take you to the booby hatch. They'll tie you up with a collar like a dog. Then you'll be jus' like me. Livin' in a kennel.

LENNIE [*furious, walks over towards* CROOKS]. Who hurt George?

CROOKS [*recoiling from him with fright*]. I was just supposin'. George ain't hurt. He's all right. He'll be back all right.

LENNIE [*standing over him*]. What you supposin' for? Ain't nobody goin' to s'pose any hurt to George.

CROOKS [*trying to calm him*]. Now set down. George ain't hurt. Go on now, set down.

LENNIE [*growling*]. Ain't nobody gonna talk no hurt to George.

CROOKS [*very gently*]. Maybe you can see now. You got George. You know he's comin' back. S'pose you didn't have nobody. S'pose you couldn't go in the bunkhouse and play rummy, 'cause you was black. How would you like that? S'pose you had to set out here and read books. Sure, you could play horseshoes until it got dark, but then you got to read books. Books ain't no good. A guy needs somebody . . . to be near him. [*His tone whines.*] A guy goes nuts if he ain't got nobody. Don't make no difference who it is as long as he's with you. I tell you a guy gets too lonely, he gets sick.

LENNIE [*reassuring himself*]. George gonna come back. Maybe George come back already. Maybe I better go see.

CROOKS [*more gently*]. I didn't mean to scare you. He'll come back. I was talkin' about myself.

LENNIE [*miserably*]. George won't go away and leave me. I know George won't do that.

CROOKS [*continuing dreamily*]. I remember when I was a little kid on my ole man's chicken ranch. Had two brothers. They was always near me, always there.

Used to sleep right in the same room. Right in the same bed, all three. Had a strawberry patch. Had an alfalfa patch. Used to turn the chickens out in the alfalfa on a sunny morning. Me and my brothers would set on the fence and watch 'em—white chickens they was.

LENNIE [*interested*]. George says we're gonna have alfalfa.

CROOKS. You're nuts.

LENNIE. We are too gonna get it. You ask George.

CROOKS [*scornfully*]. You're nuts. I seen hundreds of men come by on the road and on the ranches, bindles on their back and that same damn thing in their head. Hundreds of 'em. They come and they quit and they go on. And every damn one of 'em is got a little piece of land in his head. And never a goddamn one of 'em gets it. Jus' like heaven. Everybody wants a little piece of land. Nobody never gets to heaven. And nobody gets no land.

LENNIE. We are too.

CROOKS. It's jest in your head. Guys all the time talkin' about it, but it's jest in your head. [*The horses move restlessly. One of them whinnies.*] I guess somebody's out there. Maybe Slim. [*Pulls himself painfully upright and moves toward the door. Calls.*] That you, Slim?

CANDY [*from outside*]. Slim went in town. Say, you seen Lennie?

CROOKS. You mean the big guy?

CANDY. Yes. Seen him around any place?

CROOKS [*goes back to his bunk and sits down, says shortly*]. He's in here.

CANDY [*stands in the doorway, scratching his wrist. Makes no attempt to enter.*] Look, Lennie, I been figuring something out. About the place.

CROOKS [*irritably*]. You can come in if you want.

CANDY [*embarrassed*]. I don't know. 'Course if you want me to.

CROOKS. Oh, come on in. Everybody's comin' in. You might just as well. Gettin' to be a goddamn race track. [*He tries to conceal his pleasure.*]

CANDY [*still embarrassed*]. You've got a nice cozy little place in here. Must be nice to have a room to yourself this way.

CROOKS. Sure. And a manure pile under the window. All to myself. It's swell.

LENNIE [*breaking in*]. You said about the place.

CANDY. You know, I been here a long time. An' Crooks been here a long time. This is the first time I ever been in his room.

CROOKS [*darkly*]. Guys don't come in a colored man's room. Nobody been here but Slim.

LENNIE [*insistently*]. The place. You said about the place.

CANDY. Yeah. I got it all figured out. We can make some real money on them rabbits if we go about it right.

LENNIE. But I get to tend 'em. George says I get to tend 'em. He promised.

CROOKS [*brutally*]. You guys is just kiddin' yourselves. You'll talk about it a hell of a lot, but you won't get no land. You'll be a swamper here until they take you out in a box. Hell, I seen too many guys.

CANDY [*angrily*]. We're gonna do it. George says we are. We got the money right now.

CROOKS. Yeah. And where is George now? In town in a whorehouse. That's where your money's goin'. I tell you I seen it happen too many times.

CANDY. George ain't got the money in town. The money's in the bank. Me and Lennie and George. We gonna have a room to ourselves. We gonna have a dog and chickens. We gonna have green corn and maybe a cow.

CROOKS [*impressed*]. You say you got the money?

CANDY. We got most of it. Just a little bit more to get. Have it all in one month. George's got the land all picked out too.

CROOKS [*exploring his spine with his hands*]. I've never seen a guy really do it. I seen guys nearly crazy with loneliness for land, but every time a whorehouse or a blackjack game took it away from 'em. [*Hesitates and then speaks timidly.*] If you guys would want a hand to work for nothin'—just his keep, why I'd come and lend a hand. I ain't so crippled I can't work like a son-of-a-bitch if I wanted to.

GEORGE [*strolls through the door, hands in pockets, leans against the wall, speaks in a half-satiric, rather gentle voice*]. You couldn't go to bed like I told you, could you, Lennie? Hell, no—you got to get out in society an' flap your mouth. Holdin' a convention out here.

LENNIE [*defending himself*]. You was gone. There wasn't nobody in the bunkhouse. I ain't done no bad things, George.

GEORGE [*still casually*]. Only time I get any peace is when you're asleep. If you ever get walkin' in your sleep I'll chop off your head like a chicken. [*Chops with his hand.*]

CROOKS [*coming to* LENNIE'S *defense*]. We was jus' settin' here talkin'. Ain't no harm in that.

GEORGE. Yeah. I heard you. [*A weariness has settled on him.*] Got to be here ever' minute, I guess. Got to watch ya. [*To* CROOKS.] It ain't nothing against you, Crooks. We just wasn't gonna tell nobody.

CANDY [*tries to change subject*]. Didn't you have no fun in town?

GEORGE. Oh! I set in a chair and Susy was crackin' jokes

an' the guys was startin' to raise a little puny hell. Christ Almighty—I never been this way before. I'm jus' gonna set out a dime and a nickel for a shot an' I think what a hell of a lot of bulk carrot seed you can get for fifteen cents.

CANDY. Not in them damn little envelopes—but bulk seed—you sure can.

GEORGE. So purty soon I come back. I can't think of nothing else. Them guys slingin' money around got me jumpy.

CANDY. Guy got to have *some* fun. I was to a parlor house in Bakersfield once. God Almighty, what a place. Went upstairs on a red carpet. They was big pichers on the wall. We set in big sof' chairs. They was cigarettes on the table—an' they was *free*. Purty soon a Jap come in with drinks on a tray an' them *drinks* was free. Take all you want. [*In a reverie.*] Purty soon the girls come in an' they was jus' as polite an' nice an' quiet an' purty. Didn't seem like hookers. Made ya kinda scared to ask 'em. . . . That was a long time ago.

GEORGE. Yeah? An' what'd them sof' chairs set you back?

CANDY. Fifteen bucks.

GEORGE [*scornfully*]. So ya got a cigarette an' a whiskey an' a look at a purty dress an' it cost ya twelve and a half bucks extra. You shot a week's pay to walk on that red carpet.

CANDY [*still entranced with his memory*]. A week's pay? Sure. But I worked weeks all my life. I can't remember none of them weeks. But . . . that was nearly twenty years ago. And I can remember that. Girl I went with was named Arline. Had on a pink silk dress.

GEORGE [*turns suddenly and looks out the door into*

the dark barn, speaks savagely]. I s'pose ya lookin' for Curley? [CURLEY'S WIFE *appears in the door.*] Well, Curley ain't here.

CURLEY'S WIFE [*determined now*]. I know Curley ain't here. I wanted to ast Crooks somepin'. I didn't know you guys was here.

CANDY. Didn't George tell you before—we don't want nothing to do with you. You know damn well Curley ain't here.

CURLEY'S WIFE. I know where Curley went. Got his arm in a sling an' he went anyhow. I tell ya I come out to ast Crooks somepin'.

CROOKS [*apprehensively*]. Maybe you better go along to your own house. You hadn't ought to come near a colored man's room. I don't want no trouble. You don't want to ask me nothing.

CANDY [*rubbing his wrist stump*]. You got a husband. You got no call to come foolin' around with other guys, causin' trouble.

CURLEY'S WIFE [*suddenly angry*]. I try to be nice an' polite to you lousy bindle bums—but you're too good. I tell ya I could of went with shows. An'—an' a guy wanted to put me in pichers right in Hollywood. [*Looks about to see how she is impressing them. Their eyes are hard.*] I come out here to ast somebody somepin' an'—

CANDY [*stands up suddenly and knocks his nail keg over backwards, speaks angrily*]. I had enough. You ain't wanted here. We tole you, you ain't. Callin' us bindle stiffs. You got floozy idears what us guys amounts to. You ain't got sense enough to see us guys ain't bindle stiffs. S'pose you could get us *canned*—s'pose you *could*. You think we'd hit the highway an' look for another two-bit job. You don't know we got our own ranch to go to an' our own house an' fruit trees. An' we got friends. That's what we got. Maybe they was a time when we didn't have nothin', but that ain't so no more.

CURLEY'S WIFE. You damn ol' goat. If you had two bits, you'd be in Soledad gettin' a drink an' suckin' the bottom of the glass.

GEORGE. Maybe she could ask Crooks what she come to ask an' then get the hell home. I don't think she come to ask nothing.

CURLEY'S WIFE. What happened to Curley's hand? [CROOKS *laughs.* GEORGE *tries to shut him up.*] So it wasn't no machine. Curley didn't act like he was tellin' the truth. Come on, Crooks—what happened?

CROOKS. I wasn't there. I didn't see it.

CURLEY'S WIFE [*eagerly*]. What happened? I won't let on to Curley. He says he caught his han' in a gear. [CROOKS *is silent.*] Who done it?

GEORGE. Didn't nobody do it.

CURLEY'S WIFE [*turns slowly to* GEORGE]. So *you* done it. Well, he had it comin'.

GEORGE. I didn't have no fuss with Curley.

CURLEY'S WIFE [*steps near him, smiling*]. Maybe now you ain't scared of him no more. Maybe you'll talk to me sometimes now. Ever'body was scared of him.

GEORGE [*speaks rather kindly*]. Look! I didn't sock Curley. If he had trouble, it ain't none of our affair. Ask Curley about it. Now listen. I'm gonna try to tell ya. We tole you to get the hell out and it don't do no good. So I'm gonna tell you another way. Us guys got somepin' we're gonna do. If you stick around you'll gum up the works. It ain't your fault. If a guy steps on a round pebble an' falls an' breaks his neck, it ain't the pebble's fault, but the guy wouldn't of did it if the pebble wasn't there.

CURLEY'S WIFE [*puzzled*]. What you talkin' about pebbles? If you didn't sock Curley, who did? [*She looks*

at the others, then steps quickly over to LENNIE.]
Where'd you get them bruises on your face?

GEORGE. I tell you he got his hand caught in a machine.

LENNIE [*looks anxiously at* GEORGE, *speaks miserably*].
He caught his han' in a machine.

GEORGE. So now get out of here.

CURLEY'S WIFE [*goes close to* LENNIE, *speaks softly and
there is a note of affection in her voice*]. So . . . it was
you. Well . . . maybe you're dumb like they say . . .
an' maybe . . . you're the only guy on the ranch with
guts. [*She puts her hand on* LENNIE'S *shoulder. He
looks up in her face and a smile grows on his face.
She strokes his shoulder*.] You're a nice fella.

GEORGE [*suddenly leaps at her ferociously, grabs her
shoulder and whirls her around*]. Listen . . . you! I
tried to give you a break. Don't you walk into nothing! We ain't gonna let you mess up what we're
gonna do. You let this guy alone an' get the hell out
of here.

CURLEY'S WIFE [*defiant but slightly frightened*]. You
ain't tellin' me what to do. [*The* BOSS *appears in the
door, stands legs spread, thumbs hooked over his
belt*.] I got a right to talk to anybody I want to.

GEORGE. Why, you—

[GEORGE, *furiously, steps close—his hand is raised to
strike her. She cowers a little.* GEORGE *stiffens, seeing*
BOSS, *frozen in position. The others see* BOSS *too.*
GIRL *retreats slowly.* GEORGE'S *hand drops slowly to
his side—he takes two slow backward steps. Hold
the scene for a moment*.]

CURTAIN

Act three

Mid-afternoon Sunday.

One end of a great barn. Backstage the hay slopes up sharply against the wall. High in the upstage wall is a large hay window. On each side are seen the hay racks, behind which are the stalls with the horses in them. Throughout this scene the horses can be heard in their stalls, rattling their halter chains and chewing at the hay.

The entrance is downstage right.

The boards of the barn are not close together. Streaks of afternoon sun come between the boards, made visible by dust in the air. From outside comes the clang of horseshoes on the playing peg, shouts of men encouraging or jeering.

In the barn there is a feeling of quiet and humming and lazy warmth. Curtain rises on LENNIE *sitting in the hay, looking down at a little dead puppy in front of him. He puts out his big hand and strokes it clear from one end to the other.*

LENNIE [*softly*]. Why do you got to get killed? You ain't so little as mice. I didn' bounce you hard. [*Bends the pup's head up and looks in its face.*] Now maybe George ain't gonna let me tend no rabbits if he finds out you got killed. [*He scoops a little hollow and lays the puppy in it out of sight and covers it over with hay. He stares at the mound he has made.*] This ain't no bad thing like I got to hide in the brush. I'll tell George I found it dead. [*He unburies the pup and inspects it. Twists its ears and works his fingers in its fur. Sorrowfully.*] But he'll know. George always knows. He'll say: "You done it. Don't try to put nothin' over on me." And he'll say: "Now just for that you don't get to tend no—you-know-whats." [*His anger rises. Addresses the pup.*] God damn you. Why do you got to get killed? You ain't so little as mice. [*Picks up the pup and hurls it from him and turns his back on it. He sits bent over his knees moaning to himself.*] Now he won't let me. . . . Now he won't let me. [*Outside there is a clang of horseshoes on the iron stake and a little chorus of cries.* LENNIE *gets up and brings the pup back and lays it in the hay and sits down. He mourns.*] You wasn't big enough. They tole me and tole me you wasn't. I didn't know you'd get killed so easy. Maybe George won't care. This here goddamn little son-of-a-bitch wasn't nothin' to George.

CANDY [*voice from behind the stalls*]. Lennie, where you at? [LENNIE *frantically buries the pup under the hay.* CANDY *enters excitedly.*] Thought I'd find ya here. Say . . . I been talkin' to Slim. It's okay. We ain't gonna get the can. Slim been talkin' to the boss. Slim tol' the boss you guys is good buckers. The boss got to move that grain. 'Member what hell the boss give us las' night? He tol' Slim he got his eye on you an' George. But you ain't gonna get the can. Oh! an' say. The boss give Curley's wife hell, too. Tole her never to go near the men no more. Give her worse hell than you an' George. [*For the first time notices* LENNIE's *dejection.*] Ain't you glad?

LENNIE. Sure.

CANDY. You ain't sick?

LENNIE. Uh-uh!

CANDY. I got to go tell George. See you later. [*Exits.*]

[LENNIE, *alone, uncovers the pup. Lies down in the hay and sinks deep in it. Puts the pup on his arm and strokes it.* CURLEY'S WIFE *enters secretly. A little mound of hay conceals* LENNIE *from her. In her hand she carries a small suitcase, very cheap. She crosses the barn and buries the case in the hay. Stands up and looks to see whether it can be seen.* LENNIE *watching her quietly tries to cover the pup with hay. She sees the movement.*]

CURLEY'S WIFE. What—what you doin' here?

LENNIE [*sullenly*]. Jus' settin' here.

CURLEY'S WIFE. You seen what I done.

LENNIE. Yeah! you brang a valise.

CURLEY'S WIFE [*comes near to him*]. You won't tell—will you?

LENNIE [*still sullen*]. I ain't gonna have nothing to do with you. George tole me. I ain't to talk to you or nothing. [*Covers the pup a little more.*]

CURLEY'S WIFE. George give you all your orders?

LENNIE. Not talk nor nothing.

CURLEY'S WIFE. You won't tell about that suitcase? I ain't gonna stay here no more. Tonight I'm gonna get out. Come here an' get my stuff an' get out. I ain't gonna be run over no more. I'm gonna go in pichers. [*Sees* LENNIE's *hand stroking the pup under the hay.*] What you got there?

LENNIE. Nuthing. I ain't gonna talk to you. George says I ain't.

CURLEY'S WIFE. Listen. The guys got a horseshoe tenement out there. It's on'y four o'clock. Them guys ain't gonna leave that tenement. They got money bet. You don't need to be scared to talk to me.

LENNIE [*weakening a little*]. I ain't supposed to.

CURLEY'S WIFE [*watching his buried hand*]. What you got under there?

LENNIE [*his woe comes back to him*]. Jus' my pup. Jus' my little ol' pup. [*Sweeps the hay aside.*]

CURLEY'S WIFE. Why! He's dead.

LENNIE [*explaining sadly*]. He was so little. I was jus' playin' with him—an' he made like he's gonna bite me—an' I made like I'm gonna smack him—an'—I done it. An' then he was dead.

CURLEY'S WIFE [*consoling*]. Don't you worry none. He was just a mutt. The whole country is full of mutts.

LENNIE. It ain't that so much. George gonna be mad. Maybe he won't let me—what he said I could tend.

CURLEY'S WIFE [*sits down in the hay beside him, speaks soothingly*]. Don't you worry. Them guys got money bet on that horseshoe tenement. They ain't gonna leave it. And tomorra I'll be gone. I ain't gonna let them run over me.

[*In the following scene it is apparent that neither is listening to the other and yet as it goes on, as a happy tone increases, it can be seen that they are growing closer together.*]

LENNIE. We gonna have a little place an' raspberry bushes.

CURLEY'S WIFE. I ain't meant to live like this. I come from Salinas. Well, a show come through an' I talked to a guy that was in it. He says I could go with the show. My ol' lady wouldn't let me, 'cause I was on'y fifteen. I wouldn't be no place like this if I had went with that show, you bet.

LENNIE. Gonna take a sack an' fill it up with alfalfa an'—

CURLEY'S WIFE [*hurrying on*]. 'Nother time I met a guy an' he was in pichers. Went out to the Riverside Dance Palace with him. He said he was gonna put me in pichers. Says I was a natural. Soon's he got back to Hollywood he was gonna write me about it.

[*Looks impressively at* LENNIE.] I never got that letter. I think my ol' lady stole it. Well, I wasn't gonna stay no place where they stole your letters. So I married Curley. Met *him* out to the Riverside Dance Palace too.

LENNIE. I hope George ain't gonna be mad about this pup.

CURLEY'S WIFE. I ain't tol' this to nobody before. Maybe I oughtn' to. I don't like Curley. He ain't a nice fella. I might a stayed with him but last night him an' his ol' man both lit into me. I don't have to stay here. [*Moves closer and speaks confidentially.*] Don't tell nobody till I get clear away. I'll go in the night an' thumb a ride to Hollywood.

LENNIE. We gonna get out a here purty soon. This ain't no nice place.

CURLEY'S WIFE [*ecstatically*]. Gonna get in the movies an' have nice clothes—all them nice clothes like they wear. An' I'll set in them big hotels and they'll take pichers of me. When they have them openings I'll go an' talk in the radio . . . an' it won't cost me nothing 'cause I'm in the picher. [*Puts her hand on* LENNIE'S *arm for a moment.*] All them nice clothes like they wear . . . because this guy says I'm a natural.

LENNIE. We gonna go way . . . far away from here.

CURLEY'S WIFE. 'Course, when I run away from Curley, my ol' lady won't never speak to me no more. She'll think I ain't decent. That's what she'll say. [*Defiantly.*] Well, we really ain't decent, no matter how much my ol' lady tries to hide it. My ol' man was a drunk. They put him away. There! Now I told.

LENNIE. George an' me was to the Sacramento Fair. One time I fell in the river an' George pulled me out an' saved me, an' then we went to the Fair. They got all kinds of stuff there. We seen long-hair rabbits.

CURLEY'S WIFE. My ol' man was a sign-painter when he worked. He used to get drunk an' paint crazy pichers an' waste paint. One night when I was a little kid, him an' my ol' lady had an awful fight. They was always fightin'. In the middle of the night he come into my room, and he says, "I can't stand this no more. Let's you an' me go away." I guess he was drunk. [*Her voice takes on a curious wondering tenderness.*] I remember in the night—walkin' down the road, and the trees was black. I was pretty sleepy. He picked me up, an' he carried me on his back. He says, "We gonna live together. We gonna live together because you're my own little girl, an' not no stranger. No arguin' and fightin'," he says, "because you're my little daughter." [*Her voice becomes soft.*] He says, "Why you'll bake little cakes for me, and I'll paint pretty pichers all over the wall." [*Sadly.*] In the morning they caught us . . . an' they put him away. [*Pause.*] I wish we'd a' went.

LENNIE. Maybe if I took this here pup an' throwed him away George wouldn't never know.

CURLEY'S WIFE. They locked him up for a drunk, and in a little while he died.

LENNIE. Then maybe I could tend the rabbits without no trouble.

CURLEY'S WIFE. Don't you think of nothing but rabbits? [*Sound of horseshoe on metal.*] Somebody made a ringer.

LENNIE [*patiently*]. We gonna have a house and a garden, an' a place for alfalfa. And I take a sack and get it all full of alfalfa, and then I take it to the rabbits.

CURLEY'S WIFE. What makes you so nuts about rabbits?

LENNIE [*moves close to her*]. I like to pet nice things. Once at a fair I seen some of them long-hair rabbits. And they was nice, you bet. [*Despairingly.*] I'd even pet mice, but not when I could get nothin' better.

CURLEY'S WIFE [*giggles*]. I think you're nuts.

LENNIE [*earnestly*]. No, I ain't. George says I ain't. I like to pet nice things with my fingers. Soft things.

CURLEY'S WIFE. Well, who don't? Everybody likes that. I like to feel silk and velvet. You like to feel velvet?

LENNIE [*chuckling with pleasure*]. You bet, by God. And I had some too. A lady give me some. And that lady was—my Aunt Clara. She give it right to me. . . . [*Measuring with his hands.*] 'Bout this big a piece. I wish I had that velvet right now. [*He frowns.*] I lost it. I ain't seen it for a long time.

CURLEY'S WIFE [*laughing*]. You're nuts. But you're a kinda nice fella. Jus' like a big baby. A person can see kinda what you mean. When I'm doin' my hair sometimes I jus' set there and stroke it, because it's so soft. [*Runs her fingers over the top of her head.*] Some people got kinda coarse hair. You take Curley, his hair's just like wire. But mine is soft and fine. Here, feel. Right here. [*Takes LENNIE's hand and puts it on her head.*] Feel there and see how soft it is. [*LENNIE's fingers fall to stroking her hair.*] Don't you muss it up.

LENNIE. Oh, that's nice. [*Strokes harder.*] Oh, that's nice.

CURLEY'S WIFE. Look out now, you'll muss it. [*Angrily.*] You stop it now, you'll mess it all up. [*She jerks her head sideways and LENNIE's fingers close on her hair and hang on. In a panic.*] Let go. [*She screams.*] You let go. [*She screams again. His other hand closes over her mouth and nose.*]

LENNIE [*begging*]. Oh, please don't do that. George'll be mad. [*She struggles violently to be free. A soft screaming comes from under LENNIE's hand. Crying with fright.*] Oh, please don't do none of that. George gonna say I done a bad thing. [*He raises his hand from her mouth and a hoarse cry escapes. Angrily.*] Now don't. I don't want you to yell. You gonna get me in trouble just like George says you will. Now don't you do that. [*She struggles more.*] Don't you go yellin'. [*He shakes her violently. Her neck snaps sideways and she lies still. Looks down at her and cautiously removes his hand from over her mouth.*] I don't wanta hurt you. But George will be mad if you yell. [*When she doesn't answer he bends closely over her. He lifts her arm and lets it drop. For a moment he seems bewildered.*] I done a bad thing. I done another bad thing. [*He paws up the hay until it partly covers her. The sound of the horseshoe game comes from the outside. And for the first time* LENNIE *seems conscious of it. He crouches down and listens.*] Oh, I done a real bad thing. I shouldn't a did that. George will be mad. And . . . he said . . . and hide in the brush till he comes. That's what he said. [*He picks up the puppy from beside the girl.*] I'll throw him away. It's bad enough like it is. [*He puts the pup under his coat, creeps to the barn wall and peers out between the cracks and then he creeps around to the end of the manger and disappears.*]

[*The stage is vacant except for* CURLEY'S WIFE. *She lies in the hay half covered up and she looks very young and peaceful. Her rouged cheeks and red lips make her seem alive and sleeping lightly. For a moment the stage is absolutely silent. Then the horses stamp on the other side of the feeding rack. The halter chains clink and from outside men's voices come loud and clear.*]

CANDY [*offstage*]. Lennie! Oh, Lennie, you in there? [*He enters.*] I been figurin' some more, Lennie. Tell you what we can do. [*Sees* CURLEY'S WIFE *and stops. Rubs his white whiskers.*] I didn't know you was here. You was tol' not to be here. [*He steps near her.*] You oughtn't to sleep out here. [*He is right beside her and looks down.*] Oh, Jesus Christ! [*Goes to the door and calls softly.*] George, George! Come here . . . George!

GEORGE [*enters*]. What do you want?

CANDY [*points at* CURLY'S WIFE]. Look.

GEORGE. What's the matter with her? [*Steps up beside her.*] Oh, Jesus Christ! [*Kneels beside her and feels her heart and her wrist. Finally stands up slowly and stiffly. From this time on through the rest of the scene* GEORGE *is wooden.*]

CANDY. What done it?

GEORGE [*coldly*]. Ain't you got any ideas? [CANDY *looks away.*] I should of knew. I guess way back in my head I did.

CANDY. What we gonna do now, George? What we gonna do now?

GEORGE [*answering slowly and dully*]. Guess . . . we gotta . . . tell . . . the guys. Guess we got to catch him and lock him up. We can't let him get away. Why, the poor bastard would starve. [*He tries to reassure himself.*] Maybe they'll lock him up and be nice to him.

CANDY [*excitedly*]. You know better'n that, George. You know Curley's gonna want to get him lynched. You know how Curley is.

GEORGE. Yeah. . . . Yeah . . . that's right. I know Curley. And the other guys too. [*He looks back at* CURLEY'S WIFE.]

CANDY [*pleadingly*]. You and me can get that little place, can't we, George? You and me can go there and live nice, can't we? Can't we? [CANDY *drops his head and looks down at the hay to indicate that he knows.*]

GEORGE [*shakes his head slowly*]. It was somethin' me

and him had. [*Softly.*] I think I knowed it from the very first. I think I knowed we'd never do her. He used to like to hear about it so much. I got fooled to thinkin' maybe we would.

[CANDY *starts to speak but doesn't.*]

GEORGE [*as though repeating a lesson*]. I'll work my month and then I'll take my fifty bucks. I'll stay all night in some lousy cat-house or I'll set in a pool room until everybody goes home. An' then—I'll come back an' work another month. And then I'll have fifty bucks more.

CANDY. He's such a nice fellow. I didn't think he'd a done nothing like this.

GEORGE [*gets a grip on himself and straightens his shoulders*]. Now listen. We gotta tell the guys. I guess they've gotta bring him in. They ain't no way out. Maybe they won't hurt him. I ain't gonna let 'em hurt Lennie. [*Sharply.*] Now you listen. The guys might think I was in on it. I'm gonna go in the bunkhouse. Then in a minute you come out and yell like you just seen her. Will you do that? So the guys won't think I was in on it?

CANDY. Sure, George. Sure, I'll do that.

GEORGE. Okay. Give me a couple of minutes then. And then you yell your head off. I'm goin' now. [GEORGE *exits.*]

CANDY [*watches him go, looks helplessly back at* CUR-LEY'S WIFE; *his next words are in sorrow and in anger*]. You goddamn tramp. You done it, didn't you? Everybody knowed you'd mess things up. You just wasn't no good. [*His voice shakes.*] I could of hoed in the garden and washed dishes for them guys. . . . [*Pauses for a moment and then goes into a sing-song repeating the old words.*] If there was a circus or a baseball game . . . we would o' went to her . . . just said to hell with work and went to her. And they'd been a pig and chickens . . . and in the winter a little fat stove. An' us jus' settin' there . . . settin' there. . . . [*His eyes blind with tears and he goes weakly to the entrance of the barn. Tries for a moment to break a shout out of his throat before he succeeds.*] Hey, you guys! Come here! Come here!

[*Outside the noise of the horseshoe game stops. The sound of discussion and then the voices come closer: "What's the matter?" . . . "Who's that?" . . . "It's Candy." . . . "Something must have happened." Enter* SLIM *and* CARLSON, *young* WHIT *and* CURLEY, CROOKS *in the back, keeping out of attention range. And last of all* GEORGE. GEORGE *has put on his blue denim coat and buttoned it. His black hat is pulled down low over his eyes. "What's the matter?" . . . "What's happened?"*]

[*A gesture from* CANDY. *The men stare at* CURLEY'S WIFE. SLIM *goes over to her, feels her wrist and touches her cheek with his fingers. His hand goes under her slightly twisted neck.* CURLEY *comes near. For a moment he seems shocked. Looks around helplessly and suddenly he comes to life.*]

CURLEY. I know who done it. That big son-of-a-bitch done it. I know he done it. Why, everybody else was out there playing horseshoes. [*Working himself into a fury.*] I'm gonna get him. I'm gonna get my shotgun. Why, I'll kill the big son-of-a-bitch myself. I'll shoot him in the guts. Come on, you guys. [*He runs out of the barn.*]

CARLSON. I'll go get my Luger. [*He runs out too.*]

SLIM [*quietly to* GEORGE]. I guess Lennie done it all right. Her neck's busted. Lennie could o' did that. [GEORGE *nods slowly. Half-questioning.*] Maybe like that time in Weed you was tellin' me about. [GEORGE *nods. Gently.*] Well, I guess we got to get him. Where you think he might o' went?

GEORGE [*struggling to get words out*]. I don't know.

SLIM. I guess we gotta get him.

GEORGE [*stepping close and speaking passionately*]. Couldn't we maybe bring him in and lock him up? He's nuts, Slim, he never done this to be mean.

SLIM. If we could only keep Curley in. But Curley wants to shoot him. [*He thinks.*] And s'pose they lock him up, George, and strap him down and put him in a cage, that ain't no good.

GEORGE. I know. I know.

SLIM. I think there's only one way to get him out of it.

GEORGE. I know.

CARLSON [*enters running*]. The bastard stole my Luger. It ain't in my bag.

CURLEY [*enters carrying a shotgun in his good hand. Officiously*]. All right, you guys. The nigger's got a shotgun. You take it, Carlson.

WHIT. Only cover around here is down by the river. He might have went there.

CURLEY. Don't give him no chance. Shoot for his guts, that'll double him over.

WHIT. I ain't got a gun.

CURLEY. Go in and tell my old man. Get a gun from him. Let's go now. [*Turns suspiciously on* GEORGE.] You're comin' with us, fella!

GEORGE. Yeah. I'll come. But listen, Curley, the poor bastard's nuts. Don't shoot him, he didn't know what he was doin'.

CURLEY. Don't shoot him! He's got Carlson's Luger, ain't he?

GEORGE [*weakly*]. Maybe Carlson lost his gun.

CARLSON. I seen it this morning. It's been took.

SLIM [*looking down at* CURLEY'S WIFE]. Curley, maybe you better stay here with your wife.

[*The light is fading into evening.* CURLEY *hesitates. Seems almost to weaken, then he hardens again.*]

CURLEY. Naw, I'm gonna shoot the guts out of that big bastard, I'm gonna get him myself. Come on, you guys.

SLIM [*to* CANDY]. You stay here then, Candy. The rest of us better get goin'.

[*They walk out,* SLIM *and* GEORGE *last. Exeunt all but* CANDY. *He squats in the hay, watching the face of* CURLEY'S WIFE.]

CANDY. Poor bastard.

CURTAIN

SCENE II

Evening.

The river bank again.

Light from the setting sun shines on the low brown hills. Among the trees by the river, the shade is deep with evening feeling.

Sounds: distant barking of dogs and the quiet call of quail.

The curtain rises on an empty stage.

There is a sudden whistle of evening wind that stirs the trees and scuds the leaves on the ground.

The stage is still again. LENNIE *enters as silently as a bear. He is bent over and wary. On stage he looks behind him. Then he takes from under his coat the dead pup, lays it on the ground and, going to the river, lies on his stomach and drinks.*

He returns to the dead pup, sits down beside it.

LENNIE. George gonna give me hell . . . I bet. I . . . won't tell him. I'll bury him. [*Begins to scoop a hole in the sand in front of him. Softly.*] But I didn't forget, you bet. I come right here. Hide in the brush an' wait for George. [*Works carefully at his little grave, shaping the hole. At last he picks up the pup and lays it in the hole. Mourning.*] He gonna give me hell. He gonna wish he was alone. [*Adjusts the puppy in the hole, turning it around to make it fit better. Defiantly.*] Well . . . I can go right up in the hills an' find a cave. 'Course I wouldn't never have no ketchup. [*Begins packing sand down carefully about the pup, patting it as he does in beat with his words.*] I'll—go—away—go—away. [*Every word a pat. Fills the grave carefully, smooths the sand over it.*] There now. [*Gathers leaves and scatters them over the place. Gets up on his knees and cocks his head to inspect the job.*] Now. I won't never tell George. [*Sinks back to a sitting position.*] He'll know. He always knows.

[*Far off sound of voices approaching. They come closer during the scene. Suddenly there is the clicking warning of a cock-quail and then the drum of the flock's wings.* GEORGE *enters silently, but hurriedly.*]

GEORGE [*in a hoarse whisper*]. Get in the tules—quick.

LENNIE. I ain't done nothing, George.

[*The voices are very close.*]

GEORGE [*frantically*]. Get in the tules—damn you.

[*Voices are nearly there.* GEORGE *half pushes* LENNIE *down among the tules. The tops rustle showing his crawling progress.*]

WHIT [*offstage*]. There's George. [*Enters.*] Better not get so far ahead. You ain't got a gun.

[*Enter* SLIM, CARLSON, BOSS, CURLEY, *and three other ranch hands. They are armed with shotguns and rifles.*]

CARLSON. He musta come this way. Them prints in the sand was aimed this way.

SLIM [*has been regarding* GEORGE]. Now look. We ain't

gonna find him stickin' in a bunch this way. We got to spread out.

CURLEY. Brush is pretty thick here. He might be lying in the brush. [*Steps toward the tules.* GEORGE *moves quickly after him.*]

SLIM [*seeing the move, speaks quickly*]. Look—[*pointing*]—up there's the county road and open fields an' over there's the highway. Le's spread out an' cover the brush.

BOSS. Slim's right. We got to spread.

SLIM. We better drag up to the roads an' then drag back.

CURLEY. 'Member what I said—shoot for his guts.

SLIM. Okay, move out. Me an' George'll go up to the county road. You guys gets the highway an' drag back.

BOSS. If we get separated, we'll meet here. Remember this place.

CURLEY. All I care is getting the bastard.

[*The men move offstage right, talking.* SLIM *and* GEORGE *move slowly upstage listening to the voïces that grow fainter and fainter.*]

SLIM [*softly to* GEORGE.] Where is he?

[GEORGE *looks him in the eyes for a long moment. Finally trusts him and points with his thumb toward the tules.*]

SLIM. You want—I should—go away?

[GEORGE *nods slowly, looking at the ground.* SLIM *starts away, comes back, tries to say something, instead puts his hand on* GEORGE's *shoulder for a second, and then hurries off upstage.*]

GEORGE [*moves woodenly toward the bank and the tule clump and sits down*]. Lennie!

[*The tules shiver again and* LENNIE *emerges dripping.*]

LENNIE. Where's them guys goin'? [*Long pause.*]

GEORGE. Huntin'.

LENNIE. Whyn't we go with 'em? I like huntin'. [*Waits for an answer.* GEORGE *stares across the river.*] Is it 'cause I done a bad thing?

GEORGE. It don't make no difference.

LENNIE. Is that why we can't go huntin' with them guys?

GEORGE [*woodenly*]. It don't make no difference. . . . Sit down, Lennie. Right there.

[*The light is going now. In the distance there are shouts of men.* GEORGE *turns his head and listens to the shouts.*]

LENNIE. George!

GEORGE. Yeah?

LENNIE. Ain't you gonna give me hell?

GEORGE. Give ya hell?

LENNIE. Sure. . . . Like you always done before. Like— "If I didn't have you I'd take my fifty bucks . . ."

GEORGE [*softly as if in wonder*]. Jesus Christ, Lennie, you can't remember nothing that happens. But you remember every word I say!

LENNIE. Well, ain't you gonna say it?

GEORGE [*reciting*]. "If I was alone I—could live—so easy. [*His voice is monotonous.*] I could get a job and not have no mess. . . ."

LENNIE. Go on, go on! "And when the end of the month come . . ."

GEORGE. "And when the end of the month come, I could take my fifty bucks and go to—a cat-house. . . ."

LENNIE [*eagerly*]. Go on, George, ain't you gonna give me no more hell?

GEORGE. No!

LENNIE. I can go away. I'll go right off in the hills and find a cave if you don't want me.

GEORGE [*speaks as though his lips were stiff*]. No, I want you to stay here with me.

LENNIE [*craftily*]. Then tell me like you done before.

GEORGE. Tell you what?

LENNIE. 'Bout the other guys and about us!

GEORGE [*recites again*]. "Guys like us got no families. They got a little stake and then they blow it in. They ain't got nobody in the world that gives a hoot in hell about 'em!"

LENNIE [*happily*]. "But not *us*." Tell about us now.

GEORGE. "But not us."

LENNIE. "Because . . ."

GEORGE. "Because I got you and . . ."

LENNIE [*triumphantly*]. "And I got you. We got each other," that's what, that gives a hoot in hell about us.

[*A breeze blows up the leaves and then they settle back again. There are the shouts of men again. This time closer.*]

GEORGE [*takes off his hat; shakily*]. Take off your hat, Lennie. The air feels fine!

LENNIE [*removes his hat and lays it on the ground in front of him*]. Tell how it's gonna be.

[*Again the sound of men.* GEORGE *listens to them.*]

GEORGE. Look acrost the river, Lennie, and I'll tell you like you can almost see it. [LENNIE *turns his head and looks across the river.*] "We gonna get a little place . . . [*Reaches in his side pocket and brings out* CARLSON's *Luger. Hand and gun lie on the ground behind* LENNIE's *back. He stares at the back of* LENNIE's *head at the place where spine and skull are joined. Sounds of men's voices talking offstage.*]

LENNIE. Go on! [GEORGE *raises the gun, but his hand shakes and he drops his hand on to the ground.*] Go on! How's it gonna be? "We gonna get a little place. . . ."

GEORGE [*thickly*]. "We'll have a cow. And we'll have

maybe a pig and chickens—and down the flat we'll have a . . . little piece of alfalfa. . . ."

LENNIE [*shouting*]. "For the rabbits!"

GEORGE. "For the rabbits!"

LENNIE. "And I get to tend the rabbits?"

GEORGE. "And you get to tend the rabbits!"

LENNIE [*giggling with happiness*]. "And live off the fat o' the land!"

GEORGE. Yes. [LENNIE *turns his head. Quickly.*] Look over there, Lennie. Like you can really see it.

LENNIE. Where?

GEORGE. Right acrost that river there. Can't you almost see it?

LENNIE [*moving*]. Where, George?

GEORGE. It's over there. You keep lookin', Lennie. Just keep lookin'.

LENNIE. I'm lookin', George. I'm lookin'.

GEORGE. That's right. It's gonna be nice there. Ain't gonna be no trouble, no fights. Nobody ever gonna hurt nobody, or steal from 'em. It's gonna be—nice.

LENNIE. I can see it, George. I can see it! Right over there! I can see it!

[GEORGE *fires.* LENNIE *crumples; falls behind the brush. The voices of the men in the distance.*]

CURTAIN

THE TIME OF
YOUR LIFE

by William Saroyan

To George Jean Nathan

In the time of your life, live—so that in that good time
there shall be no ugliness or death for yourself or for any
life your life touches. Seek goodness everywhere, and when
it is found, bring it out of its hiding-place and let it be free
and unashamed. Place in matter and in flesh the least of
the values, for these are the things that hold death and must
pass away. Discover in all things that which shines and is
beyond corruption. Encourage virtue in whatever heart it
may have been driven into secrecy and sorrow by the shame
and terror of the world. Ignore the obvious, for it is unworthy of the clear eye and the kindly heart. Be the inferior of no man, nor of any man be the superior. Remember that every man is a variation of yourself. No man's
guilt is not yours, nor is any man's innocence a thing apart.
Despise evil and ungodliness, but not men of ungodliness
or evil. These, understand. Have no shame in being kindly
and gentle, but if the time comes in the time of your life
to kill, kill and have no regret. In the time of your life,
live—so that in that wondrous time you shall not add to
the misery and sorrow of the world, but shall smile to the
infinite delight and mystery of it.

*First production, October 25, 1939,
at the Booth Theatre, New York City,
with the following cast:*

THE NEWSBOY, *Ross Bagdasarian*
THE DRUNKARD, *John Farrell*
WILLIE, *Will Lee*
JOE, *Eddie Dowling*
NICK, *Charles de Sheim*
TOM, *Edward Andrews*
KITTY DUVAL, *Julie Haydon*
DUDLEY, *Curt Conway*
HARRY, *Gene Kelly*
WESLEY, *Reginald Beane*
LORENE, *Nene Vibber*
BLICK, *Grover Burgess*
ARAB, *Houseley Stevens, Sr.*
MARY L., *Celeste Holme*
KRUPP, *William Bendix*
MCCARTHY, *Tom Tully*
KIT CARSON, *Len Doyle*
NICK'S MA, *Michelette Burani*
SAILOR, *Randolph Wade*
ELSIE, *Cathie Bailey*
A KILLER, *Evelyn Geller*
HER SIDE KICK, *Mary Cheffey*
A SOCIETY LADY, *Eva Leonard Boyne*
A SOCIETY GENTLEMAN, *Ainsworth Arnold*
FIRST COP, *Randolph Wade*
SECOND COP, *John Farrell*

THE PLACE: *Nick's Pacific Street Saloon, Restaurant, and
Entertainment Palace at the foot of Embarcadero,
in San Francisco. A suggestion of room 21 at
The New York Hotel, upstairs, around the corner.*

THE TIME: *Afternoon and night of a day in October, 1939.*

Act one

NICK's *is an American place: a San Francisco water-front honky-tonk.*

At a table, JOE: *always calm, always quiet, always thinking, always eager, always bored, always superior. His expensive clothes are casually and youthfully worn and give him an almost boyish appearance. He is thinking.*

Behind the bar, NICK: *a big red-headed young Italian-American with an enormous naked woman tatooed in red on the inside of his right arm. He is studying "The Racing Form."*

The ARAB, *at his place at the end of the bar. He is a lean old man with a rather ferocious old-country mustache, with the ends twisted up. Between the thumb and forefinger of his left hand is the Mohammedan tattoo indicating that he has been to Mecca. He is sipping a glass of beer.*

It is about eleven-thirty in the morning. SAM *is sweeping out. We see only his back. He disappears into the kitchen. The* SAILOR *at the bar finishes his drink and leaves, moving thoughtfully, as though he were trying very hard to discover how to live.*

The NEWSBOY *comes in.*

NEWSBOY [*cheerfully*]. Good-morning, everybody. [*No answer. To* NICK.] Paper, Mister? [NICK *shakes his*

head, no. The NEWSBOY *goes to* JOE.] Paper, Mister?
[JOE *shakes his head, no. The* NEWSBOY *walks away, counting papers.*]

JOE [*noticing him*]. How many you got?

NEWSBOY. Five.

[JOE *gives him a quarter, takes all the papers, glances at the headlines with irritation, throws them away. The* NEWSBOY *watches carefully, then goes.*]

ARAB [*picks up paper, looks at headlines, shakes head as if rejecting everything else a man might say about the world*]. No foundation. All the way down the line.

[*The* DRUNK *comes in. Walks to the telephone, looks for a nickel in the chute, sits down at* JOE'S *table.* NICK *takes the* DRUNK *out. The* DRUNK *returns.*]

DRUNK [*champion of the Bill of Rights*]. This is a free country, ain't it?

[WILLIE, *the marble-game maniac, explodes through the swinging doors and lifts the forefinger of his right hand comically, indicating one beer. He is a very young man, not more than twenty. He is wearing heavy shoes, a pair of old and dirty corduroys, a light green turtle-neck jersey with a large letter "F" on the chest, an oversize two-button tweed coat, and a green hat, with the brim up.* NICK *sets out a glass of beer for him, he drinks it, straightens up vigorously saying "Aaah," makes a solemn face, gives* NICK *a one-finger salute of adieu, and begins to leave, refreshed and restored in spirit. He walks by the marble game, halts suddenly, turns, studies the contraption, gestures as if to say, Oh, no. Turns to go, stops, returns to the machine, studies it, takes a handful of small coins out of his pants pocket, lifts a nickel, indicates with a gesture, One game, no more. Puts the nickel in the slot, pushes in the slide, making an interesting noise.*]

NICK. You can't beat that machine.

WILLIE. Oh, yeah? [*The marbles fall, roll, and take their place. He pushes down the lever, placing one marble in position. Takes a very deep breath, walks in a small circle, excited at the beginning of great drama. Stands straight and pious before the contest. Himself vs. the machine. Willie vs. Destiny. His skill and daring vs. the cunning and trickery of the novelty industry of America, and the whole challenging world. He is the last of the American pioneers, with nothing more to fight but the machine, with no other reward than lights going on and off, and six nickels for one. Before him is the last champion, the machine. He is the last challenger, the young man with nothing to do in the world.* WILLIE *grips the knob delicately, studies the situation carefully, draws the knob back, holds it a moment, and then releases it. The first marble rolls out among the hazards, and the contest is on.*

[*At the very beginning of the play "The Missouri Waltz" is coming from the phonograph. The music ends here. This is the signal for the beginning of the play.* JOE *suddenly comes out of his reverie. He whistles the way people do who are calling a cab that's about a block away, only he does it quietly.* WILLIE *turns around, but* JOE *gestures for him to return to his work.* NICK *looks up from "The Racing Form."*

JOE [*calling*]. Tom. [*To himself.*] Where the hell is he, every time I need him? [*He looks around calmly: the nickel-in-the-slot phonograph in the corner; the open public telephone; the stage; the marble game; the bar; and so on. He calls again, this time very loud.*] Hey, Tom.

NICK [*with morning irritation*]. What do you want?

JOE [*without thinking*]. I want the boy to get me a

watermelon, that's what *I* want. What do *you* want? Money, or love, or fame, or what? You won't get them studying "The Racing Form."

NICK. I like to keep abreast of the times.

[TOM *comes hurrying in. He is a great big man of about thirty or so who appears to be much younger because of the childlike expression of his face: handsome, dumb, innocent, troubled, and a little bewildered by everything. He is obviously adult in years, but it seems as if by all rights he should still be a boy. He is defensive as clumsy, self-conscious, overgrown boys are. He is wearing a flashy cheap suit.* JOE *leans back and studies him with casual disapproval.* TOM *slackens his pace and becomes clumsy and embarrassed, waiting for the bawling-out he's pretty sure he's going to get.*]

JOE [*objectively, severely, but a little amused*]. Who saved your life?

TOM [*sincerely*]. You did, Joe. Thanks.

JOE [*interested*]. How'd I do it?

TOM [*confused*]. What?

JOE [*even more interested*]. How'd I do it?

TOM. Joe, you know how you did it.

JOE [*softly*]. I want you to answer me. How'd I save your life? I've forgotten.

TOM [*remembering, with a big sorrowful smile*]. You made me eat all that chicken soup three years ago when I was sick and hungry.

JOE [*fascinated*]. *Chicken soup?*

TOM [*eagerly*]. Yeah.

JOE. Three years? Is it that long?

TOM [*delighted to have the information*]. Yeah, sure. 1937. 1938. 1939. This is 1939, Joe.

JOE [*amused*]. Never mind what year it is. Tell me the whole story.

TOM. You took me to the doctor. You gave me money

for food and clothes, and paid my room rent. Aw, Joe, you know all the different things you did.

[JOE *nods, turning away from* TOM *after each question.*]

JOE. You in good health now?

TOM. Yeah, Joe.

JOE. You got clothes?

TOM. Yeah, Joe.

JOE. You eat three times a day. Sometimes four?

TOM. Yeah, Joe. Sometimes five.

JOE. You got a place to sleep?

TOM. Yeah, Joe.

[JOE *nods. Pauses. Studies* TOM *carefully.*]

JOE. Then, where the hell have you been?

TOM [*humbly*]. Joe, I was out in the street listening to the boys. They're talking about the trouble down here on the waterfront.

JOE [*sharply*]. I want you to be around when I need you.

TOM [*pleased that the bawling-out is over*]. I won't do it again. Joe, one guy out there says there's got to be a revolution before anything will ever be all right.

JOE [*impatiently*]. I know all about it. Now, here. Take this money. Go up to the Emporium. You know where the Emporium is?

TOM. Yeah, sure, Joe.

JOE. All right. Take the elevator and go up to the fourth floor. Walk around to the back, to the toy department. Buy me a couple of dollars' worth of toys and bring them here.

TOM [*amazed*]. Toys? What *kind* of toys, Joe?

JOE. Any kind of toys. Little ones that I can put on this table.

TOM. What do you want toys for, Joe?

JOE [*mildly angry*]. *What?*

TOM. All right, all right. You don't have to get sore

at *everything*. What'll people think, a big guy like me buying toys?

JOE. *What people?*

TOM. Aw, Joe, you're always making me do crazy things for you, and *I'm* the guy that gets embarrassed. You just sit in this place and make me do all the dirty work.

JOE [*looking away*]. Do what I tell you.

TOM. O.K., but I wish I knew why. [*He makes to go.*]

JOE. Wait a minute. Here's a nickel. Put it in the phonograph. Number seven. I want to hear that waltz again.

TOM. Boy, I'm glad *I* don't have to stay and listen to it. Joe, what do you hear in that song anyway? We listen to that song ten times a day. Why can't we hear number six, or two, or nine? There are a lot of other numbers.

JOE [*emphatically*]. Put the nickel in the phonograph. [*Pause.*] Sit down and wait till the music's over. Then go get me some toys.

TOM. O.K. O.K.

JOE [*loudly*]. Never mind being a martyr about it either. The cause isn't worth it.

[*Tom puts the nickel into the machine, with a ritual of impatient and efficient movement which plainly shows his lack of sympathy or enthusiasm. His manner also reveals, however, that his lack of sympathy is spurious and exaggerated. Actually, he is fascinated by the music, but is so confused by it that he pretends he dislikes it. The music begins. It is another variation of "The Missouri Waltz," played dreamily and softly, with perfect orchestral form, and with a theme of weeping in the horns repeated a number of times. At first TOM listens with something close to irritation, since he can't understand what is so attractive in the music to JOE, and what is so painful and confusing in it to himself. Very soon, however, he is carried away by the melancholy story of grief and nostalgia of the song. He stands, troubled by the poetry and confusion in himself.* JOE, *on the other hand, listens as if he were not listening, indifferent and unmoved. What he's interested in is* TOM. *He turns and glances at* TOM. KITTY DUVAL, *who lives in a room in The New York Hotel, around the corner, comes beyond the swinging doors, quietly, and walks slowly to the bar, her reality and rhythm a perfect accompaniment to the sorrowful American music, which is her music, as it is* TOM'S. *Which the world drove out of her, putting in its place brokenness and all manner of spiritually crippled forms. She seems to understand this, and is angry. Angry with herself, full of hate for the poor world, and full of pity and contempt for its tragic, unbelievable, confounded people. She is a small powerful girl, with that kind of delicate and rugged beauty which no circumstance of evil or ugly reality can destroy. This beauty is that element of the immortal which is in the seed of good and common people, and which is kept alive in some of the female of our kind, no matter how accidentally or pointlessly they may have entered the world.* KITTY DUVAL *is somebody. There is an angry purity, and a fierce pride, in her. In her stance, and way of walking, there is grace and arrogance.* JOE *recognizes her as a great person immediately. She goes to the bar.*]

KITTY. Beer.

[NICK *places a glass of beer before her mechanically. She swallows half the drink, and listens to the music again.* TOM *turns and sees her. He becomes dead to everything in the world but her. He stands like a lump, fascinated and undone by his almost religious adoration for her.* JOE *notices* TOM.

JOE [*gently*]. Tom. [TOM *begins to move toward the bar, where* KITTY *is standing. Loudly.*] Tom. [TOM *halts, then turns, and* JOE *motions to him to come over to the table.* TOM *goes over. Quietly.*] Have you got everything straight?

TOM [*out of the world*]. What?

JOE. What do you mean, what? I just gave you some instructions.

TOM [*pathetically*]. What do you want, Joe?

JOE. I want you to come to your senses. [*He stands up quietly and knocks* TOM's *hat off.* TOM *picks up his hat quickly.*]

TOM. I got it, Joe. I got it. The Emporium. Fourth floor. In the back. The toy department. Two dollars' worth of toys. That you can put on a table.

KITTY [*to herself*]. Who the hell is he to push a big man like that around?

JOE. I'll expect you back in a half hour. Don't get side-tracked anywhere. Just do what I tell you.

TOM [*pleading*]. Joe? Can't I bet four bits on a horse race? There's a long shot—Precious Time—that's going to win by ten lengths. I got to have money.

[JOE *points to the street.* TOM *goes out.* NICK *is combing his hair, looking in the mirror.*]

NICK. I thought you wanted him to get you a watermelon.

JOE. I forgot. [*He watches* KITTY *a moment. To* KITTY, *clearly, slowly, with great compassion.*] What's the dream?

KITTY [*moving to* JOE, *coming to*]. What?

JOE [*holding the dream for her*]. What's the dream, now?

KITTY [*coming still closer*]. What dream?

JOE. What dream! The dream you're dreaming.

NICK. Suppose he did bring you a watermelon? What the hell would you do with it?

JOE [*irritated*]. I'd put it on this table. I'd look at it. Then I'd eat it. What do you *think* I'd do with it, sell it for a profit?

NICK. How should I know what *you'd* do with *anything?* What I'd like to know is, where do you get your money from? What work do you do?

JOE [*looking at* KITTY]. Bring us a bottle of champagne.

KITTY. Champagne?

JOE [*simply*]. Would you rather have something else?

KITTY. What's the big idea?

JOE. I thought you might like some champagne. I myself am very fond of it.

KITTY. Yeah, but what's the big idea? You can't push *me* around.

JOE [*gently but severely*]. It's not in my nature to be unkind to another human being. I have only contempt for wit. Otherwise I might say something obvious, therefore cruel, and perhaps untrue.

KITTY. You be careful what you think about me.

JOE [*slowly, not looking at her*]. I have only the noblest thoughts for both your person and your spirit.

NICK [*having listened carefully and not being able to make it out*]. What are you talking about?

KITTY. You shut up. You—

JOE. He owns this place. He's an important man. All kinds of people come to him looking for work. Comedians. Singers. Dancers.

KITTY. I don't care. He can't call me names.

NICK. All right, sister. I know how it is with a two-dollar whore in the morning.

KITTY [*furiously*]. Don't you dare call me names. I used to be in burlesque.

NICK. If you were ever in burlesque, I used to be Charlie Chaplin.

KITTY [*angry and a little pathetic*]. I *was* in burlesque.

I played the burlesque circuit from coast to coast. I've had flowers sent to me by European royalty. I've had dinner with young men of wealth and social position.

NICK. You're dreaming.

KITTY [*to* JOE]. *I was in burlesque.* Kitty Duval. That was my name. Life-size photographs of me in costume in front of burlesque theaters all over the country.

JOE [*gently, coaxingly*]. I believe you. Have some champagne.

NICK [*going to table, with champagne bottle and glasses*]. There he goes again.

JOE. Miss Duval?

KITTY [*sincerely, going over*]. That's not my *real* name. That's my *stage* name.

JOE. I'll call you by your stage name.

NICK [*pouring*]. All right, sister, make up your mind. Are you going to have champagne with him, or not?

JOE. Pour the lady some wine.

NICK. O.K., Professor. Why you come to this joint instead of one of the high-class dumps uptown is more than I can understand. Why don't you have champagne at the St. Francis? Why don't you drink with a lady?

KITTY [*furiously*]. Don't you call me names—you dentist.

JOE. Dentist?

NICK [*amazed, loudly*]. What kind of cussing is that? [*Pause. Looking at* KITTY, *then at* JOE, *bewildered.*] This guy doesn't belong here. The only reason I've got champagne is because *he* keeps ordering it all the time. [*To* KITTY.] Don't think you're the only one he drinks champagne with. He drinks with *all* of them. [*Pause.*] He's crazy. Or something.

JOE [*confidentially*]. Nick, I think you're going to be all right in a couple of centuries.

NICK. I'm sorry, I don't understand your English.

[JOE *lifts his glass.* KITTY *slowly lifts hers, not quite sure of what's going on.*]

JOE [*sincerely*]. To the spirit, Kitty Duval.

KITTY [*beginning to understand, and very grateful, looking at him*]. Thank you.

JOE [*calling*]. Nick.

NICK. Yeah?

JOE. Would you mind putting a nickel in the machine again? Number—

NICK. Seven. I know. I know. I don't mind at all, Your Highness, although, personally, I'm not a lover of music. [*Going to the machine.*] As a matter of fact I think Tchaikowsky was a dope.

JOE. Tchaikowsky? Where'd you ever hear of Tchaikowsky?

NICK. He was a dope.

JOE. Yeah. Why?

NICK. They talked about him on the radio one Sunday morning. He was a sucker. He let a woman drive him crazy.

JOE. I see.

NICK. I stood behind that bar listening to the Goddamn stuff and cried like a baby. *None but the lonely heart!* He was a dope.

JOE. What made you cry?

NICK. What?

JOE [*sternly*]. What made you cry, Nick?

NICK [*angry with himself*]. I don't know.

JOE. I've been underestimating you, Nick. Play number seven.

NICK. They get everybody worked up. They give everybody stuff they shouldn't have. [NICK *puts the*

*nickel into the machine and the waltz begins again.
He listens to the music. Then studies "The Racing
Form."*]

KITTY [*to herself, dreaming*]. I like champagne, and
everything that goes with it. Big houses with big
porches, and big rooms with big windows, and big
lawns, and big trees, and flowers growing everywhere, and big shepherd dogs sleeping in the shade.

NICK. I'm going next door to Frankie's to make a bet.
I'll be right back.

JOE. Make one for me.

NICK [*going to* JOE]. Who do you like?

JOE [*giving him money*]. Precious Time.

NICK. Ten dollars? Across the board?

JOE. No. On the nose.

NICK. O.K. [*He goes.*]

[DUDLEY R. BOSTWICK, *as he calls himself, breaks
through the swinging doors, and practically flings
himself upon the open telephone beside the phonograph.* DUDLEY *is a young man of about twenty-four
or twenty-five, ordinary and yet extraordinary. He
is smallish, as the saying is, neatly dressed in bargain clothes, overworked and irritated by the routine and dullness and monotony of his life, apparently nobody and nothing, but in reality a great
personality. The swindled young man. Educated,
but without the least real understanding. A brave,
dumb, salmon-spirit struggling for life in weary,
stupefied flesh, dueling ferociously with a banal
mind which has been only irritated by what it has
been taught. He is a great personality because,
against all these handicaps, what he wants is simple
and basic: a woman. This urgent and violent need,
common yet miraculous enough in itself, considering the unhappy environment of the animal, is the
force which elevates him from nothingness to great-*

ness. *A ridiculous greatness, but in the nature of things beautiful to behold. All that he has been taught, and everything he believes, is phony, and yet he himself is real, almost super-real, because of this indestructible force in himself. His face is ridiculous. His personal rhythm is tense and jittery. His speech is shrill and violent. His gestures are wild. His ego is disjointed and epileptic. And yet deeply he possesses the same wholeness of spirit, and direct-ness of energy, that is in all species of animals. There is little innate or cultivated spirit in him, but there is no absence of innocent animal force. He is a young man who has been taught that he has a chance, as a person, and believes it. As a matter of fact, he hasn't a chance in the world, and should have been told by somebody, or should not have had his natural and valuable ignorance spoiled by education, ruining an otherwise perfectly good and charming member of the human race. At the tele-phone he immediately begins to dial furiously, hesi-tates, changes his mind, stops dialing, hangs up fu-riously, and suddenly begins again. Not more than half a minute after the firecracker arrival of* DUDLEY R. BOSTWICK, *occurs the polka-and-waltz arrival of* HARRY. HARRY *is another story. He comes in timidly, turning about uncertainly, awkward, out of place everywhere, embarrassed and encumbered by the contemporary costume, sick at heart, but determined to fit in somewhere. His arrival constitutes a dance. His clothes don't fit. The pants are a little too large. The coat, which doesn't match, is also a little too large, and loose. He is a dumb young fellow, but he has ideas. A philosophy, in fact. His philosophy is simple and beautiful. The world is sorrowful. The world needs laughter.* HARRY *is funny. The world needs* HARRY. HARRY *will make the world laugh. He has probably had a year or two of high school. He has also listened to the boys at the pool room. He's looking for* NICK. *He goes to the* ARAB *and says, "Are you Nick?" The* ARAB *shakes his head. He stands at the bar, waiting. He waits very busily.*]

HARRY [*as* NICK *returns*]. You Nick?

NICK [*very loudly*]. I am Nick.

HARRY [*acting*]. Can you use a great comedian?

NICK [*behind the bar*]. Who, for instance?

HARRY [*almost angry*]. Me.

NICK. You? What's funny about you?

[DUDLEY *at the telephone, is dialing. Because of some defect in the apparatus the dialing is very loud.*]

DUDLEY. Hello. Sunset 7349? May I speak to Miss Elsie Mandelspiegel? [*Pause.*]

HARRY [*with spirit and noise, dancing*]. I dance and do gags and stuff.

NICK. In costume? Or are you wearing your costume?

DUDLEY. All I need is a cigar.

KITTY [*continuing the dream of grace*]. I'd walk out of the house, and stand on the porch, and look at the trees, and smell the flowers, and run across the lawn, and lie down under a tree, and read a book. [*Pause.*] A book of poems, maybe.

DUDLEY [*very, very clearly*]. Elsie Mandelspiegel. [*Impatiently.*] She has a room on the fourth floor. She's a nurse at the Southern Pacific Hospital. Elsie Mandelspiegel. She works at night. Elsie. Yes. [*He begins waiting again.* WESLEY, *a colored boy, comes to the bar and stands near* HARRY, *waiting.*]

NICK. Beer?

WESLEY. No, sir. I'd like to talk to you.

NICK [*to* HARRY]. All right. Get funny.

HARRY [*getting funny, an altogether different person, an actor with great energy, both in power of voice, and in force and speed of physical gesture*]. Now,

I'm standing on the corner of Third and Market.
I'm looking around. I'm figuring it out. There it is.
Right in front of me. The whole city. The whole
world. People going by. They're going somewhere.
I don't know where, but they're going. I ain't going
anywhere. Where the hell can you go? I'm figuring
it out. All right, I'm a citizen. A fat guy bumps his
stomach into the face of an old lady. They were in
a hurry. Fat and old. *They bumped*. Boom. I don't
know. It may mean war. *War*. Germany. England.
Russia. I don't know for sure. [*Loudly, dramatically,
he salutes, about faces, presents arms, aims, and
fires.*] WAAAAAR. [*He blows a call to arms.* NICK
gets sick of this, indicates with a gesture that HARRY
should hold it, and goes to WESLEY.]

NICK. What's on your mind?

WESLEY [*confused*]. Well—

NICK. Come on. Speak up. Are you hungry, or what?

WESLEY. Honest to God, I ain't hungry. All I want
is a job. I don't want no charity.

NICK. Well, what can you do, and how good are you?

WESLEY. I can run errands, clean up, wash dishes, anything.

DUDLEY [*on the telephone, very eagerly*]. Elsie? Elsie,
this is Dudley. Elsie, I'll jump in the bay if you
don't marry me. Life isn't worth living without you.
I can't sleep. I can't think of anything but you. All
the time. Day and night and night and day. Elsie, I
love you. I love you. What? [*Burning up.*] Is this
Sunset 7-3-4-9? [*Pause.*] 7943? [*Calmly, while* WILLIE
begins making a small racket.] Well, what's your
name? *Lorene*? Lorene Smith? I thought you were
Elsie Mandelspiegel. What? Dudley. Yeah. Dudley
R. Bostwick. Yeah. R. It stands for Raoul, but I
never spell it out. I'm pleased to meet *you*, too.
What? There's a lot of noise around here. [WILLIE

stops hitting the marble game.] Where am I? At Nick's, on Pacific Street. I work at the S. P. I told them I was sick and they gave me the afternoon off. Wait a minute. I'll ask them. I'd like to meet *you*, too. Sure. I'll ask them. [*Turns around to* NICK.] What's this address?

NICK. Number 3 Pacific Street, you cad.

DUDLEY. Cad? You don't know how I've been suffering on account of Elsie. I take things too ceremoniously. I've got to be more lackadaisical. [*Into telephone.*] Hello, Elenore? I mean, Lorene. It's number 3 Pacific Street. Yeah. Sure. I'll wait for you. How'll you know me? You'll *know* me. I'll recognize *you*. Good-by, now. [*He hangs up.*]

HARRY [*continuing his monologue, with gestures, movements, and so on*]. I'm standing there. I didn't do anything to anybody. Why should I be a soldier? [*Sincerely, insanely.*] BOOOOOOOOOM. *WAR!* O.K. War. *I* retreat. *I* hate war. I move to Sacramento.

NICK [*shouting*]. All right, comedian. Lay off a minute.

HARRY [*broken-hearted, going to* WILLIE]. Nobody's got a sense of humor any more. The world's dying for comedy like never before, but nobody knows how to *laugh*.

NICK [*to* WESLEY]. Do you belong to the union?

WESLEY. What union?

NICK. For the love of Mike, where've you been? Don't you know you can't come into a place and ask for a job and get one and go to work, just like that. You've got to belong to one of the unions.

WESLEY. I didn't know. I got to have a job. Real soon.

NICK. Well, you've got to belong to a union.

WESLEY. I don't want any favors. All I want is a chance to earn a living.

NICK. Go on into the kitchen and tell Sam to give you some lunch.

WESLEY. Honest, I ain't hungry.

DUDLEY [*shouting*]. What I've gone through for Elsie.

HARRY. I've got all kinds of funny ideas in my head to help make the world happy again.

NICK [*holding* WESLEY]. No, he isn't hungry.

[WESLEY *almost faints from hunger.* NICK *catches him just in time. The* ARAB *and* NICK *go off with* WESLEY *into the kitchen.*]

HARRY [*to* WILLIE]. See if you think this is funny. It's my own idea. I created this dance myself. It comes after the monologue. [HARRY *begins to dance.* WILLIE *watches a moment, and then goes back to the game. It's a goofy dance, which* HARRY *does with great sorrow, but much energy.*]

DUDLEY. Elsie. Aw, gee, Elsie. What the hell do I want to see Lorene Smith for? Some girl I don't know.

[JOE *and* KITTY *have been drinking in silence. There is no sound now except the soft-shoe shuffling of* HARRY, *the Comedian.*]

JOE. What's the dream now, Kitty Duval?

KITTY [*dreaming the words and pictures*]. I dream of home. Christ, I always dream of home. I've no home. I've no place. But I always dream of all of us together again. We had a farm in Ohio. There was nothing good about it. It was always sad. There was always trouble. But I always dream about it as if I could go back and Papa would be there and Mamma and Louie and my little brother Stephen and my sister Mary. I'm Polish. Duval! My name isn't Duval, it's Koranovsky. Katerina Koranovsky. We lost everything. The house, the farm, the trees, the horses, the cows, the chickens. Papa died. He was old. He was thirteen years older than Mamma. We moved to Chicago. We tried to work. We tried to stay together. Louie got in trouble. The fellows he was with killed him for something. I don't know what. Stephen ran away from home. Seventeen years old. I don't know where he is. Then Mamma died. [*Pause.*] What's the dream? I dream of home.

[NICK *comes out of the kitchen with* WESLEY.]

NICK. Here. Sit down here and rest. That'll hold you for a *while*. Why didn't you tell me you were hungry? You all right now?

WESLEY [*sitting down in the chair at the piano*]. Yes, I am. Thank you. I didn't know I was *that* hungry.

NICK. Fine. [*To* HARRY *who is dancing.*] Hey. What the hell do you think you're doing?

HARRY [*stopping*]. That's my own idea. I'm a natural-born dancer and comedian.

[WESLEY *begins slowly, one note, one chord at a time, to play the piano.*]

NICK. You're no good. Why don't you try some other kind of work? Why don't you get a job in a store, selling something? What do you want to be a comedian for?

HARRY. I've got something for the world and they haven't got sense enough to let me give it to them. Nobody knows me.

DUDLEY. Elsie. Now I'm waiting for some dame I've never seen before. Lorene Smith. Never saw her in my life. Just happened to get the wrong number. She turns on the personality, and I'm a cooked Indian. Give me a beer, please.

HARRY. Nick, you've got to see my act. It's the greatest thing of its kind in America. All I want is a chance. No salary to begin. Let me try it out tonight. If I don't wow 'em, O.K., I'll go home. If vaudeville wasn't dead, a guy like me would have a chance.

NICK. You're not funny. You're a sad young punk. What the hell do you want to try to be funny for? You'll break everybody's heart. What's there for you to be funny about? You've been poor all your life, haven't you?

HARRY. I've been poor all right, but don't forget that some things count more than some other things.

NICK. What counts more, for instance, than what else, for instance?

HARRY. Talent, for instance, counts more than money, for instance, that's what, and I've got talent. I get new ideas night and day. Everything comes natural to me. I've got style, but it'll take me a little time to round it out. That's all.

[*By now* WESLEY *is playing something of his own which is very good and out of the world. He plays about half a minute, after which* HARRY *begins to dance.*]

NICK [*watching*]. I run the lousiest dive in Frisco, and a guy arrives and makes me stock up with champagne. The whores come in and holler at me that they're ladies. Talent comes in and begs me for a chance to show itself. Even society people come here once in a while. I don't know what for. Maybe it's liquor. Maybe it's the location. Maybe it's my personality. Maybe it's the crazy personality of the joint. The old honky-tonk. [*Pause.*] Maybe they can't feel at home anywhere else.

[*By now* WESLEY *is really playing, and* HARRY *is going through a new routine.* DUDLEY *grows sadder and sadder.*]

KITTY. Please dance with me.

JOE [*loudly*]. I never learned to dance.

KITTY. Anybody can dance. Just hold me in your arms.

JOE. I'm very fond of you. I'm *sorry*. I *can't* dance. I wish to God I could.

KITTY. Oh, please.

JOE. Forgive me. I'd like to very much.

[KITTY *dances alone.* TOM *comes in with a package. He sees* KITTY *and goes ga-ga again. He comes out of the trance and puts the bundle on the table in front of* JOE.]

JOE [*taking the package*]. What'd you get?

TOM. Two dollars' worth of toys. That's what you sent me for. The girl asked me what I wanted with toys. I didn't know what to tell her. [*He stares at* KITTY, *then back at* JOE.] Joe? I've got to have some money. After all you've done for me, I'll do anything in the world for you, but, Joe, you got to give me some money once in a while.

JOE. What do you want it for?

[TOM *turns and stares at* KITTY *dancing.*]

JOE [*noticing*]. Sure. Here. Here's five. [*Shouting.*] Can you dance?

TOM [*proudly*]. I got second prize at the Palomar in Sacramento five years ago.

JOE [*loudly, opening package*]. O.K., dance with her.

TOM. You mean *her?*

JOE [*loudly*]. I mean Kitty Duval, the burlesque queen. I mean the queen of the world burlesque. Dance with her. She wants to dance.

TOM [*worshiping the name Kitty Duval, helplessly*]. Joe, can I tell you something?

JOE [*he brings out a toy and winds it*]. You don't have to. I know. You love her. You *really* love her. I'm not blind. I know. But take care of yourself. Don't get sick that way again.

NICK [*looking at and listening to* WESLEY *with amazement*]. Comes in here and wants to be a dish-washer. Faints from hunger. And then sits down and plays better than Heifetz.

JOE. Heifetz plays the violin.

NICK. All right, don't get careful. He's good, ain't he?

TOM [*to* KITTY]. Kitty.

JOE [*he lets the toy go, loudly*]. Don't talk. Just dance.

[TOM *and* KITTY *dance.* NICK *is at the bar, watching everything.* HARRY *is dancing.* DUDLEY *is grieving into his beer.* LORENE SMITH, *about thirty-seven, very overbearing and funny-looking, comes to the bar.*]

NICK. What'll it be, lady?

LORENE [*looking about and scaring all the young men*]. I'm looking for the young man I talked to on the telephone. Dudley R. Bostwick.

DUDLEY [*jumping, running to her, stopping, shocked*]. Dudley R. [*Slowly.*] Bostwick? Oh, yeah. He left here ten minutes ago. You mean Dudley Bostwick, that poor man on crutches?

LORENE. Crutches?

DUDLEY. Yeah. Dudley Bostwick. That's what he *said* his name was. He said to tell you not to wait.

LORENE. Well. [*She begins to go, turns around.*] Are you sure *you're* not Dudley Bostwick?

DUDLEY. Who—me? [*Grandly.*] My name is Roger Tenefrancia. I'm a French-Canadian. I never saw the poor fellow before.

LORENE. It seems to me your voice is like the voice I heard over the telephone.

DUDLEY. A coincidence. An accident. A quirk of fate. One of those things. Dismiss the thought. That poor cripple hobbled out of here ten minutes ago.

LORENE. He said he was going to commit suicide. I only wanted to be of help. [*She goes.*]

DUDLEY. Be of help? What kind of help could she be of? [DUDLEY *runs to the telephone in the corner.*] Gee whiz, Elsie. Gee whiz. I'll never leave you again. [*He turns the pages of a little address book.*] Why do I always forget the number? I've tried to get her on the phone a hundred times this week and I still forget the number. She won't come to the phone, but I keep trying anyway. She's out. She's not in. She's working. I get the wrong number. Everything goes haywire. I can't sleep. [*Defiantly.*] She'll come to the phone one of these days. If there's anything to true love at all, she'll come to the phone. Sunset 7349. [*He dials the number, as* JOE *goes on studying the toys. They are one big mechanical toy, whistles, and a music box.* JOE *blows into the whistles, quickly, by way of getting casually acquainted with them.* TOM *and* KITTY *stop dancing.* TOM *stares at her.*]

DUDLEY. Hello. Is this Sunset 7349? May I speak to Elsie? Yes. [*Emphatically, and bitterly.*] No, this is *not* Dudley Bostwick. This is Roger Tenefrancia of Montreal, Canada. I'm a childhood friend of Miss Mandelspiegel. We went to kindergarten together. [*Hand over phone.*] God damn it. [*Into phone.*] Yes. I'll wait, thank you.

TOM. I love you.

KITTY. You want to go to my room? [TOM *can't answer.*] Have you got two dollars?

TOM [*shaking his head with confusion*]. I've got *five* dollars, but I *love* you.

KITTY [*looking at him*]. You want to spend all that money?

[TOM *embraces her. They go.* JOE *watches. Goes back to the toy.*]

JOE. Where's that longshoreman, McCarthy?

NICK. He'll be around.

JOE. What do you think he'll have to say today?

NICK. Plenty, as usual. I'm going next door to see who won that third race at Laurel.

JOE. Precious Time won it.

NICK. That's what you think. [*He goes.*]

JOE [*to himself*]. A horse named McCarthy is running in the sixth race today.

DUDLEY [*on the phone*]. Hello. Hello, Elsie? Elsie? [*His voice weakens; also his limbs.*] My God. She's come to the phone. Elsie, I'm at Nick's on Pacific Street. You've got to come here and talk to me. Hello. Hello, Elsie? [*Amazed.*] Did she hang up? Or was I disconnected? [*He hangs up and goes to bar.* WESLEY *is still playing the piano.* HARRY *is still dancing.* JOE *has wound up the big mechanical toy and is watching it work.* NICK *returns.*]

NICK [*watching the toy*]. Say. That's some gadget.

JOE. How much did I win?

NICK. How do you know you *won?*

JOE. Don't be silly. He said Precious Time was going to win by ten lengths, didn't he? He's in love, isn't he?

NICK. O.K. I don't know why, but Precious Time won. You got eighty for ten. How do you do it?

JOE [*roaring*]. Faith. Faith. How'd he win?

NICK. By a nose. Look him up in "The Racing Form." The slowest, the cheapest, the worst horse in the race, and the worst jockey. What's the matter with my luck?

JOE. How much did you lose?

NICK. Fifty cents.

JOE. You should never gamble.

NICK. Why not?

JOE. You always bet fifty cents. You've got no more faith than a flea, that's why.

HARRY [*shouting*]. How do you like this, Nick? [*He is really busy now, all legs and arms.*]

NICK [*turning and watching*]. Not bad. Hang around. You can wait table. [*To* WESLEY]. Hey. Wesley. Can you play that again tonight?

WESLEY [*turning, but still playing the piano*]. I don't

know for sure, Mr. Nick. I can play *something*.

NICK. Good. *You* hang around, too. [*He goes behind the bar.*]

[*The atmosphere is now one of warm, natural, American ease; every man innocent and good; each doing what he believes he should do, or what he must do. There is deep American naïveté and faith in the behavior of each person. No one is competing with anyone else. No one hates anyone else. Every man is living, and letting live. Each man is following his destiny as he feels it should be followed; or is abandoning it as he feels it must, by now, be abandoned; or is forgetting it for the moment as he feels he should forget it. Although everyone is dead serious, there is unmistakable smiling and humor in the scene; a sense of the human body and spirit emerging from the world-imposed state of stress and fretfulness, fear and awkwardness, to the more natural state of casualness and grace. Each person belongs to the environment, in his own person, as himself:* WESLEY *is playing better than ever.* HARRY *is hoofing better than ever.* NICK *is behind the bar shining glasses.* JOE *is smiling at the toy and studying it.* DUDLEY, *although still troubled, is at least calm now and full of melancholy poise.* WILLIE, *at the marble game, is happy. The* ARAB *is deep in his memories, where he wants to be. Into this scene and atmosphere comes* BLICK. BLICK *is the sort of human being you dislike at sight. He is no different from anybody else physically. His face is an ordinary face. There is nothing obviously wrong with him, and yet you know that it is impossible, even by the most generous expansion of understanding, to accept him as a human being. He is the strong man without strength—strong only among the weak—the weak-*

ling who uses force on the weaker. BLICK *enters casually, as if he were a customer, and immediately* HARRY *begins slowing down.*]

BLICK [*oily, and with mock-friendliness*]. Hello, Nick.

NICK [*stopping his work and leaning across the bar*]. What do you want to come here for? You're too big a man for a little honky-tonk.

BLICK [*flattered*]. Now, Nick.

NICK. Important people never come here. *Here.* Have a drink. [*Whiskey bottle.*]

BLICK. Thanks, I don't drink.

NICK [*drinking the drink himself*]. Well, why don't you?

BLICK. I have responsibilities.

NICK. You're head of the lousy Vice Squad. There's no vice here.

BLICK [*sharply*]. Street-walkers are working out of this place.

NICK [*angry*]. What do you want?

BLICK [*loudly*]. I just want you to know that it's got to *stop.*

[*The music stops. The mechanical toy runs down. There is absolute silence, and a strange fearfulness and disharmony in the atmosphere now.* HARRY *doesn't know what to do with his hands or feet.* WESLEY'S *arms hang at his sides.* JOE *quietly pushes the toy to one side of the table, eager to study what is happening.* WILLIE *stops playing the marble game, turns around and begins to wait.* DUDLEY *straightens up very, very vigorously, as if to say: "Nothing can scare me. I know love is the only thing." The* ARAB *is the same as ever, but watchful.* NICK *is arrogantly aloof. There is a moment of this silence and tension, as though* BLICK *were waiting for everybody to acknowledge his presence. He is obviously flattered by*

the acknowledgment of HARRY, DUDLEY, WESLEY, *and*
WILLIE, *but a little irritated by* NICK's *aloofness and*
unfriendliness.]

NICK. Don't look at me. I can't tell a street-walker from
a lady. You married?

BLICK. You're not asking *me* questions. *I'm* telling *you*.

NICK [*interrupting*]. You're a man of about forty-five
or so. You *ought* to know better.

BLICK [*angry*]. Street-walkers are working out of this
place.

NICK [*beginning to shout*]. Now, don't start any trouble with me. People come here to drink and loaf
around. I don't care who they are.

BLICK. Well, I do.

NICK. The only way to find out if a lady is a streetwalker is to walk the streets with her, go to bed, and
make sure. You wouldn't want to do that. *You'd*
like to, of course.

BLICK. Any more of it, and I'll have your joint closed.

NICK [*very casually, without ill-will*]. Listen. I've got
no use for you, or anybody like you. You're out to
change the world from something bad to something
worse. Something like yourself.

BLICK [*furious pause, and contempt*]. I'll be back tonight. [*He begins to go.*]

NICK [*very angry but very calm*]. Do yourself a big
favor and don't come back tonight. Send somebody
else. I don't like your personality.

BLICK [*casually, but with contempt*]. Don't break any
laws. I don't like yours, either. [*He looks the place*
over, and goes.]

[*There is a moment of silence. Then* WILLIE *turns and*
puts a new nickel in the slot and starts a new game.
WESLEY *turns to the piano and rather falteringly be-*
gins to play. His heart really isn't in it. HARRY *walks*
about, unable to dance. DUDLEY *lapses into his cus-*

tomary melancholy, at a table. NICK *whistles a little; suddenly stops.* JOE *winds the toy.*]

JOE [*comically*]. Nick. You going to kill that man?

NICK. I'm disgusted.

JOE. Yeah? Why?

NICK. Why should I get worked up over a guy like that? Why should I hate *him?* He's nothing. He's nobody. He's a mouse. But every time he comes into this place I get burned up. He doesn't want to drink. He doesn't want to sit down. He doesn't want to take things easy. Tell me one thing?

JOE. Do my best.

NICK. What's a punk like *that* want to go out and try to change the world for?

JOE [*amazed*]. Does *he* want to change the world, too?

NICK [*irritated*]. You know what I mean. What's he want to bother people for? He's *sick.*

JOE [*almost to himself, reflecting on the fact that* BLICK *too wants to change the world*]. I guess he wants to change the world at that.

NICK. So I go to work and hate him.

JOE. It's not him, Nick. It's everything.

NICK. Yeah, *I know.* But I've still got no use for him. He's no good. You know what I mean? He hurts little people. [*Confused.*] One of the girls tried to commit suicide on account of him. [*Furiously.*] I'll break his head if he hurts anybody around here. This is *my* joint. [*Afterthought.*] Or anybody's *feelings,* either.

JOE. He may not be so bad, deep down underneath.

NICK. I know all about him. He's no good.

[*During this talk* WESLEY *has really begun to play the piano, the toy is rattling again, and little by little* HARRY *has begun to dance.* NICK *has come around the bar, and now, very much like a child—forgetting all his anger—is watching the toy work. He begins to smile at everything: turns and listens to* WESLEY: *watches* HARRY: *nods at the* ARAB: *shakes his head at* DUDLEY: *and gestures amiably about* WILLIE. *It's his joint all right. It's a good, low-down, honky-tonk American place that lets people alone.*]

NICK. I've got a good joint. There's nothing wrong here. Hey. Comedian. Stick to the dancing tonight. I think you're O.K. Wesley? Do some more of that tonight. That's fine!

HARRY. Thanks, Nick. Gosh, I'm on my way at last. [*On telephone.*] Hello, Ma? Is that you, Ma? Harry. I got the job. [*He hangs up and walks around, smiling.*]

NICK [*watching the toy all this time*]. Say, that really is something. What is that, anyway?

[MARY L. *comes in.*]

JOE [*holding it toward* NICK, *and* MARY L.]. Nick, this is a toy. A contraption devised by the cunning of man to drive boredom, or grief, or anger out of children. A noble gadget. A gadget, I might say, infinitely nobler than any other I can think of at the moment. [*Everybody gathers around* JOE'S *table to look at the toy. The toy stops working.* JOE *winds the music box. Lifts a whistle: blows it, making a very strange, funny and sorrowful sound.*] Delightful. Tragic, but delightful.

[WESLEY *plays the music-box theme on the piano.* MARY L. *takes a table.*]

NICK. Joe. That girl, Kitty. What's she mean, calling me a dentist? I wouldn't hurt anybody, let alone a tooth.

[NICK *goes to* MARY L.'s *table.* HARRY *imitates the toy. Dances. The piano music comes up, the light dims slowly, while the piano solo continues.*]

CURTAIN

Act two

An hour later. All the people who were at NICK's when the curtain came down are still there. JOE at his table, quietly shuffling and turning a deck of cards, and at the same time watching the face of the WOMAN, and looking at the initials on her handbag, as though they were the symbols of the lost glory of the world. The WOMAN, in turn, very casually regards JOE occasionally. Or rather senses him; has sensed him in fact the whole hour. She is mildly tight on beer, and JOE himself is tight, but as always completely under control; simply sharper. The others are about, at tables, and so on.

JOE. Is it Madge—Laubowitz?

MARY. Is what *what?*

JOE. Is the name Mabel Lepescu?

MARY. What name?

JOE. The name the initials M. L. stand for. The initials on your bag.

MARY. No.

JOE [*after a long pause, thinking deeply what the name might be, turning a card, looking into the beautiful face of the woman*]. Margie Longworthy?

MARY [*all this is very natural and sincere, no comedy on the part of the people involved: they are both solemn, being drunk*]. No.

JOE [*his voice higher-pitched, as though he were growing alarmed*]. Midge Laurie? [MARY *shakes her head.*] My initials are J. T.

MARY [*Pause.*] John?

JOE. No. [*Pause.*] Martha Lancaster?

MARY. No. [*Slight pause.*] Joseph?

JOE. Well, not exactly. That's my first name, but everybody calls me Joe. The last name is the tough one. I'll help you a little. I'm Irish. [*Pause.*] Is it just plain Mary?

MARY. Yes, it is. I'm Irish, too. At least on my father's side. English on my mother's side.

JOE. I'm Irish on both sides. Mary's one of my favorite names. I guess that's why I didn't think of it. I met a girl in Mexico City named Mary once. She was an American from Philadelphia. She got married there. In Mexico City, I mean. While I was *there*. We were in love, too. At least *I* was. You never know about anyone else. They were engaged, you see, and her mother was with her, so they went through with it. Must have been six or seven years ago. She's probably got three or four children by this time.

MARY. Are you still in love with her?

JOE. Well—no. To tell you the truth, I'm not sure. I guess I am. I didn't even know she was engaged until a couple of days before they got married. I thought *I* was going to marry her. I kept thinking all the time about the kind of kids we would be likely to have. My favorite was the third one. The first two were fine. Handsome and fine and intelligent, but that third one was different. Dumb and goofy-looking. I liked *him* a lot. When she told me she was going to be married, I didn't feel so bad about the first two, it was that dumb one.

MARY [*after a pause of some few seconds*]. What do you do?

JOE. Do? To tell you the truth, nothing.

MARY. Do you always drink a great deal?

JOE [*scientifically*]. Not *always*. Only when I'm awake. I sleep seven or eight hours every night, you know.

MARY. How nice. I mean to drink when you're awake.

JOE [*thoughtfully*]. It's a privilege.

MARY. Do you really *like* to drink?

JOE [*positively*]. As much as I like to *breathe*.

MARY [*beautifully*]. Why?

JOE [*dramatically*]. Why do I like to drink? [*Pause.*] Because I don't like to be gypped. Because I don't like to be dead most of the time and just a little alive every once in a long while. [*Pause.*] If I don't drink, I become fascinated by unimportant things— like everybody else. I get busy. Do things. All kinds of little stupid things, for all kinds of little stupid reasons. Proud, selfish, *ordinary* things. I've done them. Now I don't do anything. *I live all the time.* Then I go to sleep. [*Pause.*]

MARY. Do you sleep well?

JOE [*taking it for granted*]. Of course.

MARY [*quietly, almost with tenderness*]. What are your plans?

JOE [*loudly, but also tenderly*]. Plans? I haven't *got* any. *I just get up.*

MARY [*beginning to understand everything*]. Oh, yes. Yes, of course.

[DUDLEY *puts a nickel in the phonograph.*]

JOE [*thoughtfully*]. Why do I drink? [*Pause, while he thinks about it. The thinking appears to be profound and complex, and has the effect of giving his face a very comical and naïve expression.*] That question calls for a pretty complicated answer. [*He smiles abstractly.*]

MARY. Oh, I didn't mean—

JOE [*swiftly, gallantly*]. No. No. I *insist*. I *know* why. It's just a matter of finding words. Little ones.

MARY. It really doesn't matter.

JOE [*seriously*]. Oh, yes, it does. [*Clinically.*] Now, why do I drink? [*Scientifically.*] No. Why does *anybody* drink? [*Working it out.*] Every day has twenty-four hours.

MARY [*sadly, but brightly*]. Yes, that's true.

JOE. Twenty-four hours. Out of the twenty-four hours at *least* twenty-three and a half are—my God, I don't know why—dull, dead, boring, empty, and murderous. Minutes on the clock, *not time of living*. It doesn't make any difference who you are or what you do, twenty-three and a half hours of the twenty-four are spent *waiting*.

MARY. Waiting?

JOE [*gesturing, loudly*]. And the more you wait, the less there is to wait *for*.

MARY [*attentively, beautifully his student*]. Oh?

JOE [*continuing*]. That goes on for days and days, and weeks and months and years, and years, and the first thing you know *all* the years are dead. All the minutes are dead. You yourself are dead. There's nothing to wait for any more. Nothing except *minutes* on the *clock*. No time of life. Nothing but minutes, and idiocy. Beautiful, bright, intelligent idiocy. [*Pause.*] Does that answer your question?

MARY [*earnestly*]. I'm afraid it does. Thank you. You shouldn't have gone to all the trouble.

JOE. No trouble at all. [*Pause.*] You have children?

MARY. Yes. Two. A son and a daughter.

JOE [*delighted*]. How swell. Do they look like you?

MARY. Yes.

JOE. Then why are you sad?

MARY. I was always sad. It's just that after I was married I was allowed to drink.

JOE [*eagerly*]. Who are you waiting for?

MARY. No one.

JOE [*smiling*]. I'm not waiting for anybody, either.

MARY. My husband, of course.

JOE. Oh, sure.

MARY. He's a lawyer.

JOE [*standing, leaning on the table*]. He's a great guy. I like him. I'm very fond of him.

MARY [*listening*]. You have responsibilities?

JOE [*loudly*]. One, and *thousands*. As a matter of fact, I feel responsible to everybody. At least to everybody I meet. I've been trying for three years to find out if it's possible to live what I think is a civilized life. I mean a life that can't hurt any other life.

MARY. You're famous?

JOE. Very. Utterly unknown, but very famous. Would you like to dance?

MARY. All right.

JOE [*loudly*]. I'm *sorry*. I don't dance. I didn't think you'd like to.

MARY. To tell you the truth, I don't like to dance at all.

JOE [*proudly—commentator*]. I can hardly walk.

MARY. You mean you're tight?

JOE [*smiling*]. No. I mean *all* the time.

MARY [*looking at him closely*]. Were you ever in Paris?

JOE. In 1929, and again in 1934.

MARY. What month of 1934?

JOE. Most of April, all of May, and a little of June.

MARY. I was there in November and December that year.

JOE. We were there almost at the same time. You were married?

MARY. Engaged. [*They are silent a moment, looking at one another. Quietly and with great charm.*] Are you *really* in love with me?

JOE. Yes.

MARY. Is it the champagne?

JOE. Yes. Partly, at least. [*He sits down.*]

MARY. If you don't see me again, will you be very unhappy?

JOE. Very.

MARY [*getting up*]. I'm so pleased. [JOE *is deeply grieved that she is going. In fact, he is almost panic-stricken about it, getting up in a way that is full of furious sorrow and regret.*] I must go now. Please don't get up. [JOE *is up, staring at her with amazement.*] Good-by.

JOE [*simply*]. Good-by.

[*The* WOMAN *stands looking at him a moment, then turns and goes.* JOE *stands staring after her for a long time. Just as he is slowly sitting down again, the* NEWSBOY *enters, and goes to* JOE'S *table.*]

NEWSBOY. Paper, Mister?

JOE. How many you got this time?

NEWSBOY. Eleven.

[JOE *buys them all, looks at the lousy headlines, throws them away. The* NEWSBOY *looks at* JOE, *amazed. He walks over to* NICK *at the bar.*]

NEWSBOY [*troubled*]. Hey, Mister, do you own this place?

NICK [*casually but emphatically*]. I own this place.

NEWSBOY. Can you use a great lyric tenor?

NICK [*almost to himself*]. Great lyric tenor? [*Loudly.*] Who?

NEWSBOY [*loud and the least bit angry*]. Me. I'm getting too big to sell papers. I don't want to holler headlines all the time. I want to *sing*. You can use a great lyric tenor, can't you?

NICK. What's lyric about you?

NEWSBOY [*voice high-pitched, confused*]. My voice.

NICK. Oh. [*Slight pause, giving in.*] All right, then— sing!

[*The* NEWSBOY *breaks into swift and beautiful song:*

"When Irish Eyes Are Smiling." NICK *and* JOE *listen carefully:* NICK *with wonder,* JOE *with amazement and delight.*]

NEWSBOY [*singing*].

> When Irish eyes are smiling,
> Sure 'tis like a morn in Spring.
> In the lilt of Irish laughter,
> You can hear the angels sing.
> When Irish hearts are happy,
> All the world seems bright and gay.
> But when Irish eyes are smiling—

NICK [*loudly, swiftly*]. Are you Irish?

NEWSBOY [*speaking swiftly, loudly, a little impatient with the irrelevant question*]. No. I'm Greek. [*He finishes the song, singing louder than ever.*] Sure they steal your heart away. [*He turns to* NICK *dramatically, like a vaudeville singer begging his audience for applause.* NICK *studies the* BOY *eagerly.* JOE *gets to his feet and leans toward the* BOY *and* NICK.]

NICK. Not bad. Let me hear you again about a year from now.

NEWSBOY [*thrilled*]. Honest?

NICK. Yeah. Along about November 7th, 1940.

NEWSBOY [*happier than ever before in his life, running over to* JOE]. Did you hear it too, Mister?

JOE. Yes, and it's great. What part of Greece?

NEWSBOY. Salonica. Gosh, Mister. Thanks.

JOE. Don't wait a year. Come back with some papers a little later. You're a great singer.

NEWSBOY [*thrilled and excited*]. Aw, thanks, Mister. So long. [*Running, to* NICK.] Thanks, Mister. [*He runs out.* JOE *and* NICK *look at the swinging doors.* JOE *sits down.* NICK *laughs.*]

NICK. Joe, people are so wonderful. Look at that kid.

JOE. Of course they're wonderful. Every one of them is wonderful.

[MC CARTHY *and* KRUPP *come in, talking.* MC CARTHY *is a big man in work clothes, which make him seem very young. He is wearing black jeans, and a blue workman's shirt. No tie. No hat. He has broad shoulders, a lean intelligent face, thick black hair. In his right back pocket is the longshoreman's hook. His arms are long and hairy. His sleeves are rolled up to just below his elbows. He is a casual man, easy-going in movement, sharp in perception, swift in appreciation of charm or innocence or comedy, and gentle in spirit. His speech is clear and full of warmth. His voice is powerful, but modulated. He enjoys the world, in spite of the mess it is, and he is fond of people, in spite of the mess they are.* KRUPP *is not quite as tall or broad-shouldered as* MC CARTHY. *He is physically encumbered by his uniform, club, pistol, belt, and cap. And he is plainly not at home in the role of policeman. His movement is stiff and unintentionally pompous. He is a naïve man, essentially good. His understanding is less than* MC CARTHY'S, *but he is honest and he doesn't try to bluff.*]

KRUPP. You don't understand what I mean. Hi-ya, Joe.

JOE. Hello, Krupp.

MC CARTHY. Hi-ya, Joe.

JOE. Hello, McCarthy.

KRUPP. Two beers, Nick. [*To* MC CARTHY.] All I do is carry out orders, carry out orders. I don't know what the idea is behind the order. Who it's for, or who it's against, or why. All I do is carry it out.

[NICK *gives them beer.*]

MC CARTHY. You don't read enough.

KRUPP. I do read. I read *The Examiner* every morning. *The Call-Bulletin* every night.

MC CARTHY. And carry out orders. What are the orders now?

KRUPP. To keep the peace down here on the water-front.

MC CARTHY. Keep it for who? [*To* JOE.] Right?

JOE [*sorrowfully*]. Right.

KRUPP. How do I know for who? The peace. Just keep it.

MC CARTHY. It's got to be kept for somebody. Who would you suspect it's kept for?

KRUPP. For citizens!

MC CARTHY. I'm a citizen!

KRUPP. All right, I'm keeping it for you.

MC CARTHY. By hitting me over the head with a club? [*To* JOE.] Right?

JOE [*melancholy, with remembrance*]. I don't know.

KRUPP. Mac, you know I never hit you over the head with a club.

MC CARTHY. But you will if you're on duty at the time and happen to stand on the opposite side of myself, on duty.

KRUPP. We went to Mission High together. We were always good friends. The only time we ever fought was that time over Alma Haggerty. Did *you* marry Alma Haggerty? [*To* JOE.] Right?

JOE. Everything's right.

MC CARTHY. No. Did you? [*To* JOE.] Joe, are you with me or against me?

JOE. I'm with everybody. One at a time.

KRUPP. No. And that's just what I mean.

MC CARTHY. You mean neither one of us is going to marry the thing we're fighting for?

KRUPP. *I don't even know what it is.*

MC CARTHY. You don't read enough, I tell you.

KRUPP. Mac, you don't know what you're fighting for, either.

MC CARTHY. It's so simple, it's fantastic.

KRUPP. All right, what are you fighting for?

MC CARTHY. For the rights of the inferior. Right?

JOE. Something like that.

KRUPP. The who?

MC CARTHY. The inferior. The world full of Mahoneys who haven't got what it takes to make monkeys out of everybody else, near by. The men who were created equal. Remember?

KRUPP. Mac, you're not inferior.

MC CARTHY. I'm a longshoreman. And an idealist. I'm a man with too much brawn to be an intellectual, exclusively. I married a small, sensitive, cultured woman so that my kids would be sissies instead of suckers. A strong man with any sensibility has no choice in this world but to be a heel, or a *worker*. I haven't the heart to be a heel, so I'm a worker. I've got a son in high school who's already thinking of being a writer.

KRUPP. I wanted to be a writer once.

JOE. Wonderful. [*He puts down the paper, looks at* KRUPP *and* MC CARTHY.]

MC CARTHY. They *all* wanted to be writers. Every maniac in the world that ever brought about the murder of people through war started out in an attic or a basement writing poetry. It stank. So they got even by becoming important heels. And it's still going on.

KRUPP. Is it really, Joe?

JOE. Look at today's paper.

MC CARTHY. Right now on Telegraph Hill is some punk who is trying to be Shakespeare. Ten years from now he'll be a senator. Or a communist.

KRUPP. Somebody ought to do something about it.

MC CARTHY [*mischievously, with laughter in his voice*]. The thing to do is to have more magazines. Hundreds of them. *Thousands.* Print everything they write, so they'll believe they're immortal. That way keep them from going haywire.

KRUPP. Mac, you ought to be a writer yourself.

MC CARTHY. I hate the tribe. They're mischief-makers. Right?

JOE [*swiftly*]. Everything's right. Right and wrong.

KRUPP. Then why do you read?

MC CARTHY [*laughing*]. It's relaxing. It's soothing. [*Pause.*] The lousiest people born into the world are writers. Language is all right. It's the people who use language that are lousy. [*The* ARAB *has moved a little closer, and is listening carefully. To the* ARAB.] What do you think, Brother?

ARAB [*after making many faces, thinking very deeply*]. No foundation. All the way down the line. What. What-not. Nothing. I go walk and look at sky. [*He goes.*]

KRUPP. What? What-not? [*To* JOE.] What's that mean?

JOE [*slowly, thinking, remembering*]. What? What-not? That means this side, that side. Inhale, exhale. What: birth. What-not: death. The inevitable, the astounding, the magnificent seed of growth and decay in all things. Beginning, and end. That man, in his own way, is a prophet. He is one who, with the help of *beer,* is able to reach that state of deep understanding in which what and what-not, the reasonable and the unreasonable, are *one.*

MC CARTHY. Right.

KRUPP. If you can understand that kind of talk, how can you be a longshoreman?

MC CARTHY. I come from a long line of McCarthys who

never married or slept with anything but the most powerful and quarrelsome flesh. [*He drinks beer.*]

KRUPP. I could listen to you two guys for hours, but I'll be damned if I know what the hell you're talking about.

MC CARTHY. The consequence is that all the McCarthys are too great and too strong to be heroes. Only the weak and unsure perform the heroic. They've *got* to. The more heroes you have, the worse the history of the world becomes. Right?

JOE. Go outside and look at it.

KRUPP. You sure can philos—philosoph— Boy, you can talk.

MC CARTHY. I wouldn't talk this way to anyone but a man in uniform, and a man who couldn't understand a word of what I was saying. The party I'm speaking of, my friend, is *YOU*.

[*The phone rings.* HARRY *gets up from his table suddenly and begins a new dance.*]

KRUPP [*noticing him, with great authority*]. Here. Here. What do you think you're doing?

HARRY [*stopping*]. I just got an idea for a new dance. I'm trying it out. Nick. Nick, the phone's ringing.

KRUPP [*to* MC CARTHY]. Has he got a right to do that?

MC CARTHY. The living have danced from the beginning of time. I might even say, the dance and the life have moved along together, until now we have— [*To* HARRY.] Go into your dance, son, and show us what we have.

HARRY. I haven't got it worked out *completely* yet, but it starts out like this. [*He dances.*]

NICK [*on phone*]. Nick's Pacific Street Restaurant, Saloon, and Entertainment Palace. Good afternoon. Nick speaking. [*Listens.*] Who? [*Turns around.*] Is there a Dudley Bostwick in the joint?

[DUDLEY *jumps to his feet and goes to phone.*]

DUDLEY [*on phone*]. Hello. Elsie? [*Listens.*] You're coming down? [*Elated. To the saloon.*] She's coming down. [*Pause.*] No. I won't drink. Aw, gosh, Elsie. [*He hangs up, looks about him strangely, as if he were just born, walks around touching things, putting chairs in place, and so on.*]

MC CARTHY [*to* HARRY]. Splendid. Splendid.

HARRY. Then I go into this little routine. [*He demonstrates.*]

KRUPP. Is that good, Mac?

MC CARTHY. It's awful, but it's honest and ambitious, like everything else in this great country.

HARRY. Then I work along into this. [*He demonstrates.*] And *this* is where I *really* get going. [*He finishes the dance.*]

MC CARTHY. Excellent. A most satisfying demonstration of the present state of the American body and soul. Son, you're a genius.

HARRY [*delighted, shaking hands with* MC CARTHY]. I go on in front of an audience for the first time in my life tonight.

MC CARTHY. They'll be delighted. Where'd you learn to dance?

HARRY. Never took a lesson in my life. I'm a natural-born dancer. And *comedian*, too.

MC CARTHY [*astounded*]. You can make people *laugh*?

HARRY [*dumbly*]. I can be funny, but they won't laugh.

MC CARTHY. That's odd. Why not?

HARRY. I don't know. They just won't laugh.

MC CARTHY. Would you care to be funny now?

HARRY. I'd like to try out a new monologue I've been thinking about.

MC CARTHY. Please do. I promise you if it's funny I shall *roar* with laughter.

HARRY. This is it. [*Goes into the act, with much energy.*] I'm up at Sharkey's on Turk Street. It's a quarter to nine, daylight saving. Wednesday, the eleventh. What I've got is a headache and a 1918 nickel. What I *want* is a cup of coffee. If I buy a cup of coffee with the nickel, I've got to walk home. I've got an eight-ball problem. George the Greek is shooting a game of snooker with Pedro the Filipino. *I'm in rags.* They're wearing thirty-five dollar suits, made to order. I haven't got a cigarette. They're smoking Bobby Burns panatelas. I'm thinking it over, like I always do. George the Greek is in a tough spot. If I buy a cup of coffee, I'll want another cup. What happens? My *ear* aches! My ear. George the Greek takes the cue. Chalks it. Studies the table. Touches the cue-ball delicately. Tick. What happens? He makes the three-ball! What do I do? I get confused. *I go out and buy a morning paper.* What the hell do I want with a morning paper? What I *want* is a cup of coffee, and a good used car. I go out and buy a morning paper. Thursday, the twelfth. Maybe the headline's about *me.* I take a quick look. *No. The headline is not about me.* It's about Hitler. Seven thousand miles away. I'm here. Who the hell is Hitler? Who's behind the eight-ball? I turn around. *Everybody's behind the eight-ball!*

[*Pause.* KRUPP *moves toward* HARRY *as if to make an important arrest.* HARRY *moves to the swinging doors.* MC CARTHY *stops* KRUPP.]

MC CARTHY [*to* HARRY]. It's the funniest thing I've ever heard. Or *seen,* for that matter.

HARRY [*coming back to* MC CARTHY]. Then, why don't you laugh?

MC CARTHY. I don't know, *yet.*

HARRY. I'm always getting funny ideas that nobody will laugh at.

MC CARTHY [*thoughtfully*]. It may be that you've stumbled headlong into a new kind of comedy.

HARRY. Well, what good is it if it doesn't make anybody laugh?

MC CARTHY. There are *kinds* of laughter, son. I must say, in all truth, that I *am* laughing, although not *out loud*.

HARRY. I want to *hear* people laugh. *Out loud*. That's why I keep thinking of funny things to say.

MC CARTHY. Well. They may catch on in time. Let's go, Krupp. So long, Joe. [MC CARTHY *and* KRUPP *go*.]

JOE. So long. [*After a moment's pause*.] Hey, Nick.

NICK. Yeah.

JOE. Bet McCarthy in the last race.

NICK. You're crazy. That horse is a double-crossing, no-good—

JOE. Bet everything you've got on McCarthy.

NICK. I'm not betting a nickel on him. *You* bet everything you've got on McCarthy.

JOE. I don't need money.

NICK. What makes you think McCarthy's going to win?

JOE. McCarthy's name's McCarthy, isn't it?

NICK. Yeah. So what?

JOE. The *horse* named McCarthy is going to win, *that's all*. Today.

NICK. Why?

JOE. You do what I tell you, and everything will be all right.

NICK. McCarthy likes to talk, that's all. [*Pause*.] Where's Tom?

JOE. He'll be around. He'll be miserable, but he'll be around. Five or ten minutes more.

NICK. You don't believe that Kitty, do you? About being in burlesque?

JOE [*very clearly*]. I believe dreams sooner than statistics.

NICK [*remembering*]. She sure is somebody. Called me a dentist.

[TOM, *turning about, confused, troubled, comes in, and hurries to* JOE's *table.*]

JOE. What's the matter?

TOM. Here's your five, Joe. I'm in trouble again.

JOE. If it's not organic, it'll cure itself. If it is organic, science will cure it. What is it, organic or non-organic?

TOM. Joe, I don't know— [*He seems to be completely broken down.*]

JOE. What's eating you? I want you to go on an errand for me.

TOM. It's Kitty.

JOE. What about her?

TOM. She's up in her room, crying.

JOE. Crying?

TOM. Yeah, she's been crying for over an hour. I been talking to her all this time, but she won't stop.

JOE. What's she crying about?

TOM. I don't know. I couldn't understand anything. She kept crying and telling me about a big house and collie dogs all around and flowers and one of her brothers dead and the other one lost somewhere. Joe, I can't stand Kitty crying.

JOE. You want to marry the girl?

TOM [*nodding*]. Yeah.

JOE [*curious and sincere*]. Why?

TOM. I don't know why, exactly, Joe. [*Pause.*] Joe, I don't like to think of Kitty out in the streets. I guess I love her, that's all.

JOE. She's a nice girl.

TOM. She's like an angel. She's not like those other street-walkers.

JOE [*swiftly*]. Here. Take all this money and run next

door to Frankie's and bet it on the nose of Mc-
Carthy.

TOM [*swiftly*]. All this money, Joe? McCarthy?

JOE. Yeah. Hurry.

TOM [*going*]. Ah, Joe. If McCarthy wins we'll be rich.

JOE. Get going, will you?

[TOM *runs out and nearly knocks over the* ARAB *coming back in.* NICK *fills him a beer without a word.*]

ARAB. No foundation, anywhere. Whole world. No
foundation. All the way down the line.

NICK [*angry*]. McCarthy! Just because you got a little
lucky this morning, you have to go to work and
throw away eighty bucks.

JOE. He wants to marry her.

NICK. Suppose she doesn't want to marry *him*?

JOE [*amazed*]. Oh, yeah. [*Thinking.*] Now, why
wouldn't she want to marry a nice guy like Tom?

NICK. She's been in burlesque. She's had flowers sent to
her by European royalty. She's dined with young
men of quality and social position. She's above Tom.

[TOM *comes running in.*]

TOM [*disgusted*]. They were running when I got there.
Frankie wouldn't take the bet. McCarthy didn't get
a call till the stretch. I thought we were going to
save all this money. Then McCarthy won by *two*
lengths.

JOE. What'd he pay, fifteen to one?

TOM. Better, but Frankie wouldn't take the bet.

NICK [*throwing a dish towel across the room*]. Well, for
the love of Mike.

JOE. Give me the money.

TOM [*giving back the money*]. We would have had
about a thousand five hundred dollars.

JOE [*bored, casually, inventing*]. Go up to Schwab-
acher-Frey and get me the biggest Rand-McNally

map of the nations of Europe they've got. On your way back stop at one of the pawn shops on Third Street, and buy me a good revolver and some cartridges.

TOM. She's up in her room crying, Joe.

JOE. Go get me those things.

NICK. What are you going to do, study the map, and then go out and shoot somebody?

JOE. I want to read the names of some European towns and rivers and valleys and mountains.

NICK. What do you want with the revolver?

JOE. I want to study it. I'm interested in things. Here's twenty dollars, Tom. Now go get them things.

TOM. A big map of Europe. And a revolver.

JOE. Get a good one. Tell the man you don't know anything about firearms and you're trusting him not to fool you. Don't pay more than ten dollars.

TOM. Joe, you got something on your mind. Don't go fool with a revolver.

JOE. Be sure it's a good one.

TOM. Joe.

JOE [*irritated*]. What, Tom?

TOM. Joe, what do you send me out for crazy things for all the time?

JOE [*angry*]. They're not crazy, Tom. Now, get going.

TOM. What about Kitty, Joe?

JOE. Let her cry. It'll do her good.

TOM. If she comes in here while I'm gone, talk to her, will you, Joe? Tell her about me?

JOE. O. K. Get going. Don't load that gun. Just buy it and bring it here.

TOM [*going*]. You won't catch me loading any gun.

JOE. Wait a minute. Take these toys away.

TOM. Where'll I take them?

JOE. Give them to some kid. [*Pause.*] No. Take them

up to Kitty. Toys stopped me from crying once. That's the reason I had you buy them. I wanted to see if I could find out *why* they stopped me from crying. I remember they seemed awfully stupid at the time.

TOM. Shall I, Joe? Take them up to Kitty? Do you think they'd stop *her* from crying?

JOE. They might. You get curious about the way they work and you forget whatever it is you're remembering that's making you cry. That's what they're for.

TOM. Yeah. Sure. The girl at the store asked me what I wanted with toys. I'll take them up to Kitty. [*Tragically.*] She's like a little girl. [*He goes.*]

WESLEY. Mr. Nick, can I play the piano again?

NICK. Sure. Practice all you like—until I tell you to stop.

WESLEY. You going to pay me for playing the piano?

NICK. Sure. I'll give you enough to get by on.

WESLEY [*amazed and delighted*]. Get money for playing the piano? [*He goes to the piano and begins to play quietly.* HARRY *goes up on the little stage and listens to the music. After a while he begins a soft-shoe dance.*]

NICK. What were you crying about?

JOE. My mother.

NICK. What about her?

JOE. She was dead. I stopped crying when they gave me the toys.

[NICK'S MOTHER, *a little old woman of sixty or so, dressed plainly in black, her face shining, comes in briskly, chattering loudly in Italian, gesturing.* NICK *is delighted to see her.*]

NICK'S MOTHER [*in Italian*]. Everything all right, Nickie?

NICK [*in Italian*]. Sure, Mamma.

[NICK'S MOTHER *leaves as gaily and as noisily as she came, after half a minute of loud Italian family talk.*]

JOE. Who was that?

NICK [*to* JOE, *proudly and a little sadly*]. My mother. [*Still looking at the swinging doors.*]

JOE. What'd she say?

NICK. Nothing. Just wanted to see me. [*Pause.*] What do you want with that gun?

JOE. I study things, Nick.

[*An* OLD MAN *who looks as if he might have been Kit Carson at one time walks in importantly, moves about, and finally stands at* JOE's *table.*]

KIT CARSON. Murphy's the name. Just an old trapper. Mind if I sit down?

JOE. Be delighted. What'll you drink?

KIT CARSON [*sitting down*]. Beer. Same as I've been drinking. And thanks.

JOE [*to* NICK]. Glass of beer, Nick.

[NICK *brings the beer to the table,* KIT CARSON *swallows it in one swig, wipes his big white mustache with the back of his right hand.*]

KIT CARSON [*moving in*]. I don't suppose you ever fell in love with a midget weighing thirty-nine pounds?

JOE [*studying the man*]. Can't say I have, but have another beer.

KIT CARSON [*intimately*]. Thanks, thanks. Down in Gallup, twenty years ago. Fellow by the name of Rufus Jenkins came to town with six white horses and two black ones. Said he wanted a man to break the horses for him because his left leg was wood and he couldn't do it. Had a meeting at Parker's Mercantile Store and finally came to blows, me and Henry Walpal. Bashed his head with a brass cuspidor and ran away to Mexico, but he didn't die. Couldn't speak a word. Took up with a cattle-breeder named Diego, educated in California. Spoke the language better than you and me. Said, Your job, Murph, is to feed them prize bulls. I said, Fine, what'll I feed them? He said, Hay, lettuce, salt, beer, and aspirin. Came to blows two days later over an accordion he claimed I stole. I had *borrowed* it. During the fight I busted it over his head; ruined one of the finest accordions I ever saw. Grabbed a horse and rode back across the border. Texas. Got to talking with a fellow who looked honest. Turned out to be a Ranger who was looking for me.

JOE. Yeah. You were saying, a thirty-nine-pound midget.

KIT CARSON. Will I ever forget that lady? Will I ever get over that amazon of small proportions?

JOE. Will you?

KIT CARSON. If I live to be sixty.

JOE. Sixty? You look more than sixty now.

KIT CARSON. That's trouble showing in my face. Trouble and complications. I was fifty-eight three months ago.

JOE. That accounts for it, then. Go ahead, tell me more.

KIT CARSON. Told the Texas Ranger my name was Rothstein, mining engineer from Pennsylvania, looking for something worth while. Mentioned two places in Houston. Nearly lost an eye early one morning, going down the stairs. Ran into a six-footer with an iron claw where his right hand was supposed to be. Said, You broke up my home. Told him I was a stranger in Houston. The girls gathered at the top of the stairs to see a fight. Seven of them. Six feet and an iron claw. That's bad on the nerves. Kicked him in the mouth when he swung for my head with the claw. Would have lost an eye except for quick thinking. He rolled into the gutter and pulled a gun. Fired seven times. I was back upstairs. Left the place an hour later, dressed in silk and feathers, with a hat swung around over my face. Saw him standing on the corner, waiting. Said, Care for a wiggle? Said he didn't. I went on down the street and left town. I don't suppose you ever had to put a dress on to save your skin, did you?

JOE. No, and I never fell in love with a midget weighing thirty-nine pounds. Have another beer?

KIT CARSON. Thanks. [*Swallows glass of beer.*] Ever try to herd cattle on a bicycle?

JOE. No. I never got around to that.

KIT CARSON. Left Houston with sixty cents in my pocket, gift of a girl named Lucinda. Walked fourteen miles in fourteen hours. Big house with barbwire all around, and big dogs. One thing I never could get around. Walked past the gate, anyway, from hunger and thirst. Dogs jumped up and came for me. Walked right into them, growing older every second. Went up to the door and knocked. Big Negress opened the door, closed it quick. Said, On your way, white trash. Knocked again. Said, On your way. Again. On your way. Again. This time the old man himself opened the door, ninety, if he was a day. Sawed-off shotgun, too. Said, I ain't looking for trouble, Father. I'm hungry and thirsty, name's Cavanaugh. Took me in and made mint juleps for the two of us. Said, Living here alone, Father? Said, Drink and ask no questions. Maybe I am and maybe I ain't. You saw the lady. Draw your own conclusions. I'd heard of that, but didn't wink out of tact. If I told you that old Southern gentleman was my grandfather, you wouldn't believe me, would you?

JOE. I might.

KIT CARSON. Well, it so happens he wasn't. Would have been romantic if he had been, though.

JOE. Where did you herd cattle on a bicycle?

KIT CARSON. Toledo, Ohio, 1918.

JOE. Toledo, Ohio? They don't herd cattle in Toledo.

KIT CARSON. They don't any more. They did in 1918. One fellow did, leastaways. Bookkeeper named Sam Gold. Straight from the East Side, New York. Sombrero, lariats, Bull Durham, two head of cattle and two bicycles. Called his place The Gold Bar Ranch, two acres, just outside the city limits. That was the year of the War, you'll remember.

JOE. Yeah, I remember, but how about herding them two cows on a bicycle? How'd you do it?

KIT CARSON. Easiest thing in the world. Rode no hands. Had to, otherwise couldn't lasso the cows. Worked for Sam Gold till the cows ran away. Bicycles scared them. They went into Toledo. Never saw hide nor hair of them again. Advertised in every paper, but never got them back. Broke his heart. Sold both bikes and returned to New York. Took four aces from a deck of red cards and walked to town. Poker. Fellow in the game named Chuck Collins, liked to gamble. Told him with a smile I didn't suppose he'd care to bet a hundred dollars I wouldn't hold four aces the next hand. Called it. My cards were red on the blank side. The other cards were blue. Plumb forgot all about it. Showed him four aces. Ace of spades, ace of clubs, ace of diamonds, ace of hearts. I'll remember them four cards if I live to be sixty. Would have been killed on the spot except for the hurricane that year.

JOE. Hurricane?

KIT CARSON. You haven't forgotten the Toledo hurricane of 1918, have you?

JOE. No. There was no hurricane in Toledo in 1918, or any other year.

KIT CARSON. For the love of God, then what do you sup-

pose that commotion was? And how come I came to
in Chicago, dream-walking down State Street?

JOE. I guess they scared you.

KIT CARSON. No, that wasn't it. You go back to the papers of November 1918, and I think you'll find there
was a hurricane in Toledo. I remember sitting on
the roof of a two-story house, floating northwest.

JOE [*seriously*]. Northwest?

KIT CARSON. Now, son, don't tell me *you* don't believe
me, either?

JOE [*pause. Very seriously, energetically and sharply*].
Of course I believe you. Living is an art. It's not
bookkeeping. It takes a lot of rehearsing for a man
to get to be himself.

KIT CARSON [*thoughtfully, smiling, and amazed*]. You're
the first man I've ever met who believes me.

JOE [*seriously*]. Have another beer.

[TOM *comes in with the Rand-McNally book, the revolver, and the box of cartridges.* KIT *goes to bar.*]

JOE [*to* TOM]. Did you give her the toys?

TOM. Yeah, I gave them to her.

JOE. Did she stop crying?

TOM. No. She started crying harder than ever.

JOE. That's funny. I wonder why.

TOM. Joe, if I was a minute earlier, Frankie would
have taken the bet and now we'd have about a thousand five hundred dollars. How much of it would
you have given me, Joe?

JOE. If she'd marry you—*all* of it.

TOM. Would you, Joe?

JOE [*opening packages, examining book first, and revolver next*]. Sure. In this realm there's only one
subject, and you're it. It's my duty to see that my
subject is happy.

TOM. Joe, do you think we'll ever have eighty dollars
for a race sometime again when there's a fifteen-to-

one shot that we like, weather good, track fast, they get off to a good start, our horse doesn't get a call till the stretch, we think we're going to lose all that money, and then it wins, by a nose?

JOE. I didn't quite get that.

TOM. You know what I mean.

JOE. You mean the impossible. No, Tom, we won't. We were just a little late, that's all.

TOM. We might, Joe.

JOE. It's not likely.

TOM. Then how am I ever going to make enough money to marry her?

JOE. I don't know, Tom. Maybe you aren't.

TOM. Joe, I got to marry Kitty. [*Shaking his head.*] You ought to see the crazy room she lives in.

JOE. What kind of a room is it?

TOM. It's little. It crowds you in. It's bad, Joe. Kitty don't belong in a place like that.

JOE. You want to take her away from there?

TOM. Yeah. I want her to live in a house where there's room enough to live. Kitty ought to have a garden, or something.

JOE. You want to take care of her?

TOM. Yeah, sure, Joe. I ought to take care of somebody good that makes me feel like *I'm* somebody.

JOE. That means you'll have to get a job. What can you do?

TOM. I finished high school, but I don't know what I can do.

JOE. Sometimes when you think about it, what do you think you'd like to do?

TOM. Just sit around like you, Joe, and have somebody run errands for me and drink champagne and take things easy and never be broke and never worry about money.

JOE. That's a noble ambition.

NICK [*to* JOE]. How do you do it?

JOE. I really don't know, but I think you've got to have the full co-operation of the Good Lord.

NICK. I can't understand the way you talk.

TOM. Joe, shall I go back and see if I can get her to stop crying?

JOE. Give me a hand and I'll go with you.

TOM [*amazed*]. What! You're going to get up already?

JOE. She's crying, isn't she?

TOM. She's crying. Worse than ever now.

JOE. I thought the toys would stop her.

TOM. I've seen you sit in one place from four in the morning till two the next morning.

JOE. At my best, Tom, I don't travel by foot. That's all. Come on. Give me a hand. I'll find some way to stop her from crying.

TOM [*helping* JOE]. Joe, I never did tell you. You're a different kind of a guy.

JOE [*swiftly, a little angry*]. Don't be silly. I don't understand things. I'm trying to understand them.

[JOE *is a little drunk. They go out together. The lights go down slowly, while* WESLEY *plays the piano, and come up slowly on.*]

Act three

A cheap bed in NICK'S *to indicate room 21 of The New York Hotel, upstairs, around the corner from* NICK'S. *The bed can be at the center of* NICK'S, *or up on the little stage. Everything in* NICK'S *is the same, except that all the people are silent, immobile and in darkness, except* WESLEY *who is playing the piano softly and sadly.* KITTY DUVAL, *in a dress she has carried around with her from the early days in Ohio, is seated on the bed, tying a ribbon in her hair. She looks at herself in a hand mirror. She is deeply grieved at the change she sees in herself. She takes off the ribbon, angry and hurt. She lifts a book from the bed and tries to read. She begins to sob again. She picks up an old picture of herself and looks at it. Sobs harder than ever, falling on the bed and burying her face. There is a knock, as if at the door.*

KITTY [*sobbing*]. Who is it?

TOM's VOICE. Kitty, it's me. Tom. Me and Joe.

[JOE, *followed by* TOM, *comes to the bed quietly.* JOE *is holding a rather large toy carousel.* JOE *studies* KITTY *a moment. He sets the toy carousel on the floor, at the foot of* KITTY's *bed.*]

TOM [*standing over* KITTY *and bending down close to her*]. Don't cry any more, Kitty.

KITTY [*not looking, sobbing*]. I don't like this life.

[JOE *starts the carousel which makes a strange, sorrowful, tinkling music. The music begins slowly, becomes swift, gradually slows down, and ends.* JOE *himself is interested in the toy, watches and listens to it carefully.*]

TOM [*eagerly*]. Kitty. Joe got up from his chair at Nick's just to get you a toy and come here. This one makes music. We rode all over town in a cab to get it. Listen.

[KITTY *sits up slowly, listening, while* TOM *watches her. Everything happens slowly and somberly.* KITTY *notices the photograph of herself when she was a little girl. Lifts it, and looks at it again.*]

TOM [*looking*]. Who's that little girl, Kitty?

KITTY. That's me. When I was seven.

TOM [*looking, smiling*]. Gee, you're pretty, Kitty.

[JOE *reaches up for the photograph, which* TOM *hands*

to him. TOM *returns to* KITTY *whom he finds as pretty now as she was at seven.* JOE *studies the photograph.* KITTY *looks up at* TOM. *There is no doubt that they really love one another.* JOE *looks up at them.*]

KITTY. Tom?

TOM [*eagerly*]. Yeah, Kitty.

KITTY. Tom, when you were a little boy what did you want to be?

TOM [*a little bewildered, but eager to please her*]. What, Kitty?

KITTY. Do you remember when you were a little boy?

TOM [*thoughtfully*]. Yeah, I remember sometimes, Kitty.

KITTY. What did you want to be?

TOM [*looks at* JOE. JOE *holds* TOM'S *eyes a moment. Then* TOM *is able to speak*]. Sometimes I wanted to be a locomotive engineer. Sometimes I wanted to be a policeman.

KITTY. I wanted to be a great actress. [*She looks up into* TOM'S *face.*] Tom, didn't you ever want to be a doctor?

TOM [*looks at* JOE. JOE *holds* TOM'S *eyes again, encouraging* TOM *by his serious expression to go on talking*]. Yeah, now I remember. Sure, Kitty. I wanted to be a doctor—once.

KITTY [*smiling sadly*]. I'm so glad. Because I wanted to be an actress and have a young doctor come to the theater and see me and fall in love with me and send me flowers.

[JOE *pantomimes to* TOM, *demanding that he go on talking.*]

TOM. I would do that, Kitty.

KITTY. I wouldn't know who it was, and then one day I'd see him in the street and fall in love with him. I wouldn't know *he* was the one who was in love with me. I'd think about him all the time. I'd dream about him. I'd dream of being near him the rest of my life. I'd dream of having children that looked like him. I wouldn't be an actress all the time. Only until I found him and fell in love with him. After that we'd take a train and go to beautiful cities and see the wonderful people everywhere and give money to the poor and whenever people were sick he'd go to them and make them well again.

[TOM *looks at* JOE, *bewildered, confused, and full of sorrow.* KITTY *is deep in memory, almost in a trance.*]

JOE [*gently*]. Talk to her, Tom. Be the wonderful young doctor she dreamed about and never found. Go ahead. Correct the errors of the world.

TOM. Joe. [*Pathetically.*] I don't know what to say.

[*There is rowdy singing in the hall. A loud young* VOICE *sings:* "*Sailing, sailing, over the bounding main.*"]

VOICE. Kitty. Oh, Kitty! [KITTY *stirs, shocked, coming out of the trance.*] Where the hell are you? Oh, Kitty.

[TOM *jumps up, furiously.*]

WOMAN'S VOICE [*in the hall*]. Who are you looking for, Sailor Boy?

VOICE. The most beautiful lay in the world.

WOMAN'S VOICE. Don't go any further.

VOICE [*with impersonal contempt*]. You? No. Not you. Kitty. You stink.

WOMAN'S VOICE [*rasping, angry*]. Don't you dare to talk to me that way. You pickpocket.

VOICE [*still impersonal, but louder*]. Oh, I see. Want to get tough, hey? Close the door. Go hide.

WOMAN'S VOICE. You pickpocket. All of you. [*The door slams.*]

VOICE [*roaring with laughter which is very sad*]. Oh— Kitty. Room 21. Where the hell is that room?

TOM [*to* JOE]. Joe, I'll kill him.

KITTY [*fully herself again, terribly frightened*]. Who is it?

[*She looks long and steadily at* TOM *and* JOE. TOM *is standing, excited and angry.* JOE *is completely at ease, his expression full of pity.* KITTY *buries her face in the bed.*]

JOE [*gently*]. Tom. Just take him away.

VOICE. Here it is. Number 21. Three naturals. Heaven. My blue heaven. The west, a nest, and you. Just Molly and me. [*Tragically.*] Ah, to hell with everything.

[*A young* SAILOR, *a good-looking boy of no more than twenty or so, who is only drunk and lonely, comes to the bed, singing sadly.*]

SAILOR. Hi-ya, Kitty. [*Pause.*] Oh. Visitors. Sorry. A thousand apologies. [*To* KITTY.] I'll come back later.

TOM [*taking him by the shoulders, furiously*]. If you do, I'll kill you.

[JOE *holds* TOM. TOM *pushes the frightened boy away.*]

JOE [*somberly*]. Tom. You stay here with Kitty. I'm going down to Union Square to hire an automobile. I'll be back in a few minutes. We'll ride out to the ocean and watch the sun go down. Then we'll ride down the Great Highway to Half Moon Bay. We'll have supper down there, and you and Kitty can dance.

TOM [*stupefied, unable to express his amazement and gratitude*]. Joe, you mean, you're going to go on an errand for *me*? You mean you're not going to send me?

JOE. That's right. [*He gestures toward* KITTY, *indicating that* TOM *shall talk to her, protect the innocence in her which is in so much danger when* TOM *isn't near, which* TOM *loves so deeply.* JOE *leaves.* TOM *studies* KITTY, *his face becoming childlike and som-*

ber. *He sets the carousel into motion, listens, watching* KITTY, *who lifts herself slowly, looking only at* TOM. TOM *lifts the turning carousel and moves it slowly toward* KITTY, *as though the toy were his heart. The piano music comes up loudly and the lights go down, while* HARRY *is heard dancing swiftly.*]

BLACKOUT

Act four

A little later.
WESLEY, *the colored boy, is at the piano.*
HARRY *is on the little stage, dancing.*
NICK *is behind the bar.*
The ARAB *is in his place.*
KIT CARSON *is asleep on his folded arms.*
The DRUNKARD *comes in. Goes to the telephone for the nickel that might be in the return-chute.* NICK *comes to take him out. He gestures for* NICK *to hold on a minute. Then produces a half dollar.* NICK *goes behind the bar to serve the* DRUNKARD *whiskey.*

THE DRUNKARD. To the old, God bless them. [*Another.*] To the new, God love them. [*Another.*] To—children and small animals, like little dogs that don't bite. [*Another. Loudly.*] To reforestation. [*Searches for money. Finds some.*] To—President Taft. [*He goes out. The telephone rings.*]
KIT CARSON [*jumping up, fighting*]. Come on, *all* of you, if you're looking for trouble. I never asked for quarter and I always gave it.

NICK [*reproachfully*]. Hey, Kit Carson.

DUDLEY [*on the phone*]. Hello. Who? Nick? Yes. He's here. [*To* NICK.] It's for you. I think it's important.

NICK [*going to the phone*]. Important! *What's* important?

DUDLEY. He sounded like a big-shot.

NICK. Big *what?* [*To* WESLEY *and* HARRY.] Hey, you. Quiet. I want to hear this important stuff.

[WESLEY *stops playing the piano.* HARRY *stops dancing.* KIT CARSON *comes close to* NICK.]

KIT CARSON. If there's anything I can do, name it. I'll do it for you. I'm fifty-eight years old; been through three wars; married four times; the father of countless children whose *names* I don't even know. I've got no money. I live from hand to mouth. But if there's anything I can do, name it. I'll do it.

NICK [*patiently*]. Listen, Pop. For a moment, please sit down and go back to sleep—*for me.*

KIT CARSON. I can do that, too. [*He sits down, folds his arms, and puts his head into them. But not for long. As* NICK *begins to talk, he listens carefully, gets to his feet, and then begins to express in pantomime the moods of each of* NICK'S *remarks.*]

NICK [*on phone*]. Yeah? [*Pause.*] Who? Oh, I see. [*Listens.*] Why don't you leave them alone? [*Listens.*] The church-people? Well, to hell with the church-people. I'm a Catholic myself. [*Listens.*] All right. I'll send them away. I'll tell them to lay low for a couple of days. Yeah, I know how it is. [NICK'S *daughter* ANNA *comes in shyly, looking at her father, and stands unnoticed by the piano.*] What? [*Very angry.*] Listen. I don't like that Blick. He was here this morning, and I told him not to come back. I'll keep the girls out of here. You keep Blick out of here. [*Listens.*] I know his brother-in-law is important, but I don't want him to come down here.

He looks for trouble everywhere, and he always finds it. I don't break any laws. I've got a dive in the lousiest part of town. Five years nobody's been robbed, murdered or gypped. I leave people alone. Your swanky joints uptown make trouble for you every night. [NICK *gestures to* WESLEY—*keeps listening on the phone—puts his hand over the mouthpiece. To* WESLEY *and* HARRY.] Start playing again. My ears have got a headache. Go into your dance, son. [WESLEY *begins to play again.* HARRY *begins to dance.* NICK *into mouthpiece.*] Yeah. I'll keep them out. Just see that Blick doesn't come around and start something. [*Pause.*] O.K. [*He hangs up.*]

KIT CARSON. Trouble coming?

NICK. That lousy Vice Squad again. It's that gorilla Blick.

KIT CARSON. Anybody at all. You can count on me. What kind of a gorilla is this gorilla Blick?

NICK. Very dignified. Toenails on his fingers.

ANNA [*to* KIT CARSON, *with great, warm, beautiful pride, pointing at* NICK]. That's my father.

KIT CARSON [*leaping with amazement at the beautiful voice, the wondrous face, the magnificent event*]. Well, bless your heart, child. Bless your lovely heart. I had a little daughter point me out in a crowd once.

NICK [*surprised*]. Anna. What the hell are you doing here? Get back home where you belong and help Grandma cook me some supper. [ANNA *smiles at her father, understanding him, knowing that his words are words of love. She turns and goes, looking at him all the way out, as much as to say that she would cook for him the rest of her life.* NICK *stares at the swinging doors.* KIT CARSON *moves toward them, two or three steps.* ANNA *pushes open one of the doors and peeks in, to look at her father again. She waves to him. Turns and runs.* NICK *is very sad.*

He doesn't know what to do. He gets a glass and a bottle. Pours himself a drink. Swallows some. It isn't enough, so he pours more and swallows the whole drink. To himself.] My beautiful, beautiful baby. Anna, she is you again. [*He brings out a handkerchief, touches his eyes, and blows his nose.* KIT CARSON *moves close to* NICK, *watching* NICK's *face.* NICK *looks at him. Loudly, almost making* KIT *jump.*] You're broke, aren't you?

KIT CARSON. Always. Always.

NICK. All right. Go into the kitchen and give Sam a hand. Eat some food and when you come back you can have a couple of beers.

KIT CARSON [*studying* NICK]. Anything at all. I know a good man when I see one. [*He goes.*]

[ELSIE MANDELSPIEGEL *comes into* NICK's. *She is a beautiful, dark girl, with a sorrowful, wise, dreaming face, almost on the verge of tears, and full of pity. There is an aura of dream about her. She moves softly and gently, as if everything around her were unreal and pathetic.* DUDLEY *doesn't notice her for a moment or two. When he does finally see her, he is so amazed, he can barely move or speak. Her presence has the effect of changing him completely. He gets up from his chair, as if in a trance, and walks toward her, smiling sadly.*]

ELSIE [*looking at him*]. Hello, Dudley.

DUDLEY [*broken-hearted*]. Elsie.

ELSIE. I'm sorry. [*Explaining.*] So many people are sick. Last night a little boy died. I love you, but— [*She gestures, trying to indicate how hopeless love is. They sit down.*]

DUDLEY [*staring at her, stunned and quieted*]. Elsie. You'll never know how glad I am to see you. Just to see you. [*Pathetically.*] I was afraid I'd never see you again. It was driving me crazy. I didn't want to live. Honest. [*He shakes his head mournfully; with dumb and beautiful affection.* TWO STREETWALKERS *come in, and pause near* DUDLEY, *at the bar.*] I know. You told me before, but I can't help it, Elsie, I love you.

ELSIE [*quietly, somberly, gently, with great compassion*]. I know you love me, and I love you, but don't you see love is impossible in this world?

DUDLEY. Maybe it isn't, Elsie.

ELSIE. Love is for birds. They have wings to fly away on when it's time for flying. For tigers in the jungle because they don't know their end. We know *our* end. Every night I watch over poor, dying men. I hear them breathing, crying, talking in their sleep. Crying for air and water and love, for mother and field and sunlight. We can never know love or greatness. We *should* know both.

DUDLEY [*deeply moved by her words*]. Elsie, I love you.

ELSIE. You want to live. *I* want to live, too, but where? Where can we escape our poor world?

DUDLEY. Elsie, we'll find a place.

ELSIE [*smiling at him*]. All right. We'll try again. We'll go together to a room in a cheap hotel, and dream that the world is beautiful, and that living is full of love and greatness. But in the morning, can we forget debts, and duties, and the cost of ridiculous things?

DUDLEY [*with blind faith*]. Sure, we can, Elsie.

ELSIE. All right, Dudley. Of course. Come on. The time for the new pathetic war has come. Let's hurry, before they dress you, stand you in line, hand you a gun, and have you kill and be killed. [ELSIE *looks at him gently, and takes his hand.* DUDLEY *embraces her shyly, as if he might hurt her. They go, as if they were a couple of young animals. There is a moment of silence. One of the* STREETWALKERS *bursts out laughing.*]

KILLER. Nick, what the hell kind of a joint are you running?

NICK. Well, it's not out of the world. It's on a street in a city, and people come and go. They bring whatever they've got with them and they say what they must say.

THE OTHER STREETWALKER. It's floozies like her that raise hell with our racket.

NICK [*remembering*]. Oh, yeah. Finnegan telephoned.

KILLER. That mouse in elephant's body?

THE OTHER STREETWALKER. What the hell does *he* want?

NICK. Spend your time at the movies for the next couple of days.

KILLER. They're all lousy. [*Mocking.*] All about love.

NICK. Lousy or not lousy, for a couple of days the flatfoots are going to be romancing you, so stay out of here, and lay low.

KILLER. I always was a pushover for a man in uniform, with a badge, a club and a gun.

[KRUPP *comes into the place. The girls put down their drinks.*]

NICK. O.K., get going.

[*The* GIRLS *begin to leave and meet* KRUPP.]

THE OTHER STREETWALKER. We was just going.

KILLER. We was formerly models at Magnin's. [*They go.*]

KRUPP [*at the bar*]. The strike isn't enough, so they've got to put us on the tails of the girls, too. I don't know. I wish to God I was back in the Sunset holding the hands of kids going home from school, where I belong. I don't like trouble. Give me a beer. [NICK *gives him a beer. He drinks some.*] Right now, McCarthy, my best friend, is with sixty strikers who want to stop the finks who are going to try to unload the *Mary Luckenbach* tonight. Why the hell McCarthy ever became a longshoreman instead of a professor of some kind is something I'll never know.

NICK. Cowboys and Indians, cops and robbers, longshoremen and finks.

KRUPP. They're all guys who are trying to be happy; trying to make a living; support a family; bring up children; enjoy sleep. Go to a movie; take a drive on Sunday. They're all good guys, so out of nowhere comes trouble. All they want is a chance to get out of debt and relax in front of a radio while Amos and Andy go through their act. What the hell do they always want to make trouble for? I been thinking everything over, Nick, and you know what I think?

NICK. No. What?

KRUPP. I think we're all crazy. It came to me while I was on my way to Pier 27. All of a sudden it hit me like a ton of bricks. A thing like that never happened to me before. Here we are in this wonderful world, full of all the wonderful things—here we are —all of us, and look at us. Just look at us. We're crazy. We're nuts. We've got everything, but we always feel lousy and dissatisfied just the same.

NICK. Of course we're crazy. Even so, we've got to go on living together. [*He waves at the people in his joint.*]

KRUPP. There's no hope. I don't suppose it's right for an officer of the law to feel the way I feel, but, by God, right or not right, that's how I feel. Why are we all so lousy? This is a good world. It's wonderful to get up in the morning and go out for a little walk and smell the trees and see the streets and the kids going to school and the clouds in the sky. It's wonderful just to be able to move around and whistle a song if you feel like it, or maybe try to sing one. This is a nice world. So why do they make all the trouble?

NICK. I don't know. Why?

KRUPP. We're crazy, that's why. We're no good any more. All the corruption everywhere. The poor kids selling themselves. A couple of years ago they were in grammar school. Everybody trying to get a lot of money in a hurry. Everybody betting the horses. Nobody going quietly for a little walk to the ocean. Nobody taking things easy and not wanting to make some kind of a killing. Nick, I'm going to quit being a cop. Let somebody else keep law and order. The stuff I hear about at headquarters. I'm thirty-seven years old, and I still can't get used to it. The only trouble is, the wife'll raise hell.

NICK. Ah, the wife.

KRUPP. She's a wonderful woman, Nick. We've got two of the swellest boys in the world. Twelve and seven years old.

[*The* ARAB *gets up and moves closer to listen.*]

NICK. I didn't know that.

KRUPP. Sure. But what'll I do? I've wanted to quit for seven years. I wanted to quit the day they began putting me through the school. I didn't quit. What'll I do if I quit? Where's money going to be coming in from?

NICK. That's one of the reasons we're all crazy. We don't know where it's going to be coming in from, except from wherever it happens to be coming in from at the time, which we don't usually like.

KRUPP. Every once in a while I catch myself being mean, hating people just because they're down and out, broke and hungry, sick or drunk. And then when I'm with the stuffed shirts at headquarters, all of a sudden I'm nice to them, trying to make an impression. On who? People I don't like. And I feel disgusted. [*With finality.*] I'm going to quit. That's all. Quit. Out. I'm going to give them back the uniform and the gadgets that go with it. I don't want any part of it. This is a good world. What do they want to make all the trouble for all the time?

ARAB [*quietly, gently, with great understanding*]. No foundation. All the way down the line.

KRUPP. What?

ARAB. No foundation. No foundation.

KRUPP. I'll say there's no foundation.

ARAB. All the way down the line.

KRUPP [*to* NICK]. Is that all he ever says?

NICK. That's all he's been saying *this* week.

KRUPP. What is he, anyway?

NICK. He's an Arab, or something like that.

KRUPP. No, I mean what's he do for a living?

NICK [*to* ARAB]. What do you do for a living, brother?

ARAB. Work. Work all my life. All my life, work. From small boy to old man, work. In old country, work. In new country, work. In New York. Pittsburgh. Detroit. Chicago. Imperial Valley. San Francisco. Work. No beg. Work. For what? Nothing. Three boys in old country. Twenty years, not see. Lost. Dead. Who knows? What. What-not. No foundation. All the way down the line.

KRUPP. What'd he say last week?

NICK. Didn't say anything. Played the harmonica.

ARAB. Old country song, I play. [*He brings a harmonica from his back pocket.*]

KRUPP. Seems like a nice guy.

NICK. Nicest guy in the world.

KRUPP [*bitterly*]. But crazy. Just like all the rest of us. Stark raving mad.

[WESLEY *and* HARRY *long ago stopped playing and dancing. They sat at a table together and talked for a while; then began playing casino or rummy. When the* ARAB *begins his solo on the harmonica, they stop their game to listen.*]

WESLEY. You hear that?

HARRY. That's *something*.

WESLEY. That's crying. That's crying.

HARRY. I want to make people laugh.

WESLEY. That's deep, deep crying. That's crying a long time ago. That's crying a thousand years ago. Some place five thousand miles away.

HARRY. Do you think you can play to that?

WESLEY. I want to *sing* to that, but I can't *sing*.

HARRY. You try and play to that. I'll try to dance.

[WESLEY *goes to the piano, and after closer listening, he begins to accompany the harmonica solo.* HARRY *goes to the little stage and after a few efforts begins to dance to the song. This keeps up quietly for some time.* KRUPP *and* NICK *have been silent, and deeply moved.*]

KRUPP [*softly*]. Well, anyhow, Nick.

NICK. Hmmmmmmmm?

KRUPP. What I said. Forget it.

NICK. Sure.

KRUPP. It gets me down once in a while.

NICK. No harm in talking.

KRUPP [*the* POLICEMAN *again, loudly*]. Keep the girls out of here.

NICK [*loud and friendly*]. Take it easy.

[*The music and dancing are now at their height.*]

CURTAIN

Act five

That evening. Fog-horns are heard throughout the scene. A MAN *in evening clothes and a top hat, and his* WOMAN, *also in evening clothes, are entering.*

WILLIE *is still at the marble game.* NICK *is behind the bar.* JOE *is at his table, looking at the book of maps of the countries of Europe. The box containing the revolver and the box containing the cartridges are on the table, beside his glass. He is at peace, his hat tilted back on his head, a calm expression on his face.* TOM *is leaning against the bar, dreaming of love and* KITTY. *The* ARAB *is gone.* WESLEY *and* HARRY *are gone.* KIT CARSON *is watching the* BOY *at the marble game.*

LADY. Oh, come on, please.

[*The* GENTLEMAN *follows miserably. The* SOCIETY MAN *and* WIFE *take a table.* NICK *gives them a menu. Outside, in the street, the Salvation Army people are playing a song. Big drum, tambourines, cornet and singing. They are singing "The Blood of the Lamb." The music and words come into the place faintly and comically. This is followed by an old sinner testifying. It is the* DRUNKARD. *His words are not intelligible, but his message is unmistakable. He is saved. He wants to sin no more. And so on.*]

DRUNKARD [*testifying, unmistakably drunk*]. Brothers and sisters. I was a sinner. I chewed tobacco and chased women. Oh, I sinned, brothers and sisters. And then I was saved. Saved by the Salvation Army, God forgive me.

JOE. Let's see now. Here's a city. Pribor. Czechoslovakia. Little, lovely, lonely Czechoslovakia. I wonder what kind of a place Pribor was? [*Calling.*] Pribor! *Pribor!*

[TOM *leaps.*]

LADY. What's the matter with him?

MAN [*crossing his legs, as if he ought to go to the men's room*]. Drunk.

TOM. Who you calling, Joe?

JOE. Pribor.

TOM. Who's Pribor?

JOE. He's a Czech. And a Slav. A Czechoslovakian.

LADY. How interesting.

MAN [*uncrosses legs*]. He's drunk.

JOE. Tom, Pribor's a city in Czechoslovakia.

TOM. Oh. [*Pause.*] You sure were nice to her, Joe.

JOE. Kitty Duval? She's one of the finest people in the world.

TOM. It sure was nice of you to hire an automobile and take us for a drive along the ocean front and down to Half Moon Bay.

JOE. Those three hours were the most delightful, the most somber, and the most beautiful I have ever known.

TOM. Why, Joe?

JOE. Why? I'm a student. [*Lifting his voice.*] Tom. [*Quietly.*] I'm a student. I study all things. All. All. And when my study reveals something of beauty in a place or in a person where by all rights only ugliness or death should be revealed, then I know how full of goodness this life is. And that's a good thing to know. That's a truth I shall always seek to verify.

LADY. Are you *sure* he's drunk?

MAN [*crossing his legs*]. He's either drunk, or just naturally crazy.

TOM. Joe?

JOE. Yeah.

TOM. You won't get sore or anything?

JOE [*impatiently*]. What is it, Tom?

TOM. Joe, where do you get all that money? You paid for the automobile. You paid for supper and the two bottles of champagne at the Half Moon Bay Restaurant. You moved Kitty out of the New York Hotel around the corner to the St. Francis Hotel on Powell Street. I saw you pay her rent. I saw you give her money for new clothes. Where do you get all that money, Joe? Three years now and I've never asked.

JOE [*looking at* TOM *sorrowfully, a little irritated, not so much with* TOM *as with the world and himself, his own superiority. He speaks clearly, slowly and solemnly*]. Now don't be a fool, Tom. Listen carefully. If anybody's got any money—to hoard or to throw away—you can be sure he stole it from other people. Not from rich people who can spare it, but from poor people who can't. From their lives and from their dreams. I'm no exception. I *earned* the money I throw away. I stole it like everybody else does. I hurt people to get it. Loafing around this way, I *still* earn money. The money itself earns *more*. I *still* hurt people. I don't know who they are, or where they are. If I did, I'd feel worse than I do. I've got a Christian conscience in a world that's got no conscience at all. The world's trying to get some sort of a *social* conscience, but it's having a devil of a time trying to do *that*. I've got money. I'll always have money, as long as this world stays the way it is. I don't work. I don't make anything. [*He sips.*] I drink. I worked when I was a kid. I worked *hard*. I mean hard, Tom. People are supposed to enjoy living. I got tired. [*He lifts the gun and looks at it while he talks.*] I decided to get even on the world. Well, you can't enjoy living unless you work. Unless you do something. I don't do anything. I don't *want* to do anything any more. There isn't anything I can do that won't make me feel embarrassed. Because I can't do simple, good things. I haven't the patience. And I'm too smart. Money is the guiltiest thing in the world. It stinks. Now, don't ever bother me about it again.

TOM. I didn't mean to make you feel bad, Joe.

JOE [*slowly*]. Here. Take this gun out in the street and give it to some worthy hold-up man.

LADY. What's he saying?

MAN [*uncrosses legs*]. You wanted to visit a honky-tonk. Well, *this* is a honky-tonk. [*To the world.*] Married twenty-eight years and she's still looking for adventure.

TOM. How should I know who's a hold-up man?

JOE. Take it away. Give it to somebody.

TOM [*bewildered*]. Do I *have* to *give* it to somebody?

JOE. Of course.

TOM. Can't I take it back and get some of our money?

JOE. Don't talk like a business man. Look around and find somebody who appears to be in need of a gun and give it to him. It's a good gun, isn't it?

TOM. The man said it was, but how can I tell who needs a gun?

JOE. Tom, you've seen good people who needed guns, haven't you?

TOM. I don't remember. Joe, I might give it to the wrong kind of guy. He might do something crazy.

JOE. All right. I'll find somebody myself. [TOM *rises.*] Here's some money. Go get me this week's *Life, Liberty, Time,* and six or seven packages of chewing gum.

TOM [*swiftly, in order to remember each item*]. *Life, Liberty, Time* and six or seven packages of chewing gum?

JOE. That's right.

TOM. All that chewing gum? What kind?

JOE. Any kind. Mix 'em up. All kinds.

TOM. Licorice, too?

JOE. Licorice, by all means.

TOM. Juicy Fruit?

JOE. Juicy Fruit.

TOM. Tutti-frutti?

JOE. Is there such a gum?

TOM. I think so.

JOE. All right. Tutti-frutti, too. Get *all* the kinds. Get as many kinds as they're selling.

TOM. *Life, Liberty, Time,* and all the different kinds of gum. [*He begins to go.*]

JOE [*calling after him loudly*]. Get some jelly beans too. All the different colors.

TOM. All right, Joe.

JOE. And the longest panatela cigar you can find. Six of them.

TOM. Panatela. I got it.

JOE. Give a news-kid a dollar.

TOM. O.K., Joe.

JOE. Give some old man a dollar.

TOM. O.K., Joe.

JOE. Give them Salvation Army people in the street a couple of dollars and ask them to sing that song that goes— [*He sings loudly.*]

Let the lower lights be burning, send a gleam across the wave.

TOM [*swiftly*].

Let the lower lights be burning, send a gleam across
the wave.

JOE. That's it. [*He goes on with the song, very loudly
and religiously.*]

Some poor, dying, struggling seaman, you may rescue,
you may save.

[*Halts.*]
TOM. O.K., Joe. I got it. *Life, Liberty, Time,* all the
kinds of gum they're selling, jelly beans, six panatela
cigars, a dollar for a news-kid, a dollar for an old
man, two dollars for the Salvation Army. [*Going.*]

Let the lower lights be burning, send a gleam across
the wave.

JOE. That's it.
LADY. He's absolutely insane.
MAN [*wearily crossing legs*]. You asked me to take you
to a honky-tonk, instead of to the Mark Hopkins.
You're *here* in a honky-tonk. I can't help it if he's
crazy. Do you want to go back to where people
aren't crazy?
LADY. No, not just yet.
MAN. Well, all right then. Don't be telling me every
minute that he's crazy.
LADY. You needn't be huffy about it.
[MAN *refuses to answer, uncrosses legs. When* JOE *be-
gan to sing,* KIT CARSON *turned away from the mar-
ble game and listened. While the* MAN *and* WOMAN
are arguing he comes over to JOE's *table.*]
KIT CARSON. Presbyterian?
JOE. I attended a Presbyterian Sunday School.
KIT CARSON. Fond of singing?

JOE. On occasion. Have a drink?

KIT CARSON. Thanks.

JOE. Get a glass and sit down. [KIT CARSON *gets a glass from* NICK, *returns to the table, sits down,* JOE *pours him a drink, they touch glasses just as the Salvation Army people begin to fulfil the request. They sip some champagne, and at the proper moment begin to sing the song together, sipping champagne, raising hell with the tune, swinging it, and so on. The* SOCIETY LADY *joins them, and is stopped by her* HUSBAND.] Always was fond of that song. Used to sing it at the top of my voice. Never saved a seaman in my life.

KIT CARSON [*flirting with the* SOCIETY LADY *who loves it*]. I saved a seaman once. Well, he wasn't exactly a seaman. He was a darky named Wellington. Heavy-set sort of a fellow. Nice personality, but no friends to speak of. Not until I came along, at any rate. In New Orleans. In the summer of the year 1899. No. Ninety-eight. I was a lot younger of course, and had no mustache, but was regarded by many people as a man of means.

JOE. Know anything about guns?

KIT CARSON [*flirting*]. All there is to know. Didn't fight the Ojibways for nothing. Up there in the Lake Takalooca country, in Michigan. [*Remembering.*] Along about in 1881 or two. Fought 'em right up to the shore of the lake. Made 'em swim for Canada. One fellow in particular, an Indian named Harry Daisy.

JOE [*opening the box containing the revolver*]. What sort of a gun would you say this is? Any good?

KIT CARSON [*at sight of gun, leaping*]. Yep. That looks like a pretty nice hunk of shooting iron. That's a six-shooter. Shot a man with a six-shooter once. Got him through the palm of his right hand. Lifted his arm to wave to a friend. Thought it was a bird. Fellow named, I believe, Carroway. Larrimore Carroway.

JOE. Know how to work one of these things? [*He offers* KIT CARSON *the revolver, which is old and enormous.*]

KIT CARSON [*laughing at the absurd question*]. Know how to work it? Hand me that little gun, son, and I'll show you all about it. [JOE *hands* KIT *the revolver. Importantly.*] Let's see now. This is probably a new kind of six-shooter. After my time. Haven't nicked an Indian in years. I believe this here place is supposed to move out. [*He fools around and gets the barrel out for loading.*] That's it. There it is.

JOE. Look all right?

KIT CARSON. It's a good gun. You've got a good gun there, son. I'll explain it to you. You see these holes? Well, that's where you put the cartridges.

JOE [*taking some cartridges out of the box*]. Here. Show me how it's done.

KIT CARSON [*a little impatiently*]. Well, son, you take 'em one by one and put 'em in the holes, like this. There's one. Two. Three. Four. Five. Six. Then you get the barrel back in place. Then cock it. Then all you got to do is aim and fire. [*He points the gun at the* LADY *and* GENTLEMAN *who scream and stand up, scaring* KIT CARSON *into paralysis. The gun is loaded, but uncocked.*]

JOE. It's all set?

KIT CARSON. Ready to kill.

JOE. Let me hold it.

[KIT *hands* JOE *the gun. The* LADY *and* GENTLEMAN *watch, in terror.*]

KIT CARSON. Careful, now, son. Don't cock it. Many a man's lost an eye fooling with a loaded gun. Fellow I used to know named Danny Donovan lost a nose.

Ruined his whole life. Hold it firm. Squeeze the trigger. Don't snap it. Spoils your aim.

JOE. Thanks. Let's see if I can unload it. [*He begins to unload it.*]

KIT CARSON. Of course you can.

[JOE *unloads the revolver, looks at it very closely, puts the cartridges back into the box.*]

JOE [*looking at gun*]. I'm mighty grateful to you. Always wanted to see one of those things close up. Is it really a good one?

KIT CARSON. It's a beaut, son.

JOE [*aims the empty gun at a bottle on the bar*]. Bang!

WILLIE [*at the marble game, as the machine groans*]. Oh, boy! [*Loudly, triumphantly.*] There you are, Nick. Thought I couldn't do it, hey? *Now,* watch. [*The machine begins to make a special kind of noise. Lights go on and off. Some red, some green. A bell rings loudly six times.*] One. Two. Three. Four. Five. Six. [*An American flag jumps up.* WILLIE *comes to attention. Salutes.*] Oh, boy, what a beautiful country. [*A loud music-box version of the song "America."* JOE, KIT, *and the* LADY *get to their feet. Singing.* "My country, 'tis of thee, sweet land of liberty, of thee I sing." *Everything quiets down. The flag goes back into the machine.* WILLIE *is thrilled, amazed, delighted.* EVERYBODY *has watched the performance of the defeated machine from wherever he happened to be when the performance began.* WILLIE, *looking around at everybody, as if they had all been on the side of the machine.*] O.K. How's that? I knew I could do it. [*To* NICK.] Six nickels. [NICK *hands him six nickels.* WILLIE *goes over to* JOE *and* KIT.] Took me a little while, but I finally did it. It's scientific, really. With a little skill a man can make a modest living beating the marble games. Not that that's what I want to do. I just don't like the idea of anything getting the best of me. A machine or anything else. Myself, I'm the kind of a guy who makes up his mind to do something, and then goes to work and does it. There's no other way a man can be a success at anything. [*Indicating the letter "F" on his sweater.*] See that letter? That don't stand for some little-bitty high school somewhere. That stands for *me*. Faroughli. Willie Faroughli. I'm an Assyrian. We've got a civilization six or seven centuries old, I think. Somewhere along in there. Ever hear of Osman? Harold Osman? He's an Assyrian, too. He's got an orchestra down in Fresno. [*He goes to the* LADY *and* GENTLEMAN.] I've never seen you before in my life, but I can tell from the clothes you wear and the company you keep [*graciously indicating the* LADY] that you're a man who looks every problem straight in the eye, and then goes to work and *solves* it. I'm that way myself. Well. [*He smiles beautifully, takes the* GENTLEMAN'S *hand furiously.*] It's been wonderful talking to a nicer type of people for a change. Well. I'll be seeing you. So long. [*He turns, takes two steps, returns to the table. Very politely and seriously.*] Good-by, lady. You've got a good man there. Take good care of him. [WILLIE *goes, saluting* JOE *and the world.*]

KIT CARSON [*to* JOE]. By God, for a while there I didn't think that young Assyrian was going to do it. That fellow's got something.

[TOM *comes back with the magazines and other stuff.*]

JOE. Get it all?

TOM. Yeah. I had a little trouble finding the jelly beans.

JOE. Let's take a look at them.

TOM. These are the jelly beans.

[JOE *puts his hand into the cellophane bag and takes*

out a handful of the jelly beans, looks at them, smiles, and tosses a couple into his mouth.]

JOE. Same as ever. Have some. [*He offers the bag to* KIT.]

KIT CARSON [*flirting*]. Thanks! I remember the first time I ever ate jelly beans. I was six, or at the most seven. Must have been in [*slowly*] eighteen—seventy-seven. Seven or eight. Baltimore.

JOE. Have some, Tom.

[TOM *takes some.*]

TOM. Thanks, Joe.

JOE. Let's have some of that chewing gum. [*He dumps all the packages of gum out of the bag onto the table.*]

KIT CARSON [*flirting*]. Me and a boy named Clark. Quinton Clark. Became a Senator.

JOE. Yeah. Tutti-frutti, all right. [*He opens a package and folds all five pieces into his mouth.*] Always wanted to see how many I could chew at one time. Tell you what, Tom. I'll bet I can chew more at one time than you can.

TOM [*delighted*]. All right. [*They both begin to fold gum into their mouths.*]

KIT CARSON. I'll referee. Now, one at a time. How many you got?

JOE. Six.

KIT CARSON. All right. Let Tom catch up with you.

JOE [*while* TOM's *catching up*]. Did you give a dollar to a news-kid?

TOM. Yeah, sure.

JOE. What'd he say?

TOM. Thanks.

JOE. What sort of a kid was he?

TOM. Little, dark kid. I guess he's Italian.

JOE. Did he seem pleased?

TOM. Yeah.

JOE. That's good. Did you give a dollar to an old man?

TOM. Yeah.

JOE. Was he pleased?

TOM. Yeah.

JOE. Good. How many you got in your mouth?

TOM. Six.

JOE. All right. I got six, too. [*Folds one more in his mouth.* TOM *folds one too.*]

KIT CARSON. Seven. Seven each. [*They each fold one more into their mouths, very solemnly, chewing them into the main hunk of gum.*] Eight. Nine. Ten.

JOE [*delighted*]. Always wanted to do this. [*He picks up one of the magazines.*] Let's see what's going on in the world. [*He turns the pages and keeps folding gum into his mouth and chewing.*]

KIT CARSON. Eleven. Twelve. [KIT *continues to count while* JOE *and* TOM *continue the contest. In spite of what they are doing, each is very serious.*]

TOM. Joe, what'd you want to move Kitty into the St. Francis Hotel for?

JOE. She's a better woman than any of them tramp society dames that hang around that lobby.

TOM. Yeah, but do you think she'll feel at home up there?

JOE. Maybe not at first, but after a couple of days she'll be all right. A nice big room. A bed for sleeping in. Good clothes. Good food. She'll be all right, Tom.

TOM. I hope so. Don't you think she'll get lonely up there with nobody to talk to?

JOE [*looking at* TOM *sharply, almost with admiration, pleased but severe*]. There's nobody *anywhere* for *her* to talk to—except *you*.

TOM [*amazed and delighted*]. Me, Joe?

JOE [*while* TOM *and* KIT CARSON *listen carefully,* KIT *with great appreciation*]. Yes, you. By the grace of

God, you're the other half of that girl. Not the angry woman that swaggers into this waterfront dive and shouts because the world has kicked her around. *Anybody* can have *her*. You belong to the little kid in Ohio who once dreamed of living. Not with her carcass, for *money*, so she can have food and clothes, and pay rent. With *all* of her. I put her in that hotel, so she can have a chance to gather herself together again. She can't do that in the New York Hotel. You saw what happens there. There's nobody anywhere for her to talk to, except you. They all make her talk like a whore. After a while, she'll *believe* them. Then she won't be able to remember. She'll get lonely. Sure. People can get lonely for ·*misery*, even. I want her to go on being lonely for *you*, so she can come together again the way she was meant to be from the beginning. Loneliness is good for people. Right now it's the only thing for Kitty. Any more licorice?

TOM [*dazed*]. What? Licorice? [*Looking around busily*.] I guess we've chewed all the licorice in. We still got Clove, Peppermint, Doublemint, Beechnut, Teaberry, and Juicy Fruit.

JOE. Licorice used to be my favorite. Don't worry about her, Tom, she'll be all right. You really want to marry her, don't you?

TOM [*nodding*]. Honest to God, Joe. [*Pathetically*.] Only, I haven't got any money.

JOE. Couldn't you be a prize-fighter or something like that?

TOM. Naaaah. I couldn't hit a man if I wasn't sore at him. He'd have to do something that made me hate him.

JOE. You've got to figure out something to do that you won't mind doing very much.

TOM. I wish I could, Joe.

JOE [*thinking deeply, suddenly*]. Tom, would you be embarrassed driving a truck?

TOM [*hit by a thunderbolt*]. Joe, I never thought of that. I'd like that. Travel. Highways. Little towns. Coffee and hot cakes. Beautiful valleys and mountains and streams and trees and daybreak and sunset.

JOE. There *is* poetry in it, at that.

TOM. Joe, that's just the kind of work I *should* do. Just sit there and travel, and look, and smile, and bust out laughing. Could Kitty go with me, sometimes?

JOE. I don't know. Get me the phone book. Can you drive a truck?

TOM. Joe, you know I can drive a truck, or any kind of thing with a motor and wheels. [TOM *takes* JOE *the phone book.* JOE *turns the pages.*]

JOE [*looking*]. Here! Here it is. Tuxedo 7900. Here's a nickel. Get me that number.

[TOM *goes to telephone, dials the number.*]

TOM. Hello.

JOE. Ask for Mr. Keith.

TOM [*mouth and language full of gum*]. I'd like to talk to Mr. Keith. [*Pause.*] Mr. Keith.

JOE. Take that gum out of your mouth for a minute. [TOM *removes the gum.*]

TOM. Mr. Keith. Yeah. That's right. Hello, Mr. Keith?

JOE. Tell him to hold the line.

TOM. Hold the line, please.

JOE. Give me a hand, Tom. [TOM *helps* JOE *to the telephone. At phone, wad of gum in fingers delicately.*] Keith? Joe. Yeah. Fine. Forget it. [*Pause.*] Have you got a place for a good driver? [*Pause.*] I don't think so. [*To* TOM.] You haven't got a driver's license, have you?

TOM [*worried*]. No. But I can get one, Joe.

JOE [*at phone*]. No, but he can get one easy enough.

To hell with the union. He'll join later. All right, call him a Vice-President and say he drives for relaxation. Sure. What do you mean? Tonight? I don't know why not. San Diego? All right, let him start driving without a license. What the hell's the difference? Yeah. Sure. Look him over. Yeah. I'll send him right over. Right. [*He hangs up.*] Thanks. [*To telephone.*]

TOM. Am I going to get the job?

JOE. He wants to take a look at you.

TOM. Do I look all right, Joe?

JOE [*looking at him carefully*]. Hold up your head. Stick out your chest. How do you feel?

[TOM *does these things.*]

TOM. Fine.

JOE. You *look* fine, too. [JOE *takes his wad of gum out of his mouth and wraps "Liberty" magazine around it.*]

JOE. You win, Tom. Now, look. [*He bites off the lip of a very long panatela cigar, lights it, and hands one to* TOM, *and another to* KIT.] Have yourselves a pleasant smoke. Here. [*He hands two more to* TOM.] Give those slummers one each. [*He indicates the* SOCIETY LADY *and* GENTLEMAN.]

[TOM *goes over and without a word gives a cigar each to the* MAN *and the* LADY. *The* MAN *is offended; he smells and tosses aside his cigar. The* WOMAN *looks at her cigar a moment, then puts the cigar in her mouth.*]

MAN. What do you think you're doing?

LADY. Really, dear. I'd like to.

MAN. Oh, this is too much.

LADY. I'd *really*, really like to, dear. [*She laughs, puts the cigar in her mouth. Turns to* KIT. *He spits out tip. She does the same.*]

MAN [*loudly*]. The mother of five grown men, and she's still looking for *romance*. [*Shouts as* KIT *lights her cigar*.] No. I forbid it.

JOE [*shouting*]. What's the matter with you? Why don't you leave her alone? What are you always pushing your women around for? [*Almost without a pause*.] Now, look, Tom. [*The* LADY *puts the lighted cigar in her mouth, and begins to smoke, feeling wonderful*.] Here's ten bucks.

TOM. Ten bucks?

JOE. He may want you to get into a truck and begin driving to San Diego tonight.

TOM. Joe, I got to tell Kitty.

JOE. I'll tell her.

TOM. Joe, take care of her.

JOE. She'll be all right. Stop worrying about her. She's at the St. Francis Hotel. Now, look. Take a cab to Townsend and Fourth. You'll see the big sign. Keith Motor Transport Company. He'll be waiting for you.

TOM. O.K., Joe. [*Trying hard*.] Thanks, Joe.

JOE. Don't be silly. Get going.

[TOM *goes*. LADY *starts puffing on cigar. As* TOM *goes*, WESLEY *and* HARRY *come in together*.]

NICK. Where the hell have you been? We've got to have some entertainment around here. Can't you see them fine people from uptown? [*He points at the* SOCIETY LADY *and* GENTLEMAN.]

WESLEY. You said to come back at ten for the second show.

NICK. Did I say that?

WESLEY. Yes, sir, Mr. Nick, that's exactly what you said.

HARRY. Was the first show all right?

NICK. That wasn't a show. There was no one here to

see it. How can it be a show when no one sees it? People are afraid to come down to the waterfront.

HARRY. Yeah. We were just down to Pier 27. One of the longshoremen and a cop had a fight and the cop hit him over the head with a blackjack. We saw it happen, didn't we?

WESLEY. Yes, sir, we was standing there looking when it happened.

NICK [*a little worried*]. Anything else happen?

WESLEY. They was all talking.

HARRY. A man in a big car came up and said there was going to be a meeting right away and they hoped to satisfy everybody and stop the strike.

WESLEY. Right away. *Tonight.*

NICK. Well, it's about time. Them poor cops are liable to get nervous and—shoot somebody. [*To* HARRY, *suddenly.*] Come back here. I want you to tend bar for a while. I'm going to take a walk over to the pier.

HARRY. Yes, sir.

NICK [*to the* SOCIETY LADY *and* GENTLEMAN]. You society people made up your minds yet?

LADY. Have you champagne?

NICK [*indicating* JOE]. What do you think he's pouring out of that bottle, water or something?

LADY. Have you a chill bottle?

NICK. I've got a dozen of them chilled. He's been drinking champagne here all day and all night for a month now.

LADY. May we have a bottle?

NICK. It's six dollars.

LADY. I think we can manage.

MAN. I don't know. I *know* I don't know.

[NICK *takes off his coat and helps* HARRY *into it.* HARRY *takes a bottle of champagne and two glasses to the*

LADY *and* GENTLEMAN, *dancing, collects six dollars, and goes back behind the bar, dancing.* NICK *gets his coat and hat.*]

NICK [*to* WESLEY]. Rattle the keys a little, son. Rattle the keys.

WESLEY. Yes, sir, Mr. Nick.

[NICK *is on his way out. The* ARAB *enters.*]

NICK. Hi-ya, *Mahmed.*

ARAB. No foundation.

NICK. All the way down the line. [*He goes.*]

[WESLEY *is at the piano, playing quietly. The* ARAB *swallows a glass of beer, takes out his harmonica, and begins to play.* WESLEY *fits his playing to the Arab's.* KITTY DUVAL, *strangely beautiful, in new clothes, comes in. She walks shyly, as if she were embarrassed by the fine clothes, as if she had no right to wear them. The* LADY *and* GENTLEMAN *are very impressed.* HARRY *looks at her with amazement.* JOE *is reading "Time" magazine.* KITTY *goes to his table.* JOE *looks up from the magazine, without the least amazement.*]

JOE. Hello, Kitty.

KITTY. Hello, Joe.

JOE. It's nice seeing you again.

KITTY. I came in a cab.

JOE. You been crying again? [KITTY *can't answer. To* HARRY.] Bring a glass.

[HARRY *comes over with a glass.* JOE *pours* KITTY *a drink.*]

KITTY. I've got to talk to you.

JOE. Have a drink.

KITTY. I've never been in burlesque. We were just poor.

JOE. Sit down, Kitty.

KITTY [*sits down*]. I tried other things.

JOE. Here's to you, Katerina Koranovsky. Here's to you. And Tom.

KITTY [*sorrowfully*]. Where *is* Tom?

JOE. He's getting a job tonight driving a truck. He'll be back in a couple of days.

KITTY [*sadly*]. I told him I'd marry him.

JOE. He wanted to see you and say good-by.

KITTY. He's too good for me. He's like a little boy. [*Wearily.*] I'm— Too many things have happened to me.

JOE. Kitty Duval, you're one of the few truly innocent people I have ever known. He'll be back in a couple of days. Go back to the hotel and wait for him.

KITTY. That's what I mean. I can't stand being alone. I'm no good. I tried very hard. I don't know what it is. I miss— [*She gestures.*]

JOE [*gently*]. Do you really want to come back here, Kitty?

KITTY. I don't know. I'm not sure. Everything *smells* different. I don't know how to feel, or what to think. [*Gesturing pathetically.*] I know I don't belong there. It's what I've wanted all my life, but it's too *late*. I try to be happy about it, but all I can do is remember everything and cry.

JOE. I don't know what to tell you, Kitty. I didn't mean to hurt you.

KITTY. You haven't hurt me. You're the only person who's ever been good to me. I've never known anybody like you. I'm not sure about love any more, but I know I love you, and I know I love Tom.

JOE. I love you too, Kitty Duval.

KITTY. He'll want babies. I know he will. I know *I* will, too. Of course I will. I can't— [*She shakes her head.*]

JOE. Tom's a baby himself. You'll be very happy together. He wants you to ride with him in the truck. Tom's good for you. You're good for Tom.

KITTY [*like a child*]. Do you want me to go back and wait for him?

JOE. I can't *tell* you what to do. I think it would be a good idea, though.

KITTY. I wish I could tell you how it makes me feel to be alone. It's almost worse.

JOE. It might take a whole week, Kitty. [*He looks at her sharply, at the arrival of an idea.*] Didn't you speak of reading a book? A book of poems?

KITTY. I didn't know what I was saying.

JOE [*trying to get up*]. Of course you knew. I think you'll like poetry. Wait here a minute, Kitty. I'll go see if I can find some books.

KITTY. All right, Joe.

[*He walks out of the place, trying very hard not to wobble. Fog-horn. Music. The* NEWSBOY *comes in. Looks for* JOE. *Is broken-hearted because* JOE *is gone.*]

NEWSBOY [*to* SOCIETY GENTLEMAN]. Paper?

MAN [*angry*]. No.

[*The* NEWSBOY *goes to the* ARAB.]

NEWSBOY. Paper, Mister?

ARAB [*irritated*]. No foundation.

NEWSBOY. What?

ARAB [*very angry*]. No foundation.

[*The* NEWSBOY *starts out, turns, looks at the* ARAB, *shakes head.*]

NEWSBOY. No foundation? How do you figure?

[BLICK *and two cops enter.*]

NEWSBOY [*to* BLICK]. Paper, Mister?

[BLICK *pushes him aside. The* NEWSBOY *goes.*]

BLICK [*walking authoritatively about the place, to* HARRY]. Where's Nick?

HARRY. He went for a walk.

BLICK. Who are you?

HARRY. Harry.

BLICK [*to the* ARAB *and* WESLEY]. Hey, you. Shut up. [*The* ARAB *stops playing the harmonica,* WESLEY *the piano.*]

BLICK [*studies* KITTY]. What's your name, sister?

KITTY [*looking at him*]. Kitty Duval. What's it to you? [KITTY'S *voice is now like it was at the beginning of the play: tough, independent, bitter and hard.*]

BLICK [*angry*]. Don't give me any of your gutter lip. Just answer my questions.

KITTY. You go to hell, you.

BLICK [*coming over, enraged*]. Where do you live?

KITTY. The New York Hotel. Room 21.

BLICK. Where do you work?

KITTY. I'm not working just now. I'm looking for work.

BLICK. What kind of work? [KITTY *can't answer.*] What kind of work? [KITTY *can't answer. Furiously.*] *What kind of work?*

[KIT CARSON *comes over.*]

KIT CARSON. You can't talk to a lady that way in *my* presence.

[BLICK *turns and stares at* KIT. *The* COPS *begin to move from the bar.*]

BLICK [*to the* COPS]. It's all right, boys. I'll take care of this. [*To* KIT.] *What'd you say?*

KIT CARSON. You got no right to hurt people. Who are you?

[BLICK, *without a word, takes* KIT *to the street. Sounds of a blow and a groan.* BLICK *returns, breathing hard.*]

BLICK [*to the* COPS]. O.K., boys. You can go now. Take care of him. Put him on his feet and tell him to behave himself from now on. [*To* KITTY *again.*] Now answer my question. What kind of work?

KITTY [*quietly*]. I'm a whore, you son of a bitch. You

know what kind of work I do. And I know what kind you do.

MAN [*shocked and really hurt*]. Excuse me, officer, but it seems to me that your attitude—

BLICK. Shut up.

MAN [*quietly*]. —is making the poor child say things that are not true.

BLICK. Shut up, I said.

LADY. Well. [*To the* MAN.] Are you going to stand for such insolence?

BLICK [*to* MAN, *who is standing*]. Are you?

MAN [*taking the* WOMAN's *arm*]. I'll get a divorce. I'll start life all over again. [*Pushing the* WOMAN.] Come on. Get the hell out of here! [*The* MAN *hurries his* WOMAN *out of the place,* BLICK *watching them go.*]

BLICK [*to* KITTY]. Now. Let's begin again, and see that you tell the truth. What's your name?

KITTY. Kitty Duval.

BLICK. Where do you live?

KITTY. Until this evening I lived at the New York Hotel. Room 21. This evening I moved to the St. Francis Hotel.

BLICK. Oh. To the St. Francis Hotel. Nice place. Where do you work?

KITTY. I'm looking for work.

BLICK. What kind of work do you do?

KITTY. I'm an actress.

BLICK. I see. What movies have I seen you in?

KITTY. I've worked in burlesque.

BLICK. You're a liar.

[WESLEY *stands, worried and full of dumb resentment.*]

KITTY [*pathetically, as at the beginning of the play*]. It's the truth.

BLICK. What are you doing here?

KITTY. I came to see if I could get a job here.

BLICK. Doing what?

KITTY. Singing—and—dancing.

BLICK. You can't sing or dance. What are you lying for?

KITTY. I can. I sang and danced in burlesque all over the country.

BLICK. You're a liar.

KITTY. I said lines, too.

BLICK. So you danced in burlesque?

KITTY. Yes.

BLICK. All right. Let's see what you did.

KITTY. I can't. There's no music, and I haven't got the right clothes.

BLICK. There's music. [*To* WESLEY.] Put a nickel in that phonograph. [WESLEY *can't move.*] Come on. Put a nickel in that phonograph. [WESLEY *does so. To* KITTY.] All right. Get up on that stage and do a hot little burlesque number. [KITTY *stands. Walks slowly to the stage, but is unable to move.* JOE *comes in, holding three books.*] Get going, now. Let's see you dance the way you did in burlesque, all over the country.

[KITTY *tries to do a burlesque dance. It is beautiful in a tragic way.*]

BLICK. All right, start taking them off!

[KITTY *removes her hat and starts to remove her jacket.* JOE *moves closer to the stage, amazed.*]

JOE [*hurrying to* KITTY]. Get down from there. [*He takes* KITTY *into his arms. She is crying. To* BLICK.] What the hell do you think you're doing?

WESLEY [*like a little boy, very angry*]. It's that man, Blick. *He* made her take off her clothes. He beat up the old man, too.

[BLICK *pushes* WESLEY *off, as* TOM *enters.* BLICK *begins beating up* WESLEY.]

TOM. What's the matter, Joe? What's happened?

JOE. Is the truck out there?

TOM. Yeah, but what's happened? Kitty's crying again!

JOE. You driving to San Diego?

TOM. Yeah, Joe. But what's he doing to that poor colored boy?

JOE. Get going. Here's some money. Everything's O.K. [*To* KITTY.] Dress in the truck. Take these books.

WESLEY'S VOICE. You can't hurt me. You'll get yours. You wait and see.

TOM. Joe, he's hurting that boy. I'll kill him!

JOE [*pushing* TOM]. Get out of here! Get married in San Diego. I'll see you when you get back. [TOM *and* KITTY *go.* NICK *enters and stands at the lower end of bar.* JOE *takes the revolver out of his pocket. Looks at it.*] I've always wanted to kill somebody, but I never knew who it should be. [*He cocks the revolver, stands real straight, holds it in front of him firmly and walks to the door. He stands a moment watching* BLICK, *aims very carefully, and pulls trigger. There is no shot.* NICK *runs over and grabs the gun, and takes* JOE *aside.*]

NICK. What the hell do you think you're doing?

JOE [*casually, but angry*]. That dumb Tom. Buys a six-shooter that won't even shoot once. [JOE *sits down, dead to the world.* BLICK *comes out, panting for breath.* NICK *looks at him. He speaks slowly.*]

NICK. Blick! I told you to stay out of here! Now get out of here. [*He takes* BLICK *by the collar, tightening his grip as he speaks, and pushing him out.*] If you come back again, I'm going to take you in that room where you've been beating up that colored boy, and I'm going to murder you—slowly—with my hands. Beat it! [*He pushes* BLICK *out. To* HARRY.] Go take care of the colored boy.

[HARRY *runs out.* WILLIE *returns and doesn't sense that anything is changed.* WILLIE *puts another nickel into the machine, but he does so very violently. The consequence of this violence is that the flag comes up again.* WILLIE, *amazed, stands at attention and sa-lutes. The flag goes down. He shakes his head.*]

WILLIE [*thoughtfully*]. As far as I'm concerned, this is the *only* country in the world. If you ask me, nuts to Europe! [*He is about to push the slide in again when the flag comes up again. Furiously, to* NICK, *while he salutes and stands at attention, pleadingly.*] Hey, Nick. This machine is out of order.

NICK [*somberly*]. Give it a whack on the side.

[WILLIE *does so. A hell of a whack. The result is the flag comes up and down, and* WILLIE *keeps saluting.*]

WILLIE [*saluting*]. Hey, Nick. Something's wrong.

[*The machine quiets down abruptly.* WILLIE *very stealthily slides a new nickel in, and starts a new game. From a distance two pistol shots are heard each carefully timed.* NICK *runs out. The* NEWSBOY *enters, crosses to* JOE'S *table, senses something is wrong.*]

NEWSBOY [*softly*]. Paper, Mister?

[JOE *can't hear him. The* NEWSBOY *backs away, studies* JOE, *wishes he could cheer* JOE *up. Notices the phonograph, goes to it, and puts a coin in it, hoping music will make* JOE *happier. The* NEWSBOY *sits down. Watches* JOE. *The music begins. "The Missouri Waltz." The* DRUNKARD *comes in and walks around. Then sits down.* NICK *comes back.*]

NICK [*delighted*]. Joe, Blick's dead! Somebody just shot him, and none of the cops are trying to find out who. [JOE *doesn't hear.* NICK *steps back, studying* JOE. *Shouting.*] Joe.

JOE [*looking up*]. What?

NICK. Blick's dead.

JOE. Blick? Dead? Good! That goddamn gun wouldn't go off. I *told* Tom to get a good one.

NICK [*picking up gun and looking at it*]. Joe, you wanted to kill that guy! [HARRY *returns.* JOE *puts the gun in his coat pocket.*] I'm going to buy you a bottle of champagne. [NICK *goes to bar.*]

[JOE *rises, takes hat from rack, puts coat on. The* NEWSBOY *jumps up, helps* JOE *with coat.*]

NICK. What's the matter, Joe?

JOE. Nothing. Nothing.

NICK. How about the champagne?

JOE. Thanks. [*Going.*]

NICK. It's not eleven yet. Where you going, Joe?

JOE. I don't know. Nowhere.

NICK. Will I see you tomorrow?

JOE. I don't know. I don't think so.

[KIT CARSON *enters, walks to* JOE. JOE *and* KIT *look at one another knowingly.*]

JOE. Somebody just shot a man. How are you feeling?

KIT. Never felt better in my life. [*Loudly, bragging, but somber.*] I shot a man once. In San Francisco. Shot him two times. In 1939, I think it was. In October. Fellow named Blick or Glick or something like that. Couldn't stand the way he talked to ladies. Went up to my room and got my old pearl-handled revolver and waited for him on Pacific Street. Saw him walking, and let him have it, two times. Had to throw the beautiful revolver into the Bay.

[HARRY, NICK, *the* ARAB *and the* DRUNKARD *close in around him.* JOE *searches his pockets, brings out the revolver, puts it in* KIT's *hand, looks at him with great admiration and affection.* JOE *walks slowly to the stairs leading to the street, turns and waves.* KIT, *and then one by one everybody else, waves, and the marble game goes into its beautiful American routine again: flag, lights, and music. The play ends.*]

CURTAIN